KISSED BY WARMTH

Batt placed a strong arm around Flame's shoulders. "You don't mind, do you?" he asked, looking down at her, a slight smile crossing his lips.

"I do." They were alone, outside, in the dark.

Batt swung her around. "Why?"

"I'm in love with Cahill."

"That kid?"

He tossed the cigar, pulled her roughly into his arms and kissed her. She couldn't break away. He kissed her hard, but his lips were surprisingly gentle. His body was granite. She felt her legs tremble.

"Does Cahill kiss like that?"

She swallowed and opened her eyes. "Batt—"

He kissed her again, and this time she put her hands around his neck—and kissed him back.

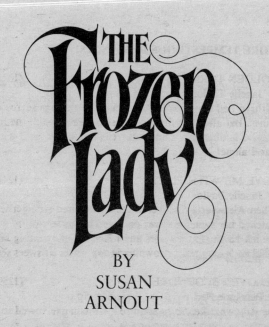

THE Frozen Lady

BY
SUSAN
ARNOUT

ZEBRA BOOKS
KENSINGTON PUBLISHING CORP.

The characters in this story are fictional, and any resemblance to real persons, living or dead, is purely coincidental.

ZEBRA BOOKS

are published by

KENSINGTON PUBLISHING CORP.
475 Park Avenue South
New York, New York 10016

Copyright © 1983 by Susan Arnout
Reprinted by arrangement with Arbor House Publishing
Company.

Printed in the United States of America

When asked the secret of her
long and happy marriage
eighty-five-year-old Aunt Frances replied:
"Put up with it!"
This book is for my husband Jim
who is doing exactly that

Acknowledgments

Special thanks to the following: Bonnie Cavanaugh and the folks at the reference desk, Loussac Library; Linda Tobiska, Alaska Historical Library; Beverlee Weston, Spenard Library; Carol Mercer, Alaska Room, UAA Library; Ron Lautaret, Peggy Michielsen, John Summerhill, UAA Library; Keith Tryck; Billie Meakok, President, Inupiat Community; Providence Hospital Emergency Room and Dr. Jim Borden; Bob Atwood, Publisher, Anchorage *Times*; John Hellenthal, for memories of the war years; the Pribilof Islands Association and KIMO TV; and the Anchorage *Daily News*; Lyman Woodman.

I'm also grateful to Laura O'Kelley and Janet Leetch, who loved my infant son while I was working; and Linda Garrett, a one-woman support system and good friend, who juggled typing, infant car seats and groceries without losing her mind. Thanks to Karen Day, who offered to fly down from Fairbanks to help and Jincy Swartzbacker. Love and gratitude to Stephanie and Doug Moen.

Special thanks to my brother, Gene Weschenfelder, for his amazing ability to find out-of-print books; my mother and father, Florence and Ernest Weschenfelder, for their tremendous support and great love; my sisters, Bonnie, Neva and Nancy, for their letters of encouragement; Thelma and Howard Arnout, my in-laws, who did a month hard time when they wandered into The Book in the middle of their vacation; and my family: Brent, one terrific kid; Aaron, who seemed to have been born knowing his mother was a writer; and my dear husband, Jim, who shielded me from interruptions and kept everybody going.

Thanks to Dawn Troup and Bill McReynolds, the very best

of teachers; and Arnold Goodman, the finest agent a writer could have.

And thanks to Darlene Bline, who fixed a casserole on my birthday so I could keep working; and Mary Fondahn, Heather Arnett, Barbara Zipkin, Diane Lake, Judy Berger and Jan Reed, for being patient when I couldn't come out and play.

Round and round the circle goes
Where it stops, no one knows
For we are never quite apart
We're bound by need and deed and heart
                                        Tareumiut circle game

The shaman picked up the stone and threw it
into the ocean. "What do you see?" he asked
the novitiate.
"A stone falling."
"And now?"
"Ripples."
"And now?"
"There is nothing. The water is still."
The shaman smiled. "Then why is it that the
ripples are seen in the mind of your son,
and his beyond him?"
                        from *The Sacred Passing of Knowledge*

BOOK ONE

Us

One

SEATTLE, 1893—It was inevitable, getting caught.

It wasn't as if she could pretend she didn't know what she was doing, either. Sundays she sat between her parents, stiff and erect in a pew at the First Baptist Temple, and listened to the preacher thumping the Bible on the altar. He smacked his fist and waved his hands and spoke of hell, and Flame knew he was speaking directly to her. Once he even leaned down over the pulpit and looked directly into her eyes and spoke of the flames of hell. She was relieved, after that. At least she would have other little girls to play with.

Flame Ryan lived with her parents in lonely splendor on First Hill. She had a white horse and two loppy-eared dogs and a tabby cat and a parakeet and no friends.

Well, almost no friends.

There was Cahill, of course.

He lived two houses away, which would have been wonderful except that all the houses were separated by three miles of lawn. Cornelius Hanford, a United States district judge, lived on First Hill, as well as Eugene Semple, a former territorial governor, and Morgan Carkeek, whose company had built the building Flame's father owned.

None of them had children young enough to be of any use on hot summer days when frogs down at the Ryans' pond pleaded to be collected and carried home in mason jars. That's how it started, really. With the frogs. It always involved hitching her skirt up to her waist and wading in barefoot. Wading in was always the easy part. The water crawled deliciously up her legs, covering her knees, then her waist, and whispering to her how much it wanted to slip up over her shoulders. Wading out was terrible. She had to close her nose to the wonderful wet smells

11

of the sludge steaming in the center of the pond and stop up her ears so she couldn't hear the siren song of all the things that crawled along the bottom.

Cahill was the only person she ever met who understood about the things that talked to her at the bottom of the pond on hot summer days.

Which is why he pushed her in.

Once her hair was wet and all the starch in her pinafore had drowned, there seemed little point in leaving on her clothes. And after they had played that way once, there seemed little point in not playing that way again. But it was Cahill's idea to take the clothes off first.

He was a year older than Flame, a year smarter, he told her, and the son of a doctor, so he was used to seeing girls naked, he said.

They had been meeting like this at the pond for four years now. Flame was eleven, soon to be twelve. She tried to explain to Cahill once about damnation and the flames of hell, but Cahill's God was Presbyterian. Cahill said he had discussed it once with his God, who said it was all right. Still the feeling persisted in Flame that what they were doing was wrong, very wrong, and that it was inevitable, the getting caught.

"Mr. Hoge said if it keeps up, the lettuce crop will dry up like dust balls." They were walking to the pond, Cahill in front of her idly dragging a stick through the chalky-looking dirt. "Yep. He says we're in for a scorcher." He liked the way it sounded on his tongue so he repeated it. "A regular scorcher."

"It should be hot enough for ya," Flame agreed. Everyone said it that summer. Once, preacher Southwick had even said it in a sermon, working it in skillfully after a particularly vivid description of hell. Flame's parents had chuckled along with the rest of the adults, but Flame had sat in rigid misery next to her mother. Flame's mother was small and precise and had mastered the art of looking disappointed to keep her daughter in check. Now, all her mother had to do was show the slightest sign—a lift of her eyebrow or a twitch of the lip—and Flame would scramble to improve herself. Her mother would die if she knew what Flame was doing—die of disappointment—and

12

if she died, she would go straight to heaven and Flame would never see her again. Right there on the pew, after preacher Southwick had asked all the grown-ups if it was hot enough for them, Flame vowed that the next time, the very next time Cahill wanted to go with her to the pond, she would refuse. She would make something up if she had to, but she would not, she could not—no, never—go to the pond with him again. Her mother's life hung in the balance.

Except that her feet never got the message.

They didn't even have the decency to drag a little. No, they ran eagerly forward in high-buttoned boots, willfully disobedient.

If Cahill sensed the inner turmoil in Flame, he never let on as he slouched out of his pants, kicked off his shoes and threw away his shirt on his way into the water.

"It's a regular scorcher," he repeated. The cool liquid of the pond hugged his knees. He jigged up and down until his sex floated on the water like a toy boat. Then he slapped back into the water and floated, pretending he was alone in the cool green universe of the pond.

The Ryans' pond. Pride of ownership flared, and Flame yanked the ribbon around her neck, tumbling her hat to the grass, her resolves landing not far behind.

"This is the last time," she said loudly. Cahill gulbed water and spouted it out like a whale.

"The bottom's squushy right now," was all he said. "You'd better hurry or you'll miss how squushy the bottom is."

It really was the last time, she told herself as she unfastened her starched skirt and stepped out of it. It settled with a sigh, a huge muttering flower on the edge of the pond. Cahill was leisurely swimming backward through the water, watching her. She hesitated over her shift, staring fascinated into the water. For a moment there, the dip of Cahill's hand into the water, the way his wrist snapped, she almost saw her mother's disappointed face staring up at her, her mother saying, "Flame, how could you do this to me? If you loved me, how could you do this? I am sooo disappointed in yew . . ."

Flame yanked the shift over her auburn head in one shuddery moment, crouched out of her bloomers and ran into

13

the water. Then they played, naked and slippery as seals.

It was the whooping and hollering that finally did it.

The Seattle Ladies' Botanical Society never wandered over to this part of the estate, especially not in this heat. But this time, homing in on the strange sounds, they flitted over, starched ships sailing majestically over the lawn.

Cahill had yanked her legs out from under her and lifted her onto his shoulders. She clung to his neck, shrieking, until he suddenly dived down into the water and threw her off. Two legs surfaced in the pond, like pale plants sprouting, and were joined by two more. It was a regular exotic plant festival. The legs grew and grew until it became clear that not all the legs were the same sex.

Dowager Wimple's cheeks got even redder under the rouge. Her mouth opened and closed like a guppy. Two ladies swooned. The others clustered together away from the pond.

Flame crouched in the water, stricken, looking at her mother. She wondered if it was too late in the day to catch a serious illness from the pond water and hover near death. Hovering near death was the only thing she could think of that could possibly put swimming naked with the doctor's son into some sort of perspective. *Please please please*, she prayed. She hoped whatever she got wouldn't be so serious she lost her appetite. They were having fried chicken for dinner.

Her mother was advancing now, not a rubbery, blubbery mass of flesh shivering and wailing "How could you *do* this to me?" No, it was worse, far worse than Flame ever imagined on the flat hard pew that had numbed her bottom on Sundays.

Her dark-haired, small-boned mother was awesomely in control.

She would remember it clearly the rest of her life: the green day, the women stiffened like paper flowers against the grass, her mother detaching herself from the others and coming closer, her face neutral, unreadable. In her arms she carried their clothes.

It was just the three of them, then. A frog gargled. The water lapped gently.

Margaret Blessing Ryan looked at her auburn-haired daughter. Flame looked back. There was a long moment of silence. Flame wanted to explain to her mother about the things that talked to her at the bottom of the pond, wanted to say "Say something to her. She'll understand then, why I had to do it. Talk to her." But the things that slithered on the bottom were curiously silent. Her mother dropped to the grass.

I was wrong. She is going to die. She's going to faint dead away and it's all my fault. All of it.

Margaret Blessing Ryan unlaced her boots and waded in.

"Too damn hot for inspecting flowers anyway," she said. "Just about right for catching frogs."

Margaret Blessing's marriage had been a double miracle. The minor miracle was that Tom Ryan was rich. The major miracle was that she had married at all.

Margaret was sixteen when her father was hit at the Battle of Seven Pines. He lingered two weeks, muttering in his sleep. Afterward Margaret dusted the room daily with talc, but somehow it always smelled faintly sweet, like rotting flesh.

He had owned several plantations and a packet along the Ohio River. The Civil War and faro took it all away.

Her mother had died so long ago she couldn't remember one clear thing about her. When she was small, she imagined her with frizzed golden hair and wings, wearing a bustle. A kindly aunt once sat her down and insisted she look at her mother the way she really was. But the woman in the gilt frame was small and dark and plain. That's when Margaret first knew that she really was the child of a phantom, golden-haired princess.

The fact that she looked exactly like her mother, with dark hair and plain features, made absolutely no difference at all.

Tom's parents were first-generation Seattle settlers, if you could overlook the Cayuse Indians, who had been there over a thousand years. The Ryans overlooked them very easily, until one Indian who had had quite enough of being overlooked shot Mrs. Ryan through the heart with an arrow. That was in 1855.

Tom's father spent the next twenty years trading land and moving up and acting as if his wife's death didn't matter, and actually, although he never really thought about it, it didn't. She had been thoughtful enough to leave him with sons.

15

Tom was the only real disappointment. He was one year old when his mother died. Of all the Ryan males, he seemed to miss her the most. There was a certain vulnerability about him. His father sensed it right away and tried, with only marginal success, to beat it out of him.

Yet, in his own way, Gardner Ryan was a fair man. In his will he divided his coal deposits east and south of town equally among his four sons.

Tom was twenty-six when his father died, and the land was the last piece falling into place. Because Tom knew something his father didn't: women love vulnerability.

He met Margaret one night when he was trying to sharpen his skills on President Hayes's wife.

He was escorted out of the banquet hall in Olympia so quickly, he left his topcoat and vulnerability behind. Margaret returned them both.

They were married quietly by a justice of the peace in 1880. She was six years older than he and the first female friend he had ever had. But he didn't really fall in love until the next year, when he wrapped his arms around their newborn child. They looked at each other steadily, the soft copper fuzz on her scalp matching his own coloring, and he knew this love would last forever.

Flame wanted to die. She wanted sweet baby Jesus to fly in through her bedroom window and take her away from all this. Maybe they could join the circus.

"Now," her mother said quietly, closing the door behind her, "I think it's time we talked."

Margaret unbuttoned her bodice. "This is what breasts look like," she said matter-of-factly. Flame stared. Her mother slipped out of her skirt and petticoat. Flame stared at the down triangle between her legs.

"You're looking at your future, darlin'," Margaret said simply. "Grand, isn't it?"

Somehow, Flame knew her swimming days were over.

What she couldn't know was that everything else was, too.

Two

The year 1893 received mixed reviews.

P. T. Barnum toured the Midwest the same week the Philadelphia and Reading Railroad went under. John Philip Sousa was the hottest thing since sliced bread, but in May, when National Cordage, the rope trust, went belly up, everybody went back to kneading their own bread, and no one felt much like whistling hit tunes.

It was the year Flame found blood in her bloomers.

The rest of the world was seized in a misery just as complete.

Banks, mortgage companies and corporations fell apart like Humpty-Dumpty. And the people who went along with all those banks, mortgage companies and corporations couldn't put the pieces back together again.

Flame's father was gone a lot that year, and when he was home, she could hear them arguing bitterly behind the polished study doors.

It was always the same. "You did *what?*" Her mother's voice. "A 95 percent margin." Her father's voice was wooden. And on and on until they were both yelling things they didn't mean, couldn't possibly mean.

Flame played elaborate games with herself to block out voices, but the same summer she was caught swimming with Cahill, two things happened—things so loud that the voices could not be blocked out any longer and her life changed forever.

They lost Hattie, to begin with.

Hattie had been with them for ten years; a gray woman of indeterminate age with a wonderfully warm and ample lap. When she wasn't scrubbing the floors or cooking supper, she lived in her own rooms over the carriage house—an apartment, she called it with pride.

Flame loved Hattie, with all the fierce simplicity of children who love whoever is kind and good to them. They would sit for hours sometimes in Hattie's cramped kitchen, Flame's auburn head next to Hattie's gray one, and talk about life and its mysteries.

Hattie didn't have much in the way of things; Flame wouldn't know how little Hattie really had until years later when she had grown up herself. But Hattie had the one gift that transcended the small dark rooms and the shabby furnishings; Hattie was continually surprised and gladdened by life.

Hattie had bad feet and wore funny misshapen shoes and walked from side to side, shifting her weight heavily. Flame asked her once about her feet, and Hattie had replied that they had grown that way because of all the dancing she had done in her youth.

One day in the same dreadfully hot summer she stopped swimming with Cahill, Flame climbed the steps to Hattie's rooms and heard the sound of her crying. She had never heard her old friend cry before, and the sound made the saliva dry up in her mouth and her chest hurt where she thought her heart must be. The sound was not like Hattie at all; she was a big woman given to large expressions of emotion—hearty brays of laughter, sudden glad bursts of song. The crying was a small, desolate thing.

Flame knocked once and the sound stopped, and she heard Hattie lumbering across the kitchen floor to open the door. And then they were staring at each other. Hattie was wearing her good dress, her Sunday dress, a blue silk that was tight where her waist would have been and generously cut over her generous bosom. She was holding her hat. Behind her, Flame could see that her trunk had been packed and the cherry-wood vanity moved next to it. Hattie's face was puffed and red. She fumbled with the hat pins.

"Could you help with the pins?" She held them out to Flame. "My eyes aren't so good."

"You're packed!" It was an accusation.

Hattie's shoulders heaved and she flung her arms around Flame.

18

"You can't leave! Is it something I did?"

The old woman rocked from foot to foot and pressed her hands into the back of Flame's head, holding the girl's face tight against her cheek. "No, child, no."

"Then why?"

"Things change. Ask your mother."

"My mother is sending you away?" Flame was shocked.

"Your mother is a good woman, Flame," Hattie said loyally. "The best." At this she began crying again, and Flame cried too.

"I'll hide you in my room. I will. I'll bring you dinner—" and then the thought, Who's going to make dinner now?

"You'll be fine. You'll see." She looked past Flame and in a rush said, "Be kind to them, Flame."

"But they're sending you away!" Flame cried harder.

"They need all the kindness you can spare. I'll be fine. I will. Going to Philadelphia," she said shyly. "Live with my sis."

"Don't go," Flame said fiercely. She could not imagine these rooms without Hattie. Hattie had brought life to them and now she was taking it away, and every time Flame passed the carriage house and looked up and saw the vacant windows, it would be like passing the open grave of a friend. "Don't go," she repeated.

"Even grown-ups can't always do what they want," Hattie said gently. "When you grow up, you can visit."

"When I grow up it will be too late! I know it! Don't go." The last was a thin wail. Flame wrapped her arms around Hattie.

Hattie took the hands away and said, "I'm ready now."

Flame's father was standing on the steps, waiting. Flame flung herself at him, pounding him with her fists and screaming how she hated him, couldn't stand the sight of him and wished he were dead. Her father stood there, and as Flame screamed, his shoulders slumped and his head sagged until his eyes, at least, yes, the dark green eyes that had crackled with fire and energy, that had melted her mother's resistance and inflamed her with desire, became as dead as Flame had wanted them to be.

Long after words, Flame would remember those eyes.

The second thing that happened that summer was even worse than Hattie's leaving. It was in August, in the last week before school started. Margaret had begun taking in other people's laundry to make ends meet. She had run out of starch, and Flame had remembered that Hattie always kept an extra bottle in her linen closet. Flame had climbed the steps and was almost at the door when she heard a small, grunting, animal sound. She stopped, curious. The door was slightly ajar. She cracked it open, looked, and looked again.

Her father's buttocks rose in the air like two pale hills, pressing furiously up and down. His pants were hooked down around his knees and he hoisted up two neatly booted feet over his shoulders. Flame didn't recognize the boots.

At dinner that night, Flame worried about hiding it from her mother, until she realized her mother knew and was hiding it from her.

Nothing that whole summer was as bad as that. Not even the day strangers came and wrapped the furniture and carried it out the door and down the broad expanse of grass into someone else's living room.

They had lost the coal deposits and the factory and the house and the fine, glittering future Tom had envisioned.

And then he took it one step further and proceeded to lose his mind.

Three

After the panic of '93, Tom was never the same. He retreated into a private world and came out only to apply for another job. He always got it, and it was always the same. He would go out full of enthusiasm the first day, and Margaret would be waiting for him when he came back. She would be eager and hopeful that maybe this one was going to work, going to do the trick, and careful not to appear too eager until she heard what he had to say. He would always be laughing and gay when he came back to the rooming house where they lived. They would go to the Arlington Hotel or a small restaurant on First Avenue and order something simple but well prepared, and over a bottle of wine he would tell her everything. The news was always very hopeful and very positive, and Margaret would hold his hand across the table and be hopeful and positive in return.

Then something always went wrong.

Once it only took three days for it to turn sour—when he was working as a salesman for a shingle company—but usually it took about two weeks. One day he would come home and Margaret would notice a change in him; he would be grim and moody, and the next day he would come home early, saying they had a light schedule or he wasn't feeling well. The day after that he would stay in bed, drinking. At first Margaret could get him up in one day, but that was before she went to work.

She was hired as a domestic for a merchant's family on Queen Anne Hill. She had to take the First Avenue line early in the morning and the last streetcar home at night. Tom would be sitting where she had left him in a chair by the window, staring over the tops of the roofs and five-story buildings, staring east at First Hill.

21

The boardinghouse was at 904 Second Avenue across the street from Globe Wallpaper and three blocks north of the department stores where Margaret used to charge. The block was crowded with small businesses. On the corner was a fish merchant, who leased the ground floor from a man who ran a laundry upstairs. Behind the building in the alleyway was a shoe repair shop. In the same block there was also a furniture repair shop, three more rooming houses, a dressmaker, a greengrocer and an alienist—a doctor of the mind. His patients never came to the front door; they used the alleyway. The doctor was always smiling and wonderfully happy. The first time Flame saw him, she thought he was a patient. Most of the shop owners lived in rooms attached to their shops. On hot nights they would open the windows and sit out on the cool cement steps, calling back and forth to one another, waiting for the rain. Young mothers would rock their babies, and the old men would smoke cigars and tell their wives about the exciting lives they left behind when they met and married them.

Tom never sat on the steps with the other men on hot nights while the rain rumbled over Mount Rainier. He sat quietly on the chair next to the plain iron bed and looked out the window. He had insisted they rent the two rooms after he had seen that the bedroom he would share with Margaret looked out over First Hill. He said he wanted it that way, to remind him of what he had lost.

"That's the last of them." Margaret put the clams into the bucket and tamped down the lid. Whitecaps were gusting in the sea as the tide began coming back into Puget Sound. It was a cold, blustery day in late September. "We could steam some for dinner. We've got enough left over."

Flame shook her head and looked at the still figure sitting on the rocks above them. "You and pa can."

Margaret picked up the bucket and looked at her sharply. "You're seeing him again?"

"We're friends, mother. That's all."

Flame started clambering up the sharp needles of rocks toward her father, but Margaret stopped her. "We need to talk."

"Ma, I'll be late."

"This won't take long."

Flame sighed and came down the beach toward her mother. Margaret had changed since they had left First Hill. In the four years since then, her hair had dulled and spidery veins of gray crept through the dark strands. It always made Flame sad to look at her, sad and guilty and angry; why couldn't her mother be pretty and gay and full of life, so Flame wouldn't have to spend one minute worrying about her? It wasn't fair.

"We'll miss the four-fifteen if we don't start soon. You know how slow pa walks."

"Flame, I know you have strong feelings for him."

Flame looked past her mother at the smooth dimples in the sand where the clams were.

Margaret touched her daughter's arm. "I'm saying you're not a kid anymore. You're a grown woman. It's time you gave some thought to your future."

"That's not what you mean and you know it." Flame turned away and started walking up the beach, picking her way sullenly over the sharp remains of butter clams.

Margaret reacted coldly and more quickly than Flame imagined she could. She caught up with her daughter and with one hand slapped her hard across the face.

Flame staggered backward, a bright streak of red flaming across her cheek.

"We may not live in a fancy house on First Hill anymore. Your mother may clean other people's toilets now to put bread in your mouth, but you *will* show some respect. Is that clear?"

Flame was close to tears. She nodded mutely.

"I'll be as plain as I can with the truth, Flame. Your father would want me to. Cahill is after only one thing."

"He is not!" Her mother was being too unfair. The truth hurt more than the accusation. Cahill had never even kissed her.

"You're not the same kind anymore. Tell me this. When the Blues have those fancy parties that get written up in the society column of the *Post-Intelligencer*, has he ever invited you as his guest?"

"My shift at the factory and with school and all—" Flame

23

faltered. Her mother had hit a nerve, and she knew it. It had been a private hurt of Flame's—something that she had always told herself she would ask Cahill about when the time came. But when things were bad between them, she didn't have the courage, and when things were good, it didn't matter. It stung, having her mother see it too. Why *didn't* he ask her to his house anymore?

"I'm the busy one." Flame wanted to sound convincing. "He kind of works his schedule around me."

Margaret put down the pail and squeezed Flame's hand. It was cold in the wind. "This is going to hurt and I'll be quick about it."

No no please no. She was eleven again and her mother was advancing toward the pond.

"Last Saturday night, I was working a progressive dinner." Her mother's voice was breathless in the wind. "You weren't working Saturday night, were you?"

"You know I had the day shift."

"The dessert course was at August Chilberg's estate. They served an elegant baked alaska. I was cutting into it, gently, so the meringue wouldn't stick, and happened to hear Mrs. Chilberg talking about a beau of her daughter's. Remember Cynthia? She starts at the university in the fall. She's lovely, Flame: small and blond with ivory-colored skin. Mrs. Chilberg was talking on and on about this wonderful young man who was courting her daughter. We were in the sitting room, and those wide double doors leading to the hallway were open, so we could see the light from the Tiffany lamps reflecting on the polished wood of the floors—"

"I don't see what this—"

"I was cutting the meringue, and Mrs. Chilberg was talking and then she exclaimed, 'Why, there they go now! They've been to the theater.' I glanced up and saw them passing in the hallway. They were a handsome couple, Flame. Two blond heads."

"It couldn't have been!"

"It *was* Cahill. I looked up and saw him, and as I was looking, he happened to incline his head slightly, and he stared into the sitting room. Our eyes met. He stared at me for a full minute and then nodded his head as if saluting me. Then Cynthia put her hand possessively on his arm, and they walked out of sight down the hallway."

The waves were gusting on the water and Flame's father was a blank gray outline against the rocks. Flame felt cold and calm and curiously numb. She stumbled and Margaret caught her.

"If we hurry we can still catch the four-fifteen," was all she said.

She didn't see him for four months, and when she did it was by accident.

The Tremain Building, where she worked nights and on weekends, was a woman's clothing factory located in the first block south of Yesler Way on First Avenue. Flame walked to work rather than spend a nickel on the streetcar. It was a miserable sleety day in January, the kind that makes you think you must have made up the whole idea of summer. The snow was gray from the soot of chimneys and factory smoke. Flame walked quickly through the slush, with her head down. She heard the carriage before she saw it.

"I thought it was you." He sounded genuinely glad to see her. He was wearing a beaver top hat and greatcoat. His companion peered around his face, and Flame recognized Cynthia Chilberg. Cynthia looked at her indifferently and turned away.

"We've got room. Can we give you a lift?"

"No, thank you." The horse stamped its hooves in the slush and shook its neck until the bells on the harness jingled.

"It's no trouble."

"I'm fine. Thank you." She began walking but Cahill was unwilling to let her go. The carriage moved along beside her.

"I haven't seen you lately."

"Yes. Well . . . I've been working."

"How's your mother?"

"Fine."

"And your father? Is he well?"

"They're fine," Flame said impatiently. "Everybody's fine." She walked faster and turned up the stairs. "This is where I work."

"May I call on you sometime?" The question hung behind her in the frosty air. Flame turned around slowly.

"My parents would be happy to see you."

"And you?" He said it lightly but his eyes were serious. Behind him Cynthia shifted in the seat and arranged her hair with one pale glove.

"I'm late," Flame said, and fled up the stairs.

A week later he showed up in time for dinner.

"Always room for one more," said Mrs. Atwood, who always had an eye for possibilities. She seated Cahill between her and Flame at dinner and kept the other boarders at the table afterward so the young couple could have a few minutes alone in the parlor.

They were awkward with each other at first until Cahill took her hand and said simply, "I've missed you. More than I can say."

"What about Cynthia."

"I'm not seeing her anymore, Flame. I haven't since the night I saw you."

Something inexplicably sweet surged up in Flame, and for a moment she thought she would cry. There was something solemn and grand about the moment, sitting stiffly side by side on the horsehair sofa and watching the snow shimmer in the lights outside the leaded window.

"I'm going to marry you, Flame."

It was almost as if he hadn't said it at all, but the words had simply appeared in her mind, clear and true. They had always known it would be this way.

There had never been anyone else for either of them, and the months Cahill had spent with Cynthia fell away and were forgotten as they sat on the borrowed sofa and held each other's hands.

The moment lasted only for a short while, if you measure time in things of substance—tables, chairs, the doilies on the arms of the sofa where they sat; but it lasted a long time in their hearts. It seemed to them both that they had answered something in themselves, and that everything else from that point forward would be easier and less dramatic, now that they were no longer searching for the essential element that would give their lives meaning.

They were still untried by love and things were still clearly black and white, but within that narrow corridor of experience, they loved each other completely and wanted nothing more than to give the other the best and sweetest of themselves.

Cahill took her face in his hands and kissed her. She closed her eyes and leaned up to him. The hairpins glinted in the firelight and her hair had the burnished gloss of rich mahogany.

He broke away and stared at her. Her eyes were tightly closed and the lashes lay in tawny curls on her cheeks. She was still bending toward him, her mouth poised in a kiss.

"Dearest, my dearest Flame." He caressed her face until the skin itself seemed to grow luminous under his touch. When touching was no longer enough, he bent his lips to hers and kissed her again. The warmth of his lips shocked her and she pulled away, unable to breathe.

"Dearest." He touched her cheek. She looked up at him, trusting him.

"I love you, Flame."

"I love you, too."

He stroked her hair and his fingers found a pin. He pulled it out and a section of her hair tumbled down.

"Cahill!" She pulled away in alarm.

"It's all right, it's all right," he murmured over and over. He took out the other pins and her hair cascaded down her back. Gently he smoothed out a snarl as she watched him, her eyes huge olive disks.

Her breath came out in a sob and at first he thought she was crying, but then he realized it was from trying to contain all the things she was feeling.

It ignited something in him. With a groan, he pressed her against him.

"Cahill, we mustn't—"

He kissed her throat, her neck, her cheek.

Across the room, next to a box of chestnuts, the door burst open.

It was Margaret. They sprang apart as she leaped across the

shabby carpet, fury blazing in her eyes. "I knew it!"

"Mrs. Ryan," Cahill stammered.

"It's not what you think, mother." Flame's face was bright red in the tumble of hair.

"It's exactly what I think. It's what I've thought all along."

"He's going to marry me." Flame said it with the confidence of a woman in love.

A silence, and then Margaret turned to Cahill, her fists balled. "Get out of here," she hissed, advancing.

"Mother—I said—"

"I heard what you said. *Get out of here!*" She lunged at Cahill.

"Mrs. Ryan, I don't understand." He looked genuinely confused.

"You understand perfectly. Stay away from my daughter, Cahill. Stay away. I won't have her tampered with. Understand?"

"Tampered with? I'm going to make Flame my wife." He stood his ground.

"Get out of here before I call the police!" she shrilled. "You might live on First Hill, but you're nothing but"—she punctuated the last by pushing him hard on the chest—"but a *bastard.*"

His face paled. Slowly, deliberately, he reached for his topcoat and hat. "Flame, I will call on you tomorrow." He tipped his hat. "Mrs. Ryan." He strode out the door without looking back.

Flame ran after him and watched him leave, and then she turned coldly back to her mother. "You had no right," she began.

"I had *every* right. He's a bounder, Flame. I told you that months ago. If I hadn't come in—"

"If you hadn't come in, what? I'm a grown woman, mother. You said so yourself."

"I thought you had some pride. Some sense."

"Did you have much sense when you met father?" Flame said it quietly, but the fight went out of her mother, and her shoulders sagged.

"I just fear for you!" Margaret mourned. "I want things to

go well for you, Flame. That's all."

Flame touched her mother gently. "He loves me, ma. And I love him."

The two women linked arms and watched the snow fall. Finally Margaret said self-consciously, "Is there anything you need to know? Young people nowadays . . ."

Her mother's awkwardness was touching. "I swam naked with him once or twice, as I recall."

"That's right." The relief on her mother's face was obvious, and stopped Flame from saying anything else. Actually she knew very little. Of course she knew about the anatomy of a male. The mystery was what a soft and spongy tube had to do with her neat and compact body. Did they work it in slowly, with their fingers? And more to the point, where exactly did they work it in? She was burning to ask her mother about it, but it was clear her mother was burning to pretend the subject didn't exist. She sighed. Life was so dreadfully complex.

She thought tenderly of Cahill, walking through the snow on this night, and wondered what he was thinking. For one heart-stopping moment a terrible picture flashed into her mind—Cahill and Cynthia embracing one another. Cynthia knowing what to do. But the picture immediately faded. Instinctively Flame knew Cahill was as inexperienced as she.

They would learn together, she supposed; awkwardly, but with great gentleness, the way lovers have always learned.

He was to think of it time and again through his life and wonder what different paths their lives would have taken had Margaret not interrupted things that evening in the parlor. As it was, sex, that triumphant, mystical joining of flesh, assumed tremendous significance in his mind. He wanted Flame worse than he had ever dreamed he could want a woman. At the same time he felt a responsibility toward her. It was confusing and alarming.

Cahill and Flame were alone often after that. He planned it that way to test himself. Little things tormented him. The pulse beating in her throat electrified him; her fragrance, the mystery of her sex, absorbed him.

The more he grew to want her, the more resolutely he

29

resisted her. He wanted only to spend the rest of his life in her arms. But he had to be worthy first.

His future had been determined at birth: his parents had decided that if their child were male, they could wish no greater honor for him than to follow his father into medicine.

And Cahill wanted to be a doctor. But he wanted to *win* Flame's hand, to wear her scarf into battle like some medieval knight and to be smothered at the end in flowers.

Barring that, he would settle for lugging a great big balooga animal to her door and grunting, "Meat, woman."

He was overwhelmed by her loveliness and fragility and then her hand would steal into his and he would feel the hot, surging power of his blood roaring in his ears and want only to tip her over backwards and nail her to the ground with his member.

If he had been less ethical, they would have married right away. Instead, they decided on a late August wedding. Cahill had chosen August because it sounded far enough away for him to make something of himself.

In February, the Blues hosted a lovely little engagement party for the couple. Everyone was happy and very gay. Mrs. Atwood from the boardinghouse was there, and two women from the clothing factory where Flame worked. Margaret had asked her employers, who came with an embroidered linen tablecloth as a gift. Tom asked no one.

The Blues were gracious and warm and overlooked the way Tom Ryan was there one moment and gone the next, as if the last streetcar inside his mind had left suddenly for parts unknown.

The high point of the evening was Cahill's gift to Flame. It was a simple gold locket, with delicate filigree embracing two hearts. The locket opened and Cahill had inserted a photograph which had been miniaturized in a new process. Cahill and Flame stared back at the camera, so tiny the curls framing her face were only specks on the paper, but their smiles were clear and radiant. Cahill had engraved their initials on the hearts. As he slipped the necklace around her neck, a hush fell over the little gathering.

"With this necklace, I swear my love to you." Cahill fastened the clasp on the chain and, with his hands on Flame's shoulders, looked around the familiar room for the faces of his parents. His mother was struggling not to cry, and his father was touching her arm in a gentle way. Margaret had moved closer to her husband. Cahill felt a deep abiding sweetness for the people in that room; those known intimately like his parents and the Ryans, and those just met, and for all lovers who had stuck by each other through the glory and pain. He looked at Flame standing next to him and thought again how right it felt to stand this way with her in front of witnesses. He thought of the children in their future, and how he wanted to raise them and raise them up.

His father held up his glass and said, "To August." And the others in the room raised their glasses high and repeated, "To August." Flame smiled, but a cold wind blew through Cahill and for a moment he felt trapped. How could he hope to prove himself to her before August? What was grand enough to win her respect?

And what was grand enough to win his?

If the *Portland* hadn't come steaming into Seattle loaded with two tons of gold from the Klondike in late July, Cahill would have gone looking for it anyway. He needed the gold strike every bit as much as the men living on the beach in shacks needed it. It was the first good news since the panic of '93 and the perfect excuse to leave.

Cahill made the best of it.

They were standing on the wharf, a small blurred island in a huge roiling sea of people. In the two days since the *Portland* had docked, stalls along the wharf had sprung up, and every boat that was the slightest bit seaworthy had been pressed into service. The water was thick with them. On the side of one small boat hung a gaily colored sign: Klondike or Bust.

The noise was deafening: horses screamed as they were shoved into cramped stalls below deck on the larger steamers, cattle squalled, and the boats groaned and clanked with the eager noises boats make in the water when they're almost loaded and a trip is in the works. Scalpers were hawking passage tickets at double the usual rate, and men were fighting each other for a place in line to buy them.

31

"You've packed your woolens." He nodded. "And your medicine kit." She was trying hard not to cry.

He felt a sudden stab of guilt. "Let's get married right now," he said impulsively. "Find a justice of the peace. Bet there are lots of them in this crowd." He was probably right, Flame thought. The city had gone wild with gold fever. Half the streetcar attendants quit their jobs on the spot when they heard the news. Even the mayor, W. D. Woods, resigned to head north in the middle of a speech urging people to stay. The instant he spoke he regretted it. What if she insisted he give up the trip?

Flame studied his face. Since he had asked her to marry him, she had harbored the uneasy feeling that it would never happen, at least not the way they had planned. She almost said, "Yes, let's get married now. Make it official."

But being married wouldn't keep him there, and she sensed he would grow to hate her if she tried. "We're already married in our hearts," she said. "I'll wait."

Cahill turned his face away so she couldn't see the tremendous relief. His parents spotted them and waved. Cahill waved back. "You know how my father is," he said. "He'd never let us live simply, and I'd always wonder if I could have—"

Flame touched his arm. "I understand."

The lie satisfied her. The truth was something he kept even from himself.

He was tired of her.

Tired of her roughened hands and serious small face; of being strong and saying the right thing. He loved her, all right; sometimes he felt consumed by love. Perhaps delaying the marriage had dulled the anticipation; perhaps he had dreamed too often of their wedding night, lying in his bed in sick wonder at his need; perhaps he loved her too much. Whatever it was, for months now there had been the nagging feeling that he could step out of his life, and things would march merrily on as before, that it would be so damned predictable.

If he stayed, he would finish school at the University of Washington, go to Cornell Medical School, and enter practice with his father. At twenty-five, he would branch out. Flame would bear children and her body would swell until the girl in front of him was no longer recognizable. And somehow, somewhere along the line, he would smother his dreams, bury them so completely that when his own son, who was still only a seed in his groin, was old enough to rave and dream and plan, he would steady the shovel as the dream was buried.

He guessed it was the love that had done him in. Of course he would marry her; he only wanted to do one splendid thing first.

"I'll write," he promised.

Her dark green eyes clouded with tears. He felt another pang of guilt at not feeling anything else.

Her face contorted and she thrust something into his hand. It was the locket.

"Flame!" He was shocked.

"Keep this for me."

"I can't do that! It's yours. It belongs around your neck where I put it." She was making him uneasy. It was one thing to go marching off on the highroad to the unknown, but a person always liked to have familiar landmarks behind him, so he could find his way home. He didn't like to think of her alone in Seattle without the necklace around her neck, like a charm warding off evil.

She stretched her hands up and put it around his neck. "You'll need it more than I," she whispered. Her words were almost lost in the sharp cry of a passing news vendor. "It will remind you of our love."

"I'll never forget that!" he said heatedly and pressed her to him.

And then there really was no time left. He wanted to say all the things he hadn't, but his parents were standing there now, so in the end, he held Flame's hand and said lamely, "You know what I'm feeling."

Something, almost a pain, shot across her face, as if she knew him better than he suspected and knew exactly what he was thinking.

Later he would think it was the sun in her eyes.

Four

He saw her right away.

She was young, small and very foreign, wearing an outrageous dress slashed down to her navel. She was standing on her trunk, peering raptly at a photographer crouched in front of her, oblivious to the thunderstruck way the men were gazing at her nipples, both of which were clearly visible through the netting holding her dress together.

She would never be mistaken for somebody's kid sister.

Cahill worked his way through the crowd to get a better look. The *Solid Gold Idea* was groaning loudly with its heavy cargo and leaving land so slowly, Cahill could still make out a row of weeping female faces on the shore. Luckily, they couldn't see what was waiting for their men on deck. He made his way through the crowds to get closer to her.

A black mole crawled high across her left cheek. Silky brown tendrils wisped around her face, framing the severe topknot on her head. Her skin shone as if she had recently been poured out of hot wax. But the best part was her expression. No lively intelligence danced across her features, marring the excellence of her function. She had been created only for this: to be a vessel, a container. As if agreeing with him, a small hand unconsciously strayed across her bosom, touching herself. A man next to Cahill dropped to his knees and groaned, "Oh, God in Heaven! Let it be me, Lord, let it be me!"

But she had eyes only for Cahill.

She reached out and touched his fair hair.

"You like?" he said. He had no plan in mind, and certainly no thought of betraying his vows, but he felt a wonderful sense of buoyancy, as if anything were suddenly possible.

"*Oui.* I like." Her voice was throaty and low. She smiled and

34

slowly leaned into him until her breasts sank across his face. He wanted to smother her to death. She smelled scented and clean and female.

"You like?" She asked it slowly, mockingly.

"Yes." His voice was high, as if it were taking that opportunity to change again, and doing it in public so he couldn't stop it.

She smiled and curled her arms around his neck. "I think we are going to be—*comment est-ce que çela se dit?*—friends. We will be friends."

Before the first night was over, they were.

Her name was Nelly and she had come from Belgium. Her passage had been paid. One way.

Cahill carried the trunk and followed her through the narrow passageway that twisted back into the bowels of the boat. The steamer could comfortably carry fifty passengers; there were 103 men, nine horses and six women of suspect virtue on board when it pulled anchor. Cahill shifted the trunk and lifted it over the hallway floor, littered with female paraphernalia.

Nelly had a room of her own. The names of an ex-governor and a general were on the waiting list for a single room, only slightly ahead of Cahill's name. His opinion of her changed. "Where do you want this?" It was a stupid question and Cahill knew it. The room was the smallest he had ever seen, no wider than a double bed. It was completely filled with clothes. He could see now why she was wearing this dress; it covered almost twice as much territory as the others. He was fascinated and excited by her. The boys in common school had always bragged about whoring around on Yesler's Wharf. Cahill had lied sometimes and claimed to have gone there too. His friends had always said terrible things about the women and wonderful things about themselves. Cahill had never dreamed a whore could look like Nelly.

She leaned against the wall and stroked the satin ribbon holding the dresses. "You like?" It seemed to be her favorite English expression, probably because it generated such enthusiastic responses.

Cahill was feeling uneasy and tried vainly to conjure up

Flame's face. Up until now he could defend his actions: he was simply aiding a woman in need by carrying the trunk for her. He knew he should turn around right now and leave; he hadn't even found his own bunk yet. He tried to remember all the reasons why he was going north—his longing to turn his hand to something fine, to toughen himself. He stuck his hands in his pocket. "Guess I'll see you sometime. The boat's small."

Nelly smiled and drooped over the trunk, her fanny in the air. She wrestled with the latches and the lid flew up. Then she smoothed out the most delicate, provocative female undergarment Cahill had ever seen.

He could see the far wall through the place where the crotch and bosom should have been.

"A girl needs a few pretties," she whispered.

Cahill knew he was lost.

She was on her back, her arms stretched lazily over her head, smiling at him. Her breasts were bigger than they had looked in the dress, the nipples large and faintly brown. The hair between her legs curved into a perfect heart. He wanted to ask her if it just grew that way, but then she might guess that he had never seen a woman naked; so he only looked at her and smiled stupidly from his vantage point on the edge of the bed. He was still in his undergarments; the clothing gave him a small surge of confidence.

"It is—*comment est-ce que çela se dit?*—the number one time for you, *oui?*"

The confidence bolted out the door and made it. Startled, he looked at her face and began to deny it, but she pulled him down on top of her and murmured, "*Merveilleux!* You have come to the right place."

Cahill had made a decision in those first delirious moments: he would not think about his life in Seattle again until the boat reached Dyea. In Dyea he would contemplate his future and weigh his past; but for now, he was traveling through a separate, unexplored country, traveling light.

She was kissing him deeply, luxuriously, squeezing his buttocks, and suddenly—Cahill was never quite sure how—he

36

was on the bottom and she was straddling him, pink flesh pouting between soft lips. She rolled down his drawers and inspected him, the way a cobbler would inspect a new bench.

"*Parfait*," she breathed. She trailed her fingers lightly along the inside of his thigh, and Cahill was afraid he might spurt onto the ceiling. Frantically he wrapped his hands around her and pulled her down on top of him, ramming his way up inside her.

The warm slippery flesh shocked and excited him. His penis tensed, and with a small cry he came at once.

Cahill thought about marrying her. Nelly thought about dinner.

She patted his cheek in a friendly way and grinned. "Welcome to the world, my friend. *On ne fait pas d' omelette sans casser d' oeufs.* Do you have a name?"

"Cahill Blue," he said. Maybe he wouldn't marry her after all. It depended.

"Well, my friend, Cahill Blue," she murmured, expertly detaching herself from him and getting off the bed. "Let's get some food."

She hummed a little tune as she washed herself. Cahill leaned on his elbow and watched her. He had fornicated. He had gone up inside a woman and come. It had been much easier than he had thought.

"How was I really?" he asked conversationally. She had one foot balanced on the bed and was squirting water up herself with a rubber tube. Cahill thought her breasts looked a little poochy, but it could have been the angle. Perhaps he'd pay a visit to those other ladies aboard the *Solid Gold Idea.* Not much privacy behind the curtain, but a good change of pace.

"How were you really?" Nelly looked at him and slipped out the rubber tube. Cahill noticed she was leaking slightly. "The truth?"

"Well, yes." She was beginning to get on his nerves.

"You know nothing about women," she said flatly. "But it's a long way to Dyea."

Cahill forgot about the women in the passageway. He forgot about feeling in charge. Horrified, he realized suddenly she could deny him access ever again. Never to see that perfectly shaped heart cracking into a pick vertical slit, those ~~magnificent breasts swelling in the air~~—

It was unthinkable.

"Teach me," he said humbly. "I'll do anything you ask."

It took ten days to make a thousand miles of sea. It took almost that long to tire Cahill out. Outside, the boat wound its way through fjords and inlets, boxed in by glaciers and wild, tangled mountains, heading always north. Inside the room, Cahill followed the curves of her fingers, the hollows of her armpits, the mystery of the tangled country between her legs. Every road led south.

For years Cahill had dreamed this dream. In his sweaty celibate bed, listening for the even sounds of his parents sleeping in the next room, he had furiously manipulated his organ. The woman seldom had a face, but she would open her legs or her mouth or any other orifice he could think of—once he had tried an ear, but that seemed to slow the dream down—and let him in. At that point, he would come in huge, silent spasms, staining his drawers or his towel or whatever was handy. The whole thing was disgusting. He knew that. He just couldn't help himself. So he limped along, cursing the deformity of his almost constantly rigid erection, vowing he could never tell anyone. Ever.

And then along came Nelly.

They used his fantasies as a starting point. Before the week was over, he had swum so far out to sea, the old dream was only a small landmark on a distant shore.

Her coming took him completely by surprise the first time. He had never considered that women could. Her coming again, right afterwards, caught her by surprise. She usually did that only when she was alone or with a particularly good customer. Certainly never with inexperienced boys.

But there was something about Cahill's eager willingness to please, to learn, that charmed her. They were probably only a year apart in age, but they were separated by centuries of experience; she was not only Nelly, but Jezebel, there since the beginning of time, teacher of the uninitiated. Cahill took the crash course and graduated with honors.

38

They spent hours joined together, in ways Cahill had never considered, his organ thrust down her throat, his mouth kissing deeply her intimate parts. It became a game. They would madden each other into a frenzy, and the first one to lose control, to come, would lose. The loser had to do whatever the other one ordered.

As the week progressed, the orders grew more lurid and erotic. They fed on each other, going farther and farther until the only thing left, the only thing that mattered to Cahill, was the wet slit between her limbs, and her tongue and breasts and hands. He wasn't himself at all. Dimly he knew that, but it didn't seem to matter. Once he told himself to pull things together and get out of that room, but before he could actually leave, Nelly had pulled him over to her and it had started all over again.

They were standing on the main deck, Cahill behind her, his hands hidden in the folds of her cape, both of them leaning over the railing. Behind them passengers played cards and talked. To the photographer watching them, they looked like lovers silently absorbed in watching the fjords. Nelly was wearing a cape with a stiff row of venetian lace on the collar. The cape buttoned down the front and fell to within an inch of the hem of her long matching brown velvet skirt. They didn't talk, but occasionally they shifted their weight and pressed against each other with the total concentration lovers reserve for one another. Sometimes the boat would rise and settle going over a swell, and the couple would shudder in unison, as if they were joined together in some secret fashion. The woman's lips were parted in the wind and her color was unusually high. The man's eyes were closed and his face wore an expression of intense pain. Under the cape his hands seemed to be moving, but that was only speculation; the folds of the cape enveloped them both. After a while their postures became more rigidly defined; hers was softer, the expression slack, while the man seemed to be pushing himself against her with a steady, fierce abandon, almost as if—the photographer shook his head. He had been working with chemicals too long. Still, there was an attitude about the two of them that was pleaning to the eye.

~~Quickly he set up his equipment.~~

The man on the deck clamped himself against the woman and with a small cry buried his head in her neck. She arched her back away from him, her lower torso still braced against his body. She appeared to be short of breath. A low moan escaped. She slumped forward and the man appeared to catch her fall. They rested quietly, his face on her cheek, their breathing uneven.

"Smile!" With a bang, in a great cloud of smoke, the photographer took their picture.

July 26, 1897

Dear mother and father,

This was a difficult letter to write; the motion of the ship is considerable and seems to have affected my ability to hold a pen. I do want you to know that I am well, although you would hardly recognize me. The old Cahill has fallen by the wayside; the new Cahill is emerging as a stouter fellow who sees what he wants and goes after it. An admirable trait, when coupled with an awareness of God's other creatures, which I am developing as well. I have spent a good deal of my time in bed, although I have been seldom idle; there has been much here to occupy my mind. Now that I have developed a certain seaworthiness, I am truly feeling fine. Yesterday I spent an hour on deck; the most exhilarating hour of my life. The scenery was magnificent: hills and valleys that defy description, glaciers with purple gashes in them. But you really would have to be here, I'm afraid.

I will post this in Dyea, although I'll wager it won't be in your dear hands before the snow flies.

My love to you all.

Your dutiful son,

Cahill

They were drowsing together. She was stroking his chest, running her hand lightly over the pale mat of hair between his nipples. She stopped at his neck, fingering lightly the hearts.

"F.R. plus C.B.," she read haltingly, from her upside-down angle on his chest. "How quaint. Two hearts."

"Knock it off, Nelly," Cahill said. He'd forgotten about the necklace. He looked around suddenly and saw the room and himself for the first time, as if he were emerging from a drugged dream. For this woman he had sacrificed his ideals? Everything he saw was a sick confirmation of his own unworthiness. This was all he deserved! An ill-smelling whore with unkempt hair and stained clothing. What had he been thinking? He pulled himself off the bed and leaned his head against the nicked metal bureau.

"Oh, an attack of the conscience," Nelly said archly. "What a surprise." She reached for the hairbrush, tilting her head upside down. "And how beastly dull."

"Who do you think you are?" His voice was harsher than he had intended, but he wanted to sting her, shake her until she took the words back, until she told him he was really a good boy after all and hadn't done anything bad. "You're a slut. A whore. A crack. A place where men come and go. That's it. That's all there is to Nelly. You don't even have a last name."

The hairbrush flashed through the curtain of brown hair, slowed and stopped. When she tossed her head back up, she was smiling. Cahill noticed something else. She was speaking perfect English. Again the thought flickered through his mind. She's not exactly what she seems.

"I am a whore," Nelly said. "And a good one. No apologies made. The real question is, who do you think *you* are, Cahill Blue? Back home, waiting on the shore, is some poor, virginal girl. Let me guess. You grew up with her and you both promised to be true until the gates of heaven opened up. The stupid little fool—"

"Stop it," he said. His voice was murderous and low. "Don't talk about Flame that way—"

"*Flame,*" Nelly said, curling her tongue around the word. "Nice, hot name. Think about what someone named Flame would be doing right this very minute. Especially if she knew

41

how faithfully her betrothed has held to his vows."

Cahill was coming slowly toward her.

"You couldn't wait to stick it in the first hole you could find," she said lightly. "And you'll spend the rest of your life denying it, justifying it, and looking for it all over again. All the time you'll be insisting your sweet, uninventive Flame cleave only to you."

He was standing over her, his face white and quivering.

"I know what you are, Cahill Blue. And you make me sick to my stomach."

He hit her hard in the face with the flat of his hand. Her hand raked up as if she were trying to scratch his face, and then she flew backwards onto the bed, taking down the rack of dresses with her. She lay there, her fists clenched, curved away from him in a gay, exotic sea of colors.

"Get out of here," she said in a low, perfectly controlled voice. "Don't bother me. Ever again. Or I'll have you killed."

The next day the boat landed in Dyea. He caught a glimpse of her surrounded by a knot of men. She was laughing.

Then she seemed to disappear and Cahill thought, Good riddance to bad rubbish. But he carried his shame like a heavy stone, and every time he thought of Flame, the stone grew heavier. He pushed Nelly out of his mind, deciding she wasn't worthy of *any* feelings, even horror and disgust. For almost a week he forgot about her, and by then it was too late.

He was high up near Chilkoot Pass, resting at the Scales, when he reached up and realized the necklace was gone.

Five

Flame believed in magic, and the shabby keeper of rabbits-in-hats and dreams-come-true rewarded her loyalty once a year. Amazing things always happened on her birthday. She could set her clock by it. The year Cahill left, Flame set her clock an hour early, to give magic a little margin for error.

She had tried to be very brave when Cahill left, but as the weeks dragged on with no word from him, keeping her spirits up ceased to be a challenge and became a dreary duty.

On the morning of her seventeenth birthday, she rose early, heel-and-toeing it over the hot floor. It rained through July and the first week in August before stopping abruptly. Now three weeks had gone by.

The heat burned off the fog; it sucked the juice out of the elms and crisped the feathers of the gulls.

From her window, Second Avenue was empty except for a milkman perched on the front of a spring wagon, his horse clopping placidly down the middle of the brick street. Seeing him reminded Flame of her own day—twelve hours at the Tremain factory, stitching sleeves. But at least she had these early morning hours, and she intended to make the most of them. She crept into the bathroom and turned on the gas light, staring intently at herself in the mirror.

She was pretty, she supposed. But her face was more angular than the ones that stared from the pages of the magazines sold on the corner. Everything about her was peculiar: her eyes were a ripe green color, like very old cheese, and her hair was just red enough to make wearing feminine yellows and pinks a disaster. She looked best in male colors—strong burgundies, rich browns. And her eyebrows were thick and straight across—not growing *together*, thank God, or she really *would*

43

have to spend the rest of her ~~life indoors hiding,~~ but straight ~~across, all the~~ same. She ran cold water in the sink and thought about whether she wanted to heat water. No, a sponge bath would work. Today was her birthday and she had important things to do.

She sat on the steps of the dormitory and felt the welcome coolness of the concrete under her. Windows jerked up and doors slammed, and students hurled good-natured insults at each other. She was trying to keep things in perspective. After all, it was still very early in the morning. She had been so sure, was the thing. Cahill had lived in the dormitory the year before he left and commuted to the new University of Washington campus north of Portage Bay. For a year he had slept in a single bed upstairs on the third floor and studied medicine far into the night. Surely something of him had to be left behind, in the walls, in the hallway, in the scattering of dust motes in the stifling room where they studied. Something. Flame wasn't sure what she expected to find. She only knew she hungered for a tangible reminder of his presence and had too much pride to visit his parents. So she had come here. *Crumbs*, she thought. *Throw me a birthday crumb.* She shifted her weight and clasped her hands. Nothing came to her. No magic appeared in top hat and tails, singing her song. It was only a very old building on a spacious and shady street.

Students were beginning to saunter out the door and down the steps. A few of them Flame recognized. They looked at her curiously as they stepped around her. A fellow from Cahill's biology class advanced and said, "Has he struck it rich yet?"

Flame looked into his soft doe eyes and said with a cheerfulness she didn't feel, "Any minute now."

The young man nodded shyly and joined a group of students waiting for the streetcar. Flame felt an impulse to run after him. She yearned to talk about anything—even the weather. It had been weeks—longer, since the day Cahill had left—since she had spoken more than a few sentences to anyone. The Latona and Brooklyn streetcar clanged down the line and pulled to a stop. The students got on, the door banged closed and the streetcar started up. Flame rose stiffly to her feet.

She didn't belong here. She would never visit again.

She was too old for magic anyway.

Flame worked in a small room on the second floor of the Tremain Building. The room held fifteen stations, thirty workers and no surprises. None of the windows worked. It smelled of sweat and sickness and soured hope. In the winter the women worked in shawls and wore gloves so their fingers wouldn't stick to the sewing machines. In the summer they stripped down to their corsets and chemises. Some still wore gloves. Metal burns skin when it's hot enough.

The job was simple. They made mutton-leg sleeves out of a yard and a half of fabric. Flame and her station partner rotated duties. One week Flame cut and her partner sewed, and the next week they switched. No one stayed more than a year. After that the muscles cramped and the fingers stumbled.

They were working now on the spring line, a brand new suit look with smartly tapered blouses underneath. Flame never saw the suits, or the blouses, either, for that matter. The little mutton-leg sleeves were stacked into a cart and wheeled into the next room, where they were attached to bodices that had come from across the hall. Flame never knew what happened to them after that, and after the first week of working there, she stopped caring.

Her station partner was already working. She waited until Flame had picked up the scissors and positioned the muslin before she leaned over, taking Flame's breath away. Sweat ringed the bodice of her corset under two hugely pale arms. "I wouldn't bother with that if I was you." Her eyes crackled with malice. "Mr. Fenley wants to see you. On the double."

Mr. Fenley was an emaciated man who seemed to take great delight in bullying the women. He wore fancy two-piece suits and mutton chops and always struck Flame as looking exactly the way a vulture would if it wore shoes and could talk. Flame hurriedly pushed herself away from the station and slowly climbed the stairs leading to his office on the third floor. In her mind she reviewed her work: she was fast and quiet and prompt. *Prompt.* Everyone was there in place ahead of her today. Her feet turned leaden. That had to be it. She was late this morning and he was going to fire her. ~~She raised her fist to the door, hesitated~~ and rapped sharply.

The door burst open and Mr. Fenley was standing there. "Well, come in, come in. I don't have all day."

She felt sick to her stomach and wondered how she could tell her mother. They needed the money.

He closed the door behind her and then magic jumped out from behind the door and chortled *SURPRISE!*

Seated across the table from Mr. Fenley was an old man with twinkly eyes and round cherub's cheeks. He was wearing a black top hat and tails.

He held out his hand and Flame shook it. It was dry, like fall leaves. "Legerdemain is my name, transformation is my game. You come highly recommended."

"For what?"

"For what? My dear girl, it's all here. All of it. The hours and benefits—yes, yes, there *will* be benefits, you can rest assured of *that*—and bonuses. All of it. Sign here. *Tempus fugit.*"

He rattled his finger against the bottom line and Flame found her fingers moving a pen across the page, leaving her signature behind.

The old man ripped the sheet back, squinted at it once, clucked approvingly and dived into his pocket. "You'll need the address. Mr. Fenley here will have barely enough time to square up with you before you leave." He wiggled his fingers in the air.

"Let's see. Never missed a day, of course, seven days a week. Produced, on the average, four more sleeves per day than the others, and the raise promised after seven months never materialized. That comes to—" his fingers danced across the air. "Why yes. Exactly fourteen dollars and thirty cents. Plus last month's salary, for a grand total of—bless my stars! Twenty-five big ones!" He sat back in his chair and beamed.

Even Mr. Fenley seemed to be beaming, seemed to be unable to stop beaming, although Flame couldn't imagine what in the world he had to beam about.

He cranked the dials on his wall safe and carefully counted out an impressive stack of ones. "Good luck to you," Mr. Fenley said as he handed her the money, "good *good* luck!"

He pumped her hand up and down.

Mr. Legerdemain took her arm and moved her through the open door and down the steps. "Run along now," he said, running along beside her.

"Who are you?"

"Adam's uncle." He sounded surprised. "Bigger job than Adam's rib, the way he carries on." He veered to the left on the second floor and she stared after him.

She sprinted down the steps and out the door. "First Hill," she told the first driver she could find. "And make it snappy."

The sickled lawn went on forever, a rolling lake of brown grass crested by small, white, dead flowers. The house squatted like a heavy-lidded toad in the middle of it. The driver looked over his shoulder and stared at his passenger, taking in the frayed cuffs and sensible skirt. "Sure you have the right address?" he asked kindly.

Flame tossed her head, clambered down the side of the buggy and handed him his money. "They're expecting me," she said.

She was almost to the door when he called to her. "Miss! I could wait. Just in case." She hesitated, but she turned and knocked on the carved door instead.

"I'll be fine. Really. Quite fine."

He whacked his horse across the rump with the switch and the carriage lurched away as the door was opened by a harried, gray-haired woman. "Yes?"

"Mr. Legerdemain sent me," Flame began confidently.

"Who?"

"Short, old. A top hat. Legerdemain."

The woman scowled and tried to close the door on Flame's foot. "Never heard of him. No one here by that name."

The carriage was rattling down the road, dust billowing behind it. Flame could never catch it now. "He sent me," she said desperately. "Adam's uncle?"

The door snapped open. "You're Flame Ryan?"

"Yes," she said, relieved.

"Why didn't you say so in the first place?" The woman grabbed Flame's arm and hoisted her through the door. "You're late. Mr. Tremain's in a snit over it, and the clients will be here any moment. Lordy! but we've got work to do on you!"

They were running down the hallway. Flame had the impression of dozens of portraits hung in gilt frames on dark, shiny wallpaper, and then they burst into a room dazzling with light.

Flame blinked, and blinked again.

Adam Tremain liked his models breasty, with willowy waists and small, rounded hips. He circled the newest one, lifting her chin, pinching her skin, checking the bones. Olive green eyes slanted over high, almost Indian cheekbones. Great hair. Yards of thick, polished red mahogany. Ripe mouth. Her body—He eyed her critically. "Strip," he commanded.

"I beg your pardon," Flame stammered.

"Over there." He pointed toward a bamboo screen covering the well.

"*Sir.*" Flame drew herself up to her full height. "The job obviously has been misrepresented. I don't know who you think you are, but I insist you find me a suitable means of transportation home *at once* or I'll—"

"You'll what?" He sounded amused. "Scream? Get behind that curtain, pronto, Miss Ryan, or I'll send you away with pleasure. And as for who I am—I'm your boss. The one who hired you. The one who is going to fire you if you don't move your little behind behind that curtain right away, is that clear? Now move."

Flame lifted her chin. "Not until I know what your intentions are," she said primly.

He looked at her dumbfounded, then threw back his head and laughed. "You really are serious, aren't you? Listen, Miss Ryan. I want you for one thing and one thing only. Your body. I want to stuff your perfect little unit into perfect little clothes. Then I want to take all those wonderful parts that Queen Victoria has told us women don't have and wiggle them around a lot, looking gloriously, radiantly *grateful* to be where you are instead of nodding off in some sweatshop. My sweatshop. And then—and there's where the work part comes in—I want you to make every woman in great Seattle *know* she could look as great, as full bodied"—he looked deeply into Flame's eyes at

48

this point and she flushed—"if only she had, could only afford, one each of good old Adam Tremain's mass-produced originals. In a larger size, of course. There will be some night work, naturally. Conventions, that sort of thing. Strictly clothes. Some traveling. And as for the rest of it"—he tilted her chin up and smiled down at her—"dream away, little girl. Stranger things have happened. But you'll have to wait at the end of a very long line, I'm afraid."

He dropped her chin and said briskly, "Now. You have exactly one minute to get out of your clothes down to the corset. I'm meeting Hanson Bluwise at the train in one hour and he's going to buy the entire spring line before the day is through. He just doesn't know it yet."

Flame stood perfectly still, her mouth open. So this was where all those sleeves ended up. The room was flanked by huge gilt mirrors. Portable oak clothes racks stood in the middle of the floor.

"Let's see"—Miss Smith was consulting a list she had pulled from the pocket of her apron—"you'll need two daytime suits, one tea dress, something more sporty and clothes for evening." As she talked, she moved along a rack of clothes until she found a row of satin gowns. She squinted at Flame, muttered to herself, and pulled down a plunging apricot dress bordered with ostrich feathers along the nipped waist. "Enhances your complexion, your hair. Accentuates the bosom, but tastefully. Now, if it only fits."

Naturally, it did. Magic things always happened on her birthday.

It was the perfect job. Flame joined a stable of four other pampered, beautiful women who were paid for making the most out of what God had given them and a healthy profit for Adam Tremain. Not always in that order.

Adam had them doing shocking things in his home. Every morning they stripped down to their bloomers and chemises and waved their legs around until they ached. A man came all the way from Pioneer Square just for that.

Good bodies don't become great bodies by accident, Adam was fond of saying, as he lounged his perfect body against the door and watched. Adam never exercised. At least not during the day.

Adam Tremain was a mover. He sideslipped into Chicago at the beginning of the nineties and squirmed his way into the local Four Hundred. None of the girls seemed to know where he'd been before that. He was a promoter, a shill with a straw hat and a bag of tricks, who always knew which walnut covered the pea. Even better, it was always his pea.

But nowhere was Adam's touch clearer than in his present line of work. He wasn't presenting clothes and fabrics to prospective buyers; he was offering romance, glitter, heat. All at a quarter a yard, plus handling.

Adam didn't actually design the clothes; that smacked too much of work. He had artists copying the latest Paris styles for that, and three floors of women churning them out. He was offering style, affordable style to middle-aged matrons. Originals-for-the-masses, he called it.

He was smart enough to know the one selling point, the one thing his kind of town had over the others, was the gold rush. Part of Flame's job was escorting visitors on a guided tour of the wharf, wearing an Adam Tremain mass-produced original, naturally.

The weeks slipped by and Flame moved between two worlds, linked together only by the clothes she wore. During the day she was pampered, given extraordinary freedom. She dressed as she chose and grew accustomed to giving orders. For this she was paid a fortune—twelve dollars a week. Then she was taken to the other world, a darker one, where her father's word was law and she needed his signature to open a bank account in both their names, and his approval to withdraw a penny.

"How can you stand it?" she asked her mother one night. They could hear Tom arguing with himself in the next room. Outside, a crew was putting up Christmas decorations in the snow.

Margaret put down her mending and stared at her daughter. "I'm surprised at you, Flame Ryan. If your father had a bad fever, or fell down and broke both his legs, would you ask the same question? He's ill. He's not himself. And it's my job— *our* job as a family, Flame—to nurse him through it the best we can."

"It's not like having influenza, mother. He might never be the way he was before." She dropped to her knees in front of her mother and wrapped her arms around her legs. "Don't you see, ma? He's getting worse. Not better."

Margaret picked up her mending and said in a tight voice, "In our house we value loyalty. Loyalty, Flame, through thick and thin. Must be going out of style nowadays."

"What do you mean?" But Flame knew what she meant.

Her mother's fingers worked through the sock she was darning, spreading the yarn. "How long you going to keep holding on?"

"That's my business, I imagine," Flame said hotly.

Margaret's fingers threaded through the sock, pulling a needle. When the yarn bunched together and she smoothed it out along the mended place, she said drily, "Do you reckon five months is long enough for a letter to reach us?"

"Keep your nose out of my business!" Flame stood up, enraged.

"You can show some respect."

"I'm *tired* of showing respect." Her voice broke. "I'm tired, ma. Just plain tired." She collapsed to her knees and buried her head in her mother's lap and began to cry.

Margaret stroked her daughter's hair and said gently, "Wouldn't hurt to give yourself a little room."

"He loves me, ma," Flame said. "I know he does. And he's coming back. Like he promised." She blew her nose and got dispiritedly to her feet. "I bet there's a letter at the post office right now for me. If it wasn't so late, I could pick it up and show you. And besides, what *about* loyalty? That's exactly what I'm doing with Cahill. What you said. Being loyal."

The yarn moved through Margaret's fingers. "Loyalty works both ways."

"That'll come as news to pa." As soon as she said it, she was sorry.

The yarn stopped moving.

"Ma, I—"

"Don't ever say that again about your father." Her mother's face was pale.

51

"I'm sorry, ma. I really am. Forgive me."

Margaret looked at her silently, and Flame dropped her eyes. Suddenly the room was stifling. Flame reached for her cape.

"I need some air." She turned at the door, wanting to say something else, but nothing came to her. Her mother's hands sat quietly in her lap, the yarn forgotten. She was staring out the window, just like Flame's father in the room next door.

Outside the Salvation Army could be heard singing faintly, "Joy to the World! The Lord is come. Let earth . . . receive . . . her King . . ." The faucet gargled in the bathroom at the end of the hall.

Love, honor, obey.

The words echoed hollowly and seemed to keep time with her steps. Flame walked through the icy fog until she found herself in Pioneer Square.

Love, honor, obey.

She shifted her feet in the snow.

He hasn't written. The thought leaped in, unbidden.

Gentlemen of the jury, would you mind explaining why he has not written once, when the accused has managed to write his parents twice? I mean, it is clear the boy still has a pencil.

She ducked her head and ran through the snow, her legs moving furiously. She couldn't outrun the thought and stopped finally, panting, in front of a glass display box outside a clothing store.

"All right," Flame said out loud. A couple passing by thought she was talking to the mannequin in the case and looked at her oddly. The man put his hand protectively on the lady's arm and steered her in a wide arc around Flame. The mannequin was wearing a hideous green-and-red traveling suit—one of Adam Tremain's, Flame noted.

"He hasn't written." Saying the words out loud made them sound flat and ugly, but it made her feel better all the same. At least the dummy in the cabinet couldn't say, *I told you he was no good for you.* She seemed to be a sympathetic listener, so Flame moved closer and continued, "It could mean Cahill Blue isn't interested any longer." Terrible thought. A crowd of women shoppers were going by and Flame fell silent until they passed.

"Or it could mean he isn't interested for the *time being*." An equally terrible thought. Flame sighed. "Or perhaps the letter was washed overboard." The mannequin looked uneasy. "Or perhaps—" Flame threw up her hands. Damn. "It could mean anything at all."

She had decided to do nothing until she knew something when a carriage rattled around the corner and the decision was taken neatly right out of her hands.

What Adam Tremain wanted, he always got. One way or another. He had decided soon after employing her that he wanted Flame. She was pretty enough, but all his models were lookers. She radiated intelligence, but that was a prerequisite. The interesting thing that distinguished her from the other four women he employed was that she wasn't the least bit interested.

It was the one thing in the world he couldn't stand.

Adam Tremain knew women found him irresistible. He took it as much for granted as the cleft in his chin or the tight tilt of his buttocks. He was born knowing the formula for melting resistance. It was foolproof and laboratory tested.

The trick lay in letting them think they were making the first move.

As the years went by, Adam refined the seduction formula until it became a foolproof masterpiece.

He had met women before who hated him once they figured him out: they were usually the ones he had rebuffed; women who blatantly offered themselves up to him, and women who ignored him with such heat he could feel his thighs burning through his tapered trousers. He had even met some who lusted after him in their hearts but were wastefully loyal when it really counted, not many, but enough to recognize the type. He had never met a woman who simply, plainly wasn't interested. And then along came Flame.

He had ignored her confidently at first, certain she would come around. She didn't. His orders to her grew more distant, colder. He made her visit the factory with Miss Smith, checking fabrics, dyes and styles against orders. Tedious work. Flame loved it, asking so many questions and remembering so many answers that even Adam grudgingly had to admit she was an asset.

It was throwing everything in his life off schedule.

He decided to take matters into his own hands. He started following her. The chill of November had deepened into December before he got his first break. He had been ready to call it a night when Flame had bolted out of the door of the boardinghouse, the pain written so clearly on her face it restored his faith in God.

It couldn't be. Adam Tremain in this part of town. Flame raised her collar and crouched next to the mannequin, her back to the street. Perhaps he wouldn't recognize her. The last thing she needed now was to have to be polite.

The carriage slowed and she heard the familiar voice drawl, "If I can tear you away from such lively company, perhaps we could have some dinner." When she didn't respond, he added, "Hell's bells. I'm not proud. Bring your friend."

His house looked different at night. All the gaudily colored work areas crackling with activity were silent, like a dress museum. She let herself be led back into the rear of the house, into his own quarters. She had never seen them before. The den was clearly masculine. Bookshelves lined the walls facing a brick fireplace. He took off her cape and sat her in a huge chair as he silently built a fire. Then he poured two glasses of brandy and watched as she drank it down. He poured her another.

"Now," he said softly, lounging on a beaverskin sofa across from her, "talk."

And much to her surprise, she did.

At the end Adam raised his empty glass and toasted her silently. "A lucky man, this Cahill Blue." She ducked her head, suddenly shy.

"No, it's true," he said, swinging himself off the sofa to stand in front of the fire. "In this modern age, loyalty is as rare as hen's teeth." He paused, looking at the fire. "And just as useless." He turned back to her, smiled and said gently, "It's late. Let me take you home."

*　　*　　*

54

It started simply. Some nights she would be working late, wrapping up last-minute things. They would go to dinner or dine in the den, his butler serving them. They would discuss business.

"The factory, Flame," he said, pouring some more wine. "What do you think?"

"Honestly?"

"Of course."

She hesitated. "I *have* been thinking about it—"

"Go on."

"I think there might be a way to utilize the smaller scraps off the bolts. If the sleeves were positioned like *this*, instead of *this* way—" she was rapidly sketching it out for him, "I figure we could get another bodice out of the yardage we now use in two." She looked up expectantly. "What do you think?"

"What do I think?" He drank slowly and his cuff slid back. Small black hairs covered the back of his wrist. He put the glass down and his cuff advanced.

"Well," she said uncertainly, "if you don't think it would work, there's another—"

"In the first place, Flame Ryan, I've thought of all that. A long time ago. And secondly, don't you think you're overstepping yourself a little? As I recall, you were nothing but a sleeve girl before this job."

"I don't understand. You asked—"

"What I *asked* and what I *expected* are two separate things. You're a smart girl, Flame, I don't need to tell you that."

"I didn't realize—"

"It's all right. Just see that it doesn't happen again."

There were *some* things about him that were appealing. He was safe, for one thing. He never touched her except in perfectly neutral places. Her elbow, the theater. At first she was relieved, but as the weeks passed and Christmas drew near, she found herself staring at his arms and wondering what it would be like to melt against him. It was a dangerous thought. She didn't trust him. Some sixth sense warned her that he could snap her in two as easily as one of the cigarettes he kept in the silver case in the den—not only could, but would.

Adam liked headstrong women. He liked forcing them to submit to his will even more. If they submitted against *their* will, why, that was even better. Flame knew that. It was clear in his insistence she share personal things about herself, and in his utter refusal to share back. In the months she had known him, she had found out only that he had never married, was an only child like herself and at thirty-five was more than twice her age.

"Have you ever been in love?" she asked one night.

He stared at her intently, his dark eyes thoughtful. "Don't ask me that again," he said abruptly.

Still it wasn't unpleasant. Her bank account was growing steadily, and it gave her a source of quiet happiness. For the first time she was feeling a sense of security apart from the troubled lives of her parents. Every Friday she would deposit the money, standing in line in the polished sanctity of the bank; sometimes, when she heard her father raving during a bad night, Flame would take out the deposit book and hold it. The money was good, the benefits excellent, the clothes lovely.

And then her good fairy ran away with a gumshoe traveling salesman, leaving no forwarding address.

It happened the day before Christmas.

She hurried into the main showroom, unbuttoning her jacket as she went. Standing there, talking animatedly with Miss Smith, was a tall, striking young woman.

"Perhaps I could help," she interrupted, advancing on the pair. "Flame. Flame Ryan."

"Oh!" Miss Smith jumped and her hands flew away. "I was just telling Amy all about you."

"Indeed." Flame smiled curtly. "I didn't catch your complete name. Amy—"

"Amy Andrews."

"Would you like to see our complete line, Miss Andrews? Are you a buyer for a store?"

The woman laughed heartily. Miss Smith laughed nervously.

"Good heavens no, Flame. Amy is your replacement."

Adam sank back in his chair, his feet on his desk, enjoying

56

himself. "I don't understand," Flame stammered. "I thought you liked my work."

He smiled agreeably, reaching for his coffee. He was dressed in a brown velvet dressing gown and matching leather slippers. Flame could see all the way up his body almost to the point where it becomes clear that he was a male.

"How dare you treat me this way?" she said furiously. "If you think because we have shared times together . . . and dressed like this! Explain yourself."

He was smiling broadly now. "It was time to replace you," he said casually, inspecting his sleeve for imaginary fuzz. His eyes narrowed, and he flicked his sleeve with a fastidious finger.

"Have I done something to displease you?"

"You are willful, mistrustful and given to large bouts of egocentricity. But no, it's nothing you can fix." He crossed his hands over his flat belly.

The day before Christmas. Only a mean-spirited man would fire someone the day before Christmas. In that instant Flame saw deep inside Adam Tremain to the place where she thought something wonderful had to be buried because he guarded it so ruthlessly.

There was nothing there.

She straightened her back. "Well, if that's all, I'll get my things."

He let her get almost to the door. "Flame."

She stopped, her hand on the knob.

"Come back inside. And close the door. Yes, that's a good girl. I have a small gift for you. A token. Something to remember the time we spent together." He pointed to the corner of his desk. There was a small package, carefully wrapped in gilt foil and red ribbons. She advanced slowly and picked it up.

"What? You're not going to open it?"

"I can still catch one of the carriages bringing the other women if I hurry, Mr. Tremain."

He swung his legs off the desk. "I insist. I want you to open it. Consider it my last command."

Flame looked at the gilt box in her hands and for some

reason thought of Hattie, who delighted in surprises and would have found some saving grace even in this one. Flame opened the package. Inside was a velvet box and inside the box was a diamond ring, the largest diamond Flame had ever seen.

"Mr. Tremain," Flame stammered, "I—"

"Adam. My name is Adam."

"I can't accept this."

"Why not?"

"It's inappropriate. It has to be worth a fortune. Do you give all the woman you fire diamond rings?"

"Only the woman I want to be my wife." He swept her into his arms. "Marry me, Flame. I'm yours. We'll travel. Go to Paris. The Far East. You'll have anything you want. Servants. Clothes. Jewels. Say you'll be mine."

It was a tempting offer. They would be comfortable together; she knew that. But could she ever love him?

Adam dropped to one knee and clasped both her hands in his, barely missing an onyx figurine that stood in front of his desk. His dressing gown snagged on it and fell open.

Flame stared at his erect penis, fascinated. The pieces fell into place. Of course. It made perfect sense. All the mysteries of sex came down to this: the man got hard and the woman grew soft.

"Goodness," she blurted out, "so that's all there is to it."

It was all so awkward. Flame tried to explain, but in the end, the only thing that mattered, really, was that Adam really didn't matter. Miss Smith gave her a last month's salary, a Christmas bonus, and a motherly pat on the arm.

On the trolley she thought about her future. She had five hundred dollars saved, enough to open a small shop of her own. Hats, perhaps. She framed the words in her mind, carefully wording them so her mother would be satisfied and her father would understand. As it turned out, her father had something much more important to tell her.

He was waving a bottle in the air, toasting the ceiling when she walked in and shook out her hat.

"We have struck the motherlode!" he sang out. "We are on the road to riches, and a smooth wide path it is, missy." He cranked open the window and pushed his head out, squinting up at the snowy morning sky. "Somewhere up there, missy, is the North Star." He pointed with his bottle, one arm draped around Flame's shoulders. "And that's what we'll follow, all the way to the end of the rainbow."

"What are you talking about?"

He smiled slyly and leaned closer to her, his breath boiling the air between them. "You think I'm crazy but I'm not. Not anymore." He shook his head. "No siree. Not good ole Tom Ryan."

Flame was filled with a terrible sense of dread. "What have you done?"

He smiled and clumsily patted his pocket. "We own a deed, missy. On Fool's Creek. Gold as big as duck eggs. No, make that goose eggs. Golden goose eggs. Laying around waiting for Tom Ryan and his burlap bag." He swung his bottle out the window and yelled, "The North Star or bust!"

Flame uncurled his fingers around the bottle, then wrenched it free and said in a quiet voice, "Now, suppose you sit down and tell me exactly what you did."

His eyes followed the bottle until it rounded the bend of her skirt and disappeared. "Oh, all right," he huffed. "You sure do know how to take the pleasure right out of a situation. Must have got that from your ma." He sat down sulkily with his arms crossed and wouldn't look at her.

"I've got all day," she said finally.

"Oh, all right," he snapped. "I wanted it to be a surprise."

"Nothing's changed," she said drily.

He brightened. "I guess you're right." He clenched his pocket where the deed was, bent forward. "It's the first good thing that's happened to me, Flame. You know what my luck's been like. And now"—he fumbled out a worn folded paper— "Here. Read it for yourself."

Flame unfolded it and read in silence. "Where did you get this?"

"Down at the snooker hall. A stranger." He held up his hand. "Now, I know what you're thinking, Flame, so just hold your horses. A mutual friend introduced us. It's all been witnessed, signed, sealed and delivered."

59

"You didn't get this for free," she said stiffly. Her throat felt sore, as if she couldn't swallow.

"Well, no, not exactly," he said uneasily. "I took out a small loan. Just enough to buy the thing." He pushed his hands out, warding off her thoughts. "I'll work it off. I will."

Flame's eyes filled with tears. "Which one of your friends loaned you the money?" she whispered. "I'll hog-tie the bastard and cook him for Christmas dinner. I swear to God I will."

He laughed. "That's my girl. Somehow I knew you'd feel that way. That's why I borrowed the money from you."

Six

Juneau was the cutoff point. It had electric lights and regular business hours. Beyond that the Lynn Canal narrowed for the next one hundred miles until the Inside Passage ended in a sorry spill of tar-paper shacks on a wet stretch of beach. Skagway wasn't known for its port of call. Baggage, food, hay and horses were unceremoniously dumped overboard and the miners were left to dig their belongings out of the mucky tide any way they could.

Mountains reared over the settlements. On the best of days, the wind scudded down the hills and whistled through the flimsy houses, rattling the bottles on the bars and reminding folks that *we all must die*. Skagway regulars killed off a lot of whiskey remembering that. A regular in Skagway was anybody who stayed more than a week.

The town attracted cardsharps, crooks and Klondike queens. Normal folks just took their chances. The town was wide open. On that private telegraph known only to criminals, the word shot around the world. It brought back opium from China, plague from Africa and Soapy Smith from Denver.

Jefferson Randolph Smith dressed in white and surrounded himself with the blackest hats he could find. It kept him alive longer. He donated to the poor, took in the homeless and established a Skagway building fund for a city hall that was never built. Soapy specialized in big scams and his associates trailed along behind, picking up the little things he missed. They were dressed as doctors, lawyers and Indian chiefs, but the most popular was *Just Plain Folk*.

The Ryans had been there two days, and Tom in particular was impressed with the quality of people he met. He should have been paying attention to the false fronts on all the buildings, but he was too busy looking at the cards in his hands. ~~He had stepped out right after breakfast on the second morning~~ to get the bulk of their supplies. When lunch came and went without him, Flame went looking.

She found him on Holly street in a place called Jeff's Oyster Bar No. 317. The other 316 didn't exist. It didn't sell oysters, either.

He was playing poker in the back. Badly. Flame could tell because he had only a tiny pile of money next to his elbow, while a burly dark-haired man in a derby had a mountain of money next to his. The man in the derby hat glared at her when she came over and crunched on his cigar. "Want something?" he growled. His eyes were a dark brown, almost black. He had a small black mustache that was clipped close.

She crouched down next to her father. "I've been looking all over for you," she hissed. "What do you think you're doing?"

He yanked his cards away. "Exactly what it looks like, missy." He pushed a silver dollar into the middle. "Call."

"Pa!"

"Go away."

"I'm not going anywhere without you. Now get up right now, tell your friends good-bye and come along." She made her voice sound soothing.

Tom appeared to consider it. "Your mother's behind this. I can tell."

"We're both behind it. Come on now, pa. Ma's got a fine dinner waiting. Fresh fish."

Tom looked at his cards. "Fish?"

Flame nodded. "The way you like it cooked. Come on now."

Tom looked at the man in the derby hat. "What do you think, Batt?"

"Maybe the little lady's right."

"Think so?" Tom appeared confused. The man nodded.

"Thank you, mister," Flame said fervently. She helped her father up.

"I mean," the man continued quietly, "if you want to be ruled by a skirt who doesn't know a damn thing, pardon my French, ma'am, about card playing, go right ahead, Tom, be my guest."

That did it. Tom scowled at Flame. "You're not too big to whale the daylights out of." He sat back down. "Sorry about the fuss, Batt."

The color left her face. Tom had taken their entire stake with him. One thousand dollars. Margaret had sold the family silver to get it. It was clear most of the money now lay in the pile at Batt's elbow. "Pa," Flame said. He didn't answer.

"How many you want?" Batt asked. Tom covered his cards and flipped up the corners. "One."

Batt peeled a card off the stack. An elated smile flashed across Tom's face and disappeared. He looked instantly at Batt, who stared blandly back. The third man playing rattled with chill and said, "I fold." He pushed his cards away, hocked up spit and shot it onto the floor.

Batt glanced at his cards.

"I raise two hundred," Tom said, reaching into his pocket. His wallet looked curiously flat.

"I see your two." Batt paused, looking at Tom's wallet. "How much you got there, anyway?"

Tom counted it out. "One hundred and some change."

Batt slapped his money down. "May as well go for broke."

"For broke!" Flame fell to her knees. "Dad, I'm begging you. Don't do it."

Tom put his cards down carefully. He looked at Batt and the table fell silent. Batt chewed on the cigar. "I didn't want to have to do this," Tom said. He hit Flame in the face, and she fell backward, stunned. A small sob escaped and her hand went to her cheek. "You made me do it, missy. I didn't want to do it." He turned back to the game.

It was over quickly.

"Call," Tom said triumphantly, spreading his cards. "Flush." Flame held her breath. For a wild moment, she thought maybe everything was all right after all. Then Batt's eyes glittered, and he smiled coldly. He flipped his cards over and splayed them out in front of her father. Tom gasped.

"A full boat," he said, pulling the money toward him. "Wouldn't try poker again, my friend," he said conversationally. "Don't have the face for it."

A hoarse cry came from Tom. He mumbled incoherently

and pushed himself away from the table. He stood stoop-shouldered and looked at the money. A sob rattled in his chest and then he turned and stumbled out the door. Flame watched him go.

Batt rifled through the bills, sorting. He hummed tunelessly. "The show's over," he said to Flame. "You can go on home now." He slapped the tens together and put them into his wallet first. He moved his gun off the stack of twenties and counted them. He looked up. "Go on home," he repeated. She had the strangest look on her face.

She raised his gun and aimed it at his chest.

Batt leaned back. "That's not a smart thing to do."

Flame clicked back the trigger. "Give it back."

"People get killed around here for less."

"Give it back. It's our money. You stole it and I want it back."

Damn, Batt thought. It had been such a good day, and now this.

He sighed, lunged forward and savagely twisted back her wrist. The gun clattered to the table. Flame burst into tears.

Batt shook his head and pulled out a chair. "Sit." He passed her his handkerchief. Flame blew her nose.

"So he lost a little money," Batt said. "So what? There's always tomorrow. Besides, maybe he learned a lesson. Maybe it saved him from letting somebody talk him out of all of it down the line someplace."

She raised her swollen eyes incredulously. "That was all of it. Every penny we had. We scraped together every penny we had, and you took it!" Her voice ended in a wail. She flung her head down on her arms and sobbed. She was beginning to attract a crowd.

He grabbed her roughly. "That was it? A thousand dollars? You came up here with your dad and only a *thousand dollars* in your pocket?"

She nodded, mumbling. "And my mother. My mother came too."

"Well, I'll be damned." He didn't know what else to say. She wiped her eyes noisily and blew her nose again.

He hoisted her to her feet. "Come on. I have something to

64

show you." He took her around the bar through a storeroom. The door opened into a small fenced yard. An eagle in a cage glared at them, its neck ruffled.

"See that?" Batt asked.

"It looks like an eagle."

Batt took her arm lightly. "That's your first mistake." His fingers dug into her arm and Flame was suddenly afraid. Batt smiled. "That's my opening to say 'Come over here, right next to him. To get a better look.'" He moved her next to the eagle, his hand tightening slightly.

"I see him fine now," she said. "Maybe it's time we went back inside."

Batt bent over her and Flame smelled the pomade in his hair and a faint scent of tobacco. He smiled, but it was a cold thing. "You're beginning to understand. Lonely. No escape. No one knows you're here. If somebody came looking for you, I have nine persons inside that door who would swear on a stack they saw you leave by yourself right after your dad." He snapped her body around and held her roughly, his dark face close to hers. Flame calculated the distance to the door. Even if she could wrench free, he could still pin her to the ground before a three count.

He was bending her arms back behind her. Flame bit her lip to keep from screaming out. "What do you want from me?" she whispered.

He stared deeply into her eyes. His own were heavy lidded, as if he had trouble keeping them open. Tiny scars cratered his face. "Want?" he breathed, and Flame's skin turned cold. "I think it's perfectly clear what I want."

She shook her head mutely, turning her face away from him. He found her ear and breathed in it. "I want to scare the living bejesus out of you; that's what I want."

He let her arms go and she fell backward, tumbling to the ground, the wind knocked out. He was standing over her, grinning broadly. She got up indignantly, refusing the hand he offered.

"You scared me half to death!" she said.

"Good." He casually unwrapped a cigar and bit off the end. "Now listen here—"

65

"Flame," she said.

"Now listen here, Flame. I'm only going to tell you this once. You never should have come here. Never. Your father attracts misery like flies on—well, you never should have come, that's all." He snagged his match on the side of the cage and toasted the end of his cigar. "But since you're here"—he turned and looked out over the trees rimming the fence—"a pretty thing like you, assuming you don't want to take the broad road—" He turned back to Flame and said hopefully, "You don't, do you?"

"The broad road? Oh. *Oh.* The broad road. No. No thanks." She shook her head rapidly.

"That leaves one choice then," he said. "You're going to have to be as mean as the country. Do you know how to use a gun?"

"My father does."

"Learn. You got to be cold, Flame. I pride myself on that. I'm the coldest SOB in Skagway. That's why I'm still around."

"But you're being so nice—"

"You have something I can live without, that's all." He peeled off a wad of bills and counted them out to the dollar. He shoved the money into her hands. "If I ever hear you gave your father back one dime of this money, I'll take it upon myself to personally show you what a mean bastard I really am."

Her eyes filled with tears.

"Now, don't go getting all weepy and female on me."

"I don't know what to say." Flame's voice was choked.

"You can try thanking me. I won't be offended."

"How rude. It's only—thank you," she said breathlessly.

"I guarantee the advice is worth lot more than the money. Stay away from the telegraph office here. There's no telegraph. Treat every person in this town like a scoundrel, starting with your father. He's proven himself. And keep clear of the minister here. He works for Soapy."

"Who?"

"Just listen. I don't have time for questions. Another thing. Don't ever breathe a word of this to a living soul, understand? My reputation would be shot to hell."

66

He was walking rapidly back toward the door.

Flame watched him go, the money tight against her chest. Then she remembered and called out, "Sir! Wait! I don't even know your name!"

He tipped his hat. "Batt Jackson, Flame. The name's Batt Jackson. And don't put that there. Don't you have an inside pocket?"

She nodded.

"The inside pocket, Flame. Always the inside pocket."

Seven

WHITE PASS, Dead Horse Trail—The thought of gold does funny things to people. It wraps itself around a person's brain and squeezes the sense right out of it. It chokes off useless feelings, like compassion, and leaves behind distilled lethal amounts of the other things: greed, rage and cruelty.

In Skagway everything had a price. Tenderness was too expensive for most folks. But when the Ryans hit the White Pass Trail, Flame knew the stakes had been raised even higher. Kindness was priced right out of everybody's range.

It had been advertised as an all-weather route, suitable for women and children and easier than the Chilkoot Trail to the north. It was a death trail, clogged with the rotting bodies of horses stuck in the mud and left to die. No one stopped to help them.

The trail was a bramble of bushes and mud slivered with rocks. It was like walking on broken glass through an endless cold shower, with the only sounds the swift rip of rain and the screams of horses and the march of boots from the man in front of you.

There was no food for the horses, and they were driven on in exhausted hunger by men senseless with their own exhaustion. The horses had been overloaded with goods, and now their backs were spiny with malnutrition and the bones in their chests stuck out. The lucky ones rolled off the ridge of the trail and broke their necks falling. The others died more slowly, thrashing through the mud, hooves bleeding on the rocks and noses clotted with yellow foam.

One man flogged his horse until it dropped and then sat down in the mud next to it and cried.

Flame saw it happening and stumbled ahead, furious at him

for his cruelty, but when she got there, he had already melted into the stream of miners crawling up the trail.

It was a brown gelding. Red stripes of blood banded its body from the beating. The owner had been in too much of a hurry to take the pack off when it fell. Flame loosened the pack. Raw sores bled underneath the place where the blanket had slipped away from the load. She looked up, searching the line of men for help. They slapped around her through the mud, rain sheeting their bodies.

Flame crouched down by the horse's head. Pink foam flecked its mouth. They stared at each other for a long moment, the girl small in soaked baggy pants, the horse busy with the hard work of dying. The gelding made whoomping noises, breathing hugely through its nose, its eyes never leaving hers. She stroked its muzzle and picked up the gun she had bought in Skagway.

"Okay," she whispered, "it's all going to be okay."

It seemed to know what she was going to do. It closed its eyes. Flame squeezed the trigger.

The gun bit back into her flesh as the bullet cracked through the horse. It punctured a neat hole above the eye and blew off the back of the head. The huge body rattled and the legs moved, all at once, as if it were galloping across some great green hill, streaking like a falling star, or a bullet, through the cold blue sky. And then it was done and the body stopped moving, and the part that was left behind sagged into the mud and the rain and Flame's memory.

She shook and sank her mouth around her cut hand. She realized she was crying. She got up shakily and backed away. A red pool stained the mud around the horse's head. Her father came up behind her on the trail and touched her awkwardly.

"I know why you did it, missy," her father said softly. He looked suddenly old and tired.

"Oh, pa," she curled herself into his arms and he patted her as he had when bad dreams had startled her out of childhood sleep.

"But you're a fool."

She looked at him. "He was hurt."

"Are you blind, girl?" he said gruffly. "Look around you."

69

For the first time, Flame did. Rain obscured a battleground of horses mired in the slime, thrashing wildly in the mud, trying to find solid ground before the stuff slowly swallowed them up alive. "You don't have enough bullets for all of them, missy," he said flatly. He dropped his arms and staggered into the line. Flame stared at the horses, her mouth dry. One of them was buried past its shoulders, its snout in the air, screaming. As she watched, the mud greedily sucked its head under. The spot bubbled and grew still.

Margaret caught her hand and squeezed it hard. The women looked at each other wordlessly and turned back to the trail.

It rained steadily all afternoon. It washed away the treacly sweet smell and covered up the grinning stillness of the horses. The trail along the river bed was so soft they sank to their knees. It was a nightmare. Her pack dug into her back. The rain stung her face, soaking her coat and hat and sliding down her body. The cold mud numbed her feet. After stepping hard on something that slid away from her, Flame was glad that her feet had lost feeling.

It had come snapping out of the slime at her, like some decomposed primeval monster. A horse's head. Flame screamed. Only her mother reacted. Her father shuddered along beside her, his eyes dull, his face a pasty gray, paler than the sky.

They plodded on, not speaking. The rain fell. Whips cracked. Horses staggered and fell, and grown men cried. By dinner they had covered less than three miles.

They pulled off the trail and clambered up a slippery bank. By the time they pitched their tent, the rain had slowed enough to tempt the mosquitoes. They swarmed around in huge hungry groups, like ants manning a picnic. The Ryans caked their faces with mud. It stopped some of them.

Everything was wet, even the wood. In the end they sat huddled together in front of the tent, eating cold biscuits and drinking colder tea.

"We could turn around, Tom," Margaret said gently. He was shaking next to her.

"Never," he rasped, his voice burred with fatigue. "Our future is up over that mountain." He jerked his thumb toward

70

the hill and doubled up, coughing. High against the sky, Flame could see a moving train of men, crisscrossing against the face of the pass. They strained under their packs, clinging to stunted pines and rocks, pulling themselves along inch by inch.

"We're going to be rich, Maggie," he said. His voice scared her.

She looked at him sharply. "You don't look well."

"Just cold," he muttered. "So cold. I'm fit as a fiddle. Let's have no more talk now." He got up abruptly, swayed against the slate sky, and dropped face down into the mud. Mosquitoes blackened his neck.

"Tom!" Margaret screamed, crouching over him and pulling him onto his back. They wiped the mud out of his mouth and nose. His breathing was shallow, as if he were running a race.

"Please!" Margaret screamed to the men moving below them on the trail. "Please! Someone. Help. My husband."

No one looked up.

Flame scrambled over to the edge. "We need a doctor up here," she cried. "A doctor."

No one answered.

They dragged him between them into the tent. Flame tried to start a fire again, but the most she got was smoke. They wrapped him in all the bedding and still he shook.

Margaret stayed with him and watched him fade away. He changed right in front of her, his cheeks deflating and his lips pursed, as if some creature were poised on his chest, sucking the air right out of him. Once he opened his eyes. They were suddenly huge in the dark sockets of his face.

"How do you feel?" she asked, smoothing the sweat off his face. His skin was cold.

He smiled faintly. "Fine, fine." He shivered uncontrollably and his teeth clacked like castanets. "The first cold of the year is always the worst," he said gamely.

She nodded, her eyes flinty with tears. He took her hand, his grip strong.

"Maggie," he whispered. She stroked his hand. "Maggie, you know in all the time we were married, I never brought you flowers." Outside, the rain picked up, rattling the top of the

71

tent. "A man thinks of things like that sometimes. Such a little thing. It would have pleasured you so much."

She took his face in her hands. "Hush, now, you hush."

"Not once. In all the time we were together. All those years you stood by me even when I was dead wrong."

"I always knew where I stood, Tom. You've been fine."

"My pack," he whispered. "Bring me my pack." Margaret turned away from him, wiping the tears, and brought it back, placing it next to his chest. He was crying, too. "You're the only part I'll remember," he said, "take with me."

"Tom Ryan, you're not going anywhere without me," she said firmly. "We've come this far together. We'll see it through."

He patted her hand gently. "Not this time, Maggie." His eyes closed and flickered open. "Turn around now."

"What?"

"Turn around, Maggie Ryan. I have something for you."

She stood there for a long time, listening to the rain skittering down the canvas, and then she finally said, "Tom? Can I turn around now? Tom?"

When he didn't answer, she whirled around. His eyes were closed, his head turned toward her back. In his hand were flowers, smidges of blue, and cranberry and deep gold, wildflowers, their brief joyous burst of life already fading.

She touched his face, his hair, and gently lifted the flowers out of his fallen hand. "I love you too," she whispered.

An hour later, Flame found a doctor, a small, wiry man in his mid-forties. "Ten bucks up front," he said, extending his palm. Maggie paid. "I'll only spend three minutes," he said curtly. "I already lost my place in line."

He displaced Maggie, who knelt next to him and said, "He's sleeping now. He's just been pushing too hard."

The doctor raised Tom's eyelids, and checked his pulse. "He's not asleep, ma'am," he said. "He's unconscious. Cerebrospinal meningitis." He got up.

"What!"

"You heard me." He turned to go.

"You can't leave just like that! There must be something we can do."

He stared back at her through small, tired eyes. He sighed. "The only thing you can do is watch him die. Preferably from a distance. You and your daughter have both been exposed. This tent is in quarantine."

Maggie sat heavily on the ground.

"I'm sorry, ma'am," the doctor said, "but you've wandered right into the middle of the worst epidemic I've ever seen."

He paused by the flap, rubbed his eyes, and looked at Tom lying on the ground. "This time for free. Bury him as fast as you can and then get the hell away." He dropped the flap and ran down the hill.

The women looked at each other. "I've got a Bible in my pack," Flame said finally. "Do you think God would forgive us if we burned it for heat?"

It wasn't a very good fire, nor very big. They split the dryest piece of wood they could find and used some papers and the Bible as a starter. It smoked thickly and finally caught. They built it right in front of the tent and shielded it from the rain with the flap, pulling wet wood next to it to dry out for later. Then they moved Tom's body next to the fire and waited.

Darkness replaced the sun around eleven that night, leaving only smoky traces of light behind. Margaret told Flame stories of a Tom young and fearless and devoted, while outside the rain thrashed through the trees like an angry wild animal.

He never regained consciousness. He died quietly around ten the next morning, his body simply getting colder and colder and the color fading away. Outside, the rain picked up again, and the wind whipped it against their fragile shelter. They moved his body to the far side of the tent, scraped in the hot coals and closed the flap.

It was warm and dry in the tent, with the coals glowing and the rain beating outside, but nothing is stiller than death, and Flame couldn't shake the chill inside her, watching her father's body across the fire. She half expected him to jump up and reach out for them both, laughing and crying and saying, "I made it up. You know what a great kidder I've always been. I really scared you, didn't I?"

But the body kept lying there, gray and sunken, and so quiet, as if it were dreaming a very important dream, a very

73

significant one, and could not be disturbed.

Flame looked outside early afternoon and gently touched her mother. "Ma, we'll have to bury him in the rain."

Margaret looked at her husband. "You know, in Seattle, they have wakes for the dead. A chance for people to give their final respects. Sometimes they go on for days." She stared at Tom. "Give me an hour." She picked up her husband's hand. "It happened so fast, is all." She looked at Flame. "I'll be fine. I will. I just need this hour."

Something in her mother's voice made Flame back away and reach for her coat and hat. She spent the hour outside, wet, muddy and miserable, looking for a place to bury him.

They settled on a flat spot in a copse of trees, with a clear view of the pass. Margaret recited some verses from memory, and then they marked it with three flat stones and a cross made from two sticks wrapped together.

Neither of them cried.

A Mountie stopped them at the customs tent. He was young, with pale features saved from total obscurity by a strikingly colorful uniform. He spread out their canned goods, bedding and outer clothing on the ground. Then he looked up sharply, taking in the bored stance of the packer they had hired and the faint air of good breeding hidden under the women's rough clothing.

"A little light, aren't you?"

"Pardon?" Flame had been peering around the canvas flap. A long line of men stood waiting. It was starting to snow.

"Supplies," he said patiently.

Margaret drew herself up. "I think we have quite an adequate amount here, sir. We don't plan on dawdling along the way to Dawson, taking in the sights."

He looked at her, then jabbed a finger at a yellowed paper tacked to the side of the tent. "A year's supply of food. Says so right here."

Margaret stared at the paper, then back to him. He was looking at Flame. "Young man." He corrected his gaze. "We spent two weeks in a boat no bigger than a wash basin. We have walked for a week through mud like quicksand. We have buried my husband along the way. And nobody, not even one of the Northwest Mounted Police, is going to turn us back now."

She was a fierce dark creature, her jaw out, her hands riding her hips. He had the uneasy feeling she meant every word she said. "Occupation?" he snapped.

Margaret pulled out the deed. "Gold seeker," she replied.

He studied it. "Where in the hell is this?"

Margaret held her ground. "That's what we came here to find out. It's in the Alaska district, anyway. We won't stay long in Dawson."

A stubby-faced man poked his head around the tent flap. "What are you doing in there, playing ball-buster poker?"

"Wait your turn," the Mountie said, pushing him out the door.

"My daughter and I can take in laundry in Dawson or do any one of a number of useful occupations. We will not be a burden on the community, I assure you."

He scratched his jaw and looked heavenward. Then he shook his head and signed their pass. "Get out of here before the sergeant comes back," he said curtly, "or you'll be tossed out of Canada and I'll be looking for another line of work." They gathered up their goods and ran.

At the town of Bennett, no one wasted wood building houses.

Everybody was building boats. Margaret and Flame had hired on with a crew of four from Minnesota. They cooked and washed clothes, drying them over smoky fires while the men whipsawed the logs and cursed the rain.

There was no bantering among the men, and no contact with the women, except at meals. It was a business arrangement. It left little time for niceties.

Winds blew off Lake Bennett and the air smelled of smoke and snow.

Calling it a town gave it a permanence it didn't deserve. When a boat was built, the tent came down and the passengers sailed away; their campground was immediately taken by an even testier group, because it was later and the weather was turning.

Flame was tired of cooking over an open fire and beating clothes on rocks. Her fingers were raw and she was cold all the time.

"When we find that claim and get rich," she said to her mother, "I'm going to hire somebody to do all the unpleasant work. All of it."

"Uh huh," Margaret said, shifting a huge pot of clothes to the side of the fire. "Just pour."

Flame tilted the pot while Margaret held the clothes in with a stick. "No, I'm serious. I really am. And I'll live in some civilized place. With indoor plumbing and electric lights. And real summers. And I'll never get married, either."

"You won't? Why not?" Margaret squeezed out a shirt and lopped it over the rope above the fire.

Flame smoothed her hair. "I've seen what it can do."

Pain creased Margaret's face.

"Oh, ma, I'm sorry," Flame said penitently. "I forgot about dad. I'm a fool."

Margaret picked up a pair of pants and wrung them out briskly, her back to her daughter. "Why don't you run along now," she said, her voice funny. "I'll finish things up here."

"Ma, I—"

"Go on, now," Margaret said, more loudly.

Flame hugged her carefully. "If you need me, I'll be down by the water," she said. Margaret nodded sharply and Flame stood there, not wanting to leave yet, with words hanging between them in the air.

"Oh, Flame, darling, darling girl." Margaret hugged her, her hands still wet with wash. She smelled like borax and the wind. "Loving someone is all that really matters. That's all we ever have." She released her daughter and said briskly, "Now run along. There's plenty of time for that."

Flame had no way of knowing that Margaret was wrong.

The sign said The Ham Grease Saloon. All Drinks a Dollar. Under it a shriveled gnome of a man danced from foot to foot, playing a mournful version of "The Man on the Flying Trapeze" on his harmonica.

76

He spotted Flame, and his bushy eyebrows stitched together across his face over eyes that talked to her, insisting that she stay. Flame was repelled and attracted by him. His body barreled into a thick chest and bull neck. His bald head glowed with mosquito welts, and his eyes gleamed like two shiny flat buttons on her winter coat. Two small, fragile legs supported the enormous weight of his upper body. He was leaning carefully against the side of the saloon, taking the weight off his legs, and Flame thought he looked just like Humpty-Dumpty.

Then the song ended and he opened his mouth and Flame forgot completely about his appearance. "I know all about you. Past, present and future. Ah, yes, most especially the future. I see pictures right here. Inside my skull. I know it all. I really do."

"What do you know?" Flame said challengingly. "Tell me one thing."

"I know you can't resist me," he said smiling at her. His teeth were rotten. "Because I have everything you want. Every last thing there is."

Flame shivered and, in spite of herself, came closer.

"You feel it too," he said. "You know it's true." He was staring at her, his eyes flat like sharks, not blinking.

"Who are you?" she whispered.

"Oh, Flame, we're old friends. Buddies that go way back. I'm a trickster. A punster. A fun guy. But enough about me. You came to hear about you. And you came to the right place."

He lived out back, behind the Ham Grease Saloon, the only wooden building in town. His room was surprisingly neat, almost chaste, with military-tight corners on the bedspread and no sign of a personal touch anywhere. It was as if the funny little man wasn't really there at all, except in Flame's imagination.

"Of course I'm real," he said, smiling at the way she jumped. "There's no hiding, Flame. None at all. I can see straight into your mind. It's right inside my skull. My body is—at best—tolerable. But there have been other, shall we say, compensations." He chortled to himself as he pulled himself onto the bed

77

and the sound made the hair on the back of her neck spring up. "I have bedded queens. And the virginal daughters of powerful men have been taught—how do I put this delicately—taught to please me in ways that still make them awaken shuddering in the middle of the night. From the horror, the delicious, compelling horror of it all."

He reached out his hand—a small plump girlish hand—and casually stroked Flame's arm. She flinched but seemed unable to move away from the crawling presence of his hand on her flesh.

Finally, even though it was like working against gravity, she pulled herself away from him and ran for the door. If she had gone without turning back, without looking at him, she would have escaped then and there. But she stopped, wanting to stun him into harmlessness. "You have nothing for me," she said clearly. "No words for the future. No powers."

He looked at her backing out of the room, her hair bunched around her face, her huge eyes never leaving his. Her fear aroused him. He chuckled throatily and squeezed his crotch, pleased at the shock widening her eyes.

"Next you'll tell me you know nothing about Cahill. Cahill Blue. Who left over a year ago seeking his fortune in the great northern unknown. Cahill, who survived a snowslide, a landslide and an even crueler slide from grace. Only to fall— ah, but forgive me, I forgot. You're not interested."

She froze, loathing him. "What do you know of Cahill?"

He laughed gleefully, clapping his two small hands together, delighted by her reaction. He patted the bed. "Come. Sit down. I won't bite. Not yet. You don't hate me quite enough for that. Women taste ever so much better when they truly, truly hate and fear you. Changes the juices somehow." He licked his lips. His tongue was deep red, almost a purple. "Tasty. Such a tasty little biscuit you will be. Oh, Flame, the ways I will defile you. Come. Sit. And we will share some wine like the two old friends we are. And in due time, I will tell you everything you want to know about your friend, your betrothed, Cahill Blue."

Flame stood next to the bed, looking down at him. "And in return?"

He stared at her, his eyes bottomless as a drowning pool for

78

newborn kitties. "You might even learn to enjoy it," he said. "Some of them do."

Her mouth was dry. She knew she should leave at once. But this misshapen, obscene little man had spoken the one name that could make her stay.

"What do you know of Cahill?" she whispered.

He smiled at her, gently, sweetly, and splayed his hand across the bed. "Sit," he said. Trembling, she obeyed but sat poised on his bed as far away from him as possible.

He moved closer. "I've always found it easier, somehow, when doing readings of this nature, to be right there in the middle of things, inhaling the special fragrance of the life I'm exploring." He lowered his head into her lap and stared up at her, the inside of his nostrils shiny with burst capillaries. He inhaled deeply, and Flame thought it was the wickedest sound in the world.

"Ah yes, that sweet, ripe odor. So fresh. Like new cream."

"Cahill," she said, her lips barely moving. "You promised to tell me about Cahill. Where is he?"

He smiled wetly, and his tongue darted out and slapped the tip of his nose. He used it to caress a tufted mole hanging on the bulb. "I've practiced my entire life for this evening," he said. His tongue slithered back into his mouth. "But enough of what you have in store for you. Tell you what. I'll even throw in some stuff about your mother."

He rolled off her lap and propped himself up on one elbow, his arm carelessly thrown across her lap. "Can't beat the price," he said jovially. "Your mother. Ah, your mother." He positioned his fat little fingers on his temples and closed his eyes. "Nice old broad. Married late. Widowed early. And the future." He squinted up at her and shrugged apologetically. "May as well tell you. You'll find out sooner or later. There is no future. Just"—he wiggled his fingers in the air—"poof. Here today. Gone tomorrow."

The room was suddenly cold. The dwarf didn't seem to notice. "In fact," he said casually, "now that I really concentrate on it, I'm picking up the feeling, the definite feeling, that *you're* not going to be here either. In the world, I mean. Just—well, just a sort of blackness. No big deal. Nothing to write home about. Life is just one big rock. And we're the bugs, crawling around, waiting to get squashed. I read that someplace in a book."

Flame got up off the bed, squeezing her hands together. "When?" she stammered. "When will it come? How? Can we stop it?"

He smiled gently. "There is one small thing that might work. Save you both. Just a try. But you'll have to do more than stand there. I think it's time you got, shall we say, more comfortable?"

Her mouth was dry and it tasted as if something had died in her stomach. She loosened her hair clumsily.

"I'm waiting," the dwarf trilled.

Flame turned to him just as the door burst open.

It was Batt Jackson. He was definitely wearing the white hat. And he was wearing something even more useful, a .44.

"Gimpy Maggot, this better not be what it looks like, or I'll snap your little legs off and use them for roasting marshmallows."

"Goldarnit, Batt, you had to go and wreck the whole damn thing," he whined. "Just when we were starting to get to know each other, too."

"Flame, I ought to turn you over my knee and spank you here and now," Batt said, exasperated. The dwarf brightened at the prospect. "But I don't want to get Gimpy here all riled up." The dwarf sat back down again.

"I bet I can tell you exactly what happened here," Batt said, prowling the room. "Good old Gimpy snagged you into coming up to his room by—let me see—probably by calling you by your name and promising to read your future."

"Yes, but—"

"It's an old routine, Flame."

"But he had names. My sweetheart. And he knew all about my mother."

"He should. He cozies up to her enough," Batt snapped. "Ask her. When you get home, ask her if she doesn't know a strange, amusing dwarf by the name of—Cyrano, wasn't that what you called yourself, Maggot?"

Flame looked at Gimpy. He looked away.

80

"And then he told you something truly evil was in store for you—and only he could change the cards."

"And that's where you came in," she said.

"What do you know," Batt said, advancing on the dwarf, who scuttled back against the wall on the bed. "I keep getting this definite feeling." He raised his hands. "Ah, yes. It's coming to me, Maggot. I get this feeling you will never, never try this little game again." He was yanking him up by his collar until they were eye level, the dwarf dangling like a frog. "Because if you do, I swear to God, I'll grind you up into guppy food and sprinkle you in the water myself." He shook him. "Understand?"

Gimpy glared at him. "Some friend you turned out to be."

Batt dropped him. "See, Flame, anybody can foretell the future. Even a slick and wonderful guy like me."

As they walked through the door, Flame took a deep breath of foggy air.

"A little cameo from the underbelly of life," Batt said. "Never trust anyone you weren't born with, and even then only partway. This country changes a person, Flame." He stared at her, the fierce look in his eyes modified by long black eyelashes. "Haven't we had this conversation before?"

"I'll remember it this time," she said. They walked in silence, Flame with her hands stuffed in her pockets. "You haven't heard of Cahill Blue, have you?" She tried to make it sound offhand.

He stopped, squinting up at the rain over the mountains. "Not yet."

The dwarf watched them through his window, his eyes as flat as Kansas during a drought. "Batt's not so wonderful," he said. "And I'm right about the rest of it, too."

The boat was ready by the end of the week. It was 20 feet long, and Simon Henry was captain. He had a wife and five kids waiting for him in Minneapolis. He had been a science teacher and on weekends he took pupils on field trips across Lake Harriet, paddling in small safe circles and inspecting the water for bugs. He had more experience on the water than all the rest put together.

81

Flame wanted Batt to take them, but he had slipped away before the week was out, muttering something about a hot deal in Circle City—nine women, a loaded deck and all the booze you could drink.

Flame thought it sounded wonderful. Batt told her it wasn't her kind of town and packed up, leaving behind a campground gleaming with broken whiskey bottles.

Flame didn't see Gimpy Maggot anymore in Bennett, but his words dogged her thoughts.

"I know it's stupid," she confided in her mother one night, "but I keep feeling that he *could* have told me where Cahill was."

"Made something up, you mean," Margaret had said. "And scared you half to death, to boot. He probably would have told you Cahill died and then offered himself as comfort. That weasel! I should have known. Cyrano, my foot."

Still, the idea lingered in her mind, teasing her. The thought that he was somewhere in the world, alive and laughing, swept a kind of craziness through her more intense than even thinking something was wrong; she preferred to think of him as if he were missing in action in the Spanish-American War, and until she heard for certain he had been killed or captured, there wasn't a thing she could do. So she chopped wood, practiced shooting, hauled lumber for the boat and washed clothes for the men. On good nights she fell hard into sleep, like an anchor plunging fast through silent water.

On bad nights she remembered the way his cheek felt against hers and the foggy hoot of boats churning through the gray water of Puget Sound, both images so clearly of home it hurt her throat, and she wondered if she would ever see either again.

The Lewes River pools into Lake Bennett in the shadow of the Chilkat Range. Between there and the place where it joins the Yukon River, at the ruins of Ft. Selkirk, it stays smooth and shallow just long enough to trick travelers into taking unnecessary risks.

The lake was dark and implacable the morning they left, but as they neared the middle of it, clouds suddenly galloped across

82

the sky. It was too late to get the wagons in a circle. They were ambushed by the worst storm Flame had ever seen. The wind keened down off the mountains and lashed the water into waves. Flame and her mother crouched down with the men in the bottom of the boat, holding on to the edge as it bucked and reared into the air. Simon had tried to guide the boat at first, but his fragile paddle was useless against the fury of the storm. In the end he was thrown heavily into the boat, still holding the paddle, and the waves batted and smashed their boat as if it were a small, only slightly interesting toy being abused by the town bully.

It lasted until midmorning, and then capriciously the storm tiptoed away, inching its way south. It terrorized Lake Lindeman the rest of the day.

"We did it!" Simon said, wiping his face and standing up in ankle deep water.

Jacob Smith agreed. A graying shoe salesman, originally from Omaha, he had seen this much action only once, from a hooker in Lincoln when he tried to write a check. "The worst is over now," Jacob said, clapping Simon on the back.

Flame wondered and said nothing.

After the storm, the weather cleared and the water smoothed. The wind was a gentle one, and blowing in their direction. The water had a hypnotic effect on Flame and the others. They didn't talk.

That night at Lake Marsh, she slept the dreamless sleep of babes and condemned men.

"Ma'am, I need to know now, ma'am."

Flame opened her eyes. A clean-shaven man dressed in a red uniform stared down at her through the flap in the tent. She squirmed out of her blanket and stood up, shivering in the cold. "Oh, I'm sorry. I was sound asleep. What did you say?"

Patiently the Mountie repeated himself.

"You're not going through the rapids, ma'am, are you?"

Flame rubbed her eyes and looked at the boat, sagging deep in the water with supplies. The water made smacking sounds, like a child practicing how to kiss.

"It's taken us this far," she said. "I expect it will carry us the rest of the way."

~~His tone changed. "You can't go," he said flatly.~~

"What's going on?" Simon stepped out of the tent he shared with Eddie, a retired plumber from the same town. Eddie had a sparkling array of grunts he used in lieu of words and at night he snored so loudly, Flame thought they were under attack.

"Sir, with all due respect, the rapids are no place for women or children. We've lost a lot of lives on the White Horse stretch."

"That a fact?"

"They can walk around them, sir. Only five miles or so. Course, it's pretty rough. Worse than the Dead Horse, some say."

Simon looked at Flame and back at the Mountie. "With all due respect, officer, if I decide to take them, who's going to stop me?"

The Mountie's lips tightened. "There's a hundred-dollar fine levied against the owner of any boat taking women or children through the canyon. You decide."

He tipped his hat to Flame and strode away. Simon watched him go and then jumped on the boat. He turned his back to Flame and hoisted out a trunk, pitching it on the sand.

"What are you doing?" Flame cried, running toward him.

"Exactly what it looks like," he said, not looking at her. He picked up a second trunk and sailed it toward its companion.

"You can't do that!" Flame shouted, dragging the trunk back toward the boat. "We worked for our passage. We earned it."

"Decide what you need and we'll carry the rest."

"Look," she said desperately, "chances are, if we get separated, we'll never meet up again."

"A hundred dollars makes one rethink basic principles," Simon said, crossing his arms.

"If we're stopped, we'll pay the hundred dollars. Ourselves. My ma and I."

And the former biology teacher, who had once let a borderline senior take home a final exam, looked down at Flame and said, "Put it in writing first."

From Lake Bennett to Miles Canyon was only ninety-five

miles. For most of that distance, between the lakes, the river spread out flat and strong. It changed so gradually that Flame couldn't say exactly when the familiar silky river sounds turned into something ominous.

It was the speed of the river that scared her.

It had been fed by small, insignificant streams along the way, fooling them by its muddy meanderings into thinking it was harmless. At Miles Canyon the entire force of the water squeezed between two high basalt walls, cresting in a furious ridge down the middle. And that was small potatoes compared to White Horse Rapids, right after it.

Simon guided his boat into an eddy before the canyon, behind a line of boats waiting to run the rapids. He sat in the stern, white-faced and tense, clutching the oar as if it had some magic property to save him. Flame and Margaret were side by side in the middle, behind Jacob and Eddie, who each held an oar. Balancing in the bow was Eric Argoneau, who had buried a rich wife the year before and fancied himself an unpublished author.

And so there they were, the six of them, entrusting their lives to strangers because they had no other choice.

The boat ahead of them slipped sideways, away from the canyon. It carried three men who strained at the paddles, pulling the boat away from the edge. "Going around!" one of them shouted.

Flame could see the fear in their faces, and something else— relief. Then Simon gave the signal and the oars bit through the water. They were next. It was too late to turn back.

"All ready?" Simon shouted.

"Ready!" the men answered. They plunged over the edge.

The boat slid down the first rock sheet and smashed into the foam. Flame held her breath and tightened her grip on the railing. The water flared around them and rushed overboard, so cold it was like an electric shock. The boat shuddered and lunged up, leaping out of the water and smacking back into it with such force she bit her tongue.

It shot into an eddy and the men dug in their oars, pulling. Then it popped out of the eddy like a cork flying out of a bottle. Within seconds they shot out from the narrow walls into an open clearing.

~~The water was remarkably still. The mile-long run had taken~~
only two minutes.

It was like winning at Russian roulette. Adrenaline coursed through her body. She felt the bite of the water, the way her muscles tensed, the wet mulch smell of the rocks. Simon hopped around, waving his oar and laughing. "Whooey!" he shouted. "We did it! We ran the Miles Canyon stretch!" All of them were on their feet, awkwardly hugging each other and laughing. They had won. They were too busy to see the water curling under into white foam just ahead.

The current snagged the boat sideways, lifting it clear out of the water. Simon fell backwards, smacking his head against the deck. Margaret screamed and clung to the tarp. The boat reeled into the trough and ground into the rocks. Water poured in. Flame knew they had been hit. Jacob stood up staggering as the water bellied into the boat and dragged him overboard, a scream drowning on his lips.

The boat was out of control now, the waves thundering in their ears and the boat splintering like a bottle in target practice. "We're going under!" Simon shouted over the furious sound of the water. "God help us, we're going under." The water hurled the boat into the air and he toppled over, still holding the oar.

Flame held on, her eyes closed. The boat shifted suddenly, as if a fist had punched it up and out away from the rocks, and then it was hurtling toward a ragged crop of boulders along the edge of the bank. Seconds later it razored neatly in two. Flame saw her mother clinging to the side of the halved boat, her eyes closed, her mouth moving as if in prayer.

And then she was swallowed up by the furious water.

It sucked her under greedily. Far above, the water twisted. But it was cool and green where Flame was.

And quiet, like the sound in a room full of people after someone screams.

BOOK TWO

Them

Eight

ARCTIC ICE, 1897—It was too cold to snow. The wind whined at the chinks of the hut and the lamp guttered out and flared in the draft.

The girls stood side by side, so close they could feel the other's thin arms through the fur kusunnaks their mother had sewn last summer. It was the proudest moment of their lives.

It was also to be their last.

They watched their mother silently, their eyes never leaving her face. They would not dishonor her by crying out.

Thirty-three winters old, she was; her hair a gray storm raging around her face. She chewed on the frozen caribou sinew to soften it, gumming it with teeth worn from so many seals and whales and caribou. So many mittens and parkas and leggings and boots. And now her two little ones stood before her, only a season apart in age, their eyes huge and their bellies pregnant with hunger. On her back she carried her youngest, not yet a year and still suckling on teats that had dried up long ago. The infant slept fitfully as she picked up the girls one by one and stood them on the high block of ice.

There was no need to speak.

She tied the strings securely to the high beam she had fashioned from a spear and looped the sinew around her daughters' necks. They stood that way, tears coursing down the furrows in the mother's face, until the older girl grasped her younger sister's hand.

Together they plunged into space.

Weeping, the mother gently lifted down the two bodies, so light they were like ptarmigan in her arms. She stretched them out side by side, their heads toward the east. She pushed their blackened tongues back into their mouths and pressed the lips together until they froze. She permitted herself one weakness: she smoothed back the hair and patted their foreheads. Death is of no consequence, she reminded herself. But she was an old foolish woman, a woman who could not help but draw the hoods close around the faces of her sleeping daughters.

She rose swiftly and pushed against the low ceiling until the center block gave way and the moonlight streamed in. Now the souls of her children could fly away. Moonlight streaked their faces deep blue. Sleeping. Only sleeping.

On her back her youngest stirred and cried weakly as she left the death house without looking back. The weight of her child slowed her steps. They had eaten the last of the dogs five days ago. She had saved the treat for last. Long after the meat was gone, she pulled the marrow out of the bones and fed it like fat worms to her children, saving none for herself.

Kannik, of course, knew.

She rested briefly, her breath warm against her face inside the hood. She could see only a tunnel of white stretching in front of her through the small hole in the cinched fur. She walked carefully, conserving her strength, until she reached a small incline overlooking the frozen sea. Satisfied, she pulled her babe out of her kusunnak and looked at her son. They stared at each other, his small mouth sucking the air fruitlessly, too weak to move his head.

Gently she sucked the mucus out of his nose and spat it out, and then there was nothing left to do but finish what had begun. She stripped him quickly and placed him on the fur scrap she had brought for that purpose. Then she rose and faced the sea.

"Oh, Tagiuk, the ocean, the sacred spring of life, take now your namesake home with you." Her eyes stung, and she scowled and blinked. "May you grant him a swift and easy death."

The infant stirred then, seeming to realize the desperateness of its situation, and screamed shrilly into the black air. The sound cut through the mother like a stone dagger. She turned her back and walked away.

90

For a few moments the tiny fists beat against the sky and the legs jerked tight against the body to warm it. But soon the movement stilled and the screaming stopped.

The wind riffled the snow then and the body became a small white mound in a sea of white, while below, the ocean lay as it always had—vast, deep, and black.

She would be honored by her family. Her name would pass into legend as the one who ended the children's suffering. She had spared them a crueler death. Already the hunger was chewing inside her belly like a live thing.

So many gone.

She put the thought behind her, but it danced ahead, rattling memories in her face. Ten children she had borne. Only two still breathed. Her oldest had died at birth. Three days she had labored in the birthing hut, kneeling over the moss bed and squeezing on the hanging strap until the effort turned her hands to clay while her husband stood helplessly at the door. On the third day, her grandmother had knelt behind her and squeezed on her belly until the sweat coursed down her body in rivers and her knees had shaken from the strain. But the child would not come. Nautchiak had straddled the moss, naked and slippery in the dim light, while the pain pulped her womb and blood leaked between her thighs and soaked the ground and she screamed. In the end her grandmother had reached up inside and pulled the child out feet first. At the first the glad cry "You have borne a son!" Then her grandmother drew a sharp breath and Nautchiak bent down and saw the truth for herself. The strong trunk. The well-shaped hands. And coiled around like an arctic eel, the birthing cord, wrapped so tightly that her dead son's face was dull blue.

The old woman stopped walking and looked sharply at the moon. A green ring glowed around it. Snow tomorrow, she thought. Good. It was always better to die with the world wrapped in snow. She was almost home now. Her heart clacked plainfully in her chest and her eyes hurt. So many gone.

She shook her head angrily. Only old women think of those who are no longer here. The hut gleamed before her in the moonlight, two small mounds with no village to surround and protect it. It was a mistake to leave the village, a small voice

91

inside her said clearly. She beat on her head, chasing away the thought. Death stalked them all. And if today it squirmed inside her hut and snapped her neck, so be it.

The bear was hungry. It had been two weeks since he had eaten his last adult seal. His stomach churned convulsively. His black tongue was slick with heavy saliva. Two days before, the rolls of fat protecting him began melting at an alarming rate. Another week and the padding would be gone.

He shuffled rapidly over the ice, his head weaving. He clambered up a pressure ridge and reared up, following a scent. He dropped down and veered away, his body a streak of pale yellow against the snow. He loped over the ice, toward the place where the ocean met the land. He stopped, his body heaving. The scent was gone. He wheeled slowly and retraced his path. There. The meat was there under the snow. Furiously he clawed a foamy trench until he snagged it.

He buried his head in the snow and crushed the small hairless meat between his jaws, swallowing it in two gulps. He snuffled in the snow and found more. No, only a scrap of fur.

He rooted for most of an hour, digging over and over in the same spot, until the scented place where the meat had hidden smelled only of bear and snow.

He needed more meat. He moved painfully away from his feeding spot. In the moonlight, he was a pale shadow gliding over a still land. He would kill anything that moved.

The old man knelt by the breathing hole, his face a scarred record of his struggles. Three weeks he had been on the ice with his son while his wife and children weakened in their hut. The hot flush of shame stained his face. He was no hunter. He was pale and mewling, like an old blind woman.

Once he had commanded a crew in the largest *umiak*, the oars flashing in the water and the harpoons singing through the air on their way to meet the whale. But now a small ringed seal was out of reach. Tears stung his eyes. Another shame. He could not brush them away. Any movement on the ice and the seal would surface somewhere else. He kept his eyes down, away from those of his son.

Nuka stared at his father, shocked by the spectacle. Eskimo men did not cry. Even in the dark days, when the Eskimos were warring with the savage Indians to the south, they went to their deaths soundlessly.

"Tears weaken a man," his father had once said. "Life is too difficult for such a luxury."

His father's secret weakness had been his children, but he had held to his words even as he watched them fall around him.

When Nuka's baby brother, Ukiak, had fallen through the new ice and drowned, it was his father who had remained strong. And when his sister, Sikinaatchiak, tripped and pierced her cheek on the barbed lure-hook, it was his father who had carried her moaning to the place where the shaman let her blood. Later still, it was he who pulled her bloated body through the skylight to prepare it for burial.

Three winters ago their hut was caught in ice too close to the shore and cracked like a duck egg. A son and daughter were lost.

His father had survived it all. And now tears disturbed his eyes. Nuka looked away. Nothing moved in the world. Not the snow nor the sky nor the tears gleaming on the face of his father.

The old woman squatted down by the door to the entryway and cracked open the whale-skin covering. The sharp smell of urine and skins comforted her, and she dropped to her knees and crawled inside, finding the storage alcove by touch. The oil for lamps had been used up before the half-moon had ripened, except for the small amount she had horded to use in the death hut. It was so cold inside that the furs snapped like spring ice under her weight as she sank down onto them.

Her teeth chattered, and she quickly yanked her kusunnak over her head and shook it out. Her strength fled before she could hang it up. She burrowed under the furs and pulled off her boots, lifting out the moss insoles and placing them carefully on the small shelf over her head to dry. She positioned her mittens alongside and listened for any breathing besides her own.

"Someone is home now after a painful journey," she said

out loud. No one answered. So Kannik, her daughter, must be gone. Nautchiak sighed, and the sound was huge under the furs. She squeezed her eyes and hugged her small, bony knees to her chest. She saw Kannik running, her black hair spreading like raven wings in the summer sky, herding her younger brothers and sisters down the spit to the marshes where the duck eggs lay hidden. She had been a good daughter, an industrious daughter, and now she was gone.

Tears burned her eyes. Nautchiak hoped her death had been an easy one.

When it had become clear that the men would not return in time to save them, Nautchiak had discussed the situation with her eldest daughter.

"It is hopeless to go on," Nautchiak had whispered to Kannik. "The little ones moan in their sleep now with hunger. Every day is worse than the one before."

Kannik had understood at once. "Do you wish my help?" she had whispered back.

"No," Nautchiak said. "The weight of such things must be borne alone."

Nautchiak stretched her legs out stiffly. Her life had been a good life, a rich life, and now it was over. She closed her eyes and waited for death to come.

Her foot brushed warm flesh.

"Kannik?"

Her daughter moaned.

Nautchiak found her daughter's body and cradled the head with her arms. "You are still here."

"The great kindness," Kannik whispered through cracked lips, "is it over?"

Nautchiak nodded, not trusting herself to speak. No longer would she carry the weight of her small son between her shoulders, his strong fingers curling in her hair. She would never celebrate the first blood of her daughters nor hold their faces while their chins were tattooed. No men would ever see the sign and take them to their huts for pleasure.

Kannik weakly patted her mother. "Life is heavier than death," she said faintly. "It took great courage."

Tears stung Nautchiak's cheek. "You are a good daughter,"

she whispered. A time passed in which there were no words.

"Mother," Kannik said, "when you were gone, someone was dreaming of the Messenger Feast. Remember how we ate for days on end?"

Nautchiak nodded.

"Fermented ptarmigan, frozen inside the raw seal. And the way the lump of blood tastes, clinging to the bird's damaged heart."

"Stop!" Nautchiak commanded. "My mouth waters to think of it."

"If someone dreamed it, it will be so again."

"First we must stay alive," Nautchiak answered.

The ivory ice pick wobbled in the snow over the breathing hole. Pana instantly tightened his grip on the harpoon and waited. Split-second timing was critical if they were to make the kill. The seal would nose up to the hole, inhale deeply and sink back into the water, all within seconds. It was going to be more difficult for Pana because the seal would never be seen. Pana would have to rely on the most subtle of changes—a quivering ice pick, a sudden indentation at the hole and the sound of the seal sucking the air. Then he must ram the harpoon through the snow and strike the seal's nose.

Pana controlled the weakness in his arms and shifted the weight of his harpoon to his right hand, his eyes on the sloping walls of the breathing hole.

The snow suddenly sucked inward and Pana heard the sharp blowing sound the seal makes. He lunged at the hole and slammed the harpoon home. The line snapped through his hands as the seal dived, dragging the float under the ice. Pana held onto the shaft, braced himself and fed out the line.

Nuka dropped to his knees and scrabbled the snow away from the hole.

"A strong one," his father said. Nuka grunted, chipping furiously to widen the hole. Striking the seal was one thing. Seizing him, another.

Pana played the line as if the seal were a big king running for miles with a hook in his cheek. You will not win, Pana told the seal.

And then the line went slack.

~~The two men stood panting, staring dumbly at the hole, the~~
line limp in Pana's hands. They had speared the seal and played
the line and lost him. And now their family would perish from
their carelessness. Pana looked very old and small in his parka.
He squeezed the line in his hands and looked at the sky. "It is
over," he said simply.

The moon said nothing.

The line whined through Pana's fingers and bit down
through the snow. Pana steadied it and fed it out. It was the
hunger that had tricked them into thinking the seal had
escaped. The men strained against the line, dragging it in hand
over hand, playing it out when the seal ran. Nuka's muscles
ached. The wind lifted off the sea and burned against their
faces, the moon threw long shafts of light across the ice and
still the seal ran. There had never been such a seal. Nuka
wanted to rest. Only a short rest, to ease the pain in his fingers
and the protests in his arms. He stood behind his father and
pulled.

When the moonlight lengthened the shadows on the snow,
the seal tired and floated to the surface. Nuka clubbed its
ruined head and both of them pulled it up.

"It's nothing but a baby seal," Nuka said. "A baby spotted
seal."

Pana stooped awkwardly, dizzy with hunger, and pushed the
seal's snout into the water pouch. "Drink, and come to us
again."

Nuka slashed its belly open and they drank until warm blood
smeared down their chins and they could hold no more. Seven
days had passed since they had last eaten.

They sawed off chunks of meat and ate in silence until their
thoughts turned to those they had left behind. They trussed
the seal in lines and walked single file, the meat skidding over
the snow behind them.

The bear's stomach clenched and spasmed, sending saliva
flooding over his elevated cusps. Fresh blood. The bear
wheeled and followed the trail. By the breathing hole.

*   *   *

96

Pana straightened sharply and listened.

"What do you hear, father?"

Pana motioned him to be silent. He stared at the endless sky and snow, listening. The wind picked up, spatting crusted snow against their faces. Across the ocean, mist floated close to the ice, like a spirit clinging to a dead body. "Something walks tonight," Pana said heavily. "Some evil stalks through the snow." He shuddered. "Come. We must hurry."

The snowhouse was pale blue in the strange light when the hunters first saw it from the pressure ridge. No dogs greeted them. The women ate as we did, Nuka thought, scrambling down the ice face. The dogs were always eaten last. The thought alarmed him. With no dogs, they were poor indeed. The men shouted until their throats burned. When no one answered, they dug away the snow by the entrance and pushed inside.

"Someone is home now," Pana said, and his voice cracked in the cold room. "Someone with a seal." The women whimpered and Pana felt a sharp stab of pain as he filled their groping hands in the dark. His wife was a good wife, an obedient wife, and he had failed her. He had abandoned her with no lamps to tend, no fat to burn for heat, no meat frozen in the tunnel. That she would not blame him for all those things, but blame instead the long winter that squeezed off the summer game this year, only added to his misery.

Nautchiak and Kannik ate slowly under the furs, grunting from the strain of chewing raw meat. "Where are the little ones?" Pana asked, though he knew by the silence.

Nautchiak squeezed his hand. "It is as it was to be," she said gently. "You are a good man. A good hunter. We still have two children. And we will make many more to warm our days."

Pana busied himself building a fire so his wife could not see his grief, while she silently filled the lamps with a lump of fat, catching the moss wicks on the flame the way she had done daily since the night they had sealed themselves to each other.

So now they were four. He and his wife, Nautchiak, and the two grown children, Nuka and the girl. Stating it so shocked him, as if his good throwing arm had suddenly been severed from his body. *Four.* His infant son's face rose before his eyes, and the secret question he had tried not to ask burst in his head. *Why her? Why was Kannik spared, with her knife tongue and independent thoughts?* She seemed to be smiling at him across the lamp, as if she knew, as if she had willed it.

Your disgrace still lives, father. He heard the words as clearly as if she had screamed them. *Even your position as whaling captain could not lure a man into wedding me. And now you must try even harder, father, for this is all that is left of your female line.*

They looked at each other from across the fire, her face a younger, softer version of his own, but still strong and blunt. Not a woman's face at all. She was smiling. As if her mother had been called upon to do work no more terrible than clubbing birds. She was mocking him. *Smiling.*

In that moment he hated her.

The fire caught a lump of fat and burned more hotly than before, and her face shone clearly. He stared at her, amazed. Her lips were pulled back wildly, not in a smile, but in a grimace of pain. At great cost, she was trying not to cry. He burst into tears.

For most of an hour he followed the scent, head down, a thin male covered with old battle scars. At the top of the ridge he reared up, his black paws taloned with claws. He sniffed the air and dropped lightly down on all fours. He crouched down and bellied over the ice ridge, a cautious stalker. The scent stopped at a curious mound of ice. He circled slowly, smelling it.

"Do you hear something?" Nuka asked. Everyone listened. "It is the wind," his mother said, covering her husband with furs as he slept.

The bear circled the mound again. The smell was unmistakable and fresh. He circled again, hunger burning his belly and goading his steps. His ears flattened against his head and the hackles lifted. Something scratched inside the mound. The bear reared up, a growl rumbling in his throat.

Then he coiled his body and sprang.

Nine

Nuka dropped the bowl of seal oil he was holding and lunged for his spear as the ice wall shattered above him. "It is not the wind! Cover yourselves!"

His words were swallowed up as the beast roared and his mother screamed. There were only frightening blurs: his father hurtling out of bed, thudding snow killing the fire, his sister crouching in the corner, the bear's immense head snapping against the sky. The lamps crashed to the ground and went out, plunging the hut into darkness. Fear shot from Nuka's testicles to his belly.

He is going to kill us. And then the second thought: food has come to our door.

He could smell the thick wet smell of the bear but couldn't see it clearly enough to risk a kill. And then the moon shadowed the animal and Nuka was staring into its flat yellow face—a killer face with black tongue and fangs, a face from a nightmare. Nuka rammed the spear into the beast. Behind it Nuka could see his father advancing, and then the beast rolled and Nuka went down hard, a scream forming soundlessly on his lips. He hit his head and went down into darkness.

There were big meats inside. Frenzied, the bear ripped into the first meat he found. It screamed and struggled. He tore off chunks and swallowed. His stomach heaved. He closed his eyes and growled with pleasure.

Pain nipped his side. He batted his paw out, pushing away the aggravation and the pain stopped. He dragged the meat away from the center and ate. The meat was very still and warm. He ate quickly, crunching bones and swallowing without chewing, his stomach still pulsing with hunger spasms. It was not seal he ate. It was sweeter, the bones thicker. The scent of its blood and fur stank the air and whetted his appetite. He ripped open its belly and sank his muzzle into the steaming organs. It was good to eat hot meat.

His chest was on fire. He jerked his head up and shook his body hard, but the pain wouldn't fall off. The pain was burning and huge and filled the black sky. He cocked his head around, his eyes a flat yellow in the light, puzzling it out. Something was trying to hurt him. He was eating hot meat and now something was trying to hurt him. He swung back toward the other meats. One was on its hind legs, holding a stick. It was coming at him. He bellowed—a good, full sound that sent the meat backward, but not fast enough. He crashed down on the meat and sank his teeth into its flesh. He ripped it open but all the time there was more pain everywhere. The meat grew still. The bear's legs were shaky. His side was matted with sticky warmth. He turned back to his first kill and kept eating.

He had taken the old woman down hard, teeth wresting flesh and trousers from her leg, the wound gaping and bare against the air. I'll freeze, Nautchiak thought in surprise and thought of her husband and children; then the blood shot out of her leg and even in the moonlight she could see it pumping like a fountain into the air, spattering the monster in front of her, and she thought sadly, no, there is no time to freeze. She dug her hands into its head, beating against it, the pain so awful she had to make it stop and then the monster closed its jaws over her belly and dragged her away and she knew then that it would never stop, and it would be best if it were over quickly.

High above her, it started to snow.

Kannik shook. Her hands rattled and her bones quaked and her teeth clacked. They were gone. She shuddered, shaking her head violently, as if by denying it hard enough she could call back the night and they would somehow all be together again, safe and warm and alive. All of them gone. Sweat had pooled under her parka and now the cold was deeper than the ice over the ocean.

The cold will kill me, she thought. Good, she deserved it.

100

She squeezed her eyes together and saw the bear feeding on her mother.

She opened her eyes wildly but she could still see it. Bones cracking, his head burrowing into her still body and then the muzzle rearing into the air, ringed with blood. Her mother's blood. Kannik sank to her knees, moaning.

Your pain will not call them back, a small voice mocked. You should have thought of that when you cowered under the sleeping ledge.

She got shakily to her feet. It was as it was to be. But the words were bitter in her throat. Her mother was dead. Her father and brother had died trying to save her.

And she lived because she was a coward. She paled, her body trembling. Cowards always die the worst deaths.

She swallowed hard and fumbled for the flint in the pouch around her neck. Her hands were so numb she dropped the sticks, and they clattered onto the ice, the noise deafening. She froze, listening for the bear, but the only sound was her own heart hammering in her ears.

Whimpering, she rasped the flint and fired the wick, grateful one lamp bowl was still intact. The light flared in front of her, casting long shadows on the ruins of the snowhouse. A black stain splashed over the wall and Kannik realized in horror that it was blood.

She moved the light along the east wall, searching for a weapon she would not know how to use. Panic will guide my hands, she thought, and felt herself growing calmer. She found a small knife her brother had used to slit the throats of seals and hooked it into the pocket of her parka, and then she looked around, not knowing what to do next.

Find the bodies. She owed them that much.

She moved the light along the wall and saw a crumpled shape in the shadows. Her belly lurched and the small of her back went wet with dread. She turned the body over.

He came slowly up. First the darkness, then a flat light on the edge of his vision, and then the night came roaring back at him and he sat up and looked around. His head throbbed. Kannik was kneeling next to him. Behind her, he saw a jagged wall in the moonlight. It was like one of those doll half-snowhouses he had built for his younger sisters so they could sit in the middle and reach everything. Only this was *his* house. Sweet Spirit, where were his parents?

There was the entryway, followed by the connecting passage with small cubicles opening off of it—the room for outer gear, the cooking room—and the sleeping platform at the far end. But there was only half of everything: half an entryway, half a corridor with rooms opening off of only *one* side, half a sleeping platform. Fear squeezed his bowels.

The sleeping ledge his father had occupied was gone, buried in a pile of rubble. And his father? Was he buried too? His mother had been in the cooking room when the bear attacked. A fine layer of snow now covered the sunken fire basin and cooking pottery. Nothing moved except the moonlight. She wasn't there anymore. He tried to wrap his mind around the enormity of it.

Once when Nuka had been a child, before the Bladder Feast announcing his manhood, a great wind had scoured the village during the night. In the morning everything had been rearranged: houses tumbled inward, sleds scattered like small sticks, birds lifted up and smashed into the mud with such force they died, their bodies forever wedged between sky and sand. The stillness stuck in his memory like sand in his throat.

It was like that now. The tools his father had so lovingly arranged in his room, meticulously hanging according to size and function, now spilled across the tundra, tangled in with harnesses and snow chunks and the boots Kannik had been sewing, while over everything the stillness beat like a frantic captured bird. Kannik stared at him, her eyes huge.

"Where is mother?" The silence hurt his ears.

Kannik turned away.

"Father?"

"There have been no cries during the night. Only the sound of the bear."

He pulled himself to his side. The blood pounded in his head and he was certain he was going to faint. The ground rushed up and Nuka doubled over until his vision steadied.

"What are you doing?"

102

He pushed himself to his knees and took the light in one hand and his spear in the other. The blood roared through his face, and he almost fell getting up.

"I'm coming too. The time for women staying at home is past."

I'm coming too. Nuka flinched as if he had been hit. He could not have been more shocked if she had blasphemed the names of their ancestors. *I'm coming, too.* He looked at the sky and waited for a bolt to strike her down. The people of the whale never use *I* out loud. It was the first lesson every child learned. It was more than the height of bad manners, calling attention to oneself. It was—he looked fearfully at the sky again, listening. Kannik knew the consequences of defying the old law. A woman hunter! The spirit of the animal would rise up against him.

"I will stay a distance behind." That word! He wanted to choke her until she cried for forgiveness. "And besides, how can things possibly be any worse than they already are? You need me."

"No wonder no man has taken you into his hut for more than a night!" he snapped. "Your tongue flies away from your face and stings whatever it lights upon."

She waited calmly, her small body tall in the light. She picked up a spear. "Perhaps my death is written tonight. But if it is to be, let me die fighting, and not cowering and whimpering alone, waiting for the snap of its jaws."

Drastic measures had to be taken. It was clear she had lost her mind. He nodded, not trusting himself to speak, and her small shoulders sagged in relief. He motioned for her to take the weapon in his hands. She took it, holding both spears. He put down the lamp and swung around and hit her as hard as he could. She crumpled to the ground with a small burp of surprise. He stretched her out and stepped into the moonlight.

He crawled over to the far wall and looked out. The snow gleamed like polished soapstone. The great bear lay on its side, its head lolling. Next to it were scraps of meat and bone. It was snoring. It had taken life, and now it was time for its life to be taken.

He turned and faced the moon.

103

"Alignuk! You who fly to the moon and guard the souls of men and animals, return now and guide my spear." The moon sailed over him, its face as smooth as an idiot's.

He tightened his grip on his spear, conscious that his hands were wet inside his gloves. The spruce shaft he had polished with his father felt thin and fragile in his hands. His head ached.

The bear was not unmarked. The left side of its neck had been grazed and now the fur around the wound was black in the light. He had almost killed him. The bear's side had been punctured and even from a distance Nuka could see the wounds were deep. His father's work. Nuka wondered what had happened to him.

The bear stirred. Nuka stopped crawling, his face slick with sweat. The bear's paw jerked in its sleep and boxed the air. Nuka was only a body length away now. He could see its chest move. His mouth went dry. He had never seen such a bear. Two bodies long. The black pads on its paws were as big as a man's head. He had one chance for a clean kill.

He moved closer. Clumps of black hair clotted the snow. His mother's hair. He swallowed the bile in his mouth and raised his spear. His mother. The beast must pay. He was standing over it now. He could see its nostrils widening as it breathed and the way the shiny wound quivered next to the yellow fur. *Pay.*

He threw his spear as hard as he could. One chance.

The bear rolled and staggered to its feet, roaring with a sound more deafening than ice thundering into ridges in the ocean. Nuka backed away. The bear reared up and the spear quivered in a small red stain next to its heart. Its claws slashed through the air and the spear snapped off and clattered to the ground.

Nuka turned and ran.

He ran blindly. He could feel the rush of the wind behind him. The faint tracing of what was left of the igloo wall loomed suddenly to his left.

Too far. The bear was closing in. With the last of his strength, Nuka hurled his body over the wall.

The bear shot toward him. It crashed over the wall, crushing

104

the ice stones and spraying ice. Nuka rolled. The bear skidded past him, so close he could smell the blood on its fur.

"Sweet Spirit," he prayed, "save me."

His hand curled around a drill his father used for fixing the dogsled. He crouched to his knees and measured the distance between them. He would have to time his attack directly to the bear's spring, coming up hard under its belly to ram the stake through its heart.

The bear turned so swiftly that Nuka was caught off balance. He flailed the drill out, knowing his timing was off, and the hit barely grazed the bear's throat.

Then the beast smashed into him and the drill flew from his hand.

Nuka and the bear were two blurred shadows as they wrestled in the ruins and clouds smoked across the moon. Kannik crouched next to the wall, fear wedged like a fist in her throat. It was a furious dance. Neither made a sound. Kannik watched, frozen, as Nuka drew back the drill and it sailed out of his hand. Then the animal was down on top of him and Kannik knew it was killing him. It shocked her into action. She picked up her father's flint axe and ran over, her crotch wet with terror.

She whimpered and raised the axe. The beast stopped eating and looked steadily at her. *It knows.* She held the axe stiff. *It knows I have never killed.* The beast dropped his head down, dismissing her. *Cowards always die the worst deaths.*

The bear was eating her brother's shoulder.

It was as if everything were slowed in time: she saw the great jaws opening and snarling back over the fangs, the thrust of its muzzle as it sank down over her brother's flesh, the huge grinding motion of its jaws.

She shook until the axe rattled in her hands and held her breath to steady it. The monster stared at her, neck bristling. She threw back the axe and buried it in the bear's skull. There was a terrible crunching noise as the bones cracked apart. Kannik saw the pinkish gray membrane of its brain and the white bone and then blood flooded over the fur. The bear fell heavily and so slowly that Kannik could see the muscles rippling under its fur and the inevitable lurch as it lost its balance and went down.

She shook violently and her teeth clacked.

Her brother lay twisted on his stomach, as still as death.

She felt the seal she had eaten rise in her throat and her stomach rush to her mouth. She stooped and threw up. Whimpering, she spat and wiped her mouth out with snow, spitting again. It won't get any easier, she thought dully. She reached down and turned him over.

Moonlight played over the planes of his face. The right side was just as she remembered it: high cheekbones accenting deepset eyes, a strong chin, thin almost cruel lips. But the left side—her body shook and she heaved violently into the snow. She made herself look again.

The left side under the eye was gone.

Nuka's head was twisted away from her, blood crusting in a pool under him. His eye was sealed shut and below it—where his cheek should have been, there was—there was *nothing*.

She reached behind her for something to hold her up. No chin, no lips, just a bloody pulpy mass hanging under the eye.

The Spirit was kind to end his life, she thought. Her body rattled with a chill.

And then his right eye fluttered and the purple hole moved where his lips had been and the *thing* that had been Nuka groaned. She reeled and the sky fell away.

Someone had lit a fire in his face and shoulder. It burned through him, the pain unbearable. He opened his mouth to scream at them to put it out but he couldn't form the words. Something was wrong with his mouth. He touched his tongue to his lips and pulled back. Hot. The fire was hot.

Sweet Spirit. The bear. He struggled to rise but Kannik hovered over him and pushed him down. Lights and shadows. He was forgetting something. What had the bear done to him? Don't panic. Panic kills. What had happened to him?

"It's not a lot of urine for such a wound, but at least it's warm." Kannik pulled up her pants and carefully raised the bowl. She wouldn't look at him. Steam rose. He struggled to see her clearly. Her face retreated and advanced. Where were they? What had happened to him? The beast had taken him down, the claws had whistled through the air and found his flesh and—He gasped. The memory came slinking back, drawn by the blood taste of his fear.

His face.

His face was—

"This is going to hurt." She soaked a caribou skin in the urine and clamped it wet against his face. Agonizing pain shot through him. He cried out but his voice only made thin gurgling sounds. He swallowed air in huge racking sobs, his heart hammering.

Something was wrong with his eye.

He strained, the good eye bulging, trying to see. Kannik was there in the right eye, kneeling in front of him. There was a tent in the eye, too. But the left one. He stopped. His heart roared in his chest. *Blind in the left eye.* From this moment on, he was only half a hunter, doomed to scraps and charity. Blind. He pushed himself up on an elbow and pain washed over him in fiery waves. Kannik held his head.

"Look at me," she said fiercely, "and listen well! It is not the way it seems. The bear has gored your face, but he has missed the eye. Your lips will never make the maidens of the village hungry for their communion, but your mouth will work for you all the same. Speech will return. Your shoulder has a deep wound. I have stuffed part of the skin of a caribou into the cavity, and for now the blood is pooling."

This time when she used *I*, he didn't flinch. The whole world had changed. Kannik paused, her hands cold against his skin. She took a deep breath and continued.

"Father lives." She restrained his body as he struggled to get up. "He has been waiting to see you. To—to die. I will help you to him, but first you must be told." Tears welled in her eyes and she whispered, "He is changed, Nuka."

"Kannik?" The voice was mushy, like rotting ice.

She stooped down quickly and supported her brother as he struggled to his feet. The blood inside his arm rushed down and his knees buckled. Nuka leaned on his sister and hobbled across the room.

It was the stench he recognized first, the unmistakable smell of dying flesh. Don't let me dishonor him by throwing up, he thought. He swallowed hard and when he was certain he had won, he opened his eyes and looked at his father.

The man's right arm had been ripped away from his body. Kannik had tied caribou string tightly around the jagged fragment of bone near his shoulder. Black streaks crawled over his father's chest, leading the poison away from the wound and toward his heart. That wound was the cleanest. The bear had ripped open his father's body and now the organs were piled loosely back into the cavity, covered only by a thin flap of flesh. His father drew a breath. The wound opened and entrails and blood oozed onto the ground. Nuka turned his head, ripped off his bandage, and was heartily and thoroughly sick.

"The Feast of the Dead." His breathing rasped through the small room and the lamp popped when the fire struck a lump of fat and Nuka was certain he could hear his own heart beating in his face. "You must take me home."

The Feast of the Dead. By which all things are righted, from which no man returns.

"You must promise me you will take me home." Nuka could feel the sweat glistening on his face. Anything but this. His father looked at him fiercely, his eyes burning like dying coals. *He hears my thoughts as clearly as if I were speaking.*

"It is true," said the old man, "the conditions under which we left the village will make it difficult."

Difficult! He had to make his father see.

The old man squeezed Nuka's good arm with a hand that still had the power to make him wince with its strength. "No. It is *you* who do not see, my son. My eternal soul is in danger. Nothing is more important than that! Not even life itself."

Behind him Nuka could hear Kannik starting to cry.

"Promise me you will take me home. My soul must not wander."

They will kill us, Nuka thought. They will scatter our bones and curse our memories. What is the Feast of the Dead compared to that?

His father stared at him, not believing. "You are afraid? My only son is *afraid?*" He smiled, and it was like a skull smiling.

108

"There are other fears that are worse, my son. There are other things more deserving of your fear."

Nuka looked away.

"You have always been an obedient son. Do you choose the burden of carrying through life the knowledge that you denied your father his final wish?"

Not a wish, Nuka thought. A command.

"A command then."

They were locked together, his father's words battling his thoughts as the sweat poured down their faces and his father gripped his arm. "It is *your* destiny too! You must consider the consequences if you do not follow the old law."

Moments passed, and over the ragged sound of his father's breathing, Nuka heard the words of a childhood rhyme, indistinct at first and then clear.

> Round and round the circle goes;
> Where it stops, no one knows,
> For we are never quite apart.
> We're bound by need and deed and heart.

The circle game. The first game he learned as a child. Why should he think of that now?

"Take me home," his father whispered.

Need and deed and heart. The children passed a stone and whoever held it at the end of the rhyme chose something to act out—a need, a deed, a desire of the heart. The person who guessed became the new leader and the game continued.

"Your life is not separate," his father said painfully.

Need and deed and heart.

"We are all bound together by our needs and obligations and love. You cannot escape, my son."

In that instant Nuka knew his father was right. Whatever happened, he had to return his father's body to the village. But the realization brought him no joy.

His father smiled at him and his hand slipped away from his arm. "Good. It is on your spirit."

His father's jaw sank back and yellow spittle flooded his mouth. His eyes clouded and he tried suddenly to sit up, his chest rattling as he coughed. His lips moved furiously and he stared at the far wall beyond Nuka, pointing with a bony finger. Nuka turned to look and when he turned back, his father's body had shrunken as if it was his spirit alone that had given weight and substance to his flesh. Now the cheeks were sucked inward and his hand curled up in a gesture of surrender.

It will be over soon, Nuka said silently. Until the Feast of the Dead, the spirit of his father would cling to the body, like a lost child clings to kind strangers.

"Come," Kannik said. "Rest." She touched Nuka and he turned and stumbled back to bed.

She stood quietly and looked at her father. He had worn his disappointment of her badly but often, as a man might wear a useful coat he hates. "Your eldest daughter always loved you," she whispered. She dressed herself, wrapped the body in skins and dragged it outside.

Clouds shrouded the moon. Violence clung to the place where she had killed the bear and skinned it. She gave it wide berth.

She dragged the body over to where her mother had died, and stared down at the bodies in the dim light.

So small. Was this the man who had carried her on his shoulders? The woman who had taught her the sacred mysteries of her sex?

She would choose them both again, next life.

She looked uneasily at the ice hut. From where she stood in the vast and silent darkness, she could hear her brother moaning in his sleep. The face would heal; she was certain the seal-gut stitches would hold. It was the shoulder wound that scared her. The caribou skin was soaked with blood. She had changed it twice already. She looked at the moon and dropped to her knees, trembling.

"Forgive me!" Her voice was low. "There is no male to intervene for me. I come to you as a child of the universe, seeking healing. Listen! Spirits of the wind, of the ice that cracks and scatters into tiny pellets seen only in the night sky, I come to you seeking relief for my brother." She waited in the white stillness; only the frosty cloud of her breathing moved.

On the rim of a gradual rise to the west, she saw it. It was only a small black spot at first, and then the spot moved and grew. Something was moving toward her across the far crest of snow, something precise and orderly.

She scrambled to her feet and ran.

The Reverend Marsh removed his spectacles and polished them. He put them on and stared at her thoroughly. Not one of the Barrow maidens, but she did wear the marks of a coastal tribe—a thin red line tattooed under her mouth, signifying that she had passed her first blood and was ready to couple. He sighed. The work was slow and difficult. He had been practicing among the natives now for over a year, sent by the Federal Council of Churches, Presbyterian Synod, to practice in the northernmost district. He was on his way to Beechey Point with a load of Bibles and medicine. He turned to his young companion.

"She tells me her brother is ill. Gored by a bear and near death."

His companion studied the girl. She was terribly thin. "What are you going to do?"

Reverend Marsh sighed. "There's an outbreak of diphtheria at the mission in Beechey Point."

"I'll stay," the stranger said impulsively. "You can pick me up on your way back to Barrow."

"My dear boy, you have no idea what you're getting yourself into! These people have different customs, you don't know the language—"

"I'll stay," the stranger said firmly.

The minister shook his head and said, "I'll be back within a fortnight." He reached out and clasped the young man's hand. "Godspeed."

"Godspeed." Cahill Blue picked up his pack and followed the girl.

Ten

Cahill took the kerosene lamp from his pack and put a match to the wick, adjusting the draft until the cotton filament glowed brightly. He motioned to the girl, and she held the light over her brother. The youth appeared to be about Cahill's age. Like the girl, he was terribly thin and was hallucinating. Sometimes he would call out, and even in a foreign tongue Cahill was certain the youth was crying for his mother. The girl stroked her brother's hand and looked at Cahill abjectly, her dark eyes silently pleading with him to do something.

He knew so little. The flow of blood would have to be staunched, but there were not even the most rudimentary of tools. The caribou cloth the girl had stuffed into the wound was full of blood. Cahill took the small bag of medicines out of his pack and spread them over the furs. How insignificant they appeared next to the young man, thrashing and moaning. There was a box of carbolic salve, a bottle of arnica, a quarter's worth of cascara bark, a good bottle of whiskey and a thick roll of gauze.

He sectioned off a wad of gauze as thick as two fingers and removed the caribou skin from the wound. His heart sank. Bright red blood was spurting in a steady stream. The brachial artery had been severed. He quickly pressed the gauze into the wound and applied pressure. On the furs the youth moaned in his sleep. The girl paled. Cahill looked around the small room. It had obviously been part of a larger snowhouse at one time. Great calamity had befallen it. He could see where two new walls and a ceiling had been built—the girl's hasty work, he guessed, after the attack. She was a few years younger than her brother, perhaps fifteen. So young to have seen so much death! He took his hand away from the wound and lifted the gauze.

The blood still hadn't clotted. The girl watched him, trying to anticipate his needs. An axe, a spear and some hunting knives had been arranged near the entryway. What he would give for a hemostat! Cahill motioned for the girl to apply pressure to the shoulder. Her hand slipped under his and she pushed hard. He got the axe and untied the thongs that were binding the stone blade to the handle. He would have to use the leather cording. The girl looked at him and understood. In a flash she left her brother's side and returned. She carried a seal-gut thread and a small ivory needle. Cahill sopped up the blood and dug down, grasping the slippery cord of the severed artery. In minutes he had finished sewing. He sat back, exhausted. The youth would never have full use of his arm again because the artery was permanently tied off, but Cahill was confident he would live. The girl stooped next to her brother and bathed his face around the stitches. Cahill examined her work. The stitches were small and even. He imagined that under the filth she might be pretty. Her hair was thick with rancid seal grease and hung in a long shiny rope that smelled. The soft skins she wore next to her body were stained with sweat and the blood from animals she had skinned. He was tired; the reverend and he had been marching on snowshoes for almost a week, the dogs and sled between them, but he knew he wouldn't be able to sleep until she was washed. The room was too close. He dug into his pack and came out with a bar of soap, a towel and a small portable stove. He lit a fire in the stove and found the cooking pot, then he crawled outside and filled the pot with snow.

The nukatpiak was crazy. To wet one's head in the middle of winter! Did he save her brother's life only to take her own? But his hands were firm against her head as he pushed it down into the water. It was warm against her head. Her hair sank and swam its own course and the blond stranger rubbed until all the color came off.

He dried her hair, dumped the water into the snow outside and heated more. When it was warm again, he made her bathe. Afterward Kannik curled into her own skins and watched the stranger. Did he wish to spear her? Was that it? He made no effort in her direction but sank, exhausted, into his own skins.

113

He was not unattractive. He was light, like the whaler. Once a
whaler named Caleb had taught her words that she now
searched her mind to remember. She crawled out of bed and
squirmed next to the stranger. She touched him. He was
wearing light pants and she smoothed her hand under them
next to his skin. He had been dozing and he jerked awake.

"My name Kannik. Snowflake. You?" Her voice was soft
and musical.

"Cahill."

"Cahill." She struggled with the word and then said simply,
"I comfort you."

She wrapped her arms around his neck and pulled him close
to her. Her breasts were small and firm.

Cahill felt a mixture of revulsion and desire. Ever since
Nelly he had been haunted by a strong sense that he was not
the good, upright person he wanted to be. His manly impulses
were not the kind that produced peace between nations or great
symphonies: they were the kind that produced children. To go
from a whore to a savage! He would never find the crown of life
promised in the Scriptures. Flame shimmered like a mirage in
his thirsty imagination, while next to him, Kannik shivered in
his bed. She touched his organ and he felt himself stiffen. He
had been alone so long! His organ throbbed and Kannik smiled.
"I comfort you," she said again.

Cahill felt himself losing control. He turned to her hungrily.

You couldn't wait to stick it in the first hole you could find.

He stiffened, pulling away from her. Kannik slowed the
rhythm of her hand but didn't release him.

*And you'll spend the rest of your life denying it, justifying it
and looking for it all over again.*

It was no use. He stopped Kannik's hand and rolled away
from her toward the wall. Kannik wrapped her arms around his
body and rubbed against him. He wanted badly to roll over and
kiss her, to bury himself in her small body. What difference
would it make? Outside, the Arctic night sky creaked with cold.
Nothing existed but this small circle of light and those hands
caressing him.

"You good man," she whispered.

A good man. He stopped her hands brusquely, shaken by

114

how close he had come to losing complete control. He threw on his clothes, furious with himself. For an hour he walked stiffly around the hut through the cold dry night, the snow squeaking beneath his boots and his cheeks stinging with cold. A good man.

The words rang in his head like a death knell. Such a bitter price to pay for goodness. To be left with ashes in his mouth and weakness in his knees. He walked faster.

He had survived this round. Endured the temptation. But the Crown of Life the Lord had promised him was still laying in a box somewhere, with the price tag hanging from its ruby centerpiece.

He had a fortnight to go.

Tears sprang to his eyes.

The full impact of what he had been thinking struck him, and it was like a blow to the head. Had he learned nothing all these months? He had wanted to be separated from all those he loved, and God in His infinite wisdom had allowed him to come here. He had gotten exactly what he deserved. There could be no one else but Flame.

It's a lie, he thought. All of it. About what makes a man a man. There was only this, over and over again.

A true man is not afraid of loving, of committing himself. To a cause, an idea, a woman. He had come full circle, and now he found himself humbled by his need for Flame, and Flame alone. It was not only a need for her body, although in the long dark months of separation that need had been constantly with him, but more a hunger for her presence. He longed not for infinite variety, but for enduring sameness. He wanted to lie with her forever, until the texture of her skin next to his was as familiar as his own, until their dreams floated easily between them in their sleep.

He stood in the night with the snow stretching for an infinity around him; the stars were sharp pricks of light. He felt alone and small and very far from home.

Loving her. That's what rooted him in the world. That's what warmed him and made his surroundings bearable. He had traveled halfway across the world and only now, from this distance, was he seeing her clearly.

He would give anything to hold her in his arms.

Daily the patient's shoulder and face improved, but he was lucid for only short periods of time. Cahill applied carbolic salve to the wounds. The salve had been made by his father out of carbolic acid mixed with vaseline and balsam of fir. Cahill always thought it smelled like a tree would if it were standing in a city park in hell: oppressive, sulphurous, and faintly woodsy. By the second day, the shoulder wound had begun to close without infection. Cahill mixed two teaspoons of brandy with a cup of hot water and thirty drops of tincture of arnica and turned the patient gently onto his side so he could swab his back. At least he wouldn't get bedsores.

Lice was another matter.

Both he and his sister were plagued by them. Kannik's solution was to go naked inside the hut. Cahill's solution was not to look. He also tried mixing two drops of carbolic acid in a half pint of water and wetting himself down. The lice moved and settled comfortably into his clothes. He tried freezing them out, smoking them out and poisoning them with carbolic acid. The fur on his parka separated in clumps; the lice stayed.

Cahill gave up and stripped down to his union suit when he was inside. He made a point of staying outside. He wasn't tempted anymore by Kannik's flesh; it wasn't that. But her nakedness was a reminder of how close he had come.

He worked hard. He rebuilt the ceiling and ice wall Kannik had hastily thrown up after the bear attack. Kannik spent her days preparing the bearskin. She used a woman's knife shaped like the outline of a horse's hoof, broader at the base and very sharp. It was metal.

"Iron," Kannik said with pride when Cahill commented on it. She held it up but wouldn't let Cahill touch it.

"Spirits," she said, groping for the right words.

What was she trying to say? *Spirits*. He thought about it. Of course, Male and female tools, neither touched by members of the opposite sex. "The spirits will be angry. Is that what you mean?"

She looked at him blankly.

"Angry." Cahill exaggerated a scowl, threw up his hands in

front of his face and advanced on her, swinging his arms like an ape. "Angry spirits!" He shouted the words. "Angry!" He put down his hands and waited expectantly.

Kannik hastily withdrew to the farthest wall, taking the bearskin with her. Nothing he could say would make her talk to him the rest of the day. That night she inched his bowl of boiled seal meat over to him and backed away, eating hers from the safety of the far wall. He hadn't meant to scare her. She worked in silence over the skin, separating bits of flesh from the fur with deft strokes. She had already dressed the bear and stored the meat in an ice cache adjoining the hut, but the skin had to be perfectly stripped and treated with urine before she could sew. Cahill wished he had a needle for a peace offering. She crouched by the wall within touching distance of a brother who could not save her, and stared often and coolly at the pale stranger.

The reverend had been right. Cahill *didn't* know anything of their language or customs. He was a failure. He wanted to get down on the ground and eat worms, except that there weren't any, and with his luck, they would probably have some sacred significance, like the cows in India.

At home it would have been easy. He would buy flowers; chocolates, too, if what he had done was *truly* unforgiveable, and he would wear his repentant look—the one that said, I'm really just a country boy, ma'am, what don't know nothing nohow, and I'm real sorry. For whatever it is. Whatever little minor thing I did to set you off.

But here it was different. Kannik spent two days glaring at him in silence, while her brother mumbled in his sleep and a parka grew out of the bearskin. She rebuffed him totally, as if he didn't exist.

On the morning of the third day of silence, he took matters into his own hands. He had a small shaving mirror in his pack. Cahill didn't use it for shaving, but he did take it out once or twice on bad nights, to prove he was really there. He laid it at her feet. She glanced at it, sniffed and went back to sewing. Cahill retreated to his pack, sat on his haunches and waited.

An hour went by. Kannik looked in the mirror and looked away, but her hand stole to her cheek to rearrange her hair.

117

She looked again, longer this time. With that peculiar hardeyed stare every female in the world has perfected by the time she is eight, studying every pore, every line, every imagined imperfection with absolute, concentrated intensity. She smiled at herself. The Kannik in the mirror smiled back.

She searched her memory and said, "Pretty."

"Very." Cahill smiled.

Kannik put down the mirror and crawled next to him. She wrapped her naked arms around his nearly naked body and pressed herself against him. "I comfort you."

It sounded like such a good idea.

He found himself wanting her again. She pressed her face against his and rubbed his beard with the flat of her hand. She had very little body hair. None under her arms and only a small dusting covering her genitals. She gently squeezed a handful of his whiskers and released them, amused at the way the hair sprang back to its original shape.

"It's a beard," Cahill said.

"Beard," she repeated promptly. She patted it with her hand, turned her face slightly and kissed him on the mouth. It was a sweet kiss, her lips soft and yielding.

How long it had been! Since Nelly. His organ stiffened. She felt it and pressed herself against him harder. He took her hands firmly and pushed her away from him. "No." It was the hardest word he had ever said. Her face was a welter of hurt and confusion.

"Kannik pretty, yes?"

"Yes. Kannik pretty."

She shook her head in bewilderment. "Kannik no see."

Cahill sighed. How could he communicate the concept of honor? They still had trouble with meat and potato words.

He thought of something. "Spirits," he said. She nodded tentatively, still hurt. "White spirits angry."

She looked away, her body sullen and rigid with disbelief. "Kannik no pretty."

Cahill sighed, exasperated. Every woman was obsessed with the same fear. He took her hand. She let him hold it, but she still wouldn't look at him.

"Kannik pretty. Very pretty."

She shook her head sorrowfully. Her hair gleamed. He had stopped her from greasing it with rancid seal oil and now it fell thickly over her shoulders.

He touched her hair. "Pretty hair." She looked at him sideways. He touched the soft curve of her cheek. "Pretty face." Her lips trembled. She looked at him then and her eyes filled with tears.

"Kannik no see," she murmured.

Kannik was nothing to him, and hurting her would not have been like hurting someone known and loved. But he knew if he couldn't fix it, didn't at least *try* to fix it, it would be one of those small things that could come back into his mind on sleepless nights, part of a long dreary line of failures that marched over his fragile self-esteem, flattening it to the ground.

He took her hand and pointed at her brother. "Brother," he said.

She nodded, her eyes down, her hand limp. Cahill pressed her hand on his chest. "Cahill brother."

She looked at him searchingly, disbelieving.

"Cahill brother," he repeated.

"Brother," she said listlessly.

"Yes," he said firmly. "Cahill brother."

She looked at her hands as if they were much more interesting than anything he could possibly say. A thought came to her. "Kannik pretty."

"Yes," he said firmly. It seemed to cheer her up.

"You could come with me, you know." He was taking everything out of his pack to rearrange it. Kannik sat quite still, her thin arms wrapped around her legs. "You could go to school at the mission in Barrow. We could wait until your brother is well. Shouldn't be much longer. You could do what I do. Heal people."

She bent her head thoughtfully and looked at the floor.

"The world is big, Kannik," Cahill said gently. "Bigger than ice. There are buildings made of brick and steel, with tall windows and flowers that grow in orderly patterns. Some men have lived their whole lives and never seen snow." He paused,

119

watching her. He knew she couldn't understand most of what he said. But he had grown accustomed, in his loneliness, to speaking to her as though she could.

She didn't say anything, and Cahill knew she was struggling with the idea. She added seal fat to the lamp; she watched her brother's sleeping face; she sat.

Cahill stretched out his blankets and slept. When he awoke, she was still sitting in the same place, but next to her were her things: snowshoes made from birch, cooking pots, tools. It was a small pile, her lifetime accumulation, and Cahill found himself touched by her courage.

"I come with you," she said quietly. She got up and dressed quickly. She didn't look at her brother.

She spent the day outside, away from the hut, dividing the bear and seal meat into piles. She would not leave Nuka hungry. At least there was that. It was small comfort.

She was defying the old law. Something evil would come of it. And for her.

It is as it was to be. She had never been like Nuka or the others. A fire burned inside her; an eagle was trapped inside her chest and longed to soar. Her future now was beckoning to her, and she had only to take up its hand to let it fly.

She walked back toward the hut, her arms filled with meat. She stopped. Nuka was standing transfixed, his head raised. The first light of the year was trailing across the eastern sky. She dropped the meat and ran to him.

"You have awakened." She felt guilty, as if she had been caught with her hand in a batch of newly made akutuk. She would have to find a way to tell him, but gently. He had removed his bandages and she was shocked by the transformation of his face. His jaw had sealed together unevenly, and now the left side of his face sank slightly under his deformed lip. The skin under his eye drooped, and the scar dividing his face had healed into a permanent purple welt. He grinned and it was the most beautiful sight she had ever seen.

"Pack your cooking pots, sister. We are leaving."

"Leaving!"

He stared at her, startled by the force of her words.

"We *cannot* leave."

120

"Cannot?"

"There—there are boots that need to be sewn still and the snares set have yet to yield game—but they will, Nuka. They will." She turned breathlessly to him. "We have everything we need here, brother. Everything."

Behind her, a blond stranger appeared, hauling bear meat. He saw Nuka and advanced, smiling as if he knew him.

Nuka backed away. "What does this man have to do with me?"

"He came one day when the bear wounded you and healed your shoulder." Kannik was smiling at the man, and Nuka saw more in her eyes than he liked.

"Get rid of him," Nuka said shortly.

Kannik paled. "Brother! The spirit of our father will rise up against you."

Nuka turned his back on the stranger and looked at the sky.

Kannik walked around him and stood in front of him. There could be no other way. "The stranger leaves today with a missionary, and they will not leave alone."

"We have a promise to our father, remember?"

"You mean you have a promise! I promised nothing!" He slapped her and she stepped back, more surprised than hurt.

"Never use that word again out loud," he said quietly. "Now pack your pots. We're leaving in the morning."

"No!" She held her ground defiantly.

Nuka thrust his left arm forward. "Look at it!" he cried. "Examine it. Hold it in your hands. And see the work the man has done! He has robbed me of my strength."

Kannik took her brother's hand in hers. Even under the aatkatik, she could feel that the hand was limp, as if it had no spirit. Her brother's killing hand. She looked up, stricken. "Your sister did not know."

"This is the man you would give up your family to follow? He has crippled me. He has sucked the power out of my arm. He is no better than the traders."

Kannik whirled away from Nuka and burst into tears.

"Your tears will not change the truth. He is one of them even though he does not come in a tall ship riding the waves. And like them, he will leave you someday, hungry and alone.

121

Who will sing songs for you then, sister, when the cooking pot is empty? Who will ~~warm your body during the next great~~ hunger?"

Kannik wept into her hands. The eagle inside her breast beat its great wings and stilled. She allowed herself to gaze once more on the face of the stranger, to see the kindness written there, before she turned and went to her brother's side.

"The pots will be packed, brother, and the furs rolled. There will be no more talk of leaving with him."

Twice more while the sled was loaded with meat and furs and Nuka readied the corpse for the trip, the stranger approached Kannik with tenderness. Both times she ignored his foreign words. The second time he put his hand on her arm and she pushed him away and ran. After that he kept to himself and watched her from a distance.

But inside, the eagle called.

"So the patient will live." The Reverend Marsh looked soberly at Cahill. "But will the doctor?"

Cahill was staring at the girl as she slipped a harness over her head and took her place behind her brother. They would pull the sled themselves. "I keep wondering what her life will be like."

"She'll live, die and go unsaved. None of that concerns you. You saved one savage. Now you must release the other from your thoughts."

Cahill strapped on his snowshoes. "I never touched her, if that's what you think. She was quick and bright." He paused. "She was going to come with us until her brother put a stop to it."

"Cahill, I baptized you myself, in your great-uncle's christening gown, still a babe in your mother's arms. Your father was a deacon in my church. You have always wrestled with the sin of impulsiveness. She is one of God's creatures, but it would go against the laws of nature, mixing blood."

Cahill looked at him sharply. "I didn't intend to marry her."

"Even more a reason not to take her along."

"What's that supposed to mean?"

"Nothing, my son," the reverend said mildly. "Only that

you couldn't take her to tea at your father's table."

The reverend eased his bad leg onto the sled and sat down. Cahill stood behind the sled and checked the straps. The dogs yanked against their harness, eager to leave. They were attached to a single trace that hooked to an iron circle. Cahill tested it. It held firm.

"I tried what you suggested for my leg," Reverend Marsh remarked. "Seems to help. But it's very hot."

Cahill nodded. "It's the cayenne pepper." He cinched down his pack. "Next time try steeping it in a cup and a half of vinegar and wrap it warm around the leg."

"Read in *Physician and Surgeon* about an electric battery a doctor build for a rheumatism patient. Attached a zinc and silver plate to the front and back of the leg, connected by a copper wire."

Cahill walked to the front of the sled and took hold of the lead dog's harness. "Surprised it didn't burn a hole through the man's leg."

"The sponges saw to that. He was cured in a week." Reverend Marsh polished his glass. "Have you given any thought to your plans?"

"You mean am I going to go back to mining?"

"The three months is up. You're free to leave."

"Heard there's a new strike, maybe; place called Rampart. Thought I'd try it out until the ice lifts. I'm getting married this year."

"You are? How wonderful! Congratulations!"

"Thank you. You'll like her if you meet her. Anyway, I'd like to take something out of this land when I go."

Reverend Marsh nodded and lifted anchor. The dogs sprang ahead, dumbly happy to be moving.

Dominion Creek had been staked for four miles, from the dome to the flats, before Cahill ever got off the boat. He worked six weeks on Cheechako Hill and found an iron nail and part of a mastodon's tooth. Then he'd wasted a month on another claim and another month packing his gear back to town.

The letter from his father had come overland from Valdez saying that Reverend Marsh was on a mission for a year, and was due in Dawson to pick up supplies.

Maybe it had been as simple as seeing somebody from home; maybe he still dreamt of Nelly at night and longed for absolution; whatever it was, he agreed to spend the deepest part of winter in the darkest part of Alaska.

He had spent three months regretting it and looking for a light.

Kannik had been that, for a while. The one person whose life he had touched and changed. He had seen something in her that struggled to rise above the poverty of her condition, and even as he thought of it now, tears came to his eyes.

Kannik was the only Eskimo he had ever met who painted pictures.

All of them were eagles.

The violence of Nuka's thoughts hung in the air. He flexed his hand. The stranger had taken more than the strength in Nuka's arm when he left. He had dried up Kannik's spirit, too. And that was infinitely worse. At least they were moving away from the path taken by the white strangers. The faster they left the circle of their power, the more chance Kannik had of regaining her own.

The ruins of the snowhouse receded. Ahead stretched an endless plain of white, unbroken by trees or hills or anything that moved. Out over the ocean, the wind bristled into clouds. It was the time of day in the Arctic that is perfectly colorless—pale yellow sky poised over luminous snow, neither day nor night but some twilight in between.

Nuka looked behind him. There was his sister, her hair a black ribbon in the wind, bent against the pull of the harness. The sled dragged behind her. It would be weeks before they met another person, yet Nuka felt only relief. He was not fooled by the kindly air of the man in black nor the yearning of the yellow-haired stranger when he looked at Kannik. He knew the men were evil brothers to the dark-souled traders who had come before. Darkness obscured their souls' path and endangered everyone they touched.

Nuka pulled the sled and remembered.

They had come to his father, bobbing and smiling and

carrying gifts.

What they brought dazzled the eye—shiny metal knives that sliced through the thickest fur without protest, white powder steamed into loaves.

And they wanted nothing in return.

Nuka smiled bitterly. How many things had changed so quickly. He wanted to remember every injustice, every indignity, every betrayal. It would fuel his hatred for the trip ahead.

The People of the Whale had traded before. Every year, during the highest point of summer, they loaded their *umiaks* with whale oil, seal, *ugruk* skins and driftwood until there was hardly room left for the dogs and children. As long as Nuka could remember, his family had traded at the mouth of the Colville River with the Mountain People from the south. When the thin ice chattered on the ocean, Nuka's family paddled home, their umiak laden with caribou skins. His father had been a skillful trader. One bladder of seal oil garnered five green caribou skins, with a wolf and fox skin thrown in for good measure.

The People of the Whale thought it would be like that with their new friends. They offered their own gifts to the white men in return: sweetly aged whale's meat, so rotted it melted in one's mouth, mukluks with soles chewed to supple whiteness, waterproof jackets to keep the water off the bodies of the white hunters as they climbed the high seas.

They were good gifts, acceptable gifts, and for a while, they were enough.

All that summer, as the sun spangled in the sky and there was no night, as the children whooped and skittered along the beach, the People of the Whale prepared for the hunt in the shadow of the great ship.

The strangers labored on a house of their own, built from driftwood and lumber they hauled from the ship, consulting the People on the best way to calk it against the wind.

As the women scanned the sky for birds and dipped their nets into the waters, the white captain laid presents at the feet of the Tareumuit: tea, tobacco, needles. Gradually the strangers acquired ears for the language of the People and a

125

taste for their women. The hunters shared them willingly.

The boundaries between the two groups softened even more until finally the day came when a gun was placed at the feet of the leader of the Tareumuit.

"I will show you," the one they called Salem said to Pana. He raised it to his shoulder, nosed it skyward and shattered the stillness with a blast that sent Pana diving backward for cover and the women flushing like birds from their houses.

Salem laughed. "No, look," he said, striding over toward the sea. He stooped, and when he stood again he held a fat ptarmigan in his hand.

Pana examined it thoroughly. Two holes punched through its body, as if from a long spear.

"A bullet," Salem said, and dropped the metal into Pana's hand.

It was heavy and small. "You tell me a bird fell from the sky from something so small?" His friend Salem was making a good joke.

Salem nodded. "And it will club seals by the breathing hole without the gun ever leaving my hands."

Pana laughed. Salem would make a good joking partner. "Teach me how to use it," he said good-naturedly. He would stretch the joke as far as the stranger wished.

Salem placed the gun in Pana's hands. "I will do more than that," he said. "The gun is yours. I will teach you things that will keep hunger from the door of your people."

And he had.

The two men stalked walrus bulls on the ice floes at the height of the summer. The magic weapon cracked their skulls and sent them crashing onto the ice from a far greater distance than the old way. The women worked furiously to temper the meat and soften the skins of so many bulls. The dogs would eat well that winter.

But there was jealousy, too, that clamped around the hearts of the villagers that summer.

"Another hunter wants a gun of his own," one of the whaling crew said. "It is not seemly that only one man feed so many from his efforts."

Pana heard the words and knew they were true. But his mind

126

had been gripped by a terrible evil—ownership. For the first time in his life, he had something he would share with no man, not even his son, Nuka. He slept with the gun next to his side and secretly traced the strange markings stamped on the butt—Winchester. When it was time to load the umiak and trade at the river, Pana could not bear to leave the teachings of his new friend, and so for the first time in Nuka's memory, his family did not trade that summer at the mouth of the Colville River.

It was the beginning of the end.

Pana's crew members finally grew bold enough to present their needs directly to the white captain instead of working through Pana, as was the custom.

"It is possible to earn a weapon," Salem said slowly, measuring his words against the hunger in the eyes of the dark men before him. "But you must answer only to me, and do exactly as I command."

Perhaps then, if Pana had stepped forward and shoved the gun back into Salem's hands, if the People had banded together and driven back the white strangers, the People of the Whale would have had a different story to tell their children during the dark nights that followed.

But the moment passed. And with it, the future of the Tareumuit twisted and slipped down a different path, into a dark, bottomless pit filled with nameless terrors.

Salem smiled.

"We will all work together and hunt the whale," he said. "And afterward we will give you more meat than you dreamed possible."

The killing went on for days.

Baleen. It had all been for baleen. Nuka saw again the bloated carnage in the water. And for what? To make corsets for white women's thick waists, women who would never know the glory of running like caribou over the tundra, who would never sense the harmony in bending naked over drying skins.

"Five dollars a pound," Salem had said, scratching his chin through his beard and watching his men jack the bowhead out of the water. "A big one like this has maybe six hundred plates of baleen in its mouth, savvy?"

No, Nuka did not.

~~The men sawed off the whale's head and~~ buried the hook into the blubber. The winch groaned and the chain creaked through the air and the massive head slowly bounced up the side of the ship, dripping blood and oil. Salem spat into the ocean and thumped Nuka on the back. "You got a ringside seat, son, savvy?"

Nuka studied his father's face. Below, in their umiak, his father and crew sat speechless, watching the strangers at work. His father stood up so suddenly that the umiak almost tipped, and shouted up to Salem. "Salem! Pi-tchailikkich!"

"The hell I'll stop work!" Salem thundered back. "You just sit tight—savak-tit-luna—and this'll be over before you can piss downwind." He scowled and muttered under his breath. "Goddamn Eskimos, more trouble than they're goddamn worth." He grinned at Nuka. "Savvy?"

Pana climbed up the side of the ship as the head of the bowhead splattered down onto the deck. Men in tall boots immediately mounted it, slicing the baleen out of its mouth in long stalks and tying them together. A ton of the stuff would be cut from just this one. Ten thousand dollars per, when the ship docked in San Francisco, and this was just the first whale. The sea was thick with them.

"*Tchaili*," Pana repeated, gesturing at the men.

"Now, Pana, you and me are friends, I think," Salem said, counting on the lilt of the words more than the Eskimo's understanding of them. "I can't stop those men. No sense to it. Besides, that's all they want. Just the baleen. Not much good to you. You can have the meat"—he flung out his arm—"all the meat in the sea if that's what you want."

Pana drew his knife. "Agvik mamianaktuk." He stepped closer and Salem backed up.

"Just a goddamn minute," Salem said. "What in the hell do you mean—the whale is angry? The goddamn whale is dead."

Pana acted without thinking. He went straight for the whaler's throat. Salem saw him coming and smashed his arms away. The knife clattered to the ground. Nuka lunged for it, and sailors swarmed over the men and grappled them down. "You want me to tie them up?" The sailor's face was next to

Nuka's, his mouth full of brown rot.

"No," Salem said shortly, "I'll handle it." The men glowered and went back to flensing the whale. "Suvich. What in the hell do you want?"

Pana stood quietly next to his son. He had learned some of the stranger's tongue and now he must summon all the words to explain. "Whale drink after hunt." He pantomined with his hands. "Drink. No drink—no come back." There. He had explained.

Salem watched his men stacking the baleen, some of it thirteen feet high. "That a fact?"

"Whale angry," Pana said. "Hunt old way."

Salem walked toward him, his hands outstretched. "We shot him, didn't we?" he said genially. "We blew him right out of the water. Took a lot less than the old way, yes? And it worked."

Pana nodded, remembering the bomb the whalers had planted in the harpooned whale. They had rammed the harpoon square in its back, below the head. The muffled whump of the bomb sounded ten seconds later and the black water was suddenly red with billowing blood. It *had* been faster, yes. And that's what worried Pana. "After baleen—go back—get new whale?"

Salem nodded. "Right. Now you're catching on. Go back. Get new whale. We just want the baleen. Some whalers—the Wegians, mostly, take the oil out. You know, boil the fat down. But we don't even need that. Just the baleen. Nice, quick work. Easy to haul. Your people can take the meat from this one, just tow it on back to shore and have your ceremonies; anything you want. Except for the head, of course." He smiled. Now the Eskimo was understanding.

Pana looked at his men in the umiak, looked at the hulking carcass of the whale strapped to the side of the ship on a wooden platform and looked at Salem.

"Blood on your hands," he said flatly. "We go now." He turned to climb down the side.

"Now just a goddamn minute," Salem said genially, his eyes narrowing. "We have a deal here, remember? Your men help in the hunt and they get guns. Savvy?"

"Eskimos follow Eskimo." He threw his leg over the side and hooked into the hemp ladder. Nuka climbed after him.

Salem lounged against the ship's railing, his hands in his pockets. "Do they follow you, really?" he said softly. "Well, let's just find out. How about that, Pana? Let's just find out. Let's call them all up here—right now—and find out."

Salem swung his body down the ladder and called to Pana's crew rapidly in Inupiaq. The men looked at Pana, but he stared stonily out to sea. They swung the boat closer and clambered up.

"Well, now," Salem drawled to Pana, "your men are stepping right smartly to my orders." It pleased him to know that Pana understood.

It was more than a battle of wills. The plain truth was, Salem Boyd needed the Eskimos. Badly. The *Derring-Do* had left San Francisco the March before, loaded to the crow's nest with sailors and supplies. They had been headed for Herschel Island. The plan had been to pick up the men whose two-year tour of duty was up, drop off the new recruits and head south before the ice jammed.

But the tender had been plagued with troubles. Before they ever made the Gulf of Alaska, the engine blew in the second boiler room, spewing steam and metal parts into the air and scalding to death the chief engineer. Then the ship got stuck in ice for three weeks.

By the time they stopped at Barrow, it was already July. That's when Salem got word at Cape Smythe Whaling and Trading Station that another ship had already slipped past them to rendezvous at Herschel Island.

This was bad news. The crew on the *Derring-Do* signed on knowing they would get paid only for what they killed. And to kill, they'd have to be transferred to a whaling ship. Salem sighed. His cut came from the whales killed, too, a split with the captain of the whaler which took the new recruits. Now they'd mutiny for sure. "What do you have to turn my ship into a whaler?"

The trading-post shopkeeper grinned and thumped him on the back. "In the back. Think we have just what you need."

Salem bought the top of the line, Danish Brojka 50-weight

darting guns with harpoons and bombs attached and second-string guns carrying only bombs. He backed it up with shoulder guns, just in case. But the real problem was boats—and for that, Salem Boyd needed the Eskimos. Badly.

Now they stood before him on deck and he jimmied open the wooden crate he had the sailors bring from the hold. He motioned them over. "Guns. Enough for each of you."

After that Pana's words were only spit in the wind. That fall the whalers took twenty-two bowheads. The village had needed only one whale to live. The Eskimos dragged the first kill back to the beach and flensed it, but the meat was bitter and tough. Then there was no time for such work. The whalers needed their boats; they needed their bodies. They killed until the whales bloated in the water like rotting fish and the gulls grew fat and lazy from the easy carnage.

Twenty-two bowheads, or enough baleen to line the pockets of the sailors with two thousand dollars cash. Salem took home enough money to start a fleet of his own. All in return for the Winchesters, rusted from disuse, cranky with age.

The whalers had wintered in afterward, the sails unbent and the yards taken down.

That spring the bowhead did not return to the waters near the People of the Whale.

Pana stood for days with his crew next to the leads, scanning the choppy ice sea, but the whales did not return. "Just a late season," Salem said. "They're bound to turn up soon."

"And the hunt this year?" Pana's crew had asked. They had grown accustomed to the whaler's method.

"Can't hunt without the whale, now can we?" Salem watched his men loading their huge ship with all the tins of food, all the white powder for making bread, all the knives and kettles. He seemed in a very big hurry to get away. "We'll be back. Just sit tight and don't follow us. We'll be back."

They sailed away. The people watched them go until they were only a small dot on the end of the world. They waited.

One day youngsters broke into the house the white strangers had built to store things. They ran screaming home and sent their fathers to look. Salem had left one man behind. He had died from hunger and cold. And from something else. Huge sores ran over his body and spilled yellow rain.

Pana knew it was a sign.

In desperation the crew turned back to the old ways, storing the sacred box of charms in the umiak and preparing for the hunt wearing newly sewn clothing and faces sooted with ancient markings. Nautchiak kept her end of the bargain. Inside the hut she neither sewed nor sang, for the Eskimos believed that any movement by the wife of the whaling captain could scare away the whales.

But the whales did not return.

More ominous still, the summer sky iced with sleet. No eider ducks nested along the marshes that year and the caribou stayed far from the northern shore.

Pana and Nuka hunted far from the village, hoarding their store of bullets and returning to the old ways of the hunt. They snared occasional hares and once even a wolf, but their catches were poor. The other men took their guns and roamed the land, practicing their shooting and squandering bullets. Pana questioned a group of them once about the wisdom of their actions, but they snapped back angrily, saying the whalers would return with a fresh supply of bullets and meat for everyone.

Pana knew in his heart that it was not so.

The men spent hours now in the karigi, the male meetinghouse, preparing for the fall hunt. They were careful to practice the old ways, singing fervent songs to the whale and blessing their harpoons, just in case. For the fear was silent but growing in their hearts that perhaps the whale *had* been angered.

The whales did not come that fall, either. The men began to camp on the ice near the leads, watching the horizon for the ship that had come to be the only hope for the People of the Whale. For on board was food and oil. And bullets.

The water stiffened into ice and pieces jammed together far out in the ocean, and still the men waited, unwilling to tear their eyes away, unwilling to face the truth.

The bullets ran out in October.

The great hunger followed. The cries of the children ruptured the nights.

132

One day men crept ino Pana's hut and dragged him out, over to the karigi.

"Your blood will purify our village," one of them said. They sat in a circle around Pana, his hands tied behind him. They had lit all the lamps along the walls, ignoring the waste. In the harsh light the men looked demented, their long hair tangled, their eyes wild. Fear had made them cruel.

"We all have erred," Pana cried out. "The whalers have altered our lives, but we still live. We still live. Do not err again!"

"It is too late to save yourself with words."

"Have you consulted the shaman?"

"There is no need. Only the need of the People."

"Do *not*—on the blood of your first whale—*do* this thing! *Do not!*"

Silence hung for an infinity and Pana knew his life was hanging there as well.

"The shaman will punish you surely," Pana said. "Revenge is a dangerous form of retribution. The pain always comes flying back into the face of the one who sent it out. It is the old law."

"Not this time," the men said flatly. "The old law is no more." They roused him from his place on the floor and marched him to the edge of the sea.

The men stared somberly at him, their eyes dead. "You were a friend once," the new spokesman said. "You may choose your death."

They stood at the edge of the sea where the whales had once played. It was galing over the ocean, that day, the way it was right now for Nuka and Kannik, and it seemed to Nuka that the wind was a bad omen; a bridge between that terrible day his father was captured and whatever lay ahead.

Nuka sighed and put thoughts of his father aside as they raised a snow hut. But that night his dreams were restless, and the next day, when they continued their journey, he couldn't shake the feeling that he and Kannik were walking into a dark and terrible future from which there was no escape.

Eleven

There were just two of them, sisters. Once there had been children and grandchildren in their hut to comfort them and warm their days. But the summer-the-game-stayed-away had shadowed their lives, too. Kannik and Nuka came upon them suddenly in the second week.

The men had left on a hunting trip months ago, the women explained. They never returned. One by one the children and the other women had died from the great hunger.

They told the story over a dinner of boiled bear meat that Nuka and Kannik provided. The women were yellowed with age, their hair floating around their faces like white clouds. But their words were strong. "What is, is," the woman called Alu said, gumming the meat and staring rheumily across the fire. "It is as it was to be."

Nuka and Kannik nodded. "But how did you live?" Kannik asked suddenly as she dipped her meat into oil. The question sent the other one, Suluktuktuk, into a paroxysm of coughing.

When she stopped wheezing, she said, "Old women do not need much to keep their bones alive." The sisters looked at each other. "Something always seems to come along."

"And what of you?" Alu asked abruptly, turning to Kannik. "A good industrious girl like yourself must have had many suitors bringing meat."

Kannik hung her head.

"My sister was not interested," Nuka said shortly.

Kannik looked away, but the old women peered sharply across the fire, their bright eyes taking in what Nuka couldn't tell.

One of them cackled, and the sound made Nuka uneasy. "You better keep her hidden when the hunters of Sippak come calling."

"Why is that?"

The woman stopped laughing. "You have not heard?"

Nuka shook his head.

The women looked at each other. "Perhaps it is best to talk of other matters," Alu said. "Let's see now, in your village—"

"No!" Nuka insisted, his voice cold with dread. "Tell me. What have the hunters of Sippak to do with my sister Kannik?"

The two sisters fidgeted. Alu nervously shredded meat between her bony fingers. "My sister speaks without thinking sometimes," she said. "It is her age."

Suluktuktuk shot her a wounded look and raised her head defiantly. "The hunters of Sippak live deep in the rocky country to the south. It is said that nothing grows in such a place and that the wind howls and clatters against the cliffs and the men forage for abominations under the rocks, putting beetles and lice-infested animals into their mouths."

Nuka's shoulder ached. His sister's eyes widened, and she gasped.

"This story has nothing to do with Kannik," Nuka said. "My sister lives with me, along the coast. Soon we will return to the village and a hunter will seal himself to her and she will bear many children. It has been written so since before my mother carried her in her belly."

The old woman smiled and a gob of spittle slipped down her chin. "Just keep her hidden when they come calling." Her sister whacked her in the chest and Suluktuktuk fell silent.

"Finish the story," Nuka commanded. Suluktuktuk looked at her sister for help.

"Well, go on," Alu snapped. "It is your place to finish. My fine words will not rescue you this time." She turned her back on her sister and gazed into space.

"Go on," Nuka said. "Words shape pictures, nothing more."

"Promise me you will not think badly of me nor scorn our hospitality," Suluktuktuk whispered. Nuka nodded reassuringly.

"Just tell me. What have the hunters of Sippak to do with

135

my sister Kannik?"

The old woman's eyes blinked and she chewed on her tongue reflectively. "The hunters have no women of their own. They capture women from other tribes to use in breeding. If the woman is unlucky enough to bear a daughter, both are killed. If she produces a son, she is allowed to live until the child is weaned, but her life is barely worth living. She must scrabble through the icy snow searching for wood. Her bare hands become frozen. The hunters insist on this in order to keep her from escaping. Without hands she cannot defend herself against attack nor provide food for her miserable life. It is said some women captured by the hunters of Sippak pray they will bear a female child, to end their suffering immediately."

No one spoke and the silence grew large and uncomfortable.

The old woman shrugged her shoulders. "You asked," she said lamely.

"Perhaps it is written so," Kannik said at last, "but they are not here. Tomorrow we will go east along the coast until we find our own kind once more. No hunters from Sippak would dare take arms against the People of the Whale."

The old woman pinched her sister's arm absently and dropped her hand into her lap. "They are Indians," she said mildly. "They are not like us. They are not civilized like the People. They are capable of great violence."

"Have you even seen them?" Nuka challenged. "Or is your information that which comes to old women in dreams during long nights?"

Alu reared her whitened head. Her cheeks were surprisingly plump, Nuka thought, for one who had suffered through the great hunger. "We have seen them," she said. She smiled strangely.

Nuka was losing patience with them. "Then share your wisdom with us so that we may avoid them in our travels."

"They move in herds," said Alu.

"Like caribou. And they—they—"

"They sweep over the coastline and strip life as they go."

"They leave behind bleached bones and tears, and children crying for the nipple," finished Suluktuktuk.

It was obvious to Nuka they were improvising.

136

Beside him Kannik became furiously busy, picking out the smallest pieces of meat from the seal oil and kneading them between her fingers. "But no women have escaped," he said. "Is that not so?"

"It is as you say."

"Then how can you possibly know what happens to them?" He rose and stretched. "Your hospitality has been most entertaining, and my sister has thrilled to your tales, but now it is time to rest."

"We will give you our best furs. The ones our children used before the great hunger."

"Thank you," Nuka said hastily, "but we have furs of our own. They are lashed to the sled. Kannik, come. The cold air will chase away the night."

She roused herself. "No. Thoughts must be followed while they dance in the air. You go."

He paused, concerned.

"Go," she said gently. "We will speak of women's things, so you will not be bored with our chatter during the night."

Satisfied, he stepped into his boots and outer clothes and picked up a stone lamp.

The night was clear and cold. He quickly checked his sled and his father's body, and yanked down the furs. Then he carefully shielded the light and crouched down. He didn't know what he was looking for, but something about the old women troubled him.

He walked once around the hut, weaving the light near the ground. When he found nothing, he widened the circle and kept looking. Nothing. He stopped. Of course! The blizzard had swept away signs of extraordinary events. He must look for strange configurations in the snow.

He found it twenty paces from the entryway to the hut. A snow wall banked higher than his head. He carved a niche and secured the light. The snow crumbled easily, like caked sand. He sank his knife into the bank and slashed horizontally. His knife cut through it. He chose a spot a foot below the first one and tried again. This time his knife struck something hard.

He shifted his weight and looked back at the hut. Smoke curled in the air over the ventilated cooking area, but no one

137

came outside. He positioned his body so that he could see any movement at the door and began to dig. The snow was harder the deeper he dug. Whatever it was had been protected by a layer of ice. He dug until he had exposed a hole two hands span wide and jammed the knife in, chipping the ice.

Then he reached in, and his hand closed around a skull.

Twelve

Alu leaned on her sister and got up awkwardly. It reminded Kannik of a newborn caribou trying out its legs. But the muscles under the skin on her arms were hard, like a boy's. How curious, Kannik thought, but then put the thought behind her. One learns to accept differences in a land of cold and death.

The women had stripped to their waists. The breasts of the two sisters hung down their chests like empty sacks. They hobbled over to Kannik, touching her. She was small, but her breasts were large and firm. Alu lifted back the thick hair which fell almost to Kannik's waist and flung it back over the young woman's shoulders. Kannik was struck again by the hidden strength in her touch.

"When did you last bleed?" Alu asked.

"Why does it interest you?" Kannik said angrily.

The sisters looked at each other. "It is your *health* that worries us. As it should you."

Something is wrong here, Kannik thought. She shifted her weight, her hands instinctively covering herself.

"Do you know what the hunters do?" They circled her like wolves closing in on a lagging caribou. "Have you seen a woman who has been forced to take the spears of many men? It tears the flesh and rots the body. Some women have lost the power to stand erect. They walk doubled over, trying to ease the fire in their bellies."

"Two weeks ago." Her voice was almost inaudible. "The last blood was two weeks ago."

"You might live then."

Kannik paled. "What do you mean?"

"You have two weeks to reach your village before seclusion.

139

Two weeks." Suluktuktuk shrugged. "It may be enough. It will have to be."

"What are you telling me?"

"In two weeks light will honor the sky longer than it takes meat to cook in the pot. Every year it is the same thing." Alu picked up the dinner bowl and fished out the remaining scraps of meat. "But enough. It is as it was to be. You will live—or not. It is of no consequence."

Kannik followed the women as they stepped up onto the sleeping platform. "This thing that happens the same every year. What is it?"

The women settled onto the sleeping ledges, their feet dangling. They folded their hands over their bellies. "The hunters come north."

Kannik sat down heavily.

Suluktuktuk turned to her sister and spoke in an undertone. "There is something we could do to—you know."

"Hush. It does not concern us."

"But perhaps it would work."

"No!"

"You are not the only one who lives in this house!" Suluktuktuk snapped. She turned to Kannik. "There is a place to hide you—but it is small and uncomfortable and still they may find you."

Kannik faltered. "We do not want to bring trouble."

Suluktuktuk spoke soothingly. "It is no trouble. It will be our way of honoring the spirits of those who have perished in this house. See the room before you decide."

She stooped and lifted a caribou-skin rug off the floor. Under it a circular door had been cut in the wood. "It is heavy. Your back is better than mine."

Kannik stooped over and lifted the bone handle.

And then she was hit from behind with something heavy, and lights exploded in her head.

Nuka raised the skull to the light. Bits of flesh still clung to it and Nuka fought down the desire to vomit. The skull was small and perfectly formed. It could only have belonged to a very young child. He put it down heavily and leaned against the

140

wall, his mind racing.

Old women do not need as much to keep their bones alive. He squeezed his eyes shut. *Eaters of Flesh.* He pressed his hands against the wall to steady himself, but a terrible picture refused to leave his eyes; old women butchering apart a child and sucking the marrow from its bones. The child screamed to him now for justice. Did they fatten it first with the flesh of another child? Or were they all killed together, during one blood-maddened night? Gasping for breath, he picked up his knife and dug.

He worked methodically, sectioning off the wall and pulling his knife horizontally through it a hand span apart. Bones. So many bones. The sheer numbers overwhelmed him. Legs, shoulder blades, breastbones split apart. The women had eaten well. Horror swam over him and he felt the wall spinning.

Eaters of Flesh. Doomed, damned for all time. The wall screamed to him in agony and his head hammered. He controlled himself and dug faster, piling skulls together. He counted them quickly once, and then once more. He moistened his lips and swallowed hard.

On the ground were eight skulls.

And Kannik was inside with them, alone.

Panic was rising inside him. His shoulder was badly weakened and the strength had fled one of his hands. The old women had not suffered during the great hunger as his family had. But they were still old, he reminded himself. And they would not expect him to know. He had to think. They had eaten well this night. He smiled sourly. Bear meat was much tougher for old teeth than children. But the meal would have served to fuel their strength. And Kannik had told them they were planning on leaving in the morning. The women would have to act tonight. A terrible thought struck him.

Perhaps they already had. Perhaps, while he was outside, they had wasted no time in clubbing his sister senseless. He had been gone a long time, and yet no woman had stepped outside the hut and called his name. Perhaps they had been busy with work just as dark as his.

What was it Suluktuktuk had said? *Something always seems to come along.*

141

His stomach lurched. The whale-skin flab covering the hut entrance cracked open and Nuka quickly smoothed snow over his grisly find. A woman stooped through the entryway. "Kannik!" He ran toward her joyfully and stopped. It was one of the old women.

"Come. You must come quickly!"

Careful now, he thought. Careful. "What is it? Is something wrong?"

"Just *come!*"

"Is it my sister? Is it she?"

"There is no time!"

A trap. It could be a trap. But Kannik. If her life was in danger, could he afford such thoughts? And besides, there was something in the old woman's voice. Urgency—no, that was not it. Panic. Something had scared the old woman. Scared her badly.

He ran after her.

She stood over the trapdoor, her breasts heaving. "Kannik gave us meat—bear meat left from dinner—and my sister went down to put it away." She wrung her hands. "Evil, evil, there is evil that stalks—" She rolled her eyes.

"Where is my sister?"

"Alu screamed. Down in the pit. She screamed and we heard the terrible sound of something down there. Something *moving* down there. A *creature.* Kannik threw herself down the pit to find my sister and now they are both gone. They are gone and the evil grows. It grows! It has taken the house and next it will come for me!"

Nuka pushed her aside and flung open the trapdoor. Cold air rushed up at him. He strained his eyes against the gloom. Somewhere a lamp flickered down below him. It looked just like any other meat locker—smooth walls cut into the tundra to keep meat permanently frozen. But it seemed larger than most. The family was larger than most once, he thought. But there was time for that later.

He swung himself onto the ladder and climbed down.

The cold struck him like a fist. He was standing in a bare room, its frozen walls green in the light. "Kannik?"

Shadows lurked along the walls. Nuka kept his hand on his knife and walked toward the light. It must be coming from a separate room, he thought. Yes. There along the far wall. An entryway. He felt along the wall until he reached the opening and stooped down to pass through. He froze, staring in mute horror at the ground. A hand curled toward him, the fingernails blue. Kannik's hand. He would kill them. He pulled out his knife and plunged into the next room. Maybe she had only fainted.

The hand was disconnected. Chopped off at the wrist.

He looked around wildly. The room was a small closet.

Another room. To the right. He crouched through the opening, smaller than the last. Here the cold air bit into him, stinging his face and freezing his lashes. The light flickered in the corner, exposing the shiny wall of ice behind it.

It was shining on a row of hanging corpses.

Kannik's face shone clearly in the light, as if the lamp had been positioned to highlight it. It was the last thing he saw before something clubbed him from behind.

"At least you're thinking," Alu sniffed as she bound Nuka's hands and feet. "If you had been like this with Kannik, we never would have had to drag her body such a distance."

"And what of *your* duties, sister?"

"Age carries certain privileges."

"Must you forever remind me that nine moons separate our births? Even mother was capable of vast mistakes."

"You are not funny. Shall we flense them?"

Suluktuktuk shook her head. "Their breathing has slowed. Let the cold end it. Besides, the organs taste better if they age slightly first. The chase has wearied me. Tomorrow is soon enough, Alu."

"Yes."

"After we eat them all—what then?"

"Why, Suluktuktuk. It is clear."

"It is?"

"Yes, dear sister. You must guard your back and never sleep."

*   *   *

He felt the cold first. It sank into his bones like metal teeth. He moved his hands and realized he couldn't feel them through the bonds. His head ached. The light from the lamp was so dim that it barely illuminated one side of Kannik's face. Her eyes were closed and her head fell forward. Nuka could see a hook in the back holding her up. His stomach felt queasy and he shook. He was lying on the ground, looking up at her through a row of legs. He dragged himself over, not knowing if she was alive or dead.

The women had hung bodies on hooks along the wall and he passed them now as he crawled toward her. One, two, three. Two naked children, a boy and girl, and a female adult. The flickering light dyed their bodies deep blue but he could still see the outlines of a long wound gaping down their bellies. They had been gutted from neck to groin and their organs removed.

Nuka tried to swallow, but something oily kept rising in his throat.

The woman's left hand was missing. At least it was not Kannik's hand that had been severed. He swallowed hard. There were only purple stumps where once had been the hands and feet of the children.

It seemed to be getting colder in the room. He wished for the hundredth time he had left his shirt on when he had come back inside.

Kannik was bare breasted. His feet were numb. "Kannik?" He pulled himself to his knees and used the wall to support himself.

At least he would pull her down. He couldn't bear to see her hanging. He hopped over to her and examined the hook, pushing away her hair.

The women had been careless when they hung her. The hook had tangled in her hair and never pierced her flesh.

"Kannik. Wake up." He punched her face awkwardly. Cold. He had to wake her up. He pummeled her body with his fists and she groaned.

"Wake up."

"So tired. Sleep."

"No." He hit her harder. *"Wake up!"*

144

"Go away."

"Kannik. Listen to me. You're going to die if you don't wake up right now. Do you want to give death such an easy victory? *Wake up!*"

He had to lift her down. His knife. He had forgotten all about it. He slapped his pockets. It wasn't there. The light was going fast. Already it alternated between sputtering out and blazing back to life. How many more times would it come back from the dead? He peered on the ground, stooping from the waist. Hurry. He couldn't see anything in the shadows.

Kannik's knife. "Kannik. Your knife. Do you have it?"

Silence. He hit her in the face.

"Pocket." She slurred the word.

He patted her leggings, his hands so cold he was afraid he would not feel the knife when he touched it. If he could only cut her down, get her moving again. There. Deep in her pocket. He cried out in relief. He couldn't reach it. His tied hands were too bulky.

"Kannik! You must help. You must!"

In the long silence that followed, the light blazed brilliantly and Nuka knew it was the last burst of fire before it died. He lunged at it and held his wrists over the flame. For an instant nothing happened and Nuka was certain he was too late, but then the sides of sinew curled and the cords binding his wrists lengthened. He snapped his hands apart as the light sputtered and went out.

"You go. It's your turn." They were standing over the cooking pot, the room so hot sweat rolled down their arms and dripped on their leggings.

"Aren't you forgetting? You traded me a turn moons ago. And the heaviest body, too! You pleaded with me and said you'd do anything. Anything, sister, if you didn't have to lift it. It was my turn at the cooking pot, but no matter. Down your poor sister went and up came the heaviest body."

Alu sniffed. "Alu does not remember. Perhaps you dreamed it."

It was Suluktuktuk's turn to be angry. "The pot is boiling, sister. We are ready for the meat."

"But yesterday it was your poor, elderly sister who clubbed the scarred one on the head."

"And *your* poor, overworked sister who tied him up. And the pretty one, as well. No. My words will not be moved."

Alu clucked her tongue and shook her head. "Mother would cry large tears to see her daughter now."

"Mother knows your tactics," Suluktuktuk snapped. "She would understand." The water in the pot made small slurping sounds, as if it were hungry for what was to come. "The meat, sister."

"All right. But from this moment on—expect no favors from me! Not one." Alu slammed down the ladder and Suluktuktuk could hear her voice echo hollowly as she moved.

"She is getting entirely too large for her own kakliik," Alu muttered. The oil in the lamp sloshed like a tidal wave as she walked—she was so angry—and narrowly missed burning her hand. She stood still until she had regained her composure and unlatched the first small door. She passed through a narrow room, then unlatched the second door and crawled through. Good. Everything was exactly as she had left it. She would have to do something with Suluktuktuk. It pained her to think of it.

The scarred one lay on his back. She jabbed his chest. Cold. The flesh would be brittle under the knife. Her sister should have gutted them while the bodies were still pliant and saved her the trouble. She raised her knife and set to work.

It was a small victory, perhaps, but still a warm one. Too often she had been harnessed by her sister for the hardest tasks. Suluktuktuk poked the fire with a stick. The water burbled. She grinned and did a little dance, belying the brittleness of her thirty-five years. She was looking forward to tonight. The soup they had made from the hands and feet of the children had been thin. Not at all satisfactory. And the bear meat for dinner had been so heavy she could barely swallow it.

Her mouth watered. Perhaps Alu would bring the pretty one up. Her flesh would be more tender. She could taste it already, boiled until the meat was flaky and smothered in seal oil. She smiled cynically. Of course Alu would bring the pretty one up.

146

She weighed less. She laughed out loud. They would eat and eat until their stomachs ached. And she would make certain that this time her sister didn't take more than her fair share.

She wiped her forehead, clearing the sweat. Her sister was trying to annoy her. She was staying down there deliberately to trick her into following. And then who will be forced to carry the body up?

Me, she answered silently. That's who. She poked the fire soundly, remembering the convenient back trouble which seemed to pain Alu only when hard work had to be done.

Her sister had tricked her in the past, but no more. The water in the pot looked a little low. She climbed onto the sleeping platform and walked around the trapdoor to the rack where water melted from the lamp's heat. She dipped her bowl, her eyes on the trapdoor.

"All right," she muttered finally. She would open it up, just in case her sister was calling. She put down the bowl and walked heavily over. The door creaked as she pulled it back. The cold air fanned her skin but only the sounds of melting water along the wall and water dancing in the pot filled the room. She looked uncertainly at the ladder disappearing into the black darkness below her. It was quiet down there, the way an animal is quiet when it watches you. She shook her head. She was a silly old woman, to be scared by shadows.

She pushed herself away from the edge of the pit, picked up the bowl of water and returned to the cooking room. Alu would let her stay down there until her nose cracked off from the cold. Why should she help her sister now? She threw water in the pot. It still looked a little low.

She crossed her hands over her breasts. Perhaps Alu *was* in trouble. But no, Suluktuktuk was the clumsy one. Once she had opened her own leg when she tripped on a knife. *Then why has she not returned?*

The water was disappearing from the pot. Something was wrong. It had to be. She lifted her knife off the shelf and moistened her lips.

"Alu, if this is a trick—"

The ladder sighed gently as she stepped onto it and steadied the lamp in her hand. The comforting sounds of her familiar

life retreated with every step until there was only the sound of
her heart beating in her ears.

The storage room was empty as always.

Then why the feeling that something was watching her?
Waiting for her? She called her sister's name but choked it off
midway. It was foolish to alert whatever waited for her. The
small closet next to the storage room was empty, too.

But the room beyond that—

Something waited for her in that room. She shifted from
foot to foot, the lamp warm in her hands.

She was stupid. She would find her sister sweating over a
body, and she would earn her dinner by carrying it upstairs.
Then why this feeling? The light wobbled on the wall, and she
realized she was trembling. She steadied the lamp in her hands
and crawled through the opening.

Even the dim light from the lamps couldn't cut through the
cold. The bodies were hung as they had left them and the
scarred one lay on the ground, his wrists bound. But where was
her sister? She looked around uneasily. There was nowhere to
hide.

"If this is your idea of a joke, sister—" Her voice quavered
in the silence. Shivering, she stooped over the scarred one. He
had not been flensed out. How like her sister to leave it for her.

She sighed angrily and put down her lamp. The angle cast
long shadows on his face until it looked as if he had grown
fangs. His face was grinning at her, a wolfish, predatory grin.

You're going to get it.

She started as if he had actually spoken and fished out her
knife. A clean cut always starts at the navel. She sank the blade
down and his hands closed around her neck.

Thirteen

Nuka seized her head in his hands and slammed her to the ground. She was clearly terrified. It pleased him. He pinned her with his body and pressed a knife against her throat.

"What do you want?" She was trembling uncontrollably. The ground scalded her back. Nuka was a madman above her, his weight pressing the air out of her chest. "Be careful with that knife."

"As careful as you have been."

"It wasn't our fault. It wasn't. Hunger took the first ones."

"And hunger took the others," Nuka finished drily. "Only it was your hunger. Yours and your sister's."

The face of the pretty one peered down at her, over her brother's shoulder. "Shall she be stripped?"

Nuka nodded, his eyes on the old woman's face. "Cold! The cold will kill me!" Already it burned her cheeks and her nipples stung. Kannik stripped off the leggings and the woman whimpered. "Have mercy!"

"We could always roast you over a fire. Isn't that the way you cooked them—your own children and children's children?"

"You know nothing of the hunger that tears apart families and leaves old women hanging on to desperate choices."

"Save your words."

"It wasn't my idea! You are harming the wrong one. My sister forced me into it. She was the one."

He bound her wrists together, ignoring her words.

"What are you going to do with me?"

He picked up the sinew and wrapped her ankles.

"You cannot leave me here."

He lifted her and stood her up, bracing her body with his arms.

149

Her eyes were huge, transfixed. Her sister was ~~hanging on the hook that had once held~~ Kannik. Her throat had been cut open.

"No," she whispered.

Nuka shrugged. "It was—an unfortunate accident. She fell on Kannik's knife when she heard what her future held."

"And mine? What of my future?"

He smiled. "We will give you a choice, Suluktuktuk. You may hang here next to your sister, or you may freeze on the ground."

She paled. "That is no choice. We are not animals."

"No," Nuka said gently. "Animals only kill what they need. They do not kill for the joy of it."

"You are mad. To harm an old, defenseless woman."

He placed her on the ground.

"Don't leave me."

"Your body will adjust to the cold as the light dims." Kannik and Nuka stepped around her and backed out the entryway.

"Killers!" she shrieked.

"One word of advice. Do not fight the cold. Welcome it as a friend. When the light dies, it is your only constant friend."

"May both your spirits wander alone forever." She spat on the ground.

Nuka smiled sadly. "It is the old law we are fulfilling, Suluktuktuk. Pain always comes flying back into the face of the one who sends it out. You know how it works."

"Then it will find *you* again, too."

He stopped, the color draining from his face.

She smiled slyly, her words fueled by desperation. "You must never turn your back. Sometime when you least expect it, the pain will come flying back into your face as well."

He shook his head. "My action completes the circle."

"It is *never* complete! Your action will bring more evil upon you!"

He pulled himself away and she jerked up her head, her eyes bulging. "You need me! There are things we have hidden from you. You have reason to be afraid! You know my words are true. Danger swarms around you and—"

He slammed the gate and latched it. He was trembling. From

150

behind the door, she was still talking to them, her words muffled.

"Make her stop," Kannik said. "She's scaring me."

Nuka rose unsteadily to his feet, his face ashen. "Come. Her life has parted from ours."

"Nuka—her words. Are you certain there is no other way?" They were groping their way to the storage room. Behind them she had started shouting.

"No other way."

"But her words—"

"No other way."

They had climbed the ladder and reached the sleeping platform when the screams began.

They used the wind to guide them as they clambered along the coast, avoiding the steep pressure ridges. A stiff breeze scudded the clouds inland that were hanging over the sea, and for the first time Nuka smelled water under the ice. Every day light stayed in the sky longer than before. The whales would be coming soon. He tightened his hold on the rope and pulled the sled harder.

His sister plodded behind him, the sled skittering over the ice like a caribou. Under the hood her hair was shorter than his. He had cut it wresting her down from the hook. She tossed her head and her hair snapped around her face. "It is much lighter," she said bravely. "All who see me will envy my daring."

"If need had not prompted it, your brother would have ordered it so anyway," Nuka said.

She stared at him in surprise. "Why?"

"It is best those we meet think you are a male."

"They will find out when we strip."

"We won't."

"But the lice and heat will consume us! Why such a strange order?" He turned and pulled the sled harder. "Surely you don't think—" She ran to catch up—"you don't think the hunters of Sippak—Nuka! Stop walking so fast! One cannot hear the words; they fly so quickly from your mouth!"

He stopped walking and waited for her to catch up. "Thank

151

you," she said crossly, her cheeks pink from the exertion. "The hunters exist only in the minds of old women. That is all."

"Perhaps."

"Perhaps? Nuka, the cold has frozen your brain. They made them up—to scare us."

"Humor me, sister."

She looked at him uncertainly. "You know something, don't you?"

"It is a feeling, nothing more."

"That they exist?"

"That evil exists, my sister. And we still have many days to pull the sled before we see our home."

"About our home. You cannot be swayed from finding it again?"

"Kannik. We will discuss it no more. The subject has been decided."

Not by me. "How much longer until—until the village?"

"If the wind does not whip us in its frenzy and the weather holds—another five days."

Five days to live. "Nuka, why are we returning? Is it only because of your promise to father?"

"Isn't that enough?"

"He does not know! He is dead, Nuka. Dead. We could as easily chant the mysteries as the shaman." She could see him wavering—she read it in his face—and then his color deepened and his face changed into something she had never seen. She backed away.

"We will both pretend you have not said those words," he said heavily. "Do not speak those words again. Ever. Do not tempt my loyalties." He raised his hand, and for one wild moment Kannik was certain he meant to strike her.

She flinched and threw up her hands to protect her face. "Never again!" she screamed.

The color drained from his face and he jerked back his fist. He turned and pulled on the rope.

Nuka stopped walking and balanced on the crest of the pressure ridge. He called her name quietly, his voice strained.

"What is it?" She climbed next to him and he pointed at the

coastline below them.

"A camp. There. From this moment on your name will be—Savik. The knife. And do not speak. My words will answer for both." He raised his hands and shouted. The strangers raised their arms in reply. Kannik counted five men and nine dogs. "Come," Nuka said, "and be constantly on guard."

They were hunters from a village west of the People of the Whale. The great hunger had forced them to forage for game at the first light, and now they flushed out anything they could find. They fell upon the bear meat Nuka offered and devoured it instantly. The dogs whined for scraps.

"Have you heard any news of my people?" Nuka asked quietly.

The leader shook his head. His eyes glowed as if a terrible fire had swept through his body and only hot embers remained alive in his head. A half-moon had been branded on his left cheek. All the men wore one. On his wrist he wore a matching emblem. "There has been much death this winter. For everyone." He looked at Kannik and she dropped her eyes. "Your brother does not speak?"

"No," Nuka said curtly. "An old injury."

The leader nodded his head, looking at her with such piercing intensity that Nuka tensed. "Very pretty," he said softly. She jerked up her head, startled. He smiled at her, his eyes burning.

"What did you say?" Nuka put his hand on his knife.

The leader roused himself. "Your brother reminds me of someone known long ago." He squinted up at the sky. "The light is paling. Build a hut with us, and tomorrow our sled will carry you back to the Village of the Whale. Our dogs have rested long enough."

"No. We will go on as before."

"It is no trouble."

"Part of the pact with our father is that we keep away from others. Isn't that right, Savik?"

Kannik nodded, not trusting herself to raise her eyes. He knows, she thought. The bear meat settled like sludge in her belly.

153

The stranger shrugged. "Suit yourselves. We are going that way anyway, aren't we, boys?" The men nodded. "We need to check snares we set two days ago."

"If we find your quarry has escaped, we will set the trap again," Nuka said gruffly.

The leader threw back his head and roared with laughter. "Yes, do that. If the quarry has escaped, reset the traps for us. Do that. Set it again. I would like that very much."

Nuka's head exploded. He reached for his knife. *I would like that very much.* He studied the strangers with new eyes. Their parkas were caribou. Not seal. *They were not from the coast at all.*

The leader looked at him stonily, his eyes narrowing. "Something wrong?"

"Where did you say your village was?"

"We didn't."

"Your words are those of the inlanders. The Indians."

"What is the difference? There are many more of us than you." Two men rose and stood next to the leader.

Nuka saw too late the impact of his words. He forced his hand to drop the knife. "No difference. Our game is different, that is all. Perhaps we could help you in the hunt."

The stranger smiled and stared past Nuka at Kannik. Nuka's throat closed. "We have captured it already. And now we are ready to go home."

"Your words have no meaning."

"We are hunters from the south. From a windy, barren place called Sippak."

Fourteen

He slammed his hand around his knife and shielded his sister with his body. "Anyone touches her, dies."

Suddenly a fist punched his groin and an arm gagged his throat, squeezing off the air. Bright streaks of pain shot up his stomach. He kicked his elbow backward as hard as he could and brought the knife up into his attacker's arm. Blood ran down Nuka's chest and the man loosened his grip. Nuka spun his body away. Something smashed into his head.

"Run, Kannik!"

Two men hurled themselves on Nuka, dragging him to the ground, immobilizing his arms and legs. Through a haze of pain he saw his sister stumble to her feet and run. She was intercepted easily by one of the strangers, who lifted her, spitting and clawing, into the sky. He carried her over to his leader who nodded curtly. "The sled."

They were going to take her away. "No!" Nuka screamed, enraged. He wrestled savagely and his right arm broke free. He hurled his shoulder around and a piercing pain paralyzed his body. One of the men was stooping over him, pressing a nerve in his neck.

And then Nuka was cracked over the head with something heavy. Sparks shot in front of his eyes and there was only the sound of Kannik screaming, the sound spiraling down into an endless white tunnel.

Nuka lurched up and looked around wildly. They were gone. The sleds. The dogs. Kannik.

He stumbled to his feet. They had wrapped him in furs and placed him on his own sled, as if the leader wanted him to stay alive, was taunting him to follow.

"You will be found!" he raged in the emptiness. "You will be

155

made to pay for what you have done this day!" He would leave the sled behind. He would stalk through the night and kill them where they slept. His supplies were piled next to the sled. He ripped back the furs covering them.

His father's face looked up at him. He staggered backward. How could he have forgotten it was there? Nuka huddled next to the corpse and talked to it.

"Once the choice was easy, father. There was only your words to consider."

The corpse seemed to grin at him, and Nuka thought for an instant the eyes blinked. "Which, father? Which? Is it not better to save the living than placate the dead?"

Nuka scanned the sky for a sign, but it was as silent as the body before him. Suddenly his father's voice came back, so clearly Nuka started.

Promise nothing you are not prepared to offer your life to fulfill. One of the sacred vows of the People.

The wind riffled his father's frozen hair and the dead eyes gleamed in the moonlight.

So be it. He would keep his pact with his father. And afterward he would keep his pact with the man who had kidnapped his sister. He would find her again.

If Kannik bore a male child, that would give him two, maybe three years to search the craters of the mountains to the south. They would not kill her until the child was weaned. And if she bore a female child?

He put the thought behind him and loaded the sled.

He stopped. Something had fallen into the cross-pattern of footprints in the snow. He stooped and picked it up.

It was a large red paint-stone, almost as big as his palm. Angrily he threw it away. What use was paint-stone now, with no female to grind it and mix it with duck blood? And for what? To trim new boots that would never be made?

He went back to loading, stopped, sighed. The paint-stone was the only tangible link to the beasts that had captured his sister. Maybe something would come of it.

He searched through the snow and picked it up.

The sled stopped suddenly and Kannik thought at first the

156

man leading the dogs was going to change places with a fresh runner. They had been traveling that way through the night. But now the man riding the back jumped off and anchored it. The second sled pulled in behind the one carrying her.

She stiffened, waiting for them to come for her, but they spoke to each other as if she weren't there. It brought home her position more clearly than if they had auctioned her to the highest bidder. She had no one in her camp. She sank down into the furs and tears sprang to her eyes. She counted the stars and traced the thin webbing of clouds across the moon until her vision cleared. She could not afford to panic. She experimented with her bonds. No. She would have to let them untie her, then she would run. She squeezed her eyes shut and prayed.

Her stomach burned and she tasted the faintly fishy taste of the meat they had eaten for dinner. Calm, she thought. She must remain calm.

The men unharnessed the dogs and fed them dried salmon, the most familiar of chores. She could get no comfort from watching it. The dogs hunkered down over the pink flesh, gnawing the heads and bones and sniffing the sky.

The men cut blocks of snow and packed them together. And then there was a hut before her. *It's not happening.* The cords in her neck constricted. She couldn't believe it.

Out of the black night the leader walked toward her. He looked down at her silently, his eyes black, unreadable. He moved his lips as if to speak, but instead he lifted her, still tied, and carried her inside.

They were seated in a circle, already naked. She was placed on the ground in the middle. The leader stared somberly at her and stripped out of his clothes. The hut stank. A powerful male smell of bodies and sweat and furs.

He stooped over her and for an instant Kannik was certain he meant her to kiss his spear, but instead he moved awkwardly down her body and untied her ankles and wrists.

She sat up, rubbing her wrists. The men strained toward her. Great Spirit, was she expected to please them all?

"Choose," the leader said quietly. "Carefully."

She lowered her gaze. "It is not right that a kidnapped

157

maiden choose which of her captors shall abuse her first."

"Choose."

Kannik looked at each man in turn, reading the hunger in his eyes and measuring the girth of his arms and the power of his spear.

"And if none of you are good enough?"

The men drew in their breath sharply. The leader stared at her, amused. "So be it." He nodded once and her body was seized. She screamed.

"We will tie back your tongue if you continue. But if you are speechless, you cannot tell us the best ways to please you. Choose. It is your choice."

She hurled a string of curses into the air. He obligingly bound her mouth and sat back, waiting until she wore down. "Have you changed your mind?" She snapped her head back and forth, growling.

He sighed. "You know your own mind but have difficulty allowing us to please it."

He grasped the leather of her tunic and suddenly tore it down her body. The skin gave way easily, exposing her breasts. Kannik could feel the heat coming from the men.

"You may help us, or you may not. It doesn't matter. Soon you will be naked and open to our suggestions. But to worship you, we need to know your secret desires. There is no escape. No calling back this night. No safety now, except that which you find here. Now. Shall I, yes, *I*, Kannik—and the word is spoken proudly among us—shall I take off your gag, or will I and my men pleasure ourselves with no thought to your comfort?"

A long moment passed. Kannik nodded, and instantly the gag came off. He sat back on his haunches, his penis flaccid between his thighs, and waited for her to speak.

The sled snagged on an outcropping of ice and the left runner twisted. Nuka scowled, furious with the sled, with his own impotence, with his dead father.

The sled couldn't be fixed. He tore his father's body away, reached for his axe and slammed it into the corpse. He severed the left leg at the thigh and chopped off the right one. The legs

158

snapped easily, like insects in a bird's beak. He hacked off the left arm and stacked the pieces like cordwood on top of the grinning head. He bound it with sinew, wrapped it in furs with the meat and lifted it to his back.

The violence helped. He felt his rage draining away, leaving behind only a dullness more oppressive than the anger. The land was as familiar now as his own footprint, yet everything was changed.

His legs worked rhythmically. He pushed himself, wanting to blunt his mind from thinking, from feeling. Here was the place where he had taken his first seal, announcing his arrival as a man. Here were the marshes where he had taught his younger brothers how to snare eider ducks and the flat plain where he had won his first footrace during the Messenger Feast.

And here, somewhere under the snow, was the deep crevice where his father had thrown away his rifle.

Nuka's temple throbbed. He took a deep breath to steady himself, and then he couldn't stop the memory anymore, and it all came hurtling back.

The whales had stayed away and the men had blamed his father. They had marched Pana to the edge of the sea, overlooking the place where once the whales had sung their fluted, mournful songs.

"You were a friend once," the new spokesman had said to Pana. "You may choose your own death."

Pana had shaken his head. "Evil done in the name of goodness is the worst kind. Do not continue along this path. Not only for my sake, but for your own. The evil shall turn and stun you with its strength."

"No more words. Enough stalling." The words had a hollow sound. "The whales will see your spilled blood and return. It is written."

Pana shook his head sadly. "The only thing that is written is that which you do. It is still not too late to write a different story to be told in the future."

"If you will not choose your death, we will choose it for you."

"There is no need."

159

The men turned. Nuka was standing there. He was holding his father's Winchester. It was aimed at the leader's heart.

"In the long months before the great hunger, when you were squandering your bullets, my father and his house were carefully counting theirs." He cocked the rifle. "There is one for each of you here, and a few left over."

The leader stepped toward him.

"You will let my family leave now. And you will not follow us. Or a bullet will end your life."

"Never return then. We will kill you surely. With stones if we have nothing else. To have had bullets that could have saved the village from starvation and to horde them!" His voice cracked. "My wife died yesterday from hunger. So do not ever return here. Ever."

The family had packed quickly amid a silence deeper than death. The villagers lined up to watch them go. They pressed together so that Pana had to push the lead dog through them to clear room for the sled, but no one spoke. Nuka stood on the sled and pointed the rifle. The faces had blurred into one: the hunger had eaten away all that was special, leaving only wide staring eyes, skin melted until the skull glowed through. There was a silence more terrible than any accusation.

The villagers stood that way until the family passed them on the sled and were still standing there when the sled moved so far away their bodies could have been birds, or specks of dust.

Nuka stared east across the marshes. In the moonlight the ice on the ponds shone like thin scabs on the knees of children. Home. He was almost home. He would throw his destiny into the sky and draw back whatever he was meant to find.

"You, then." She pointed at the leader.

"My name is Senati." He stood. His body was bronze in the light.

He could feel her shivering. "Don't be afraid."

Her body was marble. He played a hand across her shoulder and lifted her hair, while his other hand dropped to her belt. With one strong movement, he ripped open her pants and thrust in his hand.

"Don't hurt me!" she cried.

The men on the floor shifted position, watching.

"Then you must help me."

She put her arms around his neck and stepped out of her trousers, her small buttocks pale curves in the light. He lifted her against him and she wrapped her legs around his body. She trembled with fear.

She closed her eyes and clamped her teeth as he plunged into her. She would kill him. She would kill him.

Fifteen

The village lay exactly as he remembered it. The huts had been built below ground, supported by whalebone and driftwood. Now snow banked over them in rolling hills. Only the wind moved.

Nuka walked slowly through the village, pulling his father's body. High drifts covered the entryways to the huts. He stopped in front of his family's hut. It had been built on the southern end of the village, away from the mosquitoes that swarmed over the coast in the summer. He didn't go in.

It was as if he were walking in his sleep. The moonlight streamed over the snow, the huts glittered in the light, and the wind foraged for scraps in the shadows.

He pulled his burden stiffly, chilled by the silence, until he left the huts behind and reached the sea. He was too late. The village was empty. The shaman could never bless his father and free his spirit. Now he would wander forever, trapped between this world and the next.

He sat down heavily and stared at nothing. Something scratched behind him and he turned. It was a white dog, swollen with pregnancy, its teats touching the ground.

She was sitting near the feet of a man.

Nuka stumbled to his feet. It was a stranger. The man was tall and gaunt. Hunger had scoured his cheeks away. His hair bristled around his face. Nuka stepped backward, startled.

It was the shaman, changed so utterly Nuka hadn't recognized him. The mist lifted around him like dreams.

"You have brought your father home?"

Nuka nodded.

"We will take him to the karigi, the place where the anger directed toward him was the strongest."

They positioned his body so that his head pointed east and arranged his arms and legs. The shaman stooped over the lamp and shadows reared along the wall, crawling over the whale jaws and baleen charms that still hung there, as a dying man might crawl over bodies.

Pain clung to the walls and floor. Nuka crouched in the half-light near his father's head as the shaman drew a circle around them and stepped inside.

Outside the circle, spirits roamed in the dark. Nuka could feel them. Evil things grew in the shadows.

"No evil," the shaman whispered. "Only anger and fear twisted upon itself."

He raised his hands above his head. "The Feast of the Dead," he said loudly. "We welcome all who will eat with us."

The shaman reached into a leather pouch and pulled out meat Nuka didn't recognize. He tore it and placed a piece in the center of the circle near the head of the corpse. He held up the rest. "We eat this now in the Feast of the Dead as part of the mystery of life. One day others will bless us as our spirits fly away, and the mystery will be complete."

He bit into the meat and passed it to Nuka. It was bitter and salty, like tears. Then the shaman held Nuka's face in his hands and spat into his mouth. The meat the shaman had eaten was sweet and rich. "Tears and laughter. They are both from the same meat."

The shaman turned and looked into the shadows. "There is a spirit here which desires rest. And peace from the troubling journey. There are those of you who hover still, trapped by your pain in a place that is no longer home. This feast is for you as well."

He motioned Nuka to rise. The shaman sprinkled oil around the perimeter of the circle as Nuka bent over his father. The dead eyes gleamed in the light, and for an instant they seemed to lock with Nuka's, as if the corpse were trying to tell him one last thing. And then the light changed and Nuka saw that the eyes were really staring straight ahead. *Good-bye, father*, Nuka said silently.

The shaman touched his arm and they stepped outside the circle. The shaman dipped a torch to the lamp and it burst into life. "All of you who wait, all of you who relive ancient pain, look now to the light." He held the torch high and his face was red, as if he had swallowed a sunset without coming up for air. He tapped the edge of the circle with the torch, and a wall of fire leaped up. Nuka could see his father's body through the flames.

The shaman raised his hands. "Now take these spirits. We give them up to you. Their bodies will mingle with the dust of the earth and nourish the grass. Their voices will feed the winds and their breath will mist the sea forever."

The flames shot up and the heat drove Nuka back. He threw up his hands—the light was so bright—and saw his father's body consumed by fire. Something strange was happening. For an instant Nuka thought he saw faces in the fire—faces of children crying, mothers wrenched from their broods, fathers staggering blindly on the ice. And the noise. It was as if they had been frozen forever in their moment of greatest pain, forced to relive it over and over.

Nuka stepped back and covered his mouth. Just as quickly as it had appeared, it was gone. When the flames died the shaman spoke.

"They have returned to the place where winters are formed, where spring pushes its way through the snow, where evil is kept at bay by the circle of highest good. We leave them to you, and take them with us in our dreams forever."

"How did they die?" Nuka asked the shaman. They were standing in a desolate place next to the sea, the dog at the shaman's feet.

"You know that already." He motioned Nuka to sit. "Come. There are other things that need to be said." For three days the shaman spoke to Nuka of the great mysteries, teaching him how to summon spirits and leave his body and travel with his mind.

Finally he stood and touched Nuka's scarred face. "Long ago it was written that one would come wearing the mark of a great battle. It is you. You are the last of the People of the Whale, yet not the last, for from your seed will spring the rebirth of your people."

164

"And my sister?"

"You will see her again."

"Alive?"

"Some things are not mine to reveal. Your sister's destiny has changed course, like the tributary of a mighty river. Yet your lives still feed from the same waters."

"She will be found and the beasts killed!"

"You have much to learn, my son, before the prophesy is fulfilled. A hatred burns now in your heart."

Nuka saw once more the hunters of Sippak wresting his sister away from him.

"No," the shaman said gently, "there are those whose lives you value less."

Nuka closed his eyes, and instantly the whaling ship rose before him, its three masts inflating in the wind.

The shaman nodded. "Any life you diminish, diminishes your own. Before you can embrace your own life, you must embrace the lives of those you have grown to hate."

Nuka stared at the shaman coldly.

He smiled faintly. "Your strong thoughts do not dilute the truth."

"But the whalers have sailed away from the coast."

The shaman laid his hands on Nuka's shoulders and turned his body away from the sea. "South. Your path lies away from the sea you love, the land of your father's birth. Even now as we speak, armies of white strangers are marching into the land, in numbers greater than all the People combined."

"Are they traders?"

"Hunters, my son."

"There is game enough for all who do not slaughter for trading, but only to survive."

"They are a different kind of hunter. They seek things they cannot find in the far land from which they came."

"And after they find what they're looking for—will they leave the land to the People once more?"

The shaman shook his head. "The land will always bear their mark. And so must you, my son."

"Will my mate—be a strange female from across the sea? One of the strangers?" Nuka felt a sudden wave of revulsion.

"Where she comes from will matter less than what is written in her heart."

"Where does it start? My destiny?"

The shaman's voice rose and seemed to fill the sky. "It starts at your feet." Nuka looked down and saw the red paint-stone he had found when the hunters kidnapped his sister.

"But it is so common! How can such a stone—"

"Take it to the source. The beginning."

Nuka bent and picked it up. "Is it a riddle?" The shaman was silent. "Nuka does not see how a stone that is traded from the coast to the inland waters can—" Nuka turned.

The shaman had vanished. Footprints shone clearly in the snow. Nuka followed them, almost running, until they disappeared next to the sea. Nuka examined them carefully. There was no sign of struggle. The footprints just ended, as if the shaman himself had been lifted whole into the mist hovering over the ocean.

"Don't leave! There is so much that still must be answered!" Silence, and then a star splintered across the sky.

Nuka put the stone in his pocket. Above him a gull rolled over and scolded the silent sea.

Sixteen

Nuka followed the frozen Ikpikuk River south and went overland to the Colville River. Here there was a deserted village where the Mountain People came every year to transfer goods from sleds to boats for the trip down to the mouth of the Colville River, where they then traded with the People of the Whale. Afterward they would pole their boats upriver to this village and, when the ice came, go north again by sled.

Nuka looked through the rack of boat frames hanging outside the village and inspected the cache holding skins for frames. He felt sad. This spring the Mountain People would not come to this village, laughing and bringing gifts. There was no one left among the People of the Whales with whom to trade.

The dog sat in the snow and looked at him. Behind her, eight pups curled on the sled.

Nuka roused himself and touched the stone in his pocket. "It's a riddle, Maguruk." He had gotten in the habit of talking to her.

Maguruk put her snout between her paws and looked at him skeptically.

"The shaman told me to go to the source. My father and his before him traded with the inland Eskimos—the Mountain People—for red paint-stone. It is true, then, that they hold the secret to Kannik's whereabouts, is it not?"

Maguruk snapped at falling snow in response.

Nuka nodded. "Yes. That is it. We must go south, into the great mountains."

He looked through the blowing snow at the mountains rising starkly to the south. The tumble of low hills gave way to monstrous juts of sandstone rising into the sky; and furthest to the south was cloud piercer Denali, the highest mountain. He had only heard of it.

Nuka had never been this far south before, and even though his village had traded with the Mountain People since his grandfather's time, the two groups mistrusted each other.

"They are savages," his father had told him. "They move from place to place like moss in the wind. They do not live in settled encampments and think as we do. Do not trust them."

Nuka went to the front of the sled. Maguruk stretched and bit the harness.

"You are eager for the trail, eh?" He scratched her ruff. "There will be much of that. We will follow the Colville until it bends at the Etivluk, and that river, Maguruk, will lead us to the encampment we seek."

There was more confidence in his voice than he felt.

It would take many weeks of climbing to reach the pass and even then there was no guarantee he would find the Mountain People. They were nomads, following the track of caribou and the spoor of bear.

"No matter," Nuka said out loud. "If we cannot find them, they will have to find us." Maguruk yawned and wagged her tail.

For twenty days it had snowed, making progress slow through the folds of valleys and cliffs. Maguruk pulled the sled without protest; Nuka walked beside her. It was light now twelve hours a day, but the blowing snow made it impossible to see more than a few feet ahead. They held to the frozen river, going steadily south.

On the morning of the twenty-first day, Nuka crawled out of the shelter he had dug from a snowbank to find himself surrounded by a herd of caribou.

In unison their heads went up. Nostrils dilated; mouths chewed. Columns of breath hung in the frosty sky. They looked silently at Nuka for a long instant, and then the pups scrambled from the shelter and began snapping at their heels. The herd turned and bolted up the ridge. They were going north, toward the coast.

Nuka watched the undulating line until they disappeared into the gray snow. His spirits soared.

168

Mountain people hunt caribou.

He summoned Maguruk, and they started on their way.

They had been going into the wind for several hours when Maguruk flattened her ears and hackles sprang on her neck. She whined deep in her throat. "What is it? What do you smell?" He scanned the horizon. In his back, he felt a gun.

"Identify yourself," a voice commanded. Nuka turned. The man was taller than he and broad shouldered, with piercing black eyes, a thick nose and long, unkempt hair. Nuka recognized him from the spring before.

"Samqr! It is Nuka! From the People of the Whale!"

There was a moment of stunned confusion and then the mountain man said, "Why do you come?"

Samqr's village was in a deep valley next to the Etivluk River. It was a collection of tents made from poles lashed together and covered with skins. Refuse and human waste was scattered over the snow.

He had two whining children and a slovenly wife. Unkempt hair fell down over her unwashed face and something green and odious smelling was crusted on her left arm. She was stirring a pot and kept her eyes down while her husband and Nuka sat on the floor and talked.

"Nuka carries sad news from the coast."

Samqr had stuffed a pipe with moss, and now he sucked it and passed it to Nuka.

"Sad news? You dare bring sad news into our encampment. Did you not take precautions to shield us?" His voice was a low growl.

"The People of the Whale are gone. Nuka is the last of the line."

"What are you saying?"

"A great illness took them. Huge sores and great suffering. Your journey down the Colville River will be an empty one this year."

Samqr's face darkened. "There is no truth in your words."

"It is true. Perhaps another village along the coast—"

"It is not true!" Samqr snapped. He turned petulantly to his wife. "Samqr is hungry."

She bent over the pot and lifted out the meat with bare

169

hands, and Nuka wondered again at the fear her husband inspired.

The meat was a caribou fetus, small and perfectly formed, its legs curled up protecting the belly.

It was moist and tender. Samqr ate noisily, sucking the bones and splitting them apart to get the marrow. The youngest child moaned once, looked at his father and stopped, hiding its face in its mother's arms.

"Why are you here?" Samqr leaned back on one elbow.

The wife cleared the bones. Nuka had purposely left some meat on his portion, and the mother divided it among her children. They ate quickly, gulping like hungry birds. Samqr ignored them.

Nuka turned his attention to his host. "For information."

"What kind?"

He pulled the red paint-stone from his pocket. "In the spring, when you traded with us, where did you get this?"

Samqr smiled and his lips gleamed with grease. "It is important?"

Nuka nodded.

"How much?" Samqr got to his knees.

"You tell me."

"The bitch. Information for the dog."

Nuka shook his head. "No. Not that important."

He made a move to get up, knowing Samqr would counter with another offer.

But the mountain savage did not. Nuka rose, bowed to his host and backed out.

It was dark outside, and he stood for some time next to the sled and dogs, wondering what to do.

He had no choice but to withdraw. He built a small snow hut half a valley away, and then he went to bed.

An hour later he heard it—the footfall so light at first he thought it must be a wild animal. Then a woman's voice said, "Hurry! There is no time for ceremony!"

Nuka dressed and removed a section of the wall and crawled out with Maguruk. It was Samqr's wife.

She had been running and now she looked behind her. "He does not know. Come! You must come." Nuka replaced the snow block to keep the pups inside.

She ran ahead through the snow, bypassing the village, and headed directly up the next sloping ridge. At an outcropping of rock she paused, caught her breath and slipped inside. Maguruk shook her tail violently, whimpered and followed her.

Nuka found himself in a cave. A fire roared in the middle of it, and smoke obscured the far wall. Maguruk had disappeared. The woman removed the bearskin jacket and dropped to her knees. She was dressed in filthy rags. "Grandfather," she said softly.

An ancient voice cleared its throat amid the smoke. The woman spoke. "Grandfather, there is someone here who wishes an audience."

"Who comes for me?" he cried out.

Maguruk yelped and bounded to his side, grunting with joy. She whined and clicked her teeth.

The old man listened and said, "So. He is dead. Well, let's take a look at the new one." He raised his voice. "Come, son. Into the light."

Nuka came around the fire and knelt. The old man was small and frail, with a mass of silver hair and a face puckered with age. Two small dark eyes shone in his head. They stared at each other in silence while Maguruk rested her head in the old man's lap.

"The shaman from the People of the Whale has chosen well."

"You knew him?"

"Yes, before the great darkness came that scattered the tribes over the earth. But that was long ago and you have pressing business."

"My sister. The hunters of Sippak wrenched her from me, leaving this in her place." He took the stone from his pocket and passed it to the old man, who closed his eyes and warmed it between his hands.

"What do you see?" the woman asked.

The old man sighed. "There has been much death this winter."

"She is not dead? Tell me!"

171

"No, she is not dead."

"What, then."

The old man gave him back the stone. "The knowledge you receive here is the kind that is surrendered by stones and the wind, not by dreams and spirits."

"You know where my sister is! Nuka feels it!"

"It is known only where the red paint-stone comes from. The rest you must find yourself."

"Where?"

"The hunters of Sippak find the stone along a certain place on a river called the Yukon. It is far to the south, past the Deep Mountains."

"That is all?" He could not hide his disappointment.

The old man smiled gently. "That is more than you knew before."

The Yukon. It was only a word. "How does one find this— Yukon?"

"South. As the shaman directed."

"Into the Great Mountains?" The encampment of Mountain People was barely inside the first rise, so steep were the ridges to the south.

"You are protected. You know that," the old man chided. "Do you shrink now from the quest?"

Nuka bowed his head. "It is as it was to be."

"That is so."

He rose. Maguruk still rested her head on the old man's knee. The young woman was curled next to him. "Thank you, woman."

The woman looked at him directly. "My name is Aan. Grandfather has spoken of you often. You were known from the first moment."

Nuka felt a peculiar warmth. He called to Maguruk brusquely, but the dog made no attempt to get up. "Maguruk! Come now."

The dog whined and licked the old man's hand.

"Maguruk!" He was humiliated. The old man knew it, the woman on the floor knew it, and Nuka knew it most of all; so he did what was always done in such cases. "You may have the dog," he said grandly.

172

"Thank you," the old man said. He looked at Nuka intently. "After you have found your sister, or settled in your own mind what became of her, return here and the dog will go with you willingly. Maguruk is old, as the man before you is, and we have many things to discuss."

"She will be missed," Nuka blurted out.

At that, Maguruk raised her head and went to Nuka, who bent down and wrapped his arms around her.

The old man turned away from the display and gazed at his granddaughter with a fierce intensity. "You will not have to bear it much longer," he said softly.

Nuka was startled. Did he mean the girl was going to die? And if so, how? At the hands of her mate? For an instant he had a strong impulse to take her away with him, and then the old man said, "She will be all right, Nuka. Do not worry."

The girl gazed at him steadily and Nuka looked past the filthy hair and greasy clothes, into her heart.

He wasn't certain what he saw there, but time and again in the lonely days that followed, he returned to it, as a hunter returns to the warming rock after many nights on the ice.

BOOK THREE

The Lines Are Drawn

Seventeen

Forty thousand people spilled off the boats at Dawson that summer, carrying their cargoes of dreams through the steaming mud.

It was not a town of pretty faces.

There was an urgency about the newcomers that hadn't been there in Skagway. Even the flush ones felt a pinch in their wallets to match the tightness in their throats. But most of the faces were still alive with hope and dread.

They found reason for both in Dawson.

The gold was there. Two and a half miles up the Klondike, from the point at which it separates from the Yukon River, Bonanza Creek stretched for twenty-five gold-producing miles, every rocky step of which had been staked by 1898. It was the same with the El Dorado, Gold Bottom and Too Much Gold Creek. The newcomers were even too late to locate on Last Chance. But the air in Dawson was redolent of easy money and the constant news of fresh strikes, always farther away. The gold was out there, all right. And every man secretly knew he could find it. All he needed was a *plan*, and he'd slip away to Indian River or Flag Creek and bring back jingling pockets and drinks for the house. But it had to be a *good* plan. Well thought out.

So the trick was to listen in, to hear about the Big One first, to get the cache together and leave, but leave *quietly*—and first. And to hang onto what you had until you got ready to make your move. That was the trick. When everywhere you turned, people had their fingers out, trying to loop into your pouch and pull the money out, like that kid in the nursery rhyme hooking his thumb around a plum in some pie. Yeah, that was the trick, alright. Hanging onto it.

*   *   *

One of Edison's inventions had been lugged over the Chilkoot Pass to Dawson the year before, and now blaring gramophones were chained like pet dogs in front of every casino and bar. Adding to the noise was the constant bleat of whistles from the boats as they rounded the arc in the Yukon River and sighted Dawson, the shrill sounds of chickens and horses unloaded at the docks and the sound a crowd makes swarming through the streets. The smell was even louder than the noise.

The town had been built on stinking ground—a bog—and in July the temperature rose above eighty. Hauling drinking water and supplies in above eighty-degree weather can be sweaty business. The men let their clothes stiffen against their bodies like snake scales, a crusty protection against the mosquitoes that prowled the streets in packs.

Three sawmills belched smoke into the sky around the clock as workers scrambled to keep up with the insatiable need for lumber. The smell of the green wood, black oily smoke and stinking men mixed with the smells of food coming from the stalls: green peppers and chili, fresh bread, roasted moose and dried salmon, ripe vegetables. A meal of biscuits, moose stew, vegetables and pie cost as much as a month's rent for a Seattle flat. Every time a man turned around, somebody was trying to hook a thumb into his pouch and pull out a plum, yes, indeed. So it was better sometimes to smell and not touch, and listen in for the big one that would make it all worth it.

But there was another smell, a smell more ominous than the smell of winter. It was the smell of sickness and death.

There were booths in Dawson that sold opera glasses and telescopes. There were shipments of Persian rugs and lace fans. There was a lending library and fourteen churches. Dawson may have been heavy in the civic pride department, but it was a little light on public toilets.

There were two for forty thousand men.

At least the civic fathers had had the foresight to put one next to the cemetery. There was a lot of traffic to the cemetery that summer. What dysentery didn't take, typhoid would. A parade of funeral wagons pulled by dogs streamed daily up the hill, with Death twirling the baton up front. Looking down over the neat row of wooden crosses, you could see the river, where garbage and excrement floated like tiny boats bobbing out to sea.

Business was brisk at the Catholic Mission hospital. By midsummer men were placed between the occupied beds to die.

But none of that was on the minds of the men seated around the back table at Harry Ash's Northern Saloon. It was a high-stakes poker game—minimum buy-in, five hundred dollars. Seven men had drawn cards the night before, and when the smoke cleared early in the morning, only three were left sitting.

Batt Jackson had it in the bag. He knew it. He'd been shuffling the spots off of cards since the three wise men were only half smart. He bit off the end of a new cigar, leaned back in his chair and looked at the other two men left in the game. The kid wouldn't last. His smooth upper lip sweated when he got a good hand. Not a lot of sweat, but enough to tip Batt off. Sooner or later, the kid would get scared, or a little too eager, and make a mistake. Batt knew it. The only real threat came from the old man sitting across from him. He had long white piano-player hands that moved tenderly across the cards as if he were playing a difficult piece by heart. Only he didn't have a heart was the thing. And that face behind the drooping mustache belonged behind bars. His eyes were as cold as Batt's, and Batt had the distinct impression the old man could see right through him to every bad thing he'd ever done. But when Batt had made a point sometime during the night of asking the stranger what he did for a living, and when he'd smiled and said he taught school, Batt knew he'd beat the old man too.

Good poker players only lie about things that could be true. If the old man was a schoolteacher, then Batt Jackson wore a tutu and a smile to his eighth-grade graduation dance. Batt lit the end of the cigar and dunked it in the ashtray.

Harry Ash leaned against the rope cordoning off the table as if he were the referee for the heavyweight championship fight of the world. Pale and pasty looking, with hair combed carefully in front over the place where there wasn't any. He had built the bar the year before, and now the place was packed with lookers and those who looked. It was Harry's job to make

179

sure the two groups got together. But the serious stuff happened in the back of the bar. That's where the gaming tables were, and that's where the action was, especially now. He leaned over the table.

"Five o'clock in the morning," he said importantly. "One hour break before the next hand." He pulled his watch from his pocket. "Meet here at six-oh-five." He motioned to Batt. "This gent's turn to deal. What's your pleasure?"

Batt bit down on the cigar. "Seven-card stud." He pulled his pouch from the inside pocket. "Ante upped to one thousand dollars."

There was a moment of startled silence. The kid licked his lips.

"If it's too much—" Batt said to the old man.

The stranger put his money on the pile, and after a moment the kid did too, but slowly, as if he were fingering it for the last time. Batt had them, all right.

"Back here at six-oh-five," Harry Ash repeated. "Or forfeit the buy-in." Batt nodded once to the armed guard and ducked under the rope. The kid followed.

The crowd at the bar had thinned. The customers had that sullen, wooden way of walking when the night's drinking is finally wearing off. A yellow-haired woman waddled over to Batt and whined, "Looking for something, mister?"

He had seen her at three in the morning, working the crowd, but she had looked younger then. He shook his head. "I got my own stable. I get it for free."

Her eyes widened and she said, "Looking for somebody else to work for ya? I'm real good and real fast."

"I'll keep you at the head of the list." He winked and dropped a silver piece into the slot between her breasts.

"Thanks, mister," she called after him.

He walked outside, squinting at the sun. An hour. Time for a hot bath and square meal. He flexed his fingers and thought of the game ahead.

He was walking back to the Northern Saloon, preened and primed and pleased with himself. He would take the kid out this

180

round, and then it would be one-on-one with the old man. Batt strolled along the waterfront, listening to the early morning sounds. The boat people were crawling stiff-jointed out of bed and gargling into the river. Batt was fond of all of them. He wanted to buy them all dinner after the game. In San Francisco.

A stern-wheeler was pulling into dock, and Batt stood and watched it. The deck of the steamer was crawling with Mounties and more were lined up on the shore, waiting to board. He sidled over and asked, "Is it a bust?"

The Mountie shook his head. He would never get used to the vulgarity of Americans. "Dead bodies," he said flatly, and moved away.

Batt put his hands in his pockets, careful not to step in the mud and ruin the shine on his boots. He felt very much alive.

As the bodies were passing by, he had time for one more question, so he leaned over to a Mountie shouldering a body and asked him what had happened.

"Drowning." The Mountie shifted his cargo awkwardly and the wrapper unwrapped. A hand slipped out, small and too white. "Have you identified the bodies?"

The Mountie shook his head. "Only one survivor and she's delirious."

Behind him two Mounties were bringing down a stretcher. It passed next to Batt and he looked down, looked straight into the face, and that's when he lost the game.

"I know her!" he blurted out.

A Mountie put his hands on Batt's shoulders, huge ham hocks of hands. He squeezed. "Come with me." The voice matched the hands.

"I didn't know her *well*," Batt said, but it was too late.

He thought of the game, thought of the thousand dollars of his money on the table, thought of the kid who even now was sitting down with sweat on his upper lip, of the old man who lied about the wrong things, and did something very foolish. Understandable, but foolish. He swung at a Canadian mounted policeman. He missed. Three Mounties jumped him. His hands were locked behind his back. He was lifted off his feet and

181

hustled over to their tent.

At the Northern Saloon, the game was starting without him. They had held it open an extra ten minutes, to be on the safe side. The kid had four kings and an ace and bet it all. On the last card the old man drew a joker. It went nicely with the three aces he had in his hand.

Eighteen

It took Batt ten minutes to tell the Mounties everything he knew about Flame and Margaret Ryan and two weeks to get out of jail for the way he told it. The same day he was released, a woman stepped off the *Seattle I* and sailed into the waterfront crowd, a huge cape inflating around her like a mast in a high wind. Even if she had been normal size, her hair would have signalled that this was no ordinary woman. It was purple, and curled up in an elaborate pompadour popular in France a hundred years before. She had little pig eyes, three chins and BILL with a ball and chain tattooed across her right wrist. Under the cape her black dress leaped and shimmied with spangles, and her breasts pointed like bloodhounds tracking in opposite directions. When she walked, the ground moved. And so did the miners.

Her name was Silver Dollar and she came on business. She wasted no time in Dawson but immediately took the footbridge across the Klondike River that led toward the chalky face of Moose Pass. Here was another town, shabbier and smaller than Dawson. It was christened Klondike City, but everybody called it Louse Town. Sixty sagging shacks housed sixty fallen women. What was lacking in class was made up in services rendered. Gold in advance.

The main alley was called White Chapel. The footbridge was usually thick with miners eager to get religion. A light rain falling that July afternoon did little to cool them down. They stood patiently in the mud, watching mosquitoes bury the necks of the men ahead of them, and waited for the healing properties of Sister French Louise or Mabel La Rose to bring to life what had died.

The quality of miracles was astonishing.

Silver picked the shack with the longest line ~~and waited until~~ ~~the door opened and a man~~ came out. He was smiling and patting his pants, as if to make certain everything was still where he had left it. She shouldered her way to the front of the line and bellowed, "Step aside!" There was a protest forming on the lips of the man whose place she had taken. It died as he looked at her. She was half a head taller than he and would have boxed in the next class up. He stepped aside.

She punched open the door, shoved it closed and sat heavily on the bed. Then she sighed and rolled down her stockings. "Damn heat. Hotter than Hades all the way from Skagway." She reached down her front and pulled up a tin of snuff. "Chew?"

The whore shook her head. Silver nodded and stuffed her cheek. "You will." She chewed contemplatively and examined the woman in front of her. The whore's hair curled from the heat and her upper lip shone. The room smelled of yeast, perfume and sweat, as if a French baker had been holed up there for a month, vowing not to take a bath until he had perfected the recipe for hot cross buns. The whore looked at Silver calmly, her small feet curled under her hips. She was wearing a surprisingly clean dressing gown that matched the tawny color of her hair and eyes. A small locket circled her neck.

"So you call yourself Belgian Nelly," Silver said abruptly. The name had been printed in script over the door. Nelly nodded. "And your Christian name?"

"I lost it long ago. There is no need to find it again." The voice was low and musical.

Silver looked at her shrewdly. This was no common whore. It made her situation all the more puzzling.

"I'll be frank with you," Silver began. "I'm here on a buying mission. I need one more girl to round out my stable. You're indentured, or you wouldn't be here." Nelly looked at her obliquely. "I buy only good quality stock. Girls with a real future in the business."

Silver moved her shoulders expressively. "Louse Town isn't known for the class of its demimondes, if you understand my French. Klondike Kate herself is in Dawson right now—along

184

with the Oregon Mare, Diamond Tooth Lil—but the boys line up in front of your place in the scummiest part of the scummiest town."

Belgian Nelly dipped her head and gracefully rolled a cigarette between her fingers, brushing away the tobacco grains before lighting it. She inhaled deeply and the pungent smell of tobacco filled the air.

"Shouldn't smoke in here," Silver said nervously. "Last year half of Dawson went up."

"What are you offering me?"

The question startled Silver. She chewed furiously. "Most women in your position are glad to move up to a real house."

Nelly smiled for the first time. "I am not most women."

I'll have to watch her like a hawk. "Five percent of the take and your free papers signed at one year."

Nelly looked indifferently around the dingy room. She stubbed out her cigarette in the metal basin by the chair and yawned.

"I will think about it."

"Ten percent. And the papers signed at eleven months."

A change came over Nelly. She rose and licked her lips as if she were a cat polishing off a very dead canary. "Deal." She extended her hand and they shook hands formally. "You have talked to my owner?"

"I don't even know who he is."

"Oh, yes, you do." That peculiar smile flitted across Nelly's face again. "It's Batt. Batt Jackson."

Silver found him at the Palace Grand Theatre eating roast ptarmigan and watching the destruction of the *Maine* on a projectoscope. She thumped him hard on the back of his hat with her fist as she squeezed behind the machine next to his. He jerked up, ready to fight, but when he saw who it was he settled back, smiled and greasily offered her a drumstick. She took it.

"Silver, my love. How extraordinary. I was just thinking about you."

"Come on, Batt. You were supposed to be in Circle last spring, remember? Anyway, I came on business. What do you want for Belgian Nelly?"

185

The screen lit up with the front page of the *World* printed the February before. It cut to a jerky sequence of gunfire. An anonymous soldier screamed silently and fell over a cliff into the water, where shards of the *Maine* still floated. The soldier fell through the words WAS IT A BOMB OR A TORPEDO THAT EXPLODED THE MAINE?

Silver sucked the drumstick noisily and threw the bone into a cuspidor. "How much?" she said again.

His eyes hardened into slits. "She's worth a lot."

Silver helped herself to a wing. "Well?"

Batt calculated, exaggerating his movements. "In a good week she pulls in about a grand."

Silver sighed. "How long have we known each other? Ten years, maybe? In all that time, have I ever known you to be honest about anything? You'd sell your own mother if a miner asked for an older woman."

He cranked the projectoscope and it sprang to life again. "Like the lady said, 'It's business.'" On the screen was the front page of the New York *Journal*:

$50,000!
$50,000 REWARD!
FOR THE DETECTION
OF THE PERPETRATOR OF THE
MAINE OUTRAGE!

Batt squinted at the words. Silver ignored the screen. "When I first laid eyes on you, you were nothing but a scroungy loser, still whimpering from the cleaning you took in Frisco. Now look at you, in your fancy French sateen shirt and high dollar boots. I bet even your undershirt is silk."

"Makes me break out."

"I pulled you up from nothing. *Nothing.* I gave you a roof over your head. I even let you test the girls. All I want is this one little favor." Silver reached her hand over to his groin and expertly plumped the soft mound of flesh. "Come on, Batt. For old times' sake."

"Ten grand."

"Five," she snapped, and took her hand away.

"Nine."

"Six."

"For you, Silver . . . seven-five."

"Deal." They shook on it.

"Seven-five and one small favor."

She tried to get her hand away but he held on to it. "Come on, Sil. For old times' sake."

"*None* of your favors are small."

He peeled the wrapper off a Havana special and bit off the end. "There's this girl."

"You've got more skirts than a French dressmaker."

"It's nothing like that. She needs an escort north. And a job."

It was Silver's turn to calculate. She smiled brilliantly at Batt. "What does she look like?"

"Not *that* kind of job. She's not that kind of girl."

"They're *all* that kind of girl. It just takes some of them a while before they figure it out."

"She's had a run of bad luck, is all. Needs a hand."

Silver's eyes narrowed. "Bad luck?"

Batt thought of the poker game. "Very bad luck. I mean, for me. I'll level with you. Every time I see her, it costs me something. I figure this way I can get her out of my life for good."

"If she's that bad for *you*, what makes you think *I* want her?"

Batt wiped his finger on his handkerchief. "Seven thousand, five hundred dollars. But never mind, I'll play out Nelly and retire next year."

Silver's small eyes blinked. "Oh, all right," she said heavily. She nibbled morosely on the wing. "Let me take a look at her."

They were past the Chinese Laundry and Sundries Shop when Silver dug her buttoned boots into the mud and refused to go on. "She's either at Ladue's Lumber Yard or the Catholic hospital. Knowing you, she's not sawing logs."

"It's not as bad as you think."

"I won't take a sick one along. She could infect my girls and I could lose my whole business."

187

"Suit yourself," Batt said cheerfully. Silver turned and started walking away. Batt called after her. "I lied about how much money Nelly makes."

Silver stopped.

Batt smiled. "It's not a grand a week, Sil. It's two."

Silver walked a few steps, but they were slow and painful ones, as if she had eaten a whole crate full of green apples and her bowels were sloshing like a cargo ship on an oily sea.

"You saw the way Nelly lined them up."

Silver blinked rapidly. "Two grand a week."

"My word as a gentleman."

The second floor of the hospital was oppressively hot. Flies dived at the small window at the end of the unlit hallway. A tall, skinny nun watched the pair climb the steps. She crossed her arms over her sunken chest.

"Sister Marie, how lovely you look." Batt swept off his hat and bowed. A boil swelled on the back of his neck, the head already a dull yellow against the inflamed skin.

"Whatever you want, you can't have," the sister said. "Besides, none of your girls are in here."

"It's a friend, sister. Just a friend."

"And trees have wings."

"Flame Ryan."

"*That* sweet little girl?"

"Like I said, a friend. She's not expecting me, exactly. I was there when they pulled her out."

"She's in no condition to see the likes of you."

Silver tugged at his sleeve. "I told you she was sick."

"Is it the plague?"

"Something worse," the sister said soberly. "It's grief."

They had put Flame in a room with a maiden schoolteacher from San Francisco who had left her job suddenly and fled north, barely outrunning her delivery date. Now a child suckled at her breast, but there was something very wrong with it; its skin was yellow and its eyes ran. The mother crooned to it and secretly wished it were dead. Across from the door was a dancehall girl in a body cast.

188

Flame lay on a narrow cot with her face to the wall, not moving. Batt stood in the doorway and studied her. "How long has she been like this?"

"Ever since they brought her in two weeks ago. At first we thought it was the shock, but now I'm not sure."

"Has she spoken?"

"Not a word. Doesn't seem to see anyone around her. I hold her head while she eats. She's diapered like a baby."

"What are you going to do?"

It had to be faced someday. "Father Powers is being transferred to a parish in Seattle. They have places in Seattle for people like Flame."

"Places? What do you mean, places?"

The sister looked at him with no emotion. "Just what you think I mean. She's being transferred to Ridgeport Community Hospital. She leaves with Father Powers in the morning."

"A *snake pit?*"

Sister Marie compressed her lips. "Mr. Jackson. Yesterday five men died of dysentery. Another man bled to death before we could close the hole an axe made in his leg. We have enough beds and linens and medicine for two hundred patients. This morning I counted four hundred and eighteen. I am not a woman without compassion. I truly am not."

"Let's go," Silver whined. "I tell ya, she's—"

"Shut up!" Batt walked to the bed. Flame lay with her head on her arm. Purple and yellow bruises splotched her back, where the dressing gown had pulled away. She was breathing unevenly, making small, whoofling noises into the curve of her elbow. Her hair had been braided into two pigtails and fastened to her head with long white hairpins. The pins in the left braid were working loose, and the hair was tufting in small, irregular patterns on the sheet. He could stand the hospital, the strong smell of dying masked by the disinfectant. He could even stand looking down at her still body and seeing how much weight she had dropped since Lake Bennett. But the braids got to him. She was always neat as a pin. He pressed his neck where the boil was. "Let me try, sister."

"Mr. Jackson, you have no experience in such matters."

He bent down and pushed a strand of hair back into the

braid. It was matted with sweat. "Can't hurt to try, can it?" He wet his lips. "Well, can it?"

Flame moaned and thrashed her legs and Batt bent over her, suddenly hopeful. But the nun touched his arm and shook her head. "It's like that sometimes for her. It doesn't mean anything."

"Just let me *try*. Okay?"

She hadn't planned on saying yes, but something in his eyes made her change her mind. The nun leaned over Flame, her eyes still on Batt.

"Flame," she said gently.

"She don't talk," the sweaty face above the body cast explained from the far bed.

"Okay, Mabel," the nun said sharply. She touched Batt's arm with desiccated fingertips. "You have ten minutes."

Batt took off his hat and wondered what to do. Flies threw themselves at the window and died, trying to escape through a window that had been nailed shut. What could he say that she would hear?

Ten minutes. He could faster fly to the moon.

Flame was quietly dreaming, dark and insular dreams. She was eight, climbing a hill behind her house. Far away, Elliott Bay gleamed like a purple jewel. Smoke from Pioneer Square floated into the lazy summer sky and Mount Rainier rose through the clouds. Below her, in town, trolley cars moved jerkily along a toy track and the elms were smudged thumbprints of green spaced along Front Street. It was peaceful and orderly and Flame sat with her knees hitched up under her chin, absorbed in constructing lives for all the people in the toy buildings. Then, as she watched, a black and orange ball, burning and bright, burst out of the window of the courthouse. *Burning*. Flame stood up and shielded her eyes for a better look. The toy courthouse was on fire. Black smoke rolled out the windows and the orange ball was expanding. The fire skipped across the tinderbox rooftops, scraps of the orange ball flying crazily into the air. Every time a scrap touched down, there grew another orange ball. Far off a tinny alarm sounded. Her mother was bending over her, squeezing her hand, telling her it was time to wake up now, that she had slept a good long while and now she must open her eyes. Then her mother's face went away and it was Batt and he was telling her something else.

"Your mother's dead."

The words were brutal, ugly.

"She's dead, Flame. She went under and drowned. The Miles Canyon White Horse stretch took her. She's dead and nothing will ever bring her back."

Flame gasped, and for a moment Batt thought he had her. Then her eyes clouded and she slipped away.

"You can lay there all you want. You can lie there until your chest sinks like Atlantis and your hair turns gray and falls out. But she's dead, Flame. *Dead*. She's not coming back, ever. And if you let this get you, then it would be kinder if I just put a bullet through your head right now. It would save everybody a lot of aggravation."

He knew he was taking a chance, a big one. It could drive her so far inside, nobody could ever find her again. But what choice did he have? *Ridgeport, for chrissake.* He stared anxiously at her and checked her pulse. It was racing. He bent over her. *What else could he say?* He'd have to try again. Something. Behind him Batt heard the whispered sound of the nun's habit as she glided toward him. *Something, for chrissake.* She laid her hand on his shoulder.

"Just five more minutes!" He hadn't meant to shout, but he didn't have time anymore to be polite. No time. Goddamn it she could *see* that, couldn't she? I mean, even a nun with her head so far up her ass she walked lock kneed could *see* that, couldn't she?

"*Mr. Jackson.* I do *not* have to tolerate such language! *Get out of here before I have you thrown out.*"

He'd said it out loud? He'd never meant to say it *out loud*, for chrissake. "Just five minutes."

"I've already given you thirty. I really must insist. I'm sorry, Mr. Jackson. Really I am." She smiled a tight-lipped smile that told Batt she wasn't sorry at all. He looked at Flame. She was breathing shallowly and her eyes were moving under the blue lids.

Sorry, kid. I tried. ~~He felt~~ old and beaten, as if he had ~~shambled~~ into one fight too many. *I tried, Flame. I did.*

Next time I'm in Seattle, I'll stop by with my hanky and wipe up the drool leaking out of your sweet little mouth.

The nun's eyes were a cold blue under her cap. "If I have to call support personnel to assist me, they could make things very unpleasant for you." She licked her lips.

And you'd just hate that all to pieces, wouldn't you, sis? "Flame, you gotta listen to me, kid. This is it. This is your last chance." The nun was grabbing hold of his arm and pulling him away. He never knew nuns could be so *strong*.

"Flame—" he tried again, his voice cracking.

But the nun had stopped pulling on him, her movements arrested by a more startling one coming from the bed.

Flame was trying to get up.

Her face was as open as a wound. She groped blindly for support, her mouth working like a newborn animal and her head wobbly. Batt took her hand, and Flame clung to him.

"Can you hear me?" Batt asked. Her head bobbled in the direction of his voice. "Can you hear me?"

They waited in the room, the flies pinging the window like sharp pellets of gravel, the mother murmuring wordlessly to the dying infant.

Flame's face doubled onto her chest and her mouth dropped open. *Whatcha trying to do, catch flies?* Some distant teacher's voice, during his unsuccessful academic career. *Keep yer trap closed and yer ears open.* Miss—what was her name? He had almost had it. Roberts? Rogers? *Robin. Like the egg I'm gonna grow on top of yer head when I bean ya.*

"Can you hear me, Flame?"

Her chin settled into itself and she made a snuffling sound, almost like—Batt swallowed. Almost like she was snoring.

"Is your name Flame?" *Step right up, folks, step right up. Answer the question correctly and pick any prize off the bottom shelf.* "Is your name Flame?" *Come on.* A simple head nod will do. *Too much for ya? Okay. An eye twitch. Just an eye twitch then.*

The nun was gently touching his arm. "You tried."

192

He let himself be pulled away from the bed, away from Flame's wobbling head and slack mouth. Then he turned around abruptly and walked to the door, the picture of her like a pain behind his eyes. He had almost reached Silver when he heard it and it stopped him cold.

"Yes."

He turned and almost ran back to the bed.

"Yes." Her voice was fluty and faraway sounding, but it was a *voice*, a voice coming out of Flame's head, and as such, was a cause for merriment, for table dancing, for balloons in the street. He took her hand. She leaned toward him and tried to focus on his face.

"Are you Flame?"

"Yes." The same muted voice. Batt looked at the nun, hitched up his pants. *You lose.*

"I'm Batt. Do you remember me, Flame? Batt Jackson." She moved her free hand toward him. *I'm here, kid. Hit me. See for yourself.* Flame's hand thumped his jaw, and he grabbed it and placed it over his face. "Batt Jackson. From Skagway."

"Batt. From Skagway."

"That's right. You've had a bad accident, Flame. You're in a hospital in Dawson. You're going to get better. Can you hear me?" Her face had suddenly slackened again. *Flame. Are you in there, Flame.*

"My mother." It was a moan.

Her hand tightened, and he carefully held it and patted it. The veins stood up on the back of her hand like night crawlers in thin soil. Not a pretty little hand, he thought. But a strong one.

"Flame, I got something to tell you that's going to hurt." *No please no nonono.* The blue vein in her hand was beginning to pound. "It's about your mother. She didn't make it, Flame. She drowned."

No no no no. Flame shook her head and squeezed her eyes tight. *A balloon, an orange, dancing balloon, sailing across a blue sky as blue as—*

She opened her eyes and stared at him, really stared at him, and he knew then that she had come back finally, and her eyes

193

opened wider until he could see the pain and the dread and underneath, far back inside her eyes, the strength.

She sank back against the pillow. "Then it wasn't a dream."

He stroked her hair. "No. Not that part." She turned her face to the wall. It was a furious thing, her grief. She began to rock back and forth, sometimes laughing, spilling fragments of stories, then howling. He held her and patted her, feeling like his arms were too long and his legs too gangly for such a delicate job. He looked at Silver once, silently pleading with her to come over and take a turn, but she became preoccupied with scratching a furious itch inside her purple hive of hair. Finally the tears came in smaller and smaller waves. He waited until her grief had spent itself before rooting around in his vest pocket for his handkerchief. He turned it over so the side with his dinner stains was on the bottom and then held it up to her nose and commanded her to blow. She honked into it, as obedient as a child. A fly inspected the crotch of her braids. Batt brushed it away, and it lifted unsteadily into the air.

"I have got to get you out of here," he said unsteadily. "I know it's sudden. Thinking about your future and all. You were heading north when—"

He clamped his mouth shut and patted her hair before trying again.

"Still going north?" It was better that time, more casual, like he'd met her in a bar on Dugan Turner Street and they'd had a few drinks.

"I've got a mine," she said dully.

"Really?"

Flame nodded. "Off the Yukon aways. Up north."

He remembered something and reached into his pocket. "Flame, the Mounties gave me something. Told me to make sure you got it when you were feeling better." When she didn't say anything, he took her hand and pressed the object into it. "It's your mother's ring, Flame. Her wedding ring."

He swallowed the lump in his throat and motioned Silver over. "This is Silver. Silver Dollar. She and me go way back. She'll take care of you. Get you fixed up. I go up and down the Yukon, see, so I won't always be around—"

Still Flame's face was turned to the wall, and Batt saw she

194

was crying again. He patted her awkwardly. "She'll get you all fixed up."

Sister Marie stood in the hallway and watched them go. Batt stopped and walked back to her. "Almost forgot." He pulled out a small gilt box. "Rum creams."

"I can't accept those."

"I got them for you." The box had scrolls rimming the edge and the words Very Fancy French Creams embossed on the cover. "Came all the way from Paris."

She narrowed her eyes and pursed her thin lips together. "Well. For the children."

Batt tipped his hat. "For the children."

The nun waited until Batt and Silver had started down the stairs before she opened the box and ate one. It had almost disappeared, melting in sticky splendor in the jowl of her cheek, before it occurred to her to wonder how Batt had known they were her favorite kind.

Thunder rattled over King Solomon's Dome. It was one of those sudden, raw summer rains, when the sky opens up and buckets the countryside in torrents of water. From where Batt and Silver sat at the Flora Dora Saloon on Front Street, they could see the waterfront along the Yukon. When lightning cracked, hundreds of boats tied to the wharf leaped into focus, as if they had been caught by a photographer's flash. Men stooped against the rain and slipped along the wharf between the tents and the small cabins built on stilts that hung out over the water. Batt wrapped his hands around his bourbon, looked out into the rain and felt warm. *She's going to make it.* It wasn't *quite* as good a feeling as the time he got a lick in before the heavyweight champion of the world, Frank Slavin, knocked him silly—but it was close. Yes indeed, it was close. He swallowed the last of the bourbon and ordered another bottle. Silver was drinking tequila straight, salt sanding the ridge of her thumb like a high beach.

"You sure are a sucker for a pretty face." She licked her thumb and the beach disappeared.

"What's that supposed to mean?"

She looked at him knowingly. "When are you planning on collecting?"

"What are you talking about?"

"I've known you a long time, Batt. And I've never known you not to collect, one way or another. Just like the tax man. So here's this young gal, not bad looking—if you like them scrawny and strange talking—and what I want to know is, when are you planning on collecting?"

A waitress, sagging in middle-aged places, brought their bottles to the table. She was wearing a red satin skirt that was hitched up in the back by a black bow. Netted stockings burst like broken veins over her fat thighs. She smiled and her face cracked under the powder. "Two-fifty, honey." She stooped down and her breasts dipped like swollen udders. Batt pinched dust out of his pouch and rubbed his fingers together over the scale until a small gold pyramid formed. She grunted as it tipped the two-fifty mark and smiled as he kept pouring.

"Thanks, honey. Thanks a lot."

He waited until she had left and they each had a drink poured before answering. "I'm not sure why I did it," he said truthfully. "But even if I do—collect—as you so delicately put it, what's it to you?"

Silver shuffled her hands smartly on the table, and Batt could see how they'd look with cards under them. "That's what I've been trying to get at." She looked at her imaginary cards and then stared blandly back at Batt.

"What are you saying?"

"What I've been *trying* to say for the last hour, Batt. She's not a bad-looking little girl. Just needs to be fattened up, is all." She leaned forward eagerly. "I'd take real good care of her for you, Batt. Real good. Make sure she has a nice, easy time, the first time. And then when you wanted her back—she'd be primed for it, would come quietly. I could pack her north with my girls and work her in real slowly. 'Course, I'd wait until we were miles from anywhere and she had grown kind of fond of me and all." She settled back in her chair and laced her hands over her belly. "Well, what do you think?"

Batt smiled again. "Just what you knew I'd think, Sil."

She looked relieved, and her hands moved again, as if she

were pulling a high pile out of the middle of the table and getting ready to count it. "Like I always say, you have to think with your head in this business."

"Quite right."

"Then it's decided."

"It's decided, all right." He leaned forward and smoothed his hands on the table. She looked at them and her hands stopped moving. But she had to see his nostrils flare and the whites of his eyes turn a funny yellow color before she understood. She tried to pull away but his hand shot out and grabbed her collar hard, twisting it until she couldn't breathe and the red veins in her nose stood out. Batt's voice was low and pleasant. "If I ever hear of you laying one finger on that girl, Sil, just one finger, I will find you and personally take care of the problem. Personally."

His eyes were hooded and black. *Snake's eyes*, she thought uneasily. The hands squeezing into her throat were freshly manicured, but Silver was remembering how they had squeezed a little too hard one night around the neck of a rowdy drunk and how Batt had left Forty Mile so fast his chips were still on the table when he was out the door. A thought that didn't exactly soothe, and she wet her lips. *He likes this. He likes scaring the shit out of me.*

"I have this little knife, see? And it does bad things to people's faces. You wouldn't want all your girls to look funny, would you? You want your girls to stay pretty for their friends, now don't you? Don't you? Answer me, Sil. It's the polite thing to do."

She whimpered and began chattering wordlessly, trying to catch a breath, staring at him as if she had never really seen him before. Batt liked that. It warmed him up, like the bourbon. He snapped his hands and she fell back, gasping, into her chair.

Her hands massaged her neck and she was very quiet, with the tequila bottle picking up the lights from the oil lamps and the lightning sparking outside the window. She looked her years.

Even with the purple hair and the encrusted rings and high coloring, her face drooped and her neck was crepey looking and

197

her eyes, when they looked at him, were old, the way old people's eyes get when they know how dangerous it is to navigate in the world, but they still want to live a long time, so they're going to be careful. Oh, so careful.

"I don't know you at all," she whispered.

He smiled, his eyes as black and cold as pebbles thrown against the moon. "That's right."

Nineteen

It was the fastest boat on the river. Carrying four hundred tons of supplies and two hundred passengers, it raced through the water at seventeen miles an hour. The *Hamilton* had been built the year before, and its painted hull had not been scoured clean by the sandy bottom of the Yukon River. It was 2190 feet long, 36 feet across and kept alive by three tube boilers, each as high as a two-story building. Two D-valve high pressure engines consumed a cord of wood an hour apiece, and turned over 2,500 horsepower. There were electric lights in the hallways and a searchlight in the pilot house. Most rooms even had windows.

Mixed in with the gold seekers were Silver's girls, a group of Salvation Army recruits bound for Fort Yukon and a nuts-and-bolts salesman who planned to open a hardware store in Rampart.

He spent the morning after they left Dawson peddling raisin seeders, sausage stuffers and cherry stoners door-to-door on the upper deck. He sold one of each and considered it a good morning. One woman had also ordered his combination meat condenser, fruit and lard press. It was stored in a crate below deck and he'd collect payment of $2.35 when it was delivered in Circle.

There was a holiday feeling on board, as if they weren't going down the Yukon at all but were plunging down the Congo into darkest Africa. Passing before them was a constantly changing panorama: villages slanting in the sun, slant-eyed natives caught in classic tableaus, hills thick with summer colors and, below them, the Yukon twisting like a snub-nosed cobra. But the headhunters waiting with their spears raised could never harm them as long as they stayed on board. Nor could the mines that were already claimed, the rivers that were wild and nameless, and the winter frost that was crouching its way down the valley toward them.

Flame stood on the upper deck after lunch, drew her shawl around her against the cool of the afternoon and looked west to where the Yukon curved around Eagle Bluff. On the left bank sagged a collection of tents. In front of them were smoking fires and drying racks hung with pink strips of fish. The water shimmered with flashes of light. A tiny woman with a face as wrinkled as a dried apple hobbled to a net and pulled out a salmon almost as big as she was. It thrashed wildly as she lifted it chest high and held it for a naked boy who clubbed it, dunked it and skinned it. The water was red before the fish stopped moving.

Two miles west, the town of Eagle lay under the shadow of Eagle Bluff. After the Indian village the town looked orderly and substantial. Along the waterfront cabins stretched in rows like neatly planted corn. Smoke from chimneys drifted in the air, and Flame could see whitewashed buildings and a church spire.

They were taking on wood for the boilers in Eagle, and impulsively Flame lined up with the others to get off.

One of Silver's whores stared fixedly at Flame and then melted behind a parasol into the crowd. Flame made her way past miners and parents counting heads and the hapless peddler. A cloud of children swarmed around him like gnats. He lost control of his wheelbarrow and a large meat grinder thunked out and bounced down the ramp into the water. He stared furiously at the spot where it went in, while behind him, the children cheered.

The small whitewashed church was farther than it had looked and Flame was out of breath when she pushed open the door and slipped inside. It was cool and dark. A gray-haired minister was preparing the sanctuary for Sunday communion, carefully arranging the loaf of bread and bottle of wine. He looked steadily at her but didn't speak.

Flame studied her hands, thinking of her mother.

She had always been quite certain of *her* right to go away, that someday she would dare extraordinary deeds; it was her birthright from her mother. Yet there had always been the unspoken assumption that the same mother would be waiting for her when she came back, soup on the burner, the mother's life steady and unremarkable and waiting to be filled with Flame's life, Flame's glory.

How could you leave me when I still needed you so much?

She had entered the church hoping, in some unarticulated way, for a tribute, a summing up, a moving on. She guessed she had wanted to leave her mother behind on the pew, safe in the hands of God and the pink-cheeked minister, the memories neat and tidy and generous.

Instead, she was filled with rages and longings and half-finished feelings.

She wished desperately she could find Cahill.

Trust me, he had said on the dock the day he left.

Trust. She had taken the word apart, scrap by scrap, but when it came time to put it together again, it had dissolved.

"Save it, Flame. Save it all for me."

"I will if you will."

"Then it's settled. I will. No matter what. Save it all for me."

The minister picked up the silver tray and was coming toward her down the aisle, his face calm with the glory that comes from knowing his place in life, the absolute rightness of his calling. It was depressing. The only thing Flame had ever been sure about was her love for Cahill, and now she couldn't even remember his face. Is trust conditional?

I will if you will.

Maybe she had banked too heavily on it, like her father and his margin before the crash. She had put all her money down on the golden chip I Will If You Will and the wheel had spun so fast she couldn't see anymore where If You Will *was*, let alone if he was keeping his end of the bargain.

How long is enough? At what point could she open herself to the possibility of loving someone else?

And then what? What if Cahill Blue came lurching back from the dead, with seaweed lips and salty eyes, a shipwrecked prisoner off some damaged spit of land. Every bottle had your name in it, he whispers, a child balanced on each of her hips, her dull husband dozing in the parlor. What then?

201

And if she waited. Years flying by, her hair ~~blowing white behind her like bitter snow~~. I am waiting to get started on my life. Everything I do now is only to fill my hands: the linens I smooth, the furniture I polish, the flowers I cut for some drawing room that is never filled with your presence. My life is a statue erected in your memory. And if she met him then? With his children swarming across his knees, his ancient wife quietly rocking by his side.

Cahill? It's Flame! Your Flame.

The eyes turn and the mouth chews on it for a while and then the words, puzzled and friendlier than the grave.

Flame? I—I don't recall any Flame. Maude, do we know any Flame? And the light would go out of Flame's eyes.

Right before she reached her arthritic hands around his neck and squeezed until he died. She thought of it and shifted in the hard pew.

Insects droned in the thick July air, and Flame could hear the faint, serious voices of girls jumping rope.

> *one potato*
> her father was dead
> *two potato*
> her mother was dead
> *three potato, four!*
> *Face it. Cahill is gone.* Flame bowed her head.
> *five potato, six potato*
> He's gone gone gone
> *seven is out the door!*

She looked up wildly. Shadows glided near the altar. Someday I'll face it, she thought, decide it one way or another. But not yet. There had been too many deaths already. She didn't have the stomach for killing dreams.

"Psst. Oui. Come here." The woman stood in the doorway of the church and gestured frantically at Flame with her glove. It was the same striking young whore Flame had seen earlier on the boat. She was still wearing an amber dress cut away from her shoulders, and now a fringed shawl was looped over the top

of it, covering her cleavage and throat. She had threaded amber ostrich feathers into her soft brown hair.

"Hurry. It is—how they say it—important very, yes?"

Flame gathered her things and went to the door. "What is it?"

The woman was out of breath. Up close, the musk of her perfume competed with the faintly sour smell of her body. Moisture beaded her lip and she fanned her glove in front of her face. "Silver sent me to find you."

"Is anything wrong?"

"*Faites ce qu' on vous dit.*"

"I don't speak French."

Nelly shrugged. "A small thing. You come now. *Oui?*"

Flame looked down the street. Two dogs dozed in the sun. A man and woman were walking briskly down the street together, the way people walk when they are furious with each other.

Nelly took Flame's arm firmly. "We go. Silver do the nice things for you. Over and over. And now you not come to her?" She stamped her foot. "Such a girl I have not seen!"

Flame made up her mind. "Of course I'll come."

A small smile lit the whore's face. "That is the sound Nelly likes."

It was a narrow hallway deep in the belly of the boat. Here, there was no pretense of style or grace. A single oil lamp swayed high above a bale of hay at the far end of it, but otherwise, the corridor was completely dark. The whore guided her easily through a maze of boxes and baling wire until they came to a small room hidden from view by steamer trunks and crates. Nelly opened the door and motioned Flame through, and then she closed the door behind them.

It was a small, dirty room with boxes stacked to the ceiling. The smell of rancid grease clung to the air. It was evidently a supply room close to the galley, Flame thought. The light was so poor it was difficult to see clearly. In one corner boxes had been moved and a mattress squeezed into the space. Flame could barely make out the shape of a person on the bed.

"Silver?"

Behind her, Nelly laughed and pushed her closer. "Your

eyes—they need the glasses."

On the bed was a naked man.

He was balding and his belly rose like a soft slug on a Seattle sidewalk. "Hi, honey."

Flame backed away. The man reached out and caught her wrist, and in the pale light, his eyes were mean.

"Don't be shy. Nelly tells me it's your first time. Couldn't have a better man show you the ropes than good old John. Right, Nelly?"

"*Oui.* It is so, *oui.*" Her voice was soothing, like a nurse's the night before an operation when the patient isn't expected to live.

"Relax." He squeezed hard.

"You're hurting me!"

"John doesn't want to have to get rough, honey."

Her heart was pounding and her hands sweated.

"Just cooperate. It'll be so much nicer if you cooperate."

"There's been a mistake!"

He stroked her arm with his free hand. "I don't think there's a mistake. Nelly, is there some mistake?"

Nelly bolted the door.

The man licked his lower lip. "No. Nelly says there's no mistake."

Flame's mouth went dry. "Please. I'm appealing to your sense of honor."

The man laughed humorlessly. "She's a real card, that one, Nell. A real card." He grabbed Flame's wrists suddenly with both hands, and there was power and cruelty in the hands. "John doesn't like gabby women, honey. A little will go a long ways." He bent her down to him and clamped her wrists together under one of his hands. Flame caught a strong smell of urine and sweat coming from the mattress.

He grasped the back of her head. "Come on, baby. How's about a little kiss?" He opened his mouth like a huge, sucking fish and closed it over Flame's. A wave of nausea engulfed her and she turned her face away. His lips slid wetly over her cheek.

He pulled her face around until he was staring coldly into her eyes. "Let's get a few things straight. I paid Nelly to bring me a virgin. Extra for a white one. Now we can do this one of two ways. You can cooperate, or I'll just have to leave marks. But that's not a pretty way to go, honey. It'll bring the price down for the next customer."

The next customer.

Flame felt chilled, the way you get if you've been out too long in the rain and you've lost your key to the front door.

"What are you talking about?" she whispered.

"You mean Nelly didn't tell you?" He looked at Nelly and back at Flame. "She's lined them up. One every fifteen minutes." He looked at Flame and saw the way her eyes changed. He smiled in relish.

"Every fifteen minutes," he repeated slowly. "Except me. I get half an hour. Isn't that right, Nelly?"

Nelly sauntered over to the mattress and lounged against the wall, her arms folded under her breasts. She didn't speak. She didn't have to. Flame stared at her and saw the viciousness in her smile and knew with sickening certainty he had told the truth.

"I'll scream."

Nelly shrugged. "Good. John likes the screams."

She had to distract him. He reached up and unhooked the top of her green velvet bodice.

"Where you from? I'm from Seattle myself. Rains all the time there. Cats and dogs."

He was down to the second button.

"Cats-and-dogs rain. That's what Cahill called it. Cahill Blue. Can you picture such a name for a grown man? Of course, some people think Flame is a peculiar name for a woman. My daddy thought it sounded like the name of somebody he had met in New Orleans once, years before he met mama, but mother, she thought it was a strong name—you know, like fire. Just a little fire can burn holes in things, and nobody can ever wrap their hands around it for long. Nobody owns fire; that's what my mama used to say."

She was open to the waist. The corset was cinched tight below her breasts, making them appear fuller than they actually were. *Damn.* It had been a gift from Silver. She wished she were wearing her oldest chemise. He stared hungrily at her and sucked in his breath.

"Of course, there was the hair, too," Flame began again, desperately. "Flame. It *does* kind of look like—"

"*Cahill Blue?*" Nelly's voice was strangled. She was standing transfixed, her hand on her throat.

"That's right. Cahill Blue." Flame barely moved backwards testing the pressure of his hands against her wrists. "We grew up together in Seattle."

"And your name is Flame," Nelly interrupted. She still wore the same intense look, as if she were listening to something only she could hear. "It is Flame," Nelly said again. "There is no question?"

What a peculiar thing to say, Flame thought. "I know what my own name is," she said. "I've had it a long time."

"Hey! What about me?" the john was squeezing her breast as if it were a bicycle pump. "A man can't hang on forever."

Flame's mouth was dry. "I can't do a thing for it if you don't let my hands go."

"What do you have in mind?"

She wet her lips, and her tongue felt thick and cottony. "Let my hands go and I'll show you."

He leered up at her. "Say now. You *are* full of surprises."

"Even more," she said with forced brightness. "Even more surprises. Let me go and I'll show you."

He released one hand and clamped down hard on the other one. "Insurance. Now about what you had in mind."

She touched his belly and the flesh quivered under her fingers.

"That's better." His pale eyes blinked. "But lower. I want it lower."

"Lower?" Nelly was walking briskly to the front of the mattress. To watch, Flame thought miserably. Best seat in the house. She was fumbling with something around her neck.

He licked his lip. "You know. Lower."

Nelly was staring at Flame as she approached the bed, her eyes hard as glass. "I have something for you, Flame. Yes, something for Flame. From Cahill. Yes, Flame. From Cahill Blue." She held out her hand.

Now. Flame clamped her hand around the man's testicles

and squeezed hard. He screamed and clutched at himself with both hands, relaxing his grip on her for an instant. It was just long enough for Flame to wrench herself away and stagger to her feet.

Nelly was behind her. Without stopping to think or weigh the consequences, Flame curled her fist and punched the whore as hard as she could in the jaw. There was a sickening crunch of bone. Nelly crumpled to the ground.

"My face!" she shrieked wildly. "You have ruined my face!" God in Heaven. "My *dent!"*

Flame hurled herself at the door, tore it open and fled down the hallway. She hid behind crates marked NC Company and fixed herself. Her legs were trembly and her hands shook. She listened, and when she was certain nobody was there, she darted out of the corridor and sprinted up the stairs. She didn't stop running until she reached the main deck.

Nelly looked in the mirror and wept. Her chin puffed in an almost vertical line and her nose was already swelling badly. But the worst thing was her front tooth. She looked at it again and touched it hysterically. It moved easily under slight pressure.

Oh, if she lost it!

Her career would be finished.

She cried in gulping sobs and touched it again. It hung crookedly in the pink mud of her gum.

Then it slid out and fell into her hand.

She studied it quietly, as she would a stranger in line ahead of her at the bank, as if she had never seen it before. The sudden dawning. Her eyes bulged and she threw back her head and screamed hysterically.

Her tooth! Her beautiful little tooth! And all because some *avortement* named Flame had chosen to ruin her!

She wiped the tears from her eyes and tried to get herself under control. She still had her legs. And teeth can be fixed.

Fury welled up inside of her. All of it was Flame's fault. All of it. Her lip quivered and tears spilled down her face.

It wasn't enough that she had lost her beautiful little tooth. Her front tooth. No, that wasn't the worst. She sobbed and

207

paced the floor in her room and clutched the tooth in her hand, wondering what to do.

No, losing the tooth wasn't the worst.

Now she was going to have to face Silver.

"I don't care if there were *fifty* men dressed in spiked boots and Waterloos lined up to pay. What you did was *wrong. Do you hear me? WRONG!*"

Silver was pacing up and down the small berth, her jowls quivering. She stopped in front of the cowed woman. "We can't work together. That's clear. Anyone who would show such little regard for the health and safety of another human being—it boggles the mind."

Silver walked, stopped and glared some more. "I had such *hopes* for you. *Such high hopes.* And you had to go and ruin *everything.* And all because of your *selfishness.* Your own *stupid selfishness.* I want you *out* of here. Out of my sight. I never want to see you again. *Is that clear?*"

"Quite."

Flame gathered up her clothes and fled.

Twenty

Nuka crouched down in the sand along the waterfront at Eagle and watched the steamer pulling into dock. He busied himself with his dogs so he would not have to bear the looks of revulsion and horror on the faces of those who were seeing him for the first time.

In every town it was the same. Smoke from the stacks of a steamer would alert the townsfolk, and before the stern-wheeler was actually in view, the dock would be crowded with people waiting.

For what, Nuka was never certain.

He would join them quietly, his body melting in with theirs. But his face screamed to them in a language of its own: the sunken left side, the deformed lip, the purple welt of a scar cruelly dividing his face under the drooping left eye.

Once a woman had fainted, and the man with whom she was seated cursed Nuka in a foreign tongue, pushing him away when he tried to help.

In another town he had been beaten up.

But he didn't want to remember that now. He needed his senses focused on the present. He watched his dogs and waited for the boat. The pups sniffed the air, their tails stiff and expectant.

The gangplank was being lowered and Nuka stood up suddenly and raised his hands to his eyes to block out the July sun. He moved closer until he had worked his way to the edge of the crowd and had an unobstructed view of the gangplank.

His elbow pressed against the knife hidden in his shirt.

None of the whites coming slowly down the gangplank interested him. He was waiting for the Indians. It had been like this every town and village he had entered along the Yukon. He

209

was obsessed with one thought: he would find Kannik. It didn't matter that the towns had surrendered nothing to him in all the months he had been looking, that no one had heard of the red paint-stone place or the hunters of Sippak. Someday there would be an Indian with a pale half-moon scarring his cheek and the same pattern in the beadwork he wore at his wrist. He would lead Nuka to his sister.

And then Nuka would kill him.

Nuka pressed the knife firmly.

How like animals they were.

He stared hard into each of their faces as they passed dumbly before him. Nothing. They looked solid and real, but inside, they were hollow.

He would split them open like spitted geese. He would twist the knife until the screams were louder than his sister's had been that terrible day.

Nothing. Nothing. Nothing on the faces. He patted his knife, whistled for his dogs, and drifted toward town.

There had been a time, after he had left the old man and before the desire for revenge overpowered him, when he had been filled with a sense of spiritual grace. It was as if the spirit of the shaman had misted over him and he could see and hear things no men could share—whispers in the trees, faces in the river. He had been a stone in the wind then, hurled up on random beaches, open to the wonder of the world.

But that had been when he still believed.

He hitched his pants and looked over the main street. He counted four places where the trappers brought furs and tins of food grew to the ceiling, six places where the music leaped out at him like mad dogs, and one building with a red fire painted on the front. In front of the building was a woman with breasts that hung low over the mountain of her belly. She was scrubbing the window. Her hair was brighter than the sun. She looked up and smiled at him. Nuka looked away. He had little use for English, and less for the whites that spoke it. When he needed something, he trapped and traded. Other than that, he preferred to keep to himself, nursing his hatred. The woman squatted down and picked up the vessel of water, squeezing her cloth into it. It made a wet slurping sound as she slapped it against the side of the building.

He had thought it would happen so quickly. The shaman had tapped him; he was next in line. Why else the markings? The shaman himself and then the old man had recognized Nuka from the scars as the one to whom the precious vessel of knowledge was to be passed.

But ever since then, there had been nothing. No clear guidance, no voice from the heavens directing his path. There had been only a thought, a niggling, irritating little thought, squirming like a worm in the back of his mind: if the shaman is so powerful, why would he permit such terror to come to Kannik?

He could accept his parents' deaths. And the lives of his sisters and brothers were no more to him than colors rippling the arctic sky—present and then forgotten. But Kannik—to be bound and delivered into the hands of the enemy—to be forced to bend to their will—death, at least, was honorable. Slavery endangered the soul. He implored the sky, the stones, to speak.

There was never an answer.

The woman with the hair on fire took her water vessel and went inside. The street was empty. The villagers were still down at the dock, Nuka guessed. He picked up a flat pebble and skipped it across the street. It skittered against the window that the woman had been washing and fell to the ground.

Once he had thrown the red paint-stone away, hurled it onto a beach. Afterward he had been seized by a fierce chill. His fingers had become blocks of ice, his lips blue.

He spent an hour on his hands and knees, searching, before he found it.

He had taken it out a thousand times, until now its rough surface was smooth and the color dull red. He had never seen a red paint-stone like it; even now it warmed his hand.

Nuka stood in the dusty street in Eagle that day in July, his heels sinking into the soft soil and his dogs nosing the rockers hulking behind him on the sand, and he touched the stone again.

Maybe for one moment he would believe.

211

He would believe that there had been a shaman who had passed him the knowledge; that he had a mission that was important, that would change the face of his country.

But he needed a sign. Now.

"Hey, kid. Yeah, you. Come here." The pale woman who had never gone hungry came out of the building and motioned to him, her fingers bright like blood.

"Lookin' for a good time, mister?" Her hair was gold, but close to the scalp her hair was curiously black, like Nuka's. So they were brothers, really, close to the skin. He walked over and said clearly, "Nuka."

"What? Yeah, sure, sure, come on in. Nooky. You pronounce it *Noo-key*. Like that Nookey. Got it?"

He tried again. "Nuka," he said, stretching out the word.

"Whatever you say, kid. Come on, let's get it over with." She pushed him inside, and he stumbled once and righted himself. Her sleeping ledge was soft and slabbed out from the wall. It was covered with small squares of colors. He had seen a lamp like hers before; the whalers had carried lamps that were never tended. But hers was dark red and matched her wounded fingers. He touched it lovingly.

"What are you, stupid? You're supposed to touch me. Like this." She captured his hand and clamped it over her thin breast, squeezing it. "Like this, see? You don't see. Okay, kid. I'll show you. Off with your clothes."

She pulled at his clothes, wrinkling her nose, and rearing back from the ugliness of his face. "Puu-wee. Not honeysuckle rose, kid." She shook her head and unbuttoned his shirt. "But still, when a woman of my, expertise, say, reaches a certain age, she has learned to take them all. Even the ones with the bashed-in faces. Funny how gold nuggets all smell the same."

She winked and pulled off his shirt. "You got it, kid?" She hung the shirt up on a brass hook and started ."Goddamn. Something sure as hell lit into you; will you look at that?"

She was staring, horrified, at his left shoulder. Nuka didn't look at it. It reminded him too painfully of Kannik. The woman shrugged.

"My sainted mother—God rest her—used to say: 'Blessed

212

are those who take the ugly ones; they're so damn grateful. The money's not bad, either.' Get it, kid? You *do* have money, don't you?"

Nuka nodded vigorously. "Nuka," he brayed.

"Shit." She settled on the bed, lifted her skirt and spread her stout legs. "Well, hop to it. I ain't getting any younger."

He smiled hugely. He had found a friend. He would not dishonor her. He removed his pants and boots and surveyed the massive mountain of flesh he had to climb. He rubbed his penis until it rose stoutly and then he sank to his knees between her thighs. She billowed around him like dough warming on the fire rock. He pushed his way between the enormous gates of her sex. He slipped in easily, lost in the vastness of her vagina. He stopped, puzzled. It was like visiting the Karigi alone. Too vast a space for one.

"Like this kid. Ya push it in and out. In and out. See? Like that. In and out. Brother."

His new friend was afraid of disappointing him. He could tell from the way she clutched his buttocks and spoke with her mouth drooping down. He would try harder. He worked his penis skillfully around, so that it angled up, hitting the side of her female tunnel. She grunted. He kept it up steadily, waiting for the loud cry that would mean she had found the happiness she deserved. For many long moments there was no sound but fevered breathing. He worked harder, until her flesh vibrated from the exertions of his body.

"For gawdsake, kid. Don't take all night!"

Nuka moved tenderly into the lump of flesh under him. The special moment when the woman calls out always produced such feelings in him. He thrust harder. Now it was his turn. He came quickly, spurting like a whale deep in the sea.

His friend immediately pushed him off and wiped herself with a small cloth soaking in a vessel of yellow liquid. How strange to place urine back into the place from which it came, he thought. His new friend contained many puzzles.

"Nuka," he murmured to her.

"That's right, kid. That'll be five bucks in gold. Five bucks." She threw out her hand and he took it lovingly, exploring the small ponds of red on her nails. She wrenched her hand away.

213

"I know I shoulda gotten it up front, kid. But you looked so ~~damn pitiful. But if you think you can deadbeat Goldie,~~ you got your trolley untracked. Batt!" she trumpeted, his hands around her mouth. "Get the hell in here."

She tapped her foot and shook her head. "And don't try to—BATT!—run away without paying, either. I got a lot of clout for a working girl. A lotta clout. You'll see."

She narrowed her eyes and smiled at him. Nuka wondered if she wanted to visit the place of happiness again. She had much energy left after their visit. His organ was sleeping soundly. She smiled again and he sighed. He could only do his best when he climbed the mountain and see. That was all. He touched her and she shrank away.

"Oh, no. That much of a sucker I ain't. Batt! Get your goddamn gambler's ass in here and—"

A spangled curtain crashed aside and a dark man chewing a cigar slammed his hands against the door braces. He scowled at the woman. "Better be important. I'm playing seven-card stud with two aces showing."

"Nuka," Nuka said.

"Listen to him, Batt. That's all he ever says. Me, with my big heart, I went ahead and gave it to him. The house special. He took to it right off, if I do say so myself. And now he won't pay for his play."

Batt squinted at the native and spat. He was a kid, maybe nineteen, with a rangy, hungry look and a thick scar welting his face. A fighter, Batt thought, but the eyes were friendly and calm.

"That the truth, son?"

The native stood there watching him, his head cocked to one side. Batt chewed on his cigar and scowled. There were a million dialects. Batt thumped his chest. "Dinaa." The native didn't flicker. So he wasn't a Koyukon.

"Iihlangaa." Nothing. "Quht'ana." Not a Haida or a Tanaina. Batt chewed on his cigar. It would take all night. In a burst of inspiration, Batt patted his face and said, "Batt. B-a-t-t."

The native was silent, puzzled.

"Batt." Batt thumped his heart. "Batt." The kid's brow was

furrowing in total concentration.

"This is really the living end," Goldie whined. "Can't you see he's just stalling? He—"

"Shut up!" Batt roared. The kid blinked and flinched. Batt smiled at him and the native squirmed.

"Let's try again," Batt said genially. "B-a-t-t." He thumped his chest and patted his face.

The boy swallowed. "B-a-t-t."

"Yeah, Batt. Good, son. Batt." Batt smiled broadly and pointed to himself. "Batt. Now you try it again."

"B-a-t-t." His voice was hesitant and soft, as if he had spoken for months only to the wind.

"Right. Batt. That's right, son. Batt." He pointed at the native. "Now you." He thumped his chest. "Batt." He thumped the native's chest and stretched his hands wide.

"B-a-t-t."

Batt dropped his hands. "No. I'm Batt." He thumped his chest. "I'm Batt." He tapped the native. "Who are you?"

The youth scrunched his face together, concentrating so totally his face turned dark red. Suddenly his mouth dropped open and his eyes blinked.

"Nuka?" he said hesitantly.

Batt bit down on his cigar and shook his head. "I'll be a sonofabitch." He tapped the native on the chest. "Nuka."

Nuka nodded and pointed at Batt. "Batt." Batt nodded. Nuka's face broke into a lopsided grin. "Batt." He said it more strongly. "Batt." Then he pointed at the whore, a question clearly forming on his face.

Batt chomped down on his cigar, grinned, pulled it out and spat. "So you want to know her name."

Nuka waited, his hands out.

"Sucker," Batt coached.

Nuka bobbed at the woman, his face tense with concentrating. "Sook—"

"Sucker," Batt said.

Goldie narrowed her eye and trotted over. "Hey, what's goin' on here? Are you gonna make him pay or not?"

"Sook-er," Nuka said tenderly to her. He patted her arm. She jerked it away and snarled, "It's not very funny, Batt.

215

I've a mind to bean the boy and—"

But Batt was laughing. He was laughing in small hiccupy jerks and then the laugh erupted into trills of the stuff, and he lost control and cackled and whooped and guffawed until he was out of breath and tears ran down his face.

"Goldie—" Batt wiped his eyes, shook his head and lost control. Loud brays of laughter subsided finally into hiccups.

"Goldie," he tried again, "you just gave away your first piece in thirty years." He slapped Nuka on the back. "Come on, kid, let's go."

Twenty-One

Ever since she was a young girl, there had been a marked streak of viciousness in Nelly that her horrified parents had barely managed to suppress. Her father was a low-level clerk in the law courts at Liège and her mother a silly woman given to wearing the latest styles very badly. Her father, along with five other clerks, shared an office which faced out on a courtyard at the old palace of Prince-Bishops. The courtyard had an ornamental pool and Nelly's mother would sit on a marble bench and gaze motionless into the water as she waited for her husband to close up the office and come home. Nelly could never figure out why her mother found it necessary to wait for him in the same spot day after day; but wait she did, like a good and faithful dog.

She was the only person Nelly had ever known who could elevate immobility to an art form. Once a pigeon sat on her head, mistaking her for a statue of Saint Lambert.

Her mother's one remarkable talent was a dull sort of intellect that enabled her to sleep through most of life's important moments. Early on, Nelly's pity for her mother's gift had hardened into a sly awareness of its potential: not for her mother—her mother was doomed to live stupidly—but for herself. If her mother was so oblivious to what was happening in her *own* life, then perhaps with time and careful manipulation, her mother could be taught to overlook certain inconsistencies in her *daughter's* life.

At least it was worth a try.

Nelly knew she was beautiful, even before her godfather had paid her a franc at ten to show him. He took her behind one of the eight pillars in Gretry Square and propped her up against

217

the statue of the musician. Gretry's right hand, ~~his composing hand,~~ was inside his long coat as if he were patting his heart. The godfather's hand was inside Nelly's coat in approximately the same place.

That day Nelly had hit upon her true calling. It occurred to her ten-year-old mind that if Uncle Hugo had paid her a franc to find out if she was developing ahead of schedule, he would probably be willing to pay her *ten* francs to keep that information to herself.

It was the beginning of an empire.

She stayed away from groping pimply youths and concentrated herself on successful middle-aged men with good reputations and families—men with lust in their hearts and money in their pockets.

And fear written all over their faces.

Nelly liked the fear. It made her feel more important even than the way they groaned when she undressed. Besides, groans fill the air but for an instant; while fear, if she played her cards right, could last forever.

By the time she was seventeen, she was playing her cards right with five of the most influential men in Belgium, including the Prime Minister to Leopold II, and a cardinal at the Cathedral of Saint Bavo in Ghent. The cardinal and she had been working their way through all twenty-five of the chapels at the cathedral, trying a different position in each, when he began writing her ardent letters. The letters had been thin papyrus affairs with reedy handwriting, but out of them Nelly had squeezed gowns and jewelry and expensive baubles. The last letter had been the thinnest of all—a single sentence in which the cardinal pitiably implored Nelly to see him or he would surely die from desire, but out of its page had sprung passage on a first-class ship bound for the New World.

Her parents had thought she won a scholarship to a Catholic boarding school.

She had followed the rails west and then north, conscious that between her limbs lay the secret to eternal youth, the lost graves of ancient kings and a thousand other magic and mysterious things men would sell their souls to possess, if only

218

in a small hotel room between the hours of four and five.

Besides, she had great teeth.

She would *never* forgive Flame for what she had done.

And now, as she stood before the small mirror in her room on board the *Hamilton*, she comforted herself with all the terrible things she would do. She saw Flame bound at her feet, pleading for mercy. Somewhere there was a man brandishing a whip. Or an axe. That was an even more satisfying image. The axe would come down and down and Flame would pay.

But first Nelly would pull *all* of Flame's teeth out of her head, one by one. Very slowly.

She stared at herself in the small gilt mirror she shared with Angel Lee and the Cornish Cow. It would do. She was wearing a ribbed velvet corduroy skirt of deep blue edged in heavy gold braid and a matching pleated Norfolk jacket, and the bruises were almost undetectable under powder. She looked neat and presentable, but contained. She had too many things to do in Circle to risk being trailed through the town by men with rigid parts, like little doggies in heat. She smiled at her face and kept her mouth closed.

"Best I can do is take a plaster cast of it tonight and send it up river to Dawson in the morning."

"How long before the *dent* returns?"

"Depends on the supply. Pritchet just opened his shop, first of the summer. Has to send all the way to Albany for the porcelain paste. If he's got it in stock—" The dentist shrugged and put down his instrument. "Depends on how backlogged he is, too. Could get it in a month, maybe sooner, maybe later."

A *month!* Nelly dug her small fingernails into the leather upholstery of his examining chair and moaned. Already her business was dropping off. One man had stuck his tongue into her mouth, felt the gaping wound of her gum and had actually lost his desire. Bad. Very bad for business.

"But I bring the tooth to you! The very same tooth! All you must do is put it back the way it was! A simple thing for a dentist, yes?"

Dr. Admans studied her anguish-filled face and sighed. He

219

was not without great canyons of unexplored responses. He might wear a white smock during the day, and fill nothing more exciting than a vial of cloves, but at night, in his single room, he was a stallion, a stallion galloping through dark purple canyons of unexplored responses.

"I tell you what," he said gently, and was pained by the sudden hope leaping into her eyes. "I'll make a plaster cast of the tooth and send it up river to Pritchet's, like I said. But until it comes back, no harm in my fiddling around."

Nelly seized his palm and kissed it fervently. "*Merci*. Oh, thank you!" Her eyes glistened with tears. "America is—how you say it?—the land of opportunity. Let Nelly take the opportunity between her hands and show you what she thinks."

She took a deep, ragged breath and sank her mouth over his scrubbed, antiseptic middle finger. Dr. Admans forgot about Harriet Stoker in the Circle Episcopal Mission choir, who at that very minute was waiting for him to escort her to Saturday afternoon practice. Forgot about Mrs. Angela Richardson, whom he had asked to visit his office to discuss the results of John Jr.'s test, and who, right this minute, was in the outer room, flipping avidly through *Harper's Weekly*.

Dr. Admans sank against the door.

Somewhere, a stallion whinnied.

Harry Bumpee wiped the ink off his hands and read it through again. She was pale and pretty and wounded looking, and no matter what she said, Harry was certain those bruises on her face hadn't come from walking into a door frame. Her front tooth looked a little funny, too. It was ringed in gold and leaned to the side, like a reporter on a toot.

"I'll pay you whatever you want," she said. "But it has to go in the paper tomorrow."

She rested her satchel on top of the Hoe press, and it vibrated gently as she lifted out a stack of bills. Harry's eyes widened.

"Whatever you want," she said gently, and counted out enough money for a separate press run.

"How high?" He found his voice.

"Pardon?"

"It's slang," Harry explained. He picked up the money. "I mean when do you want the paper delivered?"

"Early," Nelly smacked her lips. "Put one at each door on board the *Hamilton*."

Twenty-Two

Captain Jacoby shook his head and put down his pencil. "Silver can't take your room away from you," he said crisply. "It's paid up. Besides, you'll be in Rampart in a few days."

Flame stood, vastly relieved. "Thank you, captain. Will we be in Circle overnight?"

Jacoby nodded. "Oh, Flame—"

She paused, hand on the knob.

"Tonight in Circle—" He moistened his lips and smiled brownly at her. He paused. He was the kind of man who hovered near the elbows of beautiful women, a savagely wide smile clouding his total inability to think of anything to say. He chewed on his lip, shrugged and began again. "Tonight in Circle—"

He was interrupted by the door bursting open. It was Batt.

He brightened when he saw her. "Afternoon, Flame." Batt turned to the captain. "Found a woodchopper in Eagle, if you're short a savage."

Jacoby waved impatiently. "Let's have a look at him." He was miffed at Batt. One minute more and he would have invited Flame to do the town. Naturally she would have said yes.

Batt lobbed his arm behind him and pushed the savage forward. He was young. A scar ran the length of his face and an arm curled inward.

Jacoby went over and poked it. "He's got a bad arm."

"Just a little weak is all," Batt said easily.

"He's not Indian, is he?"

"Eskimo."

Jacoby made a face. "That'll be a problem, right there. You know how the Injuns are about the Skimos."

222

Batt shrugged. "Suit yourself." He knuckled the Eskimo's back. "Come on, kid."

But Nuka wasn't listening. He was staring transfixed at Flame.

"Yeah, she is beautiful," Batt agreed. He tugged gently on Nuka's arm. "Come on."

Nuka paled and dropped to his knees before her.

Staring back at him was a white version of his sister Kannik. To him it seemed that these were the same high cheeks and blunt eyebrows and full mouth, as if Kannik had been born with a pale twin who had been separated from her until this moment.

"Kannik!"

She stared at him soberly and did not recoil from the impact of his face. He felt tears stinging his cheeks and realized he was crying. The pale sister looked at him searchingly and touched his cheek with her hand, a movement that brought fresh tears to his eyes. Everything about her reminded him of his sister— the way she pressed her lips inward when she was thinking, the fragile construction of the bones in her face, the curious dignity of her bearing.

She extended her hand and he took it and rose to his feet. He held on to her hand, not willing to let go, until the palm moistened and he sensed her confusion.

Little white sister, do not fear, he thought lovingly. I have been sent to watch over you. She averted her eyes and hurried past him out the door.

And you have been sent to lead me to Kannik.

"Any idea what that was about?" Jacoby was leaning against the door, looking down the corridor. Flame had slowed her steps and Nuka was hesitantly matching his stride with hers.

Batt shook his head. "None at all, but I can tell you one thing."

"What's that?"

"If you've got any ideas about asking Flame out, forget it."

He saluted the captain and ambled down the corridor in Flame's direction.

"You've already asked her?" The captain was outraged.

Batt smiled. He was coming up on Flame. He took her arm.

223

"Flame, I'll be in Circle tonight. I'd be honored if—"

~~The captain's fist hit the wall and he missed the rest.~~

Circle wore an air of genteel poverty around its sloped and peeling shoulders. It was a quiet town built for high life and excitement, but it hadn't seen much of either since the Dawson strike had taken all the people, kind of like a man who had been fired from a job that was exactly right for him, but couldn't believe it and kept telling the story over and over. The signs inside the bars still spoke of the big strike that had happened six years before; drinks were named the Mother Lode or the Golden Way.

Flame ordered a lemonade in one, took off her gloves and laid her satchel on the counter. Under her skirt she hooked her boots around the stool. She studied Batt. He was wearing a clean shirt and a bowler hat, and had a nick on his cheek where he'd cut himself shaving. His teeth under the mustache were white when he smiled, which is what he was doing now. "Why are you staring at me?"

She laughed. "I was just thinking; if you were a horse, you'd fetch top dollar."

He drained his glass. "Is that a compliment?"

"No, that's impertinence." She grinned. "I meant you have great teeth."

"Dimples, too. And a wonderful personality. All the girls love me."

"I'm sure they do," Flame said primly. She sipped her lemonade and stared at a man swabbing the counter. He was wearing a string tie that looped over the long apron tied over his chest. Behind him was a row of bottles that had been new when the place opened. On the mirror was a sign reading No Natives Served.

"Why is that?" she wondered out loud.

"Why is what?"

"Why is there such a fuss about the natives up here?"

"They're subhuman."

"You don't believe that!"

"Most people do."

"But you don't."

"No, I don't." He stared into the mirror at the back door. "Did you know you've had one of them following you around all night?"

Flame was shocked. "No." She looked uneasily at the door. "Where is he?"

Batt thumbed toward the window. "Out back."

"You mean that kid with the scar?"

"Nuka's his name."

"What does he want?"

"I don't think he wants to get close to you, Flame," Batt said slowly. "I think he just wants to *see* you. But I could make him go away if he's bothering you."

"Make him? How?" She stared at him and shook her head vigorously. "No. Leave him alone."

"I must say, he has remarkably fine taste." Batt raised his eyebrows over the bottle of bourbon and poured more into his glass.

Flame felt herself growing warm.

Four soldiers banged through the door and went to the far end of the bar. The military had established posts along the Yukon to keep order. Above the bar hung a sign:

Bar closed between hours of 0006 and 2100 hours every
Sunday   Order of Captain Richardson

"So. You travel up and down the Yukon taking people's money." It sounded harsher than she had intended.

He burst out laughing. "Yes. I never phrased it exactly that way before, but that's what I do. Yes. I go from town to town moving my nimble fingers across other people's wallets."

"Don't you have a conscience?"

He grinned and stared down into her eyes. His own were almost black and fringed with long lashes. Only a strongly masculine face could bring off such strikingly pretty eyes. "A conscience?" he murmured.

She felt her lips grow warm. She cried, "I'm engaged, you know!"

He looked startled, then laughed, and Flame felt uncomfortably sure he could read her thoughts.

225

"I don't recall having asked you the nature of your relationship with—Cahill? That was his name?"

She nodded and drank her lemonade, humiliated.

Batt reminded her of a darker, wilder Adam Tremain and she felt definitely out of her league. "You know the trouble with older men?" she snapped.

"What?" He was amused.

"They always think they know so much about younger women. And they don't." She flounced her skirt.

He grinned and changed the subject, but Flame had the annoying feeling he still thought he had the upper hand.

"Your claim's over by Rampart?"

She nodded. "On Fool's Creek. I have the deed here in my satchel." She pulled it out and he read:

NOTICE OF LOCATION

Notice is hereby given that the undersigned has located *forty* acres of placer mining ground situated in RAMPART MINING DISTRICT of Alaska on *Fool's Creek*, Tributary of Big Minook Creek to be known as *The Frozen Lady*.

He glanced at the exact location of the markers and handed it back to her.

"Do you know where it is?"

He shook his head and passed it back. "Shouldn't be too hard to find if it's off the Big Minook. Do you have supplies?"

"Not yet."

"Any prospects for work?"

"I'll find something when I get there."

"The Indians think if you save a person's life, it makes you responsible for them forever." He stared at her intently. "I'd like to help you get your stake together."

"I couldn't accept that. You've done enough for me already. I owe you my life." She thought of the hospital and how close she had come to falling into the pit forever. "You still haven't told me why you did it."

"It was a slow afternoon."

"No, really. You could have left me in the hospital. Why

226

didn't you?"

Batt nicked a strand of wood off the counter and clamped it between his teeth. "I had a debt to pay." His voice was curiously remote.

"A debt?" Flame pressed.

"You sure ask a lot of fool questions." He looked longingly at the pool table. A low green lamp hung over it and dust boiled off the table in clouds when the balls moved. Two men were playing.

"I've found it's the best way to get answers," Flame said.

There was a long silence. "I had a sister who was born defective." His voice was barely audible. "She was five years older than I. I grew up thinking I was an only child. When my dad died, I found it in his papers."

He took the toothpick and flicked it into the sawdust.

"They'd had her committed to one of those places. They kept them all in a room. No windows. Threw food at them once a day and the smell— They did everything in that room. For years and years. I went there—"

Flame reached out and touched him.

The words came slowly.

"—I went there to get her out. I was going to take her home. My father was rich and he left a rich son." He drank. "She'd already died. She'd died when she was fifteen. They just never bothered to let us know."

"I'm sorry." She had tears in her eyes.

"I am, too."

They were both aware of Flame's hand on his arm.

The pool players were arguing furiously. As they flung down their sticks, Batt got up. "This place is too rough for a lady. Come on." He took her arm and helped her off the stool. "You should always wear green." He fastened her cape awkwardly, his face softened with tenderness. Warmth flooded her. She felt again he was reading her mind.

"I don't take anything that's not freely offered," he said.

She flushed. The door tinkled open, and a gaggle of Silver's girls poured through. They had been drinking heavily, and they leaned muzzily against each other. Their makeup was smeared and none of them was wearing hats. Nelly smiled

227

widely when she saw them.

"Well, if it isn't Battimus Jackson the Third. When'd you start associating with low-life?" She poked Flame in the arm.

"Easy, Nelly. You're drunk."

"That's what she is." Nelly whooped into a chair and patted the table. "Come'n over here, Battimus, and give lil Nelly a big fat kiss. We're celebrating."

"Not now, Nelly." He walked Flame to the door.

Nelly scowled. "You never missed a kiss with good ole Nell before. What'sa matter?"

"I don't want to waste it, Nell. You'll never remember it."

Flame felt a flash of anger. All the tenderness she had felt toward him evaporated. It was clear he was enjoying Nelly. How could a man have felt so deeply about a lost sister in one instant and the very next be chucking a whore under the chin?

"That's all right," she said stiffly. "Why don't you stay with your friends. I can walk myself home."

"No!" Nelly cried and stumbled awkwardly to her feet. "You have to come and help me celebrate. Let bygones be bygones." She draped herself over Batt and confided, "Flame and me, we used to have a big fight. But not anymore."

"Not anymore?" He grinned down at her and his arm supported her fanny.

"I'm leaving now." Flame turned to go.

"No! Gotta help me celebrate." She fumbled through her velvet bag and dumped the contents in the sawdust, cursing. "Here." She grunted and stooped down, picked up a newspaper and smoothed it out. "Front page." She handed it to Flame. "Whataya think?"

It was an inch long. Flame read it twice.

Smith-Blue Nuptials

Jacques and Marie Smith of Belgium announce the engagement of their daughter, Nelly, to Cahill Blue. He is the son of a prominent Seattle couple, Dr. and Mrs. Blue. Nelly works in Rampart. No date has been set.

Flame's face turned ashen. "What is this? I don't believe it."

228

Nelly patted the paper. "And you thought you won."

Batt yanked the paper from Nelly's hands and read it quickly. "It's not funny, Nelly."

She was laughing helplessly. She collapsed in a chair and pointed at Flame. "You—you pathetic creature!" She wiped her eyes. "Such a look I have not seen! So much pain."

"Tell Flame right now you made it up."

"This I cannot do," she said sorrowfully, and hiccuped into her hand.

Batt said, "Flame. It isn't true. You know it isn't. Consider the source."

Nelly fumbled with a locket hidden in her dress. "Batt, you are so good with taking apart the clothes of Nelly. Help me with this."

Impatiently he unclasped it, and Nelly drew off the locket.

"No!" Flame cried.

"Cahill Blue put it around my neck himself the moment he left you. He doesn't love you. And when he marries, it will be to me."

"It's not possible!" Flame cried. "I don't believe you."

"Open it," she said solemnly. "If you dare."

Trembling, Flame unsnapped the hearts. The case sprang open.

Inside was a picture of Nelly and Cahill.

"So you see how it is," Nelly shrugged her shoulders. "Young love." She giggled helplessly and collapsed into a chair.

Flame dropped the necklace and ran blindly out the door. Batt followed her. She was weeping against the side of the building.

"Flame, I'm sorry. Believe me." He tried to hold her but she pushed him away.

"No! Please. I need to be alone." Her face was crumbling with grief, and a pin had come loose. A wave of hair fell down her back.

"Are you going to be all right?"

Dazed she turned and stumbled down the road. The sun was setting and the sky was blazing with pink and gold. In the river a moose was muzzling a pool of reflected pink sky. It came gasping up for breath, water running off its snout in rivulets.

"Flame!" he called. "Are you going to be all right?"

She kept staggering down the road. The light caught her hair and it blazed. Another pin came loose.

Nelly came unsteadily out the door and leaned against him. "Come on. Let's go play. I'll give it to you for free." She tugged on his arms.

"Knock it off," he said angrily and pushed her away. "Why'd you have to do that, Nelly?"

"Can't you take a little joke?" she said sulkily. "Jus' a li'l one."

"That wasn't a joke. It was cruel."

"She deserved it."

"I hope you're really happy with yourself." He strode off.

Nelly smiled widely and patted her hair. "As a matter of fact, I am."

When the pain came for Flame, it caught her by surprise and carried her twisting and screaming into the bowels of despair. Pain took her by the elbow and squeezed her hand gently and said, *"Come with me. We have so much to discuss."* It led her down golden streaked roads and made her stop at particularly lovely things, stop and pick them apart and reflect on their loveliness. She remembered only the finest things in Cahill: she saw only the things that were dear and unrepeatable.

"Oh, Cahill," she mourned, "how could you do it?"

She wept and remembered and Pain stood next to her and nodded approvingly and said, *"That's right, Flame. That's right. But perhaps you overlooked this."* And then she would remember something else.

It was a long, terrible night. She sat at the edge of the river. Fog was rolling down from the hills, and in the distance, she could see the steamer rocking quietly where it was moored in the mist.

Desolation swept over her. How could he love Nelly? And if it wasn't love, then how could he have given up what they had?

A solitary figure was paddling a small boat. When the boat drew even with her, a man jumped onto the bank and tied up

Dogs spilled after him. Flame rocked her knees up under her and bowed her head. She didn't want to talk to anyone.

A dog nosed her rudely and she looked up. It was Nuka.

She turned away, ashamed of her swollen eyes. He pulled her briskly to her feet and pushed her toward the boat. It was a small skin boat, the kind the Indians used. In the bottom of it was her trunk.

With a small cry she stepped into the boat, balanced herself and sat down, leaning against the trunk. How had he known she couldn't face any of them?

The dogs tilted into the boat and Nuka steadied it, pushed it away from the shore and got in. He picked up the paddle.

Flame looked back once at the *Hamilton*. It wasn't too late. She could still get on board. A crew was shoveling out ashes from the boiler room, their good-natured oaths traveling clearly over the water. They were familiar sounds, comforting sounds.

She knew that what she was doing was reckless. But if she couldn't love Cahill Blue, she would do the next best thing. She would hate him until the day she died. There was strength in that. For the first time that night, she closed her eyes and went to sleep.

The land around the river was flat and the river spread out in marshy channels, humped with islands of mud. There was an explosion of birds in the flats. Overhead the summer dawn sky vibrated with the call of trumpeter swans, their long white necks stretched gracefully ahead of enormous wings. Songbirds warbled in the brush and mingled with the cries of mallards and sandhill cranes. A pintail duck paddled near the bank, its body the same gray as the water and grass behind it; only its long white neck and brown head gave it away. Eagles cruised overhead: one of them sliced down to the river directly in front of the boat and lifted off with a salmon.

In the distance a thunderstorm flashed: the flats went on forever. The air was damp and cold. It was as if it never really believed in summer, sensing it was a charlatan anyway, and so didn't bother warming up. Winter was coming. Even though the sky pulsed with life and the woods crashed with the sounds

231

of animals, winter was coming. She shifted her position and drew a fur over her.

She would go to Rampart and find her claim. After that the future was blank.

They traveled all day and into the night. The air cooled rapidly after the sun went down. Nuka combed loose hairs out of the dogs' fur and tamped them down in the bowl of his pipe as a filter before adding tobacco. It was a good mixture: tobacco seasoned with cottonwood bark and fungi. He lit his pipe and drew deeply, inhaling the pungent aroma. Across the fire from him, Flame sat with her arms around her knees. He felt pity for her. She had cooked the salmon poorly, blackening it on the fire instead of using the steaming rock. And some of the grasses she had gathered were inedible, forcing Nuka to throw them all away to stop her from eating them. She stirred and looked west. A great horned owl was staring fiercely at her from its perch in a field of wet muskeg. She rose and went to the river. The wind kept the insects away. Slowly she splashed her face and washed her hands.

Behind her a hare thrashed through tall grasses in a hillside stand of birch. The woman crouched down, startled at the sound. The hare leaped into view, its long legs fully distended, and flashed back into the woods. Flame rose and wiped her hands on her dress. Sadness poured from her. She sighed and walked toward him, past the bed of spruce boughs he had made for her, until she was standing in front of him. She dropped beside him and murmured, "Let's have it done with, then."

The words made no sense to him, but her hands spoke a language he understood. She touched his face gently, her hand soft against the rough texture of his skin, and breathed one long wracking sigh that ended in almost a sob. He laid her gently back on the furs covering the spruce bed and looked at her.

Tears wet her cheeks. She looked once at the moon, as if hoping to find an answer to an unspoken question written across the face of it, and finding nothing, she closed her eyes and whispered a single word.

"Cahill."

It was said with finality, as if the longing and raging of a lifetime had been summoned into that single word. It reminded Nuka of winter's eves long ago, and rocking in his mother's kusunnak, nestled like a warm lump next to her neck, while around them the wind howled and the snow fell and nothing in the world could harm them.

She opened her eyes and cried, "Why are you delaying?" He knew what she wanted him to do.

"I am here!" she cried out. "Take me. Isn't that what you want? Well, isn't it?" She sobbed and tore at the buttons on her shirt, her face an ugly caricature of lust. He stilled her hands and she pulled free.

"Take me, savage! Take me." She kissed him full on the mouth and he pushed her away roughly and shook her hard. Her head snapped back and she looked at him in disbelief. And then she burst into tears and crawled into his arms. She clung to him and he tasted her tears.

She rooted against him blindly, as a suckling child or a damned soul would root; looking for sanctuary, and finding only the uneasy kind: a temporary hiding place, away from the wolves and wild beasts that circled in the darkness, calling her by name.

Twenty-Three

The Yukon Flats come together into one channel at Rampart. Fifteen hundred men and seven women lived there in 1898, not counting the Indians in their separate village, who were never counted. There were four roadhouses, six restaurants and twenty bars. No churches. Traveling ministers traveled half-price at the Mayo Hotel, along with cardsharpers. The log buildings were built along the bank, above the high-water notch of the Yukon where it flooded every spring. Army barracks stretched over a low ridge to the east; the Indian village faced the town across the river on the north bank.

Flame left Nuka at the river and went looking for work. She found it at Julius Ramsdorf's store. Or, more precisely, *behind* the store.

Julius Ramsdorf was fifty years old, with a bald head and a full white beard. He ran a friendly, cluttered secondhand store, was happily married to a sturdy, good-natured woman named Sarah and the father of six children, none bald. They all had his kindness, however.

He sized Flame up. "Tell you what. You can work for three weeks in the garden and I'll get you outfitted for a year. Can't go mining without the right things."

"Three weeks! Mr. Ramsdorf, I was prepared to offer you three months of service."

"Three weeks should bring us through the worst of the harvesting. Any time left over, you can help my missus put the vegetables up."

Tears filled her eyes. "I thank you."

He polished his head with his hand. Tears always made him uncomfortable. "Have a place to live?"

She shook her head.

234

He walked outside and took her around back.

The garden was the size of a basketball court. Peas climbed a high trellis almost nine feet tall. He looked down the rows of leaves, taking pleasure in the neat precision of the plants—the full bushy fronds of carrots, the reddish darker leaves of the radishes. On the other side of the trellis was a small cabin. He pointed at it. "You can live there, if you like. Eat dinner with my missus and me."

For the second time Flame's eyes filled with tears, and for the second time, Julius rubbed his head awkwardly, clearing his throat.

"Chickweed's heavy. I got some gloves you can use."

"Thank you."

He turned to go back inside when she remembered something. "Mr. Ramsdorf?"

He stopped. "Yes?"

"There's one thing you should know." She felt her cheeks flush. "I don't know quite how to say this."

He waited. Females had such an endearing way of never getting to the point.

"I live with a man."

Perhaps he had misunderstood. "Say again?"

"It's not how it sounds. We're—friends. He takes care of me. Watches over me."

Julius Ramsdorf thought about it. Sarah would probably have a fit. Think it was a bad influence on the girls. But if he didn't give her a job, where else could she go? Too damp to work in the bathhouse. The Dealy sisters were old biddies, anyway. They'd work her to a nub in a week. And the bars were rough. That left only Silver's.

"He's welcomed to come to dinner, too," Julius said firmly.

More tears. "I'll get right to work. Soon as I settle in."

He first heard about it an hour later, when Sarah brought him lunch. He was on the ladder, rearranging the top shelf. He'd put the hatchets under the counter, he decided. The way they were now, he always worried one of them would sail off and whack him in two.

"Hello, Mrs. Ramsdorf," he called down to Sarah. It was their little joke.

But Mrs. Ramsdorf was in no joking mood. "Julius, we've got a problem."

He dusted off his hands and came down the ladder slowly. He should have told her first thing about Flame.

She put the lunch pail on the counter and he opened it before answering. She had packed hot moose stew and half a loaf of good bread. "She and her friend will be gone in three weeks." He bit into the bread. It was still warm and covered with butter.

"Have you *seen* her friend?"

Julius shook his head. "Is he a hard worker?"

"Yes. He is that." There was something odd in her voice.

"Then what is it? Just last week you told me the carrots were coming up faster'n you and Ellie May could pull them."

"He's a savage."

Julius choked on the bread. "You're sure."

"Things like that—*course* I'm sure."

"It's not the way it looks. They're not lovers. She told me and I've no reason to doubt her word."

"Then it's even worse than I thought," his wife said. "You know how funny this town is. What it's like. I want you to do something."

He swallowed the bread and carefully put it down. "What would you have me do?"

"Ask her to leave."

"I wouldn't feel right about that." He picked up the spoon and dug into the stew. "She'll be gone soon."

"I want her gone *now*."

"Ellie May'll be eighteen, come September," he said mildly.

"You haven't heard a word I've said."

"I was just thinking. Ellie's been talking about leaving. Going south. Kind of make me feel better if I knew folks out there in the world were helping her when she needed it." He ate in silence.

"Ellie May's not a savage."

"Neither is Flame."

It was a standoff.

"What'll we tell the little ones?" Sarah asked finally.

"Don't think we have to tell them a thing. They've seen

236

mixed couples before."

"And they've seen what happens. Have you clean forgotten about Dan Carolan's wife?"

Julius swallowed. "That was different."

Sarah set her mouth in a thin line. "A gang of white men raped her, Julius Ramsdorf. And when her husband hunted one of them down and shot him, Dan Carolan was arrested—"

"I don't want to hear it."

"—arrested and charged with murder. The law says Dan's wife was a squaw and fair game for anybody that had a hankering for yellow meat."

"That's enough!" Julius said sharply.

"I'm telling you what they said, Julius Ramsdorf. No more and no less." She took a deep breath. "What they said right before they dropped a rope around his neck and hung him."

Julius wiped his mouth. "Maybe it's time somebody stood up for decency around here."

"Start with your own family, then, if you must! Start by protecting them! Somebody could get some wild idea—" She shuddered. "You got three of your girls of age now," she said.

"Becky Sue isn't a grown woman yet."

"Her change came yesterday. Four females old enough to worry about." She touched him gently on the arm. "You're a good husband, Julius, and a good father. You'll do the right thing." She turned and walked quickly out the door, leaving him behind with no chance of saying anything else.

That afternoon he thought about it while he puttered around. He always felt the store was his area, a masculine retreat away from the overwhelming female paraphernalia that surrounded him at home.

If God had wanted him to worry about stray girls and savages, He would have given Julius Ramsdorf boys.

Julius sighed and went out to the garden to talk to Flame.

The news was all over town before supper, and during supper, three men from the Jolly Companions paid a visit to the Ramsdorfs'.

When the knock came during dinner, Julius excused himself and went to the door. "Evening, boys."

237

"Evening, Julius." They were all shop owners, like him. Ray, Bill, Marcus. Not one of them looked him in the eye.

"Would you like some pie? First blueberries of the year."

"What we got to say is best said outside," Bill said.

Julius stepped outside and closed the door behind him. He could still hear the baby banging a spoon on the tray, the two older girls arguing over a hair ribbon, the clatter of dishes being cleared, squeals from the younger girls and the exasperated voice of his wife. From the door he could see the green block of garden and the store. Julius put his hands in his pockets. "Is it my turn to bring the liquids?"

Ray looked away. Marcus spoke up. "Heard you got a white gal and a savage on your place. Shacking up."

So that was it. Julius nodded cautiously. "He stays with her. But I wouldn't call it shacking up."

"They live together in the same one-room cabin!" Ray flared. "Use your head, man. All the decent folk in town are worked up about it. I'm surprised your missus hasn't put her foot down."

"Careful now," Julius cautioned. "Keep my Sarah out of this."

"It's a scandal. And that's a fact. All the boys feel the same way."

"All the boys?"

"We got together this afternoon, Julius."

"You mean the boys got together and talked about me?"

The three looked uncomfortable. "They took a vote. Thought the three of us might be able to wring some sense into your head."

"You got together and talked about me?"

Ray put a hand on Julius's arm. "Now, Julius, it was a friendly meeting. For your own good."

"A few hotheads wanted a vote right off, but we talked them out of it."

"A vote?"

The three looked at each other and looked away.

"What in the hell are you boys talking about?"

"Ask her to leave. Her and that savage. There's other towns."

238

"And if I don't?"

"None of us want it to come to that, Julius. I nominated you myself."

Julius unfolded his hands across his chest. "You won't have to vote me out. I'm retiring from the Jolly Companions. As of tonight."

He thought they'd try to talk him out of it, tell him to be reasonable. But they just turned around and walked away, three abreast. On the way down the path, he heard them talking about other things, laughing; it was the easy laughter that hurt the most.

He opened the door. Inside, the baby had just dumped cereal on her head. She was smiling.

Sarah was singing from the kitchen. Julius unlatched Edith from the highchair, tipped her like a football under his arm and sponged her down. The three younger girls were doing the dishes tonight. They were scraping dishes at the sideboard. Sarah had them organized like an all-women's army. No volunteers. He clucked at Edith and carried her into the kitchen. Sarah looked up from the pie she was cutting. "I could cut into the extra one. For your friends. Got some coffee on, too."

"They didn't stay." He gurgled at the baby.

Sarah looked at him sharply. "Something's wrong." She always knew.

He practiced his dada's on Edith. All five of the others had said mama first, but Julius still held out hope. "Dadada . . . a little wrong, maybe . . . dadada."

Sarah put down the knife, wiped her hands off and took Edith. She put the baby on her hip. "It's the girl again, isn't it?"

Julius nodded.

"I thought she was gone."

"Sarah, you know I've never lied to you."

"No, but sometimes you don't tell me all there is, either."

"I couldn't ask her to go. She's got no one, Sarah. No one at all. Both her parents died on the way. She'll be gone soon."

He embraced her and the child. Edith bucked against her parents, squealing. "It worries me, Julius."

He patted her. "Might not hurt to keep the girls close to home."

"You're worried, too, aren't you?"

"I think things will cool down. Something will come along in a few days. Another girl at Silver's, maybe, or a fight. People will lose interest."

They stood together for a few minutes, holding each other, the child between them. "What did your friends want?"

"Just to tell me they're not my friends." He made it light.

She hugged him harder. "I'm sorry, Julius. I am. I know how much you needed to get away every week."

Another revelation. Julius had prided himself on how well he pretended to hate the meetings. "It's nothing," he said gamely. He stopped. She knew how he felt. "I'm going to miss it." Suddenly he felt like he was going to cry. She squeezed him really hard, then, until the baby sputtered for air and they broke apart.

She handed Edith to him and went to the kitchen table and dished up the pie. She cut a thick slab for him and poured the coffee.

The two girls came running into the room.

"Grandma told us to share it, Annie. And the only time I *see* it is hanging from the line on wash day. Leave it *alone*. It's my *turn*."

"Girls! Enough." The two stared at their mother, then ran, stumbling over each other, out of the room.

Julius watched and shook his head. They heard stifled screams and the sounds of socking coming from the parlor. "Do you think I should step in?"

Sarah shook her head. "Get in the middle of those two and you're liable to break a nose. It's mostly show anyway. You should hear them late at night, whispering and giggling together. It's going to break Annie's heart when Ellie leaves."

Julius ate his pie and jigged Edith on his knee. "What do you think I should do?" he said finally.

She crossed her hands and leaned on them. "Maybe it is time to stand up for something," she said slowly. "It made me sick in my stomach, sick for days, when I heard what they did to Dan Carolan. Then I think about the kids and I know there's

240

not a principle in the world worth losing a child over."

He finished his pie. "It won't come to that." He took her hand. "I promise. But if a man can't stand up for what he thinks is right—"

"But is it right for them to stay together, Julius? In the same cabin? I have searched and searched my heart, and it feels wrong."

"Have you even talked to her?"

Sarah shook her head. "I don't intend to, either. How would you like a daughter of *yours* carrying on with some savage? How can we hope to teach the girls right from wrong if we don't take a stand somewhere?"

Julius thought about it. "Tell you what. A minister got into town today. Came into the store and bought some darning yarn. He's staying at the Mayo. I don't suppose it would hurt if I asked him to pay her a visit. Maybe all she needs is to see things from a different angle. Get her back on the right track."

Sarah squeezed his hand. "Julius Ramsdorf. I love you."

He patted her hand and kissed the baby on the head. "I'll do it now."

Ever since it happened, Flame had had a feeling of weightlessness, of never knowing exactly where she was. She had left behind more than Cahill that night. With him had stood a reassuring bulwark of rules and conventions.

If there were no rules in this gray netherworld, she would have to invent them. She had thrown out the wash basin, and now she was hunting for the baby she was sure she had seen once, playing with a rubber duck in the water. She had stepped outside the law as surely as if she had shot her own mother through the head. It opened the world up—not like a flower—but like a yawning chasm, boiling with fire.

So here she was, her mother prone and bleeding at her feet, looking for babies among the fireballs.

The year she had been born, 1881, the James brothers had gotten together for one last family reunion at the Chicago, Rock Island and Pacific train near Winston, Missouri. The gang went shooting the way some women went shopping: they wore comfortable shoes and didn't stop until their ammunition

241

was gone. Flame's mother had clipped the article and saved it as part of a scrapbook quaintly entitled *Flame's First Year*. Flame had always wondered how it was that *all* the brothers had gone bad and stayed that way. Now she knew.

Once they had stepped over the line, who else was there to talk to? Certainly not the Pinkertons. And once you had robbed a few banks, you built up a certain stake in justifying your actions. It wasn't enough to take the money and run. The James brothers yearned to be respected and admired by the same folks whose pockets they had just emptied at gunpoint. And the more banks you robbed, the more tellers you killed, the more the dream of the cozy little house with the white picket fence and the civic award for good works retreated to some little attic in your mind. If you kept the dream there *long* enough, nothing you could say to it would induce it to come out. It would just stay there, getting wrinkled and dry like Emily Dickinson.

Flame wasn't sure she wanted to march hand in hand with Nuka into the sunset, but the more resistance she felt from others, the more likely it looked.

He, at least, would eat dinner with her. Now if she could only get him to say something. They sat in silence on the cement step, their backs to the cabin door, and ate the fish Nuka had caught. In front of them, the garden hummed with bugs.

The first time she had heard the phrase *going siwash*, it had been muttered at her behind a shocked hand in Fort Yukon. She hadn't known what it meant, and now that she did, it was too late. Even Jesse James had a mother to critique the day's robbery.

How'd I do, ma?

Try a number two rope next time, son. Bank president thrashed around like a landed bass. And eat some more potatoes. Got to keep your shooting arm strong.

Gee, thanks, ma. Do you suppose after dinner you could read me a story? Maybe something from the newspaper about the raid.

If it's not too late, son. You've got that early robbery in the morning.

Oh. Right. Forgot all about it. What in the world would I do without you?

242

What, indeed.

He had thinning brown hair and a bad leg, but to Flame, he was a prince from another world. She took one look at him and wrapped her arms around his neck. "Reverend Marsh!"

He pulled away, embarrassed.

"You don't remember me. I'm Flame. Flame Ryan. From First Hill. I was visiting Cahill the day you came calling. We sat in the parlor, remember, and drank tea."

He studied her thoroughly, tilting his glasses back to get a better look. "Little Flame Ryan? Good gracious, child! You've grown!"

Flame squeezed his hands. "I can't tell you what it means to see you." She felt her throat constrict. She swallowed. "I'm forgetting my manners. Please sit down." She moved her trunk off the chair and motioned him into it. "Can I fix you something? Are you hungry? I have fish. And a few vegetables. Mr. Ramsdorf gave them to me. Oh, Reverend Marsh! You're an answer to prayer! Tea. No, coffee. I'll fix coffee. Would you like some coffee?" She took the pot off the back of the stove and poured it into a cup.

"I can't get over it." She put the cup in front of him. "Someone from home." She sat in the second chair. "How did you find me? How did you know where I was?"

"I didn't," he said truthfully. "Mr. Ramsdorf visited me at the Mayo Hotel." He cleared his throat.

"Of course! How thoughtful of him! He knew I was from Seattle."

It was going to be awkward. Reverend Marsh took off his glasses and polished them. Perhaps he could work into it gradually. "I saw Cahill this winter," he remarked.

The color drained from her face. "How is he?"

"Quite well," Reverend Marsh said heartily. "Thinner than I remembered him, perhaps. He doctored with me among the savages."

Flame got up suddenly and went to the stove. She poured coffee into a cup. It rattled. "I thought he was mining."

"He is. Should be around here, somewhere, as a matter of fact. If he hasn't left yet. He's getting married."

She bowed her head, her back still to him. There was a long moment of silence.

"Don't know who the girl is. Nice family, though, Dr. and Mrs. Blue. When I left, he had some heart trouble. The doctor, not Cahill. Talking about taking his son in as partner, once he finishes school."

Flame spent a long time wiping the stove. She smoothed the dishrag carefully over the front handle. She adjusted the cups on the shelf. She turned around. Reverend Marsh thought her color looked unusually high. Perhaps she was coming down with something.

"When you see Cahill—" she said carefully. She swallowed.

He really should look at her tongue before he left. A little hops bitters might be in order. "Yes, my child?"

"Tell him—" she swallowed again—"tell him I'm doing well. *Very* well." She sat down with her cup. "You won't forget what I said?"

He patted her hand genially. "I'll tell him first thing." He leaned forward in his chair and pulled a small New Testament out of his shirt pocket. "But I think now we should talk about *you*, Flame Ryan."

"What do you mean?"

He looked at her searchingly. "Mr. Ramsdorf tells me you lost your parents on the way."

"Yes." Her throat hurt.

"There is comfort to be found in God's Holy Word. Your parents were Christian, I take it?"

She nodded.

He took her hand. "Then there is nothing to fear, my child," he said gently. "They are just a little ahead of you, is all. You'll see them again."

He put on his glasses and opened the book.

"Let us read together from God's Holy Word. St. John, Chapter Fourteen, Verse One." He cleared his throat. "Let not your heart be troubled—"

She got up suddenly. The coffee spilled. "Please. Reverend Marsh."

He looked up in surprise. "What is it, my child? Are you ill?"

"I find no comfort in the words."

"Death is always harder for the rest of us." He grasped her hand. "Sit down, my dear." She kept standing, but a small sob escaped and her shoulders hitched up and down. "Sit."

She sat in the chair and put her head in her hands, crying very quietly.

"I was about your age when my parents passed away," he said. "Scarlet fever took them."

Flame wiped her eyes. "What did you do?"

"I was the oldest of six children. I did the only thing I could. I went to work at a boat factory. A dollar a week, at first. A sister was next in line. We were mother and father to the younger ones."

"Didn't you question God?"

He looked at her sharply. "Question? Of course. No one escapes. Ever. We are all touched. In my ministry, it's been my experience to examine those among my flock whose lives appear serene and unblemished. There is always a secret wound someplace. Life moves us all, in its own time. And not like a broad river, either. More like a tornado." He patted her hand. "But it is possible to pick things up and find a new order in the chaos." He spoke gently. "You have to be willing, Flame. God does the rest."

She was quiet for a long time. She said abruptly, "Did Cahill ever talk about me?"

So that was it. Reverend Marsh drank his coffee. "Would it make a difference if he had?"

"He never talked about me, did he?" Silent tears rolled down her face.

"He's getting married, Flame. He told me so himself. If a man is promised to someone else, it means God has another person in mind for you. There is always a higher plan."

She buried her face in her hands.

"In time God's plan will be clear to you. But first you must be willing to live according to God's laws." He touched her shoulder. "Mr. Ramsdorf asked me to see you because he's worried about you, Flame. I can understand how despair can fill a person up until they choke. Your parents dying. Cahill leaving— But Flame, living with a savage is not the answer. It's

245

no worse than any other sin. And while God hates the sin, He still loves the sinner. But it's time to repent and give yourself over to His holy plan. He does have a plan for your life. First, John, one-nine," he recited. "'If we confess our sins, he is faithful and just to forgive us our sins, and to cleanse us from all unrighteousness.' You must start with a repentant heart, Flame. That's first."

"But I haven't done anything wrong," she protested.

"Child, you're going against God's holy plan for your life. Do you honestly feel right about what you're doing?"

She was silent.

"In the quiet of your own heart, you hear God working," Reverend Marsh said gently.

The door opened. Reverend Marsh and Nuka studied each other. "Is this the savage?"

"His name is Nuka."

They both recognized each other at the same moment. Nuka started, and touched his left shoulder. "Ilaa-likaa anaayu-liksi!"

"Paglan! Anaayu-liksi patchisaiksauruk."

Nuka spat on the floor. "Nuka uumikliksuk anaayuliksi?"

Reverend Marsh gasped. "God nagliktuk."

"Do you know each other?"

Reverend Marsh nodded. "Cahill saved his life by closing off a vein in his arm. That one arm is weaker than the other and he blames us for it. Claims we robbed him of his spirit. He wants me to leave. Flame, I want you to come with me. It's not safe here."

Flame looked thoughtfully at Nuka. It was clear he was angry at the minister, but Flame didn't think he was dangerous. "Have you tried to explain to him?"

Reverend Marsh nodded. "When it happened, we did. He said it was another white man's lie. Flame, I really do insist."

"Ask him what he wants."

"Suvich."

"Sugriuich itkilik tigliktuktuk kannik. Nuka tuvraktuk. Nuka-pakittuk-kannik-kuak-Flame."

Reverend Marsh looked at Nuka in astonishment, then glanced back at Flame.

"What did he say?"

"His sister, Kannik, was stolen by the Indians. He's got some crazy idea you're going to lead him to her."

Nuka stared steadily at Flame, his eyes bright with trust.

"Ask him why."

"I don't like this, Flame."

"Ask him."

"Su-mman."

Nuka looked astonished. "Kannik-suli-Flame-kak-atiruk-kiinak."

Flame looked at the minister expectantly. "He says you look alike."

"I look like her? That's it?"

"In their religion, that's enough. It's a sacred connection. Broken only by death."

"Then he wouldn't hurt me, would he?"

"No," Reverend Marsh said at last. "But it's not going to help you, either. Think of your eternal soul! You were not put upon this earth to be a helpmate to a savage. Flame, if you stay with him, he will not leave your side until he finds his sister. Believe me."

"He couldn't very well find his sister in Seattle if I decide to go home."

"You don't understand, Flame. He wouldn't *let* you go home. Not without finding Kannik first. It may already be too late!" He gathered up his Bible and put it back into his jacket pocket. "Flame, I'm imploring you, by everything that is good and true, come with me."

"Ask him—"

"I'll ask him nothing! Come!"

"Just this one thing." She turned to Nuka. "Ask him if his sister is all he has left." Her voice caught.

Reverend Marsh gazed thoughtfully at Flame. "You are lost already," he said with finality.

"I need to know."

"Su-ilivich-anayukaagiitchuak."

"Suli-Kannik."

The minister turned to Flame. "There's something else you need to know—"

247

"What did he say?"

"—and that's this. You're putting Mr. Ramsdorf in a terrible position. I thought you should know that first. Before I tell you what Nuka said."

"I don't understand."

"Mr. Ramsdorf has a family, Flame. A store. This garden. He's worked his whole life and has this to show for it. He could lose it because of you."

"What do you mean?"

"The town has its eye on you, Flame Ryan. And because of you, it's got its eye on Julius, too." He walked to the door. "At least pray about it, Flame. Promise me you'll do that."

"What did Nuka say?"

The minister's face softened. "Flame, you've got the Lord. Don't turn away from Him."

"And Nuka? What does Nuka have?"

There was a beat of silence. The minister said, "Kannik is his only relative."

"Then I can't leave him, can I?"

His eyes burned through her. "I'll be back in the morning." And with that the minister turned abruptly and walked out the door, leaving Flame alone with her thoughts.

Twenty-Four

The barracks at Rampart had been built on a hill. Most of the fifty-five men assigned to the camp wouldn't get there until September twenty-second. They had been assigned from three different units: E and F Company from the Eighth Infantry and the A Battery from the Third Artillery. The camp was a group of cabins inside a barbed wire fence. The military had been assigned to Alaska to keep order during the gold rush.

Sergeant Viceroy Dillard thumbed through a magazine and sighed. Not actually *thumbed;* fingered was more accurate. He had lost his thumb in a boating accident at Camp Buckner, the year before he was to have graduated from West Point. It cost him graduation and a career as an officer and doomed him to second-rate posts forever. This one was only his for another few weeks, until Lieutenant Edwin Bell came with the rest of the men and took charge.

Dillard hated Bell and his take-charge attitude; hated his youth and most of all, hated his thumbs. There was a knock and Dillard hid the magazine, "Yes?"

It was Private Hardwick, working the front desk. He was wearing brown baggy khakis, polished knee boots and a sour expression. "Somebody to see you."

"That's it? Just somebody to see me?"

Hardwick knew there was nothing Dillard could do to him. He sneered. "That's it." He trotted back to the front desk and opened his book. He was reading A. Conan Doyle's *The Sign of the Four.*

"Hardwick!" Dillard barked, and steadied himself.

Coming across the room was an angel in a print dress. She was small, with enormous amber eyes and soft brown hair that curled tightly over her forehead. There was a mole high on her cheek. She smiled tremulously at him. Her front tooth, ringed in gold, wobbled precariously.

They stared at each other for one heart-stopping moment. All Dillard's life, he had been second best, and now before him there was this exquisite vision, staring up at him with liquid fire in her eyes.

"What do you want?" Hardwick interrupted. He was smirking at Dillard.

"Get Miss—what did you say your name was?" he murmured.

"Nelly." Her voice was wondrously rich.

"Get Miss Nelly here some coffee."

Hardwick sulkily snapped his book shut and clomped out the door. Through the window Dillard could see him slipping through the mud over to the mess hall.

"What can I do for you?" Need a mountain relocated, Miss Nelly? I'm free this afternoon. She touched his arm. On second thought, I'm free the rest of my life.

Nelly settled into her seat. "You are the person to see?" She had a charming way with words. "The one on top?"

Or on the bottom. Whatever you want, Nelly. He found his voice. "Viceroy Dillard, here." He extended his hand and she took it without flinching, daintily clasping his fingers under where his thumb had once been.

He felt a curious stirring of emotion. So accepting, she was, of other people's liabilities. He hoped whatever she needed would take all night.

"Good." She sighed and pulled a newspaper out of her satchel and passed it across the table to him. "He is—how you say it—the most important person in my life. Most important." As she drew the last words out, her tooth clicked.

Dillard read through the article and passed it back, feeling deflated. "You must be very happy."

"No, no. Not happy." She burst into tears.

"What is it?" he asked, alarmed. "What happened?"

"I can trust you? A big, handsome military man like you?"

"Of course."

"Cahill took my honor out the door with him. I met him in Seattle, after I come to this country off the big boat." She

250

twisted her hands together in her lap and stared over the sergeant's head at the head of a black bear that was mounted on the wall behind him. The bear's yellow glass eyes stared back at her in frank disbelief.

Sergeant Dillard was more easily fooled. He rose and crossed swiftly around the desk to her side, his handkerchief at the ready.

"What did he do to you?" The sergeant stood behind her and rested his fingers lightly on her shoulders.

"It is the oldest story in the world." Her voice was barely audible. "A young girl—" She paused.

"—a boat," Dillard encouraged.

"Yes, and a boat." Her voice trailed away. Sergeant Dillard walked his fingers over Nelly's shoulders. His West Point ring glowed in a shaft of afternoon light. He admired the ring: an eagle with spread wings over the words Duty Honor Country. Underneath, a sword slashed through a helmet. He unconsciously rubbed the pad where his thumb had been.

"It is terrible!" She dissolved into fresh tears.

"When you say he took advantage of you, surely you can't mean—" Sergeant Dillard's phantom thumb did a delicate dance on Nelly's shoulder.

She nodded and bowed her head. "My honor is dirty. Like yesterday's bloomers."

He squeezed her shoulders and his ring gleamed. "The cad."

"I must find him," she whispered. "Before my brothers do." Tears spattered her plump hands.

"Your brothers?"

"They want to kill him. I just want to marry him." She wiped her eyes. "You see how it is."

Oh, yes. He saw how it was. A young innocent, ruthlessly seduced and abandoned. Rage burned in his breast. They were alike, cripples, both of them. He was missing a thumb and Nelly was missing the one thing she needed to be happy in this world. He was beginning to love her.

"What do you want me to do?"

Her eyes were a bright amber. "Make him marry me," she whispered. "You have the power, don't you, lieutenant?" She looked at him helplessly.

"Sergeant," Sergeant Dillard corrected. "Although I'm due for a promotion this year."

She blinked her eyes. "So sorry. Such a man, I thought, naturally, would be a lieutenant."

He shrugged, and Nelly could see he agreed with her.

"Actually, there is a precedent," he said importantly. "Doe versus Roe. Last year in Circle a miners' association forced a man to marry a woman he had seduced. Offered him that or jail and a stiff fine. Heard they're happy." He paused meaningfully. "You're certain he's the only one who could make you happy?" He held his breath.

She touched Dillard's arm and his pulse jumped. "At this point in time," she whispered.

Then there was hope! Oh, he would sing any song for her, climb any mountain, but he refused to play second fiddle. Well, all right, even second fiddle if it got him into the band. "I could scout around and try to locate him. Every good-sized town has a claims office."

"You would do that for *moi!*" she cried. Her eyes, the color of ale, were remarkably dry for the number of tears so recently shed.

"I'd do anything for you," he blurted out. And for the moment he meant it. But if Cahill couldn't be found—if he wasn't around— His jowls quivered with desire and his pale eyes burned into her. "I mean that," he said. "Call me anytime. Day or night."

She blinked and touched his arm again. "*Merci.* But Nelly, she works the nights." She stood wearily.

Dillard stood in alarm. "Nights?" His voice was a squeak. "There is only one place in town where women work nights—"

She covered his lips with a gentle hand. "Hush. It is too awful to say outloud."

"He did this to you! He promised to marry you and then reduced you to this?"

She nodded mutely.

Anger blazed in his heart. Dillard took her elbow. "Don't worry. I'll find the cad and bring him to justice!"

She smiled tremulously. "Be as rough as you want. Just

252

don't kill him." She floated through his office door past Hardwick, who was seated in the outer office reading. Dillard opened the front door for her.

"Don't worry about anything," he promised. "Dillard's here."

She moistened her lips. "Nelly will never forgive you," she murmured.

"Forget," Dillard corrected. "Nelly will never forget me."

"Ah, yes. The English language." She shrugged and fastened her cape. "'Bye for good." She started down the path toward the main gate.

He called after her, "You mean, Good-bye for now!"

She didn't stop. Dillard sighed. Behind him Hardwick snorted into his book.

"I thought I asked for coffee?" Dillard snapped. It would have kept Nelly there another ten minutes.

Hardwick read to the end of the page before looking up. "Wasn't any," he said tonelessly.

He kept reading and Dillard found himself wishing he hadn't bothered the private so Hardwick could get back to his real job, reading trashy novels. Dillard hated people like that: little people who were good at only one thing: making the rest of the world feel lousy and responsible.

"You'll love the way the book ends. I mean, you'll really love it."

Hardwick scowled at him.

"See, Jonathan Small is an escaped convict. And after Mayor Sholto's death, Small waits until the son stumbles on the treasure. Poor young Sholto, he's killed with a poison splinter before Small can get into that locked room suspended through a trapdoor."

The private's cheeks were turning bright pink. "Don't tell me anything else."

"Of course, Sherlock was *right* in thinking it had been Small that had left the paper with the Sign of the Four—"

Hardwick screamed and covered his ears. "Shut up!"

Sergeant Dillard tenderly removed his hands. "It all ends just fine, private. Dr. Watson asks Mary to marry him, on

253

account of her not being an heiress anymore, since Small dumps the treasure in the river."

"Get out of here!" the private hissed.

Dillard walked serenely to his office. Hardwick was crouched over the book, his hands clenched in rage. "She accepts, by the way," he called out offhandedly. Hardwick gave a strangled cry and threw the book across the room.

Twenty-Five

It had beaten him down, this land. He was a veteran of two stampedes, each guaranteed, like war, to be the most splendid and the last.

He was a miner; he could call himself that now. He had sifted pans for colors, his fingers numb with cold. He had staked corners on cliffs and doubled under the weight of gravel. He'd even worked for somebody else once, when things went sour, taking his place in line with the Indians, his ankles sodden with water and his heart humbled by dreams.

It had raised him up, this land. He had stood exalted before a blue canyon of sky and watched the wind gallop through a torrent of trees below him. He had seen God, once or twice, when the sun slanted on the snow just right, and had held death in his arms the day his partner died.

And now he was going home, knowing even as he bound nuggets to his body and lifted his pack that he would be back.

He looked once around the room: there was the stove—cold now—and the iron bar he had used to hack ice off the inside walls when the temperature dropped, the faded pictures clipped from magazines he had used to spruce up the walls, the thin straw pallet on his bunk, his gold pan.

He ducked his head, stepped outside and walked quickly toward the river. The woods rang with the sound of men and equipment. An eastern conglomerate had bought him out. He had dug three thousand dollars of gold out of a hole smaller than a man's grave and the syndicate had given him six thousand more to move on.

He walked to the boat, threw in his pack and sat down. The guide said, "Ready now, sir?"

Cahill nodded. They floated in the fast current. Hunter

Creek was high this year. Another hour and they would be back on the Yukon. Cahill swiveled around and watched the cabin until he lost it in the dusk. The syndicate was going to use it to store supplies; it was too small for the men. He sat down and watched the pilot maneuver them around the sandbars and limbs. At length the man remarked, "Going to be a helluva winter, this year. Frost is early."

"Wouldn't know," Cahill said shortly. It felt funny talking out loud. They lapsed into silence that lasted until the Yukon. Here the river was flat, and in the distance Cahill could see the lights of Rampart.

"Going to have a little fun?" the pilot inquired.

"Going home." The guide left him alone after that. Cahill was relieved.

The boat pulled up at the wharf and the guide stepped out, tying up the boat. He stretched, scratched an armpit and hoisted Cahill's pack onto the ground. Cahill got out and gave the man a nugget.

"Thank you."

There was a pause and then Cahill remembered the proper response. "You're welcome."

There was a hint of smile. "Be careful in town," the man said. "The girls will eat you alive."

Cahill slung his pack onto his back. No chance of that. Tomorrow a steamer would take him to St. Michaels and there he would meet up with the *Seattle I*. In a week he would be home, home to Flame.

Nothing in the world could change that.

He rented a room at the Mayo Hotel, took a leisurely bath at Dealy's bathhouse and bought a paper at the bar, reading the front page on the way to his room. He went immediately to Silver's.

Between the Dealy Sisters' Restaurant and the office of Samuel E. Heater, general contractor, there was a two-story log cabin in Rampart for Silver and her girls. It had once belonged to an enterprising widow who dispensed advice and opium to the miners. She went south one winter and opened a blissfully quiet but peculiar smelling nursery.

256

Silver put in eight rooms upstairs for the girls and a parlor downstairs. The parlor walls were hung in red velvet. On one of the walls was a large painting of a nymph dragging a sailor down into the sea. The sailor was smiling.

Nelly came down the stairs and stared at her next customer with frank admiration. He had a well-formed head under the heavy beard and mustache, and piercing blue eyes. Young, too. There was strength in his hands, and his shoulders were broad.

"My name is Nelly and I am here only to please you." He stood up and was taller than she had expected. She led him upstairs.

She loved her work.

Their gratitude at her skill was so touching.

She walked into the room and closed the door behind the customer. She loved this room, too: the soft satin of the sheets, the velvet comfort of the spread.

All over the world, there were women bending over steaming tubs of washwater, making unimaginative meals for doltish husbands, wiping noses of whining infants. She, alone, was blessed. She had this warm and cheerful room, and the confidence that comes from knowing she could go anywhere in the world and find work in her field.

Her customer was staring at her hungrily.

Nelly knew the look well. It meant he had been alone in the woods too long. She shrugged. Ah well, perhaps the next time he would appreciate the subtlety of her art. For now, she would concentrate on relieving him of the pressure in his loins and the deeper pressure in his pocket. She curled her arms around his neck.

There was something about him that was familiar. She had indulged her senses so long that the nights were one long magnificent blur. But still— "Are you sure Nelly does not know you?" She liked to give repeat customers a special rate.

The question stunned him. She could sense him pulling away and she stayed her hands. "A stupid question," she murmured. "Only this matters." Her hands crept to his thighs. She rubbed along his crotch, traced the outline. He stiffened instantly.

He held her head loosely in his hand and she nuzzled his

257

body. He pulled gently on the chain around her neck and Nelly thought fleetingly that if it were rope, he could strangle her.

"A necklace." He had found the hearts. "A gift from a lover?"

"It is a long, boring tale, my friend." She stroked the bulge in his pants.

He tightened his hand around her neck and for an instant, she was certain the chain would break, and then his hand slipped away and he caressed her hair.

She rubbed herself against him. "What is your pleasure with Nelly?" she whispered, and worked her hands slowly down his shirt, unbuttoning as she went. "A man alone in the universe has only his thoughts to fuel his dreams. But now there is Nelly and all your dreams are flesh."

She kissed him deeply on the mouth. He was perfectly still, and then a long shudder escaped and he crushed his mouth against hers and carried her to bed.

She rolled gracefully out from under him.

"Nelly is expensive."

He sat on the edge of the bed, pulled a pouch out of his jacket and rolled a nugget in his palm.

She smiled then. "Where would you like to start?"

"Wherever you say."

She rolled off and knelt before him, untying his boots. She had lost a spread once, from muddy boots. She pulled them off and still kneeling, smoothed her hands over his thighs. His pants were tight over the thick bulge in his crotch.

"Tell Nelly your secrets," she whispered.

He swallowed hard, his eyes closing into slits. "There is one thing—"

She smoothed her fingers lightly over the outline of his member. Such a shame it would be over so quickly.

"Anything," she prodded.

"I always wanted—" He swallowed again.

"Yes."

"It is vile."

"Nothing is vile to Nelly. There is only pleasure."

She moved closer and kissed the front of his pants lingeringly.

"Anything I want?" His voice was strained.

"Anything," she murmured in a muffled voice.

"Would you mind holding—"

Dear boy. Such an ordinary request.

"I mean, in your mouth."

She rolled her fingers over his crotch toward the buttons. "Of course."

"You don't think it's awful?"

She smiled. That's all they ever wanted. "No. Nelly does not think it is awful."

"Good." He sounded genuinely relieved. "I've never seen anybody suck on a nugget before."

She paused. Perhaps she had misjudged him.

"A nugget."

He held it out. "If you just sort of—rest it on your tongue, Nelly." He looked at her anxiously. "I knew it was vile." He turned his head away and started to get up. "You were my last hope."

She pressed him down. "No. Please. Nelly would be— honored to do such a thing."

She had sucked on worse things before. Besides, the nugget was a generous one. And if it would relieve something in this handsome stranger's mind— She took it firmly out of his hands and popped it into her mouth. It was unbelievably heavy and the metal made something ache in her tooth.

"It's good," she said gamely. The words were blurred.

He was watching her carefully, the way she had seen men watch her working, as if he were memorizing something beyond her features. Nelly felt regret. Perhaps she would not see the secret world under his belt after all.

He withdrew a bottle from his jacket and unscrewed the cap. He passed it to her. "It'll go down easier if you take a long drink."

Perhaps she had misunderstood.

"Go down?" The words were a gargle.

He nodded. "I want you to swallow the nugget, Nelly."

That was not exactly what she had in mind. Nelly spit the nugget carefully into her hand.

She said gently, "Nelly has other things in mind to swallow."

He didn't appear to be listening. He opened his pouch and

259

pulled out the biggest nugget Nelly had ever seen. An ostrich egg. He weighed it in his palm. "This is yours, if you do it."

What was a little inconvenience, compared to such a thing of wonder? She took a long swallow of whiskey and squeezed the nugget in her palm, her eyes never leaving the rock of gold in his.

"Look at me," he ordered. "I want to see your eyes change."

She smoothed her gown around her body and fluffed her hair. Even a pervert deserved the best performance money could buy. Nelly prided herself on her ability to rise above the little things that would have cooled the ardor of a lesser whore.

She held the nugget briefly, saluted him with it, and threw it into her mouth. It clanked against her back teeth. She rolled it into position, held the bottle gingerly, and then threw back her head and drank.

Her throat closed.

She smiled at him reassuringly. "Almost." She timed it better this time, taking a deep belt and letting the whiskey wash the nugget down her gullet. It felt terrible.

He was watching her with great interest. She kept her eyes on his. The nugget was working its cold way down her chest, through the soft warm passages of her body. She felt a piercing pain, and then it settled in her body with a sickening thud.

She smiled sickly. "There. Nelly has done the thing." She held out her hand.

But he was standing up now, putting the pouch in his pocket.

Perhaps he had forgotten, in the ecstasy of the moment. "There is a little matter of a nugget," she coached gently.

He looked perplexed. "A nugget? I already gave you a nugget, remember?"

A small pain nudged her stomach. "That is so," she nodded. "But I did as you requested. Nelly swallowed the nugget."

He stood and put his hands gently on her shoulders, caressing her neck. "That was a pretty stupid thing to do." He snapped the necklace off. "Goodbye, Nelly."

And then she saw him for the first time. "Cahill." She picked up the lamp and threw it at him. It shattered against the door.

He turned around, smiling. "I just came back for this,

260

Nelly." The necklace lay like a dead bird in his hand. "I'm going home now. There's a lady, a proper lady, who will expect it around my neck when I come calling."

He opened the door. "You really are a bitch."

She hurled the pillow at him.

"And scared too. Only an aging whore would do something so stupid."

"Scum!" she shrieked. "*Avortement!*"

"Live it up, whore. I'll come back next year and find you gumming strangers in alleys for table scraps."

She let him almost get away before she said it, the words so full of loathing they were almost unintelligible.

"Flame is not in Seattle."

He stopped. "What did you say?"

His face paled and Nelly knew she would win after all. "She is not in Seattle. She is here." She rubbed her throat. It felt raw and swollen.

"It won't work, Nelly."

She looked out the window, dismissing him. "Ask any of the whores, Cahill. We all know her."

He moved swiftly across the floor and jerked her around. "Where is she?"

Nelly laughed. It was good to see him in pain. She hoped, as the years went by, she would not become dulled to the joy of hurting this man.

"We taught her everything, Cahill. Everything a good whore should know. But she was such a disappointment."

He shook her violently, and her hair loosened and fell down her back. "What have you done to her?"

"*I* have done nothing. Flame has done it all—with so many men we have lost count."

"Where is she?" His voice was deadly.

"We threw her out. Even whores had standards."

His face under the beard was blotched and his voice was strangled. "*Where is she?*"

"She's in bed with a savage."

"*Liar.*" His hands closed around her throat.

"A savage—"

"*Shut up.*" He struck her and she sprawled backward onto

261

the bed.

"Ask your dear Reverend Marsh, if you don't believe me. He's at the Mayo Hotel. Ask him what everybody in town is saying about Flame. Everyone knows. It's all the men talk about."

He stood over her for a moment, his hands balled up. His voice quivered and Nelly knew he would kill her if he could. "I hope to God I never see you again. In this life or the next."

She laughed. "You might want some company in hell."

Carefully he put down his hands. "You're not worth killing, Nelly." He walked out the door.

Nelly smiled and got off the bed. She stretched and yawned. So tedious, this future husband of hers. She went to the closet and found something sensible, a brown wool dress with all its parts. She dressed quickly, fastened a cape around her shoulders and walked swiftly downstairs and out the door.

It was raining and she put up the hood. She walked rapidly through the town toward the army barracks.

It was all a blur. He had gotten very drunk in some bar, singing old fight songs in the ear of a good buddy.

Someplace along the line, the buddy had let Cahill in on a little secret: he had a few fight songs of his own, and he sang them with his fist. Cahill had slipped in the mud in the rain, and then somehow he was at the wharf and he had fallen in the water and life sobered up. He pulled himself out and made his way, chattering and subdued, to the Mayo Hotel.

He dripped up the stairs. In his room he toweled off and rubbed down his legs. His watch had stopped at one-fifteen. Then he said, "No time like the present."

The night clerk at the desk was thin and had bags under his eyes. Cahill was sure the clerk would tell him Reverend Marsh wasn't there and that would be the end of it.

"He's in room three." He pointed upstairs. "End of the hall."

So what? Cahill told himself. So what if that much was true? The rest of it wasn't. Not the part about Flame. He climbed the stairs. He stood at the door. It was three in the morning. Reverend Marsh would be sound asleep.

He knocked. The door opened immediately. Reverend Marsh was standing in his shirtsleeves, his Bible open. His face was more deeply lined than Cahill remembered. "Yes?" Then recognition. "Praise God! I asked for help, and here you are!" He took Cahill's arm and led him into the room. "Sit down, dear boy." Cahill sat heavily on the bed. It hadn't been slept on. Something was wrong, and Cahill had the terrible feeling it was about to get a lot wronger.

"Son," the minister said without preamble, "I'll get right to the point. A serious matter has come to my attention. A soul is in jeopardy. God in His infinite wisdom sent you here to help." He looked keenly at Cahill. "You are truly the only one who can help, my son."

Cahill wanted to get out of the room. "What is it?"

Reverend Marsh took off his glasses and polished them. A bad sign. He always did that when he had something difficult to say.

"A childhood friend of yours has strayed from the path. Flame Ryan. She is here in Rampart, living with a savage."

Something roared in Cahill's ears. From far away, he heard the sound of his own voice shouting.

"I don't believe you!"

Reverend Marsh restrained him. "I'll take you there and you can see for yourself."

It felt like someone had died.

They walked in silence through the rain. The sun was coming up. They passed Silver's, the Dealy Sisters' Restaurant. At Julius Ramsdorf's store, they took the path that led around back. There was no light coming from the cabin. On the high fence next to the cabin, peas gleamed with water. The rain and long days had created an explosion of vegetables.

The minister paused at the door and turned kindly to Cahill. "Are you all right?"

"Yes."

Reverend Marsh knocked and opened the door.

Soft light was streaming through the windows. The room was small and furnished only with a table and chairs and stove. In the corner of the room were blankets, and on the blankets were two people.

She was sleeping. One arm flung over her head. Her hair was undone, and it glowed like a copper river in the sun.

The other sleeper was laying on his stomach, his face covered by hair.

It's a woman, Cahill thought. Has to be.

And then the other sleeper rolled over and jerked awake and Cahill found himself looking at a face from a nightmare.

"Nuka."

"Aggun!" Nuka reached for his knife.

Flame stirred in her sleep and her hand rested on Nuka's arm.

Such a small thing.

Such an intimate thing.

"Flame! What has happened to you!" Cahill dropped to his knees and buried his head in his hands.

Reverend Marsh touched Cahill's shoulder and whispered sternly, "Remember the sin of impulsiveness, Cahill. Don't do anything rash."

Cahill groaned loudly. "But it's Flame!" he cried. "You don't understand."

She opened her eyes and stared at the ceiling, half-awake. "Cahill?" she said wonderingly.

He groaned and dug his hands into his head.

She sat up swiftly and drew the blankets around her. Nuka flexed the knife and looked from the minister to Cahill and back again.

She stared at Cahill. The silence grew enormous. Finally she said, "A beard. You have a beard."

She was so beautiful, with the light washing over her, her arms pale and sculpted against the blankets. Cahill tried to speak and found he couldn't.

Reverend Marsh spoke rapidly to Nuka in Inupiaq.

Nuka stared at Cahill and shook his head, and Cahill could see the savage hated him still. Reverend Marsh said something else, gently. Nuka turned inquiringly to Flame.

"He doesn't want to leave you here with Cahill, Flame. He thinks he has to protect you."

Flame touched Nuka on the arm. "I'll be fine."

264

Nuka stared at her quietly—*into* her—and then flung the blankets away from his body and stood up. He was naked.

Cahill turned away. Something cold twisted inside him. Nuka dressed and walked outside without a word.

Reverend Marsh squeezed Cahill on the shoulder and followed Nuka, closing the door behind him.

Cahill looked around the room at everything but her. The silence grew.

He had never known such misery. A year had gone by and now they were alone. He thought of Kannik, of her simple eagerness to please him and the fight he had put up, resisting her. Oh, he had been so proud of his little victory! His head hurt, his stomach hurt. His heart hurt.

"I'd like to get dressed, please. If you don't mind."

They were strangers. He got up and sat down in a chair, his back to her. He heard her dressing and the sounds of the stove coming alive. He turned and looked at her.

She was indifferent to him, as if making coffee were much more absorbing than anything he could possibly say. She put the pot on the back burner.

"I missed you." It came out in spite of himself.

He watched her back, the way she held her shoulders, her body thin and sullen under the clothes. She had a bucket of sourdough started. She lifted out the dough and rammed her fist into it.

"You never wrote."

The arrogance of her words stung him.

"And you're right where you promised to be. Waiting in Seattle."

She didn't answer him at once but kept slamming the dough down, raising it up, hurling it down. "You didn't do much waiting, either."

"What's that supposed to mean?"

"That boat. Nelly."

He felt again the sweet sickness of his shame, and so picked it up as if it were a slimy mud ball and hurled it back at her, as hard as he could.

"You're a fine one to talk about Nelly! No decent woman would carry on the way you do. I've got half a mind to tell your parents myself. Your father'd whip the hide off of you."

Her hands stilled. She patted the dough in quick darting motions. "They're dead."

"Dead?" It wasn't possible. He got up and stood behind her. He touched her awkwardly.

She stiffened. "Do not touch me, Cahill. Do not."

He took his hands away. She punched down the dough.

"I'm sorry." He felt helpless. "What happened?"

She still hadn't looked at him. She put the dough in the pot and shifted it to the back of the stove. She pressed her finger against the coffeepot and jerked it back. "Coffee's ready."

She got two cups off the shelf and poured. She carried them back to the table and sat down across from him.

She said it with no expression. "Father died on the Dead Horse Trail and mother drowned in the White Horse Rapids."

Tears sprang to his eyes. She looked away. "I'm over the worst of it." She drank her coffee. "How are your parents?" It came out stiffly.

"Fine." Both parents dead! And he hadn't known.

"Your father's health?" The words came from a stranger who was determined to be pleasant.

"Failing. He had one attack, last spring. Just got the letter last week." He reached for her hand and stopped. "I'm so sorry about your parents."

Her face was hard and still, but her remarkable eyes looked at him with a softness he didn't expect. He felt his anger sliding down into hopelessness. "Why'd you do it, Flame?"

Her eyes flashed and she bit her lips hard and fiddled with the oil tablecloth. "People got tired of waiting for something that never happens."

"I was coming back!"

She looked at him quietly. "You never let me know."

"But the way we left— You had to know how I felt, Flame."

A vein quivered in her neck where the first button closed her shirt.

"I thought I knew how you felt. Once." She bent her head and drank, and Cahill saw the auburn curve of eyelashes against her cheek and felt the thick agony of arousal beginning.

"But living like an alley cat, Flame! Curling up in doorways,

266

going from man to man like a stinking, rutting animal. I can't stand to be near you, knowing what you are."

"Then get out of here." She said the words calmly, as if his life were no more important than a stray crumb on the table.

Fury welled up in him. For this he had suffered the agony of guilt-wracked nights? This was the woman for whom he had forsaken all others?

He rose and scattered the cups. They crashed to the floor. "No, Flame. I'm not leaving yet. Not by a long shot."

She got up and backed away from him. "What gives you the right to tell me how to live? Were you there when my father strangled on his own scum? Did you give your hand to my mother and pull her into the air? Or were you too busy trailing after a two-bit whore to write and tell me how faithful you were? You make me sick."

"At least I didn't crawl into bed with a savage."

She slapped him hard in the face. "You're a bastard."

"And you're a whore."

He stood perfectly still and the blood roared in his head.

He knew he had to get out of there, right now. Get out. Because if he didn't, he wouldn't stop until he had crushed her completely. He went to the door and opened it. It was raining hard. "Good-bye, Flame."

She went after him. "I'm not through."

"Nothing you say could change a thing. I've seen women like you. They're as common as weeds." The garden stretched ahead of him, through the rain, and he went into it.

"You might think you have the corner on fine words, Cahill Blue, but you haven't heard mine yet. And mine have something yours don't."

She was behind him, pulling on him.

"Let me go." He jerked his arm away and almost fell in the mud.

"Honesty."

"I'm warning you—"

"Did you think truth was something you could invent every day, Cahill? I'll tell you the truth, and I'll make it plain and clear. I loved you once, loved the man I thought you were. But you're not him anymore. Maybe you never were."

He whirled suddenly. "And Nuka is? I'll tell you something, Flame. I saved Nuka's life once. And I wish to hell I had let him bleed to death. He's nothing. He's worse than nothing."

"Leave Nuka out of this."

"You didn't."

She was soaked, her shirt clung to her breasts and her hair was matted against her head. "All right, if that's the way you want it. Nuka and I are lovers. He's wonderful. I should know—"

Cahill stalked away from her, deeper into the garden. "I don't want to hear it."

"When he takes me in his arms, he makes me do the most shameless things. He makes me forget I'm civilized—"

"*Shut up!*"

"You're nothing compared to him. I could never be satisfied with you. Nuka's a real man. Go back to your whores. It's what you deserve."

She stood snarling, her slight body and twisted face taunting him. The rage came boiling out. He pulled a nugget out of his pocket and hurled it at her. It struck her leg and bounced away. She flinched, and he saw the fear in her eyes. For an instant there was a small voice inside, telling him to stop, that what he was doing would take him into some swampland of the spirit, but then he looked at her face again and felt only bruised outrage at her betrayal. She backed away.

"Pick it up, Flame. The nugget. It's yours."

Her mouth worked and her small hands flew out from her body. He could see her nipples through the shirt. "Cahill—" She stumbled and righted herself. His rage mingled with desire.

"Pick it up. I always pay first. Just like any other john."

She whirled and ran. His hand shot out and grabbed her arm and he twisted her down. She clutched at a broken root, but it came up easily in the soft mud.

She would pay.

"Stop now." Her voice was hoarse and much too late.

"There is some honor among us, Flame. I never take anything that's not mine."

He lay on top of her and she struggled hard, beating him with

268

small fists. *"Please—"*

She was crying. *Good,* he thought grimly.

He separated her legs with his knee and pinned down her hands. Her hair tangled in the plants. She bucked under him, and he felt the length of her body. He was instantly hard.

He would show no mercy.

He ripped open her pants and wrenched them down. She had closed her eyes and she was sobbing.

"Tears won't work, Flame," he whispered. He ripped apart his buttons and pulled out his organ, pressing it roughly into the soft slit by touch. Her eyes widened with shock.

"You're hurting me." Tears coursed down her face.

She was trying one last lie. "You're wrong, Flame. Whores don't have feelings."

He rammed his way in and she screamed. His organ went in easily and stopped. He pushed again, harder, and felt her soft flesh slipping around him until he was lost in the awful sweetness of her body.

She will pay, he thought. She will pay and pay and pay.

He rocked over her, knowing she would want it to end quickly, and delaying it.

I loved you once, Flame Ryan. And now look what you are. Her hair was clogged with mud and she was sobbing soundlessly.

This is for all the nights I dreamed of you.

He shoved harder.

This is for the life we never had.

He felt his breath ragged in his throat.

This is for the love that died.

She wasn't moving anymore, and he felt a vicious satisfaction. He came hard, exploding in spasms. She lay under him, her face ashen. He kept coming until he could feel his own seed like a warm wound around his penis.

He was suddenly tired. His mouth felt dry. The rain was picking up. Flame sagged away from him.

This is for—. But the pictures had gone away. The rage was gone and the only thing he could see was her face, the way it had been that day on the dock with the cannons popping behind them and the balloons in the air and people cheering like he was a hero going off to war.

He looked at her now and knew he was going to cry, that no matter how he tried to hold down the sob it was going to rise up and strangle him. She lay beneath him, subdued, quiet, her breathing shallow. He had broken her. But there was no victory.

"Why did you do it, Flame, why?" he cried hoarsely, his voice foreign. He held her against him, his penis still inside her, and rocked her wildly until his shoulders shook and he sobbed. It was the harshest sound he had ever heard, and the loneliest.

"I loved you. I did. But whoring around, Flame—" He buried his head in her body and cried until he felt his penis stiffen again and he knew that no matter what she had done—what she had been or meant to someone else—he loved her, now, forever, always.

Still crying, he picked her up and carried her inside.

Twenty-Six

The rain cleared while he slept. He whuffled and snorted in his sleep, his hands flung out and one knee tucked up as if he were springing from dream to dream. He woke suddenly and reached for her. She wasn't there. He couldn't have dreamed it.

He sat up. Flame was sitting in a chair next to the stove. She was wearing a shirt and nothing else. He felt a stirring of desire. Her hair had dried and it fell in auburn waves over her shoulders. She was staring out the window.

"Darling." It felt wonderful saying it. "Darling Flame."

She turned and looked at him, her eyes green pools of light. He could stare at her forever and never tire of her face. The night came back, and with it, the memory that she had been weeping. He got up and put on his shirt and pants. Today was a splendid day—a day to right wrongs, a wedding day. He stood in front of her, dropped to his knees and took her hand. "Flame, about last night—"

Her hand trembled.

"I'm sorry if I hurt you. I'll never hurt you again. Ever. I swear it."

She was perfectly quiet, almost as if she hadn't heard him.

"Let's go to Reverend Marsh. I always wanted him to do the service. Ever since I was little."

She sighed deeply and twisted her head so that she was staring out the window. She took her hand away.

"I'm asking you to marry me, Flame, the best way I know how."

But still there was that awful silence. A whistle blew on the river, three long mournful notes. His boat. He had forgotten completely about it. They could book passage on a later one, one with married quarters.

271

"Listen to me, Flame," he said gently. "What I did on the boat with Nelly was just as bad as whatever happened between you and the savage—or any other man. But I'm carrying out almost nine thousand dollars. That's enough to help us both forget the past. We'll never talk about it again. Ever."

He wanted to touch her. But she pulled stiffly away from him when he tried. "No one will ever know what you were. That's all behind us."

She fitted her chin into her knees and Cahill marveled at how soft and rounded they were compared to the angles of her face. He wanted to write sonnets for her, climb mountains or snatch a child from death in her name, not knowing that all men feel that dizzying wave of splendor at the first. He only knew that she was fragile and lovelier than any dream, and that the miracle of her made him suddenly powerful, grand and immortal.

He touched her and she didn't pull away, but she bowed her head and started to cry. The sound was chillingly quiet, as if she were alone, not only in the cabin but in the world, with nothing to hope for.

"Flame, I'm here. There's no reason to cry." But that only made her cry harder. He fumbled for her hand and missed.

"Talk to me." It was a plea, not a command, borne on a wave of growing alarm. Something was wrong.

"Flame, I love you. I always have." There it was. He had thrown down his last card, squandered his final nickel and now he stood waiting, a beggar at her door.

After a long silence she turned and her eyes were bright red and green. Fear clutched his heart. "Do you love me?"

She stared at him soberly, and then past him out the window.

Her face was horribly neutral and he felt the way he had when he was ten and his mother had come into his room to tell him his grandfather was finally dead.

He had known already, before his mother spoke, that the life had gone out of the upstairs room. When he saw her, he could feel it in her body, the way she composed her hands, but until she actually said the words, there was the wild hope that maybe at the last moment, she could change the words into flowers.

It hadn't worked then and he knew with a dreadful certainty it wouldn't work now, so he waited for Flame to speak and hoped she never would.

She opened her mouth and uttered the most terrible words he had ever heard.

"I used to love you."

"And now?" His heart pressed wildly in his chest.

She looked at him with infinite sadness and shook her head. That was all. He felt as if his chest had been crushed in. He stumbled against the window.

"Is there anything I can do to change your mind?"

She looked at him and lowered her eyes.

Tears blurred his eyes. He sat down heavily and planted his hands to steady himself. She couldn't be gone. He couldn't live if she were gone from him. "Tell me what I can do," he beseeched, holding out his hands. She sat perfectly still, her head bowed, her hands folded, the way a widow would sit. Then he saw it. Blood on the bottom of her shirt.

"Flame, are you bleeding?" His voice was stiff with wonder. "Did I hurt you?"

She didn't speak, but something—the bruised look in her eyes, the way her head lowered—made him suspect the truth.

And then he knew.

He had taken something fine and broken it. Flame had been what she claimed to be: sterling, solid, pure. But it wasn't the fact of her virginity that made what he had done so wrong. It was that he had even tried at all. She was *Flame,* and he had forgotten it. He sensed in that terrible moment something rare and unrepeatable in her, and knew that if he lost her, he would spend the rest of his life looking for her in every woman he met, and never finding her again.

He learned then what lovers always come painfully to know: the world is not full of limitless possibilities. The world is full of people you could never grow to love, not in a deep abiding way. Among them are a few whose heart could answer your own, but only a few, and they are hidden and hard to find. The lucky ones find that one other person, whose heart strikes something in theirs. If they're luckier still, they realize how lucky they are, and spend their life protecting what they have

273

from all comers. For they will come, the lonely and heartsick and jaded, who see the love shining and want to squirm somewhere inside the magic circle.

Cahill wanted then, wished it with all of his heart, to be one of the lucky ones.

"I love you," he said again. But it was said mournfully this time.

She reached for him and wrapped her thin arms around him and he held her tightly. He thought that maybe it would work after all, and something leaped inside him, but then she shifted her arms and patted him and he knew. She was comforting him, nothing else.

He pulled away from her. "Will you ever change your mind?" he asked hoarsely.

She stared at him tenderly, and Cahill sensed that even now she was considering his feelings. It occurred to him that he could use her goodness to force her to stay, but immediately he threw the thought out. No, this was her choice, and hers alone.

In the end it was her goodness that spoke.

"There is no hope for us, ever."

He dropped his hands to his sides and she released him. She got up and went to her pack and sorted through until she found a pair of pants. There was a sexlessness about her movements. In her mind she was already somewhere else.

He watched her button her pants. Brush her hair and wind it into a braid. He watched her walk through the door and into the garden, her steps confident and remote. He watched the sunlight construct patterns on the table.

The sun was hot, and by ten the water had burned off the garden, but Flame was cold inside, bone cold. Her body ached. Not just the place between her limbs, but her head and throat and chest. She felt tears behind her eyes and thought, I'll never cry again, after today.

Nuka came back midmorning and sensed she wanted to be left alone. He immediately retreated to the river to fish. Mrs. Ramsdorf carried a bucket down the hill at lunch and went home again. Children screamed with joy in far-off games; the river whispered.

274

Only the mine was left. When things got bad, she'd think of it over and over until she stopped thinking again.

It was gone. All of it gone. Ahead of her stretched nothing. Years of nothing. So she worked in the garden, pulling radishes, and thought very hard of nothing at all.

Cahill stumbled to the dock. He remembered that he was supposed to go home; his father wasn't well. He repeated the words, but they didn't make sense. His steamer had already left. He sat on a crate by the river and watched the boats come and go. Midmorning, an old man timidly asked him to help him unload some boxes. Cahill was too absorbed in his own misery to protest. He hauled the boxes off the steamer and loaded them in a horse-drawn wagon the old man had rented to take him to town. Then he sat back down. Late in the day, an army man found him.

"Cahill Blue?"

Cahill nodded. The sergeant pulled out handcuffs and clicked one around Cahill's wrist. It happened so quickly he didn't have time to respond. The sergeant clamped the second set around his own wrist. Cahill saw he didn't have a thumb.

"What is this about?"

"I am arresting you, sir, on charges of breach of contract."

"I demand you remove these cuffs at once!"

"You will be taken before a jury of your peers and judged."

"I don't know who you are, but if you value a career with the United States Army, remove these cuffs at once. My father personally knows Lieutenant Edwin Bell, commander of this post."

"You should have lots to discuss then. Lieutenant Bell ordered this himself."

It was a long march up the street from the dock to the army barracks, made longer still by the crowd of men thronging behind him.

Sergeant Dillard took Cahill into the mess hall where a small platform had been built. The room filled up. They sat on tables.

Sergeant Dillard led Cahill to a chair on stage and removed the cuffs.

He walked to the podium and cleared his throat. Bodies

shifted, boots scraped. "The defendant has been charged with seduction under promise of marriage."

Cahill sprang to his feet. "Seduction—"

"*Silence!* You will have your turn." Sergeant Dillard rubbed the pad where his thumb had been. "The plaintiff wishes only fair retribution. She seeks not money nor a prison term for the defendant, but the sacrament of marriage." He turned sideways and said gently, "All right, Nelly. You may come forward."

Nelly walked out of a side room and onto the platform. She was dressed simply in a demure brown wool, and even her curls lay more smoothly against her head. The effect was a stunning combination of sensuality and modesty.

"Nelly—" He held out his hand in a kindly way. "Don't be afraid. We're going to get to the bottom of this, once and for all."

She kept her eyes down as Sergeant Dillard led her to the podium. He looked intently into the faces of the men.

"Some of you might know Miss Nelly in another context. Know her well. But remember as this testimony is given that we judge women hastily and remember how few avenues are open for honest employment after a victim is seduced and abandoned." He turned to Nelly. "I'll ask the questions. Please answer them as thoroughly as possible."

She nodded. Sergeant Dillard turned and pointed at Cahill on his chair. "Do you know this man?"

Nelly stared soberly at him, and Cahill watched in utter disbelief as her eyes filled with tears. "*Oui.*"

"In what context?"

"I met him on the boat, coming from Seattle."

Dillard snapped a handkerchief out of his pocket. He presented it formally to Nelly. "Tell me what happened."

Nelly's lips trembled. "I just want a happy family. That has been my only dream. Since a little girl." She looked helplessly at him and fluttered her eyelashes. "I am new in this country. Forgive my English."

"You speak beautifully," Sergeant Dillard said. "Go on with your story."

"Nelly was—how you say it?—going to teach French. And

276

then she meets this—" She paused and dabbed her eyes. "It is too painful!" she cried.

Sergeant Dillard glared at Cahill and patted her shoulder. "I'm sorry to put you through this, Nelly, but it can't be helped."

Cahill sprang to his feet. "I demand this farce be stopped at once! She was a whore when I met her, and a whore she'll be until she dies!"

Two miners leaped onto the stage and pushed him back into his chair. "We got a code here," one of them explained. He had a flat nose and an even flatter fist. He thumbed Cahill on the forehead. "You're not doing your side any good at all."

"If Mr. Blue will permit," Sergeant Dillard said crisply. He turned to Nelly. "So what happened on the boat?"

She clasped her hands together. "Everything."

Five men moved off the back tables and sat closer.

"Everything?"

Nelly nodded and looked down at her hands.

Sergeant Dillard paced around the podium, his hands clasped behind his back. "Nelly, how old are you?"

"Twenty."

"What kind of a family do you have in Belgium?"

"The best," she said fervently. "My father is a law clerk at Liège and my mother is a saint."

"So from this law clerk and this saint was produced"—he lowered his voice dramatically—"a fallen angel."

Nelly stared at Cahill, her face stricken. "Yes," she said bravely to Dillard. "It is true. After Cahill, I fell in with, how do you say it—"

"Bad company," Sergeant Dillard supplied. He glared at Cahill again. "Yes. I can see how that would happen. A young, naive girl, new in this country—"

"Cahill seemed like such an honest man. When he told me he loved me"—she shrugged helplessly—"of course I believed him."

"Of course."

"Sergeant, you don't understand!" Cahill blurted out. "She's a tramp, a whore, a lying, cheating—"

This time Sergeant Dillard didn't have to respond. The men

on either side of Cahill bent his arms back until the sockets hurt. "Another word from you, and your arm goes home in a box," the one with the boxer's nose whispered.

Cahill snapped his mouth shut.

"So, Cahill Blue promised to marry you and on that basis, he took advantage of a pure young girl. He *seduced* you. Not *once*, but over and over again." His voice dropped. "He didn't marry you, did he, Nelly?"

She shook her head, dry eyed. "He left me in Dyea. At first I waited for him, until my money went. And then there was nowhere else to turn—"

She began to cry in earnest.

Dillard put his arm gently around her shoulders and led her to a chair. He walked erect toward the audience. "You may bring the defendant forward."

The men lifted Cahill to his feet and brought him to Dillard. "You are Cahill Blue?"

The two miners still had hold of Cahill's arms. He nodded.

"Speak up, man!"

"Yes. My name is Cahill Blue." He shook himself free and rubbed his wrists.

"Do you know the plaintiff?"

Cahill stared at her with hatred. "I knew her, all right. She's a—"

"Mr. Blue," Sergeant Dillard said coldly. "This is a historic meeting. This is the first time the miners' association and the military have gathered to mete our justice. May I suggest that you are not garnering sympathy by your continued abuse of the plaintiff. So, you don't deny you know the plaintiff."

"No."

"Do you deny that you used this woman for your own pleasure?"

Cahill thought quickly. Who was to say what had happened? It was his word against hers. "I didn't do anything to her." He straightened his back and looked out over the audience.

Nelly gasped. "It is a lie!"

"*Nothing?* You did *nothing* to this woman?"

"I carried her trunk to the room, it is true."

Dillard smiled incredulously. "You honestly expect us to

278

believe that was all there was to it?"

Cahill remained silent.

"You never saw her again?" he prodded.

"The boat was small. Naturally I saw her—"

"But never alone. You never put your arms around her, say, or kissed her—"

"Never." Cahill's voice was firm.

"I'm going to ask it one more time," Dillard said. "And I want you to think very carefully before you answer." He circled Cahill. "Did you *ever* kiss Nelly Smith?"

"Never."

"Did you ever put your arms around her?"

"Never."

Dillard walked to the edge of the platform. "I would like to call Jacob Plenut to the stand."

The miners looked around expectantly.

From the side door, a graying stoop-shouldered man backed onto the platform, dragging boxes and a tripod. It was the man Cahill had helped earlier in the day.

He pulled the equipment next to the podium and straightened up, his cheeks pink from exertion.

"Jacob Plenut, would you tell these men your occupation."

"Photographer."

"Have you ever seen the defendant?"

Jacob looked at Cahill and said easily, "Yes, sir. I saw him today."

"You saw him today." Dillard walked around the podium and looked at the ceiling.

"Yes, sir. He was at the dock, watching the boats. He helped me take my gear off."

Cahill was getting impatient. "Sergeant, I fail to see what this has to do with—"

"Was today the first time you saw the defendant?"

Jacob Plenut tweaked his nose and the gray hairs in his nostrils quivered. "Oh, no, sir."

Dillard faced the audience. "Would you tell this body on what other occasion you saw the defendant?"

Jacob turned and said to Cahill, "You know, it bothered me. I pride myself on never forgetting a face. I knew I had seen you before, and all day long it ate at me. I was at Silver's today, taking portraits, and that's where I put it together."

A feeling of dread was growing in Cahill. "Get to the point."

"All right," Jacob said humbly. He pointed at Nelly. "It came back when I saw her. I remembered then where I'd seen you before." He turned to Cahill. "It was on the boat."

"The boat?"

"The *Solid Gold Idea*." He turned to the audience. "I came across from Seattle on the same boat. I remember thinking they must be newlyweds, since we saw them so rarely, and when we did, they could never keep their hands off each other."

The color drained from Cahill's face. "That's a lie."

"Let me get this straight," Dillard said. "You saw Cahill Blue and Nelly Smith—" he pointed at each in turn—"these two people on the boat and they appeared to be very much in love."

"Very much."

"Did you take any pictures?"

Jacob Plenut nodded. "There was the tintype, of course."

"Tintype?"

"It's a cousin to the ambrotype, which, of course, is the daughter of a collodion-based, light-sensitive emulsion—"

"I'm sure it's all very fascinating," Dillard said. "But perhaps you could move along."

"Yes, of course." Jacob began dismantling the box on the floor. "The tintype is small, and it's exposed inside the camera. On the plus side—" He was setting up a huge bulky tripod, snapping it into place. "It's inexpensive, easily produced and small enough to fit inside a piece of jewelry."

Cahill put his hand in his pocket and felt for the locket.

"So you took a tintype of the two of them together."

"That's correct." Jacob opened a smaller box and lifted out a camera. He positioned it on the tripod.

"What happened to the picture?"

"I gave it to Miss Nelly. As a present."

Dillard turned to Nelly. "You still have the picture?"

Nelly lifted her tearstained face. "Cahill took it from me."

Cahill sensed the crowd turning on him. He was running out

280

of time. He sifted through his pockets and found it under his watch and a few coins.

"I don't know what she's talking about."

"Hand it over!" Dillard said.

"I don't have it! I never *did* have it." He worked his fingers around the heart and squeezed. The locket sprang apart. Why hadn't he looked inside? Of course Nelly would have put the picture there. How else would Flame have known about them? He scraped the tiny picture with his finger.

Dillard was watching him. "What are you doing?"

"What do you mean, *What am I doing?* I'm defending myself against slanderous lies." He scraped harder.

"No. There. In your pocket."

"Nothing."

"Go through this man's pocket," Dillard ordered. The two hulks on either side of Cahill obliged.

"Aha!" Dillard sprang at the locket and lifted it triumphantly.

"That is it!" Nelly cried. "That is where the picture went!"

Dillard examined the photograph in the locket. His look of glee faded. In the photograph Cahill's face was still visible, but through the face of the woman was a long scratch.

"It was my mother," Cahill explained. "Best she ever looked."

"The negative then," Dillard said to the photographer. "What about that?"

Jacob Plenut shrugged regretfully. "That's the negative part about tintypes. There's no negative." He paused. "Get it? The negative thing about tintypes is that there's no—"

"Then there's no way of proving they were together." Dillard stalked up and down, whapping his fist against his palm.

A wail went up from Nelly. For the first time that day, Cahill felt hopeful.

Jacob Plenut opened a thin metal box and removed a large glass plate. He rested it carefully on the podium. "Here is the proof you seek."

The audience murmured.

"The tintype was only one of the cameras I brought. This is

281

the negative for a mammoth wet-plate camera." He paused. "It was developed in a bath of pyrogallic acid and fixed in sodium thiosulfate. Washed in clear water, of course, afterward."

"This negative—what is on it?"

"Why, Cahill and Nelly, of course."

Cahill reached over and thunked against the glass.

It wobbled on the podium. Then it fell crashing to the ground and splintered apart. Jacob Plenut ran around and tenderly cradled the pieces in his arms. *"Murderer!"*

"It was an accident," Cahill said.

The miners on either side of him lifted Cahill and carried him back to his seat.

"Gentlemen of the jury," Dillard said. "You have seen for yourself the way Cahill Blue has tried to obstruct justice—first by denying his involvement with Nelly Smith, and then by destroying the only solid evidence against him."

"That's not the only evidence," Jacob interrupted. He was scraping the silver nitrate pieces into a pile.

"It isn't?"

He lifted the glass pieces into the box. "I took the liberty of printing one up."

"You have a picture of the two of them?"

"Of course." He wiped off his hands and went through another box. The miners leaned forward.

"Why didn't you say so in the first place?" Dillard said.

Jacob looked at him with dignity. "You never asked." He pulled out a long paper tube. "If I could have two volunteers from the audience—"

Two miners stepped onto the stage.

"Hold up your arms." The men held up the paper and Jacob unwound it.

It was large: 5-1/2 by 7 feet. In 1869, the union of the Central Pacific and Union Pacific Railroads at Promontory Point, Utah, had been documented with the mammoth wet plate camera.

Jacob Plenut had documented another promontory; another union. Cahill had his arms around her. She was backed into him. There was a look of total ecstasy on his face. It also showed clearly that his hands were in a place where they shouldn't be, where they certainly *wouldn't* be, if Nelly and Cahill hadn't known each other very well.

The crowd grew perfectly still. Cahill felt the sweat roll down his arms.

"I rest my case," Dillard said. "The jury may now convene."

It was getting dark when Julius came down the hill. He poked in the radish barrels, checked the lettuce.

"Brought you a sandwich." He handed it to Flame. "Chicken."

As she bit into it, she realized she hadn't eaten since noon the day before. Julius settled himself down and cleared a spot for Flame. It felt good to sit in the cool dusk, the air heavy with insects, good to sit and feel nothing.

"All right," Julius said finally. "Out with it."

"Out with what?" But the sandwich was suddenly dry.

Julius picked a leaf apart. "I haven't been the father of six girls for nothing. I know misery when I see it, Flame."

He waited some more, and they sat and watched a raven picking apart a fishbone on the edge of the garden. It shifted from foot to foot, watching them with a bright eye.

"Has anybody ever hurt you so badly it changed you forever?" she asked suddenly.

"You mean a woman?"

Flame nodded.

"Once."

"Did you leave her?"

He was quiet, his thick hand nubbing a stem. "No, Flame. I married her."

"Why?"

Julius smiled briefly. "Why does anybody get married?"

"But she hurt you," Flame persisted.

"Flame, loving somebody opens up a person to all the glory and wonder of the universe. It also makes them bleed. Can't be much of a love if it doesn't have the power to kill you."

"But that's terrible! It gives everybody a license to hurt the people they say they love the most."

"Oh, but that's where the glory comes in. Real love is

283

knowing you have the power of life and death over somebody, and being very careful not to use it. Most people use it once, by accident, but if they're lucky, the love survives and mends over the bad place. It's never the same as new, Flame. But it can hold together, even stronger sometimes than it was."

"But what if she had hurt you so badly there was no going back?"

"None of us can ever go back. If you can't go forward, that's another story."

Flame mulled it over in her mind and said finally. "But how do you know it won't happen again? I mean, if you go forward."

"You can't. That's what makes love such a risky business."

A raven sailed by, its beak drooping with secondhand food.

"I wish there was some way to know."

"Have you tried asking yourself some questions and taking hard looks at the answers? That one works for me."

"All I ever *do* is ask questions, but nothing comes."

Julius looked at the clouds. The sky was turning red between the slats in the fence where the peas grew. "Might be you're asking the wrong questions," he said mildly.

Flame tore off a piece of crust and threw it toward the raven. "What kinds of questions?"

"Well, does the person you picked to love make you feel grander and more yourself, or mean and small and afraid?"

"And should he feel the same way about you?"

"No, that's where things start to go wrong. Only the other person can ask *himself* questions. You've got plenty to do just answering your own."

"Then maybe he'll never know how much he hurt you."

"In a good love, the pain he caused should rattle his teeth and loosen his grip on life momentarily."

"I don't understand." The raven lifted off again, the crust in its beak, on its way to some hoarding place.

"If he can't feel what you felt when he hurt you, then it's no good either. If he doesn't see how hard it was for you to come back and take up his hand again in yours, if he doesn't feel humbled by your love and courage, then it's no good."

Flame took another bite of sandwich. "I've seen some pretty

weak people pretend to be mighty hurt, just to keep somebody."

Julius nodded. "It happens like that, sometimes. A weak person clings to somebody stronger. Whining, always whining. But when that happens, the truth is that the stronger one only *looks* stronger. He needs the misery as much as the weak one; otherwise, he'd throw off the thing and get on with his life. That's just fear, Flame. Not love."

Flame finished her sandwich in silence. "Say a person loves somebody else," she said slowly, "another strong person, and hurts her— And if his teeth rattle like you said. What then?"

"It's anybody's guess," Julius said gently. "Love is a peculiar journey. It's different for everybody."

"But it's so different than I thought it would be!" she protested.

"It always is, Flame. It always is." He got up and wiped off the back of his pants. Flame got up too.

"Tomorrow—" she said slowly.

"Yes?"

"Tomorrow I might be late, Mr. Ramsdorf. I have some business to take care of."

He didn't seem surprised. "Take the whole day, if you like. You're ahead of schedule as it is."

She walked quickly out of the garden, turned, and called to him. "Mr. Ramsdorf!"

"Yes?"

"Thank you." She turned and ran down the path.

She found him at the Mayo Hotel, in the bar. She worked her way past the crowded gaming tables: craps, chuck-luck, studhorse poker, blackjack, faro. His back was toward her and he was in the middle of a roistering group of men. The bar was walnut with a brass footrail. Heavy gilt-edged mirrors hung behind it, and Flame could see his face reflected in the dim light. He didn't look happy. A soldier was standing next to him, laughing. Cahill took a long drink and looked in the mirror, idly. Their eyes met. He put down his bottle and turned around. The soldier pulled on his arm. Cahill shook him off and pushed his way over to her.

Flame wrapped her arms around his body and kissed him hungrily. There was only the two of them.

His face was going through rapid-fire changes: she could see the love there, but it crumbled into pain and twisted wildly into something else.

They had to get out of there. Had to talk. She pulled away from him. "Let's go outside."

He looked around once, as if he was trying to get his bearings, and then stumbled after her.

It was cold outside and she pulled both his hands into her pockets to warm them. They stood facing each other.

"Flame, I— There's something I have to tell you." Lanterns had been strung above the door of the Mayo Hotel, and Cahill's face was unnaturally pale.

"Hush, darling. First hear what I have to say." She squeezed his hands. "I love you, Cahill. Nothing can change what happened between us, but now I want to go on with our lives. I love you. I want to be your wife and have your children." She reached up and kissed him tenderly and it was like they had never been apart. "Let's get married tonight. Just like you wanted, with Reverend Marsh doing the service."

Tears came to his eyes. He pulled his hands out of her pockets and crushed her against him. "Remember that I love you," he cried hoarsely. "I always will. Only you."

The door to the hotel opened and someone came out.

"*So!* It is *you!*"

Flame looked over Cahill's shoulder. It was Nelly. She advanced on them, her face white with fury.

"Hello, Nelly." Even she couldn't spoil this moment. Flame saw her for what she was: the garish mouth, the flounced skirt muddied along the hem, the shrill whining voice.

"For one minute, Nelly leaves to visit the powder room, and poof! You are gone! And to think Nelly finds you *here* with this—"

"Nelly!" he said sharply. He looked sick.

Flame patted Cahill's cheek. "It's all right." Love made her reckless. "She won't be in our life at all, after tonight."

Nelly looked sharply from one to the other. "Tonight? What is happening tonight?"

286

Flame smiled coldly. "I am getting married tonight. In a very small, very private ceremony."

Nelly licked her lips. "A marriage always has two."

"You're very good at math, Nelly, but you're still a loser."

"Flame—" Cahill's voice was strange.

Flame touched his arm. "Don't worry, sweetheart. She can't hurt me, not ever again."

"What do you mean, loser?" Nelly's eyes narrowed.

"You didn't get him after all. We're going to be married tonight. Cahill and I."

Nelly regained her composure. She fanned her face with her hand. "That's quite impossible, I'm afraid."

"What do you mean?"

Nelly smiled at her indulgently. "Even Rampart has laws against such things. Cahill is already married to me."

Flame felt herself falling. Someone caught her and laid her gently on the planks covering the muddy ground. She could hear voices coming in waves.

"You mean you didn't tell her?" Nelly laughed. "Cahill, how truly wicked! We are alike, you and I."

"Stop it, Nelly." His voice was full of loathing. "You got what you wanted."

"Almost. It would have been wonderful if Flame had died just now from the shock. But even Nelly cannot have it all."

"You are a monster."

"*Oui*," she calmly agreed. "But you have a lifetime, Cahill, to get used to it."

"Leave us alone, Nelly." It was a command.

Nelly sucked in her breath. "All right." She minced back a step. "But I'll be right here. A wife's place is near her husband. Yes?"

Flame opened her eyes. It had to be a mistake. A terrible mistake. Cahill was bending over her.

"It's not true," she whispered.

He had tears in his eyes. He nodded.

"Why?" she burst out.

He picked up her hand and told her what had happened.

*   *   *

287

The jury had been out ten minutes. The foreman read in a monotone: "We find the defendant, Cahill Blue, guilty as charged of breach of promise, and rule in favor of Nelly Smith." He raised his eyes. "There's a precedent here we took into account. Doe versus Roe in Circle City last year."

He resumed reading. "The undersigned jurors order that said defendant marry Nelly Smith. If he doesn't, this jury orders him fined nine thousand dollars and held one year in the barracks at Rampart, and in case he doesn't pay the fine, that he be jailed in same for a period of no less than five years."

Cahill felt the blood leave his face. Nine thousand dollars! Or five years in jail. He got unsteadily to his feet.

"Well, man, what will it be?" Vindication shone on Dillard's face.

"Reverend Marsh is staying at the Mayo Hotel," Cahill said heavily. "Room three."

Flame was perfectly still. "Reverend Marsh performed the ceremony?" She was trying to understand.

Cahill looked back once at Nelly and said urgently, "Listen to me. I don't have much time. I'm leaving tomorrow for Seattle. I'm going to have the marriage annulled. I'll be back for you. I swear it."

He kissed her and then Nelly was standing there, and he shuddered and took her arm.

Twenty-Seven

In Julius Ramsdorf's store were barrels of potatoes and rolled oats, bags of flour and tins of sugar. Dog harnesses hung on the wall next to the door, and on the shelf behind the filigreed cash register was a locked cabinet. On it was the sign:

Any one giving whiskey to the Indians
will be Hung
Order of the Rampart Miners Association

There were boots and belts and bolts of calico, jars of chewing tobacco and bars of lye. On the sides of the window were shelves holding mining equipment: chisels, jack planes, gold pans, granite buckets, hammers. The floor was banked with crates of supplies that had just arrived on the NC Company boat.

Julius looked up briefly when the door tinkled open and thumbed toward the stove. "Put it over there."

Nuka threaded his way through the crates and dropped the armload of kindling into the box. The stove was smoking slightly and the air was acrid. He went back to the door, pretended to open it, and when Julius started working out the nails on the far side of a crate, he crept quickly through the crates to the neat row of guns hanging under a sign:

No Dogs, Drunks or Indians allowed
Order of the Rmpt. Mnrs. Ass.

He had been planning it for a week, since the first time he saw the guns. It took less than a minute to shove the gun and a box of bullets under his jacket, steal through the crates, pinch

289

the bell quiet and escape.

The Indian came down out of the iron red hills, scattering gold leaves and crushing wild cranberries and celery underfoot. On his back he wore a leather pouch of skins. He stayed clear of the army barracks. He went to the door of Julius's store and knocked. Then he withdrew and arranged the skins on the ground. He had four wolfskins, a string of marten and ten red foxtails. Also a box of red paint-stone. The whites were fond of drawing.

Now he reviewed his own list: a copper teapot, sewing thread, a hatchet, flour and a bolt of calico. Was there something else? Oh, yes. The tea.

A native was working in a bank of birch nearby, cutting firewood. He favored his right arm and Senati looked at him curiously. Not an Indian. He wasn't big enough and his cheeks were broad. Eskimo—had to be. He was familiar looking, too, but then, all Eskimos looked alike.

Senati picked up a red paint-stone and examined it idly as the Eskimo carried a load of firewood to the door. They stared at each other; the Eskimo dropped the wood and drew a gun from his pocket, and then Senati remembered where he had seen him.

Julius walked outside, wiping his hands on the paunch of apron.

"Senati?" He took in the tumbled wood and abandoned furs buzzing with flies. "Senati?" he called again. He sighed and picked up the furs and carried them inside.

The rain had turned to *apun* before they crested the first rise. It was only a light dusting, a *katiksunik*. Below them in the valley was a swollen creek. Tethered nearby a canoe.

"I will not run," the Indian said quietly.

"You are filth," Nuka spat. "There will be no words between us except those that are needed for life's functions. You are my prisoner. Once we find the encampment where my sister has been held hostage, a trade will be made. Your life for hers. But do not run. This is a warning. My life had no meaning apart from this. If you run, you will be hunted and trapped like the caribou you run into fences. The first time your tongue will be cut out. If you persist, the digits of your hand will be severed. And know this, Indian, you will be found. There is nothing ahead, all the years of my life, but to find you and kill you slowly."

"Do you not wish to hear how she is?"

"There is only one wish that burns in my heart. To see her and hear from her own lips which of you deserves to die." Nuka pressed the gun into his back. "Indian, someone has dreamed of this moment and the moment is sweet. Where is she?"

The Indian looked at him in silence.

"Where is she?" Nuka prodded him with the gun.

"She is at the fall encampment. Two miles above Morelock Creek and six miles below the rapids."

"How far?"

"One sleep."

"We will move through the night and be there tomorrow."

"As you wish."

"And do not expect me to be taken in by your meek words!"

The Indian did not answer, but Nuka thought he smiled slightly. It enraged him.

"Do not make me kill you now."

The Indian laughed. "Do it. And then you will never find her."

Nuka butted him hard with the end of the gun and the Indian staggered and almost fell.

They moved single file through the sifting snow, the dogs plunging down the tall grass to the boat. Senati untied the boat from the tangle of willows and got in. Nuka and the dogs followed.

"Does the Indian have a name?"

"Senati." He raised his head proudly.

"Be swift, Senati."

It was the last time they spoke.

The cliff of red paint-stone reared over the moss-covered huts. The first snow had melted and the ground sank under

291

them as they pulled the canoe ashore. Ice ran in the creek. The huts had been built along a lip of sand. It was dim, dark, unwholesome. So this was where Kannik had survived the terror of the kidnapping. Here, with no airy expanse of ocean, no marshy freedom for wandering. His anger surged and he pressed Senati's hands together, pushed the Indian to his knees and held the gun against his head. "One sound and you die."

They crawled forward.

A bearskin covered the entryway; the floor was moss, the walls birch bark. Caribou fat glowed in stone bowls on either side of the main room, giving off a thick and pasty yellow light. Light glowed through the caribou-gut skylight. In one corner an iron stove balanced on four flat rocks and the stovepipe jutted through the sod ceiling. They stood up in the main room and Nuka saw a woman on skins in the corner.

She turned, exhaled her breath, sighed in her sleep.

Tears sprang to his eyes. He had found his sister. He blinked rapidly. It was not seemly to meet her in tears.

Nuka lashed Senati's hands to the stovepipe and went slowly to the furs and knelt down.

She opened her eyes. She turned her head. They stared at each other. And then he pulled her roughly to him, and she cried out and clung to him. They embraced, and he pushed her away and looked at her. She was older and thinner than he remembered and there were bruised shadows under her eyes. She had threaded quills and beads into her hair.

"I knew you would come." She spoke Inupiaq.

"Kannik, someone has come to take you home."

She looked tenderly at him. "I am home, Nuka."

"Here?"

She looked past him at Senati. "You have met Senati. You understand." Then she saw he was tied, and she scrambled to her feet. "How can this be? What have you done?" She ran to him.

"Leave him, Kannik. Give me the slightest reason to kill him and it will be done. He is an animal."

"He is my *husband.*"

The words caught Nuka with the force of a bullet and he

292

sagged backward. "Your eyes have been blinded. When we reach the sea, you will see them as they are."

She was untying the rope around Senati's wrists. "I will never see the ocean again, or the place where the whales play. I have left my other life behind, and it has melted from me, like a skin of ice that no longer can contain the rushing water beneath. Believe me, I would have killed him gladly once. But that was long ago."

A faint whimper came from the corner. At last Nuka understood. Kannik went to a box behind a stretching rack and carried back an infant.

The baby stared fixedly at Nuka. It had perfect features and no hair.

"See? He knows you already." She touched the delicate amber cheek and the babe turned blindly toward her finger, sucking. "His name is Pana."

Nuka looked sharply at her. "You summon the spirit of father to live in this child?"

"If father lives again in his grandson, it is a second chance for me. So many things were left unhealed the last time he lived."

"Wrap him. We'll take him with us."

She shook her head. "This is my home, and here I will stay."

"You will do as you are told!" Nuka flared. Senati moved toward him and Kannik stepped between them. "Stop! Both of you."

A man was crawling through the entryway and when he stood up in the main room, Kannik went to his side and gave him the child. He swung the infant into the air and said in Athapaskan, "And how is my son?"

Nuka looked from one man to the other. "Nuka does not understand."

Kannik kissed the second man. "This is Shanyaati. My husband."

Nuka stepped backwards, steadied himself. "Kannik. *Two* husbands?"

She spoke rapidly. Shanyaati handed her the infant, and the men bowed and left the room.

Kannik sat on a caribou hammock and unfastened the quill

293

buttons on her tunic. She put the child to her breast. Nuka looked at her as if she had grown talons and a tail.

"Remember the time father shared mother with the whaling captain from the next village?"

"Of course," Nuka snapped. "It was the old way."

"Then you will understand. This is still the old way. To share the wealth." Her infant was staring at her over the pale expanse of breast, its eyes large, unblinking. She stroked his ear and cooed.

"But—are you passed around from hand to hand like—a dog bone?" He was beside himself.

"Of course not, silly. *I* decide. *I* choose. I picked the two best hunters, the two best lovers in the village. Senati is chief," she said proudly. "And now I sleep between them, so I never get cold at night."

She shrugged and stroked her hair languidly. "*I* going to stay here my whole life."

Nuka didn't know what to say. He felt sick. The baby was sucking greedily; the milk was coming out so quickly he was making little gulping noises as he swallowed.

"What happens when your child is weaned? Remember the words of the eaters-of-flesh? You could still die."

"Those women were wrong, Nuka. Senati and his men did not want them, and they were jealous."

"Then what happened to their own women?"

Kannik worked her finger into the small fist. "Senati lost his wife when the missionaries came. Measles, it was called. The men had to find women to suckle the children or the village would have been lost."

She lifted her child, wiped spittle from its mouth with her finger and burped him over her shoulder.

"There are closer villages. Other women."

"Shanyaati and Senati are tied by blood. They wanted to make strong children from undiluted blood."

"There is nothing that could be said to change your mind?"

"I love them," she said simply. She took her brother's hand in hers and squeezed it. "Your arm is strong, almost healed."

"Every day Nuka pushes it more, to lift, grasp, strike." He spoke numbly.

294

She got up and laid the sleeping infant in the birch-box cradle. It was packed with a deep layer of sand and covered by moss to absorb excrement. She tenderly covered him with a light moose skin.

When she came back to Nuka, he was deep in thought. She sat on the ground and put her head on his knee. "What are you going to do now?"

He shook his head. He felt drained. He had lived for only this since the kidnapping—to find her and kill the captors. He looked at the gun next to him on the floor.

She gently took his hands. "There will be new dreams. You will see."

He stayed ten sleeps with them and, by the end, was resigned to leaving her behind. His chest hurt constantly, and Nuka knew it was the place where his heart had died of grief. To go from choking on the Indians' smell to breaking food with them was too much pain to bear. Only his love for Kannik helped him through it.

Now they grouped around him as he harnessed the dogs in the snow. Kannik gave him mittens and Senati and Shanyaati each gave him parcels of food, still frozen from the meat cache. "On this spot was the last war between to Kobuk Eskimos and the Koyukuk Indians," Senati remarked. "But now it has a new meaning. It is here that the first bond has been made between our peoples. You are tied to us as surely as though you yourself wore the mark of the moon on your face." He held Nuka's face in his hands and they touched foreheads. "Now our thoughts meet."

He stepped aside and Kannik flew into Nuka's arms. "Will I see you again?"

He didn't answer but embraced her roughly. "Take care of your son."

They held each other hard.

Nuka sledded down the frozen Yukon to the Koyukuk River and then headed his dogs north, until the river became a frozen marsh of hundreds of channels. They crossed the Zane Hills and the Kobuk and Noatak rivers.

They were still many sleeps from the coast, but the air itself spoke of the sea, and at night when he camped, the wind brought messages from the whales. He was going home.

Two days of plunging down valleys and crossing frozen creeks and he began the climb to the valley of the Mountain People. One sleep later and he was there.

It was snowing and the wind howled. Nuka stopped every few minutes and wiped snow from the faces of his dogs. The tents were gone; the Mountain People were only there during the spring caribou hunt. He went straight up the ridge to the cave of the old man.

"Are you in there?" he shouted.

Silence. The dogs sniffed and whined.

Nuka took the axe off the sled and hacked a hole in the snow.

There was a fire going in the cave, and a figure poked at it with a stick.

Nuka put his hand on his knife. "Who goes there?"

The figure straightened, the hood fell back, and Nuka saw a mane of white hair and a gaunt face. It was the shaman. There was a rabbit on a spit and the shaman turned it smartly. Behind him stretched a row of dried salmon, and hanging high in the cave, bats slept upside down.

"Someone is lost!" Nuka blurted the words out.

The shaman looked at him sharply as he divided salmon and threw it to the dogs. "Let us eat first. Then talk."

They ate in silence. The shaman sucked the bones and threw them to the dogs. "You found your sister."

"That is so. But nothing has changed in my life."

"Ah, but that is not so. Remember?" The shaman put his hands on Nuka's shoulders and together they gazed into the snow. In front of them, a mist burned and became two persons and Nuka found himself looking at the man he had been.

Any life you diminish, diminishes your own, the shaman told the man who had been Nuka. Nuka could see clearly the disbelief and loathing on his previous face as he contemplated the Indians and whites in his future.

Your path lies south . . . away from the land of your birth . . .

"Please!" Nuka cried, "it is painful to watch!"

"But there is your answer. You have changed, Nuka. You have made peace with the Indians you hated and have reached a deeper truth—that because a man is white, he is not necessarily evil."

"Flame taught me."

"Yes, Flame. And others." The shaman waved his hand and a mist trailed behind; the woman was fat and brassy and deeply angry.

*Batt! Get your goddamn gamblerman ass in here and—*Nuka saw again the spangled curtain crash aside.

"Batt."

"Yes, and even the woman called Goldie shared what she had, in her own fashion."

Nuka lapsed into silence.

"What is it, my son?"

"With nothing to hate, what will fill the void?"

The shaman touched him. Already he was beginning to shimmer, and Nuka could see the sweep of valley and the outline of the cave through his body. "You are learning to be human, Nuka, not a god. It is much more difficult."

He raised his hand once, in a small salute, and then he was gone.

The pain in his chest continued. By the time he reached the coast, Nuka knew something was wrong. The air burned as it went down and it hurt to breathe and when he coughed, he spit yellow clots onto the snow. He tried the old incantations, swallowing dried dog dung mixed with the blood of a newly killed caribou, but the pain would not die.

He decided not to avoid the encampments of whites.

At Barrow he stopped at the Presbyterian Mission, where a doctor told him he had tuberculosis.

Nuka placed his dogs with a local family and moved into the hospital, where he was issued a cotton shirt, pants and slippers. He slept on a tiered bunk in a room with twenty other men. Two heating stoves provided warmth, and except for the ice weeping along the crack between the floor and outside wall, the room was dry.

Nuka sat on his bed. The man above him, Appyouw, told him they were all required to eat together and attend services afterward.

"Services?"

Appyouw was carving an ivory. "You'll like it. Lots of singing."

Nuka stared at the door. Where was his life leading? In the hallway, he heard light footsteps, and then a woman knocked cautiously on the open door before peering around it. The men looked up and went back to what they were doing.

She walked slowly into the room, looking. Nuka stared at her in wonder. It was Aan. She was unnaturally pale. She coughed and doubled over.

Nuka got off the bed and went to her. He put his arms around her, and when the coughing subsided, she looked up and said, "They told me you were here."

"How long have you been sick?" He led her back to the bed and they sat next to each other.

She wiped her eyes and the corner of her mouth. "A moon. A month, I mean." She looked up shyly. "The first time I said *I*, it caught in my throat, but I am over it now."

"Are the others with you?"

"Grandfather and the children died from it. Maguruk lay down next to their bodies and wouldn't leave. I had to leave him there, Nuka. They were inseparable."

"And Samqr?" The thought of her cruel husband stirred him, and he reached for her hand.

"He left when the first ones weakened. Missionaries found us." She squeezed his hand. "I have to go. I'm not supposed to be here. They keep us apart at dinner, but afterward, we can sit together in chapel."

The service was given in Inupiaq and in the middle of it, the congregation stood and sang lustily along with a small pipe organ. Nuka stood in awed silence.

Aan stood next to him and held the hymnal, singing in a clear voice. Her dress was tightly cinched in around her frail, narrow waist. Afterward Nuka helped her collect the hymnals and deposit them in a box next to the minister. He was wearing a black robe and his dark hair was cropped close. "What do you think?" he asked Nuka.

He shrugged. "The stranger in the sky—"

"Jesus."

"This Jesus is only one of many gods who perform miracles."

"We believe He is the only God, Nuka," the minister said gently. He put the box away. "You are interested in the Spirit?"

Nuka nodded.

"Perhaps you could assist me at services."

Fear gripped him. "No. There will be no more services for me."

And then Aan grasped his hand and exclaimed, "Oh, Nuka! We will be working together!"

And so it came to be that Nuka assisted the minister and learned a great deal about the Stranger in the Sky and how love for a woman changes man. He longed to know she loved him back, but she never spoke. It troubled him.

Then one day in chapel, while on his knees praying, the Holy Spirit entered his heart and he put away the man he had been and the gods that had belonged to him.

The day he was baptized in the chapel and sprinkled with holy water, Aan learned she was being transferred to another facility farther south. They sat on a bench in the back of chapel and she hung her head, weeping uncontrollably. "Everything in my life I have lost. But this is the cruelest loss of all!" As she sobbed into his shoulder, joy surged up in him. He put his arm around her and held her close. "I won't let them take you. I'm going to marry you. And when we're well again, we will live here in Barrow. I will hunt, the way my father did before me, but with no rage for the white men who live beside me. We will make strong children and raise them up in the Holy Spirit. And I will treat you with great kindness and love. Now dry your tears."

She dabbed her eyes with the sleeve of her dress. Nuka bent his head and kissed her gently. "Come. Let's find the minister."

They were married a week later. She was dressed in white muslin, a gift from the minister's wife, and Nuka stood at her side, wearing a suit and a new name.

"Nick Snow, do you take ~~this woman to be your wedded~~ wife, to love and honor, until death do you part?"

"I do," Nick answered in English, proud of his new skill and no longer afraid of offending the old gods by using the *I* out loud.

"And you, Aan? Do you promise to love, honor and obey this man, until death do you part?"

She looked searchingly at Nick and his heart froze until she whispered, "I do."

"Kneel, please."

They knelt and received the sacraments of marriage and the minister blessed them.

Nick thought he would remember these things forever; the hard wood against his kness, the way the collar choked his throat, the sharp scent of evergreen coming from the candles, the patients coughing in the pews, the warm stillness of Aan's hand in his.

And then it was over, and their friends emptied out of the pews and rushed toward them. Presents were pressed into their hands: an ivory fishhook, a steel knife, a needle and thread, and then arms lifted them up and they were carried down the aisle.

A strange old man still sat in the last row, wearing a bowler hat, a suit and a string tie. Nick stared at him curiously and felt the blood drain from his face.

It was the shaman. He looked penetratingly at Nick, shook his head slightly and smiled. It was the saddest smile Nick had ever seen.

Someone clapped Nick on the back and his leg slipped and they pushed him up again, and when he craned around to look, the pew was empty.

"The old man—" he shouted down into Appyouw's ear. The patients had started singing.

"What?"

"The old man. You were in the last row. What happened to him?"

Appyouw looked at him strangely. "There was no one there but me."

300

Twenty-Eight

Winter came a week after Cahill left. Frost scalded the trees, ropes of crystal webbed the rocks, mountain valleys stopped breathing under an avalanche of snow, and the air itself froze where it hung in the cobalt sky. In the Yukon River chunks of ice butted heads like rutting rams, and Rampart reverberated with the cries of the river freezing.

Inside the Ramsdorfs' kitchen, Flame worked furiously, canning vegetables with Sarah and the oldest girls. The room was moist and humid. Steam ran in rivulets down the inside of the window and hardened into washboard ice while two feet away, the women worked with their sleeves rolled up, hair curling from the heat.

Flame had never had sisters and, until now, hadn't realized what she was missing. She was amazed at the vigorous power that comes to women when they're alone and don't have to consider the needs of men. It never occurred to anybody to mention men: in this world, they simply didn't exist. Not that they didn't all adore their father and cuddle him relentlessly. They did, but the way a museum curator might care for a creature from outer space: taking exquisite care and patience with it, not knowing which of its appendages was fragile and could break off in their lands.

Men were mysteries, and their father, the biggest mystery of all. They knew their mother had a separate relationship with him, but that was strictly between the two of them. The girls ran together.

The girls were used to sharing and goodnaturedly made room for Flame in their conversations, and by the end of the week, room for her in their house.

"What's one more girl?" Julius had said.

But Sarah had wiped her hands on the apron and asked, "When are you planning on going to that mine?"

Flame flushed. "I'm not sure where it is. I keep asking—" Her voice trailed off. She hadn't expected the weather to turn so quickly.

Sarah polished the glass cannisters in the kitchen, and Flame knew instinctively that Mrs. Ramsdorf would never completely trust her, even if Nuka was gone for good.

They fell silent and heard nails popping on the porch from the cold.

Julius went over to Sarah and squeezed her shoulder. She smiled up at him and then at Flame. "You can stay with Ellie May and Annie, but I guess they've already told you."

The two oldest girls whooped and put on their boots to help her move.

"I'll do extra work. Take the load off. I promise—"

"It all comes back," Julius said easily. "Just pass it along sometime."

The three girls went chattering out into the night, gasping as the cold air struck them, their boots squeaking in the snow.

For the first time since she left Seattle, Flame felt safe.

The Ramsdorfs did not have indoor plumbing or running water, and the first thing Julius would do when the river froze was cut huge blocks of ice and borrow Samuel Heater's horse to drag them up the hill to the house.

"Easy, boy." He steadied the horse and walked around to the block, shoving his shoulder against the freezing weight of the metal hook and yanking it free. He yanked the other hook free and lifted the block onto a stack by the door. His nose pinched from the cold, and he clapped his hands together and stamped his feet. Another trip and then firewood.

He wished again he had a boy; Sarah was a stickler for segregating chores according to the sexes. He sighed fondly, slipped the hooks off the chains and on to his wrists and went to the front of the horse.

When he was almost at the river he saw the man. He was sawing out a block of ice, his arms swinging like a young man's. He straightened then he saw Julius. Ice crusted his mustache.

302

"Been watching you. Thought you could use a hand."

"Much obliged." Julius stuck out his glove. "I'm Julius Ramsdorf."

"Name's Batt. Batt Jackson."

They worked well together. Batt steadied the horse while Julius slammed the hooks out of the last block. After they returned the horse, they hiked across the river and snowshoed a mile up the hill overlooking the Indian village. It was brutally cold work. Sweat ran down the inside of their jackets and froze if they stopped moving. By suppertime a respectable stack of kindling had grown up the side of the cabin, and Julius asked him to stay for dinner.

Flame almost dropped the wild-berry pie she was carrying in from the kitchen when she saw the back of his head in the parlor.

"Heard Congress has given the go-ahead for men to build roads and collect tolls in the district." Julius swirled his brandy.

Batt shook his head. "They're going about it all wrong. The cost of clearing road would price the tolls out of reach, or keep the return on the investment so minimal nobody but a fool would be interested. Folks would use the Indian trails, same as always, when they had to leave the rivers. No, we need a railroad. That's the key."

Flame set the pie down quietly on the sideboard and ran upstairs to the room she shared with Annie and Ellie May. Her hair was a mess. The steam in the kitchen had ruined it. She curled it frantically around her fingers, and settled finally for tying it back with a brown ribbon that matched her skirt.

Mrs. Ramsdorf looked sharply at Flame as she took her place at the dining table. She slipped between Ellie May and Laura, nodded at Batt and looked primly at her hands.

"Why, Flame Ryan, I didn't expect to see you here."

"You know each other?" Julius beamed.

Flame flushed and Ellie May looked sideways at her. She knew they were expected to say something. A long moment went by.

"I met her family in Skagway and saw her again in Dawson, after she lost her parents."

Sarah changed the subject.

"Mr. Ramsdorf, would you ask the blessing."

"For these and all Your gifts, we give Thee thanks. Amen."

"Amen," the girls echoed.

"Amen," Batt said.

A meal at the Ramsdorfs' table was a thing of splendor: hot biscuits swimming in butter and gravy, moose stew, salmon patties, stewed tomatoes, green beans and corn on the cob grown in the garden and flash-frozen outside. There was honey and bread and canned milk. When they'd eaten their fill, the men retired to the parlor while the dishes were cleared.

Over cigars and whiskey Batt said, "Since you've taken Flame in, I feel I should ask you. I'd like to court her, Julius."

Julius built a fire and stretched his legs out. "Have you talked to her about it?"

"Not yet."

Julius drained his glass. "I've no objections, if she doesn't."

"Well, I do." It was later, and they were alone, outside, in the dark.

Batt swung her around. "Why?"

"I'm in love with Cahill."

"That kid?"

"You met him?"

"On the boat downriver at Ruby. Flame, I'm telling you, you could chew him into breakfast wafers in two minutes. He's weak."

"He is not!"

He tossed the cigar, pulled her roughly into his arms and kissed her. She couldn't break away. He kissed her hard, but his lips were surprisingly gentle. His body was granite. She felt her legs tremble.

"Does Cahill kiss like that?"

She swallowed and opened her eyes. "Batt—"

He kissed her again, and this time she put her hands around his neck and kissed him back. A shudder passed through her. "I'm going to marry him," she said weakly.

"Listen to me. I know Nelly. She'll never let him go. Not until she's sucked all the juice out of him."

"That's a lie!"

"It's the truth. He'll never marry you. Besides, he had his chance. And right here, right now, this is my chance, Flame Ryan, and I plan to make the most of it. Do you think it was an accident, my finding you? I could have found you right away. I wanted to give you a chance to get over him."

"It's not just Cahill—"

He started kissing her again but she pulled away. "Then what?"

"It's the way you live. Buying and selling women. It would never work between us."

"Buying and selling women. Is that what you think?"

"That's what you do, isn't it?"

"I manage them. That's all."

"Are you telling me they enjoy it?"

"Some of them, yes."

"Batt, stop kidding yourself. You're making money off the pain of other people."

"Did I tell you I've put three of them through school? Gotten them out when they were tired of it?"

"Does that make you feel better about the ones you still have working for you? Is that it?"

They walked in silence up the hill. At the door Flame held out her hand and said stiffly, "I am grateful to you. I really am. But I think it would be best if we didn't see each other again. A future between us isn't possible."

He looked thoughtfully at her. "Anything is possible, Flame. You just have to want it badly enough."

The Ramsdorfs kept chickens in a heated shed. Every night and the first thing every morning, the stove had to be stoked. Ellie May hated the job and Annie flatly refused to do it, so Flame quietly took it over. She liked the gray stillness of the coop, the humped shapes of the chickens, the rustlings and cluckings.

After breakfast everybody but Flame and the two youngest would line up in the parlor, the older girls winding scarves and checking the mittens of the younger ones, and Sarah would kiss them and send them off to school. It was one room on the top of the hill across from the Army barracks.

A strange sort of peace would descend, and that's when the real work began.

It was endless—the polishing, scrubbing, dusting. The family generated an enormous amount of laundry, and each piece was scrubbed by hand, boiled and wrung dry. Julius had built a lean-to next to the cabin and heated it with a potbellied stove, and it was there that the laundry was hung.

It occurred to Flame that having six daughters was only an asset when they were home working, and she grew to admire Sarah for her calm efficiency, and to like her as a friend.

The day before Halloween, Flame was hanging wash when Sarah came in, Edith balanced on her hip. She closed the door behind her.

"Flame, you've been here almost two months, and I was wondering if there was anything bothering you."

"Not that I can think of." She snapped a petticoat flat and pinned it up.

Sarah transferred Edith to her other hip. "With so many females, it's not easy to hide things. I'll come right to the point. I haven't seen you wash any pads for yourself and hang them to dry."

Flame was stunned. Until this moment she hadn't been keeping track. My God. How long had it been? She thought quickly back, her anxiety turning to dread. Since Cahill. She covered her mouth and sat slowly down at the folding table. Sarah sat next to her.

"Just as I thought." She sighed. "Tell me it's not that savage, anyway."

Tears streamed down her face. "It's not true. It can't be. It's the strangeness—"

"Is the father white?"

She nodded numbly.

"Does he know?"

Flame bowed her head and shook it. "He's in Seattle. Married to someone else." There wasn't any reason to withhold that information; the rest was hopeless anyway.

"Well," Sarah said gently. "I'll be in the kitchen if you want to talk."

306

But what was there to talk about? She was two months pregnant.

She would go overland to Valdez and take a steamer back to Seattle. She would stay there and raise the child alone. A child, spinning in warm darkness, deep in the sanctity of her womb. Oh, Cahill. Out of the pain of our union has sprung this miracle.

She found herself watching Edith at dinner—the wide blue eyes, the blond fluff of curls, the small fat fingers painting the tray with mashed food. At night there was the agony of listening to Ellie May whispering innocent dreams to her from the next bed and falling into peaceful sleep, while Flame turned and thrashed in bed, thinking.

She would have to make a decision, and quickly. In school, years ago, she had shared a desk with a new girl. She was all elbows and ducking head, as if she were fielding blows only she could see. One day, walking home from school, Flame found out why.

The boys had pinned her down by the pond, stuffed her mouth with mud. They stood chanting, "Bastard, bastard, bastard."

Never would a child of hers slink through life apologizing. Never. Whatever else, her child would not have to be stronger than she. The night passed, and with it the last of Flame's girlhood. There were no more tears—only a grim determination and the frightening knowledge that time was running out.

"Anybody home?" Batt knocked with one hand and opened the door with the other. Outside, the mercury had frozen solid at forty below and cracked the container.

Annie stopped playing the piano when she saw him and smoothed her corn-silk hair. At fifteen she had dreams of marrying someone just like him, only with thicker hair.

"Don't know why they get like this," Sarah said, pulling her off him.

"Oh, ma'am, it warms my heart, it does." He had a pumpkin under one arm and a canvas bag in the other and stood while the girls fussed his coat off. He looked at Flame, and she turned and busied herself at the table.

"For all you kids." He handed the pumpkin to Becky Sue. "Happy Halloween."

She left awkwardly, certain that Batt could see into her belly.

Flame slowed work on the pumpkin, haggling endlessly with Laura, Gracie and Becky Sue about what the face should be, where the cuts would go. Afterward Flame polished the kitchen, feeling trapped. She would have to go through the parlor to get to the stairs.

Sarah came in, her eyes flinty. "I want you to talk to him, Flame."

"I don't want to! He'll know! He will! Besides, I don't even want to see him."

"Nobody knows but the two of us," Sarah said fiercely. "I want you to speak to him. Just a few minutes alone. That's all."

She left Flame standing there and in a while, Batt came in. He sat at the kitchen table and looked at her. "Do you see anything different?"

"What do you mean?" He did know. Had to know.

"In my face—my eyes—anything at all?"

"Are you mocking me, Batt?" She was close to tears.

"No. It's me, Flame. I'm different. I'm the one who's changed, and I want to tell you about it." She sat down, watching him, not believing.

"Could I have some coffee?"

She got up, relieved to have something to do. When she sat down again, he said, "I disbanded the business."

"What do you mean?"

"I got out of it. Let the girls go. Thought about selling it. Had a buyer all lined up—Silver Dollar. Then I thought, 'What would Flame say about it?'" He chipped a splinter of sugar off the blocks and dropped it into his coffee. "You know, I think you're the first woman whose feelings ever mattered to me. Thirty-two years old, Flame, and you're the first one." He looked up. "You know what that means? The more I looked at myself, the less I liked. Look, I'm no do-gooder. I'll never be great with children, and dogs hate me. I gamble sometimes, and smoke cigars, and sometimes I fool around." He looked at her.

308

"Okay, I won't do that either. I promise I really won't."

"Batt—"

"Let me finish." His voice was quiet. "I'm falling in love with you, Flame. It started in Dawson, in the hospital. You haven't been out of my mind since. I'd be good to you, Flame. I swear it. I have a claim in a place called Nome. It's right on the beach. The town is just opening up. Rumors of strikes. It's going to be the big one, Flame, I can feel it. I want you to come with me. Marry me."

He stopped talking and Flame stared at her hands. Finally she looked up. "I need to think about it."

He got up. "I'm giving you fair warning, Flame Ryan. I'm going to marry you. I'm the only one who can match you, strength for strength. We're builders, you and I. And you need me, too."

He turned and walked away without touching her. It was more physical than if he had swept her into his arms again. Her body had expected that; maybe even wanted it. She was left shaken, too warm. She took a deep breath, tried to remember all the things she hated about him. But instead, she remembered how, in Skagway, he had held her roughly against him, and the elegant, masculine smell of his body.

"Maybe I need you a little, too," she whispered.

The question was, did she love him? And not in the absence of Cahill, either, but *him*. She would never marry a second choice. But could she choose Batt? Without knowing what Cahill was planning?

All the women she had ever known had been the clay upon which men's stories were written, and now life looked at her and said, *"Ah, Flame. Play it with the cards in hand, my friend, the cards in hand."*

If tomorrow Cahill sent money to get her home, would she drop everything and go? Yes. Oh, yes. And if he didn't—if there was nothing there but the swell of her belly under the apron, harder to deny every day—what then?

But she knew, deep in her heart, what she had to do.

Becky Sue leaned on her knees and studied Flame in the mirror. Why did she look so sad? She was marrying the handsomest man Becky'd ever seen. Flame twisted thick ropes of auburn hair over her ears and pinned them on top of her head. Becky's hand strayed to her own pale hair.

"What're you thinking?" Flame's eyes met Becky's in the mirror and then she turned sideways in the dusky rose dress and sucked in her stomach.

"Nothing." Becky Sue traced her name idly on the quilt with her finger.

"Something. I know it." Flame sat down next to her. "What?"

Becky's eyes filled with tears. "I'll never be pretty. I'll be thirteen forever. Nobody will ever—"

"Oh, pooh." Flame hugged her. "You'll have them falling over themselves. Besides, you do what *you* want to do, Becky. Don't wait for anybody."

"Is that what you're doing?"

Flame thought about it. "Yes." She got up. "That's exactly what I'm doing."

"Then why do you look so sad?" She said it quietly.

Flame stilled her hands. Becky Sue was pinching up her blue flowered dress and watching it flutter over her rounded knees.

Flame sat next to her. "You can be sad and happy at the same time. Maybe I'm sad for the girl I used to be. You know how you dream things—all sorts of things?"

Becky nodded.

"I'm starting a new life today, and that girl is watching me go on without her. And that's kind of sad. We've been friends a long time. But I'm happy because I'm getting on with my life. Can you understand?"

"I think so."

Flame kissed her briskly and stood up as Ellie May ran up the stairs. "They're here, and you'll never guess who's best man!"

She was wearing the blue velveteen and her dark hair was braided and looped.

"You know that old guy with the handlebar mustache who works at the Mayo Hotel slinging drinks?"

"Ellie! I'm shocked! Such language."

She shrugged. "I sneaked in there one night. Besides, I'm eighteen myself now. Your age. Anyway, you know how

310

everybody thought he was a derelict?" She turned to Becky Sue. "This gets too much for you, just close your ears."

"Never."

Ellie May grabbed Flame's hand. "All this time—it's really been—you're not going to believe this—"

"Who?"

Wyatt Earp."

"Wyatt Earp? OK Corral Wyatt Earp?" Ellie nodded. "Earp, as in Virgil, Morgan and Wyatt Earp."

"One and the same. And right now, he's standing next to Batt, big as you please, wearing a clean shirt. He's real skinny, with the lights on. You'll be amazed."

"I'm amazed already."

"Who's Wyatt Earp?" Becky Sue said. Downstairs the reedy strains of Sarah's soprano filled the air, singing, "Oh, Promise Me" to Annie's piano.

The girls looked at each other a long moment. Finally Flame squeezed Ellie's hands. "If anybody asks if I have sisters, I'll think of you."

Ellie May's eyes grew bright. "I love you, too," she whispered.

And then it was time. Becky Sue and Ellie May marched down the stairs and Flame looked one last time at herself in the mirror. Her color was high, her cheeks the same dull pink as the gown. She smiled.

The music ended as she came downstairs. The furniture in the parlor had been pushed against the wall, and the group was standing. The Ramsdorf girls, starched and plaited, stood in reverse order of birth: there was four-year-old Laura; six-year-old Gracie; Becky Sue; Ellie May; Annie at the piano; and Mrs. Ramsdorf with Edith asleep on her shoulder. Flame loved them all.

Across the room the minister stood, Bible open. Batt was behind him with Wyatt Earp. Julius stepped forward and took her arm, and into this deep and holy silence, Flame walked toward the man she would marry. He straightened his neck and clasped his hands in front of him.

She looked steadily into his eyes as she walked, the rest a blur. This man. Yes, this man. She felt a flood of tenderness for him. Not a perfect man, but a good man, and that was enough. She knew with a deep sense of certainty that whatever life did to them, Batt would never settle for little truths, easy outs. He had tossed out the things in himself that were no good, and what was left behind was real and true. She believed in his dreams and, even more important, knew that he believed in her right to dream, too.

Yes, my friend, we are good together, she thought silently. She stopped in front of him, and they smiled at each other. His dark hair was closely cropped and his mustache trimmed. He was wearing a silk shirt and three-piece suit, and across his pocket was a watch chain. He smelled of soap and pomade.

"Dearly beloved, we are gathered here together in the presence of these witnesses . . ."

It was a rite of passage, as familiar as the grandfather clock striking the hour in the corner.

". . . to join together this man and this woman in holy matrimony.

"The ring please," the minister said, and Batt turned to Wyatt. He was giving her his own mother's ring—a cluster of emeralds, rubies and diamonds. There was an awkward moment as Wyatt shuffled through his pockets.

"Got it here somepl—" He brightened the pulled it out of his coin pocket, handing it to Batt with flourish.

Batt took her hand. "I, Battimus Jackson the third, in the presence of these witnesses, take thee, Flame Ryan, to be my lawful wedded wife." He'd memorized it.

His voice cracked and he broke down and wept. There was nothing childlike about it: it was as if the last thing separating them was dissolving away—as if Batt was risking something even he wasn't sure of—and was still terrified he would lose—but risking it all the same.

It moved her more than anything else that day, and severed the last of the strings to Cahill. She was taking *this* man, this day, from this time forward. And oh, she would be good to him!

The minister quietly filled in the words, and Batt looked deep into her eyes and repeated them.

It was Flame's turn and in a firm, clear voice she bound herself to this man.

The ring slipped on her finger, the minister prayed for guidance and protection, and Batt drew her to him and kissed her. The littlest Ramsdorfs sucked in their breaths and Edith started wailing. Then Julius uncorked a bottle of champagne and Annie played Mozart and they celebrated.

He wanted everything to be perfect for her. He had planned it all out. At the cabin door he lifted her and carried her in. The cabin Flame had once shared with Nuka had been transformed. Julius had given them a brass bed; Sarah had made quilts. Ellie May had embroidered pillowcases for the chicken-down pillows Annie had stuffed. On the clean stove Becky Sue had left breakfast fixings for morning. And the room was finally warm.

"Do you like it?"

"Batt. It's beautiful." She took off her coat, boots, scarf, and went slowly to the table. Six-year-old Grace had written in block letters the word *HAPPY*. Four-year-old Laura had contributed a gold leaf she had pressed into a book. She picked up the scrawled word. Yes, she was happy.

Batt was hanging up winter things. "Wyatt gave us a bottle of wine." He took off his gloves.

"Wonderful."

He unsnapped a leather case and lifted out two goblets and a corkscrew.

"Have you known him long?"

Batt smiled and poured. "Involved in a high-stakes poker game with him in Dawson."

"He won?"

"I was—called away. Couldn't get back to the game in time, so yes, I guess you could say he won." He was thinking about identifying Margaret's body and how white Flame's face had been when the Mounties carried her off the boat. "I didn't know who he was until I met him again in Rampart at the Mayo, working the bar. Funny old guy."

He carried the drinks over and gave her one. "To us."

"Always."

They clicked glasses and drank and then looked in companionable silence at the fire.

313

"Is he still a lawman?"

"You know he never shot anybody—except that day at the OK Corral? And then later, when his brother Morgan was killed, he went after them. But that was it. He's just drifting now."

"Did he ever marry?"

"Twice, I think. First wife died. Separated from the second."

She looked in his eyes. "That's sad. Thinking of him alone."

He took her drink gently out of her hands and wrapped her to him. "Then let's just think of us tonight."

She was still dressed in rose silk and it was like water spilling under his hands. He bent down and kissed her throat.

She closed her eyes and he carried her to bed.

He looked at her luminous face in the firelight and wished suddenly he had never touched another woman but her. The sweaty couplings with anonymous strangers, the dead desire, and now his body was going to meet hers the same way it had met those others. Here were the hands, smoothing down the buttons of her bodice, caressing her soft breasts, the swell of her belly. Here were the arms, lifting free the dress and laying her gently down. The same mouth kissing the soft folds of flesh, the same tumescent knob of flesh rising—but oh! it wasn't the same! It was more, so much more!

And when he entered her, he felt that he was entering her soul, and he wanted to go deeper and stay longer, stay forever, until the world burned into dust and Flame and he were consumed in flames, or ice or whatever it is that comes next, after all is over, but this: this union of flesh, this need to be one.

She was a Botticelli painting, an angel of God and he pressed himself into her and lost himself in the miracle of her body.

With deep sweetness, she took him into her, this man, this husband. Her body shifted around his and she wrapped herself around him and buried her face in his neck and cried out sometimes, with pleasure; and after a long time, the thing that happens between a man and woman built in her and she tightened around him and screamed and into that scream, her husband poured himself, like holy water.

314

She sensed then the fragility, of this man, of all men. It was not the power of her sex over him, but the need men have of women: to help them release the sweetness the world has them lock away.

With their contemporaries, they pretend: each one stronger and more superbly equipped than the last to storm the barricades and field the blows.

In bed, they are one of two and their strength comes in letting go.

BOOK FOUR

Need

Twenty-Nine

The town had been preparing for weeks, which was only proper, since the district had been preparing for years—four years, to be exact.

It started in 1909 when the Alaskan delegate, James Wickersham, introduced his first bill in Congress to create an Alaska legislature. It was a simple document, carefully thought out. Wickersham had even conferred with President Taft before deciding on twenty-four members—eight in the Senate and sixteen in the House. Six members would be elected from each of the four judicial districts.

It was a nice, quiet sort of bill, but it created thunderous opposition among the ones who had the most to lose, big Eastern businesses. For years they had been busily going to Alaska and taking things out: fish, furs, copper, gold. They neglected to leave behind things that Alaska needed, like a few roads or schools. They would bring up their own workers, cheap Chinese labor for the canneries, say, and then after the salmon run, they would pack everybody up and go home. Laws written by people who lived there all the time were unthinkable. What if they decided to tax corporate businesses? Set quotas on how much they took? It couldn't be allowed to happen.

So the corporate attorneys hurried to their local congressmen, and over an expense and expensive lunch, they reminded them how only hooligans lived in Alaska, and then only part-time. The congressmen talked to the president, and before long, Taft was urging Congress to vote down the bill Delegate Wickersham offered. After all, Wickersham couldn't vote anyway, since he was from Alaska.

It went on. Wickersham would doggedly present his bill,

which was looking more sickly all the time, and somebody would think up a wonderful bill, the perfect bill, really, that would take care of the Alaska problem. President Taft wanted to appoint nine men, the way he had in the Philippines, who could go in there and straighten things out. Make a few laws. Senator Beveridge, chairman of the Senate Committee on Territories, thought there might be a spot for Alaska in the War Department. Let them worry about it. Or maybe somebody in the Alaska Roads Commission could step in and do the job.

In the House Congressman William Sulzer stood up one day and said if that happened, he thought Alaskans had the right to revolt, just like the original thirteen colonies. He was pulled to his seat.

When Congress met in January of 1912, Wickersham was there again, little bill in hand. The debates were bitter. Even Alaska Governor Clark stood up and argued against it, which made sense, since he was appointed by the president. Maybe an elected legislature wouldn't like him. What then? He left that part out of his speech, concentrating instead on how large and unwieldy the land mass was and how much government cost.

Everybody nodded. It was right after lunch and that always cost a lot.

But Wickersham was prepared. He had facts and figures and a fury that made the congressmen uneasily decide he would keep bringing it up until he got what he wanted. He had also taken his case to the press.

They compromised. The little bill went from committee to committee, like a lost and lonely child, and at every stop, it was examined and pulled on and spiffed up, until it finally staggered through the House and Senate, burdened down with layers of restrictions, its small face sweating and strained. But it passed, clothes and all, and that was the beginning. Alaska was ecstatic, and Juneau most of all, for the little bill was coming home to it. It wasn't until later, in the privacy of those newly hallowed session chambers, that the legislators undressed the law and saw how small it was. They were furious.

Flame leaned on the bell and tapped her foot. Where was

320

Lucille? Eight hundred guests expected tomorrow night and no water. She'd told that girl about it yesterday. She sighed and looked through the mint green sitting room toward the bathroom. The manager of the Lewis-Juneau Water Company insisted the water faucets stay open to keep the pipes from freezing. A lot of good it did. The water table was so low now that nothing came out but a drip, and it was staining the porcelain with rust.

She rang again. Footsteps flurried on the steps, down the Persian-carpeted hallway, and Lucille ran into the room, bobbing and beaten looking. "Yes, mum?" The brown hair was messy under the cap, and there was a crumb hanging on her wilted collar.

Flame looked at her in distaste. "Fetch James, please."

The maid curtsied and went out. Flame turned back to the gold-and-ivory desk and ran her finger lightly over the embossed stationary: *Senator and Mrs. Battimus Jackson III.* She sat down and picked up a pen and wrote:

Dear Delegate Wickersham:

Batt and I are so looking forward to seeing you and your dear wife—Deborah, again. It's hard to believe almost twelve years have passed since you served on the Nome bench. As you know, we are throwing open our doors to greater Juneau to honor your accomplishments in Washington. Finally, a legislature of our own! And, if you will forgive a measure of wifely pride, what better man representing the Interior than Batt? He will be so pleased to see you.

She sighed and chewed on the end of her pen. He wouldn't. That was the problem. He had been furious when she'd told him.

"Wickersham, the guest of honor!"

"I thought you would be pleased," she stammered.

"Haven't you been listening to anything!" he thundered. "He sold us out! Home rule, my foot! It's a kangaroo legislature with a governor that's appointed by the United States president. Our delegate to Congress, the honorable James Wickersham, played right into their hands." He paced up and down the bedroom, counting them off. "We have no control of land, minerals, or fisheries. That stays in federal hands. No rights to form county governments or borrow money—even divorces have to be approved by Congress on a case-by-case basis. And if we do, by some miracle, pass significant legislation, it's still subject to veto by a governor who's a puppet of the president."

She looked at him, stricken. "I've already sent the invitations out."

Mount Katmai had erupted the year before, creating the Valley of Ten Thousand Smokes and blanketing Juneau under a haze of white ash. It was second only to the explosion in the Jacksons' bedroom. Flame sighed and signed her name to the bottom of the letter, creased it and slid it into an envelope. She tore off a two-cent stamp and hesitated over the glue pot. No. It would be faster to hand deliver it.

There was a discreet cough and knock on the mahogany door.

"Mrs. Jackson." James had the professionally neutral look of all first-class servants.

"James." She rose and gathered her black silk kimono imperiously around her. "Something must be done about Lucille. Her personal habits are slovenly, and I find it distasteful to have her handling my personal effects."

"Certainly, Mrs. Jackson. Perhaps Adrienne or Nancy—"

Flame waved impatiently. "Whoever. Please handle it. Thank you." She pointed at the rusting sink. "I can't stand to look at it."

"Do you wish Lucille terminated?"

"Put her to work polishing silver. If Mrs. Harris can't straighten her out, fire her."

He bowed slightly. "Is that all?"

"Heavens, no," she snapped. "I want a full report on the dinner preparations. And have the floors in the reception hall been stripped yet?"

"They finished stripping yesterday. They're waxing now."

322

He pulled a list from his pocket. "I thought perhaps you might want a status report on the banquet preparations, so I took the liberty of bringing this along."

He handed it to her and Flame scanned the list:

2,000 sandwiches; ham, turkey, chicken
60 cakes; cream, chocolate and assorted
garden salad and vegetables, 60 gallons ea.
   (from greenhouse)
400 pounds cracked crab
30 pounds crackers
150 cases beer, Eagle Brewery
200 bottles spirits
100 gallons punch (dry)

"What about mints?"

"The kitchen is preparing them now. Mint, spearmint and butter, as you requested."

"Thank you, James, you have been most helpful."

He bowed slightly. "Anything else?"

She went to the desk and took a bill out from under the inkpot. "The light bill, James. Have we suddenly acquired bulbs in the house of which I am not aware?"

"Mrs. Jackson. I keep you personally apprised of—"

"One hundred and eight dollars this month! Power and Light is still charging by the bulb, is it not? One dollar for every sixteen-candle bulb and we have exactly one hundred and three bulbs in our house, counting the servants' floor. An error of five dollars a month may seem insignificant, but over the course of a year—"

"Perhaps they made an error in their accounting department—"

"Perhaps! Of course they did!" She pressed her fingers to her head. "And please, I don't care what it costs, but do get the walkway cleared." She sighed and looked out the window at the snow. From the second-story window in the sitting room, she could see the tops of passing carriages. No snow removal in the capital city! A crime.

James looked at her cautiously, waiting.

"Did that little Auke village boy bring round the smoked salmon?"

James nodded. "Forty Kings. I paid him eighty dollars out of household monies."

"Very good. Oh, and have Harold ready in twenty minutes."

"Do you wish the Ford?"

"The carriage will do."

"Anything else?"

"Is Jennifer home from school yet?"

"Begging your pardon, Mrs. Jackson, but I thought you gave her permission to attend the legislative session today. To hear Delegate Wickersham."

"Yes. Of course. With so much going on—" She waved her hand. "That will be all, James."

He nodded and was leaving when she said, "Oh. Yes. This letter. Have one of the boys deliver it personally to Delegate Wickersham."

"Certainly."

Flame closed the door and walked from the sitting room into the dressing room. Lucille had laid out a waist of pale silk and a dusky rose serge suit with a hobble skirt. She took off her wrapper and dressed quickly, dreading the afternoon.

The new legislature had convened for the first time the day before and both keynote speakers had sharply criticized Delegate Wickersham's compromises in Washington that had led to the creation of an Alaska legislature. It wasn't fair, she thought: Wickersham couldn't vote in Congress, since he represented a district—he could only *suggest*. After *years* of suggesting, Congress finally changed Alaska's status to a territory, which meant that someday it could become a state. Instead of praising Wickersham, both speakers had condemned him. Representative Ingersoll, a Ketchikan attorney, had gone so far as to ask what the legislature was even *there* for, since it couldn't *do* anything. She stepped into her baby Louis heels and wondered again if the guest of honor would be killed today before she had a chance to honor him at the party. Maybe she could serve two thousand sandwiches at the wake.

There was a timid knocking. "Come in." She sat down at the

dressing table and inspected her face. A few fine lines around the eyes, and one in the forehead. Thank God her hair was holding. Legislator Ransom's wife was a year younger than Flame—only thirty-two—and already her hair was streaking.

Nancy dipped a curtsy. "I would be honored to serve you, Mrs. Jackson." She was broad shouldered with a meaty smile and thick brown hair parted evenly down the middle.

"Did James explain what is expected?"

She nodded. "Yes, Mrs. Jackson."

"Very well." She turned back to the mirror and pulled the combs out of her hair. "Fix it."

The legislature had rented the Elk's Club on South Franklin Street. Flame leaned against the carriage window and studied the view. Douglas Island rose in drifting fog across Gastineau Channel. The Treadwell Hardrock Mining complex was built on the island, and even in Juneau, one could hear the muted roar of the enormous stamp mills. The harbor was full of halibut and salmon boats. Icebergs rose like dollops of granite whipping cream. They were being towed out of the bay to Mendenhall Glacier, fourteen miles away.

Flame saw a flash of the Alaska Sea Cannery she and Batt were negotiating to buy before it was obscured by the Juneau Ironworks. Chapped-faced men stood in front of the iron-works, banging hammers into molten metal to temper the molds. The freezing temperature hardened the metal on impact. A row of finished boat parts and harness rings hung on a rack by the door.

The carriage stopped and Harold helped her out. "Should I wait?"

"Please."

He held the door of the building open, and she walked between the high gray drifts into the building. An American flag hanging from a second-story window slapped the snow in the light breeze. Harold closed the door behind her, pulled an apple from his pocket. "Here, Bossy." The mare nickered.

Flame went up the stairs to the third floor. At the door to the joint assembly, she pulled her face veil down and smoothed her gloves. The room had been done in early patriotism:

national flags covered the walls. Jenny was sitting alone in the last row. Flame tensed the way she always did when she came unexpectedly upon her daughter. There was something lonely and inexpressibly sad about the slope of the enormous shoulders. At fourteen, Jenny made a chair look small. She brightened when she saw her mother.

"I was hoping you'd make it," she whispered. "It's thrilling, isn't it?"

She had Flame's wide green eyes and her grandmother's dark hair, but the body was hers alone. She had cut her first tooth at six months and hadn't stopped eating since. A navy blue sailor dress stretched across her belly where there should have been pleats. Her gloves were crumpled on her lap and the ankles of her white stockings were soiled.

"Has Delegate Wickersham been up yet?" Flame took off her beaver Eton jacket as she took a seat next to her daughter.

Jenny shook her head. "Any time. Governor Clark has been introducing him for *hours*. After *he* was introduced for hours by somebody else."

"That's enough, Jennifer." Flame looked through the desks of delegates and found Batt midway through the second row. A wave of pride surged through her. She was glad she had talked him into wearing the new gray pinstripe. It brought out the faint gray in his dark hair. Very distinguished looking. He looked over and saw her and nodded slightly. She smiled back.

At the podium United States Delegate James Wickersham was starting to speak. He had a strong, square face and a slightly receding hairline. His clipped mustache was flecked with gray. Flame leaned forward.

"Ordinarily, a legislator who has succeeded in enacting an important law should treat criticism of the law with patience. Time will vindicate my judgment."

Flame clicked her tongue. She could feel the legislators stiffening in their seats. Batt shifted his legs and set his mouth in a hard line.

Wickersham stared coolly at the legislators and went on.

"When, however, the representatives chosen to act under the law put forward a keynote speaker to denounce the act with

326

unmeasured and hostile criticism, a different situation is presented."

Flame slowly covered her mouth with her gloved hand. He was going for the throat.

"When the gentleman from Ketchikan, a lawyer of wide repute, in forceful phrases condemned the act of Congress creating the legislative body, one must wonder at the motive."

"*Delegate Wickersham.*" Senator Bruner jumped to his feet, his face flushed and his fists balled. "You have not been invited here to lecture the legislators or to criticize a member of our group."

"And who started it?" Wickersham said. "You're here today because I fought a bill through Congress, *creating* this body. And fought not once, sir! Not even twice! But year after year—"

Bedlam. A senator from Nome, in baggy tweed and walrus mustache engaged in a clumsy hands-on with the representative from Wrangell. Three men threw their jackets aside and leaped in. Flame covered her eyes.

"You're missing the best part, mother."

"I can't look. Tell me."

"It's father."

Flame shuddered and took her hands away. Batt was striding to the podium. "He has the right to speak!" he shouted. "Let him finish!"

Senator Bruner pushed Batt aside and rapped for silence. "A vote. We will put it to a vote." Bruner's face was blotched, and he was breathing heavily. "All those in favor of allowing United States Delegate Wickersham to continue with his speech—"

Four hands went up.

"Those opposed." Four hands. Bruner threw down the gavel and stalked out. With him went five sandwiches, two helpings of salad and a plate of vegetables from the menu, along with ten pounds of mints. Flame had known Bruner and his hearty appetite in Nome. Then he was an attorney, heavily into mints. Now he was just heavy.

Striding behind him out the door were two senators and

a representative.

Wickersham clamped his hands around the podium and grimly went on. He left motherhood and apple pie alone, but managed to hit everything else before a fire alarm interrupted him and the senators and representatives became volunteer firemen. Batt went with the rest.

Wickersham looked at the men scrambling out of the hall and his sentence trailed away.

He sighed, rubbed his head and picked up his papers.

"Is it over already?" Jennifer was amazed. The speech was shorter than the introduction.

"Yes," Flame said absently. "Put on your gloves, Jennifer. I think we've seen enough for one day."

Delegate Wickersham hadn't the faintest idea who Jenny was, even after Flame prodded his memory, but Flame, of course, he remembered. They all did. Jenny reclined like a beached whale on three chairs while the adults conversed. Delegate Wickersham had gray eyes and a mustache and inhabited that netherworld of age—over sixty but not yet dead.

Jenny sighed. On the way out, Delegate Wickersham clapped Jennifer on the shoulder and said, "It's so good to see you again, Melinda."

"Jennifer," Jennifer said.

"Yes, of course. How foolish. Good-bye, Flame." He looked deeply into her eyes, and Jennifer knew he was trying to tell her something.

Flame stared at him, flushed, and said, "My husband is so looking forward to seeing you again."

Wickersham nodded glumly. "Yes. Of course. Your husband."

"And your wife—Deborah—"

"She's not here this trip."

There was that look again. Jennifer knew someday she would understand what the delegate had been trying to tell her mother. For now she noted that her mother looked sympathetic but not interested.

He shrugged and smiled at Jennifer. "See you tomorrow night, June."

"It's *Jennifer*," Jennifer said to his retreating back.

Jennifer hated riding in the carriage with her mother; her side always sank down like the heavy end of a teeter-totter. It was a silent ride. Jenny adored her mother with the abject adoration of a peasant gazing at a passing princess. She also hated her. What right did a mother have to be beautiful? It was embarrassing, and deep down, when she wasn't thinking about food, it hurt. All the remarks from well-meaning friends of the family about how at least she had inherited her mother's intelligence. The cruelty of classmates—since they had come to Juneau last year, she had been tagged Bimbo, the Dancing Whale: She walks . . . She talks . . . She eats!

Elsie, the German cook, was the only one who understood. Weighing well over 200 pounds herself, she would cluck over Jenny like some monstrous hybrid chicken, shoving soft bits of food into her mouth and watching her reaction. Between sampling in the kitchen with Elsie and eating with her parents, Jenny polished off six meals a day, which left her barely enough time to trot heavily down to the kitchen for a last snack at night.

Flame couldn't understand it.

"She has to be feeding you. She has to be."

Jenny's eyes widened under the pouches of fat. "It's my glands, mother."

"She'll outgrow it," Batt would say, and pat Jenny's hand fondly. He hadn't really looked at her since she was three years old, and now, at fourteen, he still imagined her with dimples only in her little hands, and not her behind.

The carriage turned off Franklin Street and up East Sixth Street. The houses climbed up the hills toward steep mountains. Still they hadn't spoken.

"Are you and dad fighting?"

"Whatever made you say that?" Flame looked at her daughter, stunned.

You never talk to me, Jenny wanted to shout. She shrugged. "No reason. I was only wondering." Another pause. "You don't laugh very much."

Flame stared at her thoughtfully. What a curious child. "Married people are still two people, going through different things," Flame said slowly. "Marriages change when people change. Some times it's easier to love a person than other times; but we'll always love each other." She looked at Jenny. "And what about you?"

I'm dying inside, Jennifer wanted to scream. *I hate myself.* Instead she swallowed slowly. It was the first time her mother had really talked to her in years, and she didn't want to wreck it by opening her mouth. "I'm fine."

"Good," Flame said absently, and patted her hand. She turned and looked out the window.

Jennifer felt tears behind her eyes. She wouldn't cry.

Tears were for people who still thought there was hope.

Thirty

The Wickersham-haters came to the party to see what he would say next so they could hate him more, and the Wickersham-lovers came to defend their king. The common folk just came to eat. Wickersham moved through the crowd, sipping Scotch, remarkably untouched by it all.

Flame wore a bronze satin hobble skirt with a pale chiffon bell. The top of the dress was cut in a low V that emphasized her breasts. She was wearing a diamond dog collar and matching earrings and there were diamond combs in her pompadour. Jennifer wore the only thing that would fit—a hideous blue-black dress that made her look like a giant tick.

The floor of the reception hall glowed in the soft light of hundreds of electric candles. Flame had ordered a brass quintet to play outside the house as Wickersham and the other guests arrived, but the cold jammed the instruments, so the players moved inside. Now they stood along a brocaded wall, eating the way they played, in unison. Extra staff had been hired, and maids circulated with silver trays of sandwiches and drinks. A buffet table next to the kitchen supplied guests with cracked crab, salmon, salad and desserts, and there was a full bar with two bartenders filling drinks. Jennifer stood miserably by the refreshment table, a living testament to the bounty of the table. Next to her, two legislators argued about home rule.

"It's true the federal government has shamefully limited the powers of this territory; it's also true that Delegate Wickersham was there when Congress did it. But the deed is done. And we get a territory in the bargain—no longer district status only—and some powers. The criminal code of the state of Oregon doesn't work for Alaska, for one thing. We need our own criminal code, with laws that apply to a land mass twice the size of Texas and a shoreline almost thirty-four thousand miles long. We can fix it. We should fix it. We're losing time, man, arguing among ourselves." The speaker was a small intent man with nervous fingers and no chin.

His partner harrumphed and crossed his thick arms over his chest. "Harry, you always were a bleeding heart. I'm surprised you're not pushing a measure through giving women the right to vote."

"I plan on it."

"Harry."

"It's 1913, man!"

Christian Degmont, one of two representatives from the Nome judicial district, glanced significantly at Jennifer, and his tufted eyebrows lifted like clouds. "Think about it, man. Women have—certain spells, when perhaps their judgment is not *perfectly clear*. Do you understand?"

Jenny did and wanted to crawl away, except for fear that someone would mistake her for a bench and sit down. Harry waved his fingers gaily. "I've already drafted it up. I'm introducing it in the House tomorrow."

"Why bother? They still won't be able to vote in federal elections."

"Christian, neither can we." They went away, and Jenny stole her hand behind her and found a sandwich.

A hand squeezed her wrist. She jumped and dropped the sandwich. Standing there was the most perfect boy she had ever seen. He was the same height—they were both already taller than her mother—with rangy arms and a slow smile. He had combed his brown hair carefully over a wide forehead and there was a small cleft in his chin. His eyes were clear blue. "Gotcha."

"Leave me alone." She tried to get her hand free and succeeded only in spilling her glass of punch down the linen tablecloth. "Now look what you made me do!" She was close to tears.

He looked at her calmly. "I think you're the fattest girl I've ever seen."

Jenny had never been so humiliated. She picked up the closest thing she could reach and hit him with it. It was a slice of Boston cream pie. He wiped his eyes, licked it off, and hit her with a second piece. With a cry of rage, she picked up an entire German chocolate cake and threw it at him. It splatted apart and fell to the ground like droppings behind a horse.

"*Jennifer!*"

"*Logan!*"

Two parents simultaneously pulled them apart.

"I am shocked. At your father's *party!* Go to your room at once!"

"Mother, he—"

"*At once!*"

"Logan Blue, I insist you apologize immediately. I'm so sorry—"

They looked up then. The color drained from Flame's face.

"Cahill."

"Flame—" He instinctively moved to embrace her but stopped and held out his hand instead. They shook formally.

His body was still lean and well muscled, the body of an athlete, but there was gray in the hair and a slight, almost imperceptible, softening along the jaw.

Cahill thought he had never seen a more beautiful woman. There were still the frank green eyes, the wide mouth and high cheekbones, but with maturity had come a new confidence.

Cahill remembered his son and pushed him forward. "This is Logan Blue. Logan, this is Mrs.—"

"Jackson. And my daughter, Jennifer." The glower on Jenny's face lost some impact beneath a sloppy layer of custard. Flame reached for a napkin and dabbed her face.

"I didn't realize— Then this party is yours."

"And my husband's. He's a senator."

"Yes, of course." He turned to Logan and said harshly, "I expect you to make amends to Jennifer. Squire her around tonight."

Jenny straightened indignantly. "Certainly not!"

Flame leaned over and said in an undertone, "It would be more fun than this. Somebody your own age. You could go skating at Evergreen Bowl."

"I don't like him," Jenny whispered urgently.

"I don't care," Flame whispered back.

Jennifer pressed her lips together. With fifty extra pounds, ~~maybe she could still hurl him to the ground and pummel him~~ to death. "Follow me. James will find you skates. And remember, this wasn't my idea."

Logan looked beseechingly in his father's direction and dragged after her.

"Is it really you?' Cahill's throat hurt.

She turned to the table and began filling his plate with food. "Are you staying long in Juneau?"

He shook his head. "We read the open invitation at the boat depot. I had no idea it was you. In the letter you never said who you were marrying—" His voice trailed off. "We're going to Valdez in the morning, and then taking a coach-sled over the Richardson Trail to Fairbanks. I'm the physician working with the Alaska Engineering Commission. The men are surveying alternate sites for the railroad."

The orchestra was playing "Only For You," and Cahill set the plate down carefully. He couldn't eat. He couldn't stop staring at her, and it hurt to see how casually she accepted it. She was adept at handling stares.

"You must talk to Batt. My husband. He strongly advocates a line from Seward to Fairbanks—from an open port to the interior of the territory. Transportation costs are prohibitive, especially since coal lands were closed to entry by Roosevelt."

There was another conversation going on, under this one. There was the familiar beating of her pulse in her throat, the high flush of her cheeks. "Has it affected Alaska?"

She nodded. "Terribly. Things have come to a standstill. Not one ounce of Alaskan coal can be mined. Everything has to be imported from Canada—at ten times the cost. No fuel for homes or gold dredges— And even with their rift, President Taft never rescinded it. At least President Wilson is more flexible. In his inaugural address, he suggested a leasing arrangement, twenty-five cents per acre for the first year and a royalty of two cents per ton. It's going to get things moving again." She shrugged and smiled. "Anyway, you'll find Fairbanks quite a change from Seattle."

"You've been there?"

"Batt and I lived there for ten years after we left Nome."

Ten years. Yesterday he had left her in Rampart, and now she was describing this gap in her life, out of which had fallen a fourteen-year-old child and a fifteen-year-old marriage.

"I'll probably be moving around."

"That's even better. This is an extraordinary land. Fairbanks is an arctic desert, you know. Has the highest shift of temperatures in the world. In summer it gets up to ninety degrees or more, and I've been there in winter at seventy below. It's flat. And the trees are stunted from cold. Not like here, where everything's so—immense."

Oh, Flame. I don't want to talk about Fairbanks, about coal or the blazing cold. I want to take you in my arms and never let you go. "Were you gold mining? I understand there was quite a strike in Fairbanks after the Nome rush."

She nodded. "We went there in oh-two, right after the Pedro strike. We own five dredges along the Cleary Summit."

"You'll be going back to Fairbanks, then, after the legislative session?"

"This is our home. It's not only the enormous expense of moving, either. Imagine moving a household three hundred and fifty miles over two mountain passes using mules! We went ahead by commercial dogsled, naturally, and stopped at roadhouses along the way. Probably by now they have a real building at the top of Thompson Pass, rather than a tent. Men were hauling lumber up from treeline a year ago. And the winds! Gales and sleeting snow. It never ends. Last year a man fell asleep with his face exposed and lost his nose and part of his chin. And then putting all the boxes and crates and furniture on a steamer to come here."

"Yet even as you say that, Flame Ryan—Jackson—I can tell you love the land. More even than the last time I saw you." Cahill was embarrassed at the slip, until he glanced at her face and saw she hadn't heard him at all.

A faraway look came into her eyes and the mask dropped. "How can I explain it? You can stand in the middle of Fairbanks on a summer night and it's blinding bright outside, and so quiet you're certain you hear the stars moving. The highest mountain on the North American continent stretches up through clouds, and the mountain is purple and violet and violent looking, and everything between is washed with blue and gold and green. And you say, This is Alaska. I have finally held it in my hands. And then, when you come *here,* to the Southeast, you can stand on the deck of a boat and feel the sea surging under you and you know the only thing that is real is the bite of a line flying through your fingers, connected to the biggest fish in the world. And you say, I dreamed the other. This is real."

She turned apologetically. "I'm sorry. I get started and—"

"Please go on. It's fascinating. Really. Especially here, I'll wager. With the legislature."

Her eyes glowed. "It is! Imagine! Here are men who *live* here finally making laws! You know what that means? It's the beginning of civilization! We've been a colony of the United States, really. It's taken what it wanted and ignored what we needed."

"Flame, we were here during the gold rush. There is an argument for federal control. The unstable population base, the vast distances—even the differences in cultures. You and I both know the Eskimos I doctored along the Arctic Ocean are as similar to the southeastern Tlingit as—golden Labradors are to the Cincinnati Reds. They've never gotten along and they never will." He was deliberately reminding her of the common history they shared from the gold rush, but Flame went on without him.

"Oh, fiddle. You know that's a ridiculous argument. In the first place, the two groups have never met. There's over a thousand miles and a bunch of Athapaskan Indians between them. Not to mention the sea, unless you expect your Eskimos to leap from southeast island to southeast island, like poor Eliza hopping ice cakes."

Now she was doing it. They had read *Uncle Tom's Cabin* together.

But she was going on. "In the second place, you know the federal government is the ward of the natives, anyway. The white laws don't apply as long as they keep to themselves. That's why they have separate schools. Anyway, that's the whole point! It *has* been boom or bust, ever since the beginning. And now there are doctors, lawyers—people of

336

substance and quality staying here, Cahill. *Staying!* And I'm right here in the middle of it. There's such vitality. Movers and decision makers sit at my table and discuss partitioning off Southeast as South Alaska and pushing for statehood, and it's glorious to be part of it! It's the best year yet!"

Her eyes were shining and her lips were parted slightly and Cahill couldn't stop himself from saying, "But have the other years been good?" If he could only hold her.

She faltered and blinked her eyes. He could see the flush of her cheeks through the amber net of lashes. When she looked up, her eyes were clear. "Come, I want you to meet my husband."

They were clearly in love.

Nothing stays the same. Two sides of land collide and shift under the sea, and a mountain folds its doughlike way out of the chaos; smoothly ordered lives shift and collide and rupture apart, and something alien springs from the rendering.

He liked the husband and hadn't remembered meeting him before.

"It was years ago," Batt said. "You and your wife were just leaving Alaska. By the way, how is Nelly?"

"We're separated," Cahill said shortly. He changed the subject. "Nice place you have here."

"Flame is forever fixing it up. A tuck here, some wallpaper there." He looked fondly at his wife. "I'm married to quite a woman."

"Yes, you are." Something passed between the two men, and it was as if Batt were saying, *I know what you want, but it's quite out of the question.*

Flame held out her hand to Cahill, and he stared at it momentarily, as if he had forgotten what was expected. They shook hands. "It was nice to see you again. If you'll forgive me, gentlemen, I have to confer with the cook."

She went through the crowd, and Batt clapped Cahill on the back. "Come on, old man. Buy you a drink."

Flame walked through the kitchen without stopping.

"Everything all right, ma'am?" Elsie's face was pink from the oven. She was pulling out a tray of sandwich rolls.

337

"Everything is fine," Flame said carefully. "Excellent. The food is very nice." She went out the far door, closed it behind her and climbed the stairs to the greenhouse. The door stuck slightly as she opened it. She walked between the dim rows of flowers, the moist beds of vegetables. The air was humid and buzzed slightly from the lights. Very carefully, so she wouldn't spoil her gown, she leaned over a tray of begonias and cried hoarsely into her hand. Her knees trembled.

Cahill. After all this time—what right did he have—even innocently—to come back into her life? And why this feeling? The strength of it surging up amazed and frightened her. She loved Batt. She and her husband had built a good life together. Never once in all the years of marriage had she been unfaithful, and something about the easy peace between them told her he wasn't hiding anything either. Oh, Batt would know! He would know! He probably already did. She went back over everything that had been said when she was standing between them—the way she looked. Her heart was pounding. She looked wildly around. In the corner the gardener was trying a great experiment; miniature oranges glowed like Christmas balls.

Cahill, Cahill. My friend, my love. *No*. Not a love. That was long ago. *Long* ago. Now her life was Batt and Jenny and this place.

God! Was their life so easily broken into, like a summer home? Was it a lie, all these years? If only her heart would stop pounding. She took a deep breath. Another. Cahill. If she could be two people! Not forever, but for now. If she could still love her husband and child and the life they had made and yet sit with this man from her past and give herself over totally to the delight of meeting him again. A dangerous thought. There could be no sharing of confidences. If she couldn't hold the line here, how much worse would it be after she had listened to his stories, held his dear hand in hers? Then there would be the desire for an embrace, only one embrace, and after that—

She whirled, and squeezed her eyes shut. No. It would not happen. Ever. And if she went to Fairbanks again, it would be with Batt.

Her husband's face rose before her. She had been lucky

338

when she married him. Over the years she had found more in him she liked and respected. How many women could say that? And Jenny—troubled, lonely Jenny—Jenny needed her, too. They were always missing each other, it seemed; but at least their arms were out, when they stumbled past each other, in the dark.

She wiped her eyes, arranged her skirt and took a deep breath.

She was Flame. Fire rising from ashes. She would survive this, too.

She hated him. No one *ever*, through all *time*, had hated another person as much as Jennifer Jackson hated Logan Blue. Even the name—*Logan Blue.*

They were taking the sleigh ride to Evergreen Bowl. James had suggested the covered carriage, but Jennifer had noted viciously that Logan didn't have a cap and insisted on this. "You'll like it," she assured Logan.

And he did. She hated him even more for that. He was leaning over the side, oblivious to the stinging wind, and watching sparks trail from the runners. Two huge horses galloped in front, bells ringing, snow flying, and the twelve passengers screamed and held on to the rail. Jenny alone sat in dull silence in the hay. How could it be? Logan Blue was a stranger, and already he was one of them.

James had found a pair of skates for Logan; dutifully he skated with her. On the shore huge bonfires had been built.

"You don't have to skate with me," Jenny said stiffly.

Logan looked at her coolly. "Good," he said, and skated away.

Oh, how she hated him!

She caught the next sleigh home, crept past the reception hall and up the stairs to her bedroom, where she locked the door, took off her clothes and planted herself in front of the mirror.

She was a monster—a blubbering mass of jelly flesh. She wanted to die. She combed her hair, put on a clean nightgown and lay down. She took a last breath and held it.

And then she remembered that after the party, there would

be leftovers.

The session adjourned. In sixty days, the twenty-four men in the House and Senate had passed laws creating eight-hour work days in the mines, old-age pensions, safety regulations governing stamp mills and changes in the civil and criminal codes. Women were given the right to vote in local and territorial elections, even though their counterparts in the nation could not.

The day the session ended, Batt and Flame bought the Alaska Sea Cannery for $4,000. It included six gill-netters, the cannery and housing for fifty employees. A counteroffer of $4,500 had been made, but it came too late to be considered. What had bothered Batt was not the offer, but who had made it.

The Alaska Syndicate was made up of the international banking houses of J.P. Morgan and Company and the Guggenheim brothers. Already it owned twelve canneries in Southeast, and a controlling interest in NC Company, the largest supplier of goods to the territory. Along with that went bits of steamers and pieces of copper; wherever there was money to be made there was the stink of syndicate. Three years before, a scandal erupted nationally when it came out that the Syndicate at one time had an option to buy all the coal lands in the Bering River area. It was the main reason the enduring friendship between Taft and Roosevelt was severed beyond repair. Roosevelt accused President Taft of knowing and approving of the potential monopoly, since a member of his staff, while still a civilian attorney, had helped draft claims for the group in the first place. It was messy and nearly endless and culminated in firings and resignations and lots of walking off in huffs.

It also split the Republican party in two and helped put Wilson in the White House. But even after all but the most zealous civics teacher had confused Pinchot with Ballinger and had forgotten exactly what it was that old what's-his-name did to the other guy that made the two presidents so mad at each other, the syndicate was quietly grazing on Alaska opportunities, getting fatter by the minute. The Syndicate came to

340

represent all that Alaskans thought was corrupt and corruptible in Washington. It had money to buy powerful votes and the power to forge dynasties. And now the Syndicate was sniffing around their cannery.

"I don't like it, leaving you here." Batt was staring out the window at the snow, smoking a cigar.

"Nonsense." Flame inspected a pair of tweed peg-top trousers and added them to the stack on the bed. "Do you think you'll need your cutaway?"

"Shouldn't think so. I'll be at the mines most of the time." They were negotiating the sale near Fairbanks of a dredge that had fallen under production. Batt sighed and smoked. "You can always send word with the mail run, if there's trouble."

She took down his Norfolk jacket from the shelf above the clothes rack, went over and kissed him. "I'll be fine. Anyway, you'll be home in a few months. It's not forever."

He held her tightly, and Flame looked at him in surprise.

"Have I told you, Mrs. Jackson, how fond I am of you?"

"Once or twice." She laid her head on his chest.

He stroked her hair. "You know what I was thinking the other day?"

She kissed his hand. "What?"

"It was strange. I couldn't remember a single thing that happened to me before I met you. Not one. Isn't that odd? But I can remember the smallest detail of our first meeting. You were wearing gray flannel, and there were pink buttons going down the front."

Flame looked up and laughed. "I'd forgotten."

"Oh, and on the table, when you picked up the gun and pointed it at me, there was a joker lying face up."

"That was appropriate."

He held her tightly. "Do you love me?"

She raised her head, startled. "Where did that come from?"

"Do you love me?"

"More all the time. Always and forever, and if I believed in reincarnation like the Indians and a few Eskimos, instead of my lapsed Baptist heaven and hell, I'd choose you again, next life."

"Would you?"

341

"Batt." She stood back and looked at him. "For fifteen years, I've lain next to you, listening to you snore. You do, by the way. I can't imagine life without you. You know that. Why are you asking this now?"

He pulled her close and kissed the top of her head. "Just a fool in love, I guess."

"No, really."

He was silent for a while, stroking her hair. Then he said, "Sometimes I look at you, and I can't believe how lucky I am. You're moving through a room of people, and all the men are in love with you and all the women hate you until they realize how wonderful you are—and then they can't bring themselves to hate you anymore, and that makes them feel even worse; but by the end of the night, they're giving you secret family recipes and telling you the darkest things they've done, knowing somehow it's *safe* with you. And they're right. And I watch you and just stand there thinking, 'I get to go home with her.' It's funny. When I had nothing, the world wasn't enough. And now that I have it all, all there is, is you."

She tightened her arms around him. "I love you, Batt."

He picked her up and there was the old fire in his eyes. "Prove it."

Old love is the best kind. You know where the arms go, the legs. When to exert gentle pressure, when to take it away. There is the rapid breathing, the slight arching of the back, eyes half closed. The power of sexual union doesn't dim with age.

It was familiar, Flame thought—this weight pressing her, the curve of his neck, the soft down of hair leading to the scalp. And the way the bodies fit, like sky against sea. They rocked in their familiar dance, and Flame thought there was more passion now between them than the first time they made love. Not the razzle-dazzle kind of passion—that's mostly show anyway, full of loud groans and deep frenzies—but a quiet complex sort of passion that comes from living with somebody else forever.

That's the kind no one talks about, because it's so much a part of you, you can't know it's there until the loved one dies or goes away.

342

But it's there, all the same.

She loosened her arms and he kissed her face and their bodies grew intent, listening to things only they could hear, and afterward, they held each other and slept.

Breakfast on a tray. A single rose. Orange juice, coffee and Batt singing wildly off key in the master bathroom. Flame opened her eyes, squinted at the sun streaming through the curtain lace and collapsed backward, groaning.

Batt lathered his face, brightened and said, "Morning, darling."

Mumbled response, then the recollection that today he was leaving.

There were a few minutes of quiet conversation, details about the cannery and final paperwork. Flame sipped coffee and sat up in bed while Batt shaved and dressed. And then as he stared intently at himself in the mirror, tying his ascot, he said casually, "If I see Cahill in Fairbanks, is there any message you want me to deliver?"

Her hand froze on the cup. *He knows.* "Nothing at all."

Thirty-One

It snowed until May, and then it started raining. Every day, fog lifted off the water, and the air was filled with the screams of gulls, the sharp scent of hemlock and cedar, and fish smell from the wharfs. Mountains climbed steeply behind the town, and moss grew up the sides of enormous trees, latched with heavy branches that kept the water from falling. Moss grew over the rocks; the ground was thick with needles. There were boat rides across the channel to Douglas Island, and a swimming pool at the Treadwell Natatorium. There were concerts and traveling minstrel shows and fights at the Opera House, and baseball games at low tide on a driftwood-strewn beach.

Jenny missed it all. She had a job during the day that kept her very busy. Every morning after breakfast her mother would leave for the cannery and Jenny would change into a smock and go to the kitchen where Elsie would feed her chocolate eclairs soft with custard, crisp fried chicken, plates of fudge and peanut brittle. Sometimes, Jenny's breath caught when she walked into the kitchen and saw the food, but mostly, her breath caught when she tried to climb the stairs. She wished she could move into the pantry: so convenient.

And then one morning, something terrible happened. Elsie had a heart attack and died.

They had to bury her in a piano crate in adjoining plots. Immediately afterward, Flame began interviewing potential cooks.

Jenny insisted she needed to be present since she would have the most contact with her anyway, but Flame firmly marched the candidates one by one into the kitchen and closed the door behind her.

And Jenny found herself getting very hungry. The merchants in Juneau had been ordered by Flame not to sell Jenny any food, so she found herself in the humiliating position of having to bribe children to make buys. The second day, the eight-year-old she had hired came out with fists of licorice and refused to give them up.

"But I paid you for them!" she cried, frantic.

"Too bad." He stuffed the longest stick in his mouth and bit off another. Jenny lost control and threw him to the ground. He screamed, he shrieked, he beat the ground and howled.

The store owner came running out. "What do you think you're doing?"

Jenny was eating as fast as she could.

"Young lady, I'm shocked! I'll call your *mother*."

Jenny's hand went down, the mouth reluctantly closed. "Here." She threw the candy at the boy, who immediately began howling again.

"She's eaten off it!"

The owner's eyes narrowed, "Buy this child some more."

Jenny had slunk home, empty-handed and hollow-stomached.

At the end of a week, Flame emerged from the kitchen with the thinnest woman Jenny had ever seen. "Jenny, I want you to meet Mrs. Obie. Our new cook."

The two looked each other over. Mrs. Obie smiled a brittle smile. "I see," was all she said.

The meals were small! So small! And where was the gravy, the rich butter sauces, the brown betty, the lemon meringue? Gone! All gone! In their places were vegetables. Not one of them had a nut or the thinnest glaze of chocolate to make it more palatable. And the meats! Broiled, baked—never fried. This woman had obviously never had a doughnut as a best friend or looked deep into a vat of grease and called it her own.

Jenny tried talking to her. Mrs. Obie picked up the knife she was using to chop yet more vegetables, pointed it at Jenny and told her to get out. In the middle of the first night, Jenny's hunger woke her up and she crept downstairs. She turned the knob to the kitchen door cautiously, listening to the quiet ticking and settling of the house. What was this? The knob was stuck! She turned it harder. No, locked! They had locked the door! She slapped the butt of her hand against it. She shoved her shoulder against the door. There was a cracking noise and the door gave way.

Mrs. Obie was standing on the other side, a blanket on the chair behind her. She smiled a thin-lipped smile. "Looking for something?"

The next morning at breakfast, Flame ignored Jenny's sullen silence and chattered brightly about the cannery. "I have a surprise for you," she said finally.

Jenny looked at Mrs. Obie in the kitchen cleaning, and thought she had been surprised enough.

"You're coming with me today."

Jenny was shocked. "Mother! You know that place makes me sick to my stomach! I can't eat."

Flame smiled.

It was awful. The workers were drenched in blood, blood to the elbows, slicing blobs of entrails, pouches of eggs, the floor slimy with scales, blood, fish eyes. Far overhead men sorted salmon and threw them down chutes. Flame got Jenny a pair of rubber boots and a rubber apron and gloves and left her in care of a Tlingit trainer. Jenny wished she had been left for dead. By midmorning, she was certain that she had.

Fish. Quick chopping motions severing the head, the mouth still opening and closing. The long slicing motion spilling fish organs, the guts smoothed off the wooden table to the floor, the fish thrown onto the conveyor belt that ran down the center of the table, to be carried to the canning room.

Another fish. Another. Her nose itched, and the bloody hand went up and stopped. Glazed eyes stared up from the table. Above her, fish spilled down a chute onto a pile of fish. A stooped Tlingit man with white hair picked up a fish in each hand and threw them down the conveyor belt. Jenny stood across from her Tlingit trainer and they lifted their fish off the assembly line and put them on the cutting table in unison. Guts and fins and tail and head, whack whack whack whack.

"Lunchtime," the foreman bellowed. He waded in hip boots through reeking guts. Men stooped, and shoveled intestines,

fins, heads, into buckets that were dumped into the bay.
"Lunchtime."

Jenny couldn't eat. Her apron was covered with slime and
scales, and clinging to her arm was a fish eye.

At dinner that night a scrubbed and subdued Jennifer picked
at the lonely arrangement of vegetables on the *hors d' oeuvres*
tray, watching the kitchen door and thinking murderous
thoughts about her mother. She was a slave, an indentured
servant. Oh, when her father found out! Her mother had
planned this for his absence—maybe even hoped Elsie would
die. The coroner had said it was a heart attack brought on by
obesity, but he was a *thin* coroner. They were all in this
together.

Her mother was talking: "I'm going to modernize the
system. Install machines to cut and clean the fish. The Iron
Chink, it's called. It's coming next week."

Jenny put an entire carrot stick in her mouth sideways and
made a face at her mother. Where was *dinner?*

"It means you won't be working inside anymore."

Jenny crunched and swallowed. "What will I be doing?" She
looked warily at her mother.

Flame smiled. "Fishing! On a boat. Isn't that wonderful?"

The door to the kitchen banged open and Mrs. Obie came
out, bearing an enormous platter. On it was an enormous fish.
It still had its head and tail attached. It stared at Jenny and its
baked eye seemed to be winking.

The Alaska Sea Cannery, which the Jacksons bought, packed
twenty-five thousand cases of salmon each summer, and each
case had forty-eight 1-pound cans. The cannery owned
outright six 38-foot gill-netters which were based near Point
Baker, seventeen hours from Juneau. The men gillnetted four
weeks straight, and then came to Juneau for two days rest.
Every night a tender came to the boat, picked up the catch and
took it to the cannery. The Jacksons leased three tenders that
worked rotating shifts: when one was leaving for the cannery,
another was leaving Juneau. The tenders also bought fish from
independent fishermen.

Jenny's boat was captained by a gruff Swede named Bjorn

who had fished for thirty years, ten with the same partner. But now Jake had an active conscience and a dying wife, so he waited in Juneau with her for death to come, and dozed in the rain, dreaming of the sea.

Bjorn got room and board and fifty dollars a month, plus a cent for every case that was canned. Flame paid him double for taking Jenny, and a cent extra for keeping her out of the galley.

It was easy money. The first morning, the boat headed out at five for the northern point of Prince Wales Island, and before six, the boat rose and fell in eight-foot swells. Bjorn drank coffee in the engine room. Jenny's face turned green, and she stumbled up the stairs onto the deck, where she hung onto a rope and threw up. She missed the water altogether. Bjorn made her wash the deck herself. She spent the rest of the day huddled on a narrow bunk in the fo'c'sle, forward of the galley, wan and shivering.

Jenny threw up at the swells, threw up when the nets were raised, threw up at the sight of fish. After a week Bjorn threw his weight around and made her get up and work.

They were gillnetting, using a finely webbed net that trapped fish by the gills. Jenny learned to roll the net out, dropping it carefully over the side with weights. For two hours they would drift, the net marked by buoys, keeping one eye on the tide. When the tide changed, bits of driftwood, tangled fishing lines and junk fish would rush into the net, so the trick was to lift the net right before rip tide, pulling it up on a cylinder drum shaped like a giant fishing reel, one foot on the pedal. They could catch six thousand fish that way each day. At night, when the sky deepened, a ninety-foot tender would sweep like a shadow across the water, butt up against them and lift out the fish. The giant kings and smaller reds went into a brine tank on board the tender; halibut, cod, candlefish, silver humpback whitefish and dog salmon were thrown into the bay to rot. Gulls followed the tenders, and on board was a fat dog.

"Why do they waste so many?" Jenny was staring out the engine porthole at the tender, moving away in the fog.

"It's what they like to eat in the United States. Only the pink flesh, never the white." He shrugged and leaned forward,

348

calloused hands around a cup of coffee. "You want to hear a good joke? The whites taste better! *Ja!* It's true." He leaned back and laughed, and his bony shoulders moved under the slicker.

She shrugged. "I don't know. It's a lot of waste."

He had grown fond of this lonely, peculiar-looking girl.

"Jenny, I am a fisherman. That is what I am. Fish. That's all for me. And clouds and sea." He spread out his battered hands, and his blue eyes glistened like pebbles under water. "Hard work, *ja*. Hard. But the hands pull fish, and the mind dreams. And when I look up, I see stars." He shook his head, and Jenny could see pink scalp under the white hair. "There is waste, *ja*. But there is respect, too. We never take so much there will be nothing left. We are not like the packers who use traps."

The twelve canneries owned by the Syndicate used fishing traps—mazes of webbing and piling that stretched over acres of sea. The traps were positioned directly in the path of spawning salmon and could trap twenty thousand fish in a day. The fishermen hated traps because they were ruthlessly efficient; they worried about next year's run and jobs; but the packers loved the traps and had the money to attend federal meetings in Washington, where they spread the love around. So the traps stayed.

There were nights when Bjorn's face would darken and his strong hands would pound the wheel in the engine room as he talked about traps. But there were other nights when he would play his harmonica in the galley and tell Jenny stories of sprites and elves and the magic that lived only in the foggy glades of home.

Every kid should have somebody like that, but if choices have to be made about such things—since people like Bjorn aren't spread like butter evenly across the world—then Jenny perhaps deserved him most of all. He was fierce and totally uncompromising when it came to work and what life expected of you—"You must work hard, Jenny, very very hard. Till the bones ache"—and yet wildly extravagant when it came to dreams—"Everything's in there, right there, inside of you girl! Anything you imagine you can be. But you must work hard.

349

Very very hard. Till the bones ache."

And Jenny did. A shy confidence began building in her about the way she handled things on the boat. She knew Bjorn depended on her to steady the nets when his fingers worked the delicate threading next to the giant spool. A slip and a finger could be lost. They never had an accident, and she was proud of that. She also knew that they were friends. It pleased her. It astonished her. The difference in age helped. With boys her own age, she was so miserably certain they were in her presence against their will, it made all the things she hated most about herself come lunging out. She had been born into the world uneasy, needing reassurance about her place in it, and now this lovely old man with scarred hands was teaching her how to *be*. There were vast stretches of silence that matched the slate gray sea and pale sky, rolling on forever. Far off, humpback whales grazed in the sea and spouted water, and sometimes sea otters and ducks splashed and gamboled in the waves. They would sit together on the deck, or apart, contemplating a separate sky. And the books! Bjorn had a library that rivaled her parents', if not in size, in quality. There was Edgar Allan Poe and James Fenimore Cooper and Stephen Crane's description of a sea, and Jennie could see that Cuba, and hear that other sea rumbling in its throat.

Twice there were bad storms that churned the sea and came roaring up from nowhere. Twice Bjorn guided the boat to shore, only the high white patches across the ridge of his cheeks betraying his fear. At those times they would go to the only building nearby, a dangerously decrepit bar built on stilts in the water. The men treated Jenny as one of them. They would sit in the bar and there would be the rich smell of fish and wind and wet wool, and they would talk of fish and catches and prices; and for the first time, the hard knot she had lived with for so long seemed to be loosening.

There was something else happening too, something under the shapeless woolen sweater and green rain slicker. The tall hip boots no longer encased her calves like sausage skins; the slicker no longer bulged across the slab of rump, the mound of stomach. But it was a private thing, and if Bjorn noticed it, he never brought it up. There was no mirror on board the boat and no mirror in the bar, and Jenny found herself thinking of her mirror at home, and wondering what she would find.

"Look at you." Her mother was waiting on the dock and rushed into Jenny's arms, hugging her tightly.

"Mother." A welter of feelings came rushing up: she wanted to tell her mother how it had been and what she had learned. She had been away forever. "Oh, I have so many things to tell you!" She clutched her mother's hand. Where had she ever gotten the idea her mother was hard to talk to?

"It's going to have to wait until dinner, but we'll share everything then, I promise."

Then Flame saw the familiar hurt on Jenny's face, the sullen mask falling. What had she said? She made a decision.

"No. Not tonight. Right now. You and I are going to spend the day together, talking. How does that sound?" She was taking Jenny's arm, her other arm around the girl's waist, and walking her up the boards to the cannery. "You can soak in a wonderful tub and wash your hair, and then we'll tell each other everything. I do have to talk to Bjorn first, though, but only for a few minutes. You're welcome to join us."

Jenny was beside herself. *You're welcome to join us.* She was being treated like an adult. And the whole day! She would have her mother to herself! Bjorn met them in the cannery, and after he was paid, Flame took them on a tour. Everything had changed. Most of the people were gone, and the floor was clean. One man now stood where Jenny and ten workers had cut fish. His job was to lay the fish headfirst evenly on a conveyor that carried them into a chopping machine where they lost their heads. Another worker pulled out the roe and put it gently on a separate conveyor to be specially processed. The headless fish was carried along and clamped up by a machine that divested it of fins, tail and innards, and then scoured it clean.

It was when they were looking down on this machine that Flame turned to Bjorn and said, "I have some news, Bjorn. There is no easy way to say it. You will always have a job with me. Always. But I have bought fish traps. They are being constructed right now in the Lynn Canal. I have sold the gill-netters, including the boat you use. I want you to work a trap

351

for me. There's no one more dependable or better with fish than you. The trap only takes one man working it. A tender will still come by every night to lift the fish, and I'll give you a bonus at the end of the season and a raise. What do you say?"

Jenny glanced up in time to see it all on his face—the stunned disbelief, the anger, the pain. More than the boat he loved, it was his life. And now it had all gone away. She wanted to run to him, take his gnarled hand, tell him her mother didn't mean it, didn't know what she was saying. She did none of these things. Bjorn stared quietly at the floor, over the railing at the workers in the room below and the shiny new machines, quiet and clean. "I don't think so, Mrs. Jackson." He stared again over the railing and then he said, "I'll get my things off now."

Flame made no attempt to stop him and no attempt to hold Jenny to her, but Jenny felt it, the tug. She wanted to run after him to thank him for everything he had done. She had already done that—time and again on the boat—but it seemed important to do it here, on land, in her mother's world. And then she thought of the fragile peace she and her mother had made, and felt it was too new for such a giant risk. So she stood and watched the man who had pulled fish from the sea and laughed at the elements walk down the ramp and out the door, his back straight and strong, without once looking back.

And then her mother grabbed her hands and laughed like a child. "We're going to have fun today!" And nothing else mattered.

Jenny stood in her underwear in front of the mirror and felt tears spring to her eyes. She was still immense, but less immense than a month ago. And she had eyes. Not little pig eyes, either, but *eyes*; green, like her mother's. Liquid pools of light. And not wading pools. Swimming pools. *The kid's got eyes.* And a waist. Nothing she'd care to accentuate at this point, but a waist, nonetheless. A slight valley in the fatty kingdom.

"Honey, listen to me." Flame's eyes were shining. "You're going to be beautiful; you really are. I'll be helping you every step of the way, and so will Mrs. Obie. It'll come off slowly, and that's the way it should. It will give you time to get used to it, develop healthy eating habits. If you like, we can work on fashions together—Mrs. Millner's dress shop has afternoon shows—and take walks in the woods. I've found a manager for the cannery and I'm going to be home, now. How does that sound?"

Angels sang in Jenny's world, trumpets sounded, and for the first time, God leaned down from His heavens and gave her a big kiss. "It sounds wonderful."

Batt couldn't believe the change when he came home in August. "Whatever you're doing with her, Flame, keep it up. I've never seen her so happy." They were unpacking his bags in the bedroom. He had sold the dredge and one claim for thirty thousand dollars and made a clear fifteen-thousand-dollar profit which he had immediately put into coal-lease options. "Did the Syndicate bother you?"

She shook her head. "Not at all. As a matter of fact, Mr. Morgan himself helped me get a good price on the traps we bought. He's really a very decent man, Batt. I don't know what all the fuss was about."

"It's a question of labor versus capital."

"You're right. I had more trouble with the fishermen and cannery workers than the Syndicate."

Batt was back on Jenny. "Did you know she's going swimming tomorrow? I can't get over it. The change in that girl. She hasn't gone swimming since she was a toddler."

"That was the last time she could find a swimsuit that would fit."

"She's a new person."

Flame smiled. "Wait until next year."

Thirty-Two

"It sounds awfully primitive."

"That's because it's a brand new town."

"There probably won't even be running water."

"Then you can run down to the water and get some." Flame went over and kissed her daughter on the forehead. Jennifer was curled up in the window seat of her parents' bedroom staring moodily out at the summer fog.

"It's not funny, mother." Jenny stretched her long legs up against the window frame and inspected them critically. "I'll probably have to leave these lounging pajamas here. I won't get much lounging done in a tent."

Strength, Flame murmured to herself, as she packed the turtleneck sweaters in the trunk. *God give me strength.*

Jenny swung her legs down. "I still don't see why I can't stay here with dad for a month while the house is sold."

"Jenny, we've been over this a thousand times. First of all, as you perfectly well know, the house *has* been sold. Your father signs the papers next week. And then he's off to Seattle to meet the Detroit shipment of steel rails. You know how important that order is to us. All the seventy-pound rails for the new track and sixty-pound rails for siding are being ordered through our company. It's a very big deal."

"The only big deal is that I'm sixteen and my life is finished! It's over! Why can't I stay in Juneau by myself? You could leave James here with me and Mrs. Obie. All my friends are here."

"You know James and Mrs. Obie are getting two months off while the new house is being built."

"It's going to be dirty in Anchorage. I know it. I hate dirt." Flame sighed. Think of a beach, a calm and peaceful beach.

354

"Jenny, on July ninth there is going to be a land auction in Anchorage for house and business lots. And you and I are going to be there. It's going to be fun."

"Why don't you take me to the motion pictures instead? Or Europe. Now *that* would be fun." Jenny got up, walked to the door and said dramatically, "I'm not kidding, mother. My life is finished."

A beach rose in Flame's mind, a calm and peaceful beach, and on the beach was a very large land mine. Toward the land mine she pushed the house and Jenny and the Ford and the dog that was sometimes housebroken. They all went in together. It made a very satisfying explosion. Lots of smoke.

Flame smiled serenely at her daughter. "Things will look different in the morning."

"*Which* morning, mother?"

Flame kept smiling. There was a little fire now curling around the edges of the mine. "Jenny. Don't pin me down. I've had a hard day. *Some* morning. Yes. Some morning soon. You'll wake up and things will look different."

"*Worse!* That's how they're going to look! Worse!" She flung herself down the hall.

Flame closed the door. Maybe one land mine wasn't enough. Maybe tanks were the answer.

The Railroad Act had passed in 1914 empowering President Wilson to build up to 1000 miles of railroad in the new territory. Eleven survey parties roamed the enormous wilderness, levels in hand, and finally agreed that the best route would connect the ice-free port of Seward, on Resurrection Bay in the Kenai Peninsula, to Fairbanks, some 467 miles to the north. A coal seam tunneled through the hills near Fairbanks, and the government thought the railroad could help get the coal out of the mountains and down to customers in the United States. Going south, the railroad could also stop for gold shipments in Glacier Creek, Sunrise and Hope, and for quartz mined near the Kenai River.

The government needed a place to dump supplies for the railroad between Seward and Fairbanks, and that's how the town of Anchorage started. Before the railroad came, the area along the Cook Inlet at Knik Arm was called Ship Creek and had two families. After the government unloaded equipment and lightered it to shore, some two thousand men—the kind that are always on the heels of opportunity—dropped down on Ship Creek, looking for work. They pitched tents on the beach. Eventually the government put in a hospital, school, water and sewer systems—but when Flame and Jenny arrived on a cloudy morning in late June of 1915, Flame's overwhelming instinct was to turn and flee.

"It's a wilderness, mother."

"I can see that, Jennifer."

The steamer *Mariposa* that had carried them from Juneau was now stalled in shallow waters; everything was being transferred to a smaller boat. Flame leaned on the railing and adjusted her felt hat.

Tents covered the mud flats. A small section of track had been laid, leading to the steep banks of the inlet. Short stacks of rails were piled with lumber and scrap metal along the track. There was a large horse barn and a few wooden buildings interspersed among the tents. A partially cleared bluff rose behind the flats to the south. The place was swarming with men. It reminded her of Skagway, except this town was younger and she was older. A lot older.

"Mother, there's still snow on those mountains. Look." Jenny decided to hold her mother personally responsible.

"Well, Jennifer, why don't you take a little spoon up there and shovel it all into the bay if it bothers you so much."

"I'm not going to like this. I'm not."

"Jennifer, someday you can tell your children about your hardships and get a lot of mileage out of it. 'If I could go into a savage wilderness, alone and friendless,' you'll tell them, 'then *you* can eat your peas and pull up your socks.' You'll see."

Not in the least mollified, Jenny stepped into the boat with her mother and was ferried to shore. Flame had booked reservations at the Crescent Hotel through Federick Mears, the chief of construction for the project. Batt had met him several times in Juneau when they were negotiating the rail shipment.

The hotel was a one-story building made of rough planks and

covered over with canvas. It was located between two stores: J.J. Ross, Signwriter, Painter and Paperhanger on the left, and on the right, Finkelstein & Shapiro: Clothing, Tents, Tarpaulins and Furniture. The hotel had been built on a platform off the ground, balanced on logs. The owner was expecting them. He had gray side-whiskers and gold-rimmed glasses and a large, pink nose set in a dead white face. His name was Crescent, as in Hotel.

"You'll have adjoining rooms, and there's a bath at the end of the hall. I'm sorry things are so primitive, Mrs. Jackson, but I trust your accommodations will meet with your approval. I assure you the hotel is the finest in Anchorage. Ours is the only one with a hand pump inside. We're hopeful hot water will be installed by September, but you'll probably be in your own home by then. Have you had a chance yet to go over the plans of the new town? There's some good property going on the block."

Flame shook her head. "I'm on my way to the Alaska Engineering Commission offices now. Mr. Mears is expecting me. When the trunks arrive, please put them in our rooms."

"Certainly, Mrs. Jackson."

She went down the hall to her room, which bore a large iron three on it, went in and closed the door. She was dreadfully tired. She could hear Jenny next door through the canvas walls, singing tunelessly. She wished she had time for a nap. She took off her hat, sat down on the edge of the double iron bed and unlaced her high shoes. She rubbed an arch and looked around the room. There was a fringe on the gasoline lamp, and the bureau next to the window had a lace doily under the basin and pitcher. She leaned over and rapped the wall gently. The canvas quivered.

Next door the rustling stopped. "Yes?"

"Jenny, it's your mother. I'm going to see Mr. Mears. Do you want to come along?"

Long pause. "No." Jenny managed to squeeze into the single word utter boredom and a sense that her life had ended several minutes ago, only nobody had bothered to see it.

Flame kept her voice level. "All right. It's"—she consulted the watch she wore around her neck—"about two o'clock now.

357

Let's meet back here for dinner at seven. How does that sound?"

How could her mother think about dinner, when her life was over now? "Fine," Jennifer said. "Just fine."

Flame saw the beach again and on the beach Jennifer was criticizing the quality of sand. Next to her were crates of furniture. The dog piddled happily on her shoe. Over the rim of the hill rumbled a little line of tanks. "Good," Flame said, and put on her shoes.

"Mrs. Jackson, how good to see you again!" Federick Mears was a large vigorous man with dark hair and a firm handshake. He came around his desk and guided her to a seat. "You must be exhausted after your journey."

"Actually I'm feeling rather well."

"Splendid. I was just readying the Ford for a reconnaissance mission. There are four miles of road, so far, and a primitive one at that, but I thought I'd see where the new town is going to go. If you'd care to join us—"

"I'd like that, thank you."

Mears looked behind her to the open door, a look of delight on his face. "Oh, good, right on time. Mrs. Jackson, I'd like you to meet Dr. Blue. He's the physician for the commission. He is going with us."

Flame should have expected it. She felt the familiar tightening. She extended her hand. "Dr. Blue." They shook hands. "You're looking well."

"Mrs. Jackson, what a surprise." He looked as uncomfortable as she. There were lines around the blue eyes. He had grown a mustache.

"You know each other?"

Neither of them knew what to say. Finally Cahill said, "I attended a party she and Senator Jackson gave honoring Delegate Wickersham. How is your husband?"

"Quite well, thank you. Busy." She glanced at Mears. "He's ferrying a shipment of rails for the new line up from Seattle. We expect him next month."

358

The silence grew. Mears said, "If everybody's ready, let's go."

Flame couldn't think of a graceful reason not to.

She sat next to Mears in the front seat; Cahill was in back. The Ford bucked over stumps and root systems. The trail ended on the bluff to the south. The three got out.

From the bluff the tents looked like fallen handkerchiefs. A steamer was anchored in the inlet and a lighter slowly moved toward it. The water stretched in placid blue-and-purple patterns. An arm of land jutted a mile into the water; on it were low chalk cliffs and spruce. The ocean spread out to the west, and in the distance indistinct smudges of soft white-and-blue mountains rose against a pale wash of sky. But to the east was the Chugach Range, angular and immediate, high hills of tan and purple patched with snow and fronted with low rolling hills of spruce and birch.

"Fourth Avenue is going in here," Mears said, pacing it off. "It's going to be the main business street in town." Small survey markers had been placed in the ground every hundred feet. The area had been newly cleared and smelled of loam and leaves. "Careful of the stumps now." Mears took her arm. "I've hired ninety men to clear the townsite. It has to be finished by the ninth. One hundred sixty acres. The blocks are three hundred feet square. There they are—see them? To the south." He pointed toward a grove of trees out of which was emerging a group of men, hauling logs.

"How big are the lots?" Flame picked up her skirt and stepped carefully over an exposed root.

"Fifty by one hundred forty feet. The town is thirty-two blocks." He grimaced. "Engineers aren't the most creative sources for street names. We numbered east-west streets and put letters on the north-south ones. Everything's up for bid except the lots we reserved for the school, federal and municipal buildings, and city parks. The cemetery's on the southwest edge of town. And the wharf. We reserved space for that. It's going in first."

"What do you expect the lots to go for?"

"I don't know. Hard to say, really. The Cook Inlet *Pioneer*

359

predicts the lots will sell cheaply, in the neighborhood of a hundred dollars, but I think they'll go higher."

He was walking along the edge of the bluff, stooping every so often to inspect the ground. Cahill lingered behind. Mears pointed down the hill. "That present track is temporary—from the dock to the office building. When your husband's shipment comes, we'll lay the new line. It's going to run from the main track just east of the Crist house. That's where we'll build the engine house."

"All the tents are going, then."

Mears nodded. "As soon as the auction. And just in time, too. Dr. Blue is worried about typhoid, with two thousand people living on the flats. Ship Creek is off limits for dumping refuse, but there's always the threat of it. We're already negotiating for a permanent system from Crater Lake." He pointed down the hill. "See that? Work's starting on the commissary. A shipment of lumber just arrived from Seward. The freight yards are going in north of the present track. Eight tracks and a storage building for the six thousand tons of steel rails your husband is bringing. The first thing, though, is a cribbed stone wharf for coal."

"Cook Inlet is salt water, isn't it? It shouldn't freeze easily."

Mears nodded. "The problem is the creeks. Ice builds up in the winter and slabs of it settle in the inlet and freeze. Then the tides lift the ice, along with tons of mud. It puts the ships in great danger."

"What are you going to do?"

"Build a wharf sturdy enough to withstand the shifting tides. It's going to be eighty feet high and a thousand feet long and can take tides up to forty-two feet. Getting technical, the reentrant angle is a crescent shoreline. Anyway, it's perfect for freight traffic, even after the railroad is built. Passengers, of course, will prefer the railroad, since it will cut fifteen hours off the trip."

"Are you concerned about snowslides?" They were walking back toward Cahill.

Commissioner Mears shook his head. "There are some heavy snows between here and Seward, but for the most part, no. We'll have to build some snowsheds, I expect. The real problem is the north side of Turnagain Arm. It could cost as much as one hundred thousand dollars a mile, just for grading and bridging work! It's the quartz."

"Do you pay workers by the hour?"

Mears shook his head. "Piecework. The stations—every hundred feet—are bid on by different crews. They're paid when they do the job. Specific projects are handled the same way. I have eight men building a wagon road and crossing; another two laying a waterline, add another man painting. I do pay hourly wages to men laying track and building bridges. We expect to have thirteen miles laid this summer alone, thirty-five more cleared and graded and another forty cleared. It's a slow process." He looked up. "I say, Anderson!" He motioned to a man who was coming from the woods, carrying a toolbox. Anderson wiped his forehead and waved. "Cahill, would you mind taking Mrs. Jackson home?"

Cahill shook his head, "Of course not."

Mears turned apologetically to her. "I'm sorry for the inconvenience, Mrs. Jackson, but since I'm up here—"

"I quite understand." Flame's heart pounded.

Commissioner Mears shook her hand. "So good to see you again, Mrs. Jackson. Please stop by for tea when you're settled."

"Certainly."

He was off, scrambling down the gravel embankment, dust rising behind him.

Flame and Cahill walked in silence back to the car. They didn't look at each other. Before he opened her door, he said, "Would you like to see the docks? It's really quite interesting."

Perhaps if she and Batt had been going through a hard time in their marriage, she would have said no automatically. If their relationship had needed careful attention, maybe something would have warned her away. But she was a happily married woman. The little she and Cahill had shared happened a lifetime ago, to someone else. It was time to put this ghost to rest.

"Yes," she said. "That sounds interesting."

They never made it to the docks, never walked along the

mouth of Ship Creek. She settled on the seat and Cahill closed her door. He cranked the car and got in. They sat in silence. The noise of workmen clearing land was muted, far away. A robin warbled. Flame looked at him sideways and felt the familiar dull ringing in her ears. Her heart. Her heart was bursting. He looked at her wonderingly and then without a second's thought, they fell into each other's arms.

They couldn't stop kissing each other. They knew what would happen, where it would lead, and yet they were powerless to stop. He loosened her blouse and kissed her throat and she closed her eyes and groaned. All her life she had been afraid of this, wanting this, knowing somehow it would end in this.

He pushed her away first. "I want to make love with you, Flame. But not here. Not this way."

"Tell me." Her voice was foreign, heavy.

"I don't want you to look back on this and wonder how it happened, or feel that you fell into it. I've loved you too long, Flame."

"What do you want me to do?"

He turned in his seat and shifted the gears. The car lurched forward. "I'm taking you home. I want you to think about it. About what it could mean to your life. Your marriage."

There was a long pause. The car bumped down the road and Flame held on to the side. She felt faint. "And then?"

"And then if you choose to, Flame Ryan, if you *choose* to, I'll be waiting for you tonight, at the docks. Eight o'clock. Where are you staying?"

"Crescent Hotel."

He took her there and opened the door for her. He wouldn't look at her. "Mrs. Jackson." He tipped his hat.

She went down the hall and knocked on Jenny's door and was relieved when nobody answered. She closed her door carefully behind her, took off her shoes and hat and coat and lay down. Her body was leaden. Either way she would perish. Either way. If she never saw him again, her heart would stop beating. But would it? Would it truly? Ever since she was small, they had been promised to each other. It had been taken for granted. Oh, how had things ever gotten so tangled? Men build laws and institutions and lives go along quite happily, sometimes forever; then something—a chance thing—an innocent meeting, a conversation, and the lives change course and no institution in the world can hold them in. But she loved Batt. More than that. They had broken through the terrible constraints that keep people apart; they trusted each other. What if she never saw *him* again? Wouldn't that be worse? Her body was aching. Her head. She was cold. She got under the covers and curled up, like a child. She dozed. Jenny knocked on her door at six-thirty and came in, concerned. "Are you all right, mother?"

"I think I've got a fever. I'll skip dinner, if you don't mind."

"Can I bring you something?"

Flame shook her head. "Sleep. That's all I need. Just some sleep."

Jenny sat and held her mother's hand, and Flame slept.

She woke suddenly and looked at the clock. Five of eight. Jenny had left. There was something— It came back. She sank against the pillow. She would get dressed and tell him she couldn't see him anymore. She owed him that much. Don't lie to yourself! Flame thought fiercely. She put on her shoes. No more attempts at trying to justify it. No more tries at understanding. It simply was.

Cahill had hired a dray and wagon and was staring over the water at Mount McKinley when she came up. He looked at her steadily. "You're sure it's what you want?"

"It's what I've always wanted," she said. He thrust down his hand, and she stepped up the ledge and sat next to him.

He picked up the reins, and the horse began plodding. They went south up the road and then east toward the Chugach Mountains. There was a faint Indian trail they followed. The mountains were purple with patches of brown and snow. They held hands. "How are your parents?"

"My father died in oh-six. Third heart attack took him. Mother took it hard. Knew she would. Spent a year in black, refusing to go out of the house except to church. And then the first Sunday she came out of mourning, she met this man from the downtown Synod—he was just visiting the congregation—

and boom!"

"You don't mean it!"

Cahill nodded. "Darnedest thing I ever saw. But they seem to be very happy with each other. He's quite devoted to her. They've been married eight years already. He raises weimaraners. Ugly things. Shows them all over the Pacific Northwest. And mother's still painting on china. She has an outlet in Seattle she sells cups through—gets a healthy commission. Amazing, the stuff women buy! Some of them come in and get cabinets full of it! Anyway, she's happy. She dyes her hair blue, now, can you imagine? My own mother. They still live in the house." There was a pause. "Nelly left."

"I'm sorry."

"It was never good between us. Reverend Marsh passed on—did you know?"

Flame shook her head.

"He went before dad. Let's see—oh-two, I think. It was very odd. Blood poisoning. He was suffering from arthritis the last years and had read somewhere that lead relieved the symptoms. He was rubbing it into his skin, Flame. A terrible thing. I kept thinking—if he'd only told me—"

They lapsed into silence. The trail became fainter and fainter and the birches thicker. Finally the horse stopped. Cahill got out and tied him up. The sky was gray and quite light. There was a slight wind.

Cahill had brought a down comforter and a mosquito-netting drape and a picnic basket, and he spread the comforter under the tree and arranged things neatly before helping her down. There was a bottle of wine with two glasses, a loaf of bread, cheese.

He stood quite close to her, without touching her, and they looked at each other. She unbuttoned her blouse. It was peculiar. They hadn't touched each other, yet they were breathing heavily. She hung her blouse neatly on a tree limb and unfastened her skirt. She stepped out of it, took off her shoes and stockings and slip and unfastened her brassiere. It was as if they had been doing this forever, this way, with each other. When she turned back to him, he was naked and aroused. She felt a thrill of fear. What was she doing here?

364

"Flame." He came to her and slipped his hand inside her silk drawers and rolled them down over her hips. They fell to the ground, and she stepped out of them. He opened his mouth and kissed her without touching her body and then she leaned slightly in and felt the shocking heat of his penis touching her belly. They groaned together and fell to the ground.

It was physical, this physical thing between them, this hunger. In chemistry there can be found elements that are irresistible to each other, that almost bore through the glass tubes holding them, and when they combine, they meld into a new thing. It was like that here; they needed the other to live. Over and over again they made love. Once she leaned against the birch tree, dreamily watching the sky turn dusky—it never was completely dark this time of year—while Cahill thrust himself into her from behind, steadily, gently, hypnotically. She took him in her mouth and drank, as did he, and it was dark and sweet and tender. She held him in her hands while he came, cradled him in her breasts, between her thighs, inside her. Over and over, before the last erection had died, he grew again, until their bodies were slippery and sore but impossible to separate. Finally they fell into exhausted sleep, curled spoon-fashioned against each other, Cahill still deep inside her.

In Alaska in the summer, there is no dawn—just dusk and a gradual lightening turning to more light. Flame awakened to feel Cahill thick inside of her. She sighed slightly and exhaled her breath, watching the breeze lift the bottom of the netting. They were inside a cloud and she was possessed by this man. He shifted against her, holding her hips, and her body warmed around him. She began trembling. Such an intimate thing, to be joined to another. And if the space in her body would never feel the same, never feel completely, utterly hers again—then it was equally true that Cahill's penis would always feel incomplete without Flame around it. It was this physical thing, yes, but more.

They had ridden together, over the dark and purple landscape of their imagination, to a country seen, yet not known. They had lain together in dappled silence, in a thousand barely forgotten dreams. He was of her and for her and nothing savage or civilized in this world or the next world would ever separate them. They had been born together, in a green dawn long ago, and they would change forms together when the time came.

Laws were nothing in the face of it. Rules, foundations, marriages. All crumbled to dust against this truth: they were the same, in separate bodies.

"What are we going to do?" she whispered.

He kissed the back of her neck. "When is he coming to Anchorage?"

"Next month."

"Then we'll think about it next month."

"I think it would be a very nice gesture," Cahill said firmly. He was standing in his sleeveless vest and shorts, shaving in front of the mirror.

"You mean I *have* to, don't you?" Logan narrowed his eyes and rolled a cigarette in the ashtray by his bed.

"Yes, as a matter of fact, that's exactly what I mean."

"She's a pig, father! She is! Would you want to be saddled with a beast like that for the night? And on the *fourth*. I'd have to put her in a choke chain to take her from party to party."

"Logan, that's enough."

He snapped a match to the cigarette and inhaled.

"When did you start smoking?"

"When I got to be the same height as you, father. Last year. You lavish a great deal of attention on your only child." He examined the cigarette. "Let's negotiate this thing. If I take her with me—just an if, you understand; I'm not locking myself in at this point—will you put the roadster on order?"

Cahill considered it. "Wrong. Your old man can still take you to the ground."

Logan stubbed out the smoke. "Really?"

Cahill put down his brush. "Really."

Logan came at him hard, and Cahill was surprised at the strength his new twenty pounds gave him. They grunted in silence, and then Cahill broke the hold Logan had on his arms and neatly buckled his legs with a sure thrust of his foot, at the same time pinching a nerve in his neck. Logan collapsed to the floor.

366

Cahill turned back and picked up the brush. "So we're in agreement? You will take Jenny to the ball game and the dance?"

"I'd rather throw myself under a train."

"You'll have to wait until next year, I'm afraid. The track hasn't even been laid."

"I have other plans, father. I'm interested in someone else."

"Have you asked anyone else yet?"

Logan sighed. Cahill went over and clapped him on the back. "It's just for one night, old man. Think of it as an errand of mercy."

"Everyone's going to be laughing at me."

"With you," Cahill said heartily. "With you."

"She really is a pig." Logan got up angrily and stomped out the door. Cahill stuck his head out after him.

"They're staying at the Crescent Hotel. I told Mrs. Jackson you'd pick Jenny up about six."

Logan stuck his hands in his pockets and walked angrily outside. Damn his father! He wasn't a kid anymore, somebody to order around. Do this, go here. He scuffed a rock savagely and started aimlessly down the street, avoiding the stumps. He went to the Montana Bar to shoot pool, and it was there that the idea came to him.

The bar was in a canvas tent; inside were the regulars. One of them was a hulking farm kid from Nebraska, with freckles and buck teeth. Logan liked Stanley because he lost a lot, and he always did it agreeably. They had been playing nine-ball for an hour, using quarters, when Logan told him, "Tell you what, I'll give you the chance to win back everything you've lost."

Stanley's interest perked. "What do I have to do?"

Logan racked the balls and broke them. "Nothing. If you win, you get everything back—and if you lose—you still win." He studied the table. "Left side pocket, one." It fell in. "Whatcha say?"

"Tell me how I still win."

"You get to take this girl to the game. And to the dance. You know how scarce girls are." He called the 2, 3, 4 and 5 balls correctly.

"So what's wrong with her?"

367

Logan shrugged. "Nothing. She's just not my type, is all. I'm only trying to do a buddy a favor."

Stanley chewed his lip. "What does she look like?"

"You mean is there anything wrong with her? Nothing. Nothing at all. She's—healthy looking, Stan. Very healthy."

Stanley's eyes narrowed. "You mean she's fat."

"I didn't say that."

"You didn't have to."

"Cross my heart, I swear to God, she's not fat." *She's immense, ole buddy. She's tremendous. She's in a category all by herself, along with a heifer I saw once at an auction.* "She's got brown hair and light-colored eyes. Green, I think. Cute little smile." The balls kept rolling into the pockets. "I'll even double with you. How's that? I'm going to ask Amanda Clemons myself. We'll meet you there. How does that sound?"

The balls were in now and Logan lined up the cuestick. "Middle left pocket." He stroked the nine-ball gently and it rolled in.

"She's not fat?"

"You can pick her up at six, at the Crescent Hotel. Ask for Jenny Jackson."

Logan whistled as he bathed and shaved, whistled as he dressed. Amanda was skimpy in the brains department, but had a set of mammaries that would have brought her a blue ribbon in a 4-H fair. He was teaching her to kiss with her mouth open. It was going to be a splendid night. Stanley wouldn't think so, of course, but that was Stanley's problem.

Logan and his father were staying at the Two Sisters Hotel and Waffle Shop, which was only a row of tents away from Amanda Clemons's place. Her father was an engineer with the railroad and her mother was active in the newly formed Women's League. Amanda had six married sisters and a brother who owned a car dealership in Cincinnati. Mrs. Clemons thought Logan was a very nice boy, which ordinarily would have rung a death knell for the relationship. Logan had put Amanda's fears to rest on the first date with some very fancy hand action. They had been inseparable since.

Amanda was ready for him, and as Logan took her arm, he

368

thought again what a striking couple they made. He was tall and broad through the neck and shoulders, with dark curly hair and brown eyes. Amanda was light in color and on her feet; everything about her was pale, delicate, fragile. The baseball diamond had been laid out between the tent city and the docks, and from a distance they could see a sizeable crowd already gathered in the bleachers. The wind started and Amanda's hand flew up and anchored her straw hat. Logan was feeling better and better. He'd never find Stanley in such a crowd. Of course, afterward Stanley would probably come looking for him with a gun, but that was afterward. This was tonight, the Fourth of July, and there would be fireworks. He squeezed Amanda's arm and she smiled up at him and moistened her lips.

But luck was not in Logan's corner. He had barely settled Amanda in the bleachers, his jacket padded under her, when there arose the most incredible din. Ballyhoos. Amanda nudged him. "I think that person over there is trying to get your attention."

"Where?" Logan jerked around. Stanley was standing up three rows back, waving his arms. "Maybe he's rooting for the women. The bases are loaded." He turned back and hunched forward. "Go, Sailors!"

Amanda watched Stanley for a while and then said, "No, he's coming this way, Logan."

Stanley was blazing with good cheer. "Hi, there. You didn't hear me calling?"

Logan and Amanda were making room in the bleachers. "Well, well, Stanley," Logan said heartily. "Well, well." He affected surprise. "So Jenny isn't with you? What a shame."

"Oh, she's here all right." He stood up and motioned. "Down here!"

Logan looked behind him. Threading her way through the crowd was a tall, statuesque brunette with shapely legs. "That's Jenny?" Logan blurted out.

"I thought you knew her."

"It's been a long time—" She was coming closer, and the closer she came, the more striking she looked. She had very

369

dark eyebrows and full lips that curved up insolently and vivid green eyes that looked Logan over once and coolly looked away.

Stanley leaned over to him. "I owe you one, old man, I really do."

"Jenny!" Logan whinnied.

She stared at him. "Oh. Hello, Logan." She settled back in her seat and said something to Stanley. He said something back and they both laughed.

"Jenny," Logan repeated.

Amanda shifted in her seat and squeezed his hand. "Introduce me," she whispered.

"Jenny"—he had to wait until she ran out of things to do with Stanley and finally looked his way—"this is Amanda Clemons. Amanda, meet Jenny Jackson."

"Nice to meet you," Amanda said. Her voice was full of suspicion, and Logan knew she didn't think it was nice to meet Jenny at all.

Jenny smiled as if she understood. "Nice to meet you." And that was it. Jenny sat on the end next to Stanley, who monopolized her attention telling stupid jokes. Jenny laughed a lot, but Logan thought she was probably only being polite. Amanda sat on the other end, telling incredibly long-winded stories in a whiny voice. Why hadn't Logan ever noticed the whine before? Her adenoids should have been buried at sea. The game went into extra innings and the people around them were hoarse from yelling.

"I've got a good idea," Logan said brightly, "let's take the girls to the Model Café for dinner. How does that sound?"

Amanda dug her fingers into his arm and hissed, "I thought we were going walking. Alone."

Stanley said, "Sorry, old man. Jenny and I have other plans."

"What other plans?" He felt suddenly protective.

"Just—other plans." Stanley smiled possessively at Jenny, and Amanda sighed and her fingers relaxed.

By all counts it should have been a red-letter night. He walked with Amanda up the hill to the bluff where the new town would be, and together they watched the fireworks explode over the flats. He kissed her a lot, and she let him wander freely under her blouse. But then he would remember Jenny, and the thrill would go out of the night. When he walked her back, she chattered brightly about tomorrow, assuming he would be in it with her. He told her he might be busy soon—he wasn't sure, but probably—with the auction and all.

A pain came into Amanda's eyes, and then a bitterness. "She's cheap, you know!"

How had she found him out? He didn't even have Jenny yet, and already he had lost Amanda. Her chin trembled, and as if emerging from a coma, he saw it was a very weak chin indeed.

"I don't even know her!" he defended himself.

"But you knew exactly who I was talking about!" She dissolved into tears and flounced into the tent. He walked disconsolately down the street. They were impossible. All of them. He found himself standing in front of the Crescent Hotel, looking up at the windows and wondering which one belonged to Jenny.

He tried steadily for three days. She was busy. She wouldn't see him. She was out. Mrs. Jackson relayed the messages. The auction had been delayed a day and finally on the tenth, the day of the auction, he caught up with her.

It was a warm day, with high reedy clouds and a light wind. Jenny was sitting on a blanket near the edge of the woods, reading a book. Her hat fluttered next to her. The soft blue gauze of her dress drifted over her long legs; the dark, glossy hair tumbled down her back; the pink ribbon lifted off the hat.

"Jennifer?" He came closer.

She glanced up and then back at the page, reading to the end; she marked the page with a bookmark and closed the book. "It's quite lovely this time of year, don't you think?"

He stood in front of her, his hands clasped. "Jennifer, I'm sorry. Please forgive me."

"Whatever for?"

"For being a cad. I was awful and I'm sorry."

She smoothed her dress and Logan saw the shape of her knees. "There was a person inside all that fat."

"I see that now."

"Why was it so difficult to see it then?" ~~she flared. "I needed it *then*.~~"

"Do you think you've changed at all? I mean, inside, when you lost the weight?"

She considered it. "In some ways, yes. I have changed."

He motioned to the blanket. "May I?"

She deliberated; nodded barely. He dropped to his knees. "I've changed, too, Jennifer. I have. Two years have passed. And I look at the terrible things I did to you—awful things, really—and I'm deeply sorry. Please accept my apology. Please." He held out his hand.

"All right," she said finally, and picked up her book. "Now leave; I'm busy."

"Jennifer," he placed his hand gently over the book. "Please. Let's start from here. Fresh."

She appeared to consider it, and Logan thought he would never take anything for granted with her. There would be nothing easy about Jennifer Jackson.

"What would you like to do? We could go swimming. I found a lake not far from here. It's a hike, actually. But we could take a lunch— How does that sound? I could bring a pistol to scare away bears. Or something here. Did you know there's a funny old woman in purple shoes who gives readings? Really. She has a crystal ball and everything. What do you say, Jenny?"

He looked contrite and sincere, and in spite of herself, Jenny began to warm to him.

Slowly, she put down her book. Logan stood up, offering her his hand. She took it this time, and he pulled her to her feet. Then he picked up the book and blanket, and they walked into town.

The woman was ancient, with baby-smooth cheeks and wrinkled fingers. She wore plumes of feathers in her hair and over her shoulders. A wide part separated plaits of thin white hair she had dyed black. The white had grown out an inch making her look like a molting bird.

The inside of the tent was covered with spidery drawings of planets and constellations, but next to the bed was a serviceable coat. "Ah, welcome, welcome, children. Such a welcome." Her voice was dry leaves.

Logan grinned at Jenny and held out a bill. "Two, please."

The woman's hand darted out, fingered the bill, and thrust it deep into the feathers. "Ladies first."

Jenny sat across the table from her. The tent smelled of incense. A fly droned against the flap. The woman stared intently at Logan, and then back to Jenny. "You've known each other a long time. Yes, yes, a *long* time." Jenny smiled into her hand. She was wonderful.

In front of her on the table were tarot cards, a crystal ball and tea leaves. The woman fanned her fingers out and brought them to rest on the ball. She stared into it intently. Logan leaned over Jenny's shoulder, trying to get a look.

"Ah, you spent time on the sea." She shook her head. "Quite a different person, I see in here. My, my." She looked pityingly at Jenny and Jenny flinched. "Strength, though. Solid steel. What's this? What do I see. Oh, ho! So you have *that* on your mind, do you!" She smiled at Logan. "Well, she's a strong-willed one, she is. She'll—" Her face turned white. Her hands came up. "No," she whispered. "No."

"What is it? What do you see?"

"No!" It was a shriek. The woman's eyes grew huge, and she looked from one to the other. "Sick! Defiled filth!" Her hands came up to her throat. "Leave at once!"

"What is it? What's wrong?"

"At once!" The woman stood so suddenly that her table upset and sent the crystal ball and tea cup and cards crashing to the ground. The ball cracked apart. A wisp—a vapor— something puffed out of it and was gone. "My pretty, my pretty, no no no." The woman cradled the ball in her lap like a child, crooning to it. Logan and Jenny backed out of the tent and ran.

They ran half a block, then collapsed, laughing. "What a witch!" Logan said.

"And the part about knowing each other a long time. Imagine." They smiled at each other. "Too bad you couldn't get your money back."

"It was worth it. Just to see that look on her face. She looked like she swallowed an egg, shell and all." His hands went to his throat and he staggered. ~~Jenny laughed. They walked a while and Logan said,~~ "All the shops are closed today. The auction, you know. The restaurant packed a lunch for me this morning. We could take it up the hill. Doesn't look like rain." He seemed shy.

"All right," Jenny said at last.

By the time they climbed the hill, the auction was starting on the flats next to the inlet, directly in front of the Montana Club.

They sat on the blanket and watched, eating sandwiches.

"Do you look like your father?" Logan asked abruptly.

She nodded. "He's dark. Wavy hair like mine. Very handsome looking. I have my mother's eyes, though." She turned to him. "What about your mother?"

"She's dead." He had told that lie for years, and it fell easily from his tongue.

"I'm sorry."

Logan shrugged. "I was very young. Six. It was quite sudden." He had trotted out the story like an obedient dog doing tricks over and over again. It never failed to get a response with women. Usually she died of scarlet fever; twice she had drowned; once he even had her captured by a band of Nez Percé and scalped. But this time the words stuck, and he found himself needing to tell her what it had really been like. "Do your parents get along?"

Jenny nodded. "That's the one thing I've always been sure of. It's embarrassing to see them together. Dad can't keep his hands off her."

"You're lucky." There was a long pause and Jenny didn't interrupt. "My earliest memory was of them fighting. I don't know how they ever got together. I really don't. Sometimes they wouldn't speak to each other for months. In the same house. Can you imagine living like that? It was awful. She would look straight through him, and talk to granny or gramp. Gramp was her favorite."

He had said too much. He had never told anyone these things.

Jenny was silent, waiting.

"It was—unhealthy, how they got along. She would spend

days with gramp, especially after dad took over most of the practice. Granny never trusted her. She was always walking into the office next to the house without knocking. I don't know what she thought she'd find, but one day she walked in and there it was."

He stared over the inlet. Clouds were banks on the bluff.

"She's not dead, is she?" Jenny's voice was gentle.

"I was home from school with a sore throat the day—the day she left. Granny found them in the office. My own mother." He turned to her. "It sounds tawdry, doesn't it? I hated her for years."

"What happened to her?"

"I don't know. Maybe dad does. He doesn't talk about her. After it—after it happened, no one ever brought her name up again. And that was hard. She was my *mother*. And suddenly I was supposed to not think of her anymore, or miss her, or wonder how she was. I've wondered, too, why she's never tried to contact me. I'm her only son. Did I mean so little to her that she could walk out and never think of me again?" He found tears coming to his eyes. "I've never told anyone—"

And then Jenny held him.

It was not at all the first date Logan had envisioned. He found himself at a terrific disadvantage. He had told a perfect stranger the blackest thing in his history and had cried like a baby, to boot. He never wanted to see her again. That wasn't true. He was embarrassed, and very much afraid she might tell someone what had happened. She seemed to sense immediately what was going through his mind.

"I'll never tell another soul," she whispered. "I promise."

There was a moment, then, when he could have leaned in and kissed her. Ordinarily he would have. But his balance was off, and by the time he thought of it, she had already moved slightly away and the moment was lost. She shook the crumbs from lunch off her skirt and stood up. "Race you to the auction."

Thirty-Three

Six hundred lots sold in two hours for $148,000. Flame bought two lots for $725. The office would go up on Fourth and E, next to the Sydney Laurence Company, owned by a young photographer and painter. The office was sensibly placed in the heart of the business district, but the house would overlook the sea. Cahill tried to talk her out of it, reminding her that K Street was the outback of Anchorage, that it would be the last street to get water and sewer; but Flame liked the peaceful expanse of sea stretching out and the view in the distance of Mount McKinley.

The day after the auction, the Montana Club Café moved its building to its permanent site, and in the week that followed, the tents along the flats came down. Work started on the post office. The Odd Fellows and Masons met, and a jury found Ed Wilston not guilty of grand larceny.

There were reminders. A black bear and cub scrounged for garbage behind the White House, and the proprietor, Mrs. White, put down her skillet and shot them both through the head with a 30-30 lever-action Winchester carbine. But at Finkelstein and Shapiro, a new order of men's and women's khaki suits arrived, and Pilger's was selling gold-buckle Sunkist oranges for forty cents a dozen. Roots were sunk, and in the brief Alaska summer, took hold. A town was growing out of the wilderness.

Flame was changing too. She had always worked at her marriage like a job, never taking vacations. But now, with great relief, she played. The lines smoothed in her face. She laughed a lot. She knew she should feel badly, should end it, but it was past that. There was no ending it, only going deeper into a love she had needed all her life. She should have followed Cahill to

Seattle. He never should have left. Together they should have shot Nelly through the head and buried her body. The years they had been apart fell away. How easy it was to love this man. The odd thing was, she didn't love Batt less. It was that the contrast was so great. It wasn't the novelty of it either; it was the essential bond between them. Her body relaxed and made her aware of how rigidly she had been holding herself for years. What had she been so afraid of? And how many things had she given up, holding the marriage together? This thing with Cahill was hers alone, possibly the only thing she had done in her life that *was* hers alone. She knew she could never go back.

The rains came and the house along the bluff went up. It was a clapboard frame, two stories, with a basement and attic peak. A balcony extended off the master bedroom on the second floor. It was nothing like the mansion in Juneau, but seemed to suit the spare wilderness. Flame was indifferent to it; she'd never live there. Still, it was a nice place to visit. Sometimes at night when the crew left, Flame and Cahill would spread a blanket on the second-story floor and watch the sky through the gaps where the windows would go.

"What are you going to tell him?" Cahill asked her one night. Outside it was raining. Lightning streaked over the Chugach Range.

Flame pulled on her shirt. "I don't know. The truth. I couldn't go back to him. I do love him, though, Cahill. Can you understand?"

"You can't have lived with him as long as you did and not." They had both lapsed into speaking of her marriage in the past tense.

"I hope he finds someone else. It makes me sad, thinking of him alone."

Cahill pulled her to him and she put her head on his chest. "Do you think he'll try to stop the divorce?"

She shook her head. "Not when he knows how I feel."

"Have you thought about the settlement?"

"I don't want anything. The house, property, mines—the cannery. None of it. He'd trade it all if he could have me back. I'm all he's ever wanted. I have to leave him with something."

"Good. I didn't want to influence you—but I want to start

377

fresh. Just the two of us building it together. I'm a good doctor, Flame. We'll always be comfortable. I don't want anything of his. I know that sounds odd. I've taken you. But the rest—"

They were silent a while. Cahill said, "I wonder how Jenny and Logan are going to like being brother and sister."

She almost told him then. It was right there, on her tongue. She paused. The decent thing to do was to tell Batt first, give him that little dignity. So instead she said, "They seem to be getting along."

"Really?" Cahill looked at her, astonished.

"They're not serious, of course. Jenny thinks of him as—a brother. She told me herself."

But Jenny was sixteen, and subject to fits and flights of fancy.

Ordinarily Jenny would have been furious with her mother and taken her long absences as a personal affront. After all, *she* was the kid; it was her mother's job to *be* there. But Jenny was busy herself.

Logan was the most interesting boy she had ever met— equally at ease chewing tobacco with dock workers or holding an umbrella over her head at the first band concert in the newly cleared park. They went on expeditions. Once, they hired horses and rode to the brickyard on Chester Creek. Charles Young was mucking about in the red loamy soil, his pants wet to the knees. He wore glasses and had big ears. They were the first visitors at the new yard, and Young held them captive most of an afternoon, showing off the new kiln and insisting they sniff the clay and roll it in their hands.

They took picnics out to Lake Spenard, hiking for hours through the birch and spruce. They would leave early in the morning and spend the afternoon swimming in the cold clear water. Jenny wore a daring one-piece suit that exposed her knees. It was at the lake that he first kissed her, or more accurately, it was in the lake and they kissed each other.

He swam over to her and they treaded water and traded swipes and then they leaned together and their lips brushed. They stared at each other, open eyed; up close, his lashes were a thicket. "Jenny," he said, and coming from him, it sounded like a prayer.

She pushed away from him and they raced to shore.

The rains started the third week in July; the sky was gray and the trees constantly dripped. It reminded Jenny of home. They stayed inside, playing bridge in the Two Sisters lobby and drinking hot chocolate. Sometimes they went to the White House and looked at magazines. In *Collier's* there was an article about triplets born in Bora Bora.

"I'd hate it," Jenny sniffed. "Two other people just like me."

But Logan read the whole thing before Mrs. White came over and told him to buy it, if it was that interesting. "I don't know. I've always wanted brothers and sisters," Logan remarked as he held open the door.

"Whatever for?"

"You haven't?"

"I'd rather have a stuffed fish."

"It would be somebody to talk to."

"Somebody to share your things with, you mean."

He put his collar up against the rain and looked at her sideways. "There are worse things in this world."

"Like what?"

He fished a stick of gum from his pocket and tore it in half. "Like not sharing at all."

Jenny grinned. "Does this mean I get the whole piece?"

Flame tightened the lid on the thermos and packed it next to the sandwiches. She went over the list: mosquito netting on the hat, light jacket in case of rain, the book she was reading. Cahill was bringing a blanket. She checked her watch, put everything in the satchel and closed the door.

She was going down the steps, satchel slung over her shoulder, when Batt stepped around the building. He was wearing a wool cap and tweed jacket. "Surprise." Big grin. Flame was so startled to see him she froze. He walked up and embraced her. "I got away earlier than I expected." He kissed her, and she recovered and kissed him back. "I missed you."

She didn't know what to say. She had betrayed him, betrayed the marriage, and the sooner she got it over with, the better. She had never lied to him before, and she wouldn't now.

He was climbing the steps. "What room are we in? I'd love to get out of these things. Take a little nap." He grinned again.

She stopped him from walking inside. "No. No. I need to talk to you. It's important, Batt, and anyway, you can hear right through the walls in there."

The smile faded and he put down the bag. "It's not Jenny, is it?"

"No, no. We're fine. Both of us." She looked down the street. Any minute Cahill would come strolling up. She needed to talk to Batt alone. She felt perfectly calm, as if she were in the middle of a terrible accident that was happening to someone else. "I know. Let's walk up K Street and I'll show you the house. How does that sound?"

"How's it coming?"

"It's almost up. They're putting in windows today. A shipment just came from Seattle." Her voice was subdued. This was awful. She had been certain he would know, and now they were chatting about ordinary things. Oh, God, what was she going to do?

They left the bag in the room. There was an awkward moment when he pulled her to him and kissed her lingeringly, but she pulled away, protesting about the walls and how the crew would be leaving soon, and there would be time for that later.

Batt took her hand on the way, and they fell into easy step with each other. They had been together a million years. Oh, there were so many little things she had overlooked!

"The whole thing was like clockwork, Flame. All of it. Brady was waiting for me in Seattle with the rails; I spent two days going over everything. The shipment is clean, Flame, really clean. No defects. All six thousand tons will be stored at the yard here. The Anchorage leg is the biggest. Commissioner Mears is planning on hiring almost three thousand men in Anchorage. Only nine hundred will come from Seward, and another seven hundred from Fairbanks, so of course it made sense to ship it here. I got the freight cost down to—"

She stopped walking. Tears streamed down her face.

"What is it? What's wrong? Are you ill?"

"I want a divorce."

He stopped, stunned, puzzled, unbelieving. "What did you say?"

"I said I want a divorce."

His voice was quiet. "Flame. I don't understand."

She hadn't expected the gentleness in his voice, the concern. He touched her shoulder, smoothed her hair.

"This isn't easy for me. Please believe me." She began sobbing as if her heart would break, and now that she thought of it, it was.

He pulled her off the street into the woods so the men hauling supplies wouldn't see her weeping. "Start at the beginning." The gentleness in his voice.

She doubled over, crying and holding her stomach. She dropped to the ground.

"Flame." He sank next to her and pulled her to him.

"We have nothing in common." She wiped her nose with the back of her hand. "Do you know I haven't been to one art exhibit since we married? I *love* art."

"You want a divorce because you haven't been to an art exhibit?" He was incredulous.

"It's what that means. What's behind that. For seventeen years, we've done what *you* wanted; gone places *you* wanted to go. My whole life has gotten absorbed up in yours."

"I never made you—"

"You never had to. You had all the power! Always. Don't you see? If I wanted to see you at all, I had to go where you wanted, do the things that pleased you. I learned to love boxing, I learned to love curling, but they were always *your* loves, Batt. Never mine. And in all that time, I can't recall once you asking me what I wanted to do."

"I never stopped you—"

"It was lonely! Incredibly lonely. If I wanted to do something you weren't interested in, I had to go alone. You flatly refused to enter my world, and after a while, I stopped going there, too. I want a companion, a mate. With you, I feel like all the effort has to come from me."

He was stunned. "I took you to the fair that time in Fairbanks. I didn't want to go."

381

"And all day long you reminded me of that, of the sacrifice. Maybe you didn't mean to, but you did. I darted around the fair, trying to find things that would interest you. Just once I'd like you to do something because *I* want to do it, and throw yourself into it with enthusiasm. Just once to have you as interested in finding out about me as I've been about you all these years."

"I've always taken care of you. I've had responsibilities. I've never let you down."

"You've always taken good care of me, Batt. Always. But shouldn't a marriage be more than that?"

"I thought ours has been. I look around at my friends—Flame, people have to do what they want to in a marriage. What would it have been like if I never did anything I wanted?"

"I never asked for that. I never wanted that. I only wanted you to share. To see how many times I had bent your way, and *once in a while*, to bend back. Would that have been so hard?" She raised her tearstained face. "I'm tired of trying, Batt. It occurred to me, it's only been my trying that's kept us together. And I'm tired of it. I'm thirty-five years old and I want to start living life the way *I* want to live it, while there's still something in there of me!" Fresh tears came to her eyes.

"Flame. I'm not going to let you go. I'm not. We can work this out. I never knew."

"I've told you! You never listened."

"Maybe I didn't, but I'm listening now. I don't want to lose you. I won't lose you. We'll build a new relationship. A better one. But we've had seventeen years together. Don't throw that away."

"It's too late."

"There's something you're not telling me. I can tell. What is it?"

Her eyes widened with pain. She took a deep breath. "You're going to think what I just told you was made up to justify it. And it isn't like that at all. What I said is at the bottom of everything. How I feel about the marriage. That trapped feeling of never going my own direction anymore, but veering off course because it's the only way to save things between us.

That's under everything, Batt."

His voice was low, wary. "Tell me. Tell me the rest."

She took a deep breath. She couldn't breathe. "Cahill is in Anchorage. I want to marry him." Batt grew perfectly still. "How long had this been going on?" Her voice was dead. "Since the day we landed."

He curled his fist and smashed it into the ground.

"It's not his fault," she said, frightened. "It isn't. It just happened."

"Oh, that sounds easy. It just happened. Heart attacks just happen, Flame, and earthquakes, not falling into bed with some—" He grimaced and covered his face with his hands.

Flame put out her hand to touch him, paused and put it down.

A long moment went by and when he raised his head, his eyes were red. "Where were you when this just happened? Didn't you think about me, Flame? Not once? About what we have?"

"Batt—"

"Seventeen years, Flame!" His voice dropped. "Seventeen. And you want to throw it all away after a month with someone else. That says a lot about our marriage, doesn't it?"

She was crying again. "I'll do whatever you want. Make it as easy as I can. We'll leave Anchorage if that would help—"

"You gave him a month. All right, Flame, I want you to give *me* a month. A month with you not seeing him, with you really *here* in this marriage, trying to work it out. That's not too much to ask, is it? After seventeen years?"

She was drowning. She was smothering. She buried her face in her hands. God, she had no idea it would be like this! So hard.

"For God's sake, Flame, I love you. I love you. You're my *wife*. Did you think I would throw up my hands and say, 'Fine, leave. Have a good time, dear?' You're my wife. I'm not going to let you go. I'll fight for you. I will. With everything in me, I'll fight. A month. That's all I'm asking. At the end of it, if you still want a divorce, I won't stop you."

She was dead inside. Her mouth trembled. "I'll need to tell him."

383

"*I'll* tell him."

"No!"

"A month, starting now. That's all I'm asking."

"Don't hurt him. Promise me—"

"I won't touch him."

"Promise me."

"You have my word. And do I have yours—that during this month you will be my wife, and mine alone? That you won't see him?"

"Batt, I do love you, I do."

His mouth worked. He pulled her up. "Where can I find him?"

"He's staying at Two Sisters. At Fourth and I."

Cahill was in the lobby, buying a magazine, when Batt came through the door. For a beat, Cahill's composure cracked, but then he extended his hand and said jovially, "Batt Jackson. This is a surprise."

Batt ignored the hand. "Step outside, Cahill."

The man behind the counter glanced curiously at the two men and went back to polishing the brass cash register. Batt walked out the door and down the steps without checking to see if Cahill was following him.

The street was wide and muddy, and there were still stumps in the middle of it. A store frame was going up across the street, and down at the corner, two boys wore sandwich boards advertising their father's laundry.

"I'll get right to the point. If you touch my wife again, I'll kill you."

"Isn't that Flame's decision? She's not a piece of meat, Batt."

Batt flexed his fist. "I swear to God, I'd smash your face in right now if she hadn't made me promise not to touch you. But I promise you, you set one foot near us, and you better hope there's a second doctor in town, because you'll never get your bag open."

"I'm going to marry her, Batt."

"You'll have to kill me first."

"She wants it, too."

Batt's face grew old. "Flame has decided to try our marriage for one month. The exact length of time she's given you. After that, she can do whatever she wants."

A month. "Let me talk to her."

"I'd like to think that under it all you're a decent man, Cahill. Leave her alone."

"And after that, you won't stop her?"

Batt's eyes were bloodshot. "One month."

Time stopped for Cahill. He watched Batt striding down the street. A crumpled paper skittered over the mud and caught on a root. Something roared in his ears.

He threw himself into his work. There were the usual things: a cold ran through Anchorage, followed by sore throats and influenza. Molly Bate's boy fell out of a tree and broke his arm. A pile driver smashed his thumb. The first child, a girl, was born to Mr. and Mrs. Ray Starks.

But all of it was unreal. He had to force himself to concentrate. He was always checking the time, and was amazed that only a few minutes had passed since the last time he had pulled out his watch. He couldn't sleep. Eating was out of the question. A month.

It seemed the closer he got to Flame, the farther apart they were pulled. Through all the bad years with Nelly, there had been one recurring dream: he was standing on the dock in Seattle, waiting for the boat. Flame was young and very beautiful, and she lifted her face to his and said, "Let's get married now, before you leave."

He always said yes.

It wasn't so much learning from his mistake as learning how much that mistake had cost, and knowing there was a good chance he would never stop paying for it.

They were supposed to be together! That was the worst part. Out of all the rest, they had been made to love each other. If he had been mortally wounded, he could not have hurt more. Flame was always on his mind.

In times of extreme pain, one finds extraordinary ways to keep living. In Cahill's case he began to see with luminous clarity into the heart of love, to know finally what it means when you say you love someone. In love there is that need to unite, to be one, but until you can separate yourself from the

loved one and see her apart from you, with her own dreams and
desires, the love will always be immature, ill formed. He loved
Flame. With everything in him, he wanted her with him. But
he loved her enough to see that what was best for her might not
always be best for him. And if there was no other way, enough
to let her go.

Flame hadn't much experience in rupturing marriages, and
even less experience trying to patch them up. There is a point
in a relationship when things can go either way: if the couple
clings to the rock face, they can inch their way forward to
safety. But they could just as easily slip and fall into space,
losing each other forever. The Jacksons clung to the cliff,
huddled together against the rain, and they talked. They
peered over the edge at the chasm below. Were there flowers
down there, and shady trees? It was too far to tell. Would it
hurt much—the fall? Would they die from it? Or if they felt
their way over the rocks, hanging on to the other when one of
them stumbled, would there be a house waiting on the other
side of the mountain, with a roomy front porch and a tire for a
swing and their name on the mailbox? Was home only around
the corner?

"I want us to try, Flame. I want it more than anything I've
ever wanted before. I don't want to give up on us. Think about
it. Ten years from now, we'll look back on this as a rough spot
in our marriage, nothing more."

"But I was unfaithful to you! Doesn't that mean anything?"

"What is this? Scream a little louder, husband? What do
you want me to say? That I'll never forget it? That every time
I've touched you since then, I've been burning to ask you how
it was between the two of you? Because I have. I think of it and
I go crazy inside."

"Do you want me to tell you? We promised each other at the
beginning of the month we would be totally honest with each
other."

He put his face in his hands and thought about it. "No," he
said finally. "I don't want to know. I couldn't handle it. All I
want to know is that it will never happen again." He looked up.

Tears came to her eyes. "I can't promise that."

"Flame, don't I mean anything to you?" It was a cry.

She came to him and held him. "I'm afraid," she whispered at last.

He stroked her hair. "Of what?"

"Of going the wrong way."

"Then come with me. You already have, all this way. You only *think* you know Cahill, but it's some romantic wisp of dream. I'm real. I'm the one who's been here for you all these years. I may not be perfect, but I've loved you the best I could, and I'll keep on loving you. Our marriage has a solid foundation, Flame. It was built on love and trust. We have a child. That other thing is just fantasy."

She grew still. "I need to tell you about that." Her voice was small. "There's something you need to know."

Don't tell him, a small voice said. Don't. It will change things forever. But the marriage *was* the lie, and the lie was the most central thing to the marriage. She had to tell him. It was the telling that would decide the rest, whether she stayed or went.

She unclasped his hand and moved toward the edge of the cliff. "Jenny is not your child. She's Cahill's. I only told you she was early— All these years—" Her face was white. Below her the ground retreated, drew close.

He had never been so quiet. The eyes were quiet, the muscles in the lips, quiet. "So." He blinked his eyes. "So."

She stepped into space. Her body was light, weightless. "I'll pack tonight."

"So," he said again.

She had the sensation of hanging in space, as if it still hadn't occurred to her body that she stepped off solid ground forever.

"I have something to tell you myself." His voice was odd. He stared at her. His eyes were cold. "I knew all along Jenny wasn't mine. I can't have children. I'm sterile. Sarah Ramsdorf told me you were pregnant. I married you anyway."

"My God!" she cried. She felt herself falling, the room falling away. He reached out and caught her and held her fast.

"Can you ever forgive me?"

He held her tightly and they both wept.

*   *   *

He knew the answer even before she sat down across from him. He could see it in the way she walked.

"Flame."

She slid opposite him into the booth. There were snow crystals on the shoulders of her coat. She left on her gloves. Her face was ravaged. "I've come to say good-bye."

"I know."

They stared at each other. It was there between them. It would never go away. There was that, at least. There was nothing to say, and he knew it would be harder on her if he started, so he pushed himself out of the booth and drew on his coat. "It doesn't change anything, does it?"

Tears came to her eyes. He bent and brushed her cheek with his mouth, and then, because he didn't have much left and it was going quickly, he straightened and pushed himself away from her, made himself walk to the door, open it and move into the soft September snow. In the alley a dog foraged for scraps and a raven called. Flame stared after him, dry eyed. "Good-bye, my love," she whispered.

"Batt, I only found out myself today! God, what are we going to do?" She was pacing up and down the bedroom.

"We can't tell her, that's clear. I won't. She's my daughter, and that's all there is to it. I won't have her whole life torn apart, and I certainly won't give Cahill another opportunity to hurt my family." He whirled abruptly. "Promise me you'll never tell her."

"Of course I won't. She adores you. It would break her heart. But what are we going to do?"

"How serious is it?"

"I don't know. They saw each other this summer. It's only late September. The dance at the Elks Club is in two weeks."

"It's just going to have to be one of those things parents do that kids don't like and don't understand. She's never disobeyed me. She'll get over him. A half-brother! Who would have thought—"

"I'm worried."

He pulled her to him. "It's the first boy she's ever liked. She'll remember everything about him when she's ninety. I still remember Agnes in the second grade—fluffy-haired Agnes with a nose that dripped—"

Flame sighed. "We better do it right away."

"Why *can't* I see him? Why? Give me one good reason. That's all I want. Just one." She was furious and in tears.

Batt was firm. "Jen, it's one of those things. I'm really sorry. I am. Please believe me. But I won't even discuss it with you. Your mother and I are in total agreement. You are going to have to tell Logan you can't see him again."

She was crying. "But I like Logan! We have fun together! We're friends!"

"Has he kissed you?"

A silence. The parents exchanged looks.

"Jenny, it's over. That's all there is. You can meet with him now, since you already arranged it and there's no way of contacting him, but only this once, and only for an hour. If I ever catch you together again, I'll tan your behind and have him arrested."

Jenny grew white. "How dare you!"

"I'm not going to talk about it anymore. The subject is closed."

"I can't stand either one of you!" Jenny bolted out of the house without her coat.

Batt stopped Flame. "Let her go."

"It's snowing."

"She's young. Let her work it out of her system. It's a tough pill. I know I was hard on her—I don't see any other way."

Flame stared worriedly out the window. "I just hope it works."

Jenny ran from K Street to Fourth and I without stopping. Logan was already in their booth at the Model Café. "Jenny, no coat?" He took her hands and rubbed them.

"They won't let me see you anymore."

"What?"

She started to cry. "They want me to tell you I can't go to the dance."

"Then we won't."

She cried harder. "I thought you loved me."

"Madly." He leaned over and kissed her hand. "But if they don't want you to go, we won't."

She wiped her eyes. "Our parents probably had some falling out. Remember how mother used to visit your father a lot? That never happens anymore. It makes me so mad! Why do they make us pay for things they do to each other? Why? And what are we going to do? I can't *not* see you."

"There's only one thing we can do."

"What's that?"

"We'll see each other secretly. And at school, of course."

"Logan, and lie?"

"Of course not. We'll just never tell them."

She settled against the red seat. "I knew you'd think of something."

Thirty-Four

If it had ended with the railroad, things might have been all
right. Not the same, but all right. But the railroad wouldn't be
the ending, and the Indians knew it. Of all the natives, they
were the first to see that. They heard the faint sounds of boots
and hammers and progress, and all along the Yukon, their
heads lifted like alarmed deer. At first they ignored it, hoping it
would go away; but gradually, at the sand cliffs below Tanana,
in the sod huts of Coschocket, they gathered to talk about it,
sensing that even the uttered words gave shape and substance
to their fears.

They were coming. The whites were coming. Worse than
that, they were staying.

At the fish wheels below Rampart, Senati and Shanyaati
heard it too. It didn't matter that the town of Rampart had
shrunk to nothing, that the whites still there rattled through
the deserted stores like beetles inside a skull. It only meant that
the whites were someplace else; not gone, but here, in numbers
too enormous to count.

Kannik alone was unconcerned. "It's a big land," she
shrugged. "Let them have a little." But she had five strong
children to occupy her thoughts, and a daughter to prepare for
the seclusion that would transform her into a woman. The men
worried in silence.

Out of deference to the missionaries, Kannik had named her
oldest girl Eve. Out of respect to the true gods in the wind and
land, she held to the ancient rites. Like any convert, Kannik
was much more zealous in her adherence to Indian rituals than
most Indians. She loved the pomp and ceremony and somehow
the gods in the rivers and hills seemed kindlier than the Eskimo
gods of the endless sea and ice. One of her proudest moments

had come years before when a pregnant woman asked Kannik about what was to be done with the umbilical cord at birth. Is it tied with sinew and cut before the black soot is rubbed into it, warding off evil? And is a part of it then placed in a skin bag and attached to the babe's cradle? Yes to both questions, Kannik had told her with authority, pleased that the woman had forgotten completely that Kannik had not been born Indian.

And now Eve was in her first blood, and life was taking on another dimension. She dressed her daughter in a menstrual hood of soft caribou skin; the leather fringe was cream colored against the glossy black hair. It was a solemn moment. The seclusion hut had been ready for months. Eve could eat only cold foods that had been properly aged. She herself had gathered moss to absorb her blood, and the moss was stacked along the wall of the waiting hut, next to sleeping-skins. She would be in seclusion five months. Kannik would be the only visitor permitted, bringing her daughter food and teaching her the things she would need to be a good wife. A boy from the village of Coschocket had been chosen. He was the son of a chief, and the union would cement the two villages. It would be a good match. He was an excellent hunter and well liked. Next month he would move into their hut, fishing and hunting with Senati and Shanyaati in the ritual service due to the bride's family. Five months from now he would claim his bride.

Kannik went to the wall and lifted down a new cup and bowl and a swan's leg bone, attached to a long necklace of goose down. Eve dropped her head forward and Kannik worked the fluff necklace over her head. Eve would drink only from it during seclusion. The two women studied each other. Tears came to Eve's eyes.

This, more than anything else, signaled her entry into the female mysteries. Every menstruating woman had her own cup and bowl that was used for eating during the sacred days of the month. She would use the same bowl and cup until her body ceased its monthly course.

"Welcome, daughter." Kannik's voice trembled. No one had told her it would go so quickly. This babe suckling at her breast—this young woman with doe eyes. They embraced, and Kannik brought the hood forward until it shadowed her daughter's face. Eve took a last look at the hut she would enter again as a bride, and then they walked quickly to the seclusion hut, careful to use a path not taken by hunters so she would not risk angering the spirits.

At the entrance to the hut they embraced again, and Eve went in alone. Kannik ran down the path, jubilant. Shanyaati and Senati had the three youngest lined up at the river, fishing. "It is done, husbands! Eve is in seclusion!"

Troubled faces stared back at her.

"What is it? What's wrong?"

Senati took her hand. "I know you have been preparing the ritual feast for months, but I have to leave today."

"Why?" Kannik was shocked. It was not seemly one of the fathers of a secluded daughter be absent when the guests were welcomed.

"Yokah sent a runner from Minto. A high person in the white government, Delegate Wickersham, has invited the Tanana chiefs to meet with him the day after the white man's holy day, the fourth of July. I cannot refuse."

Kannik clutched his hand. "Don't go! Ignore the whites. They have nothing to do with us! Nothing!"

Senati held her tenderly. "You know when our eldest son, Pana, was matched to the daughter of the best hunter in Minto?"

Kannik nodded.

"How proud we were of him. The last time we hunted together, he told me that the geese stay away from the flats."

Kannik raised her head. "They have always been there. Since the beginning of time, nesting and raising young."

"Not any more. There are cabins now, and the air rings with the clamor of men trapping beaver and muskrats. Don't you see, Kannik? It will not stop until the whites have covered the earth. I must go to the meeting, and Delegate Wickersham must listen to what the Indians have to say. It is the only way."

Shanyaati cut Senati's hair above the ears and unwrapped the suit the runner had brought. It was stiff and scratchy, and when Senati put it on, he couldn't breathe.

They came to Fairbanks because they were invited, and they came because they were scared. But the fear didn't show on the faces of the chiefs as they sat in a row at the Thomas Memorial Library.

They were proud men, strong men, Athapaskans.

Hawkfaces, Wickersham thought as he joined the whites across from them. The Indians had the high cheekbones and craggy noses of Navajos. Not at all like the moon-flattened yellow faces of Eskimos. Taller, too.

Wickersham cleared his throat and the native interpreter, Paul Williams, leaned forward. "State fully what is on your minds and I will carry your words back to the secretary of the interior in Washington, D.C." He gestured down the row, introducing his side.

"I am glad to see you here from Salchaket, Chena, Nenana, Tolovana, and all up and down the river. I have been elected by the people of Alaska to go to Congress in Washington, to represent all the people of Alaska, including the Indians. I can say, as your friend, that I want to do everything I can to help you. Railroads are coming. White men are staking homesteads, cultivating the land, raising potatoes and all kinds of crops. Oh, there are many, many white men in the United States—as many as there are trees on hills here, and in a few years, many of them are coming to Alaska, and they are going to take up land. Mr. Richie, from the Land Office, is surveying the land and he is going to survey all the good land. They are running lines so that they can tell where the good land is, and so they can tell how much three hundred and twenty acres are, on the ground. And the white men coming from the United States are going to keep taking up this land until all the good land is gone, and the Indian people are going to have to move over. The white men are going to keep on taking more land. After a while, the Indian will have no land at all. He cannot live in the water, and he will have nothing to do, and this is what we want to talk about. We want you to have a home, we want your people to take land, we want you to take good land, and we do not want you to be pushed aside. We want you to do something before it is too late."

He took a drink of water while Williams finished translating.

The Indians had grown watchful; nothing flickered in their faces.

Wickersham explained their choices. They could homestead 160 acres or be put on a reservation.

He said, "Now you can get the best of it. When the white men come into the country, the land will be taken up quickly, so we want to help you now. We want you men to get your land before it is all gone. That is all."

Reverend Madara ran his finger along the inside of his clerical collar. It was hot in the room, close to ninety. "Mr. Wickersham, what you say is all true. It had been done with the Indians outside and it will be the same here. Forced back and back until there is no place to go. But the one hundred and sixty-acre idea doesn't fill the bill. When the Land Office investigates a claim, they look to see if a cabin has been built and they look to see if a garden has been made, and if they don't find these things, they believe the Indian does not intend to occupy it permanently. The Indians hunt and fish. They move around."

Paul Williams finished translating and immediately said in English, "If you gentlemen will kindly allow me to say a few words. If they should make a big reservation, these Indians would have to move from their tribal relations, and not live where they have been used to and in places which are their homes."

"Suppose several smaller reservations could be made," Wickersham suggested.

Williams shook his head. "That would be about the same. It would take them away from the old habits and homes where they have been used to living."

He sat down, and the oldest chief, his face a welter of furrows capped by hair that had gone completely white, motioned for help in rising. He leaned on an arm and stood stooped over.

"I remember ever since the ground was bought from Russia by the United States government when we used the stone axe and the flint match, when I was a small boy." His voice stopped and started in fits. "We have never had a chance to see the government officials and tell them what we wanted. I have heard that the United States government was supposed to be a good government, and according to reports that I have heard, they even protect dogs in the streets. And if the government is able to protect the dogs in the streets, it should be able to look out for us."

With great dignity he lowered himself into his chair.

Wickersham studied the faces. Impossible to know what they were thinking. "We will meet with you men at four o'clock. In the meantime, you can talk it over among yourselves and tell us what you want."

He stood and the others rose and they all shook hands.

"What do you think?" Richie asked. He represented the federal Land Office.

Wickersham stared thoughtfully out the window. The Indians were walking down the steps. One of them was pointing at the Pioneer Hotel. They had never seen a two-story building before. "I don't know. But whatever they decide, they'll go as a group."

Richie folded his maps and charts and unwrapped a toffee. "They better go as a group straight to a reservation while they have the chance." He turned to the railroad representative. "How many folks you think will come up because of the railroad?"

"Workers, or families and store owners, too?"

"All of them." Richie rolled the toffee delicately between his teeth.

"Five—seven thousand. Hard to say."

Richie sucked the candy. "That's my point. Those chiefs, all together, represent maybe fifteen hundred Indians in the midsection of Alaska. They don't know it, but it's a done deal. July fifth, 1915, the Indians have already lost the war. We're only negotiating the settlement now, tying up a few loose ends."

Wickersham was getting impatient. "I don't see it that way. I've worked with Congress; you haven't. We're dealing with a separate intellect here, a separate culture, but the Indians are making great strides in becoming Americanized. This is a chance for the United States to treat the Indians more humanely than they have in the past."

"Ho!" Richie crunched down on the toffee. "So it's Take a Savage to Lunch and Save America Day, is it? It's not going to work. They're not going to listen and they won't let you save them, no matter how much you assure them it's really quite all right, won't hurt a bit, and it's for their own good. They're going down, Wick. This meeting is only a nicer funeral than most, a classier way of saying good-bye than shooting them through the head. But it doesn't change things. The railroad will do that very nicely, thank you." Richie nodded at Riggs, the railroad representative. "But if it wasn't that, it would have been something else. The only primitive state was the garden of Eden, and look what happened to it."

"Are you through?" Wickersham's cheeks were bright pink. Richie shrugged. "For now."

"I hold my obligations as delegate to Congress in sacred trust. I will not let those people down. I will not."

Richie looked dubious. "Nice words. Sincere. But when the whites start marching in front of your house, good friend, demanding Indian land, remember that it's the whites that voted you in as delegate, and the whites who can vote you out."

"Are you saying I'd compromise my office—"

"Not at all," Richie said mildly. "I'm only reminding you that intentions sometimes butt heads with reality, and the reality is that the Indians couldn't vote your mother in as tooth fairy. They're so far off the power scale they're hanging on by their fingers, dangling in the air."

"Which is why I'm their advocate in Congress."

Richie smiled blandly and reached for another toffee.

The Indians were adamant and extremely polite. They went down the line of chiefs, and each one said the same thing: no reservations, and reservations about homesteads.

Chief Alexander of Tolovana said, "I tell you that we are people that are always on the go, and I believe if we were put in one place, we should die off like rabbits. I ask you not to let the white people come near us. Let us live our own lives in the customs we know."

Another chief agreed. "Every one of us here is just like one man. We are suggesting to you just one thing, that we want to be left alone. As the whole continent was made for you, God made Alaska for the Indian people, and all we hope is to be able

397

to live here all the time."

Senati stood, spread his hands on the table and smiled. He had listened and given considered thought to it, and now had the solution. "It is the whites who are causing problems, yes? The whites who are creating turmoil and churning the land and rivers into alien deserts. Very well, let the *whites* live on reservations. The Indians have done no wrong." He sat down.

Wickersham adjourned the meeting until the next afternoon.

"I still think the reservation idea is the best thing," Wickersham said as he walked with Richie toward the Land Office in Cushman. It was dry, and dust rose in the street. They stood to one side on the high wooden sidewalk and let a woman pass. She was pushing a pram. Inside was a baby teething. Drool puddled the front of the infant's dress.

"Ma'am." Wickersham tipped his hat.

"You'll be lucky if you can talk them into homesteading," Richie said, "let alone the reservation."

"They want to keep their villages," Wickersham itemized, "come and go at will, and if they homestead, they don't want to have to live on the land all year, as the law now stands. I don't think any of those things are out of the question. It's a matter of carefully recording what the Indians want and then letting the secretary of the interior know."

"It's not that easy. You and I both know that, Wick. There's a war going on. We'll be in it soon, mark my words. That's not all. Congress is lusting after the Virgin Islands and it's got ants in its pants over the Panama-Pacific International Expo, trying to make sure everything goes just right. The states' senators and reps are worried about unemployment; they're worried about inflation. Worrying about a small band of Indians along a couple of rivers in the middle of Alaska is about ninety-fifth on the worry list, right under house training puppies. And to be perfectly honest, it's not even number one on *your* list. You are still planning on introducing a statehood bill this year, aren't you?"

Wickersham nodded. "California was admitted with less. When they see how stable we are—"

"*Aha.* Stable. Then don't bring up the Indians. Don't mention them. Pretend they went the way of the dodo bird and the last of the Mohicans. Talk about roads and schools and church box lunches, but leave the Indians out of it."

Wickersham shook his head. "I'll just work harder and do both."

"Or maybe neither."

It was a strange paradise. Water gushed from small metal tubes into large white bowls in their rooms. In the lobby there was a wooden box, and if you cranked the side and put your ear to it, a woman you couldn't see would talk to you in a language you couldn't understand.

Piles of logs were stacked neatly in front of every house, and around the houses were fences. They were amused to see the fences. Even caribou could have escaped from them. There were wooden planks on the sides of the wide trails, and people rushed along them at high rates of speed, even though the trails were softer to the feet.

Candles had been captured inside glass bottles. The front of every store had them, even though it was blazing light this time of year. Inside there were shelves of bottles full of colored water—sometimes pink, sometimes green. There were hard clear boxes with nuggets inside like moose pellets, but the pellets were sweet. Chocolate taffy, the man said.

Indians were not permitted inside stores in Fairbanks, but Wickersham had written notes explaining how these were special Indians. Each chief carried his note slung low in the hip pocket of his wool suit and brandished it like a magic sword when attacked. The paper was read, the eyes changed, the store spilled its goods. There were fans and whistles and combs. There were papers for tobacco and pipes and sailor hats. Wickersham had given them each a dollar and they deliberated; they bargained, discussed; they haggled. Eventually they bought and carried their prizes back to the Third Avenue Hotel, where they dumped them in a pile in the room Senati was sharing with Chief John of Chena.

The pile looked smaller, somehow, on the floor.

*   *   *

"We have decided on allotments, on homesteads, provided our villages remain intact and that we can hunt and fish as we please." Senati was speaking for them all. Paul Williams translated.

Wickersham nodded, pleased, and told them he would visit the villages and survey out the areas where they hunt and fish. "When I know all those things, I will go to Washington and tell the men there what you want to do. Are there any other things you want to discuss?"

They brought up the need for doctors and schools, and talked about jobs on the railroad. Wickersham added those to his list. "But tell them, Paul," he said to the interpreter, "that it all depends finally upon the Indians themselves. If they work good, they will be employed. If they work bad, they won't be employed."

Williams told them and added in English, "The Indians say that the next time you run for a delegate, you want to be sure and notify us and be sure you accomplish this before you run again for delegate."

Wickersham smiled wanly. "Tell them, Paul, that as soon as they have established homes and live like white men and assume the habits of civilization, they can have the vote."

Senati strode past the children playing cup-and-pin games and ducked to avoid a buzz toy whirring in the air. He found Kannik coming down the path from the seclusion hut.

"Husband!" She flew into his arms.

He took a deep breath. "Kannik, this is the last ritual of blood. The last. We must give up those things. I will build a cabin and the children will learn to write."

"Senati, what did they do to you in Fairbanks? What?"

"There are many whites. More than—more than the blueberries that come soon to the hills. They are everywhere. The white high person, Mr. Wickersham, told us how to take care of things, how to keep our lands from them. But we made promises, too, in return. We must live like they do to get the protection of the law. It is the only way."

Kannik detached herself and looked at him soberly. "The

400

whites—do they have more than one husband?"

He hadn't thought of that. "No," he admitted.

Kannik's eyes were bright. "What do you suggest, dear husband?"

Senati considered it. Shanyaati was like a brother to him, but Kannik was his wife. "Shanyaati will be able to find another. I will tell him myself."

Kannik put down her head and lifted it. Her eyes were bright brown. Tears gleamed on her lashes. "No, husband. If you wish the white way, *you* leave. Leave us here, to our old ways."

She was trembling. Senati knew how much she loved him. And yet Wickersham had said— "Very well," he said boldly. "I will leave."

She packed him in silence as the children wailed and Shanyaati pleaded with him. Only Kannik's words could move him and she never spoke.

He went to the winter camp, but it was lonely with no one there. With no children laughing and no wife saying idle words in his ear, it left much time for thinking. He thought and thought and finally remembered something that would save them all.

"It is your husband, returning from the hills." His hair had grown long, and there was snow on the shoulders of his suit.

With a small cry, Kannik flew into his arms. "Husband, husband, how I missed you! But how can this be? Shanyaati is here. And you—"

"I heard once about a white custom," Senati said heartily. "A man marries a woman, and then one of them—sometimes the man, sometimes the woman—either one, takes another person to themselves, while still being married. It is called"—he searched his memory—"adultery. Yes, that is the word. Adultery. I think we will keep things as they are. You will be married to me, or you will be married to Shanyaati, and the other one will have this adultery thing. It is all the same. But after this time, there will be no seclusion hut. I will build a cabin and the children will learn to read. We will keep our villages and our hunting and fishing grounds and we will have

401

this adultery thing."

Kannik shrugged. "Some bad, some good."

In the spring of 1916, Wickersham presented a bill that would give the natives rights to their villages and subsistence privileges: a statehood bill; bills giving the Indians doctors and schools.

But nothing passed; Congress had other things on its mind. That was the year it introduced sweeping legislation making it a crime to spit on public sidewalks and prohibiting camels within city limits.

Thirty-Five

There were people who didn't know about the railroad, and if they did, they wouldn't have cared. It was far to the south. It had nothing to do with them.

For Timmy it was the best time to be a kid, and the best time to be living on the edge of the world close to the Arctic Ocean—the best time to be Eskimo. They were safe in the cycle of the seasons, wandering at will over the endless marshes. Timmy loved summers best. That's when they camped at the mouth of the Okpiksak River, where it joins the Meade from the southeast. They were sixty miles south of Barrow, away from wooden houses and white people and books.

There were sandy stretches along the rivers for leaving definite footprints and dense thickets of willow for hiding. The rivers glinted with whitefish and grayling, and the huge burbot cod. You could roll your pants up past the knees and plunge into the icy water, so cold it took your breath, and catch fish with your bare hands, like Daniel Boone. Summer was one endless day, as bright at midnight as it was at noon. The sun rose in May and didn't set until August. You only slept when your mother caught you.

There were chores, of course, but Timmy was lucky. His father, Nick Snow, didn't make him help dry fish on racks, like Naomi, or poke them into seal oil pouches to preserve them, like his sister Ruth. He didn't have to cut willow branches, like Matthew, or bundle them, like Mark, so they would have fuel for heat. As the eldest, he was his father's right-hand man, and like him, he would herd reindeer when he grew up.

Together they chased wolves away from reindeer fawns, and trained the adults to pull the sled. First they fed moss to the deer. They would choose one with a fine rack and glossy coat,

single him out and feed him from their hands. The third day
they would slip a rope around his neck and anchor him on a
long tether to the mossy bank.

"Free him in the morning," his father instructed, "so that
he knows his bondage is temporary." They would untether him
and attach a long rope and gently pull him behind. "Don't
frighten him," his father exhorted, "and he will serve you
willingly."

Soon the deer was following docilely and they would attach
the harness. Timmy's mother, Aan, was known in Barrow for
her sewing skill. The harnesses blazed with red and orange
ribbons.

She had made them from caribou sinew, but when the Lapps
came to train the Eskimos in the art of herding, Aan saw how
drab hers were in comparison and surreptitiously made her own.
Now they rivaled any Tim had seen.

Once the deer were adjusted to the harness, they attached
the sled. Tim or his father would run ahead, and the empty sled
would bounce and skid behind. Then they jumped on, guiding
the deer as they would dogs. Nothing beat it. The air was sharp
with moist green smells and the deer's huge muscular back legs
moved rythmically under the rack of antlers, while the world
spread out around them, soft as gauze.

Timmy had seen enough of life in Barrow to know he didn't
want any. It wasn't right for him, didn't sit well. He hated
school. Books didn't tempt him as they did Matthew, the next
oldest, or the two girls, Naomi and Ruth. Even Mark was
lisping out English words. They would sit on packing crates in
their sod hut in Barrow, reading by lantern until their mother
dimmed the light to save fuel. Timmy couldn't wait to close the
book. Life wasn't happening inside those pages! It was out
there, with the deer.

Matthew had begun reading Beacon's *Sixth Reader* last
winter. Timmy had been in *Third Reader* for five years. It was
humiliating. Even when he could figure out what the words
meant, they had nothing to do with him. His family didn't sleep
with sheets in high beds like the Smith children; their mother
didn't bake cookies, and they didn't keep tiny fish swimming in
their house in clear buckets. So tiny, those fish. One bite and

404

they would be gone.

And geography! The smallest Eskimo child knew the world was flat and supported by four pillars. Lost hunters had fallen off the edge of it. The teacher knew it, too, even as he earnestly pointed at the map. After all, wasn't the map itself flat?

Soon it would be over. Next spring Timmy would hand back his Beacon's *Third Reader* and *Songs of School and Flag*. He would give his *Primer of Sanitation* to Naomi and Ruth. Let *them* wash their hands every time they ate! He was thirteen, and he would eat with the deer.

There hadn't always been reindeer in Alaska. A white missionary, Dr. Sheldon Jackson, got a Congressional appropriation in 1899 to bring them in. He figured that if the Siberian natives could herd just across the Bering Strait on the Chukotski Peninsula, so could the Eskimos.

He set up a herding station in Barrow and brought in Laplanders to run it. They were small and spare, like Eskimos, and wore bright purple-and-red skirts and felt shoes. Their job was to teach the Eskimos about reindeer.

But there was a problem. The Lapps would be in the middle of a lesson, and the cry would go out that the whales were running in the open water next to the ice pack. The Eskimos would drop everything and go. That was in the spring and fall. In winter there were seals to harpoon at blow holes, and ice fishing. There were traps to set for white fox. In summer there were a thousand more distractions.

The Lapps loved the deer and explained that they had to be watched, like children, and protected from wolves. But the Eskimos knew that was crazy. The caribou didn't have to be watched, and yet every year they returned to the same feeding grounds. So did the whale. Could reindeer be much different?

The Lapps petted and patted the deer and started herds of their own which grew fat. The Lapps grew fat. They prospered.

But the Eskimos were new at parenting deer. They insisted that the reindeer would conform to *their* lives, and that being parents wouldn't change a thing. The deer died.

Eleven herds were allotted to natives in 1903, the year Timmy was born, and by 1916 only five herds were left, not counting the Lapp herds, which had quadrupled in size. It wasn't the Lapps' fault; it really wasn't. They nursed calves and sutured wounds. They stumped over the tundra, waving sticks to keep the deer together. Everything they got they earned.

It was just hard to be a herder and Eskimo too.

Which was why Timmy's father needed him so badly. In the spring at the first sighting of whales, Timmy would bolt gladly from school to mind the deer while his father hunted the whale. In winter he would abandon the stifling hot schoolroom and march the length of the corral, peering through ice fog, looking for wolves while his father crouched on the ice by a seal's hole. His father's shoulder still ached, sometimes, from an old bear wound, and Timmy used that as an excuse on days when school was too deadly to be endured.

In summer, after they established the fish camp on the Okpiksak River, Timmy and his father herded deer to the slaughter grounds, where they were killed, skinned and traded for flour, coffee and tobacco. It took ten days herding to get from the fish camp into the mountains to the south where the deer were killed.

It was miserable work. They led deer into a corral where the throats were cut. Timmy's father, Nick, would slash the throat and Timmy would hurl himself onto the deer's chest, kicking out the air and crushing the lungs. The pelt was valuable; no marks could be left. By the middle of the day, their hair stank of blood. Mountain People hired on as skinners for a share of meat and pelts. The NC Company trading post on the Colville River had everything, and Timmy thought of that as he hacked off reindeer heads and carried away dripping pouches of stomach, still warm in his hands.

This year he would ask his father for a rifle. He had seen one in the locked cabinet behind the counter at the trading store, and all year the vision of its shiny face had hypnotized him. He knew his father would balk. Countless times he had heard the story *How a Gun Spelled Doom for the People of the Whale*. He meant no disrespect, but it *was* a long time ago. Even his father used guns now. Besides, he was entitled.

He waited until the pelts were stacked, the meat cached, and his father's own bartering complete, before asking. They were outside, next to the tent. The lead reindeer was grazing placidly in the distance, near the corral still shiny with blood.

"I'll take good care of it, I swear. I'll keep it dry."

His father glanced at the brown rolling hills and snuffed mucus from his nose onto the ground. "I need to say words to you."

His father had only used that voice once, when he pulled Timmy onto his lap and told him his brother Andrew was dead.

"What is it?"

His father rubbed the scar along his cheek. "Come. Let us walk."

They climbed a small hill bright with yellow and orange poppies. Then his father said abruptly, "Did I ever tell you I first met your mother near here? She had another family, you know."

"I never knew that."

"Yes. Well." His father sighed and sat on a rock. They were overlooking the river. The trading post was a neat brown box. "I have tried not to favor one child over another."

"That is so." Timmy was puzzled. His father usually got right to the point.

"She does love you, you know."

Below them their deer lifted her head. The harness was a small slash of color against the rich brown of her coat.

"If you think I'm too young for a rifle, I'm not. Really. I need it. You're gone hunting so much, and you need a weapon of your own, rather than leaving yours with me. You have good friends. Strong friends to loan you guns. But a gun of one's own—" Timmy fell silent, contemplating how it would feel.

"I have decided to send you away." The words were unnaturally loud.

Timmy's mouth opened. "What?"

The muscles in his father's scarred cheek rippled like the flank of a deer. "Your teacher, Mr. Riley, has discussed it with me. He can't teach you anymore, but there's a school—"

"I'm done with school—"

"—in a place called Dakota. The Indians go there. And now it's time for an Eskimo to go there, too—"

"I won't go! I hate school! I hate it! I hate reading and

407

everything white! This is where I belong. Right here, working with you."

"It's time Matthew helped."

He wasn't hearing right. "Matthew tires quickly, father. You know that. Send *him* to this place called Dakota. Let *him* go to school. Matthew loves it. I read and all I think about is escape."

"Did you know sometimes your mother and I have differences? Ah, well. You're young. Anyway, we have them, sometimes."

But all Timmy heard was that he was being sent away. "Don't do this to me."

"In this place called Dakota, there are tall buildings and I have heard there are metal sleds that carry men without deer or dogs pulling. Can you imagine?"

"Don't send me away. Please."

"Mr. Riley opened my eyes. He told me how I robbed you of your chance to learn."

"Books have taught me nothing! Everything I know, I learned from you or the country."

"Mr. Riley explained it to me. It was very clear."

Timmy put his head in his hands.

"We're going to Nome. A boat is there—a steamer. It will take you to another country, and in this country is Dakota." His father fumbled in his pocket. "It's all here. Mr. Riley wrote it down so you could read it, or have someone read it to you." He held the paper out and finally stuffed it awkwardly into Timmy's coat pocket.

"Your mother thought it would be best if we left from here."

At that, Timmy raised his head. "I won't get to say good-bye to them? My own sisters and brothers?"

"Your mother thought it would be best." The vein in his father's temple throbbed.

"How can you do this to me?"

"I want you to be someone!" his father burst out. "My whole life I've worked hard, and for what? For my sons. I want you to be someone."

Tears streamed down Timmy's face. "I am someone, father. I'm your son. I thought you loved me."

"I love you too much."

At last Timmy understood. His mother. His mother was sending him away.

"Why does she hate me?" he whispered.

"She doesn't hate you," his father said helplessly. "She loves you. When you're older, you'll see how things are. It's not her fault. If I had loved you less, if I had spent more time with Matthew—"

"When will I see you again?"

His father's eyes were dull. "I signed papers. You stay in this place called Dakota four years."

Thirty-Six

The train hurtled past trees and rolling fields. It was alive, this train. It breathed fire and roared and ate track for breakfast, lunch and dinner. It was insatiable. Day and night, the train ate its way through the forests of Washington, the potato fields of Idaho, into the vast prairies and mountains of Montana. It choked to a stop in small towns to take on the same passengers over and over. They had children and paper bags and put the window down on their side when they climbed into the compartment with Timmy. He had been ten days on the steamer in the same clothes and it was hot that summer on the train. When they got on, he always obligingly moved over his fermented fish and aged meat to make room, but no one ever sat next to him on the bench.

It was a milk train, and most of the people were only going to the next town to visit the folks. Timmy would smile and sometimes a woman smiled shyly back, before quickly turning her head.

In Montana a family of five got on in the dark. The youngest cried himself to sleep while his mother mechanically rocked him, her knees slack with fatigue. She had blond hair that stuck out under a yellow hat, and fine hair on her delicate arms. The husband caught Timmy staring and said something sharp to his wife in another language. She put on a sweater and stared sullenly out the window.

Timmy waited until her head lolled backward on the seat. He opened the window, knelt facing it and unbuttoned his fly. It was important to aim down, at an angle. The first time he tried it, he had sprayed his shirt.

He had only begun urinating when the woman shrieked and the man socked him hard on the arm. The child toppled to the

410

floor, its sleep-drenched face crumpling into a wail. The woman covered her mouth and pointed at him.

The man ran and got the conductor, who said angry words to Timmy and dragged him down the shaking, clanging corridor. He threw Timmy into a small vault. "Use the toilet. The toilet." The conductor showed him what he meant. Timmy was puzzled but polite. He didn't have to go anymore; the conductor knew that.

The family got off at the next stop. There was a high round tower with the words:

WELC ME TO SOU H DAKOTA

Timmy opened the window again. The night was balmy and hummed with insects. The air smelled like baking bread and rubber.

Dakota, Dakota. He said the word over and over, trying to get a sense of it. It was all new. Everything that had been a part of his life was gone. He wasn't sad. He was stunned. As if his heart had been cut out of his chest and now he held it in his hands, disbelieving, and watched the blood seep away.

But there is a marvelous thing that happens with children. They can be in the midst of war, with bombs exploding and heads bursting apart, and feel a sense of buoyancy creeping through their veins. Timmy felt it. He was stunned, and he had learned to use the toilet, and out the window a thousand incredible things flashed and were gone, and every day, there was a surer sense that he would never find his way home again; but in his veins, something surged.

Dakota. Dakota. He said the word over and over as he took off his coat and punched it into a ball. There would be trees and toilets. He put down his head and slept.

It happened during the night. The train carried them out of the prairies and into the desert. The air steamed. Timmy's shirt clung to his chest. Rivulets ran down his back and dripped in the creases of his buttocks. His toes slid in their socks. The train clanged through yellow fields, scattering fat, hornless beasts and raising clouds of dust. It still stopped in towns, but they were parched towns with cracked and peeling porches. Women adjusted babies on their hips and squint-eyed men spat and stared at Timmy going by them on the melting seat. He stared back.

They were in the Bad Lands where the ground was red clay and even the air was dead. It was yellow dust. Timmy kept the window up. In the middle of the day, a flash storm burst from the sky and Timmy opened the window and put his head out as far as it would go. The rain ran down the cracks in the ground and small white flowers sprang open. The ran stopped abruptly and the ground blazed again. The window frame burned when he put his head against it. Sometimes in the summer at home, the temperature climbed to fifty degrees. They stripped and plunged into icy streams to cool down. Oh, father, Timmy mourned. What have you done to me?

At Interior, South Dakota, the conductor took him off and threw down his food bag, wiping his hands afterward on a handkerchief. The train left immediately, as if glad to be rid of him. Timmy picked up the greasy sack and looked around. The station was a faded wooden building with a rail and porch. Three white elders sat on kegs, their feet on the rail. Timmy took the paper out of his pocket and studied it. He turned it right side up. The teacher in Barrow had printed:

INTERIOR, SOUTH DAKOTA. ASK FOR MISS BLACK.

He looked around. The men on the porch chewed and spit. On the horizon a cloud of dust appeared. It got bigger the closer it came, until it turned into a metal box charging over the road. It shuddered to a stop in front of him. A woman peered out. She had enormous brown eyes behind thick glasses and soft blond hair that hung to the waist. "Timmy?"

He couldn't speak.

"Timmy?" Her voice was gentle.

Dumbly he handed her the paper. She read it and pointed to herself. Her nails were clean. "I am Miss Black. Get in."

The Pine Ridge Reservation is as big as the state of Connecticut and, in 1916, was home for eight thousand Oglala

412

Sioux. In it were nine cars, seven districts, four counties and three million dry acres of dust, clay and prairie. The Indians raised cattle and corn. The Little Wound Boarding School was in the southern part of the reservation in the town of Kyle. Children from the outlying districts stayed year-round, going home for holidays. Miss Black explained that to Timmy on the way, but stopped talking when she realized he didn't understand a word.

They went through the towns of No Flesh Creek, American Horse and Medicine Root. Sioux children ran along the car, their hands out. "They want candy," Miss Black explained.

The towns had a hopeless air about them, as if they were dying from neglect. Chickens scattered and goats bleated as the car went by, while lank-haired women in scarves slid into shadows, watching.

The only trees were in the dry bottoms of creeks. They were small and twisted and chalk colored, like the earth.

The top of Miss Black's head was turning pink by the time they got to Kyle. It had a store, a district farmer, a church, a community center and a policeman who owned the only café. The café was adobe, and a flag was anchored in the roof next to an enormous cement cup of coffee with the words EATS.

Miss Black stopped the car in front of a two-story building. She got out, went around and opened Timmy's door. "We're here."

On the ground she was taller than Timmy by four fingers. He wondered how old she was and if her husband was a good hunter. There were no animals here. He got out warily.

Miss Black smiled. Her teeth were very white. "No one will hurt you."

It was the first lie.

The hair went first. Black drifts piled up on the white linoleum. The two white men ignored him as they flicked on a small, metal box that buzzed and ran it over his scalp. The rest of his hair fell away. A bald eagle with eyebrows glared back at him from the gleaming line of mirrors.

"Now the clothes." The man wiped his hands on the front of his shirt. His hands were speckled, like duck eggs. He mimed taking off the shirt and Timmy reluctantly unbuttoned it and

413

handed it over. They had already taken the suit jacket.

"The pants." The man held the shirt away from him, between his thumb and forefinger.

Timmy untied the rope around his waist and undid the pants. He gave it to the man. He wasn't wearing underwear. He stood uncertainly, naked except for socks and shoes. "That, too. Everything."

Timmy sat down slowly. The glossy finish of the new shoes had given way to mottled stains and clay. They were still the handsomest shoes Timmy had ever seen and the only ones his father had ever bought him.

"You'll get them back," the man said. Timmy untied them and took them off. Then he rolled down his socks and put them neatly into his shoes. A louse jumped.

"Sonofabitch." The men kicked the shoes into a white-tiled corner and threw the clothes after them. The man with glasses went away and came back with a box. He gingerly put in the clothes and shoes and socks and slammed down the lid while running out the door. The man with speckled hands soaped Timmy's head with purple medicine.

"It's all right; it's all right," the man murmured.

Timmy stared at himself. He looked like a missionary Easter egg.

"How can I teach him?" she exploded. "He's not even supposed to be here. All the boarding Eskimos go to the Chimewa reservation in Oregon."

The principal offered her a lemonade off the tray. She shook her head. He lifted a glass and erased the dew with his finger. "I know you're upset, Nancy. Anyone would be. But he's stuck here for at least a year. I got the papers on him this morning. The Chimewa school is full."

"I don't know the least thing about him! I don't know Eskimo—I don't even know what their language is called. I have seventy students to civilize, Mr. Vaden. Seventy."

He drank half a glass and set it down. "Now you have seventy-one."

"It isn't just one more, it's a different culture entirely."

He stared thoughtfully at the globe next to his desk. "Do you

414

know where Alaska is?"

"Don't insult me," she snapped.

"I wasn't intending to. You'd be amazed how many people don't. My own sister put it off the coast of South America." She didn't smile. "There is a segregated school system in Alaska. The territory has schools for white children and those of mixed blood. Natives go to federal schools, but they're not like the ones here, in America. Anybody can teach, as long as they've finished the eighth grade. Most of the teachers have no educational background whatsoever. They also"—and here he peered at a list in front of him—"are required to sew wounds, assist in childbirth, and in the northern sector, where Timmy's from, help with reindeer herds. From tooth rot to hoof rot, they get it all."

"How awful."

"That's why none of them stay. The average length of time for a teacher in the northernmost sector is a little over a year." He looked at her kindly. "He does know a little English, you know."

"Really?"

"He swore quite adequately when he was shaved and deloused. We had to burn his clothes."

She squeezed her eyes shut. He looked at her carefully. He hadn't misjudged her. She sighed. Her eyes were lovely behind the lenses. "Are there any teacher aids?"

He handed her a book. "It just came at the first of the week. A phonetics guide from the Chimewa teachers."

She riffled through it. It was thorough and for the first time she felt a glimmer of hope.

"Nancy, remember you are only one person. Don't let yourself get too tired. And remember, anything you do for him will improve his lot."

She nodded wearily and reached for a lemonade.

Forty heads lifted from workbooks when they came in. Timmy kept his eyes on the floor.

"Children, I have a surprise. We have a new student. His name is Timmy Snow and he is from Alaska. Can anyone tell me where Alaska is?" She looked around the room, her smile

415

never faltering. "Yes. Jack Yellow Thunder."

The boy had acne and skinny wrists. "Miss Black?"

"Yes, Jack?"

"Why he have purple head?"

The class tittered.

Timmy jerked his head up. The class grew deathly quiet. He walked over to the boy and leaned on his desk. He had longer arms and more muscle. "I like it," he growled.

"Oh," Jack said, and sank back in his seat. "Good."

STATUS REPORT
December 20, 1916

Timmy Snow
Height: 5'3"
Weight: 122 pounds
Binet-Simon Scale for Measurement of Intelligence: 83

Timmy Snow is Eskimo, approximately thirteen years old (birthday unknown). He has made remarkable progress in four months. He is learning the distinctive sounds of the English language and his vocabulary has grown to 15,000 words. He exhibits extreme reluctance in speaking up in class, but that is due largely to the emphasis Eskimos place on not calling attention to themselves. His best friend is Jack Yellow Thunder. Timmy has the most trouble differentiating between the English p and b sounds; in his native language, they are sometimes interchangeable. Also, the sentence structure is quite different than Eskimo and is a source of frustration. (An example: his language has many words which must be joined like a caboose to others in order to make sense). His usage of written words has improved and he is now reading at the fifth grade level. This is due primarily to our discovery that he badly needed glasses. He is quite farsighted: 200 over 20. He assisted in the fall carnival and especially enjoyed helping construct the pastry booth. The other boys consider him a leader; he taught them to play an Eskimo game—like horseshoes but using an enclosed ring. The winner always gets a prize. Timmy has been caught masturbating in bed and was punished. Only one outbreak occurred. He is extremely friendly and exhibits common sense. There has been no word from his family. In reference to the Binet-Simon score, the general cultural and educational background of Timmy is different enough to render the results imperfect. I do not agree with the newest information released by Garth, insisting that Eskimos are genetically that inferior. I have enclosed a sample of Timmy's work.

THE REINDEER

You lift your head and listen
The wind blows, you smell it
Is there still a trace of me
In the wind

Thirty-Seven

June 5, 1917, was Logan Blue's eighteenth birthday, and the day President Wilson had set as registration for the draft. Men between the ages of twenty-one and thirty-one were required to sign up at polling places. Logan celebrated his birthday by getting quietly smashed at an underground Seattle bar. At first he thought the coincidence with the draft was mildly interesting; after three beers he was slobbering over strangers, insisting it was extraordinary, but by midafternoon, Logan was certain God Himself was talking to him. He signed up.

Later, when he emerged blinking and sobereyed into the street, the full impact hit him of what he had done. He felt like he'd been tattooed. Why did he do it? Why? He touched the green card in his pocket. It was smaller than the thick vellum folded next to it, congratulating him on his acceptance to the University of Washington. The draft card was hardly there at all. Logan took it out and stared at it. His signature careened across the bottom. Steady old man, he told himself. The odds were only one in five that he'd be picked.

But if he'd wanted a long shot, he should have gone to the track.

Ten million men registered and 687,000 of them were called up right away. The numbers were pulled out of a hat. There were 4,500 local draft boards across the nation, and each draft board had assigned numbers starting with one. Logan's number was 258.

It was the first one called.

Logan eased by the draft office and inquired pleasantly if his induction was legal, since he was a territorial resident and all. The woman behind the desk was wearing an enormous red, white and blue bunting. She studied his passport again.

"Quite legal," she said frostily.

Logan stumbled out. His roommate arrived from Michigan, a quiet, bookish youth who plotted his courses as carefully as a general.

"What are you taking?" he inquired of Logan, when he finally came up long enough to realize he was sharing a room with someone.

"Army," Logan said.

The owl blinked and went back to his books.

The papers from the school stacked up on Logan's desk, unopened. He grew a beard. The same day a schedule of the courses he wouldn't be taking came in the mail, a white card came, ordering him to report for his army physical. Hope flared. Maybe something was wrong.

They checked his nose, his feet, his rectum.

"Check for fear," Logan said.

"What?" The doctor straightened.

"Nothing, sir."

The doctor slapped his back. "You're healthy as a horse. Congratulations."

"Thank you," Logan said faintly.

After that it was a race between getting the final green card and seeing Jenny. She was coming on the twelfth of August, on her way to college in upstate New York. Her parents wouldn't permit her to go to school in the same state as he, let alone the same university. Jenny, Jenny. He chewed his nails and started gnawing his fingers. He checked the mail. He sat on his bed, hands clasped between his knees, and thought of her.

She ran down the ramp into his arms. He caught her up and they embraced. "Logan." She pulled away from him. "Let me look at you." She frowned and he grinned foolishly.

"It's the beard."

"You've lost weight."

"It's nothing." He took the claim check from her hand.

"You eating right?"

"Not really," he confessed. "Oh, Jen. You're here."

She leaned up and kissed him soundly. "That's for all the

419

months apart." She kissed him again. "That's for—" The rest was lost as he crushed her to him. Behind him two girls whispered and nudged one another.

"That's him. I'd swear it." They were young, possibly eleven, slouching the fashionable way their older sisters did, but with no breasts to flatten. The blond tapped Logan on the arm. "Excuse me, mister." She was blushing to her scalp.

Jenny and Logan separated, and Jenny smiled at them. They smiled back.

"Yes?" Logan said.

"Aren't you the hero who was in the papers last week?" Jenny looked at him curiously.

"I'd swear it—"

"You're too young to swear," Logan said gruffly.

"But aren't ya? Aren't ya?"

"What's this all about?"

It was all wrong. He was going to broach it gently. The girls blurted it out. "He enlisted and his number was called first and now he's going to save America—aren't ya, mister? Aren't ya? Wait'll I tell Corie! She'll split, I swear it, she will."

Jenny stared at him. "Is it true?"

He hadn't wanted it to come out this way, with pigeons cooing on the archways, the steamer making flatulent noises near a grimy dock.

"Will you marry me, Jenny? I love you." He kissed her again and the girls clapped.

"Of course. Let's go right now."

It was a simple ceremony. They stood in front of a justice of the peace at the Seattle Municipal Marriage Chapel. The justice's wife had frowzy hair and ancient arms that swung to their own music. She sang "Oh, Promise Me" in a rich contralto and her ugliness melted away. Jenny was still wearing her traveling suit—a chemise of soft pink under a short bolero jacket. She wore her long hair simply, rolled at the back and curled around the eyes. The hat was the same soft pink. She carried roses that the justice had cut from the front lawn and sold Logan on the spot.

"You're a beautiful bride," the woman said afterward. Her

eyes were wet, and Jenny wondered if she cried at all the weddings.

Then they were walking out the door and down the sidewalk. "I have a room in the dormitory." Then he remembered. "And a roommate."

They were both thinking of it, wondering what it would be like. Married. Jennifer Jackson Blue. She was married. She touched the ring on her finger. It was solid gold. The justice had a side-order business of rings and wedding pictures. They had gotten one of each.

They took a trolley out to Lake Washington and rented a cottage along a heavily timbered stretch of shore. In the distance they could see flat-topped Mount Rainier. The other cabins were full of vacationers.

"You're lucky, Mr. and Mrs. Blue. We had a cancellation last minute; that's the only reason we have room. Man leaving for basic."

The Blues glanced at each other. He had gotten his final green card that morning.

"How long will you be?"

"One week," Logan said with deep regret.

The justice had sold them a bottle of wine under the counter, and Logan opened it while Jenny took a bath. When she got out, she stared at herself a while; it was a momentous occasion; and then she remembered he would be gone in a week—less now, because of the long bath—and she threw open the door and went to him dressed in a towel. Her hair was damp along the neck.

He was in bed. His chest was naked. He had a mat of dark hair on his chest. His body seemed long under the spread. It was the middle of the day and they heard children screaming. A dog barked.

"You locked the door?" she asked.

"Check it again. Just to be sure."

She went to the door and rattled the knob. Locked. The ring glowed on her finger. She straightened the curtains, smoothing away the small crack of light that had been there.

"No one can see." He held out his arms.

421

She hesitated. The sum total of her mother's instruction were the terse words "You sleep with a man. That's how you get pregnant."

She walked over to him and sat on the edge of the bed. "Logan, have you ever—I mean, that is—"

"No, Jen." He grasped the towel gently and it fell away. Her breasts were sculptures in the light, soft slopes of light and dark. She was rounder than he'd imagined. He kissed her throat and felt her pulse beat. "Jenny, Jenny."

He pulled her to him and held her. They were separated by the spread. "Are you afraid?" he asked at last.

She shook her head. "Are you?"

He stopped tracing circles on her back. "Yes."

"You mean of war?"

"Of this."

It was very quiet in the cabin. The faucet dripped in the tub and Jenny thought idly she should have turned it harder. "You mean because it's the first time?"

"I always thought the man should be experienced." He said it as if he were ashamed.

Jenny hugged him. "I'm glad. Really. It makes it special. Something we only do with each other."

He kissed her again and turned out the small light on the nightstand. Then he opened the covers and took her in.

For eighteen years Jenny had lain alone at night. Her mother had never smothered her with hugs; her father had never hoisted her onto his shoulders as a child, or tussled her to the floor. The sheer warmth of another body was magical—to feel skin next to hers and arms around her! And then to open her eyes and see that it was Logan's arms and Logan's mouth.

She would have been happy with that. Logan touched her, tentatively, as though she would stop him. Her body tensed and then she remembered that she was married and this was her husband and it was all right.

He started with things known: the hollow of her throat, the solid shape of shoulder, and then moved his hands wonderingly over her body. "Beautiful," he whispered in awe. "You are so very beautiful." His hand found a breast and he touched her with the gentlest of touches, amazed at the effect. Her nipple bloomed under him.

"Jenny." He said it over and over. At last he touched the part of her that was least like himself. She gave a small sigh and her body shuddered.

"Am I hurting you?" he asked in alarm.

"Don't stop," she whispered. Her voice was strange and fearful. He took her hand and placed it on himself. The hand spasmed around his penis and touched it. Her hand was warm silk.

"Jenny." Instinct took over. Blindly they embraced. Blindly he guided himself into her. Nothing had ever felt so good.

Her body stiffened. "You're hurting me!" she cried out.

Immediately he stopped pushing. He wanted to withdraw, with everything in him he wanted to, but he couldn't; so he lay on top of her, breathing shallowly, and stopped pushing. "Jenny, I'm so sorry. I didn't know. I didn't mean to hurt you." He was murmuring to her while down below, in another world, his penis was pushing by itself. "Is it all right? Is it okay, now? I can stop. I'll stop."

"It hurts." There was fear in her voice.

He grimaced with effort and stopped moving.

Jenny's face was very quiet.

"How are you feeling?"

"I didn't know it would hurt so much. No one ever said it would hurt."

"I didn't know either," Logan confessed.

"It hurts you too?"

"Oh, no. No. It feels wonderful. Wonderful. But I don't want to hurt you," he added anxiously. "We can stop for a while."

"You wouldn't mind?"

"No," he said gamely. "No, I wouldn't mind."

But he was pulling against gravity. He would almost get out of her and then something irresistible pulled him back. How could it feel so wonderful for him and hurt so much for her? He found himself going faster, until all the blood in his body was in that nob of flesh and there was nowhere else to put it all, except into her, and he exploded with it.

For a long delirious moment, he was absorbed in his own

pleasure, in the total concentrated joy of it; and then he became aware of Jenny again, how quiet she was. He raised a flushed face.

"I'm sorry. Forgive me. Can you forgive me?" He kissed her.

"Is it over?" she said in a small voice.

"Does it still hurt?" He pulled out now, in haste, as if he could rectify what he had done.

"I just thought—" Her voice trailed away. "In the movies—" It was a dirty trick. "Maybe only the man is supposed to enjoy it."

"No," Logan said stoutly. "No. I don't believe that. Maybe in other marriages, but not ours. It was the first time, and it hurt, but we'll find what you like. We will." He kissed her. "Only now I have to sleep. Forgive me. Oh, Jenny, forgive me!" And he was gone.

Jenny covered him up and went into the bathroom. Her legs were wet and when she washed, there was a trace of blood on the cloth. She rinsed the washcloth thoroughly until she rubbed out the stain; embarrassed that some anonymous hotel maid would have discovered it and known something intimate about their lives. She studied her face in the mirror. She was very pale. Her hair was a dark nest around her face. She found her hairbrush in the overnight case and leaned over the sink, brushing it out. It had hurt, there was no way around that, but she was married to a good man. Married. Jennifer Jackson Blue. The brush moved through her and behind the quiet curtain, tears came to her eyes.

They filled every minute. They barely slept at night; it seemed such a waste. Is it possible to wrench time from its orbit, to stay its course? They tried. It wasn't only the wonder of the bed, although that held them well into the day. It was the love that went with it.

They were unabashedly romantic with each other. They held hands at restaurants and kissed on the beach. Once they rented a Pierce-Arrow and drove around Lake Washington. With gas rationing they weren't supposed to get any for pleasure driving, but when the owner found out Logan had enlisted, and they were newlyweds, he silently gave them a gallon. It lasted all day. The road was a mire. Twice Logan got out and put logs under the wheels. The second time there was a breathless minute as the wheels spun and mud flew, but Logan got them out of it; and Jenny knew he could get them out of anything. Fear overcame her. She pressed herself closer and put her arm around his shoulder. "You promise you'll come back?"

His Adam's apple moved and he took one hand off the wheel and patted her knee through the dress. He didn't speak.

"I think we shouldn't tell the folks yet. That's my gut feeling. What do you say?" They were on a ferry going to Mercer Island. The water swirled placidly behind them in gray green waves. Ahead, the island was a rolling valley of trees.

"Why?"

"Your folks have each other. I'm worried about dad. Coming on top of my enlisting."

"You know him better than I do."

"You're not disappointed?"

"No," she lied. She raised her hand and examined the ring. She was married and she wanted to tell the world.

"Thanks, Jen. Just for a while, until I'm home."

The fear gripped her. "You won't be gone forever?"

He held her tightly. "Nothing can separate us."

She went with him to the train. The station was crammed with men and weeping women. The women were thrusting baked goods into their men's hands, and Jenny felt a flash of disappointment. She wished she could have baked something for Logan.

A band was playing a jaunty version of "Over There" and went right into a solemn rendition of the "Marine's Hymn." A small choir began singing:

> *From the halls of Montezuma*
> *To the shores of Tripoli*

Protect him, protect him, she thought. Don't let anything bad happen to this man. She thought of the orphans in France, the starving hordes in Belgium.

*We will fight our country's battles
On the land and on the sea.*

What right did she have to keep him? He was the hope of the world, he and the other men on this platform—American boys, American men, with wide open faces and hands that had thumped balls and whistled for dogs, legs that had carried them over the wide shady spaces of summer and dragged them into fall schoolyards. Now they would carry them into battle, into the grim courtyards of fallen villages and into the trenches; and everything they touched, they would bring to life again.

*First to fight for right and freedom
And to keep our honor clean*

They all felt it. On the platform the women clutched their men to them, and the men were straight and tall and scared and proud. They were going away, into the unknown, into something terrible called war; and behind them, behind them, the women would be fighting, too.

*We are proud to claim the title
Of United States Marine.*

"I love you, Jenny." He kissed her again, hard, and she clung to him until the last possible moment, until the force of the crowd behind them took him to the edge of the platform, up the stairs and away from her.

She waited for him to materialize in a window. The last of the men got on and the conductor gave another call. The whistle blew.

She couldn't find him. She twisted her ring. Frantic, she ran up and down the platform, searching for him. A thousand men waved back. Logan, Logan. Tears streamed down her face. She brushed them away. The men were a blur in front of her, the train a blur of its own, picking up speed.

Logan, Logan. She waved to them all, knowing that Logan

426

was in there somewhere; knowing he would feel it with his heart, and hoping he was close enough to a window to see *some* woman waving good-bye, some fresh-scented sweetheart or wife. So she waved to the others on board, waved gaily, waved until her arm was tired, and then she changed hands and waved some more; while behind her, the choir started singing, the words floating high and clear into the sky like colored balloons:

> *Keep the home-fires burning,*
> *While your hearts are yearning,*
> *Though your lads are far away.*
> *They dream of home*

She had hoped she would be pregnant. With everything inside her, she had hoped it, *willed* it. She thought, somehow, if she were carrying his child, he'd have to come home, alive and well. The day her period started, she sat on the tile floor in her bathroom at the YWCA in New York and wept. It was a private grief. How could she tell her roommate what it was like? Corinne had never been married.

When she got control of herself, she powdered her nose, went down the stairs and out the door, past the public library on Forty-Second and Fifth Avenue to the first beauty parlor she could find.

The first cut was the hardest, and she closed her eyes against it. She couldn't explain why she had done it, except that Logan was gone from her, and she needed a tangible mark separating the old life from this one. She stared recklessly into the mirror. Her head was curiously light. The cut came mid-cheek and accentuated the bones in her face. She gave the barber a dollar, hesitated and tipped him a quarter. "Come back again," he said from the door, pleased.

School was out of the question, with Logan gone. She and Corinne both worked with the YWCA in the United War Work effort. There were seven organizations in it: the YWCA, YMCA, Salvation Army, National Catholic War Council, Jewish Welfare Board, American Library Association and War Camp Community Service. That first summer, eighty-five hostess clubs were built and stocked with books and papers.

Women volunteers made cakes, sang birthday songs, wrote letters. In France they started social and welfare programs in munitions factories, manned telegraph lines and held the hands of dying men. YWCA nurses were sent to the front.

Jenny worked in the local branch. Ten thousand military men slept in War Camp Community Service quarters in New York each week. They served 80,000 meals, gave 300 to 500 sightseeing trips and gave away over 80,000 tickets to Broadway shows. Every time Jenny danced with a young soldier, she saw her husband's face. Every time she gave a man coffee, she was giving it to Logan. She had relived their week together in her mind a hundred times, poring over every detail. Even though she wasn't a religious person, at night before she slept, she got down on her knees next to the lumpy bed and prayed to God. She was praying for Logan's safety; and because they were tied together, because she would die without him, in the quiet of her heart, she knew she was praying most of all for her own.

Thirty-Eight

He was in the army now; everything told him that, from the spit polish of his boots to the loudspeaker blaring orders. He had been sent to Fort Benning, Georgia, a sweaty armpit of a place. The first night, something wet and vicious slid across his ankle and was gone. The barracks were on a low rise called the Hill, surrounded by pine and swamp. Moisture hung in the air; shirts clung like wet sheets; and mosquitoes nicked through ponchos and lifted off with flesh.

All of which seemed to please the sergeant major.

He was the first small, mean-spirited man Logan had ever met, and he used his small powers relentlessly. The first week, an ashcarver from Ashtabula had hanged himself in quarters after the sergeant major had made him stand at attention for three days and nights for mislacing a legging. The man had a terrifying way of sniffing out any recruit with a shred of leadership, a spark of life. Logan sank into the shadows; he drilled and ran with the pack.

The first week, the company practiced the Manual of Arms; they learned how to care for their feet and uniforms and about the perils of VD. They heard about a man whose whanger had turned black and fallen off after a night in a local brothel. "At least it got him out of the army," a recruit muttered. But mostly they learned to duck down, cover their ass, ask no questions and stay out of Sergeant Major Dillard's way.

The second week, they sighted the rifle and aimed it. They went over how to care for their uniforms and feet, and added cleaning the teeth and rifle. They thrust bayonets into stationary dummies. They pitched tents and dozed through lengthy explanations of why they were at war. They cheered each other up with statistics: only eleven out of a thousand would die. They learned to shoot craps and call it African golf, mend their own pants and peel potatoes.

The third week, they fired the rifle, and it was then that it occurred to Logan that he was being trained to kill people. That was what war was about—aiming and flexing a finger on the trigger and blowing a man to smithereens; a man with a blond German wife making strudel for dumpling red-cheeked children. He wondered why he was the only recruit that saw it.

The last week, they learned about the mustard gas the Germans had invented, and the bombs they would use, and it was then that it occurred to Logan that the Germans would be firing back.

"Private Logan Blue reporting as ordered, Sergeant Major Dillard." He stood at attention.

"At ease, private."

Logan spread his legs and put his hands behind him. He looked straight ahead.

"Sit down."

"Thank you, sergeant major."

"Cigar?"

"No, thank you, sergeant major."

Dillard studied Logan. "Do you have any idea why I summoned you?"

Logan had several, but none he wanted to share. "No, sergeant major, I have no idea."

Dillard nodded as if that was what he expected. Resentment flooded Logan as he watched Dillard fish a card out of a file box. It was made more complicated because Sergeant Major Dillard didn't have a thumb. Logan didn't volunteer to help; the army had taught him that much.

"Yes. Here it is." Dillard squinted at the card and finally put on his glasses. Logan recognized it; it was his personal history card. Dillard smiled and looked up. "How is your mother, Nelly?"

"Excuse me?" Logan was so startled he forgot army protocol.

Dillard didn't. "What did you say?"

"Excuse me, Sergeant Major Dillard."

"That's better." Dillard leaned back in his chair. "You seem surprised, Private Blue." His head glinted through the thinning hair.

"Well, yes, sergeant major. If you wouldn't mind my speaking frankly, I'm shocked my mother—"

"Would have known an SOB like myself?" Dillard finished drily. "Attila, I believe the boys call me behind my back."

Logan fell silent. Attila was the mildest one. He stared straight ahead.

"You haven't answered my question, private."

"She's dead, sergeant major."

There followed such a silence, Logan thought maybe Dillard hadn't heard him. He glanced at the sergeant major and his mouth gaped open in astonishment. The old bastard was weeping openly. Wait'll Logan told the boys. They wouldn't friggin' believe it.

"How—how did it happen?" Dillard blubbered.

"Suddenly, sergeant major. She was kidnapped by a band of Nez Percé while riding a trolley in Seattle."

"Nez Percé?"

"Yes, Sergeant Major Dillard," Logan said crisply. "They drowned her."

"She was—drowned?" At that he launched a fresh wave of tears.

"Yes, sergeant major. But perhaps it was a kinder death."

"Kinder?" He was wiping his eyes. His nose was leaking.

"Yes, sergeant major. The autopsy revealed she had scarlet fever. Probably wouldn't have lasted the night, Sergeant Major Dillard." Logan felt quite pleased with himself. It was the first time he had managed to work all three lies into one story.

"Scarlet fever." Dillard reached behind him, found a handkerchief and blew his nose.

Logan waited politely until it became clear Dillard wouldn't get a grip on himself in the near future. "It's always good to meet people who knew dear mummy, Sergeant Major Dillard."

"You called her mummy?" Dillard's voice was foggy.

"Yes, sergeant major. She was never mother to me. You must have met in Alaska."

Dillard's eyes took on a faraway look. "I was stationed in

Rampart, a bawdy, brawling frontier town on the edge of civilization."

Logan sensed a long-winded story coming. "About mummy—"

"Into this Arctic wasteland, a small flower was thrown and struggled for life."

"Mummy." Logan wondered if Dillard was writing this down.

"Dear, sweet Nelly. She had a delicate beauty that transformed the squalor of her rough surroundings. She came on a mission, private. A mission of love."

"She was pretty?"

"She was beautiful," Dillard said reverently. "I worshipped her. From a distance, of course. It was all very proper. That was one thing about her. Your mother was a perfect lady." His voice quivered with feeling. "Despite everything. You understand? Everything. She was a lady."

"I'm sure." Logan purposely left off his title. After all, they were getting quite chummy.

"Yes. She was skilled in many things." A yearning smile came and went.

"So you helped her?" Logan prodded. He wasn't sure why he was doing this, except it was wonderful to see his enemy squishy with emotion.

"I helped her, much against my better judgment. Everything inside me spoke out against it, but I am, above all, a gentleman, with a code of honor."

"Quite right. So you helped her. Helped her do what?"

"Why, track down your father, of course. I forced him to marry her."

"You did what?" Logan blurted. The story had been going along very nicely and then it suddenly swerved off the road and careened down a cliff.

"Your father didn't want to marry her. Imagine. But I tracked him down like the common criminal he wa—" He remembered Logan. "I get carried away, son. Sorry." He shrugged. "It was a long time ago, but I've never forgotten her. I always thought—if things had been different—" He got hold of himself and cleared his throat. "I have the power to fix

432

orders, you know. In special cases."

Logan's eyes narrowed. "What do you mean, sergeant major?"

Dillard half shrugged, embarrassed. "A son of Nelly—"

"I'll go where I'm sent, sergeant major. There's a war on."

"But you're Nelly's son!"

"And Cahill Blue's son, too, sergeant major." The words came out without thinking. There was a long pause. Horrified, Logan realized what he had done. If Dillard could fix orders to get a man out of combat, couldn't he as easily fix them to get a man *in?*

Dillard's face grew black. "Dismissed," he barked.

Logan stood up. "Sergeant Major Dillard, if I might—"

"Dismissed."

Logan's head was ringing. He stumbled out the door. What had he done? He stopped in the hallway and calmed himself. Dillard couldn't have that much power. He was only a sergeant major. With more bravado than he was feeling, he walked back to the barracks and told the boys everything. They all laughed.

The orders came the next day.

War is relative. Let the generals examine boards and move players and endlessly discuss odds over old bourbon. To Logan, the war was a burned scrap of farmland somewhere in France. It was raining, that first battle, and all the Germans he shot had gone down in a merciful blur. On the land stood a gutted house and Logan ducked into it at the end, to check.

The only furniture left was a charred table leg in the fireplace. The plastered ceiling had collapsed in the parlor. On the floor a stuffed chair was missing a leg. Logan climbed the stairs cautiously, rifle in hand. His heart hammered. He couldn't hear clearly. He made the top of the stairs. The hall was papered in roses. Something scrabbled in the closet, back in a hole. A rat? Must be a rat. His heart was roaring now. He shifted his gun. His hands were wet.

"I'm taking you prisoner." His voice roared. His ears roared. Something moved in the closet. A gun. Logan flattened against the wall. He could see the gun and behind it, he could see eyes. They were dilated and very black. The gun went off

and the wall splintered above Logan's ear. He raised his rifle
and fired. He saw the man's eyes in that dreadful instant, and
the pinched fear in his face. The shot exploded the man's chest,
and he crashed backward. Logan trembled. He wiped his
mouth. The room was very still. He pulled the body into the
room. A streak of blood smeared the floor. He had shot him
through the heart. He was a boy, maybe fourteen. He was very
thin and his knuckles were scabbed, as if he'd been playing
marbles right up until the second he had aimed and fired.

Hideous business, Logan thought. Hideous. Hideous. He
turned his head and threw up.

A year went by and Logan never threw up any more over
Germans. He had seen far worse things: in Lorraine, a nun
raped and tortured before she was killed; in Alsace, a baby
thrown against a wall, its fragile head smashed like an egg. Yes,
Logan knew what war was, now. War was waking up wet and
shivering and knowing the shakes were partly there for that
other thing—that fear down in the groin that never quite went
away. It was staying alive. And so far, he'd won.

He was in the Argonne, in the shadow of the Ardennes, an
ancient cropping of broken hills and heavy forests. It was
ambush country, the kind of war the Germans liked. Every
clump of trees had a nest of machine guns. The forest itself
breathed. The Americans were advancing toward the Metz-
Lille road. Behind it the Meuse River meandered to the sea, and
a railroad track stitched over the rolling ribbon of brown earth.
The primary objective was to smash the railroad artery that
carried supplies and reinforcements to German troops. If they
could do it, several key branches connecting the German
armies in the north and south would also be cut.

The war would stop.

Logan crouched beneath the trees, eyes darting. The heavy
trees breathed in and out. His skin prickled. There was
something there, in the dim greenery. Something not quite
seen but sensed. He raised his rifle. Something was wrong. He
ran backward. No. It wasn't his feet running. It was the impact

of a bullet. He hit the ground hard. The wind went out of him. He looked at his body in surprise. Something red poured out of him. Fire slugged into his chest. The gun fell away. "No!" he screamed.

It is useless to expect that we have accomplished the truly great results of the last two months without paying a heavy price. Not an exorbitant price, it is true. But a heavy price has been paid—much higher, indeed, than has yet been indicated by reports. But this is inevitable. Every position or series of positions has its value as expressed in casualties. And our contribution to the general success in bringing the war so near an end justifies the expenditures we have made, and shows that we have obtained value received. It has been infinitely cheaper to fight the war as has been done. More men are consumed every day, but the total required to complete the task is immeasurably lower.

Jenny stopped reading out loud.

"Is that the *Times?*" Corinne was dabbing paste on her lips. She pressed her lips together, blotted them on a tissue and examined herself critically.

Jenny nodded. "The military expert again. His usual column: 'The War Situation.'"

"I wonder if Logan would agree with that business about casualties being cheaper." Corinne flounced her skirt. She had dance duty at the Y.

"Of course he would," Jenny said loyally. She folded the newspaper.

"Have you heard from him lately?"

Jenny shook her head. "He's still somewhere in France." The censor deleted more specific information.

"Could I borrow the green glass beads again? Please."

"Sure."

Corinne went to Jenny's side of the room and got them from the jewelry box. "Thanks." She dropped them over her dark head and got a light coat from the closet. "I don't know."

435

"About what?"

"Have you noticed how they always talk about numbers, and never the men behind those numbers?" She put on her hat and gloves.

Tears came to Jenny's eyes. "It's the only way to get through it," she whispered.

Corinne pasted the last thrift stamp in her booklet and put it in her purse. "I wish you'd come with me, Jen. It's a glorious day out there. I bet you haven't been out in weeks. The store's only seven blocks away, and besides, you need a new suit. You've worn the War Service Oxford forever. What will Logan say when he sees you?"

Jenny frowned and looked at herself. Corinne was right; her suit was an uninspiring gray that bagged at the knee.

"It's your lunch hour," Corinne coaxed. "Look around you." The other three desks in the small green office were deserted. "Even Mr. Perkins has to eat, doesn't he?" She held up the ad enticingly.

BEST & CO.
Fifth Avenue at 35th St.
FIRST REDUCTION SALE
Women's Tailored Suits
33.00
heretofore 42.50 to 49.50

"They're from Paris and London," Corinne said. "Velour." Jenny laid down her pencil. "All right, you win. But only for an hour. Mr. Perkins is counting on me to give him the statistics right after lunch."

"How's it coming?" Corinne glanced out the window. Across the street, a couple was swinging down the marble steps of the library, laughing. The elms were blazing gold. Jenny picked up the sheet in front of her and cleared her throat. "Financial Statement for the National War Work Council, from the entry of the war to July 31, 1918, submitted November 1918. The YMCA-YWCA has handled $54,354,034, of which over $400.00 is accrued interest on contributions. Up to July 31, 9,500 uniforms were furnished—" She put the paper down. "Are you alseep yet?"

Corinne laughed. "It is beastly. And I thought totalling area contributions was awful."

"Is that what they have you doing this week?" She straightened papers.

"I'm filling in for Sal. She's got it, Jen."

They stared at each other. "Influenza?" It was a cruel killer, on top of the war. Thousands had died in New York alone.

Corinne nodded. "And with all those kids and her husband in France. She's quarantined. Her mother's in from Jersey to sit with the kids."

"That's terrible." Jenny hunted her pencil and stuck it in her purse. She had been careless with the last one and someone had stolen it. Graphite came from Germany; pencils were hoarded. "We should send her something." She turned out the light.

Corinne nodded. Jenny locked the heavy oak-and-beveled-glass door. "Do you have to go to the room, Jen?"

She shook her head. Living and working in the same building was convenient, in a claustrophobic way. They linked arms and went down the linoleum-tiled hallway to the main door. The heat blasted them as they opened the door.

"Can't believe it's already November," Jenny remarked. "We still haven't seen Al Jolson. He's been at the Winter Garden for thirty-two weeks."

Corinne made a face. "I'd rather see *A Woman's Experiences* at the Rialto. Mary Boland is supposed to—"

She never finished.

The street erupted with newsboys thumping hoods of cars, dealing papers to frantic pedestrians. Horns blared; a woman screamed and fainted, and an elderly man with a small flag in the band of his hat put down his head and wept. Jenny paled and clutched at a racing newsboy. "What is it? What's happened?"

"It's over! Read for yourself!" He thrust an extra edition into her hands and she gave him a cent. He sped away, and the crowd swarmed over him. It was a single sheet of paper. Trembling, Jenny read:

UPI BREST

ARMISTICE ALLIES SIGNED ELEVEN THIS MORN-ING   SEDAN TAKEN THIS MORNING BY AMERI-CANS

details night final

THE EVENING POST

Relief swept over her and she shook. The crowd melted into delirious tears. Sirens blew, church bells rang wildly, factory and steam whistles keened. Everything that could make noise, did. People streamed out of buildings, hugging strangers. Confetti poured down, flares shot up. Traffic was diverted off Fifth and they danced in the streets. The city was overcome with joy. It was over. The boys were coming home. At the Barge office, buglers trumpeted from the roof. The Stock Exchange closed a half hour early. Spontaneous parades swept down Fifth Avenue, igniting pedestrians to join in. Broom-factory workers strutted behind a sign We Made the Broom that Swept the Hohenzollerns OUT! Nobody went back to work. A barber in Park Avenue quit mid-customer, his hands too shaky to finish. Columbia University students snaked across the lawn, kicking their feet as a plane loop-de-looped in the bright sky. They wandered aimlessly; euphoria carried them along.

All Jenny could think about was Logan. He was coming home. She stumbled and cried and Corinne caught her and they laughed. They waited for the final edition. They were going to take the paper to the Ritz-Carlton and celebrate. The newsboys fell out of trucks and scattered. They ripped a paper from one and gave him two cents. Eagerly they read:

REPORT ARMISTICE SIGNED, CITY IN WILD DEMONSTRATION: STATE DEPARTMENT AT 2:15

Jenny was stunned, dazed from disbelief. She read it again. "It's not over?" she asked wonderingly. The crowd grew still, the faces gray and watchful. They looked at each other, hoping to read something different. "It's not over." She doubled over. "How could they do that! Who's responsible? This is the cruelest—" She broke down and sobbed.

Corinne took her arm. "It's all right, Jen. It's all right."

Fear clamped around her. "Then he's still there. He still could be—"

"Hush, now."

They stumbled home through a mire of confetti.

"I still don't believe it." Jenny put down the November 8 edition of the New York *Tribune*. "The *Trib* is right, you know. In the editorial. The edge really has been taken off. The president of UPI should be shot."

Corinne clamped an earring on and came over. "Oh, baby, when we hear the news, you'll be fine. It was a miserable mistake is all, but when those bells peal and it's for real—"

"I won't believe it," Jenny said flatly. "Not until I see him."

Noise. So much noise. Her hand came up in sleep to brush it away, like a fly. It kept up. She nosed the pillow, thrashed her legs and opened one eye. She could barely see the outline of posters: Uncle Sam was a black blob inside the words Uncle Sam Wants YOU! Next to him the Victory Liberty Loan lady clutched her slip with a slim right hand. Corinne staunchly maintained she was wearing a gown, but Jenny knew a slip when she saw one. She opened both eyes then sat straight up and turned on the light before she remembered it was a lightless day in New York. She checked the time and snapped it off. Three on the nose.

"Corinne." She was a lump in the covers. It was a coalless day, too, and the room was cool.

Jenny put on her robe and crawled out of bed. She went to the window and raised the shade. Fifth Avenue was jammed with people and the *New York Times* tower was lit. Lit. On a lightless day. She shoved up the window and leaned out. "Is it over? Is it really over?" Tears sprang to her eyes.

"It's really over!" The man raised a newspaper. It was too far away to see.

She slammed down the window and ran to Corinne.

"I heard."

They were subdued, trembling. They dressed in the dark and gripped each other's hands going down the stairs. The streets echoed curiously the celebration of four days before. Confetti fell. Strangers kissed.

"It's over?" Jenny asked over and over again.

"Yes!" strangers told her.

"It's really over?"

"Yes."

It was over. It was over. Jenny stopped next to a peach stone barrel out of habit and fumbled through her purse. The sign on the barrel said:

> The Government needs **PEACH STONES!**
> SAVE THEM! and put them in this barrel.

The army ground down the pits and used them to filter poison out of gas. Jenny had two pits wrapped in tissue. Corinne stayed her hand. "They don't need them anymore, Jen."

Jenny stared at the pits.

"It's over," Corinne said gently.

The coffins and wounded went first. Two hundred thousand Americans died in the war. Most of them were buried in France, but when the fighting stopped, boxes were made in munitions factories and the lonely cargo made its way across the ocean on its final trip. The coffins were carried on the decks of German ships with new American names—ships that had been idle in the ports of Hamburg, Bremen and Trieste, and now were pressed into active duty on the last detail. The ships dropped the bodies off in New York and picked up grain and food to feed the living in Germany and Austria.

If the men inside the cabins could have peered outside, some of them might have wished they could trade places with those bodies, but most of the wounded were too ill to care. This was the real immediacy of war: the tortured breathing through a tube, the pounding blood in limbs that were gone, the gradual realization of how much was wrong, and how long it was going to stay that way.

A few years before, eternity was summer—warm dappled days and easy laughter. Nobody thought what it would feel like to be gray-lipped and hollow, to have food cut up for them into bite-sized pieces. They were young and fearless. Who could have known that starting now, from this moment on, forever and ever, there would be only this bed, this ancient pain, this terrifying reliance on strangers?

Of course, if they had known that, back in those mud-drenched, dew-drenched days, perhaps none of them would have gone. That's the hideous joke of war, played over and over on new, fresh men, men who still have fingers and toes and dreams.

She read it again, not comprehending. It couldn't be. Had to be a mistake. It was the sixteenth of November. The war was over. She read it again:

CASUALTIES REPORTED BY
GENERAL PERSHING

WASHINGTON

Angelini, Giovanni. Mrs. M. Salili, 120 W. 4th Sea. KA

Barlow, G.A. Mrs. E.A. 46 Turner St. Sea Ka

Blue, Logan. Mrs. Jennifer Y.W.C.A. 42nd St. N.Y. WA

Broilovic, Ivan, J.F. Brunner North Yakima, KA

She dropped the paper. Her face went white.
"Jen?" Corinne went to her. "Jenny, what is it?"
Jenny covered her mouth with her hand. She was trembling.
Corinne opened the paper and read silently. "Oh, God."

Fog held them up at Sandy Hook for twenty-four hours. Jenny and Corinne waited through the night, stamping their feet, drinking Red Cross coffee and eating sandwiches.

441

Thousands huddled in blankets in Battery Park. Would he still have a face? Could a man live, and not have a face?

Over ten thousand soldiers were coming home on the *Leviathan*. One in eight were wounded. Could he still hold her? Could a man hold a woman with one arm? No arms?

"There it is! I see it!" Corinne cried out.

Jenny shielded her eyes.

"Next to the Statue of Liberty, Jen."

Tears sprang to her eyes. It was a scuffed bullet of a ship, steel gray, the camouflage erased. A New York police boat motored toward it, its pale light glowing through the fog. Fireboats flanked it as it sped toward the pier. A roar went up. A hundred bands began to play. Soldiers crowded the top afterdeck, waving. The ship nosed into Pier 4, Hoboken, and the crowd emptied the park and ran.

"Come on, Jen."

Jenny adjusted her hat. "How do I look?" Her face was pale.

"Beautiful," Corinne said, and hugged her in a rush.

Jenny squeezed the wrapped package she had brought, fussed with the ribbon. It was a silk smoking jacket from Saks, trimmed in burgundy cord with silk frogs. It was the safest thing she could think of to buy. She wished she were braver. The park was nearly deserted. Scraps of paper and damp sandwiches littered the tables. Somebody had left a blanket, and a child was wandering near the garbage cans, crying for his mother.

"Jenny, tell me one thing. Do you love him?"

Jenny's eyes filled up. "Very much," she whispered.

Corinne touched her hand. "Then don't be afraid."

The tugboats in the harbor shrilled a welcome as the gangplank lowered and the first soldiers filed down, blinking in the pale light. Red Cross workers threw chocolates and cigarettes. The Camp Merritt band played "Home Sweet Home." Everyone cried. Soldiers rushed into waiting arms. Jenny strained to see him at the skyline of the ship.

The bad ones came off last, a steady stream of stretchers with fluid bottles bobbling overhead. The faces were slack and gray and shared the same extraordinary pain. Jenny leaned on

442

the rope and looked down at each face, relieved when it wasn't Logan, and horrified at what that relief meant; that somehow she was less human not to have enough tears for them all.

The stretchers ended and the men in wheelchairs began the slow procession down the ramp. Jaunty smiles above savaged bodies. Here was a missing leg, there a missing arm. One man was only a torso; everything else was gone. His wife screamed when she saw him, and instinctively covered her child's eyes, and the last part of him that was still whole shattered apart. Logan, Logan. Jenny glanced at the top afterdeck. Coffins rose in somber walls. Was he dead? Had he died?

And then there he was, not sitting, but limping slowly down the ramp, steadying himself on a crutch, looking frighteningly thin and old. He stooped over, twisting toward his left side.

"Logan!"

He stopped, puzzled, trying to locate her.

"Logan!" She ducked under the rope, scrambled up the ramp and threw herself into his arms.

He was a week in the General Debarkation Hospital on Ellis Island; the day before Christmas, he mustered out. She had found a room for them on Central Park West.

"What do you think?" she asked shyly, when he unlocked and opened the door. A small, fat pine tree glowed with lights in front of leaded-pane windows. Foil packages glinted on the floor, and outside, the park sparkled with snow.

He grunted, and hobbled through the door, banging his bags awkwardly against his knees. He had insisted on carrying them himself. Jenny checked her disappointment. She closed the door and locked it.

"What would you like?" she asked uncertainly. "We have lemonade. I made cookies." She was remembering how he had gone away with nothing to eat.

He held out his hand. "Come here."

The bullet had pierced a lung, punching a hole the size of a man's thumb through the front of his chest and biting out three pounds of meat in the back. But the real wound was inside his head.

He mounted her quickly, coldly, his physical need more pressing than any tenderness. She needed him too; she had been as long without a man; but she found herself responding slowly. She had spent so many months extinguishing any flash of desire that now she found it hard to summon up. Afterward he was remote. He rolled onto his back and smoked.

She groped for his hand in the dark, couldn't find it and settled for patting him awkwardly on the shoulder. They were strangers.

"I asked Corinne for Christmas dinner tomorrow. I bought a ham."

Next to her a pin of fire burned in the dark. She rolled over and kissed his shoulder, resting her chin on the curve of his arm. "Was it bad over there?"

"Not bad," he said automatically.

A long silence. Snow floated lazily past the window. A dog barked.

"It's going to take time," Jenny said finally. "That's all. You've been gone a long time."

The ember glowed hotly on the tip of his cigarette. "I'll say." His voice was peculiar, hard.

"What's that supposed to mean?"

"Why'd you cut your hair?"

Her hand went to it. "You don't like it? I thought you said you liked it."

"And the face paint! Like a common tramp!"

Tears slid down the corners of her eyes. "All the women wear it now, Logan. It's the style."

"Not my wife. I won't have my wife painted up like a whore. All the actresses your friends at the War Council sent us were nothing but whores."

"Logan, I've never heard you this way!"

"And you won't be working, either." Angrily he stubbed out the cigarette and shoved the ashtray against the wall on the nightstand. He rolled away from her.

"Logan." She knew he was still awake. "Logan, honey. If you don't want me to work, I won't. That's fine. I'll stay home and keep house." She clasped her arms around his shoulders. "The important thing is that you're home and we're together.

We can work the rest out."

He rolled over so suddenly he pinched her arm under him. "And get rid of Corinne. I don't like her!"

"Corinne's my friend!"

"I don't like her," he repeated. "She's a bad influence." He turned over and went to sleep, leaving her staring in stunned silence at the wall.

Thirty-Nine

Flame looked up from her breakfast tray and grinned. "Well. This is an honor. Mrs. Caruso herself."

Batt groaned and rubbed his chin. "I was that bad?" He sat down across from her and poured coffee. Flame spidered the window of the breakfast nook. It was winter black outside.

"Why, you were the hit of the show, darling." She leaned over and kissed him.

"I was that bad."

James carried in a tray of steaming scrambled eggs and bacon and set it down in front of him. "I liked the high kick myself. Losing your balance and falling off the stage was a real act of genius, Mr. Jackson."

Batt groaned. "Don't remind me."

"It was all for a good cause, darling. We raised five hundred dollars for the French orphans."

"Wonderful. I didn't know we could get that many into Roberta Hall."

"I didn't know we could get you into that little dress." She wiped his cheek with her napkin.

"I missed something?"

"There. Just a little rouge. Brought color to your cheeks. You know, Mrs. Robarts has already requested the honor of your presence at next year's cabaret."

"Really?" He sipped coffee. "Well, darling, inform Mrs. Robarts I might have taken my act on the road by then."

The phone rang in the kitchen and James answered it. "It's for you, Mrs. Jackson." He put his hand over it. "Mrs. White."

Flame rolled her eyes and took it. "Hello? Yes. Of course. How nice. Certainly. Oh, no. No trouble. What? Oh, fine. No, his leg's not broken. Yes, I think he was wonderful last night,

446

too." She raised her eyebrows and Batt snorted. "Oh, fine. We're all fine. Yes. I'll see you soon, then. Good-bye." She made a face into the phone. "Yes. I agree. Well, good-bye, Mrs. White." She put the phone determinedly back in its cradle, while Mrs. White's voice trailed like a meteorite, still talking.

"Trouble, darling?"

"That woman loves to talk."

"What did she say?"

"Nothing."

Batt laughed.

"Are you touring with Mr. Ryan today?" W.A. Ryan represented Secretary of Interior Lane. He was carrying back to Washington an itemized report on Alaska's resources.

Batt nodded. "We're riding Engine 606 to Seward. The slide's been cleared at mile 54."

"That was the worst, wasn't it?"

"Twenty-five feet deep and three hundred feet long. Took two crews half a day."

"At least the weather's nice. It was only fifteen below yesterday." They sipped coffee in companionable silence. "When are the new rails due?"

"Tomorrow in Seward. The Anchorage crew is stalled north of Talkeetna."

She glanced out the window. The first sun washed over the Chugach Range: black shadows lightened to purple, violet and pink, and a slash of gold spent itself on the peak. "I thought I'd give your old flannel bathrobe to the Red Cross. A relief train is going to Wasilla in the morning and by dogteam to Susitna. The Indians have been hit hard by influenza."

"My old bathrobe? The one you gave me on our fifth wedding anniversary?"

"It's falling apart. The last time in the wringer, a sleeve disintegrated."

"I love that bathrobe."

"All right, darling, and when it dies, we'll bury it in a little box in Cook Inlet."

"Good." He got up and kissed her.

"Oh, our lessons start tonight."

"I can't dance, Flame."

"That's the whole point," she said sweetly.

"Okay. I win on the bathrobe and you win on lessons. But I will say a fox trot is a stupid name for a dance."

"Agreed. Do you have any mail to go? I'll be down that way."

He shook his head. "Should be home about six."

She put her hand on his arm. "Take your pills along."

"They give me heartburn."

"You know what Dr. Beeson said."

"Dr. Beeson is wrong," he said flatly. "I'm going to live forever."

"Then take your pills." Her voice followed him to the coat closet and out the door. She looked at his retreating back. His neck bulled into muscular shoulders. Only his hair gave him away. Gray was winning the war; every year it advanced and the black retreated. Except for a weak heart, he was in better physical shape than most twenty-year-olds.

"More coffee, Mrs. Jackson?"

"No, thank you. I have errands to run."

"Mrs. White?" he asked sympathetically. Flame nodded. "I could ready the Packard."

She shook her head. "I think I'll walk."

She went quickly east, the snow squeaking under her boots. To the north, the railroad terminus was an intersecting maze of tracks and buildings, stretching to the inlet. The mosquito fleet of boats crowded the shoreline, locked in by ice. Thick black smoke rose from the Alaska Engineering Commission machine shops. Men labored like ants across the flats, carrying machinery from the warehouse to the tracks. The town was growing, even though the war had slowed railroad construction.

Fourth Avenue had a sidewalk; there was talk of paved streets. Flame could almost believe she was in the States, except for the Indian slouching down the street, squatting by his dogteam, and the sparse cropping of buildings, spaced far apart, she thought, to make the town seem bigger. Only a heartbeat of territory had been wrested from the wilderness; outside the fragile protection of the streets, girded in civilized lines, the mountains loomed like hulking trolls and the wind chittered and lashed and howled. She glanced uneasily at the Chugach Range and almost missed the house. Mrs. White lived alone at Fourth and I. The Red Cross's special cause was the Indians; the Ladies' Aid Society had the French orphans, and Flame had Mrs. White.

She eased the gate open over the crust of snow. The door opened before she could knock. Mrs. White, dressed in a cowgirl suit, looked like a Kewpie doll with white hair. She smiled happily and extended her arms. Her mouth was a purple slash. "Come in. I have so much to tell you!"

"Yes, Mrs. White." It was death, these hours. Sometimes Flame thought it would be easier to give at the office.

Loussac's Drug was having a 25-percent-off sale on Libby's cut glass, and Flame browsed, looking for something for Jenny. She kept coming back to a bronze vase, elegant in its simplicity, and finally bought it and had it wrapped. She addressed it from memory and went through the blinding snow past the federal jail, telephone and telegraph office and into the post office.

"Noon, Mrs. Jackson."

"Hello, Jerome. Anything for me?"

"Jenny wrote you." Jerome's hair prickled from his scalp like a first beard. He frowned. "I thought you said she lived in New York."

"She does." Flame took the letter. It was postmarked Seattle. She put the package on the counter and ripped open the envelope, vaguely disturbed.

He picked the package up and set it on the scale. "You want this to go?"

"Wait, Jerome." It was a single page. Jerome hung over the counter, waiting. He loved postcards best; much easier to read. "How's she doing?" he pressed.

Flame put her hand to her mouth. She stared blindly at the federal Wanted posters.

"Mrs. Jackson, are you all right?" Jerome came around the counter.

"I need to call my husband." She went past him around the counter without waiting for a reply.

Batt and Flame sat together in his office on the third floor of

449

the hospital, amid his books and papers. A picture of Logan hung on the wall next to the diploma from Cornell Medical School. Three stories below, an Indian on Barrow Street screamed furiously at a cowering dog. It was early afternoon and in the dimming light, the dog blended with the gray snow.

The door opened. He was wearing a surgical coat, his stethoscope draped around his neck. It was the first time she had seen him face to face since the day they said good-bye. Her mouth went dry.

"Mr. Jackson. Mrs. Jackson." His voice was cautiously professional.

"Close the door," Batt said.

Cahill closed it. "What can I do for you?"

Batt handed him the letter. Cahill read it and gave it back. He sat slanted on his desk. "It might not be the marriage we would have wished, under the circumstances, but Logan's a good boy. He'll make Jenny a fine husband."

Flame stared out the window, stared at her hands, raised her face and stared into his eyes. They were crystal blue and wary.

"What is it?" Middle age had toughened his features; he was extraordinarily handsome.

"We never wanted to tell you," Batt said. "We wouldn't have told you—"

"What is it?"

"I've raised her like my own. She *is* my own." His face was anguished.

"What is it?" He had come off the desk now, come closer. "Batt?"

Batt dug his hands into his face.

"Flame?"

The look that passed between them! Always and forever, it said forever. "Jenny's your daughter," she whispered.

His pupils dilated. It took all his control not to touch her. "Rampart?"

She barely nodded.

Batt fumbled for a pill and ate it, his voice gruff. "So what we want to know is, are you sure you fathered Logan? Nelly being what she was."

"That's one thing I am sure of," Cahill said bitterly.

There was a throb of silence and Batt put his head in his hands. "Poor Jenny."

"Who's going to tell them?"

Flame swallowed. "I am."

"God help her," Batt groaned.

Cahill said, "God help us all."

He came screaming out of sleep, sweating and shaking. Jenny reared up, disoriented. She had been dreaming she was in New York still, with Corinne. Now she looked around the bedroom and remembered. They were in Seattle, in their house. Someone had left the light on in the bathroom and Logan's suit rack loomed like a scarecrow over the bed. By the window the azalea blazed with red orange petals.

It was a familiar pattern: first the screams, then the rasp of match lighting the cigarette; the awful silences; and the next day, Logan would march woodenly home and compose himself behind a newspaper. What terror waited there, behind his fierce composure? What had they done to him?

She had thought time would heal it, but three months had gone by and now she wasn't sure. Next to her the cigarette blazed and dimmed, blazed and dimmed. Her heart pounded. She touched him. "Logan—"

"I don't want to talk about it."

She sat up. "Well, you're going to." Her heart was beating so!

"Who in the hell—"

"Your wife." She snapped on the lamp. His face shone with sweat under the stubble of beard. He smoked in silence. "You haven't been yourself since you got back."

He leered at her. "Maybe you're just seeing me the way I really am, Jenny."

"What happened in the Argonne?" she said quietly.

He stared abruptly at the ceiling. "You know what happened." A vein pounded in his neck. He passed his hand over the scar. "Your husband was shot and miraculously nursed back to health."

She leaned over him. "Who was Jack?"

He flinched. "Where did you get that?"

451

"You scream his name in your sleep."

"It's not important."

"Did he die? Was he a friend? Is that it? He died and you're still alive. Are you going to punish yourself forever?"

"Shut up." His hand trembled. Jenny gently took the cigarette away and rubbed it out. She turned out the light and took his hand.

"Tell me about Jack," she whispered. Outside the window a robin landed heavily on the feeder, its throat a triangle of color. Logan's hand grew warm in hers, then wet. Please God, she prayed. Please.

The silence grew. Finally he said, "We were attached to the Headquarters Company of the 304th Infantry." His voice was so low she could barely hear him. "I met him in basic; we went the whole way together."

"He died?" she whispered.

There was a long silence. Logan's chest moved convulsively. "I saved him."

She waited. He dug his nails into her hand. "We had a deal, Jen. Do you know what that means?"

Mutely she shook her head in the dim darkness. In the bathroom the toilet seat was up. A towel lay crumpled on the tiles.

"It means we'd pull the other out, save him."

"Then you followed through."

Logan jerked his head back and forth. "No, no. There was another part to it, Jen." His chest heaved. "If things looked bad—real bad—we promised to shoot the other one through the head. Kill him." He swallowed hard and his eyes closed and opened. "It was raining. We were storming a machine-gun nest in a pocket of trees. Jack was right next to me. Everything exploded in our faces. The impact threw me back and I crawled into the smoke and fire. He'd stepped on a land mine, Jen." His voice shook, his body shook. She reached for a cigarette, lit it and gave it to him. He inhaled, his breathing ragged. "I pulled him out, dragged him back. I only wanted to save him. Get him to a safe place. When we were behind the line, I put him down and got my first good look at him. The bottom half of his face was gone." Logan's voice was full of wonder. "He was still

452

conscious—I don't know how—and his eyes pleaded with me above the shredded— I knew he wanted me to kill him. His body was mangled. A foot gone, his groin bloody. I put the gun to his head. He jerked and closed his eyes. It was raining, Jen. I couldn't do it. I couldn't bring myself to do it." He started to cry and she held him.

"What happened to him?"

"He's in the Red Cross hospital at Neuilly. They're building a freakshow face for him, using a rib bone, a sliver of shin, another soldier's teeth. Out of scraps. They say he'll live a long time." A smile twisted his face and ended in a sob.

"There's more, isn't there?"

He took another breath. His heart pounded against her chest. "His genitals were shot off." Outside, the robin snapped into sudden flight, hovered, and shot away. "He has a wife, a young, pretty wife. She looks a little like you—"

They held each other tightly and he buried himself in her body, his head in her breast. She clung to him murmuring, "It's all right, it's all right, it's going to be all right."

His teeth rattled. He shook. Then wondrously, he felt an erection building, and for the first time in almost two years, they made love.

It was a wonderful neighborhood. The frame house clung to the side of the hill, and from the front window, the roofs of other houses were colored boxes leading down to Green Lake. Tennis courts stretched in neat squares to the southwest, the cement shiny with rain, while to the west, over an undulating rise of hill, jaguars and cougars banged against steel fences, spitting at spectators visiting the zoo. They were leasing with an option to buy; Logan made good money as mill foreman: almost two thousand dollars a year. He deserved the promotion. She cracked open the window, inhaling the rich loamy smell of earth. Tightly curled flowers were thrusting their way through the mud. It was spring, and everything was burgeoning. She patted her belly, tapped the iron with her finger and hummed absently. Rain dripped down the eaves. Logan was fishing for bass, using minnows for bait. She was glad he had splurged on the rowboat; a man needed an outlet.

453

She tightened the crisp bow of her apron and patted herself. Why couldn't her mother be happy for her, just because she was happy? The letter had been strained, peculiar. Jenny slapped another shirt on the board. A child would fix it. What grandmother could resist? She smiled serenely. Next week Flame Ryan Jackson arrived, not as a mother, but a grandmother-to-be. That would fix it. She would be, stunned.

Jen finished the shirt and hung it still warm on a coat hanger before checking the roast. Spicy aromas filled the kitchen. The mail slot clanged and she heard the soft thump on the carpet. Two bills, a flyer from Wards and a letter for Logan. The envelope smelled of violets. Curious, she turned it over and checked for a return address. There was none. She smiled to herself, her mind on her belly, and set the letter by his plate.

It was from his mother and right to the point:

Dear Logan,

I saw the picture of you in the paper. Congratulations on your promotion. I know I haven't been the best of mamas, but I so wish to see you and meet your new wife. Please, Logan, dear, please say you and your wife will meet me at Pierre's in the Public Market next Tuesday at one, as my guests of course.

Your mama,

Nelly

He threw the letter down, furious. "I won't. After all these years! How dare she!"

Jenny gripped his hand across the table. "Logan, I don't ask for very much. Would you do it for me?"

"Why?"

Jenny was thinking what it must feel like to have a child and lose it, and suddenly find it again; it was a treasure, a second chance. "Maybe it wasn't the way you remembered it exactly," she said slowly. "She has to love you. Why else would she risk it? Think of it from her side, Logan. How terrible for her if you

454

refused. At least give her a chance to explain her side."

He cut into the roast savagely.

"Please, Logan."

The first thing that struck Jenny was her delicacy: everything about Nelly was soft, fragile, luminous. She had to be in her late thirties, but from a distance, she had the body of an adolescent. Her arms glowed through champagne-colored chiffon sleeves. The front of her blouse sparkled with tiny pink beads, the whorls and drifts reminding Jenny of sand inside a shell. Small ankles crossed neatly, the champagne crepe skirt exactly eight inches above the floor. A small, antique locket banded her throat: two intersecting hearts. Amber hair waved softly over her ears; amber eyes scrutinized her. Jenny's hand went instinctively to her abdomen and Nelly smiled. It was a secret thing, just between the two women. Jenny couldn't be showing; she was less than three months along.

Nelly extended a small, manicured hand. "Sit down, my dear." The voice was perfectly modulated and slightly foreign. The waiter held the chair as Jenny sat, while Nelly extended her cheek to Logan.

He kissed it stiffly. "Mother." He said it without emotion.

She studied him with that smile again—catlike, knowing, but gently, too, as if she were sorry for him, sorry that it still mattered so much, after all these years. "Sit, my dear boy, and Jacques will fuss over you."

They were at a corner table arranged with cut crystal and bone china on a heavy linen tablecloth. A small bowl of perfect cut flowers glistened in the center.

"Do you come here often?" Jenny inquired politely. There was familiarity in the way Jacques bent to take the order.

Nelly shrugged. "Whenever I'm in town. Jacques, raspberry ice, please, three of them, and escargots."

"You don't live here?" Jenny felt the need to keep the conversation flowing over Logan's stony silence.

"I spent winters in Phoenix. The air is dry there, you know. But with the war over, I'm buying an estate near Paris. The papers are already drawn up."

Overhead, the brass-and-oak fan whirred softly. "It sounds

as if you are doing very well," Jenny remarked.

"I own three dress shops, half ownership in a chain of restaurants—Ah, but I can see Logan is bored with such details. Tell me, how is your father doing?" Her tongue flicked out and back.

"Do you care?" He burst with hatred.

Nelly smiled and shrugged. "Not really," she confessed. "So, you married before the war?"

She was making an extraordinary effort, Jenny thought. "Right before he was sent over." As an afterthought she said, "We grew up together, in Alaska."

"Ah. I thought he would go back." The appetizers came. Jenny busied her hands. Still Logan hadn't spoken. "You look very good together, you know," Nelly remarked, patting the side of her mouth with an embroidered napkin. She studied her son. "You probably wonder why I left."

His eyes were wary. "Don't go into it."

"Did you know your father loved someone else, when he married me? I hear he fathered a child by her. The man who married her told me himself, years ago. Please don't look so shocked, Logan. Life is too short. Have you looked at the menu yet? The *côtelette de veau* is quite good—served with a light butter sauce; and the curried shrimp is fresh daily. They roll the noodles by hand."

"You could have seen me, you know." His voice was raw. "You didn't have to divorce me, too."

"Dear boy." She looked genuinely surprised. "Your father never told you? He had a court order, forbidding it."

He didn't believe her, couldn't believe her. "You could have written, then."

"I did. Every birthday and Christmas until you moved. I didn't know where to send it after that. I am not a monster, Logan, whatever you might think." She put another snail on her plate and delicately pronged the soft meat.

Hope and fear struggled on his face. He wanted to trust her! Nelly looked discreetly away. "Tell me about yourself," she commanded Jenny.

"There's not a lot to tell. My father was a legislator—"

"No. Tell me about *you*."

456

Jenny was starting to like her. "I'm an only child. I grew up in Alaska, in one boom town after another. I was born in Nome, during the rush, and then we went to Fairbanks. My father was a legislator in Juneau one term, and when the railroad started, we moved to Anchorage. I married your son, and spent the war in New York, working for the United War fund."

"Oh. Did you know John, Jr.?"

"Mr. Rockefeller?" He headed the Great New York organization.

"Yes."

"I met him once, in a receiving line. Did you?"

"We're old friends." Nelly smiled and touched Jenny's hand. Her fingers were ice cold and Jenny involuntarily flinched. "But we were talking about you. Tell me," she said abruptly, "who is the person you most admire?"

"Why do you ask?" Jenny was startled and amused. Nelly was full of surprises.

"It says so much about one, don't you think? I mean, after whom one patterns oneself."

"Who do I pattern myself after," Jenny said slowly. "I suppose—I suppose I'd have to say my mother."

"Ha." Nelly leaned back in the pink-and-gold brocaded chair and nodded slightly. "A safe choice." She nibbled the escargot.

"No, a good choice. You don't know my mother. She's all concentrated energy. She burns holes in things with her enthusiasm. I always thought she was the most perfectly named person I ever met. Her name is Flame, and besides having hair the color of—"

"Flame." Nelly put down her fork. Her face was a ghastly paste color. "Flame, you say? It couldn't be Flame Ryan?"

"Why, yes," Jenny said in surprise. "Now she's Flame Jackson, but how did you—"

Something wickedly victorious blazed across Nelly's face. "I have dreadful news for you both." Her voice quivered with emotion, and startled, Jenny realized what it was: not sorrow or pain—but *joy*. This was a supremely happy moment for Nelly. Jenny had never been so frightened. She groped for Logan's hand.

"I'm not feeling well at all. Could we leave?"

457

"Dreadful news," Nelly spat. The mask dropped. The cultivated lady was gone, the vulnerable softness obliterated. There was a killer in there, and the knife had just come out.

"Now!" Jenny pushed herself up from the table. "Now, Logan! Let's leave now!"

Swiftly the knife slashed the air. "Jenny's your sister, Logan." Her voice caught him between sitting and standing up. He staggered backward.

"No!"

Her voice was so low only they could hear. "You married your own sister, Logan. Your father and Flame had Jenny."

He regained his balance. "I don't believe you. Lies! All lies!" The room grew quiet around them. Nelly unfastened the necklace.

"Here. Look at it. Their initials. He gave it to her." She held it out. "Are you afraid? Afraid to see the truth?"

"Logan, let's leave now! Please, Logan—"

Logan's hand was shaking. He took it, his hand stiff with dread. He turned it over. His eyes rolled. The necklace dropped to the floor. He tottered.

"Logan!" Jenny instinctively put her hand out to catch him.

"Don't touch me!" He backed away, stumbled into a waiter, righted himself, fell against a table and ran out the door.

"Logan!" Jenny cried out. She whirled towards Nelly. "You are a monster!"

Nelly shook her head sadly. The great ones were always misunderstood. "It is your mother," she said softly. "Your mother is the monster. She should have told you years ago."

Jenny turned and fled.

Nelly picked up the menu and motioned to Jacques. "I seem to have lost my guests, but my appetite has grown enormous. Could you reach that for me? It's under the chair. Ah, thank you. And fasten it around my neck? You are such a dear. Now. Tell me something amusing; my friends were so tiresome."

Brother and sister. Brother and sister. She had married her own brother. Logan, Logan. Flesh of my flesh, bone of my bone. The most terrible of all sins. They could leave. They could go away somewhere. No, even in the most primitive

458

worlds, it was the strongest taboo, the only sin. Logan. She squeezed her eyes shut. His naked body glowed behind the irises, imprinted on her brain. She rode the streetcar for hours, not knowing what else to do. Could they pretend they didn't know? Just go on? Her hand went to her belly. What abomination grew there? What had she done? Her own brother.

The worst was that Nelly was right: her mother should have told her. Why didn't she? She saw Flame in a new light, not loving and generous, but selfish; not nurturing, but saving herself first. It explained the strained letter; the visit. Her mother was coming tomorrow to tell her; too late, it was too late.

Jenny groaned. The conductor came toward her. "It's the end of the line, miss. Are you all right?"

Jenny walked home through a flash storm. Logan, Logan. The door stood ajar. She pushed it open, knowing what she would find. Every trace of him was gone. Everything. His clothes, his books, his favorite records. She sank to her knees and put her head against the carpet. Her eyes shut. Logan squirmed behind them, in the throes of passion. She beat her fists against her head. He mocked her, his eyes slits.

She had to stop it, stop the pictures. Shuddering, she got to her feet and swayed out the door. Rain lashed her face. The boat was a muddy oblong near the pier. Logan had gaily painted on its side, *The Other Woman*. She slipped down to it, through the mud. The lake churned with gray foam. To the right of the boat and pier, the bank dropped suddenly twenty feet to a gravel beach. She stumbled over it, wavered on the edge; then closed her eyes and jumped.

Something snapped in her legs and she sprawled on her back, her arms spread like a fallen angel. Her throat clicked and she chattered to herself. Pain wormed its way through her belly, her legs. She gasped. It burrowed through her, raking a hole in her stomach. A scream whistled through her teeth and was lost in the wind. She clutched her belly as the pain gutted her stomach and smashed her into darkness.

Jenny was dreaming. She was dreaming she was still young

and her mommy and daddy wrapped their arms around each other all the time. Her mommy was hanging little paper lanterns high, high in the sky.

"It's for you," her mommy whispered. "It's your birthday and it's all for you." And there they all were. Her mommy and daddy and Logan and her best friend, Neva. They floated toward her, across the damp grass, carrying presents; and in all of them was everything she had always wanted but never told anyone.

Now all her secrets were spread out over the grass, and they looked even better in person than they had in her heart. Her mother kissed her sweetly, and gave her a package she had overlooked. "We've been saving the best for last. Open it," she murmured, and they all nodded gently, their heads waving like wheat in the wind.

"Open it, Jenny," they chanted. "Open it."

The package was silvery with spun ribbons curling out like angel hair and tiny bells that tinkled when she shook it, which she did over and over to make it last. It was like the sound in your head after a long nap, when you wake up and the room is still sleeping and the only sound is the ocean in your ears.

Then she touched the ribbon and it sprang apart and the paper melted away and she lifted out the most beautiful doll she had ever seen. It was small; she could hold it in her hand, its little feet no bigger than a thumb. Fine hair fluffed around her face and her skin was white, like old cheese. It was wearing—Jenny looked again. It was wearing nothing at all. It opened its eyes and stared at Jenny. The foot thrummed against her wrist. She screamed and dropped it in the grass.

They squeezed around her and the sun dimmed. Her mother shook her shoulders. "Bad girl," she hissed. "Bad girl," they chanted, shaking their heads like a machine working. "Bad bad bad—"

She woke up, sweating and chattering and wondering where she was. Then the pain chewed her again and she remembered.

"No," she whimpered. "No." She pressed her hands to her belly. Something was moving down, down; boring a hole through her. "No, no," she chattered.

The pain muscled down her belly, bunched like a thick

snake. Terrified, she realized it was down *there*, at the place she hardly ever looked, not even when she washed. And then the pain stopped.

It's gone away I won't let it come back I'll be good, mommy; I'll be so good—She was babbling out loud. Whimpering and whispering, she rolled onto her knees. Pain shot up. She had to go to the bathroom. In the worst way. She had to go *now*. Crying, she rolled to her side and hiked down her panties. Then she closed her eyes and pushed.

Something huge and steaming plopped out of her and settled on the ground. She shook the way old Doc Watson did with palsy. It was very quiet. Her tummy had knots in it; sweat rolled down her. She thought fiercely of her house and crawled painfully one yard; then two. She stopped. Something stirred on the ground. Behind her. Her throat clacked. Something small and alive. The silence beat. There it was again. Jenny laughed and took a deep breath.

It was just a kitty. A small, tiny kitty. She leaned toward it, crooning, "Here, kitty, kitty. Come to mommy." But it stayed there, mewing pitifully, the smallest alive sound she had ever heard. She crawled back to it and touched it. She lifted it up.

It was a doll.

Her skin was white, like old cheese.

It was wearing—Jenny looked again. It was wearing nothing at all.

Flame sat next to the bed. Everything was white: the walls, the sheets, the blanket, her daughter's pale leg above the cast. Her heart ached for Jenny. If she could have thrown herself into her daughter's body, borne the pain, she would have done it gladly. Gladly.

"Jenny please try to understand. It happened so long ago. We never thought you and Logan— Your father loves you dearly. He couldn't bear the thought of losing you. Neither could I. We were fools! We were. I admit it, Jennifer. I do. But nothing changes the way we feel about you, how sorry we are."

Jenny turned and looked at her mother. Her face was pale, composed.

"Will you forgive me? Say you forgive me, Jen."

461

A tear rolled from her eye and was absorbed in the sheet. "I never want to see you again."

Flame clung to her hand. "You're upset. You don't know what you're saying! Jenny, Jenny. You don't mean it. Say you don't mean it."

"I hate you," she whispered.

A sob chocked in Flame's throat. "Jenny!"

A nurse trotted in, concerned. "It's time for her pill, Mrs. Jackson." She drew Flame gently away.

"Jenny! Please!"

Jenny turned her face away.

"Come, come. You can see her after dinner," the nurse said impatiently.

"Jenny, I love you." It was a strangled cry, unanswered, unheard.

Flame knocked. No response. "Jen?" She quietly opened the door. The bedspread stretched tautly over the frame; Jenny's flowers were gone. Puzzled, Flame checked the number on the door. Fear washed over her. She ran down the hall to the nurse's station.

"Room three-oh-nine," she said loudly. "Where is the patient in three-oh-nine?"

A bland moon face arranged itself under a starched cap. "She's gone, Mrs. Jackson. Checked herself out an hour ago."

Flame gripped the counter, knuckles white. "Did she say where she was going?"

"We thought she was with you."

"Fool!" Flame cried. "Does she look like she's with me!" She burst into tears.

The nurse hurried around the counter. "Mrs. Jackson." She held her shoulders. "Get five milligrams of Haldol on the double," she commanded a nurse who had just come from the elevator. The nurse turned and ran.

"No!" Flame cried. "No. I have to find her!" She was hysterical.

"Calm down. You have to calm down." The nurse firmly moved her to a chair, still holding onto her arms.

"Jenny!" Flame screamed. Doors opened along the hallway.

462

A doctor came running out, his stethoscope bouncing on his shirt.

"What is it? What's wrong?"

Flame struggled to her feet, pushing hands away, frantic. And then someone held her arm tightly and she felt a sharp stinging sensation and everything calmed down.

Forty

Outside Alaska the twenties roared in, a dizzy blur of short skirts, coonskin coats and bathtub gin. Anchorage did its best to keep up. The Women's Christian Temperance Union organized patrols to scour Cook Inlet for bootlegged alcohol. Once a week they smashed bottles against the only bridge in town, while around the bend, boys leaned into the mud with cups, scooping out scotch and water.

Every afternoon women dressed in gloves and hats and went calling, wobbling unsteadily down the unpaved streets to leave gilt cards at the doors of absent mistresses. Calling was a serious occupation in the summer of 1921. Guests would be met at the door in a long skirt and served the laborious result of days in the kitchen: iced petits fours, scones with melted cheese, flaked pastries marbled with nuts and pudding. It was here that recipes were traded, sitters located and reputations finished off. Flame was an easy target: she never came.

"It's not as if she doesn't know we called, either." Mrs. Warner settled herself in the largest chair and dove for the mixed nuts. "I can feel her, lurking behind those awful curtains. Nobody has corded silk anymore. It's so untrés chic." She rolled her hand across her mouth and worked the nuts in before licking the salt off the palm.

"What do you think is wrong?" Mattie Humbard had the body of a ten-year-old boy and the face of a retired accountant; glasses and regrettable hair. Once she had dragged herself out of bed with a blazing temperature to attend a calling, terrified that if she didn't, they would all be talking about *her*. Now she arranged a plate of bacon-rolled oysters on a paper doily and carried the silver tray around the room. Mrs. Warner took four and ate one before leaning conspiratorially forward.

"My little Harry saw her."

"Really?" Mattie murmured, interested in spite of herself. Little Harry, as Mrs. Warner so tenderly called her immensely fat son, had been suspended ten days last year from Anchorage Public School for lying. She leaned in. "What did he say?"

"I'll have a few more of those mints and another helping of chicken, if you don't mind."

Mattie fetched them and stood respectfully to one side, so the other women's view wouldn't be blocked. Mrs. Warner ripped the meat off a wing, sucked the bones and delicately rolled her fingers across a napkin. She looked expectantly around the room. She had everyone's attention. "Flame has a hump."

"A hump!" A cry from the sofa.

"Shocking!" A hand to a heart on the cushion by the mantel.

Mrs. Warner nodded happily. "That's not the worst of it."

"There's more?" Fingers delicately whiffed salts under a nose by the hanging begonia.

"Something terrible's wrong. She's growing huge. I don't mean on the heavy side, either. I mean, huge. Like a house— huge."

The women shuddered. Mrs. Warner popped the rest of the oysters in and washed them down like pills. She drained the tea glass and set it down. Her hand rummaged through the nuts, as if she were going through an enemy's closet.

"Well, gracious sakes, maybe we should pay a neighborly visit on her."

"Might cheer her up," Mattie agreed. She placed a tray of candied oranges on Mrs. Warner's knee.

"Waste not, want not," Mrs. Warner said, and emptied the tray into her pocket.

They traveled to the Jacksons' house in three cars, giddy with excitement. Trees crowded up to the house on three sides; not pretty trees bought at a greenhouse, either, but wild trees—scraggly scrub pine and birches warted with disease. A small sidewalk barely held its own. Past the gate a poppy defiantly bloomed in a crack of cement. On the fourth side, away from the street, the house faced a drop down to the water. Mount McKinley was a soft blob of purple on the horizon. An unfriendly house, the women agreed. No welcome mat greeted them at the steps. No woman leaned over the absent back fence, waving a glad hello. Nothing stirred. And yet—"

"Go on," Mrs. Warner nudged Mattie. "Knock."

Mattie tapped timidly.

"No," Mrs. Warner instructed. "Like this." She made a fist and pounded. Mattie thought she saw a dent forming. Mrs. Warner paused expectantly. Upstairs, behind pale curtains, something moved heavily. The curtains exhaled gently; the women exhaled, too.

"She's up there. Got to be."

Mattie said, "There's a curtain open over here." She hesitated; then shored up by the eager way the women crowded around her, she led the calvacade through the garden. It was dry and patchy looking, looped with bristling cords of dead plants. The window was high and nailed shut. The curtain fluttered slightly, as if something very old breathed in the room beyond.

"Here goes," Mattie whispered. She gripped the sill and leaned on her toes. It was a bedroom; a girl's bedroom. Stuffed toys sprawled on a crocheted bedspread; a Raggedy Ann doll stared vacantly from a rocker. The closet door stood open and Mattie could see a neat line of clothes and shoes. But there was something wrong. The clothes were wrong. Old. Very old. And the Raggedy Ann doll hung from the ceiling, caught in a spider web.

Mattie's arches got tired then and she dropped down to flat feet and let Mrs. Warner take a look. One by one the women peered in and dropped away, not looking at each other. It was almost like a museum.

"It's about five," Mattie said a little too loudly. "We'll leave a card. That's the neighborly thing to do."

They fled through the garden, brambles pulling at skirts, and Mattie fumbled for a card. "One ought to do, don't you think?"

She peeled off her gloves and separated one card from the pack. She crept toward the door, the women behind. Everything was heavy, oppressive: the hot afternoon, the bees glistening with pollen, the leering gargoyle on the metal face of the mail slot. Mattie licked her lip and raised the lid.

466

Behind the door, something stirred.

There was an eye, an eye behind the slot. "Get out of here," a voice hissed.

Mattie shrieked and toppled backward, scattering cards. The slot clanged down. The women scattered like alarmed birds.

On the street they stopped, collected themselves and giggled nervously. Mrs. Warner reached into her pocket and bit into an orange slice.

"Some folks don't know an act of kindness when it hits them in the face."

Grief feeds on guilt in darkened rooms; shades carefully drawn, lamps dimmed, music stilled, grief grows monstrous. After a certain point, simple sunlight can't kill it, life can't touch it. Laughter dries up, voices hush, visitors tread softly, giving it the respect due the dead.

Flame sat in a chair in the parlor and stroked a lock of Jenny's hair. James stood in the doorway leading to the kitchen.

"Mrs. Jackson, I don't mean to sound presumptuous, but I am concerned."

"About what?" Flame asked in surprise.

"Annie and I could look in on you, you know."

"You mean a social call? Really, James, I expect more sensitivity than that from you." She put the lock back in a brocaded box and set it restlessly down. "Three times a week cleaning will suffice."

Sadness came off of him in waves.

"Is there anything else?" Her voice was neutral.

"No, Mrs. Jackson, I guess not. It seems a strange end to our association."

"Oh, yes. I'm forgetting my manners." She rose from the chair and came toward him, blinking in the light. Lines gouged her forehead and the bony eye sockets were pale blue. She extended a hand, wiping the other on her black dress. "Good-bye and good luck."

"Thank you, Mrs. Jackson."

She nodded and went back to the chair.

"I could make some soup, before I leave," James said,

moved by her appearance.

"I'm fine, thank you. Oh, and James—" She waved a hand vaguely around the room. "Take whatever you like. As a wedding present."

"I couldn't."

"Well, then—" She went to the sideboard and banged cups into the punch bowl. Everything was sterling silver; it clanged like a mine. From the wall Jenny stared down in silence, smiling. When Flame had all the cups inside, she wrapped her arms around the bowl and brought it to him. "Here," she said, thrusting it into his hands. "Take it. I'll never use it again."

"Mrs. Jackson—"

"Go on, now. Take it. One less thing I have to worry about."

"Thank you," he said, touched. "And please—"

"Yes?" She was already moving away from him.

"If there's anything we can do—"

"There isn't." She sat down again and stared at the wall.

"I'm home," Batt called loudly. No answer. He banged through the hall, bellowing a curse when he clunked a shin, and stamped in the parlor, needing to cover the awful quiet with noise. "Oh, so here you are." He kissed the top of her head. "I have a surprise for you."

"Jenny!" she cried out, rising, a terrible hope flashing through her heart.

"No, no," he said quickly. "Not Jenny. But this—" He dropped it into her lap. She touched it dully. "It's a swimming suit. I got it at Loussac's. We're all going swimming at Lake Spenard and you're coming too. It's great there, Flame. It really is. They have awnings and a boat dock and this funny old man who sells fried potato slices. Quite tasty."

Her hands drifted to the chair arms. "You go. I'm not feeling up to it."

He went to the window and flung open the curtains. "It's a beautiful day out there. Look at it."

Her hands came up against the light. "I don't want to."

"You're going to," he said grimly, his patience gone, and took her out of the chair.

"I'm not feeling well!" She stiffened, her voice harsh. He studied her; his hands dropped. She arranged herself in the chair. "I'm a little under the weather. That's all. When Jenny writes—" She stared at the flowered wall. When had the paper started fading?

"Stop it, Flame. I can't stand it anymore. It's all you ever talk about. We don't exist for her anymore."

"No!" Flame cried out, frightened. She clapped her hands to her ears and Batt slammed them down.

"She's as good as dead, Flame. She is. Grieve for her and go on. Come back to life."

"Show me the grave, then."

He pressed her hand to his chest. "It's right here. In our hearts. She's gone. Nothing you can say to the wall in the middle of the night can change that."

"But I'm her mother! I can't stop thinking of her! If I could only hold her in my arms and tell her—"

"Tell her what?"

"How sorry I am!" Her voice broke. "We never meant to hurt her."

"Flame, Flame." He drew her onto his lap and caressed her hair. It was still a burnished copper, thick and luxuriant. "We did the best we could with what we had. That's all any parents can do."

"But it wasn't good enough!"

"Maybe not, but it doesn't change how hard we tried." He looked helplessly around the room. Jenny was everywhere: a mooseskin diploma from high school hung next to the sideboard; a five-legged purple reindeer looked down from the dining-room wall. It had green and orange antlers and a missing front tooth. Jenny had painted it in first grade. "Jenny lied to us all through high school about her and Logan. Did you ever think about that? She stared straight into your eyes and lied."

"She was a child," Flame protested.

"And now she's grown. How long are you going to carry it?"

"Forever," Flame whispered.

"Then you'll do it without me." Batt's voice was flat. He pushed her off his lap and stood up.

"What do you mean?"

"I can't stand it anymore, watching you kill yourself. I thought it would help, the trips. God, I really did. Do you

469

remember one thing about Yosemite? How about the Grand Canyon or Niagara Falls? But, no, you only came alive when you pored through one of those damn directories, looking for Jenny's name."

"If I could just find the right one. I know she's out there, Batt. I can feel it." He walked angrily from the room. "Where are you going?"

"To pack." He climbed the stairs.

"Batt, listen to me," Flame said eagerly. "I'm going to offer a reward. Something small. Maybe five thousand dollars— Batt, listen to me." She ran up the stairs, after him.

He snapped open his trunk and dumped his stocking drawer over it. His undershirts. Underwear. Tears rolled down his face.

"Batt, I know it's a long shot, but I have this feeling she's in the midwest—"

He stopped, his face a mask of grief. "I'm leaving you, Flame," he said distinctly.

Nothing flickered. "Then again, maybe New York. I've tried contacting that old friend of hers, Corinne. The YMCA is helping me. Did I tell you?"

"Over and over." He shut the lid hard, snapped the hasp and lifted it to his shoulder. "Good-bye, Flame." He waited an instant by the bedroom door, then ducked the trunk through the door and walked quickly down the hall and down the stairs.

"Wait!"

He had opened the front door. His eyes were dry. "What is it?" Outside, the trees rustled.

"Where are you going?" She was poised at the top stair, hand on the rail.

His face contorted, then grew still. "I don't know." He walked outside and down the steps. A boy of about six trotted happily down the road, fishing pole bouncing over his shoulder. A puppy snapped at his summer bare toes.

"No!" She ran after him, shielding her eyes from the light.

He broke stride at the gate, opened it and kept walking.

"No." She caught up with him and clutched his sleeve.

They studied each other, Flame winter-pale in a black dress. Finally Batt said quietly, "She is gone, Flame."

She buried her face in her hands and sobbed. "I know. I know."

Batt put down the trunk and held her. A woman with a berry basket and white Hoover apron wandered by. She stared at them, then looked studiously away.

Finally Flame wiped her eyes. "Will it ever go away?"

"You mean the feeling?" He stroked her hair.

She nodded into his chest.

"Probably not. Maybe the only thing time really teaches is to be a little kinder to ourselves. We were good parents, Flame. Remember that."

Parents. Flame had always thought God had been especially clever when it came to children: terrifying helplessness softened by sculpted ears, translucent eyelids—who could turn away? In those sleep-drained first years, when Flame had rocked her wailing child and marveled at the clutch of tiny fists, Jenny's needs had been dramatic, insatiable. It had never occurred to Flame that parents need their children even more.

Somebody else could have raised Jenny and Jenny wouldn't have known or cared, but Flame had needed her from the first; needed to hold Jenny in her arms; hungered for that whirring nubbin of flesh sucking the life out of her breast. Nights she had watched Jenny sleep—small perfect body sprawled in the crib, a rosy hand spread flatly over the stomach, toes curled, snoring gently, her mouth a soft, slack O. Who had prepared her for the rich sensuality of holding a child, cheek against cheek, the irises huge unblinking moons, staring into her eyes forever?

She had needed Jenny to help her grow up. She could admit that now. Her adult heart had sometimes hammered in the night when things went bang and thump, but her voice was always steady when she sat on the edge of Jenny's bed, pulled the covers up tight and told her it was only the wind.

She raised her head. "We'll start with the hardest. Jenny's room."

"There's a trunk in the attic. We can pack her clothes."

Flame shook her head. "Let's get rid of them. Get rid of everything."

*   *   *

471

There's no business like war, and no business that had liked it better than the canneries. They had embraced war with a greedy enthusiasm, asking no questions and filling all orders. In ten years, the number of canneries in southeast Alaska doubled; by 1919, eighty of them butted up against each other. If space along the wharf in Juneau had grown crowded, it was even worse in the water.

Trollers crawled through the fjords of Southeast, huge spider legs delicately snagging salmon. Purse seiners payed line out around entire schools, tightening the net bottom and brailing hundreds in at once. But mostly the war years had belonged to traps, the traps belonged to canneries, and the canneries belonged to corporations owned by conglomerates in the States. It was not a decade for the little guy.

What salmon lack in imagination, they make up for in loyalty. Silvery chum fry slip their way to the ocean after they hatch and wander among the plankton for three years; then something stirs dimly in their primitive brains and they lurch their way back to the mouths of rivers, fighting upstream to spawn on the same rock or hollow they were spawned.

The canneries wove nets of wire and logs across the water and waited. In late June the chum flash through the ocean in thick calico-colored schools, the males snouted like sharp-nosed old men with receding gums, all teeth and hooked noses; the females a faint splash of pink. A thrust of the caudal fin and thousands tangle in netting, woven in such a way the fish can only go forward, through smaller and smaller openings, until they meet the pot at the end of the rainbow. The pot tunnels into a spiller, and the chum are hauled up to a skow: no mess, no fuss and no little fry to repeat the cycle. If more salmon were making their way onto tables and into mess kits of Americans everywhere, it was because fewer escaped.

At first the canneries ignored it; there was a war going on and they were doing their patriotic duty, feeding soldiers. Making money hand over fist was of course, incidental. But after the war, the army and navy and marines and army air corps took all the tins of fish the soldiers didn't eat in France and dumped them on the open market back in the States, at ridiculously low prices. The military, the main buyer of chum, turned on the canneries with chilling ease and became their biggest competitor. Prices were slashed from nine dollars a case to five and a half.

The big canneries reeled with the punch, but the little canneries were knocked flat. The corporations could handle it: they shifted books and ledgers and upped the output of Fords in the Michigan branch, or dug deeper in the opal mines in Australia, but the little guy with a family boat and a box of lures was finished. The medium-sized guy—the Alaskan with a trap and a shoestring cannery—wobbled back and forth, lighting candles and praying to gods he'd never heard of. Anything was worth a try.

If there could be an antidote for grief, perhaps it's ruin, approaching at a gallop. The Jacksons began fighting for their lives.

During the war they had shifted holdings from gold and copper into fisheries. They had lumped almost everything into one enormous egg and it was very fragile nest, indeed. The problem was this: fewer fish were spread among more canneries at bargain basement prices. If life is a crapshoot, the Jacksons had just rolled snake eyes.

"We still have the coal deposits." Flame propped her elbows on the desk and gazed at Batt.

Wordlessly he handed her the latest report from the mines and looked out the window. Orange and gold poppies floated like parachutes over the grass. A wild rosebush drooped petals by the front door, the violet and pink flowers making way for rose hips. The air was bursting with summer.

He turned back. She was scanning the report, frowning. "They talk in charts and graphs when English is too painful." He tried smiling.

"What does it mean?"

"The Mat River field is flawed."

"Flawed? It tested out equal to the highest grade Pennsylvania coal."

"Only in steaming, Flame. In mining they're finding nasty problems. Folds, faults, underground water, coal marbled with bits of bone like fat on a rump of round."

"We'll sell the newest cannery. Tighten our belts."

473

He shook his head. "I don't think belt tightening's enough."

"What do you mean?"

He looked steadily at her. "I think we'll have to start lopping off limbs."

It's easy to get religion when the boat's going down. The corporations got it right about the time the market and fish supply dried up. For years they had lobbied Congress against making laws prohibiting traps, claiming they would be ruined without them. Now they claimed they had been ruined with them; the fish had been leeched from the water. Not that they wanted traps banned; what they wanted was for Congress to ban everybody else and to give them exclusive fishing rights.

In February 1922 President Warren G. Harding created the Alaska Peninsula Fishery Reserve, by emergency executive order, followed by the southwest and southeast reserves. Nobody could fish, can or fix salmon commercially without a permit from the secretary of commerce.

It was done ostensibly to save the fish, but what it really did was save the megacanneries. Only the big canneries got the permits. Overnight it turned the small Alaska operators, like the Jacksons, into indentured servants. The only way they could legally fish was to work for somebody who owned a permit, and the only ones with permits were the big corporations owned by conglomerates outside. It gave a virtual monopoly to foreign businesses with no stake in the growth of Alaska, especially if it meant taking less out.

By late 1922 the Jacksons had been forced to sell two canneries, the dormitory, four traps and a tender to the Alaska Pacific Cannery, one of three outside corporations that made up 80 percent of the permits Harding had issued.

In the summer of 1923, when women in tights and belted suits strutted down the boardwalk in Atlantic City, Flame and Batt sat in an office in Juneau and signed over the last cannery. They wrote their names swiftly, not wanting to prolong it, and stood up immediately. Behind the desk the man gently adjusted a brass tabletop plaque reading *Everyday in everyway I am getting better and better. Dr. Émile Coué.* He smiled benignly.

"Nice doing business with you."

He glanced at the Mah-Jongg game resting on a low stool next to his desk, and Flame knew he was only waiting until they were at the door before starting to play. From the window she saw strangers carrying equipment into the cannery. She looked quickly away, took Batt's arm and got him out of there before Batt could show the nice man what he thought about doing business with *him*.

They had failed. They had gambled everything and lost. After paying the bank creditors and buying tickets home, they had exactly a thousand dollars in cash.

It's one thing to lose everything when you're young; it's another to be in your fifties, like Batt, winded, a little paunchy, waking up tired after grappling demons in your sleep.

"Is it because we're so far away?" Batt wondered out loud. "Is that it? Absent corporations own us and absent government protects us. This couldn't have happened if we were a state, with the powers to set our own laws on fisheries and the muscle to enforce them. If somebody had tried this in California, Washington would be outraged. I'd like once to give somebody a piece of my mind."

"Is the president of the United States high enough?" Flame inquired.

"What are you talking about?"

She pulled a letter from her purse. "I was going to save it. We have an audience with President Harding."

The earth's crust is fragile, sliding over ground as blubbery as pudding. It took eight years to build the railroad through the mountains, up the sides of cliffs, and climbing grades so steep the heart sank to the belly; but underneath, the ground shifted and melted and rearranged itself. Mud flowed like lava over the track; streams surged and dug away sand; rails collapsed, engines snapped off and flew into the air. There were eight hundred bridges and trestles to maintain; dwarf spruce pilings rotting in the rain can't last forever, especially under the weight of 230 tons per train. The cold buckled the track like a metal pretzel, snow buried it, sudden drops in temperature

475

cracked the track apart and slammed it unevenly together, and yet the railroad was a work of art; a triumph of man over environment.

Think of what it meant to a land with 34,000 miles of coast and only one main road, a road built torturously through mountains and muck and petering out in the interior, not half the way through it! A railroad: from the salty sea town of Seward—drifting kelp and churning water—to Fairbanks, bedrock and boardwalk, a town stranded deep in the interior, surrounded by dome hills and the far pinnacles of Mount McKinley. Crates of canned goods, pianos, even cows, could be shipped by rail, and what had taken weeks before, by road, now took a day. Still to the north, the Brooks Range loomed in terrible unexplored triumph, and past that, tundra stretched to the Arctic Ocean, but a railroad even halfway through the country spelled civilization. No fly-by-night towns stoked railroads across America, only real towns, towns of substance with jails and schools. If the federal government was willing to invest 65 million dollars in a railroad, could statehood be far behind?

So with great anticipation in the summer of '23, Alaskans got ready for a visit from the man himself—President Warren G. Harding. That too, was reason for hope: no president had ever visited Alaska in the fifty-six years America had owned it. Harding was coming to bless the railroad.

At the south end of the Hulitna River, near Hurricane Gulch bridge, the Riley family changed in the bushes and waited by the track with a pie they had packed ten miles on foot and baked in a wood-burning oven. At mile 49, rail crews creased Sunday suits under mattresses at the same place snow had pitched two engines and a rotary plow into a gully two winters before. In Kashwitna, all twenty-five residents lined up holding a letter apiece, blank sheets between words, and spelled out WLECOME PRESIDENT HARDING. The L holder nudged the E and they changed places as the train pulled in; while on board, Batt and Flame sat in green leather bucket seats in an observation car and waited.

He had a doughy face, but kind. Thin white hair lay to one

476

side over a broad forehead; thick brows angled over pouched eyes. Deep lines creased from his long nose to the edges of a full mouth. His cheeks had slid long ago from the high bones and settled into jowls on either side of a round chin. His hand jutted forward slightly, over a mound of belly, and his back sloped with age.

What do you say to a president? It's one thing to mutter and rave at his picture in the paper, dressing him down for being so stupid in Washington, and it's another to be standing in a shaking railcar, shaking his hand. And then Batt remembered he didn't have a job anymore, and it got easier.

"Mrs. Jackson," President Harding said. "Mr. Jackson."

"You have five minutes," Secretary Hoover shouted over the train, and left the car. Outside the window, the Susitna River spilled through a gorge far below and the train shuddered toward Mount McKinley, rearing through a break in the clouds.

Harding glanced out the window and deliberately sat with his back to it. "What can I do for you?" He had kind eyes and sour breath, as if some hidden sickness crouched in his chest.

"The reserves have got to go; it's inequitable to the people here. We're the ones with investments: homes, children, futures. If we can't make a living anymore, how can we stay?"

"What do you suggest?"

"When the sixty-eighth Congress convenes, we need a bill introduced giving the secretary of commerce power to create fishing areas, regulate the size and kind of gear, even limit or outlaw fishing in places where things are bad. But no more of this assigning exclusive rights to outside canneries! And put specifics in the bill, insisting a percentage of fish be released to spawn. And give the locals some teeth so they can enforce whatever it is the boys in Washington dream up. Alaska for Alaskans, Mr. President. And statehood. We need to be a state. We deserve it. We more than pay our way. Over 15 million dollars worth of gold and timber and fish leave Alaska every year, clear profits for outside investors, and yet only six towns in the whole territory have sewer systems. And this is 1923! Think of it. And there's more. Tell him, Flame."

She opened the paper in her lap. "I have it written down, Mr.

President. The government spends less than half a million dollars here every year compared to the 15 million taken out. That's everything: schools, road, even this railroad."

"May I keep it?" Harding asked.

"We'd be honored." She handed him the paper and he carefully folded it and put it away. And then Hoover clanged open the door and said, "Sorry to interrupt, Mr. President, but others are waiting to see you." He gently helped the president up.

It didn't change anything; the Jacksons had still lost everything, but for both of them, it was a better ending than the bitter one that day in Juneau. They shucked it off, that day on the train, all the failure and fear. They had a thousand dollars, reasonably good health and each other, and for five minutes on a trail near Mount McKinley, the undivided attention of a president of the United States.

"Pig heaven," Batt murmured, and unwrapped a cigar.

Harding drove the golden spike into the track near the Indian village of Nenana, signifying the completion of the railroad; then dug the spike out and hammered in the real one. Afterward, everybody cheered, and he tottered back to the train and collapsed until Fairbanks, where he addressed two thousand people at the ball park. The news was good from the top; Harding planned to change the fishing laws, press for statehood and pour money into industry.

Which would have been wonderful except that he died promptly following the Alaska tour.

But that afternoon ovations shook the bleachers, bands played and three horses dragged a plane onto the field.

It was a Jenny with an OX-5 engine, a wicker seat and open cockpit. The pilot loped toward it and bowed to Harding, who was still alive enough to wave back.

Flame leaned forward as the pilot clambered up its side, thrusting his legs into the cockpit. The plane shuddered down the short field and lifted seconds before striking an enormous pile of wood. Everybody cheered.

It stormed over the president, twisted upside down, circled the field and glided gently to a stop, tipping slightly and righting itself.

The plane could go 150 miles in an eyeblink: toss down mail and meat and quaff fuel like a drunken sailor on leave, and soar home again.

She gripped Batt's hand. "Let's get one."

"What did you say?"

"Let's get one. Let's take the money we have left and gamble it all."

"Are you serious?"

"Never been more. We can bid on a mail run with the government—has to be faster than dog teams—or just haul people where they want to go."

"Flame, we don't know anything about flying!"

"Then we'll learn. I bet we could pay that guy, there, to teach us."

He stared at her, amazed, and finally said, "All right." He thrust his hand into hers. "You have yourself a partner, partner."

There was nothing small in this world. The plane roared over a crust of valley, red as Mars, and lifted over a lip of mountain. Here rivers foamed down granite slabs, ice cracked and shuddered and smashed into valleys, heaving snow forty feet into the air. The plane trembled, jacked up and fell like a handball. Hands steadied gears; the plane calmed and tilted through a notch in the mountains. A valley rolled out, summer brown and gold and threaded with spruce. Caribou swept over the ground, a horde of insects. A river system sprawled below, gray arms muscling through flat green prairie. It was summer and the land bristled with winter colors: gray green tundra, purple gray rivers, slashes of green spruce and skies washed with winter white clouds. It looked cold from the air and wet; snow burrowed in crevices scrubbed out by the wind.

Sometimes, far below, a cluster of houses huddled together near a cliff or gash of river; but mostly there was only the fluid rise and ridge of hill, the sharp canyons latched with rotting snow; the splash of sun across a pink violet lake that winked once and shuttered to black. Grizzlies streaked like gold comets, rams slammed into each other, splintering horns, fish pounded their way upstream. The land pulsed with terrible life. Here were glaciers, oozing like old wounds and ancient ice scabbed over terrifying black pits, so deep and cold the snow steamed. Lightning hurtled down and a hill exploded, a valley ignited. Winds boiled down mountains, thunderclouds rubbed out sky landmarks, and man guided his fragile craft across the sky, praying the weather held and nothing broke he couldn't fix.

The plane was an old Standard, banged up in the war, with a Curtiss OX-5 engine that coughed like a man with emphysema and a gas tank smaller than a pregnant dog's bladder. They paid $900, as is, in Seattle for it and spent the last hundred getting it shipped up. They mortgaged the house to take lessons, bumping over the new dirt runway and wobbling into the sky. The prop was taller than Batt, and the engine needed a shot of ether to get it going in the morning. The altimeter rattled, the compass veered wildly to the northwest and the cockpit was as naked as a baby's behind, but to the men waiting to be lifted from isolated camps into the bright lights of Anchorage, it was prettier than a fat woman after closing time.

The Jacksons invested in a Curtiss OXX-6 water-cooled engine, attached a working compass, located a reasonably accurate map and sailed away, certain they would fall off the edge of the world. They did, once or twice, but they learned to crawl their way up: banging dents out of the prop with a tree trunk, roping struts with wire, shoring a wing up when it tipped into a sandbar.

They crashed into buildings, sank in rotten ice, bounced off the ball park in Fairbanks and finally developed a certain confidence in finding their way back home.

They hauled everything: traveling salesmen—men with encyclopedias and women in fishnet stockings; engineers from the Colorado School of Mines; miners from Nyak, Polly Creek, Livengood and Kennicott; the dead and nearly dead. So, when that next year in late August, a man shifted out a fat wallet and thumbed two hundreds onto the table at the Jackson's Flying Service office, Batt only said, "Where you want to go?"

The man smelled like rotting meat and he leaked clots of mud onto the carpet, but he was soft in the wrong places, with sloping shoulders and a face that had spent too much time indoors. "Chelatna Lake." He slid out another three. "Two trips."

Batt leaned back and swiveled the chair, staring at a map. "Chelatna Lake. That's up by McKinley, isn't it?"

He nodded. He had built a cabin there, he explained, and wanted Batt to fly in his family and supplies.

"You had experience, living through a winter?"

The chin went up. "My business, I 'magine."

Batt put the money in a cigar box in the drawer and held out the flight log. The man looked startled, gripped a pen and finally wrote: John Smith. California.

"What part?"

"Excuse me?"

"What part California?"

The man stiffened and his hand went to where a gun would be, twitched and relaxed. "Less said, the better."

"'Magine," Batt said drily.

They were waiting by the plane the next morning and got off the crate of canned goods when he drove in. The woman was wearing a cotton dress and sweater and heels and stockings, and Batt knew she had just come off the train. She had a beaten look about her, as if life had spent a long time teaching her to heel. She patted the hump of bedding next to her and a hand thrashed out and disappeared. "Wake up, now, Roybob. Come on, honey."

She pulled up a dark-haired toddler, limp with sleep.

"Let him sleep," Batt said. "Nobody's going anywhere until you've got decent clothes."

Her hand darted to her hair, touched the seed pearls on the sweater.

"Boots, pants, heavy jackets," Batt said gently.

"Oh," the woman said in relief. "Sure."

"It's in the bag," her husband said gruffly. He pointed to the middle duffel bag rising from a small sea of supplies. She waded over, crouched down and rummaged awkwardly through it until she had a set of clothes for herself and the boy.

"You can change over there." Batt gestured at the outhouse. "Faster than taking you back to the office."

"Be quick about it," her husband ordered.

She slunk from him and fled toward the outhouse, almost running, and appeared moments later fully changed, the dress folded around the underwear, shoes hooked on a thumb. Her husband yanked the clothes away as if he were separating a child from its mother and threw them in a trash bin.

"Harry, those are my new things!"

"You don't need them."

"Harry, I got them special—"

"I said you don't need them."

Her eyes were flat with misery. She went to the child, roused him hard and his head snapped back. He started to cry and his mother whispered fiercely, "Hush your mouth or I'll beat your face."

He sucked it in, staring at her. She punched his limbs into pants and a slicker.

"Hi, Bud," Batt crouched down and snicked his fingers through the boy's hair.

The boy stared at him with round brown eyes. Freckles smattered his nose. "My name ain't Bud."

"It isn't? What is it?"

Shyness overwhelmed him, and he rolled his face into his mother's leg.

"His name's Roy," his mother said proudly. "After his grandaddy."

"How old are you, Roy? Three?"

"Four," his mother said, automatically smoothing his hair. "He's small for his age."

"Good thing, too. Plane only carries four-hundred-and-fifty pounds."

The boy didn't smile.

"Well, Roy, you're going to do something probably no other four-year-old gets to do. Fly like a bird." He picked the boy up and lifted him into the cavity of the plane.

"Jimbob flew like a bird off the roof of the barn back home," Roy said solemnly.

"That a fact? Did he like it?"

Roy shrugged, losing interest. "Don't know. Now's he's

flying with the angels."

"Oh, well. Sit right there and don't move."

"Cute little guy," Batt said to the woman.

She brightened. "He's a handful, he is. Do you have any?"

Something sad came and went. "One. She's grown and gone."

"Don't take long," the woman agreed.

Her husband said, "Get your butt over here, Lizbeth, and give me a hand sorting stuff out. Can't take much this trip 'sides us."

She smiled tremulously at Batt, as if thanking him for a small moment of kindness, and scurried away. They had stowed the first load, bedding and canned goods, and locked the rest in the shed before Batt realized the bundle in her arms was another child.

"She don't take up no room." She pressed the child to her.

"Hold her tight," Batt instructed. "Don't strap her in with you."

Clouds blew over Cook Inlet as the plane climbed to the northwest, hurtling over shaggy forests. He put the plane down twice for gas before he picked up the gleam of the Yentna River and banked to the right, following it through rubble-strewn glaciers and mountains that signaled the beginning of the rise to Mount McKinley. Columns of granite spiked the sky, and Batt leaned on the controls, hand light and easy. He spotted the shiny mouth of the Kahiltna glacier, swept over a spiny ridge of exposed rock and dropped down over Chelatna Lake, looking for a place to land. He nosed it down on a sandbar finally, 400 feet long, the plane bouncing gently and dipping a wing into the sand like a shovel at the beach.

"Sonofabitch," Batt muttered. He unfastened his seatbelt and glanced at the woman behind him. She was unnaturally pale. "Ever seen anything like it?"

"Not in Leavenworth." She looked immediately at her husband; he studied his hands. The cockpit grew quiet.

"Harry, I'm—"

"Shut up."

She buried her face in the infant.

Batt turned to the man. "Think the wing's sheared?" He

stood and swung his legs out. "Saw it like that once; looked like one of those tins of corned beef with the lid rolled back."

It didn't need an answer and Batt didn't expect one, so he was almost surprised when the man finally said, "Don't know," and got out to take a look.

Batt was lucky; the trailing edge of the wing had scallops now but the rest was fine. He patted her, unlatched a can of gas and filled her up. "One thing about a country like this," he remarked. "Gives a man a second chance."

They studied the scenery. The lake was a blue as cold as a dead man's eye. Freezing wind gusted down from the snowfields rimming it; the grass blazed with cranberries.

"That's the way I had it figured," the man said at last.

They trotted back to pull off supplies. The woman teetered in the cockpit, the babe in her arms, the oldest asleep at the rear on a crate of supplies. "Harry, I—" she tried again.

"I said shut up." He held up his arms for the infant, and Batt saw the woman instinctively pull back. "I won't hurt her." His voice was unexpectedly gentle. The woman nuzzled her once, smoothed the blanket and passed her carefully down.

She leaned over the boy and shook him gently. "Wake up, Roy, honey." She reared her nose into the wind, gasped and buttoned Roy's coat. "Come on, now."

It was a respectable cabin, sturdy and low, with moss banking the roof and firewood stacked on two sides. Inside, three chairs and a table leaned up against an oil-drum stove, and spruce boards supported a mattress in the corner.

The romantic notion of living in a cabin in the wilds gave way to reality: she saw wind spitting dirt across a floor, filtering it in her socks, piling it in gritty castles inside her bed; wind leaking through the chinks in a wall, whistling to itself; cold, damp, dirty; the feeling in your belly the first time water freezes solid in the kettle overnight.

The boy looked once around the room, chewed on a thumb and announced, "Time to go home."

His mother sighed, lifted him up. "We are home, Roy."

She set him down on the bed next to his sister and opened the first crate, taking out Dutchboy cleanser, Fels Naptha soap and Moon Rose soap-for-fine-fabrics.

"You coming back tomorrow with another load?"

Batt knew she wanted to step into the plane and fly back to Anchorage, back to the warm comfort of beds with clean sheets and toilets that flushed.

"Maybe. Weather's starting to turn." He dropped the last crate down and peeled a sleeping bag off his shoulder, glancing at the sky. Clouds cartwheeled to the west, like tumbleweeds across a blue prairie.

He rapped the stove pipe with his knuckles. "Check the chimney before you fire her up. No telling how thick the creosote is."

"Chimney's fine," the man said.

Batt was almost to the plane when he remembered something Flame always did. "Need anything special?" he asked her. "A mirror, maybe, or some face paint? My wife knows what to buy."

The woman stared at him; her mouth dropped open. "Here?" It was an ugly laugh.

The glacier rose next to Chelatna Lake, feeding it melted bits of ice and slush. The plane lifted over it, engines rattling like gunfire. The glacier muttered. Something anciently cold, viciously fluid, shifted in the core. On the face of it, nothing moved; but underneath, timbers of ice collapsed like a rotting mine shaft and tons of water flooded it. The shell of the glacier trembled against this underground avalanche; trembled and held firm. Then the rains came.

The plane skidded down in Anchorage, butt up against a rain squall that had smacked it from McKinley like the backside of a boy. He tied her up and was smoothing out the canvas when Flame drove in.

"Been looking for you. Weather report's bad. Six days of this, at least."

It rained steadily for a week. Winds lashed and gusted down the Chugach; the Cook Inlet thickened into a swollen gray wave and water streamed down the mountains. At mile 40, a bridge went, and on Turnagain Arm, a railcar slipped into the sea.

Far to the northwest, at Chelatna Lake, the rain mixed with

sleet; the glacier creaked and trembled.

Lizbeth put another pan under a drip, wiped her hands and shifted Jody to the other breast.

"Want to know how I did it this time?" Harry asked suddenly.

"No," she said flatly, glancing over at Roy. He was sleeping hard.

Harry gripped her arm. "I didn't kill nobody, Liz. That counts for something, don't it?"

"That'n five'll buy you a cup of coffee."

"I didn't want Roy here to grow up without a dad."

"You should have thought of that before you robbed the Piggely Wiggely."

"I wanted the best for you, hon."

She looked at him dry lipped. "I only wanted you."

He put his arm around her. "And now you got me, Liz. Good deal."

"I'm tired of running, Harry."

"We won't run no more, I promise."

"Save it."

"We won't." He laughed. "There ain't no other place to go, Liz. This is it. The end of the world."

But he was wrong. The world didn't end for several more days.

Rain lashed the cabin, the roof wheezed, and in Roy's sleep, a shaggy beast caught him in its teeth. Three nights in a row, the thing ate him and he screamed out of sleep. On the fourth night his father climbed out of bed, came to Roy's box by the stove, raised his finger and fired into the wall.

"What happened?" Roy blubbered.

"I shot him," his father said. "Now go to sleep."

But the next night, the thing was back, teeth bubbling blood, a hole in its chest. "I'm going to get you for this," it told him.

Roy moaned. "No."

"Too late," it said. "Too sad, too bad, too late."

The sun came out the beginning of the second week and everybody put on boots and coats and ran outside. The air

486

smelled of snow and the cranberries had turned black. "Let's go exploring," Liz said, eager to stay outside. "Want to? I'll pack a lunch."

They clambered over wet sinking bog, climbed through the trees and slid down to the gravel bed of the glacier. Every year it inched backward, retreating up the mountainside, exposing ground frozen for three thousand years. It was like walking on the moon; huge chunks of boulders shifted underfoot and rock shattered like glass.

Liz looked nervously up the hill. The glacier rolled down to the lake in convoluted blue ridges, like the humps of some enormous prehistoric animal. "Could that thing fall on us?"

Harry squinted up at it and shook his head. "Naw. It's backpedalin', hon."

They clambered up a grassy slope, and she arranged sandwiches. "Don't wander off now, hear?" she said sharply to Roy, who wandered off.

"Maybe the plane will come today with the hole in the weather." Harry bit into his sandwich.

"Harry, what if it don't?"

"He'll come."

"I mean—"

"I said he'll come. Now drop it, Liz." He sprawled backward and picked up a pebble. "Besides, this place is crawling with food. Come on." He tossed the pebble. "Gonna get some hot meat for dinner."

He rolled to his knees, picked up his 12-gauge and sprinted down the slope. "Come on, Liz." He stepped lightly onto the glacier face.

She glanced at the baby. Jody slept in a ball inside the blanket, like a puppy. Next to her, Roy was inspecting the ground for bugs.

"Come on," Harry yelled.

"Stay with Jody now, hear? Right here until I get back."

"Mom, what if Jordy—"

"It's Jody, hon. Joe-dee. If she hollers, give her this juice." She wiped the nipple off carefully on her sleeve and gave it to him. "Don't move or I'll beat your face." She kissed him and ran down the hill.

Geese lifted against the sky, gray on blue, and Harry raised the shotgun and fired.

Under them the ice rumbled, shifted and splintered apart. Something roared. Harry dropped the gun.

"Run!" he screamed. "Run!"

Lizbeth stared at him, uncomprehending. The gun capered across the ice and slid into the open water. A split second later the ice opened like the gates of hell, swallowed Harry to the neck and slammed shut. His neck turned dead white, then bright red. Blood fanned across the ice, drizzling the glacier like icing on a cake.

"Harry!" she screamed and stumbled to him. He was staring at her, pink drool foaming from his nose. His mouth worked and his eyes bulged.

The ground rattled and she scooted backward, terrified. The geyser shot into the air green and pink foam, shards of ice, slabs of concrete snow. Harry's body hurtled with it, twisting in the air.

"Harry!" she screamed again.

It ran over her like a train.

From the grass, Roy saw it all: the pretty colors, the water shooting up. He patted Jody and she whimpered and Roy said affectionately, "Be quiet, Jordy, or I'll beat your face."

A bird landed on the grass, bright eye staring at him. Fascinated, Roy followed it until it clacked into the air. He found a twig, then, and bits of things. A bug trailed across a sliver of grass and Roy built a mud wall; the bug changed direction busily. Excited, Roy dammed one end. The bug bumped into it, feelers out. Roy dropped a clot of mud, another, then a rock. He peered at it expectantly, frowned, poked it and said, "Come out now or I'll beat your face."

It was late when he remembered Jody. Guiltily he trotted over, rolled her into his lap and plugged the crying with the bottle.

It seemed his mom had been gone a long time, but it was like when he was waiting for Christmas and his mom said it was really only two weeks of waiting but it seemed a lot longer. So he held Jody and she drank half and then he rumped her up on his shoulder and patted her, the way his mom did.

Then he remembered the other thing and put her down to check. Wet as rain.

"Just a minute, Jordy," he said, and got up. His mom had packed a few diapers and he pulled one out. Her sandwich was there on the ground, with a bite out. He looked at it a long time, mouth watering. He'd keep it safe in his pocket. He tasted it to make sure it was still okay. The rain started and he changed Jody. His slicker had a hood but Jody only had that little blanket, so he wrapped her real tight and stuck her inside his jacket. She squirmed and nosed around his chest like she expected to find something and finally fell asleep.

He tried singing out loud to keep his spirits up but Jody moaned, so he switched to just thinking songs and finally he slept.

Jody wet all over him, through the T-shirt and everything. "Jordy!" he cried irritably. And then he remembered and opened his eyes. Everything was white. It was snowing. Frightened, he stood up and peered around.

"Mom!" He shivered. Jody stirred against his chest. He ran a ways down the hill and stopped, terrified. The cabin wasn't there. Did he dream it? Dream where it was? He looked around wildly. Chunks of ice slabbed unevenly out. It was like the skating rink back home, but it weren't smooth and there weren't no pretty lights. He backed up the hill and sat back down, not knowing what else to do.

Jody thrashed next to him, furious. "Stop being so mad, Jordy," he said helplessly. He wrapped her in another diaper and stuck her back inside, shifting up the bottle so she could eat.

He remembered the sandwich. The jelly had squished out of it and it was flat as a pancake from sitting on it, but he ate it all anyway; licked his fingers and then his thumb and left it there, hanging out of his mouth like a baby.

Batt scraped the ice off the wings and studied the slate sky. Winds funneled off the Chugach.

"I've got to try it, Flame."

She gripped his arm. "I know." She kissed him hard. "I do love you."

"I've always known that." He clamped on earmuffs and fastened his helmet. He checked the skies one more time and climbed up.

It was dark. Darker than his closet that time Jim Paul locked him in. And freezing cold. Roy's teeth chattered and his body twitched.

Jody had cried herself to sleep, finally, but she was cold as ice.

"Mom," Roy said quietly, to himself.

Behind, something scrabbled down the hill. *I'm going to get you*, it said over his shoulder. Roy squeezed his eyes shut.

Two creeks flashed by, rimmed with trees, and Batt banked to the left and climbed. Fog spiraled around him and he studied the compass, adjusted his course. His hands were wet in the gloves and his feet smarted with cold. He stamped them and peered down.

Through a rip in the fog he found a landmark and eased through the gorge, shifting the stabilizer back and slowing the ship to a crawl. The fog was thicker here. Walls of granite whipped past. Two hard turns to the right, a box canyon on the left, and he pulled the ship up and out.

He almost missed the first gas-up; the cabin looked so different in snow. He circled, dropped down and eased onto the bank, tapping skis to snow and veering wildly, almost sliding the nose over the bank into the river. He filled the tank on the run, not daring to shut the engines off.

Smoky Joe lumbered out of the cabin toward him, shaking his head. "Thought it was you. Only a goldarn fool would try that in a storm. Shut that durn thing off and sit a spell."

Batt shook his head. "Can't, Smoke."

"And why not?" Bright blue eyes studied him through a shag of hair.

"Just can't, that's all."

"Then take a squirt of this." Smoky thumbed the lip of a bottle and handed it to him. Batt drank it, choked, and drank some more.

"Good God," he said, handing it back, "what is it?"

490

"Fermented muskrat juice mixed with grain and a pinch of snuff."

"Don't you know it's prohibition?"

"Don't you know it's twenty below?"

But Batt was already climbing back up.

Roy wasn't cold anymore; Jody either. He could tell because she was fast asleep and couldn't care less that she had wet clear through. He knew he should change her, but he was warm now, so he dreamed he was changing her instead and that worked real fine and then he stopped dreaming altogether.

At first he thought he had the wrong lake, and then terrible comprehension came and he banged his fist against the door. "No, no."

Green-and-blue ridges marbled with pink cracked under him, shoved up against the woods. Trees and rocks poked from the rubble like bones through skin. He dropped down, looking.

Once, twice, three times he circled. His mouth drew dry.

He banked up a bouldered moraine, frowned, peered down. Something yellow blinked on the slope. Cautiously, he gauged the angle, white on white: where did the sky end and the slope begin. He bounced down hard.

The plane skittered over the ice, chewing it. He wiped his mouth, got out and ran back. Roy was motionless, face down in the snow. "Roy," Batt said.

He took down the hood. Roy's face was cold.

"Hey, Bud," Batt said gently, pulling him into his arms.

"I ain't Bud," Roy said sleepily, and closed his eyes.

By the time the hospital released the baby, Roy was calling Flame "Mom" and refusing to let her out of his sight.

"What do you want to do?" Batt whispered. Roy's fanny flagged the air in Jenny's old bed.

"The truth?" She adjusted Roy's blanket under his chin and they linked arms into the hallway. "Batt, it feels so good to have kids in the house. But there's got to be grandparents—aunts, uncles—"

"We don't even know who they were, Flame."

"We should write the prison, at least. They could tell us."

"Tell us what? That John Smith didn't escape because he was never there?"

"Harry," she said mildly. "And his wife was Lizbeth."

Batt tightened his arm around her. "All right, Flame, I'll write the prison. But I'll tell you right now, God gave us those two as another chance. Even the baby's name—Jordy. Roy calls her that all the time. Bet they named her Jordan, like the river—and Flame, that's what she is, she and Roy. They've carried us home like that river, across to the other side."

Flame's eyes filled with tears. "Do you think really—"

"I think they needed us as much as we needed them and God just kind of worked it out."

Forty-One

"Do you think she'll like me?" Aan peered critically at herself in a mirror, sighed and put it down. A lifetime of herding reindeer, coupled with sewing in dim light, had given her radiantly glowing skin and terrible eyesight.

Nick Snow patted his wife affectionately. "I think Kannik and you will be chattering like ptarmigan in two minutes, leaving the men and children to fend for ourselves."

Aan looked at him sideways. "Is it true—she has two husbands?"

"Two husbands, seven children and ten grandchildren, all coming to Nome."

Aan leaned over the spit cup and expelled green mucus, put the lid on and drank her medicine, a mixture of creosote and water. She choked and made a face. "Did you know in America, they use this stuff to keep the rain off roofs?"

"Where did you hear that?"

Aan shrugged. "I read it someplace." She had been learning to read at night along with the grandchildren.

A coughing attack seized her and she held the cloth to her mouth. Nick felt again the pain in his own chest.

His wife was dying. Every year the tuberculosis got stronger and her breathing weaker. Through the Presbyterian missionary in Barrow, Nick had planned the family reunion, motivated by the fear Aan would go first. He had told her he picked Nome as a halfway point because of a missionary translator there, fluent in both Athapaskan and Inupiaq; but the real reason was that the hospital was better than the one in Barrow.

Nick picked up the spit cup, emptied its foul contents into the fire and refilled the cup with carbolic acid.

493

"I'll bet you're glad to be running dogs again," Aan said suddenly. Nick had borrowed a team from a friend to carry them to Nome. He nodded.

Altogether they were taking three sleds, the family had grown so. Out of his four children in Barrow, two of them had families of their own.

"I can't wait to get started," Aan said, and reached for the spit cup.

"Neither can I," Nick said, and tenderly held her head as she used it.

The day before the families arrived in Nome, six-year-old Dickie Stanley lay in bed, eyes glassy, staring at the Wright Brothers model twirling over his bed.

"Come on, Dickie." His mother opened the door and switched on the light. "You're going to be late for school." She picked up his Babe Ruth mitt and stray sneaker and put them in the closet.

Dickie groaned. He thrashed. He chattered his teeth. He had been working all night on a sore throat, nursing it into a reason to stay home. A spelling test was waiting to get him at school.

"Dickie," his mother said sternly, and fluffed the pillow under him. She had nursed five children through measles, mumps and chicken pox, and had found that mysterious, paralyzing illnesses only happened on test days.

"I'm sick!" Dickie protested.

She sat next to him. His face was blazing hot.

"All right. You can stay home. But only today. And *study*."

Dickie nodded, moaning, and wondered how his mother had found him out. When the door closed, he sat up immediately, pulled a Speedo action-train set from under the bed and built a track in the covers.

But his throat felt funny—scratchy like his daddy's chin in the morning, so he scooched back his pajama top with the boats on it and rolled the cars across his bare chest, and then his *chest* felt funny, like it was a real train instead of a play one and he had been squashed on the track, so he wrecked the train into his knees and rolled over on his side.

His mother spooned chicken soup into him and pretended to

494

go along with it, but by the next afternoon, she didn't have to pretend anymore and went to get old Doc Welch.

It was diphtheria.

Kannik's family got there first and set up housekeeping along the south wall of the community center, arranging Coleman stoves and sleeping bags in family groupings, discreetly separated by sheets hung on clotheslines.

The kids tumbled outside to play, climbing the scraggy slabs of ice that had piled up in frozen Norton Sound. The only ocean they had seen was in *Boys' Life,* and they had all been furious when this one turned out to be gray washboard, frozen as hard as the Yukon back home, instead of blue and warm with boats and wading children.

Her grandson, Cliff, immediately torpedoed the beachball he had bought with his own money and arm wrestled his cousin into buying him peanuts at Brown's General Store on Front Street.

Then they horsed around the brass scale, feeding it pennies until they each got a fortune they liked, and Cliff scratched a mustache on the Coca-Cola lady with his penknife before the owner ran them off.

Cliff felt an enormous need to run in place, spit in the snow, blubber his lips like Jack Dempsey. Afterward he said casually, "What do you think granny's relatives will be like? Eskimos. It's *weird.* Being related to *Eskimos.*"

Samuel nodded. Their fathers had worked on the Fairbanks section of the railroad, benching and trestling near the Nenana River Canyon, and now had jobs on rotary plows clearing slides.

They lived in log cabins, wore boots and ate Spam, and Cliff refused to play anything but a cowboy when the kids at the mission chose sides. They might have looked Indian, but they *felt* about as Indian as the wooden one standing in front of the Nome Bank and Trust Company.

Samuel shrugged. "I don't know, but mom says I have to be nice to them anyway, or I won't get my allowance."

Cliff sighed, got down on fours and bit a chunk of snow off the sidewalk.

"Hey, Cliff, getta loada this." Samuel nudged him.

Trotting down the snowpacked street past the Bohemia Hotel, three dog teams trailed red and green ribbons like electric Christmas streamers, bells jangling, horns tootling; the sleds bellied over the snow, sagging with children, reindeer skins, bags of grease and antlers.

"I got a bad feeling about this." Samuel shook his head.

"Gotta be," Cliff agreed, and slouched into the street.

"Hi," he called, waving his hands.

"Hi," a kid brightened and waved back.

The two boys glumly watched the sleds bounce down the street. "Ooh, they speak English," Cliff moaned under his breath.

Samuel viciously slammed the snow with the toe of his boot. "Anybody thinks it's easy, being a kid, oughta try it once."

Doc Welch counted the vials, closed the cabinet and carefully locked it. He sank his forehead against the cool green metal. "We've got problems," he said finally.

Bertha Seville studied his face; kind gray eyes, gray hair, a roadmap of lines. They had worked together a long time.

He banged the cabinet. "Damn it, I knew it would happen. That's the worst part. Two months ago, Bertie, I wired the federal health office in Seattle for more serum. *Two months.*"

"How bad is it?" she asked quietly.

He put his head in his hands. "We're going to lose the Stanley boy." He looked up and his eyes were bloodshot.

"And it's even worse than that, Bert. If it breaks out, we'll lose a lot more. I only have serum for twenty people."

"Oh, my God." Bertie clapped a knobby hand over her mouth. Tears came to her eyes.

"Quarantine the town. Stop school, meetings, churches. Tell everybody to stay home."

"But that big group—that family reunion at the center—"

"Keep them together and hope to God none of those kids has found a way yet to bring it in. And don't let anybody leave Nome, Bertie—or it'll spread like a fire over the territory."

"Anything else?"

"Pray."

He walked out the door and ran down the steps. Bertie clasped her hands together. She bowed her graying head. Tears leaked over her hands.

Nome calling . . . Nome calling . . .

Earphones adjusted, fingers tapped: *Go ahead Nome . . . we're standing by . . .*

In Juneau, Anchorage, Fairbanks, across the wide, winter-dark landscape, radio operators with the United States Army Signal Corps translated the dots and dashes into misery.

Diphtheria epidemic . . . need serum . . . repeat . . . need serum . . . town in trouble . . . please help us . . . over . . .

In hospitals so small the kitchen doubled as an operating room, in villages where the whole drug supply could be locked inside a tackle box, Alaskans looked, and looked again.

McGrath to Nome . . . McGrath to Nome . . .

Go ahead, McGrath . . .

Still looking . . . we are with you . . . repeat . . . we are with you.

"Hah! My sister!" Nick hugged Kannik, kissed her cheeks and squeezed her hard. "Twenty-five years it's been."

Her eyes glowed under crepey folds of flesh. Gray streaked the black hair, and she had grown fat.

"Twenty-six," she corrected. "I counted."

He squeezed her again, then pushed her away to look at her. She was wearing western clothes—heavy pants and boots and a pink sweater fluffed out like the minister's cat.

"You have all your teeth," he accused.

Kannik grinned. "My boys, Joey and Frank, have good jobs. White jobs, Nuka. I have my own toothbrush," she added proudly.

She fingered open a jowl. "Only one pulled. Not bad."

Nick embraced his wife and pushed her forward. "Aan, this is my sister, Kannik." He hugged one on each side and laughed and kissed the top of one head and then another.

The two women gripped hands and Aan said, "You are

prettier than he told me."

And you are sicker than I thought, Kannik thought sadly.

Aan's face had the luminous quality of the very ill, as if she were staring into God's face.

"She looks well, doesn't she, Kannik? Doesn't my wife look good?"

They had to know. Aan stared at Kannik and suddenly Kannik understood.

Aan and Nuka both saw Death and were protecting the other from the sight.

"Your wife is quite beautiful," Kannik said gently. "Now come, I want you to meet the others."

It was a moiling, boisterous crowd. Shanyaati and Senati stood like ancient ravens, backs sloped, shoulders rolled inward, a ruff of feathers and beads on mooseskin jackets; separated as much by their clothes as the Athapaskan they spoke. The middle and younger generations spoke English, and casually mixed clothing styles: Hudson Bay shirts, mooseskin pants, heavy nail boots and fur parkas. Nuka's side was different.

"Are they poor relations?" Cliff whispered to his mother.

"Whatever made you say that?" Eve wiped her hands off and picked up another potato, working the knife against the flat of her thumb.

Cliff shrugged. "They didn't bring one store-bought thing."

"That's not true." The peel spiraled to a paper bag at her feet. "There's some Folger's over there. And granny's brother, Nick, chews like grampa Sen."

"But their clothes are funny," Cliff insisted. "Greasy looking."

"It's the skins," Eve explained. "You don't run them through the wash."

He shrugged and trotted off, rump jouncing over slim legs.

"He's a corker, that one." Kannik spoke Athapaskan with her daughter. It was their private language, away from the children.

"Did you have any favorites, mom?" Eve asked abruptly.

Kannik looked around the room, matriarch of a dynasty. "Still do," she said mistily.

And then the outside door burst open and it was the nurse from the hospital and everything changed.

In Washington, Territorial Representative Dan Sutherland padded for the phone and knocked it off in the dark. He grunted into it and snapped on the light. A little after three in the morning.

"Dan. This is Leif. Over at Public Health. Found that serum you need."

Sutherland sat up, instantly alert, and reached for a pad and pencil.

"Checked through all the pharmaceuticals. Finally found it at—"

"How much?" Sutherland interrupted.

"A million units. It's being flown to Seattle now, on Uncle Sam's dime. So I guess when it hits Seward, you can throw it on a bus or something."

"Railroad."

"What?"

"Railroad. As far as Nenana." Sutherland was breaking down the units into shots.

"Okay then, throw it on a bus at Nenana."

"Excuse me?" It was enough for 330 shots.

"A bus," the public health man explained patiently. "To Nome."

"Only one problem with that."

"What's that?"

"There are no roads to Nome."

"No roads! Then how in the hell do you plan to get it there? Dan? Dan. Hello?"

Sutherland laughed maniacally and slammed down the phone.

"It's not fast enough." Governor Strong paced the floor, a burgundy terry cloth robe flapping open over dead white knees. At the table sat his commissioners, summoned out of bed.

"It's the end of January," Strong said. "The fastest time from Seattle to Seward in those seas is almost two weeks. The whole town could be dead before the serum even gets to Alaska. We've got two problems. We've got to find closer serum—"

The phone rang and Strong's secretary glided across the floor, gray efficiency packaged in a modulated voice. She put the phone down. "Anchorage just wired the Juneau telegraph office. Dr. Blue's found three hundred thousand units. Enough for one hundred shots."

"Thank the Lord. Maybe it'll hold things in check until the Seattle shipment comes. So now we just have one problem. How to get it there."

"Pilots," the commissioner of transportation suggested. "Ben Eilsen could fly it from Fairbanks."

Strong shook his head. "Eilsen's in Washington working on an airmail contract with the federal government."

"Then get Batt Jackson. He's the best in Anchorage. It's farther to fly but—" The commissioner glanced down and realized he had misbuttoned his shirt.

Surreptitiously he worked on the buttons as Strong stopped pacing and stared out the window into the pitch-black night. Ice cascaded down the tall windows.

Strong turned and said harshly, "In an open cockpit at seventy below? Toss-up which'd freeze first, Batt or the oil. With no radio over the mountains in a blizzard—It's too risky." He shook his head.

The men looked at each other in silence.

"We're going to have to use dogs," Strong said finally. "Thelma. Wire that doctor in Anchorage and tell him to get the serum on the first train to Nenana. Then wire the operators along the Nenana to Nome stretch. Tell the best musher in each district to stand by. We'll relay it in."

"But sir!" postal liaison Browning protested. "It takes two weeks by dog team to work that route."

"Nome doesn't have two weeks," Strong said.

That night in Nome, Doc Welch used the last vial.

In Anchorage, Cahill Blue was wrapping serum. He cushioned it in flannel, bundled a blanket around it, checked to see that the instructions held under the twine. Then he stood in the steaming fog and put it on the train.

500

At Johnny Campbell's roadhouse in Minto, Edgar Kalland hunkered over a second piece of pecan pie, mailbag asleep at his feet. Outside, the wind skated across the flats and hurled chunks of ice against the window.

The phone rang and Johnny answered it.

"Hey, Edgar," he yelled. "They want you back in Tolovana tonight."

Edgar polished off the pie. "Just came from there this morning. Supposed to be in Nenana with the mail tomorrow."

"Forget the mail," Johnny said. "Leave it here and we'll send somebody else. You've got more important things to carry."

Edgar took off his moccasin, rolled down a sock, peeled off two more and snaked his fingers down the last one. He pulled out a pebble and chinked it onto the table. "And what might that be?"

"Serum," Johnny Campbell said. "They're dropping like flies in Nome."

"Spend yourself extravagantly," Kannik said in English. The room was quiet. Parents rocked children between knees, babies cried in fits and starts, and outside, the snow creaked in Norton Sound.

"But granny, what if—" Cliff looked uneasily around the room. "What if it gets in?"

"You mean the diphtheria?"

Cliff nodded and hugged his bony knees to his chest.

"Fight it," Kannik advised. "Smack it hard right between the eyes. You know what it is, really, Cliff, that gets a person?"

He shook his head.

"It's fear. That's all. Fear. It squeezes more lives than any sickness. Fear. If this diphtheria thing comes for you, Cliff, stand up to it. Tell it it's going to have to fight to get you. And then you fight harder. Give it everything you've got."

She pointed a twisted finger at him, swollen with arthritis. "But don't let fear wrestle you down first. Don't let fear rob you of your strength. Do you hear me? Do you understand?"

He nodded. Through the room, Kannik could feel a softening, a coming back to the place where they had been before the sickness had announced itself.

The room shifted into sleep.

Across town, Dickie Stanley died.

Bill Shannon stamped his feet and smacked his face against the cold. The conductor clanged open the door. Ice cracked off in a sheet. He passed the package down.

"Good luck, Willy."

Shannon lashed it to the sled, stepped onto the crossbar. The dogs shot into the night.

He couldn't swallow; and then he could swallow, and it woke him up. Cliff remembered about fear. I'm not afraid of you, he told the diphtheria. You come for this kid, you got a fight on your hands.

He closed his eyes and willed himself to sleep.

Aan woke Nuka. She was fully dressed in the only white clothes she owned: a printed dress, ankle socks and boots.

"Dear one," she whispered. "Dear one." Moonlight rode the high flat planes of her cheeks, across the small flat nose.

"What is it? Here is the spit cup. Do you need it?" He held it out to her. The tenderness in those scarred hands!

"I am old and tired, Nuka."

"Aan. What are you saying?"

"Nuka, my love, you have protected me for no reason. I am not afraid."

"I'll take you to the doctor."

Aan shook her head. "No, my love. I will die in my own way. The old way." She got to her feet.

"What are you telling me?"

"You already know." She held him tightly.

"But the serum! It's on its way. There is no need for this."

"We both knew how the story would end."

She parted the curtain separating their sleeping quarters from the children and entered Naomi's world. She touched her grandchildren one by one. Naomi sat up next to her husband.

"Mom?" She crept out of bed. "Mom, what is it?"

"Hush, Naomi. You'll wake the babies."

"Is there something wrong?"

Aan squeezed her daughter's hand. "I needed to touch my little ones. And tell my oldest daughter I love her."

"Oh, mom." Naomi hugged her. "I love you, too."

"Go back to sleep," Aan whispered.

And then into Matthew's cubicle. Such a stern, solemn little boy he had been! Growing into such a quiet man.

Herding reindeer had never been right for him. With one of those terrible insights that comes too late, she knew it wasn't a stillness she had sensed in him, but a lifelessness, as if he had given up. She should have sent him to school instead of Tim.

Ah, Matthew, she trembled. What have I done. His wife's dark head shifted with dreams.

She touched his shoulder and he jerked awake, saw her and relaxed.

"Matthew. Do what you want in life."

"Mother?"

"Hear?" she whispered hoarsely. "Do what you want."

She pressed her hand to his face and he held it against him and then she turned and went swiftly through the curtain into Ruth's chamber.

Alone and almost twenty she was. Proud and independent, the poverty of reindeer herding rankling her most of all.

"Ruth?"

"What is it, mama?" Ruth asked sleepily. She pushed a braid from her eyes.

"Don't settle for anything," Aan said.

"Is there something wrong?" She sat up.

"Nothing. Nothing at all. It's been on my mind to tell you that. Don't settle for anything. Go your own way and the rest be damned."

Ruth hugged her, alarmed at how light her mother felt, as if the bones were hollow. "I love you, mother."

"I'll always love you. Now go back to sleep." Aan started out.

"Mom?" Ruth whispered.

"Yes?"

"Do you think we're all going to die?"

"Sooner or later, paniga."

"But I mean, now. Do you think we're going to die now?"

"Not you, Ruth."

"You don't think so?"

"No, darling, no. Now go back to sleep."

Mark was the hardest to release. Her baby at fourteen; glad darting energy. He loved the reindeer with the simple instincts of a natural herder.

She hugged him and he groaned in his sleep, woke up. "What is it?"

"I needed to hug my boy, that's all."

"Mom, I'm fourteen. I'm not a boy anymore."

He endured the hug and Aan stretched it out. "Mark, take care of your father. He needs you so much."

But Mark was already asleep.

Sighing, she got to her feet, dropped the curtain and walked into the main part of the room. Across from her the curtains of Kannik's tribe fluttered like a friendly camp.

Nuka was waiting for her by the door. "You won't do it alone."

"You can't, Nuka, they need you too much."

He was crying. "I can't let you go."

"You must," she whispered.

"Then let me help."

They put on parkas and slipped outside, walking along Front Street. They climbed the high ridges of ice in Norton Sound. The night was bitterly beautiful. Stars winked like diamond chips.

Too soon she stopped. "Right here."

Nuka took his knife and went to work.

It was a small hut, only big enough for her. She put her arms around him. They kissed.

"You know how we always thought we could see into the curve of heaven, when we reached the rim edge of life?"

"Do you see anything?"

"Only your face."

He embraced her, buried his face in her.

She patted him. "I'll always be with you."

She crawled inside.

Nuka walked a distance. Sat down on a keg of ice; stared at

the stars. An old star fireballed across the sky.

"Aan." He put his head in his hands.

Inside the hut Aan curled into a ball. Her body was empty, light. There was no hurry in her, no rush. She thought she heard a child crying; a dog snuffled along Front Street. Her children were red balls of memory behind her eyes. She thought of Timmy, sentenced long ago to a white world and felt remorse. Gone. Her oldest was gone utterly. Nine years and not a word.

Is this a sacrifice? she wondered. Am I sacrificing myself to an old god, hoping to save my family?

Her feet were turning numb. No, she thought.

Tears slid from her eyes. Here is only an old woman, who loves an old man too well to see the pain in his eyes any longer.

Freezing to death is not bad, she thought suddenly.

It's just drifting, deeper and deeper into a dream.

Shannon hated the wind. It roared up the frozen Tanana, tearing the scarf from his mouth. He moved it again. Half the scarf crackled with ice from breathing on it.

The dogs were ghostly ships bobbing in a sea of fog. It was quiet; only the soft whump of breathing dogs, the sled running. Away from the towns there was only fog and gloom and darkness, going on forever. Sometimes he imagined he was running over the same spot endlessly, dogs' breath hanging like stationary clouds, wind lashing his face.

Shannon shifted the scarf again away from the ice shield he had made. His hands began to smart inside his gloves.

Green light washed over the snow and filtered to lemon. The sun climbed over the edge of the world as if it were an exceedingly old man hooking one foot over a tall saddle. The snow blushed to pink, deepened to dusky rose.

Light bounced inside each crystal of snow.

Shannon's eyes hurt. His feet hurt. His face hurt where it took a beating from the wind.

And then, there it was: Tolovana. He braked the sled and staggered off.

He had gone fifty-two miles in thirteen hours.

505

Dan Green warmed the serum by the stove, whip-tied it to the sled and pushed off.

The torch was passed.

"What is the meaning of this?" Doc Welch demanded.

The natives looked at the floor.

"An old woman frozen to death in a hut."

"Tell me," Kannik said quietly. "Have you stopped the epidemic?"

Welch shook his head. "What are you getting at?"

"Let us take care of ours. You do your job. And let us take care of ours."

He sat down tiredly and put the medical kit on the table.

"It's all right," Kannik said gently. "It is. We have customs you find strange. But there is no time now to ponder them. How can we help you?"

He said finally, "I'll have to call the mayor."

"Fine. And he will tell you she was an old tubercular woman who chose to freeze to death."

"Who is the next of kin?"

"My brother, but English does not come easily to him. And besides, do you wish to disturb a man in his hour of grief? It is a private thing, doctor. Save the living, if you can."

Welch expelled a breath. He stood up. "How many here with sore throats?"

No one moved.

"Nothing?" Welch said, unable to keep the glad hope from his voice. "None of you has sore throats?"

Cliff raised his hand, not daring to look at his mother's face.

Around him, bodies shifted. He looked up.

It was a sea of hands.

They moved the sick to one end of the community center. Doc Welch had decided at the start not to send diphtheria patients to the hospital, for fear they would infect the other patients. Almost every house had someone sick now, but this was the worst.

Bertha Seville immediately started administering a grain of quinine every three hours, and tincture of iron mixed in five drops of water. Kannik worked alongside her.

"You're not afraid?" Bertha asked.

Kannik looked down the row of faces. Senati and Shanyaati lay side by side, eyes closed, silent warriors. She could feel the thoughts moving between them; was it sharing the same woman for so long that had given them this special ability to read the other's mind? Or was it relying on the other's instincts in the hunt?

Beyond stretched more dearly beloved faces, now flushed, throats swollen with the unspeakable.

"They are my family."

Bertha looked steadily at her. "Help as long as you can stand it, then."

She gave Kannik sterile canisters of hydrogen peroxide for gargling and Kannik distributed one to each person. When she got to Cliff, he clutched her hand.

"Granny," he whispered.

"I'm here."

"Tell me again about fear."

"Are you afraid?"

He nodded.

"It's not a bad thing to admit that." She held his hand quietly. "The thing is, what do you plan to do about it?"

"Fight it," he whispered.

She gripped his hand. "That's my boy."

Hour by hour, carried from one swift sled to another, the serum made its way west. From Manley Hot Springs to Fish Lake, from Fish Lake to Tanana, past Gold Mountain and on to Nine Mile, drivers stumbled off sleds and passed the package to the next one in line.

The Seward Peninsula—the land stretching out from Nome into the interior—bristles with winds spitting sand and snow. The Eskimos say some evil long ago was thrown out of heaven and forced to do time eternally on the wind-scoured peninsula.

Leonhard Seppala knew it was true. Togo ran by instinct now, not command. Seppala couldn't see a thing. A ghost line of dogs almost ran into them.

It was Hank Ivanoff. He braked hard and the sled leapt across the ice. He lunged off, braking the sled manually before it slammed into the dogs.

He unlashed the serum and limped over. His face was purple and his lips cracked from cold. "Here it is." He thrust it into Seppala's hands.

In Nome, three more died and Senati lapsed into delirium.

At Golovin, the phone rang at Josh's Roadhouse.

"It's coming this way," Josh reported, "but there's a helluva storm out there. Fifty miles an hour." He looked around the room.

"Hey, Smiley, you want to run the serum into Bluff?"

Smiley stuck a thumb up his nose, pulled it out, flicked it off. "How much you pay me?"

Charlie Olson got to his feet. "I'll do it."

Across Norton Bay, the wind had slicked the ice to glass. The gale picked up the sled and hurled it on edge. Seppala banged down his body, straightening it. The dogs didn't lose a beat.

In Nome, Kannik's throat began to hurt.

Seppala staggered off the sled, dazed from the cold. His dogs collapsed in the snow. "Serum," he roared. "Warm it up."

Charlie shook his head. "No time, Len. The town's going under."

He snapped the package to the sled and was gone.

Cliff crawled painfully past the rows of makeshift beds. Kannik lay like a doll on the last one. He squeezed her hand.

"You fight it, granny," he thought fiercely. He couldn't speak. "Fight it." He crept into her arms and died.

Gunnar Kaasen was waiting in the mail cabin at Bluff; outside, snow whipped the side of an abandoned mine and his dogs whoofed in the snow.

Balto barked. The door slammed open and Olson fell face down into the cabin.

*   *   *

The wind cuffed him. The sled faltered; lines tangled. Gunnar worked swiftly. This was the last stretch, the final distance. His ears rang with cold; he couldn't feel his cheeks. He checked the serum.

"Mush." It was a scream of agony. Balto leaped forward; the dogs leaped forward into a scalding cold night. Gunnar closed his eyes and groaned.

Her eyes fluttered open. Such a dear face staring at her. Her oldest friend. Her soul loosened inside her, like a warm cake coming out of a pan.

"You know what I was thinking?" Nuka said in Inupiaq.

She couldn't move her head so she moved her eyes back and forth.

"How mad I was the first time I heard you say *I*." He laughed. "This brazen woman, my sister. And now my own granddaughter wears skirts, sometimes to the knee. Tell you what. In heaven we'll find a warm spot, a hot spring, maybe, and soak our tired old feet. How does that sound? Kannik? Kannik?"

She soared freely, staring down at her brother kneeling by an old woman. She looked lovingly around the room, turned her face toward a blinding light and was gone.

He bent down and put his cheek next to her nose. She wasn't breathing, but her face was rosy and soft. He pulled the covers up, smoothed her hair, and held her hand until it grew cold.

Topkok Hill was six hundred feet of ice overlooking the Bering Sea. Winds scoured it as Gunnar pushed the sled up the hill. His right cheek was a block of marble. At the summit he groped in the darkness for the sled and got in. He closed his eyes as the dogs plunged into the eye of the storm.

Past Solomon Roadhouse, past Spruce Creek, Gunnar Kaasen drove the dogs through snow so thick he couldn't see more than a few feet ahead. At Bonanza Flats the wind hurled the sled over, tangling the dogs. Gunnar stumbled to the front, righted things, and patted once for the serum.

It was gone.

Frantic, he ripped off his gloves and thrust them into the

snow. It couldn't be gone. It couldn't. His right hand bumped it. With a cry of relief, he tied it securely on and put on his gloves. His hands burned with cold.

Can't stop, can't stop. On past Point Safety, following the beach. High drifts, rock ice, and then the lights of Nome.

Weeping, the dogs stumbling with cold and fatigue, Gunnar dropped off the sled and banged on the doctor's door. He cried and banged and screamed, and finally the doctor opened it and Gunnar fell inside.

The serum was frozen solid, but they thawed it carefully.

By two that afternoon they started shots, and by the next night, they knew that they had won.

Nuka looked slowly around the room. So many gone. His own beloved youngest son, Mark—eager hands, busy feet—gone; four grandchildren, a daughter-in-law. His sister, Kannik. Half her brood. And Aan, always his thoughts went to Aan.

How could he live without her?

He loaded the sled in silence.

He was an old man and he had seen much pain. Is it time yet? he wondered. Can I go now? So many gone.

He felt a presence behind him and turned, expecting to see one of his children. It was the shaman.

Nuka cried out in surprise.

"You cannot leave," the shaman said. "Not yet."

"Why?" Nuka cried hoarsely.

"Your work is not finished."

Nuka dropped to his knees imploringly. "I am an old man! I have no mysteries! No light for the world! Why do you bother me now? Leave me alone! Let me die quickly, and in peace!"

The shaman touched his forehead. His hand was cool. In Nuka's mind he heard the words: *for from your seed will spring the rebirth of your people.*

"I don't want it!" Nuka cried. "Give it to someone else!"

But the shaman only smiled, his body growing fainter and fainter until it disappeared, leaving only the snow and sky and sea.

*　　　*　　　*

Thousands of miles and six months away from Nome, a summer school class shrieked and hollered past the balloon man at the Forty-second Street entrance to Central Park.

The teacher limped behind, long dark hair swinging in the sun.

Down a winding path, past a playground, she paused at a statue of a dog. It was a bronze cast of Balto, the lead dog on the last trek of the Iditarod diphtheria run. The inscription underneath read Endurance, Fidelity, Intelligence. A lump came to her throat. Alaska. It was her home and she had lost it forever.

Jenny Blue turned quickly and limped away.

BOOK FIVE

Deed

Forty-Two

If Alaska had been mostly overlooked during the gaiety of the twenties, it was largely untouched by the great terror that followed.

Congress insisted the railroad raise its rates between Seward and Fairbanks to ten cents a mile; work slowed in the mines and the canneries had troubled years, but for the most part, Alaska dozed through the early Depression as a woman might doze through early labor: there was a twinge here and there, but not enough pain to scream.

And then something quite wonderful happened.

It was President Franklin D. Roosevelt's idea, and it fired the imagination of the nation.

He suggested taking dirt-poor farmers from Michigan, Wisconsin and Minnesota—farmers already used to cool climates and toughened by hard work—and relocating them in the fertile Matanuska Valley, fifty miles north of Anchorage. No charity cases either: they would be expected to pay for what they got with an easy payment plan over thirty years. Everybody wanted to go, or knew somebody who did.

So in early January of 1935, Roosevelt sent agents into the red clay farms of Minnesota, into the sharp fusty stalls in Wisconsin, looking for couples the way the marines looked for a few good men—couples who wouldn't quit when things got tough, folks with a yen to colonize the moon.

"I'm that type of person," Sadie Jean spoke right up. "Me and my husband, both." She glanced at Earl sitting ramrod straight next to her, and he nodded.

Even though the government-relief man had come all the way from Le Seur in a Nash 400 to sit in their kitchen, boots

515

steaming and trousers leaking with melting snow, he still read Monkey Wards in the outhouse, same as they. Sadie wasn't afraid of him. She was more afraid of the way the shelves in the root cellar looked without cans on them.

"Only eighty-six families will be chosen from Minnesota, so you understand this shouldn't be a rash decision," the agent warned.

He had big blubbery lips and sagging eyes, and reminded Sadie a lot of a dog they'd had once, only he smelled better. The agent, not the dog. Spot smelled like pig turds and wet wool and would have lived forever except crazy old Tibbins shot him through the head when he was busy making mongrels with Tibbins's registered Lab. At least he died doing something he really liked.

"We understand," Sadie said primly, and folded her hands in her lap.

"Could I get you something? Our daughter Emily could sing for you. She's real good."

He whumped over his boots to buckle them, and his belly slid over his knees.

"I would enjoy that immensely," he said, and it sounded like he meant it, "but I'm supposed to be in Le Seur at two for a meeting with my higher-ups."

"Higher ups." She nodded. "So, what'a think?" she said shyly, and thumbed a spot off the Universal combination range.

The agent found his hat, dumped the puddle of melted snow from the brim carefully into the sink.

"You have"—and here he looked around the kitchen as if he could find the word he was looking for in the Mason jar of pickled beets—"remarkable vitality."

"Does this mean we're going?"

"It means you've got as good a chance as any. Maybe better."

"Thank you," Sadie said fervently, and wrung his hand.

She walked him to the kitchen door and opened it for him, because the real front door stuck where it warped and you could skate across the porch on your knees, if you weren't careful. Besides, the kitchen was the warm room and she

516

thought it would leave a better impression.

She and Earl leaned against each other, hands around each other's waists, and watched him plodding through the high, wet drifts toward the main dirt road where he'd parked the car.

"Do you think we're going?" Earl had baby-soft hair that whuffed in his eyes and his shoulders drooped from where he'd tried to catch too many things that had gotten away.

"I don't think, I *know*." Sadie always talked like that. She pressed her shoulder blades back and pinched a strand of hair. The crimp would have stayed in longer with a dab of Vaseline, but she was lucky to have Lifebuoy, and glad of it.

"I *know*," she repeated and went to the stove to dish up the chicken-neck soup.

All along the way they had been treated like Bing Crosby or Shirley Temple, people rushing up to the platform and shoving papers through the train windows for autographs.

Emily had been on her best behavior, Sadie had seen to that. The first time she'd bellied into the aisle and scrapped with the little Cleaver boy, twisting his ears and boffing his nose, Sadie had hauled her off to the lavatory, tipped her over the commode and blistered her bottom, but good. Emily started squalling and wouldn't talk to her until Salt Lake.

Afterward, Sadie gave her a Sears catalogue to cut up, and Emily tried to put clothes on all the women modeling underwear.

Earl sat and stared out the window a lot and read clear through Pearl S. Buck's book *The Good Earth* and then traded it for Walter B. Pitkin's book *Life Begins at Forty* even though for the life of her she didn't know why, since Earl was only going to be thirty-three next birthday and hardly looked a day over twenty-five. Except for the bald spot he pretended wasn't there and the way his hands got from thrashing, all scuffed and scabby looking.

Then Emily got that bloodlust in her eyes again and no amount of Sadie telling her what ladies did and didn't do seemed to help. Emily wanted to kill the Cleaver boy and would have, except Earl leaned over from across the aisle and said quietly, "That's enough."

Sadie could never understand it. Emily wiggled back in her seat, smoothed down her dress, locked her knees together. If she'd tried saying that's enough, Emily would have shot over her seat like a rocket.

"Yeah, Emily, that's enough," Sadie repeated with authority.

She wanted Emily to know she and Earl weren't about to be divided and conquered by one scrawny, runny-nosed freckle-flecked seven-year-old with jug ears and a missing front tooth. But Emily was staring out the window and after a while, Sadie forgot how exasperated Emily made her all the time and stared along with her.

"Glory be," Sadie said, under her breath.

Anchorage had gone all out.

Flags waved like hands from the platform and everybody in town had to have been there. Sadie wasn't sure how many that was exactly, but everybody was there all the same, hooting and hollering and clapping and carrying on and moving back respectfully to let them up the platform; while a MovieTone cameraman got the whole thing.

"You be good now," Sadie hissed, and squeezed Emily's hand real hard when they went by the camera, so Emily wouldn't have any thoughts about sticking out her tongue.

They shook a line of hands. On the way to the community hall for dinner, Earl told her they were the mayor, the president of the chamber of commerce, the head of the booster club and the organizer of the car committee, but Sadie thought the hands looked about the same.

The dinner was something else again.

Fifteen tables—Sadie counted them twice—covered with white linen and frippery.

The most interesting thing about the dinner was that everything had been grown right there in Alaska: there was beef and pork and potatoes and spinach and tomatoes and cabbage and sweet churned butter and raspberry jam and blueberry pie; but the best part was that Sadie didn't have to do the dishes.

She pushed herself back a little from the table and worked her thumb into the button under her belt and then Colonel F.

518

Ohlson, general manager of the railroad, was introduced by the mayor as "the father of the great movement which brought you here."

Sadie dropped her napkin accidentally, and Earl stooped over to pick it up, but his face turned a pasty gray color and sweat popped out on his forehead and his hand fell away from the napkin like his brain had forgotten what it had asked it to do.

"Earl, honey. What is it? What's wrong?" Sadie leaned over and clutched him, and they were whispering but nobody could hear them anyway, since they were all clapping for Colonel Ohlson, who was about to speak.

"I don't know," Earl mumbled, "but my arm feels funny. Hot and then numb."

Earl wasn't a pantywaist, that was one thing about him.

She leaned him back up in his chair and said, "I'm going to get the doctor. Meet you at the depot."

"No!" Earl said fiercely, but then the clapping stopped and she pushed back her chair and Colonel Ohlson said "Welcome home" and a lot of other things as Sadie ka-bump ka-bumped across the floor in her clunky shoes.

She knocked timidly, but there was nothing timid about that face. She had wide eyes and high, wide cheeks, and hair the dusky gold color that always reminded you of childhood summers, the gold of long wide roads, infinite days and your mother's voice floating across the hot throbbing air, calling you in for supper.

Her eyes were a vivid blue and she was underfed and taller than average. Cahill had the distinct feeling she didn't know she was pretty, and that added to her charm.

She was wearing a red beanie, a long serviceable plaid skirt and a heavy jacket, even though it was close to seventy outside. He suspected two children, or one messy one: the remnants of peanut butter and jelly trailed across her sleeve like an army of ants, and what appeared to be the bottom end of a scantily dressed cutout poked from the pocket of her skirt.

"Excuse me for bothering you, but I am looking for a doctor." Her voice was husky, a whiskey voice without the ruined face.

"I'm a doctor." Cahill closed the American Medical Association Journal he had been reading. The Richards girl suffered acutely from acne vulgaris, and in the latest issue of the journal, Dr. Jeffrey Charles Michael had written of the excellent results obtained from treating the infected area with X rays.

She looked at him doubtfully.

"What's the matter? You look as if you don't believe me."

"You're very handsome for a doctor."

Cahill burst out laughing. The sound was foreign in the room full of diplomas and plants and portentous books.

"Well, I am." He stood up and extended his hand. "Cahill Blue."

She shook it firmly. "Sadie Person."

"Please, sit down." He offered her a chair. "What can I do for you?"

"Well, Dr. Blue, it's for my husband. I can trust you, can't I?"

Again he was flummoxed. Twice in one minute. She was an amazing woman. "Certainly, I'm a doctor."

"Well," she settled back in her seat, hefting her bag up like a cranky child, "in that case, here it is. Earl and me—Earl's my husband—are colonists. You have heard of the colonists haven't you?"

"Oh, yes," Cahill reassured her. The town hadn't slept in a week, from the excitement.

"Well, good, practically everybody has, you know, but just about the time you get to counting on that, somebody will look at you and say 'Colonist who?' and you want to die, so I like to ask. Anyway, Earl's been feeling kind of poorly since Seward with his neck and all—"

"His neck?" Cahill interrupted.

"You know," Sadie patted her own uncertainly as if she was wondering what kind of a doctor he was, not to know a neck when he heard one. "Anyway, he wanted to hush it up, on account of the land drawing coming up and how all the colonists are supposed to be in the pink of health, but Earl usually is, which is why I came." She looked at him

520

breathlessly, as if waiting for a diagnosis.

"I'll have to see him."

"I figured that," Sadie said, pleased. "He'll be at the depot in a little while, and maybe you can kind of scoot him between two railroad cars or something and get it over with quick."

He found himself laughing again. "What?"

She sighed, "You're as exasperating as Emily, I do believe. He can't very well come here, can he? Not with those reporters tripping over themselves for a good picture. They'd blow it into something major, sure as I'm sitting here, and then we'd have to spend the next year working twice as hard as everybody else, just to show them how healthy we are. No, sir," she shook her head vigorously, "we'll put him between us and take him down across the tracks and make him stick out his tongue. You better bring some pills along, too, because we'll be leaving right away for the Mat Valley." She got up and went to the door. "Ready?"

He laughed, shook his head and got his bag.

Sadie wanted to walk, so they started up Barrow Street toward the railroad.

"You're not very happy, are you?" she said before they'd gone a block.

"Whatever made you say that?"

She shrugged. "I was born with a caul. You know what that is?" She put her hands uncertainly over her face. Any doctor who had trouble knowing where his neck was certainly needed all the help he could get.

"Yes."

"Well, anyway, you're not," she persisted. She looked at him slantwise. "What happened to your wife?"

"Excuse me?" He had trained himself never to think about Nelly; it filled him with terrible rage and loathing and longing for that other life he'd never had.

"Your wife," Sadie said patiently. "It wasn't a good marriage, was it?"

Cahill stopped walking abruptly and his bag banged Sadie in the shank. "I'm sorry," he said, and started walking fast. "I really don't think it's any of your—" He sighed distractedly.

Down below in the depot, a floor sweeper was taking the

opportunity before the colonists came back to tidy things up. Cahill saw him stoop down, pick something up, examine it and pocket it. A dime or something.

"No," he said finally. "It wasn't a good marriage."

"Want to talk about it? Sometimes it helps."

"Young woman, I've never talked about it."

"Then I expect you're way past due," Sadie said. She plopped to the grass and smiled widely, as if sitting with a perfect stranger discussing personal problems was an everyday occurrence.

Maybe it was, for her.

"They're not back or anything. It's more interesting than watching that man scrape the gum off the bottom of the depot benches."

Cahill laughed again and sat down. "I guess it is," he agreed. "It can't hurt anymore, if that's what you're worried about. They're only words and they just tell what you remember, but it happened a ways ago. Do you know what I mean?"

He leaned back and surrendered himself to the warm fragrance of the clover.

"Her name was Nelly. No. Her name was Flame."

"You can't remember which?" Sadie laughed, and Cahill found himself laughing too.

"I can remember which."

And then he told her about Nelly and how much he hated her, and about the woman he loved but could never have. He even told her about Logan.

Sadie listened, and after he had run completely down and lapsed into silence, she shook her head and said, "Seems to me you're doing a whole lot of belt whipping."

"What do you mean?"

She touched him gently on the arm. "Unhappiness is only a state of mind. Not a state to live, like Missouri."

And then the cars with the colonists came back and they started down the hill.

Cahill could see right away she was the strong one, even though Earl had muscles like the haunch of a deer.

"Bend your neck," he commanded, and Earl bit his lip when he did it.

522

"Earl, honey!" Sadie cried, and gripped his arm. They were using an office in the depot Cahill had discreetly borrowed. The shapes of the colonists outside moved and shifted across the clouded door.

"Have you had a fever lately?" Cahill asked shortly.

Earl shrugged. "Maybe a little one—"

"You never told me!" Sadie accused.

"It was just a little one, Sade."

"Did you throw up?"

"I thought it was bad chicken in Seward."

"How about a headache?"

"An axe through my head."

"It's nothing bad, is it, Doctor Blue? Tell me it's nothing bad," Sadie said.

Cahill looked from one young face to the other and his heart ached. "Could be nothing bad," he said cautiously.

"Or what?" Sadie sensed. "Or what?"

"Or it could be polio," Cahill said quietly.

Emily pulled on her mother. "Mommy, I—"

"Hush. Go sit down over there."

For once Emily obeyed her. She sat in a chair by the window and drew circles in the dust on the sill.

"It can't be," Sadie said flatly. "We're going to the Mat Valley today, to start a new life." She picked up her purse, clutched her husband's arm and said, "Emily, come along now. It's time to go."

"I can't let you," Cahill said quietly.

"What do you mean, you *can't*. Of course you can."

"If it is polio, Earl here needs to be in the hospital, you know that. And nobody really knows how the virus spreads, but it could be by breathing the same air as Earl." He nodded at the door. "We can't risk infecting everybody out there."

"No!" Sadie cried out. "I don't believe it! It's not happening. It's not."

"Sadie, he's right." Earl's eyes were fearful. "I need to be in the hospital."

"Now don't you quit on me, Earl Person." She flung herself at him, beating his chest. "We're going to the Mat Valley and we're going to start a new—" She slid sobbing down his body and clutched his knees.

Cahill touched her gently. "Come on now, come on. Not everybody gets the really bad kind anyway. He could be up and out in a week. The worst part doesn't last long; we'll know by next Friday."

He helped her up and she honked her nose into his handkerchief and squared her shoulders.

"Don't know what came over me," she said. "Everything's going to be fine. Just fine."

Only before the week was out, it wasn't.

Cahill knew by Monday that things had taken a turn. All Earl's limbs ached and his back roared with fire.

Earl knew it too. His face grew even more gaunt, and his eyes beseeched Cahill to save him. Cahill kept him in bed, motionless, frustrated by the lack of anything else he could do, and let the disease burn itself out.

"Hon." Earl's voice was a croak. "I'm scared."

"Earl Alvin Person." Sadie only called him that when she was especially mad at him, and of course she wasn't now, but, she needed him to snap out of it, but quick.

So she sat straight up until her knees bumped under the metal tube railing on his bed and said again, "Earl Alvin Person, you cut out this nonsense right this minute, hear?"

Tears rolled down his eyes and his nose got real wet, but he never said a word.

"We've got a homestead to think about. The drawing's next week as soon as the Michigan and Wisconsin farmers get in."

He shook his head from side to side, but slowly, like he was a horse flopping. "I can't walk, Sade."

"What do you mean, you can't? Doctor Blue says you can get out of that bed any time you want now and give it a try. Your knees'll be wobbly at first, but don't worry. By the time we get the potatoes going—"

"I said I can't walk."

"What do you mean?"

He stared savagely out the window.

"Earl, honey, what do you mean?" She got up and leaned over him.

524

"Get away from me."

"Earl, you're acting might peculiar and I'm not going to put up with it. Now you tell me right out what you mean."

"I tried walking today." He swallowed, blinked fast like there was dust in the air, only there wasn't. "Walking." He cackled. "That's a good one."

He rolled his head and looked her square in the eye, and Sadie thought suddenly he needed a haircut.

"I can't move, Sade. My arms or my legs."

A week—only a week. They were going to be farmers. Settle the valley.

"Doctor Blue says sometimes there's an amazing comeback. After you give yourself a chance to heal."

"I said I goddamn can't move my goddamn legs and arms." He rolled his head back and forth, pounding it on the pillow. His eyes were closed and his mouth was open in a scream, only he wasn't screaming, only making little noises deep in his throat, and for the first time, Sadie was afraid.

"Listen to me, Earl." She sat on the rail and leaned down on him, holding his shoulders. "Listen to me," she said fiercely. "Don't you quit on me. Don't you quit. You can do anything you set your mind to. Anything. But don't you quit on me."

His shoulders shook in silent agony. "You're wrong, Sade. You're wrong. The only one I ever met who could make things come out of the air was you."

"It's because I believe! You've got to believe. Just believe it and you can do it. You can."

"Sadie, I can't walk. Get that through your thick skull."

"You watch your mouth," she said tartly. "I don't deserve any abuse and I won't tolerate it. There's got to be a plan in here someplace. Something good will come out of this."

"Sure there's a plan," he cracked. "Plant me in the potato patch. You won't believe how they'll grow."

"Your brother. I'm going to send for your brother."

"I hate Morris! I hate him."

"He'll come, that's the main thing. Beggars can't be choosers."

"I'm not a beggar, Sade. I'm a cripple. A pleege. A baseball stop."

"Listen to me. We're going to build this place and plant those crops and ~~you're going to walk and maybe we'll even make another baby.~~ Like Emily, only quieter. A son. How'd you like that? That would be something, wouldn't it?"

"You've got it all planned out, don't you?" he taunted. "You've got the future all wrapped up, Sade. Hooray for you. Except for one little thing. I goddamn can't move my goddamn body."

"Don't you take the Lord's name in vain."

His face crumpled and he opened his mouth wide and started to cry. Sadie pressed herself to him, held his head, murmured to him, kissed him.

When he was calmer, she whispered, "You remember one thing, Earl Alvin Person. I love you. And there's nothing in this world we can't rise above. Nothing. Now try to sleep and I'll be right here. Right here."

She stood up, right by his head so he could see her, and stayed there until he closed his eyes.

Her hair was in braids pinned to the top of her head, and that's all he saw for the first fifteen minutes while she got it out. Finally he passed her a tissue and she blew her nose.

"I just can't believe it. Why Earl? Why?"

"I'm so sorry. I was going to tell you myself. Gently. I had no idea he'd try to walk on his own."

"Gentle or not, it doesn't change a thing. My granddaddy always used to say, 'What is, is, and what ain't, ain't.' Course he's dead now, God rest his soul." She blew her nose again, took a deep shuddery breath and said, "I want us to go to the valley right away. I think the faster Earl gets there, the faster he'll heal."

"He might never walk again."

"Now you're talking like he is!" she flared. "I won't hear it. I won't. Earl Alvin Person is going to get out of the chair under his own power and walk. I know it." She clutched and unclutched the tissue.

"It's going to take a lot of work," Cahill said finally.

"I've worked hard before. I can do it again."

"He's going to need therapy."

"You tell me what to do, I'll do it."

"He'll need hot, moist packs applied to his arms and legs four times daily for a half an hour. And you're going to have to manipulate the limbs for him. I'll type up a complete list. Another thing you can try is exercising him under water, in the tub."

"In the tub," Sadie repeated.

"I don't mean to sound negative, but I seriously question taking him away so soon."

"Doctor Blue." She hunched forward and her eyes bored into him. "If I don't take him away *right now*, he's going to die here. I can feel it. He's already given up. I can't allow that to go on. I cannot. I will not."

She had lost even more weight during the last week and Cahill felt a flood of compassion. "One thing, Sade. You can't run on Empty. You've got to start eating right and sleeping. You'll be no use to him at all, otherwise." She nodded her head as if that was part of the treatment she was memorizing.

"How are you doing, Sadie?" he asked gently.

She nodded her head in little jerks. "Think I'm over the worst of it." She stared out the window, then back, and for the first time, something almost bashful came into her face. "I have a question."

She reddened and Cahill guessed. "I don't know what your marital relations will be like," he said gently. "Or even if you can resume genital intercourse. It depends on how much recovery there is. In my opinion, based on his condition now, no."

There was a slight tightening around the mouth, that was all.

She got up, extended her hand and said, "I surely do hope you'll see us soon, Doctor Blue. And I can't thank you enough for your kindness to us, and the way you saved his life."

She picked up her beanie, arranged it over the glowing ribbons of hair. "I'll pick up Emily now at the hotel and come back for Earl when I've worked out the arrangements."

Cahill had a full day of appointments afterwards, and an emergency appendectomy, but he couldn't stop thinking of her and wondering what would happen.

She was the strongest woman he'd ever met.

There was endless light, which Sadie was grateful for since it went along with the endless work. They were in Camp 9, south of Palmer, and if you could eat and sleep scenery, they'd have been fat and sassy instead of owing their soul to the company store.

The colonists bought everything on credit: land, barn, livestock, household goods, house and food. It was supposed to cost about three thousand dollars, payable over thirty years, but Sadie figured out right away they'd have to eat less and plant more, or she'd have to live to a hundred to pay it all back.

Morris, Earl's brother, got there right about the time the transients were roughing in the root cellar and foundation, and immediately took off his suit jacket and rolled up his sleeves, claiming the more he did for free, the less the transients would charge to their bill.

Earl added that to his list of reasons for hating him.

They designed a one-story, flat-roofed house everybody said was modernistic, but Sadie just called it practical. A wheelchair can't get upstairs.

She hoed, and Emily and she planted potatoes, carrots, radishes, asparagus, turnips, peas, string beans, oats and cabbages. The soil was sandy loam, better than the red clay of home.

She milked the cow they had drawn in the lottery—a spine-sagging, udder-swaying Guernsey of indeterminate age with foul breath and a fouler temper—built a pen for the pigs and shod the horse. She split logs for wood, washed and dried and ironed; she weeded and carried water and made meals; and when she was tired of that, she manipulated Earl's limbs.

At night she fell asleep instantly, which helped take her mind off the other thing; and besides, all living in a tent, with the walls so thin you could hear Elvi Kertulla singing a lullaby two tents over, they couldn't even if Earl could.

Which was beginning to look less and less likely every day.

Not that he wasn't getting feeling back—he was, in his hands, and Sadie would give him things to hold like a can of beets or a potato. It was his listlessness, like he was always about to apologize but couldn't find the words, so he ducked and bowed his head instead, with his eyes red and watery, like he had ragweed for eyelashes.

By the time the frame house went up on their forty-acre tract, and the crops leafed out, Earl could wheel himself across the floor and use a fork strapped to his hand. Sadie still had to cut his meat for him, but what was that, compared to how still his hands had been?

"It's everything," Earl had snapped. The dinner table got quiet and Morris said "Pass the butter, Sade" like he hadn't heard Earl and seen the way his eyes flashed.

Earl shoved himself away from the table, trying to make the length in one move, and the chair rolled away by itself, clicking over the planks, before he shoved it hard again and went over next to the front window to stare out over the radishes.

Emily had gotten real quiet the past few months, and now her eyes shifted from Sadie to Uncle Morris and back to the corned beef and cabbage stuck on her fork. She put it up, checked it, and put it down again.

Sadie had had about all she could stand of it and so she said, "Clear the table now, Emily, and then you and Uncle Morris can do the dishes."

Morris didn't think much of the idea, but when he saw Sadie's eyes, he got up right away and cooched Emily under the chin, chucked her in the belly and hauled her off to the kitchen.

Sadie waited until she heard the screen door bang and knew they were going for water, and then she put her hands on her hips and said, "You cut this out right now, Earl Alvin Person. I'm not going to stand for it."

"Stand for what?" He thought something was funny then, and he laughed, and said again, "Stand for what, Sade? Stand for what?"

She got down and gripped the chair arms. "I'm not going to put up with you feeling sorry for yourself. You're not the only one that got polio. Armstrong's littlest got it twice as bad as you. They had to cut a place for a tube in his throat, just to breathe, so you count your blessings and stop this right now."

"Sadie, don't you see what you have here?"

"Hells bells," she said. She never swore. Earl's interest perked.

"Hells bells," she repeated, "you've got a blind spot as big as the great divide, and I don't mean the Grand Canyon either. I'm talking about the one between your ears. You've got your mind, don't you? You've got your hands, your arms? What's wrong with you?"

"I can't walk." He pushed himself away from her and rolled the chair across the room, until a knee banged the sheet-iron fireplace. His crazy bone would have ached something awful, only he couldn't feel it.

"Listen to me, Earl." She marched over and put her hands on his shoulders. "I married you til death do us part, and that's exactly how long I plan to stay."

He bowed his head and began to weep. "You'd be better off without me."

"You cut out that kind of talk. You work on moving your body and never give up." She wrapped her arms around him and kissed his neck. "Everything will work out. You'll see."

"You really believe that, don't you?"

"Absolutely. Faith brought us this far. I expect it'll carry us the rest of the way." She fell silent. "You know what I do sometimes, right before I fall asleep? I close my eyes real tight and I can see you walking. You look so good, Earl, tall and proud and not an ounce of fat, just striding through the potatoes." Her eyes wet.

She tightened her arms around his neck. "It's going to happen that way, too. You'll see. Just that way."

"It's funny." Earl's voice was bitter. "When I close my eyes to sleep, all I see is nothing."

He'd been seeing them for the past week, out of the corner of his eye. At first there was only one, then two, and then by the time Sadie rolled out the dough for the Fourth of July pies, he could tell by the stealthy scrabbling that the walls were riddled with rats.

Nobody believed him.

Morris maintained there weren't any, because this part of

Alaska didn't have rats, but Earl knew Morris was only trying to bring him down a peg in front of Sadie.

That's why he couldn't go to the picnic.

He didn't tell Sadie, of course; she would have insisted, and then he would have had to sit there for hours, locked in his chair, while Morris played his tomfool banjo in the Glee Club and everybody looked through Earl and smiled at something behind him, like he wasn't really there, and asked Sadie in hushed undertones how everything was.

I can hear fine, you idiots! he always wanted to scream. It's my legs that're bad.

"I'm leaving lunch right here on the stove for you. It's hot."

"So be careful?" he taunted. Everybody treated him like a kid. Sometimes he didn't know if he hated Sadie because she could walk or because she still loved him.

She flushed and said evenly, "We'll be home by supper."

"Don't hurry on my account." He rolled himself to the front window. Wimmer's Ford was churning dust on the road toward them, and Earl called over his shoulder, "They're here."

Behind him, Sadie put three blueberry pies carefully in a box, one on top of the other separated by dish towels and Morris and Emily divided up the Bell jars full of carrots.

"Everybody's got everything?" Sadie asked. "Emily?"

"Yeah, mom."

"You got your doll?"

"Course."

Sadie came over and bent down and kissed Earl real fast on the cheek, more kissing the air than anything, and Earl grunted and looked out the window.

"Better hurry. Wimmer's getting out."

"You'll be okay?"

He didn't bother answering and after a minute, Sadie said, "Well. We'll be going then."

She clunked across the floor in those awful green shoes she had bought on sale in Le Seur, the fabric so cheap she'd already had to stitch up the straps twice.

He didn't turn his head but he could feel her there, watching him from the kitchen doorway, "Better hurry," he called shortly.

She went out the screen door and came around the front, handing over the pies to Morris inside the car. She waved. Earl pretended to get real busy with his chair and when he looked up, the door had slammed and Wimmer started up the car.

Earl didn't waste any time.

He rolled himself into the bedroom. Morris had carved a piece of diamond willow, punching the knots out and polishing the yellow wood with linseed oil until it shone like satin. It was propped up in the closet. Sadie was going to make it into a floor lamp.

He rolled the chair around the brass bed. The wheel caught on the quilt and it yanked the spread down some, but Earl didn't stop.

The rats were louder now.

His gun was hanging up high in its holster, on a nail inside the closet next to his church clothes. He experimented with the willow stick and finally hooked the holster belt. The gun dived into one of his good shoes. He grunted, straining, and picked it up.

He was sweating. It rolled down the inside of his cotton shirt, only up high where he could feel it. It probably rolled from the ridge of his spine clear down to the crease in his seat, but he couldn't feel that so it didn't count.

He ducked his head down, lifting the gun between his arms and unsnapped the holster with his teeth.

He was panting.

Something scrabbled in the living room.

"Dirty bastards," he muttered. He dropped the gun to his lap and rolled hard into the living room. He stared wildly.

He could feel their hard shiny eyes watching him.

He ducked his head again and pulled the gun out with his teeth. It was a long-barreled navy Colt .44, with six brass shells.

Such a pretty gun. A clean, lean, mean gun.

He whapped back the hammer with his arms and shifted it around until he was staring down the barrel, mesmerized.

A rat scuttled across the floor and leaped onto the chair. Earl sank his teeth around the barrel. It was salty and smelled of hunts through the Minnesota woods, of gray squirrels with burning fur dropping from trees at his feet; of old Spot whoofling through the sharp leaves.

He shoved his finger awkwardly through the trigger cavity. On the dining room table, Morris had left a pack of Lucky Strikes. The smoker's best friend, the ads said. It'll never let you down.

The rat was chewing through his scalp. Earl could feel the sharp teeth, the soft, delicate tongue.

He pulled the trigger.

In the microsecond before the bullet smashed into his head, spraying bone and scalp and hair and blood across the front window, Earl thought, I don't want to die.

They came back full of pie and speeches around supper time, arms smarting from sun and mosquitos. Morris got out of the front seat and pushed the seat up for Sadie. It was bright as noon, and the sun glanced off the front window like a mirror, only the window was cloudy.

Morris patted for his smokes, crumpled the empty pack, looked again.

Sadie was saying, "We surely do thank you, Mr. and Mrs. Wimmer. Thank them for the ride, Emily."

Morris clamped his hands on Sadie's shoulder. "Listen to me."

"What is it?" She straightened and smiled at Mrs. Wimmer in the front seat and slammed the door shut.

"Take Emily and go for a walk."

"What is it?"

"Just do as I say." He strode up the path.

"Is it Earl? Has something happened to Earl?"

She ran after him, caught the screen door before it slammed shut. Emily had started crying outside, running up the path.

"Don't come in." Sadie commanded. She was looking at the gun on the linoleum, right inside the kitchen.

"Oh, my God. Oh, no. Oh, my God." Morris backed into the kitchen and gripped her arms. "Don't go in there, Sade. Easy now, easy now."

But she threw off his arms and ran in.

Earl sat in his chair, knees sagging apart. The shot had blown off the back of his head and splashed it across the room.

Sadie dropped to her knees, hysterical. "No!" she screamed. "No!"

It was a gay drift of blood and white bone and brown hair and gray brain chunks, but the front of his face was the same old Earl: mouth opened in a puzzled smile, as if he couldn't understand what all the fuss was about.

Forty-Three

The same summer the Matanuska farmers came, Jordy Jackson turned twelve and changed her name to Natasha, refusing to answer her mother, Flame, when she forgot. Natasha spent a lot of time in front of the mirror trying out expressions; and when she wasn't there, she was in the front row of the Empress Theatre, watching Cary Grant make moony eyes over Jean Harlow through a blizzard of popcorn thrown at the screen.

But Jordy was tall and wiry and never remembered exactly where she'd left her body, only that it was around here someplace, the last she'd seen it. It usually went on without her, anyway. Once she whacked herself on the head, walking into the gun cabinet, and dropped an entire angel food cake with heavenly frosting into the head judge's lap at the 4-H show. She didn't win. Once she caught an innocent thread on a shard of door frame as she sauntered past, and by the time she noticed it, two trips around the dining-room table to dip into the jelly-bean jar and a half an hour examining herself in the reflection of the china cabinet, most of the hem was out of her skirt and her petticoat had a close relationship with her scabby shins.

She sensed things were in the wind, inevitable as the tide and a spelling test every Friday—incomprehensible things that would change her into someone beautiful, who knew the right thing to say to a man in the moonlight.

But Roy just couldn't see it. "You're hopeless," he announced with finality.

It was the summer before he turned sixteen, the third year in a row they weren't speaking.

Oh, they said things like "If you don't change your underwear, next week, you can teach it to stand up and

535

do tricks."

Or "Major Edward Bowes called and says ~~he's got a place for you on Amateur Hour.~~ One of the baboons died."

But that was about it.

Roy hadn't grown since he was twelve. Nobody brought it up except Jordy when she was really mad at him, and then she always felt bad and tried to make up for it, only he'd scowl and tell her to beat it, he had important things to do. For a while, the folks had taken him to doctors, but nobody seemed to know what to do.

Their dad and mom owned Jackson's Flying Air and Roy had tinkered with the Lockheed Vega seaplanes since he could make a fist around a wrench. Four of the twenty-one planes that flew out of Anchorage belonged to the Jacksons, and Roy loved them all; patting the props like the backside of a woman, gently, with the flat of his hand.

He had never smarted off to grown-ups, and the plane mechanics accepted him as half-grown, even though Jordy knew better, and never failed to tell him so. Around the men, he wore Aqua Velva, even though there wasn't any earthly reason, and stuck his hands in his back pockets, thumbs out, while they talked over Roosevelt's New Deal.

At home Roy waited until his father was lighting a cigar, his eyes clouded with smoke, and his mother got up from the table to turn on "Amos 'N Andy" on KFQD. Then he'd take a gob of mashed potatoes mixed with catsup, stuff it in his mouth, expand his cheeks and punch them together, squirting it out in a disgusting glop, whispering to her that that's what the pimple on her nose looked like, when he'd caught her squeezing it.

She didn't hate him. She tolerated him the way she tolerated measles when she was five and getting glasses when she turned ten. Roy was one of God's adversities, sent to make her a stronger person.

Occasionally she lapsed into eye gouging and finger bending, and once she tied all the strings on his shoes together in a line and knotted the cuffs of his pants and stood at the end of his bed and yelled *FIRE!* but mostly, they grunted when they were forced to and pretended they were each an only child.

By summer the habit of ignoring him was so ingrained that

Jordy almost let what happened next get by her. The only thing that alerted her was how nice Roy was, all of a sudden. He only did that when he wanted something, and it didn't take her long to figure it out. Roy wanted to be left alone.

It was a Saturday night. Usually Roy would be out in the backyard, working on his model airplane. Calling it a model made it sound small, and that was one thing it wasn't. It was longer than Roy was tall—of course, you have to remember that he was short for his age—but the plane had flat wings that rounded at the tip and slanted up like the wings of a butterfly, supported by a truss of balsa wood and wheels he'd bought at Loussac's that had once girdled the big wheels on a five-year-old's bike.

Training wheels, Roy had explained patiently, as if anybody could see by looking at them that's what they'd been. Then Jordy'd say, "Well, excuse me for living" and kind of innocently lean her palm up on the real glass windshield.

Then he would jump up and chase her down to the fenceline overlooking the drop to the railroad on the flats, and that would give Jordy the excuse to beat him up. That would take them until nine o'clock, when they would trot inside to listen to "The Jack Benny Show."

But this Saturday night, Roy cleared the table without a word and disappeared. It was Jordy's turn to do dishes. Her mom had said that a long time ago they had had a servant, and Jordy couldn't figure out why they had used him up then when anybody could see they really needed him now. But her mother said it built character. Jordy thought she could get along with a little less, if it meant never using another Brillo pad.

Anyway, sometime after the glasses but before the frying pan she'd let soak, Roy banged down the stairs and Jordy came out of the kitchen to look.

His face was flaming pink, as if he'd scrubbed the skin off, and he was wearing a tie. His hair was damp and skinned back and he'd managed to get most of the grease out from under his fingernails. Actually, Roy didn't have fingernails, since he bit them down to the quick, but the raggedy nubs of cuticle weren't as black as usual.

And he smelled to high heaven—a mixture of Aqua Velva

and talcum powder and Listerine. If he had been a radio, he'd be turned up loud enough to bring hearing back into old man Witner's ears.

"Peeeee-yuuuuu," Jordy bleated, honking her nose. "Somebody forgot to take out the garbage."

"That's enough, Jordy," her father said from the sofa by the mahogany radio. Jordy was amazed what he could hear when he wanted to. He'd bought a hearing aid two years ago, but usually it sat in a blue velvet box upstairs on his dresser. "That's enough," he said again.

He and Roy exchanged a conspiratorial look, and then Roy ambled over to the dormer window, hitched his shoulders and buttoned his suit.

He slid his wallet out, counted his money and patted it back in place; then he said grandly as he banged out the door and strode down the steps, "Don't wait up for me."

Jordy slung the dish towel over her neck and said, "Where's he going? To a funeral?"

"On a date," her father said and smiled into the paper.

"A date? Who'd go out with him?"

But her father didn't answer because her mother came out of the kitchen then, with a glass of cherry Kool Aid and said, "Our little boy is growing up," in a teary voice and her father put down the paper and put his arms around her.

An arm around her. Out of the question, totally. They were halfway through the Paramount newsreel and had seen Haile Selassie of Ethopia appealing to the League of Nations for more arms. Roy only needed one, but it had to work right, so he could identify with the old emperor's position.

He shifted his body and felt Stephanie in the dark next to him. She was taller than he was by about three inches, but she carried it in the legs, so sitting down it didn't matter. Stephanie had fiery red hair and a soft bosom that had hit him squarely in the throat the one and only time they danced in the gym.

She was beautiful, and she didn't seem to mind the difference in height; at least they never talked about it. They hardly talked at all.

But Sissy was something else again. Sissy was Stephanie's younger sister by two years, which made her barely thirteen. She was chaperoning them, and so had the upper hand when it came to ordering supplies. For starters, she demanded jawbreakers, Tootsie Rolls, a caramel all-day sucker and a Butterfingers; and those were just for her. She had brown hair and a hollow leg.

Stephanie ordered popcorn, but Roy wasn't hungry.

Stephanie could pack away more popcorn than any girl he'd ever seen. She had kind of a rhythm going; hand rummaging through the bag, popping it into her mouth, chewing, swallowing and reaching, her eyes never leaving the screen. Roy counted how long it took, like a prisoner counting how long it took the guard to go to the east wall and back, and when he had it down, he plunged his hand in.

Their hands collided in the bag.

Roy had it planned so that would happen. He was going to follow it up with some casual maneuvering, until maybe their slippery fingers locked in the salty darkness. After that was a blur, except that somewhere in there, the organ music would majestically swell and Stephanie would stop eating popcorn and turn her greasy mouth to his and they would kiss, ignoring the announcer telling them about hog prices soaring to a new height.

Roy would do the soaring for everybody.

What happened was that his fingers touched hers and jerked away so fast the bag exploded, and Stephanie shrieked, "It's all over my skirt!" and spent the first reel of the new comedy *In The Spotlight* dabbing out the butter. It never completely came out and it looked like she'd wet her pants.

Roy shoved his hands in his pockets and cursed himself while Stephanie stood at the drinking fountain and rubbed and Sissy stared through the red velvet curtains at the movie.

He was going to get more popcorn, but Stephanie suggested a Baby Ruth, so he got three of those and some Red Hots for Sissy and three Cokes. They got back to their seats right about the time the famous stage dancer Hal Le Roy was dipping and diving across the stage in a spectacle of balloons.

Stephanie ate right through the first Babe Ruth and had started in on the second when the main feature came on, and she settled back in her seat to watch Jean Harlow, tossed into the swirl of penthouse and Palm Springs gaiety in *The Girl from Missouri.*

Roy knew his chance when he saw it, so he lopped his arm casually across the back of the crimson velour seat. Stephanie didn't seem to notice; she kept watching and eating, watching and eating, so he inched his hand next to her back and left it there.

Right about the time Jean Harlow met Lionel Barrymore, his hand started going to sleep.

Pins and needles. It was agony. He couldn't concentrate on the movie, so he shifted closer to her and dropped his numb hand on her shoulder.

Afterward he walked her home. Sissy was a real pest, hanging on him and chattering, but Roy tolerated it on account of her being Stephanie's sister. Maybe she'd put in a good word for him.

At the door Stephanie said in a mean voice, "You go on in right now."

He could see Sissy wasn't about to miss anything, so he said, "It's all right, Sis. My hand's still asleep from the movie."

She cheered right up and Stephanie opened the door for her and shoved her in.

He grinned at Stephanie and scuffed his foot into hers. "I sure had a good time," he said.

Stephanie's eyes filled up and she stared off somewhere. "I was kind of wondering—" Her voice trailed away and she looked down the street.

"Wondering what?"

"I couldn't help noticing how you had a hold of Sissy's shoulder all night long." Her voice trembled.

"Sissy?" He was dumbfounded. "Sissy," he said again. He couldn't think of anything to say.

"Good night, Roy." Stephanie walked inside and turned off the porch light.

Roy stumbled home in a daze. Sissy. Sissy.

Upstairs, Jordy's door was open across the hall and she

called in the darkness, "Well, how was it? Did you do anything stupid?"

That next Wednesday, Jordy and Roy were walking down Fourth Avenue toward the Anchorage Grill, and Jordy was twitting him, trying to find out who the girl was, when Roy stopped dead in his tracks and his mouth fell open; not in wonder or shock, but more in hurt surprise.

Jordy turned and stared. Going by in a Dodge was a girl with curly red hair. She was nestled into the neck of a big fat-lidded, flat-nosed boy nine feet tall who weighed three hundred pounds.

The girl rolled off of him and over to the window. Jordy noticed her nail polish matched the color of Roy's face: a kind of rich mahogany.

"Afternoon, Roy," the girl said.

"Afternoon, Stephanie."

"Would you care to take a spin? There's room in the back seat."

"No. I'm due back at Merrill Field in half an hour."

Jordy knew it was a complete lie; he had the rest of the day off. But when she started to remind him, he elbowed her and kept walking, only faster this time, and didn't stop until he hit the grill at 429 Fourth Avenue and slid into a stool at the counter.

The wood counter ran along the entire east side of the grill, and Tony Cravalini, a loud, affectionate, emotional Greek, ran it like boot camp: throwing orders and hamburgers around with snappy precision.

"What'll it be, hah? You look a little pale, a little pale, my friend. My short friend. What'll you have? Chicken's not bad. Fixed a batch for the chamber today. There's some left."

The Anchorage Chamber of Commerce met once a week at the grill for lunch on Wednesdays, but they always sat at oilcloth tables near the window.

"He's not feeling well," Jordy said cautiously. She wasn't used to sticking up for her brother, and found herself swimming in dark water.

"Whatsa matter? Lose your best friend? Lose your girl, is

that what happened? Hey, Fredo, the short kid here lost his girl."

~~He leaned in~~ confidentially. "Fredo wishes he could trade you problems, you better believe it. Straight across the board." He straightened and bellowed, "FREDO!"

"Yah, yah, yah," Fredo said good-naturedly. The rush was over for the time being and he was polishing catsup bottles in the booths.

"Fredo's got too many girls and not enough energy." He winked at Roy. "He'll give you one—how's about that? How do you like that?"

Roy didn't say anything, just kept staring at the big sign proclaiming We Serve Fresh Matanuska Eggs Daily.

"I think he'd rather have a Coke," Jordy said, then turned to Roy. "It's on me."

The Cokes came and Roy looked at his like it was his last meal.

Jordy didn't know what to say. "You can't win 'em all," occurred to her, but in the end she said, "Kinda quiet in here for a change. Course, maybe somebody's in the back room having a banquet or something. Getting married or something."

As soon as she said it she put her face in her hand, then sucked the Coke noisily.

The door banged open and Jordy hoped they'd all sit in a booth, but they came right over and sat next to Roy.

She stabbed a chunk of ice with her straw and lifted it out.

"We serve fresh Matanuska Eggs daily," the voice recited. "What the sam hill kind of bird is a Matanuska?"

Tony roared, and Jordy and Roy stared at each other in wonder. The voice. That wonderful soft Oklahoma twang of a voice. They'd heard it a million times before on the radio.

They turned in unison. Sitting next to Roy—

"Will Rogers," they said reverently, in unison.

"Pleased to meet ya." He stretched out a warm hand, shook each of theirs and said to the man behind the counter, "Do you have any lamb? I've had a hankering for it ever since we flew over McKinley and I saw it on the hoof."

"Of course, Mr. Rogers." Tony spatulaed off the grill and

put down sliced potatoes and both sides of a muffin.

All they could do was stare. He was wearing grease-stained yellow corduroy pants, a gray open-necked shirt, and his hair was sticking up in tufts under the punched-in hat.

The door opened and a crush of people crowded in, but not too close; except the reporter, a crepey-skinned, gray-haired lugubrious man who had been old even when he covered the gold rush as a young man. He leaned right over Will and watched the way he cut his roast leg of lamb and put catsup on the potatoes.

"Where are you going, Mr. Rogers?" His name was Charlie Settlemeier and he worked for the Anchorage *Times*.

"Wiley Post and me are on the way to the Matanuska."

"The Matanuska," Settlemeier repeated, scribbing ponderously. "And what do you plan to do there?"

"Why, I plan to see if they've run out of committees."

The crowd tittered. The federal government had been sending people to investigate the colony for months.

"Committees for what?" asked the reporter. His elbows were covered with mosquito bites, and he slouched under the felt hat.

"Committees to investigate the Matanuska. We heard they were coming so fast, the supply was about exhausted, and I met a revenue cutter man at Juneau. A woman was on the way and was the last of the tribe they could find to send."

Tony guffawed behind the counter. Charlie Settlemeier thumbed back his glasses and wrote it all down.

Will turned to Roy and said, "So what's the problem, son?"

"Problem?" he whispered.

"I can spot a troubled man. What's eating you?"

It was funny. It was like they were all alone. Will turned and said nicely to the reporter, "This part's off the record." Charlie hooked the pen in his pocket and stepped back into the crowd.

"I'm short, Will," Roy said softly, so only he could hear. "I'm fifteen, pret' near sixteen, and everybody takes me for my sister's younger brother."

Light glanced off the pie case at the end of the counter and the Frigidaire ice maker hummed. Will's face glowed. He tipped back his hat.

"Heck, son, how tall do you think I am?" he said in an undertone. "I'll tell ya, last time I checked, about five foot eight. That doesn't have anything to do with what's inside. If you think you're a man, you are. It's that simple. If you *feel* short, you are. But if you can get comfortable with it, like an old shoe, maybe joke about it, nobody's going to think twice about it. You understand?"

He looked straight at him with kind gray eyes.

"Thank you," Roy said humbly.

He leaned over to Jordy. "And what do you want to be?"

"An actress like your daughter, Mary," Jordy whispered. Even Roy didn't know, but this was like talking in the presence of a priest; everything was sacrosanct; no, a priest if he had the power to right all wrongs, correct evil, bestow gifts. Will Rogers shone with a light and Jordy felt as if she were being touched by a great wind.

"Mary?" Will's face lit up. "You know about Mary?"

Jordy snapped open her purse and pulled out a clipping. "It was in the *Times* last week," she said shyly. Mary was in a summer-stock production of *Ceiling Zero*. Jordy liked the whole review except the part about the ending: in the last act was a fatal plane crash. With both parents pilots, Jordy lived in mortal fear of it.

Will read through the review and asked, "Could I keep it?"

Jordy nodded.

"Thanks." He put it in his pocket and reached for a piece of pie.

"You've got some growing to do," he said to Jordy, but this time Roy didn't fill up with despair, the way he usually did when people talked about height. He knew Will meant growing inside, and certainly Jordy had plenty of that left.

"I'm twelve," she said. "Last birthday."

"Work hard, and give me a call when you reach eighteen. Maybe I can help you."

"Really, Mr. Rogers?"

"Sure." He clapped Roy on the back. "Now you remember what I said?"

"Always," Roy said.

Charlie Settlemeier saw a rip in the conversation and dived

544

in. "Will you go fishing for some of our trout or try for a bear?"

"Nope. Don't fish, don't hunt; wouldn't know what to use for bait or how to shoot or what to do with the victims. Just don't have the urge."

"You're out for a good time, then?" Charlie turned the page in his notebook.

"Never had such a good time in my life," he twinkled. "Mrs. Rogers is thousands of miles away, headed for New England on a visit—and am I enjoying myself! Don't know just where I'm going, probably as far as Bering Straits with Post, and then back. Course he's been around the world twice, and I wouldn't mind going myself again if Mrs. Rogers didn't send the dogs after me about the time I hit China."

"Have they heard about the Matanuska project outside?" Charlie inched closer.

Will nodded, thumbing his jaw. "The papers have been full of it, and I will add my daily shot when I get there."

The door opened and someone said, "Your taxi is here, Mr. Rogers." He and his friends got up. He clapped a friendly hand on Roy's shoulder.

"So, adios, until we meet again. Glad I came. Here's hopin' to come again and linger longer."

He clasped hand after hand until he reached the door, turned and waved his hat.

Charlie slid into the still warm seat next to Roy and slapped down his pad. "So what did he say to you, son?"

But Roy only smiled and said to Jordy, "A piece of pie would go mighty nice with that Coke, if you're still buying."

Forty-Four

Will Rogers wasn't the only one on his way to the colony that Wednesday in the middle of August; Cahill Blue took the train in the morning, carrying a stack of patient files he was bringing to Nurse De Foras in Palmer. The manila folders were only an inch deep, but they spelled misery and disruption for thirty families. Two epidemics had swept through the small colony. Six children had died from scarlatina, and three little ones lay paralyzed with polio. And, of course, there was Earl.

Cahill had met the families, given what comfort he could, and felt the pain of knowing it wasn't enough. Cahill sighed, leaned back and let the scenery seduce him.

The conductor was on the loudspeaker, relating the history of the colony to tourists. They peered out the windows through their Kodaks, snapping the wild tumble of trees and foaming rivers. Most of them were on their way to Mount McKinley, where they would tour the park in a bus. But in Palmer the conductor announced a half-hour rest stop and everybody scrambled out.

Gamely they snapped pictures of dogs scratching in the dirt in front of Felton's General Store and crazy Juice Suet, the octogenarian who kept himself going by charging tourists who wanted to take his picture.

De Foras was out on rounds. Cahill left the files with her assistant and walked through the dust back to Felton's. Juice had a knot of tourists hooked, and they all had their wallets out.

Once he'd taught accounting at Stanford, but he had dropped out, grown long hair and purchased a pair of red suspenders to go with his army fatigues. He was telling them all how he had been raised by wolves and rescued by nuns and needed money to support his mother.

It was mail day at Felton's, and the rear of the store was crammed with colonists. Cahill raised his voice and asked if anybody was going toward Camp 9.

"Sure," Felton said. "Give me a chance to finish this up and I'll take you myself." He was dark and ruddy with naturally red lips and quick hands that darted over the letters.

Cahill poked around the store. The colonists had their own well-stocked commissary down the road where they could charge things; after they picked up the mail, they went right by the meager supplies on Felton's shelves and back out into the sun.

Felton slammed down the mail fence, bolting it to the counter, and hung a sign Post Office Closed. Come Back Next Week.

"I got a disc harrow in this morning for Armstrong," Felton said. "He lives out that way. I told him I'd run it over. Who do you want to see?"

They walked outside and Felton locked the porch, flipping over the Open sign to Closed.

"The Person family."

Felton shook his head and slid into the driver's side of his black Dodge pickup. "Sure a shame what happened."

Cahill's heart quickened. He got in and slammed the door. "What happened?"

Felton backed up the truck and shifted into forward, driving past government transient workers unloading crates of Booth's broiled sardines and Del Monte canned corn from a freight car.

"What happened?" Cahill asked again.

"Don't know how I'd handle it myself, if it happened to me."

"Did something happen to Sadie? Is she all right?"

"Sadie's fine. It's Earl. Say, who are you anyway?"

"I'm a doctor. Earl's doctor. I took him through the polio."

"Well, you took him as far as he went."

"I don't understand."

They bumped onto the main road. It hadn't rained in a week, and dust rose in clouds behind them.

"He killed himself on Independence Day. Put a bullet through his head."

Cahill sagged against the green vinyl seat. A bullet. "Poor Sadie," he murmured. "How's she doing?"

"Sadie? She's tougher'n shoe leather. She's fine."

They were quiet the rest of the way.

She was pulling chickweed. She straightened when she saw Felton's truck, waved and went back to work. Her hair was braided and pinned and she wore a long apron over the sundress.

"Need a ride back to town? I could swing by," Felton volunteered. It was five miles to the depot.

"Thanks. I'll take my chances."

"Suit yourself." Felton shrugged. Cahill slammed the door shut and stood on the road, the house behind him, watching her.

Sadie put a hand to her eyes, studied him and then husked off her gloves. She was half an acre of crops away, and it gave him time to analyze the graceful way she walked, the high line of her chin.

Up close her face had toughened and the eyes were brilliant blue against the tan.

"Got some lemonade inside, squeezed this morning." It was like he'd seen her yesterday, rather than a month and a half ago.

He nodded and followed her through the kitchen. The dining room-living room was like Sadie, strong and spare with graceful splashes of color. The walls were whitewashed and the floor was oak planks. She had hung plants along the window, her irresistible green thumb spilling over into the house. It felt light and airy and clean. There was a good Van Gogh lithograph on the wall—his sunflowers.

"Got it at a farm auction for fifty cents," she said, following the gaze. "Nobody knew what it was, except me."

"It's beautiful."

"Sit." She handed him a frosty glass and he sat at the table. "Suppose you heard?"

He nodded. "I'm sorry, Sadie."

She drained half her glass. "I weighed a turnip yesterday on the kitchen scale. It was over eighteen pounds. All this sun, I guess."

There were new lines around the eyes. The arms sticking out from the sundress were brown and lean.

"How'd it happen?"

"I don't know, Cahill. I can't honestly say." It was the first time she had used his Christian name, but that, too, seemed natural. "He didn't seem any more upset than usual, although he kept talking about rats. Rats. For weeks after it happened, I'd lay awake at night and think—rats. Did he mean live rats, or rats like an expression, or what?"

Her eyes reddened and she dipped her head and drank. "It happened over there." She jerked her head toward the front part of the room where the sofas were. "Morris found him."

"Morris?"

"Earl's brother. I don't know what I'd have done without him, Cahill, and that's the honest truth. He stepped right in and helped me every step of the way."

Of course. Did he think Sadie would have been waiting for him here? Fool.

"Say, would you stay for supper?" she said shyly. "It's nothing fancy. Morris caught some grayling and I could fix biscuits."

"I couldn't," he said stiffly. "I only stopped by for a minute, Sadie. I don't want to intrude."

"Intrude? I'd be honored." She touched him tentatively. "Please say you'll stay. Emily'll pitch a fit if she hears you came by and she didn't see you. She's quite fond of you, you know."

"How's she doing?"

Sadie shrugged and bit her lip. "It comes and goes. I take it one day at a time with her. Morris caught her before she saw Earl; but the first week, she had nightmares, steady— sometimes two or three a night—and after the funeral, she's been scared to death something will happen to me. She's always saying, 'Mommy, don't let God take you to heaven and leave me behind.'"

"How are you doing?"

She rubbed her temple. A long silence went by. "I guess I should have expected it," she said. "He'd started crumbling long before we left Le Seur. There were signs. I never wanted to

see them, was all. You keep playing things over in your mind—
going through the whole thing, thinking, 'If I'd said something
here, maybe it would have changed things.'"

Tears splashed down her cheeks. "I'm sorry," she muttered,
and fled to the kitchen.

He went after her. She was sobbing silently into a dish towel
over the porcelain sink.

Without a word he took her in his arms and held her. "I love
you, Sadie," he whispered finally. "I didn't mean to say that.
But I do. I haven't stopped thinking about you since we met.
Not one day. Not one minute. You are the most amazing
woman I've ever met. The most hopeful. The strongest. I'm
sorry about what happened to Earl. I really am. But remember
what you told me the first time I met you? I had been belt-
whipping myself for years. And I would have gone on doing it
for years more if you hadn't pointed it out to me."

He stroked her glowing hair. "Don't make the mistake I did.
Don't waste years of your life, Sade."

"But I should have seen it! I should have been able to stop
it!"

"Sadie, I've lived a lot longer than you, and about the only
thing I've learned is that folks have a way of doing pretty much
what they want. Don't beat yourself over the head with it. You
have a child, and you're young. And Morris is devoted to you."
He said the last bleakly.

She pulled a hanky from her apron and wiped her nose.
"You're right," she said. She wiped her eyes and looked dully
around the kitchen. "I don't know what I'm going to do when
he goes home."

"He's leaving?" He couldn't keep the glad hope from his
voice.

She nodded. "Next month. He left a sweetheart to come.
She's flat run out of patience, so he's going home. I don't
begrudge him his life; I honestly don't. I only wonder—"

She stared through the screen door at the garden. A car
lumbered by, and dust filtered through the room. Cahill saw it
all in her eyes: planting, hoeing, caulking leaks, hauling
water—the endless effort to stay alive.

She squared her shoulders. "Stay for dinner," she commanded.

And he did.

They spent a lot of time laughing, although when he thought of it later, Cahill could never remember what it was they had been laughing about.

Morris and Emily cleared the dishes, and Sadie took her guest through the fields, as proud as a new mother.

"You love this life, don't you?"

"It's hard work." She laughed. "Yes, I love it. When the hail pelts down, I fret and stew; if it's cold at night, I worry—" She looked at him blandly. "I'm trying to figure out right now how to send all the radishes to the college of their choice. I think they're lots smarter than the cabbages."

Cahill laughed, reached for her and stopped.

"Why'd you stop?" She stuck her hands in her apron and kept walking.

"I feel like a kid," he confessed.

She squinted up at him. "What's that supposed to mean?"

"I'd like to do something frivolous in your name. Or something. You know how some church groups will write you a card, saying they've contributed a Gideon Bible to a poor savage in Tibet in your name?"

"Easy now, Cahill," her eyes flashed. "I'm a religious person myself."

"All right then, I could stand under your window and serenade you."

She laughed. "It's on the ground floor, right off the living room."

"In that case, I'd like to—" He stopped abruptly. "Do I have a chance, Sade?"

"For what?"

She wasn't being coy.

"Sadie Person, a light came into my life the day you walked in. Something loosened in my heart. You make me feel young and hopeful again, and I don't want to lose that." He added softly. "I don't want to lose you."

"What are you telling me, Cahill Blue?" She smiled shyly,

glowing. Her hair gleamed in the soft evening light, the color of summer wheat.

"I know this is sudden. Coming right on top of what happened—" He stopped helplessly.

She put a hand gently on his arm. "Spit it out, Cahill."

"I'd like to court you." He stopped again. "No, that's not true. I want to marry you, Sadie Person. I love you and I want to marry you. Will you marry me?" He had tears in his eyes and he was laughing.

"You've got to marry me, Sade." He wiped his eyes. "Because if you don't now, I'll keep after you until you do."

"What about your house?"

"I'll sell it. I've hated that house anyway."

"What about your practice?" She was laughing now.

"I'll sell that too. Just like an insurance man with a list of clients. Some doctor'll want to buy them." He took her in his arms. "No, they'll be fine without me. They haven't needed me in the hospital for years. Ever since they got Dr. Romig."

He bent and kissed her squarely on the mouth, hard and fast, and then they studied each other and something wonderful happened inside their bodies, and he shifted his hands down her body and she held onto his neck and he bent his head and kissed her. She trembled and her mouth sagged open and they kept on kissing.

Finally she detached herself gently. "Goodness," she said softly.

He smiled. "Goodness gracious sakes."

"Alive," she said, and kissed him again.

She snuggled into his body and he kissed her hair. "I always wanted to be a country doctor married to a gentleman farmer," he said.

She giggled. "Mighty peculiar, if you ask me. Besides, I'm a working farmer, and proud of it."

"Then the answer's yes?"

Everything glowed: the peach colored skin, the lashes flecked with light, the strong teeth.

"The answer's yes."

"Oh, Sadie." He held her close. "Sadie, Sadie."

Cahill looked over the shimmering rows of crops into their

future and saw a family there—strong and fearless and full of positive light. Like the earth and rain, they would endure, they would triumph. Nothing could harm them; they would build a circle of light and protect each other forever.

And then the screen door banged open and Emily shrieked outside, Morris diving after her, scuffing up dirt, and the spell was broken.

Forty-Five

Twelve miles south of Barrow village, a bluff rises twenty feet over the Chukchi Sea. Below it a long finger of sand juts out into the Arctic Ocean, separating it from Walakpa Bay to the west. Rivers and streams meander through this marshland on their way to the sea.

It is here that travelers start east to reach the Meade River, here that runners stop on their way to Barrow, and here that a large red plane bounced gently out of the sky on a summer afternoon, settling on a river that cut along the bluff.

The noise scattered the reindeer, and Nuka got warily to his feet. He poked the fire and turned the Arctic char he was frying.

Out of the huge red bird stepped two men wearing boots.

"Howdy." The man smiled and extended his hand. "Name's Will Rogers and I'm pleased to meet ya."

Nuka remembered his English and responded, "I am Nick Snow. How are you?"

"Couldn't be much better and that's a fact." The man had a seamed face and was chewing gum. He grinned and thumbed at his partner. "This here's Wiley Post and I'm embarrassed to say it, but we don't know where in sam hill we are."

"Why, you're here," Nuka said in surprise, as if that answered it.

"Yes, well, I appreciate that information, but we're on our way to Barrow."

"Old Barrow or new Barrow?"

Will cocked back his hat and scratched his head. "There's more than one?"

"Old Barrow—Barrow village—Eskimos live. New Barrow—Point Barrow—Eskimos and whites. I live," he added proudly.

"I tell you, I don't rightly know which it is. I'm goin' to visit a friend of mine, Charlie Brower. Old Charlie used to run the whaling station. Been there about a million years, I imagine."

Nuka nodded his head vigorously and smiled. "A good man. I know him. Point Barrow." He pointed north. "This way. Not far. Day, maybe, on foot, two hours in boat."

The reindeer crept closer again, nibbling on the sparse covering of lichen along the river banks.

"Thank you kindly," Will said. "We surely do appreciate it." The wind shifted, and the odor of fish drifted tantalizingly into the air.

"Look," Nuka said, "you hungry? A friend of Charlie Brower is a friend to me."

Post and Rogers looked at each other, and Rogers grinned. "We're starved," he confessed.

Clair Oakpeha and three friends clambered up the bluff. "Big bird!" he cried.

"It's a plane," Will explained.

Clair was young and lean, with great grave eyes. He and his buddies got as close to the plane as they dared and studied it from the bank.

Nuka dished up the fish. "Clair, you hungry?" he called in Inupiaq.

Clair shook his head, fascinated. "We ate."

Will sauntered back to the plane, rooted around and dug out chocolate bars and plates. He presented each boy with a bar and brought the rest back, giving one to Nuka.

"For dessert," he explained.

He hunkered over his plate and made little grunty sounds. "I tell you, there's nothing better than fresh fish in the wilderness."

After he finished, Wiley got up and went back to the plane. He pulled out a tool kit and began tinkering.

"Get many planes up this way, Nick?" Will asked.

Nuka shook his head. "First one."

"That a fact? You're mighty calm."

"Thank you," Nuka said.

"How do you do it?"

"Do it?"

"How do you stay calm? I've met a lot of folks in my life, and boy, some of them are running around like chickens. There's not a calm bone left in their body. You tell me, and I'll write it down and tell them. Everybody wants to know the secret to staying calm. It's right up there with the secret to the pyramids or how to live long."

"Calm," Nuka reflected, lifting the backbone out of his fish in one piece.

Fog swirled off the inland ponds and blew over the bluff on its way to the sea, giving the stranger the look of a prophet, not quite there, yet there.

"You live. You die." Nuka shrugged.

Will grinned and crossed his arms. "That's it? You live, you die? I'll tell them, Nick, but I imagine they'll try to form a committee to make it more complicated."

There was more Nuka wanted to say. "Live inside the skin you have," he added. "It is as it was to be."

"It is as it was to be. That's pretty deep for a country boy. You mean you think somebody sits up there and decides who's going to live and who's going to die?"

Nuka shook his head. "No. But the wind shifts. Snow falls. Ice comes to the sea. A man gets caught and dies. But if he worries, if he never left his ivruluk from fear of it, there would be no meat in the winter and his family would die. It is as it was to be," he repeated.

"In other words, enjoy it while you got it. Make the most of it. Don't be afraid of what's gonna happen next. I can go along with that." Wiley Post sauntered over.

He leaned back, patted his belly and said, "Well, Wiley, what time you got?"

Wiley squinted at his wrist with his good right eye. "Ten after eight."

"That late? This sun fools you. Got an appointment I can't put off."

Will got to his feet and clasped Nuka's hand. "Been nice talking with you. Enjoyed the fish and liked the man behind it. I think you got something there, Nick. Think you should bottle it and sell it. Make a fortune."

He waved, and ambled toward the plane. The men climbed

up the pontoons, got inside. The engines started. The plane lifted, hovered, choked and seemed to waver in the air for a moment. Then it banked steeply to the right and plummeted to the ground, crashing at a sickening angle, the right wing buckling under it. It flipped over into the water, shifted, bounced gently twice, and stilled.

Nuka dropped the last fish and ran over. Clair was already in the water. He wrenched open a door. A body fell out. Clair caught it. The hat fell off. It was Will Rogers.

"Quick," Nuka commanded. "Carry him to the bank."

His head was bloody.

Nuka knelt next to him and held his hand. It was limp.

Clair screamed. He ran back to the plane. His friends darted back and forth in the water. Wiley Post was still inside.

"He's crushed inside!" one of them cried. "Under the front. He's not moving. We can't get him."

Clair barreled through the water. The engine had slammed into the cockpit. There was no way he could still be alive.

Clair stumbled through the water and ran back to Nuka. Tears streamed down his face. "He's dead. He's dead." He stared, agonized, at the body on the ground. "Him, too? They're both dead?"

He dropped to his knees and put his face in his hands.

"Listen to me," Nuka said. "Listen. Run to Point Barrow, Clair. Tell the telegraph man. He'll know what to do. Now go! Quickly!"

Clair stumbled blindly to his feet and ran sobbing into the north.

Nuka patted Will's hand. *It's all right, my friend. You're not alone. I'm right here. I'll be right here.*

Clouds feathered across the sky; the fog deepened, and when the ground grew cool, Nuka covered him up with a sleeping bag. A light rain fell and Nuka stayed next to him, while in the soft summer sky, the mystery of life-to-death completed itself.

Can you feel the soul leave? Can you see the spark of life slip from the bonds of flesh? Perhaps not, but no one should pass from one world to the next unaccompanied, so Nuka sat and held the stranger's hand through the soft summer night that never darkened, while down below, on the sandy spit, a walrus cub bleated for its mother, its cries going on forever, across the flat, gray sea.

At first, Stanley Morgan thought it was a bird, tapping at the door of the U.S. Signal Corps station, but when it kept up, he climbed over the wastebasket he'd been using to shell peanuts and popped it open.

A native stumbled in, gasping for air.

"Whoa, son. Take it easy."

"Bird men," Clair wheezed. "Dead."

Sergeant Morgan only looked at him.

"Dead," Clair repeated. "Red bird smashed."

Morgan rang the doctor at the mission. "Hi, Henry, it's Stanley." Stanley kept his voice down, glancing at Clair who had collapsed in a chair.

"Got a report of a plane down. Maybe. Not sure yet." He nodded into the phone and turned to Clair.

"Where is it?"

"Walikpaa."

Stanley raised his eyebrows. "He says Walikpaa. Yes, I know it's fifteen miles away." He turned to Clair. "How did you get here?"

"Run," Clair said, his chest still heaving.

Stanley turned back to the phone. "He says he ran, Henry. Yeah, I know." He listened for a minute and said thoughtfully, "Okay," and hung up the phone. "Doc's got a boat we can use. Think you can lead me to it? The fog's come up. We'll go through the marshes, hitting the ponds."

Clair stood and tears came to his eyes. "Yes," he said. "Yes."

It was three-thirty in the morning when they got there. Morgan climbed out of the umiak and went up the beach to where the body was being attended by an old Eskimo.

He glanced at the water. The plane was a hybrid—Sirius wings, the fuselage from an Orion. It was upside down in the river.

He put a hand on the old man's shoulder. "It's all right," he said, and gently took down the sleeping bag.

He stared at the man's face. Tears ran down his face. "Oh, no. Oh, no." He looked helplessly at the sky. "Oh, my God, no."

On the ground next to the body was a piece of paper. Stanley picked it up.

"It fell out of his pocket," Nuka explained.

Stanley unfolded it.

It was a review of Mary Rogers's play.

It was early in the morning when their mother woke them and told them to come downstairs, she had to tell them something.

Jordy knew right away somebody had died. Her mother only used the tone of voice when something really bad happened. She felt her way into her bathrobe and slid into her slippers, colliding with Roy in the hallway.

"Who do you think got it this time?" she whispered.

"Beats me," he answered. His hair stuck up and he had sleep in his eyes. "I thought all of Dad's relatives bit the big one a long time ago."

Jordy padded downstairs into the kitchen and poured herself a glass of orange juice before she went in.

Her mother had brushed her auburn hair, but her face was deathly pale without makeup. She looked like she'd been crying. "I have some bad news for both of you," she said, composing her voice. She looked from one to the other. "Your friend—" her voice shook and she paused briefly. "Your friend Will Rogers died last night in a plane crash."

"No!" Jordy cried.

"It's not true!" Roy insisted. "It can't be." He stood up, fists clenched. Tears rolled down Flame's face. "I know how you feel. We all feel exactly the same way. I thought especially since you'd met him—"

She swallowed and looked out the window. "Your father is sending a telegram to the family now, and Radio City Music Hall is beaming a memorial at four, our time. President Roosevelt will be talking to the nation."

She wiped her eyes and clasped her hands. "I think we should bow our heads in a moment of silent prayer."

Jordy inched closer to Roy. They ducked their heads and squeezed their eyes shut. They both were crying. For a moment there was only the muffled sound of sobs filling the room, and then Flame said in a steady voice, "Dear Lord: You must have had a plan we don't know about when it came to Will Rogers." Her voice broke and she steadied herself. "Maybe You needed to be cheered up. If so," and here her voice trembled again, "If so, dear Lord, then You called up the right person. Nobody can do it like Will."

She wiped her eyes and said, "So Lord, take care of him. Enjoy him. We surely did. Amen."

"Amen," Roy and Jordy whispered.

Forty-Six

A year after the bird crashed out of the sky, Nuka got a letter from Timmy. It was the first letter from his son in almost twenty years.

Nuka took it to the teacher at Point Barrow, who read it aloud:

Dear mother and dad,

I am working for the government in the Interior Department, helping enact the Howard-Wheeler Act, which has recently been extended to Alaska. In that capacity, I will arrive in Point Barrow around the 23rd of July, and expect to stay two days.

I am looking forward to the trip with great anticipation.

Your son,
Tim

"Well, congratulations," the teacher said. He folded up the letter and gave it back. "I didn't know you had another son."

"Yes," Nuka said proudly. "He's going to stay for good now."

"But I thought the letter said—"

"He's staying for good now," Nuka repeated and rose, a small scarred man in a shabby suit with flint for spine.

The teacher banged an eraser against the blackboard and said brightly, "When he comes, be sure and bring him around.

I'd love to meet him."

He came on the revenue cutter on a blazing day in late July, his seersucker jacket draped across the rail and a lump in his throat as big as Kansas. The one-story building was new; a hospital or school, Tim guessed, but the huts still slanted with sod and the flat marshes extended as far back into the horizon as his memory.

A skin boat moved swiftly toward the cutter, and Tim strained over the side, hoping to see his father. It was a kid ferrying the boat, and Tim swallowed his disappointment.

He threw down his suitcase and put on his jacket, then he gripped his briefcase with one hand and clambered down the ladder into the boat.

"You Tim?" the boy asked. He had a flat face and rotten teeth and spoke with the peculiar inflection of natives speaking English, expelling the words in heavy guttural breaths, like a German tourist thumbing through a guidebook.

Tim nodded and sat down, gripping the sides. The boat waffled in the noisy swells, and he felt a surge of fear before the boy sliced the paddle through the water and got them away from the cutter and pointed toward home.

His father was smaller than he remembered. Where was the thunderous laughter, the economy of gesture, the swift iron justice carving brisket out of his behind? It was as if time had collapsed him inward, his cheeks, his legs, the thrust of his scarred head.

He recognized his father's suit, baggier in the seat than it was twenty years ago, and shiny at the elbows, but the same gray serge with black flecks.

"Timmy," his father said, and held out his arms.

Tim embraced him and felt tears come to his eyes. He patted his father sharply on the back, hard little pats, and blinked his eyes. "Dad," he said. He patted him some more, then pulled away and said, "Where's mom? She waiting for us?"

He looked swiftly down the line of people. There were five grimy black-eyed children, fingers in mouths, two fat women who looked old but Tim guessed were probably in their mid-twenties, and a short elderly man with few teeth.

"She died, Tim, oh, maybe—how long has it been now, Matthew?"

"Thirteen—"

"Thirteen years. During a diphtheria outbreak in Nome."

Thirteen years ago. His father socked him on the arm. "Hey, but it's good to see you. Don't you recognize your own brother? Look. Here's Matthew. Not your little brother anymore, is he? And here's Naomi."

Tim was shocked. Matthew was five years younger than Tim, but looked at least twenty years older. Lines creased his papery cheeks and his few remaining teeth jutted from his mouth like yellow tusks.

"Matthew?" Tim said.

Matthew nodded but didn't speak.

There was nothing recognizable about Naomi: she could have been any fat woman wearing her hair in a bun, her pendulous breasts sagging on a belly blessedly covered by a shapeless dress. One of the sleeves had pulled loose, exposing a nest of underarm hair.

"Timmy," she cried, and embraced him, her body odor so strong he stopped himself from pulling away.

"Here's some of my brood," she said good-naturedly, and stuck a small child forward. "Say hello to your Uncle Timmy," she instructed. "He's kind of shy, but if he don't say much, I'll beat him but good when we get home."

"No, no," Timmy said, alarmed. "It's all right. Nice to meet you," he said, and hurriedly turned away. The boy had an enormous goiter on his neck.

"So, you come home," Matthew said. He spat the words through the gaps in his teeth. The hostility hissed through the air like a snake.

"Only for a few days."

Tim tried to infuse some regret into his voice, but Matthew eyed him maliciously and Tim stepped back, embarrassed.

"You hungry?" Nuka asked. "You come home and get settled and we'll have a nice meal. Naomi cooks for me and is she good! She fermented a ptarmigan in our *argagniq* for a month, using rancid seal oil. We have all been hungering for it, I tell you! And that's the truth."

"Oh. I ate on the boat. But please—I know the little ones have raging appetites. Don't hold off on my account."

Even to his ears, it sounded insincere.

Matthew blew air through his teeth and shook his head, but Nuka gripped his arm and exclaimed, "Good to have you home!" He squeezed harder. "Good," he repeated.

"What happened to your legs, dad?"

Nuka shrugged. "Old age. The joints are not what they used to be. Naomi makes a poultice of wild celery and willow in a batter of fermented fish eggs, but it doesn't do much."

"I have some Ben Gay in my briefcase."

"What?"

"Ben Gay. It's a medicine. I'll give it to you."

They were coming up on the hut.

It was like a sharecropper's shanty, Tim thought, stunned. In his memory, he had built rooms, added a veranda, a screen door, real glass in the windows, and sometimes a slide in the front yard; but here was a dark, wobbly structure, sloping and sloppy, its walls tamped with crumbling dirt and its yard blooming with rusty cans.

"Who lifts and packs the ice now, dad?" he asked suddenly. In his childhood, his winter job was insulating the outside walls with snow.

"Oh, it depends," Nuka said vaguely. He pushed open the peeling door and stood inside. Tim crouched and went in, blinking in the dim light. His family crowded in around him.

The room smelled like something had died in there.

His father was smiling broadly. "Well, what do you think? It's a lot different, eh, son? Eh?"

"Different—" Tim said cautiously, not knowing exactly what his father was getting at.

Nuka limped over to the bed platform, dipped under the worn Hudson Bay blanket. "An alarm clock," he said triumphantly. "Pretty good, huh? Pretty nice."

He pulled himself over to the stove. "Remember when we had only a cooking fire? Now we cook the old way only at the fish camp." He patted the stove lovingly. "It came all the way from See-at-all."

"That's Seattle, dad."

"You've heard of it?" Nuka was astonished.

Tim nodded. "I've been there."

"Hey, Matthew. Your brother's been to See-at-all. That's something, huh?"

"I heard him, dad." Matthew said softly, and went to stand by the table.

"Remember how we borrowed books from the teacher?" Nuka pulled a crate from under the table.

"We have *five* books in this house." He recited the title and put each on the table: "*McGuffey's Fourth Reader*, the *Holy Bible*, the *Sears-Robuck* book, the *Presbyterian Hymnal*, and this one, this is a good one, *The Call of the Wild*. It's about dogs, Timmy."

"I've read it," he said gently.

Nuka smiled at him with pride. "I knew you'd turn out this way. I knew it. Matthew will help you build your own place. We'll get started on it right away. If we work hard, we can still be in the summer camp for a couple of weeks good fishing before the snow comes."

"I told you I'm not staying, dad. I only came to visit a few days."

Nuka appeared not to have heard. "We could use that ptarmigan, Naomi." She waddled to the door and ducked outside.

"Where's Ruth?" Timmy asked suddenly.

Nuka shrugged. "Your sister's living inland. She met a nice boy, a teacher. He's white. They have three little ones now. Good boys, but none of them can hunt. Can you believe it? None." He paused. "Mark died, though. Your little brother. Same time as your mother."

Nuka sat at the table and ruminated. "Things have been pretty good for me. Yes, they have. Come on. Let's take a walk before dinner. I have some things to tell you."

Matthew said, "Can I come?"

Nuka shook his head and said flatly, "These are private

things, between Timmy and me."

Nuka limped blindly past Matthew, but Tim saw the despair and hunger on that face, and felt again the injustice. Tim, who had loved reindeer and rain, had left, while Matthew, who had loved books and hungered after beauty, had been forced to stay behind, to grow old in poverty, in squalor, and pass it along to his sons.

Tim followed his father into the kelp-smelling air. They passed Naomi, squatting over the fermenting pit, pulling out a ptarmigan with its feathers still on. The bird smelled revolting. Tim moved to the opposite side of his father.

"So, you work for the government?" Nuka inquired.

Tim nodded. "The Interior Department. They sent me to tell everybody about something called the Howard-Wheeler Act. Basically, it means all the Eskimos here can get together and form a corporation. That's like a business."

"A business?" Nuka said. "What kind of business?"

"Any kind you want. If you want. And you could borrow money from the government."

"How long it take to get this money from the government?"

"I'd say a couple of months to process the request and another month to get it—say three or four months, depending on the time of year. If it's winter, it will take longer, because of the Arctic Ocean freezing."

"Four months." Nuka nodded his head and pulled himself along. "If I get broke, I ask Matthew for money, and I get it right now!" He laughed.

"But you could borrow more money from the government than Matthew has," Tim explained.

"I'd have to pay it back."

"That's right."

Nuka shrugged. "I am an old man. I would not risk dying in shame, owing somebody money. What else does this law do?"

"If everybody wants it, you could all get together and vote to stay on a reservation."

"What's that?" They were leaving the last of the village behind now, walking along the beach toward the west.

566

"It's land. It's your land. You would stay on this land and that's what you would have. You wouldn't be able to sell it, and you wouldn't have title to it—that's a piece of paper saying it's just yours—the land would belong to everybody in the village, but you could stop other people from coming and living there."

"Why would I want to do that?" Nuka asked in surprise.

"So it would be just yours, yours and your family's."

Nuka shrugged. "What's so different about what we do now."

"Right now, somebody—some white guy—could come along and put his house on top of yours and you wouldn't have any rights."

"I have my fist," Nuka exclaimed, and shoved a gnarled hand into Tim's face. "Besides, who would do that, anyway? Nobody I know. You know somebody that would do that, you point him out to me, and I'll show him a thing or two."

Tim grew quiet.

"So, is there anything else the government wants you to say?"

"Dad," Tim said cautiously. "I don't mean any disrespect, but I'll leave some papers with the teacher, and he can go over it with you. With all of you, after I leave."

"Who's leaving?" Nuka said confidently.

They had reached a sandy bluff that stretched over the Arctic Ocean. Nuka went down stiffly on one leg, then another, and sat in the cold sand.

"Dad, I told you I'm only staying a few—"

"Sit," Nuka commanded, "and hear me."

He waited until Tim dropped heavily next to him.

"There is something burning in my heart. Magic lives there. Spirits melting in the wind, voices."

He jabbed at his scar with a chewed finger. "You see this? It's a sign, Timmy. I was picked. I was chosen; in the dark days when Kannik was taken from me, before books and schools, the shaman recognized me by the scar, as the one chosen to receive the sacred knowledge. I studied—"

"Dad—" Tim said.

"I studied three days and three nights. He told me many things and the time has come to share them with you."

"You've got the wrong son!" Tim cried. "Tell Matthew these things."

Nuka shook his head. "The light is in you. I can see it around your face. Besides, you're wearing glasses. That's a sign. A mark."

Tim laughed helplessly. "Dad, that's not a sign of anything except poor eyesight. I bet Matthew would be wearing them, too, if there was anybody here who could give tests."

Nuka shook his head serenely. "No," he said flatly. "It is as it was to be. You are the one. The shaman told me—"

"I don't want to hear it!" Tim leaped to his feet.

"The shaman told me that from my seed will spring the rebirth of our people. You are my seed, Tim. You are the one that will change the course of our people's history. You. From you will spring a great people, strong as winter ice."

"Winter ice gives way to summer winds, father," Tim said.

"The day I sent you from me was the saddest in my life, second only to the day my wife, Aan, died. But I had to do it, Timmy. I had no choice. And now you have come back. We need you here, Timmy. I need you. You cannot leave. This is where you belong now. Here with us. And here you are."

"Dad," Tim beseeched, "please don't make it hard for me."

"Hard for you!" Nuka snapped. "You don't know what hard is." He thrust his hands out; they were brittle and fragile, like spokes of a wheel.

"All my life I've worked with these hands, scraping out a living. And for what? So my sons can have it easier. So *you* could have it easier."

"You think I wanted to leave? I loved it here! I loved you! But I can't stay now. I can't."

"Why not?"

"I can't stand anything about this life." The words were out before he could take them back.

His father staggered to his feet. "No!"

568

"Dad, I'm not Eskimo anymore. I'm not white, either. I don't know what I am, but I tell you this, no spirit of our ancestors ever whispered to me in my sleep. I'm not the one you thought I was. I can't be any clearer than that."

He stumbled down the bluff back to the house, and as soon as it was decently possible, he left.

Forty-Seven

The first annual Matanuska fair was scheduled for Labor Day weekend of 1936. There was going to be baseball and boxing and wrestling, marathon jitney dances and a picture show every night. There would be prizes for canned goods and baked goods and delivering the goods.

Roy Jackson patted and polished and buffed his model airplane to a high-gloss state of excitement; he whispered to it, fed it bits of string and spit, tweaked the trim tabs and waxed the elevator.

"I know I can take the educational class," he confided to his father.

They were wading single file through tall, wet grass, the plane hoisted over their shoulders. Roy planned to test it on the bluff.

It was opening day of duck hunting, and since Roosevelt's restrictions were still in effect, banning the use of any larger weapon, Batt carried a 10-gauge. Roy had his toolbox.

The Jacksons hiked in companionable silence, the father gray-haired and thick-shouldered, the boy short and muscular. The leaves were turning gold and the grass drifted waist high, sharp smelling like the sea.

Fingers of Knik Arm rolled like wet, gray carpet out and up the flats. High tide, these fingers were submerged in eight feet of sea, and then the inexorable force of nature pulled the water back, exposing oozing black mud, shiny and slick and deep, slanting into a bottomless V of muck.

They came up on one and gave it wide berth, hip boots slipping through the grass, arms shifting with the precious cargo of Roy's exhibit.

Finally they reached a pond rimmed with reeds and set the

plane carefully down.

It was early morning, barely eight, and a wet fall fog hung in the air. Batt checked the wind direction and they waded into the pond and lined up decoys in a pipe formation.

"You could test it over there." Batt jerked his head toward the east bluff. "Or for the matter, on the west bluff, but you might dunk it in Ship Creek or get it killed by a truck." Anchorage lay on the other side of the west bluff.

Roy uncorked the thermos and poured coffee into the cover.

"Naw, it's coming down right on top of me. I got it planned out. But I'll go east anyway. Don't want to alert my competitors."

He drank and passed the coffee to his dad.

Batt said, "You think you'll have competitors?"

Roy shrugged. "Not like mine," he admitted. "Saw one the other day that looked like somebody'd sent away for it on a Post Toasties box. No imagination."

"Well, you earned it," his father said, and tossed out the rest of the coffee. He screwed the lid securely on and put the thermos down.

They heard the unmistakable quack of mallards, and Batt and Roy sank back into the high grass and waited.

Thirty seconds later, they spotted them angling down the bluff through the fog, three females and a drake, his head a dark green against the gray sky.

Roy curled his fists and did a credible call. They dropped five feet and answered.

Batt aimed and gently pulled the trigger, shattering the stillness. The ducks cried an alarm and scattered. The drake crashed heavily into the marshes.

"This is when always I think we need a dog," Batt said, and clambered after it.

The bag limit was down to ten a day per person, and they were in no hurry, so Roy caressed the plane, checked the fuselage and, when his father tossed the duck down, he said, "I'm going to try it out. Want to come?"

Batt shook his head. "Maybe later." He unwrapped a cigar, lit it and took off his wool jacket, bunching it under his head.

"Gonna lay down my troubles," Batt intoned. "Contemplate

the changing seasons. The gray of hair. The scuff of hand." He puffed. "You get the idea."

"Don't think anything too strenuous," Roy said. He hefted the plane to his back and hiked across the flats. The sun was burning off the high fog when he climbed the east bluff. The Chugach Range humped up behind him, green and gold. The wind gusted, and a pond glinted below, then a black furrowed finger of Knik Arm. The wind shifted and fog smoothed it all away, a gray thick cloud under him. He opened his tool kit, took out the bulb and gas can, and started feeding gas into the filler tube. The tank only held a pint, but squeezing it laboriously by hand, it took fifteen minutes before the gas spilled out the overflow tube.

Roy patted her as he went to the engine with the battery and leadwires. The breeze was from the sea, spelling the start of high tide.

He cranked the prop until the single cylinder dropped into the bottom of the crank case, then leaned down and squirted gas into it. The glow plug sizzled.

Satisfied, he whapped the prop, pulling his fingers away when it grabbed and bit him. He sucked on his finger and kept turning.

The prop roared to life, spitting air like a fan, and Roy tossed a rag into it to still it. He hadn't perfected it; he hoped it wouldn't act up for the judges.

He squirted in more gas and tried again. Ten minutes more and the prop hummed a deep throaty tune. Roy toyed with the fuel adjustment until the plane whined.

"First prize, baby," Roy muttered.

He bent the moveable elevators up and twisted the rudder to the left; then picked it up, ran to the edge of the bluff and threw her overboard.

She lifted into the sky, doing exactly what he'd planned: he'd arced the elevators for maximum rise, and now she was spiraling in a high circle to the left, directly overhead.

He jumped up and down, raised a fist and cheered. His father answered with a single shot from the flats.

She took his breath away. Her wings glinted through the fog, the silver flash going higher and higher. For ten minutes he watched her, totally absorbed. When she started to wind down, he followed on the ground, trotting in a circle on the bluff.

He frowned. The wind was gusting in from the sea and it sent her into a pattern over the flats. He skidded down the bluff, eyes up, and tracked her. The wind batted her farther across the flats, and Roy started running.

He had worked for two years on that plane. But it wasn't just for the fair; it was all his free times and good times tied up in that silver-painted balsa body, with rubber wheels and a glass-covered cockpit.

She was starting to shake now, from lack of fuel, and Roy ran faster through the silvery fog. He needed to catch her. If she crashed, it could shatter the fragile internal plumbing. The fair was less than a week away.

He lost his footing, grunted, slipped and rolled heavily down a gully.

The plane glinted overhead and floated off into the woods, cut off from view by the high cliff of mud above him.

A sudden awareness came, and with it, a terrible, paralyzing fear. Frantic, he clawed the mud, scrabbling for a toe hold.

His boots sank to the ankles.

"Dad!" he screamed. *"Dad!"*

The gully chewed for half a mile to the sea, and Roy stared in hypnotized horror at Knik Arm.

The tide was coming in.

Half a mile away, a gray wall of water slid over the mud.

Think, Roy. Think.

The mud sucked up to his knees.

"Dad!" he bellowed.

Something crashed through the grass. "Where are you?"

"Down here."

His father's head appeared, eight feet over him. "Get out of those hip boots," his father barked. "Move!"

Roy unbuckled them at the hip and tried shifting. "It's like concrete."

"Give me your belt."

Roy took it off and heaved it up. Batt caught it as it was slipping back down, snapped off his own and buckled them together. He dropped to his belly and snapped down an end.

573

A foot short.

The tide was creeping stealthily forward, like a shiny gray leech.

The mud was to Roy's thighs now.

Water innocently trickled over it, foaming and swirling.

"Oh, God," Roy cried.

Father and son stared at each other, sober eyed. "It's not over yet." Batt scrambled away from the edge.

Roy stared at the water lapping his hips. It was ice cold. He squeezed his eyes shut.

Batt dropped to the sand on the edge of the pit, yanked out the forearm clip on his 10-gauge, and snapped the switch on top to the right. He knocked out the pin and cracked the gun open. The double barrel fell away from the stock and trigger housing and forearm rest.

He tore at the buckles on his hip waders and peeled them down. Then he picked up the double barrel and the stock and plunged over the edge.

He slid down and carefully treaded water, staying clear of the mud.

The water slid over Roy's waist.

"Hold this," Batt ordered. He thrust the double barrel into Roy's hands. Roy raised it over his head.

Batt held his breath and ducked under, shoveling mud with the stock. The water burned like melting mercury. Batt worked silently, furiously.

Roy sank to his hips in mud. The water swelled to his armpits.

Batt dug the mud away from his son, fueled by terror. He had to break the seal. The instant he gouged out a pocket, mud slipped around his fragile shovel and filled it up.

"When it gets to that, use the barrel to breathe through."

"What about you?" Roy cried.

His father took another breath and went under.

Ten minutes of digging, of pulling, of Roy sinking deeper. Batt's legs slowed; his hands numbed.

A sudden, terrifying pain shot up his left arm, scoured his chest and squeezed his heart. Batt dropped the stock into the water and plunged backward, groaning.

574

"Dad!" Roy bent and supported his father's head with his hand.

Batt's face was slack and gray. He pushed himself feebly away from Roy.

"Dad!"

"Listen to me, son," Batt whispered. "Don't panic. Keep your wits."

"What happened to you?"

Batt swallowed with effort. "A little twinge. Don't drop the gun."

"I won't, dad," Roy whispered. They were quiet. "Dad?"

"Yes, son." Batt's legs were fiery blocks treading the water.

"I love you."

"I love you too."

The sea inched up Roy's face.

"I'm right here," his father said.

Roy swallowed hard, closed his eyes and lifted the barrel to his mouth, breathing through it like a reed.

A second pain roared over Batt, a crushing, breath-stopping pain. His heart—that old, reliable friend that had carried Batt over the Chilkoot into Flame's arms—convulsed, faltered, roared to life.

"Flame!" Batt screamed in agony.

Something inside him galloped, burst, stopped.

The water took him.

Breathe slowly, Roy commanded himself. In and out. In and out. He squeezed his eyes shut against the silt and gripped the barrel hole tightly, creating a seal for his mouth.

In out. In out.

It went on forever. How much longer for high tide?

How much higher?

He saw his mother's face. Jordy. His dad. I love you all, he thought. Oh, God, please, he bargained. Please.

In and out.

The air inside the barrel grew moist.

Oh God Oh God.

Roy took a deep breath and held it as the water shot down the barrel. His lungs were on fire.

Please God please.

He opened his mouth and drank.

When they weren't home by supper, Flame paced the living room, staring out the dormer window into the trees. Restlessly she walked to the front gate and checked the street.

"Maybe they went for a beer or something," Jordy volunteered.

"No," Flame said. "No. It doesn't feel right."

"You worry a lot," Jordy observed.

Flame didn't answer.

When they weren't home by dark, she called the police, and when they couldn't find them, she organized a search party to scour the flats.

It was dawn. The fog drifted over a brilliant splash of leaves. The sea murmured and whispered in the ocean. The searchers fanned out through the tall grass, silent, somber, sharp eyed.

Ten minutes in, Cam Combs spotted Roy's plane sticking nose down in the reeds. Three minutes later, the bones of the gun on the crest of pit. Batt's boots.

He tested the ground cautiously and inched over.

Batt's body lay spread-eagled in the mud, face down. Roy's twisted at a sickening angle, his feet stuck, the bones in his ankles snapped.

Cam fired his gun twice, the prearranged signal, and wiped his eyes.

Bill Hollowell from First National was the first there. He stared in silence down at the bodies. "We're going to have to stop Flame." He blew his nose hard. Cam nodded. They stood in heavy silence, waiting.

She burst through the grass. "Did you find them? Are they all right?"

The joy on her face faded. She looked from one man to the other.

They gripped her arms. "Flame. Flame."

"What is it? What happened?"

"They got caught in the tide—"

"They're not dead. They can't be dead!"

"They're gone, Flame." Cam's face crumpled.

"You're lying. It's not true." She yanked herself free, and Bill held her back.

"Flame, they're gone."

"No!" she cried. "No. I don't believe you." She started sobbing. She brought her hands to her face, squeezed off the sound. Tears streamed down her cheeks. "It's not true. Maybe it's somebody else."

"Flame." Cam's shoulders shook. "Flame, I'm so sorry. I loved that man like a brother." He broke down and sobbed.

"No!" She was hysterical. "No." She kicked her way free and ran toward the edge.

"Don't look," Bill pleaded. "Don't." He ran after her.

She was shaking her head with her hands up to her face, crying, "Oh no oh no oh no."

She sank to her knees and rocked, her hands around her, holding herself, holding it in. The bodies so silent, covered with fine gray silt.

Her husband her love her child.

"Oh no," she cried. "No."

She dug her head into her lap. "Batt!"

She raised her face to the sky and wept.

Forty-Eight

A year of grief, of getting used to it, of realizing she would never get used to it.

The silent house Jordy and she couldn't fill up, the still bed next to her at night.

"Let's go to the fair, mom," Jordy insisted. "Let's get out of here. We'll ride the rails, and I'll make lunch."

She kissed her mother squarely on top of the head, still amazed by the fine threads of gray in the rich auburn.

Since the men had died, Flame seemed more fragile, and for the first time, it occurred to her that her mother wasn't young anymore; was in her fifties; would die someday.

It brought out the kindness in her. At least her mother would die knowing Jordy loved her. She told Flame every day.

Now she went briskly into the kitchen. "How does peanut butter sound?" she called.

"Terrible." Flame laughed.

Jordy nodded agreeably and opened a shelf door, studying the contents quietly. She had stopped growing tall, finally, for which she was fervently glad, and started growing out.

"Corned beef or tuna fish," she called. "Take your choice."

"How about neither," Flame said, and got off the couch. "How about my taking you to lunch on the Alaska Railroad's finest—"

"You mean only."

"Finest and only. The infamous, Bismarex popping, Alaska Railroad grill, where you pay twice for grease: once in your wallet and then on your hips."

Jordy banged the cabinet door shut. "Ready in two minutes."

*   *   *

Blue-and-white mountains rose over the fairgrounds and people swarmed through the hot, dry dirt of the parking lot, checking for purses and cameras, children corralled in sweaty adult hands.

Sheep trotted in circles, led by nervous owners, inside a fence to the east. An enormous barn housed livestock exhibits: cows calmly chewing, horses stamping, a lynx darting from one end of its pen to the other. An enormous sow had given birth to ten hairless piglets; they sucked noisily while she sniffed the air and growled at spectators.

Inside a long, cool building were stalls filled with carrots, turnips, squash, paintings, ceramic pots, aprons, mono-grammed towels, pies and a cake decorated to look like President Roosevelt.

"Glad you came?" Jordy nudged her, her arms filled with jars.

"Very." Flame hugged her daughter.

"Blueberry and raspberry, since we didn't go berry picking this year." She dropped the jars into her mother's purse.

"I wonder if they have mint? It would go nicely with lamb."

She walked to the booth. A striking young woman with bright blond hair sat behind the counter, hands folded over the swell of her belly.

"Can I help you?" The woman smiled widely and her skin gleamed.

"Do you have mint?" Flame asked.

"Sure do." She pulled down two jars. "The sixteen-ounce size is the better buy. Ten cents."

"I'll get two." Flame pulled money from her coin purse. "When are you due?"

"January." The woman grimaced. "A ways to go." She patted her belly fondly. "I don't mind the team captain. It's the basketball he's packing with him."

"It agrees with you," Flame said and picked up the jars.

"Sadie, honey, there's a—"

Flame dropped a jar and it cracked open; green jelly heaved in a broken-sharded pile.

The woman leaned over the counter. "Oh," she cried. "Here. Let me help you."

"No! It's all right."

The woman lumbered around the side with a towel. "I'll give you another one."

"No, please. I was clumsy. It was my fault."

"Flame." Cahill stared down at her.

"Cahill."

He was graying, but his eyes burned with remembered intensity.

"You know each other!" his wife said in delight. She extended a jelly-covered hand, wiped it and said, "I'm Sadie Blue. Cahill's wife. Very nice to meet you."

Flame shook her hand warmly. "My name is Flame Jackson."

Sadie glanced at Cahill. "Not *the* Flame."

Cahill nodded.

"My husband's told me a lot about you. I'm glad we've finally met."

The two women studied each other.

"And I'm glad Cahill's finally happy," Flame said. "He deserves it."

Sadie smiled widely. "He is a love," she said.

She started awkwardly to her feet, and Cahill helped her up.

Flame stood. "Congratulations on your child."

"Thank you," Cahill said. "How's Batt?"

"He died last year."

"I'm so sorry."

There was nothing left to say. Finally Sadie added lamely, "If you have time, you could stop by for a piece of pecan pie—"

"No, but thank you."

Sadie seemed relieved.

"Well, good to see you," Flame said briskly, and clasped Cahill's hand.

"And you," he said.

She turned and walked back to Jordy, who was studying a large, bulbous, purple ceramic ashtray.

"Who was that man you were talking to?" Jordy asked.

"That man I was talking to"—a thousand images crowded into her mind—"that man, Jordy, was my oldest friend."

"Older than dad?"

Flame nodded. "Even older than dad. We grew up together." In so many ways.

"Well, we'll have to have them over for dinner some night. I bet he's got great stories."

But Flame only said, "I can't believe it, but I'm hungry again. Race you to the hot dog stand."

BOOK SIX

Heart

Forty-Nine

It suited her.

Jenny had been trying for nearly twenty years to leave herself behind, and now she had finally found a place as stormy and bleak as the inside of her mind.

It was Atka, an Aleutian island overrun with reindeer and blue foxes; fifty-five miles of sponge muskeg; home of Korovino Volcano, thick fog and violent gales.

A long, southerly tail of islands twisted out from Alaska in a fiery arc pointing toward Russia. Atka sat in the middle of these volcanic islands at almost the lowest point in the arc.

Jenny discovered it just past her lowest point, and immediately knew she belonged.

Atka was battered on the north by the freezing Bering Sea, but on the south side, the silky drift of the Pacific Ocean fed the island warm water and summer breezes.

The currents met over Atka in a clash of air power—a rattle of hail, bombs of fog, bursts of rain. No trees grew in Atka, but terrible winds were born and died there.

Children rode the gray and choppy seas as confidently as their city counterparts rode wooden horses.

Whales, sea lions, otters dunked and played, cod and halibut finned, while along the bottom, ancient creatures crept in smarmy silence, forgotten since the dim start of time.

There was no running water and no sewer and no post office on Atka; the hospital had been built in 1822 by the Russians, and the high point of Jenny's day was wandering down to Sandy Beach and watching the children crack open the eggshell skins of sea urchins and eat the yellow roe raw.

On the island was a Russian Orthodox Church, with a high twisted cross on its cupola. Inside were tall arched windows, paintings gilded in twenty-four-karat gold, and scrolled and scalloped icons of immeasurable value, brought to the islands hundreds of years ago by Russian sealers.

On Saints' days, the candles were lit, and the priest covered himself with gold-threaded robes and hats. During the three days of Christmas, carolers carried a spinning star centered with an ancient nativity of gold, but nobody bothered them or thought about stealing them. Nobody spirited them away in the middle of the night and buried them behind one of the wind-chapped houses.

They belonged to everybody, the way the fog did.

They left Jenny alone, too, this strange middle-aged, serious teacher with one leg shorter than the other.

She was a familiar figure, silhouetted against the rolling green muskeg and gray sky, her body as humped and magnificent in its thick coat and scarf as a sod barabara; a house half in, half out of the earth.

She would stand on a hummock and stare for hours out to sea, over the small islands squandering themselves in the sea; staring until the sky turned pearl gray and pink and the islands were only there in her dark imagination.

Nobody knew where she had come from or why. Only that she never smiled.

The stranger came in mid-June of 1938. Jenny watched him from her hummock perch as his trunk was carried up the wooden wobbly slope by two children.

He was as dark as an Aleut, but he walked like a white man. He was wearing a woolen cap and glasses, and a pen stuck from the pocket of his rain slicker.

He passed within yards of her, stopped, nodded and said, "Hello."

"Hello," Jenny said.

She immediately limped down the hill away from him, her long dark hair glistening in the wind.

"Who is that?" the man said in English.

"Teacher," Vasily Tartakoff said.

"What's her name?"

"Miss Blue."

"Miss Blue," he repeated, and looked thoughtfully after her.

He was collecting vegetation samples for the government, and Jenny didn't see him again for almost a month.

It was in the middle of a drowsy afternoon and Jenny was saying to her class, "All right. Tumanin Adaq 'aman akuxtxin inin kungin; assan amcug asadag'ta."

She paused, looked around the room. "Who can give me the literal translation of that? Vasily?"

Vasily started and stared at his hands. "Excuse me?"

The class tittered.

"Vasily, keep your mind in the confines of the room, not on the halibut in your father's net."

"Yes, Miss Blue. Sorry, Miss Blue."

He ducked his head and gazed dreamily out the window.

"Vasily."

"Oh. Sorry."

"Not sorry enough. Ten sentences from *McGuffey's Reader*, starting with page ten. Due tomorrow."

"Yes, Miss Blue."

"Now, who can give me the English literal version of the Aleut I recited?"

Narnia Chichakoff raised her hand.

"Yes, Narnia."

She was wearing a brilliant red wool shirt and purple skirt, embroidered with yellow and green flowers. She stood by her desk and recited: "For-us, father who thou art heavens on them; thy name it-to-be exceedingly praised."

"Very good, Narnia."

The girl looked shyly pleased and sat quickly down. She glanced toward the door.

The stranger was poking his head around. He knocked. He was carrying a large fabric bag.

"I hope I'm not intruding."

It was a stupid thing to say. Of course he was intruding. The students looked at him with interest, delighted with any interruption.

"As long as you have," Miss Blue said stiffly, "please come in and introduce yourself."

He grinned and strode into the room. He took off his wool

cap and stuck out his hand. "I'm Tim Snow and I work for the Biology Survey Division of the Interior Department. And you're—"

"Miss Blue," she said crisply. She was furious with him.

"Well, Miss Blue, if you think your class might be interested, I have collected samples of flora on their island. I'd be more than happy to—"

"I am quite certain my students know a great deal already about the flora on Atka, since their ancestors have lived here four thousand years, compared to the month of your tenure."

She knew she was being unforgivably rude. But she didn't care.

His eyes twinkled. He turned to the class. "You're a fair woman, Miss Blue," he said. "Let's put it to a vote. How many want to see what's in this bag?"

Everybody raised their hands.

He turned to her. "There? You see? Your fears were unfounded."

"Mr. Snow, I am not afraid of anything; but much to my regret, and I am quite certain the regret of the twelve students before you, we have a mathematics test next; or more precisely, three mathematics tests, for different grade levels."

Lower lips dropped in unison, but silently.

"That's fine," Tim said smoothly. "I'm not busy tomorrow. I can come back."

Lower lips went up in unison, but noisily.

He walked out.

"Mr. Snow," she called after him, "come back in one hour. I wish to speak to you."

She was furious. She paced up and down the empty classroom, between the first row of seats and her desk. "How dare you defy my authority in front of my students? Who do you think you are?"

"Miss Blue," Tim said, "I have been observing you on your solitary walks. And I have decided you are too solitary for your own good. That needs to be rectified by the government. And as the government's representative on this island—"

"Young man, I do not find your impudence attractive."

Tim laughed. "I don't know how old you think I am, but we can't be more than a few years apart. Why don't you call me Tim."

"I wouldn't even call you to supper," she snapped.

"That's fine, because I'm taking you out."

"You'll do no such thing."

"Not out exactly," Tim said. "In, really. But don't worry, it's all very proper. They have me living with Nikoli Kasinoff. He's almost deaf, but his eyes are very sharp and his tea is wonderful. You'll be fine."

"Why are you doing this to me? I don't like it."

He said seriously, "Because we're alike, you and I. Neither of us fit—anyplace, maybe, I don't know. But I can spot people like us; I knew you the instant I saw you, I could feel that thing in you, that uneasiness. The loneliness. Jenny—"

"How did you know my name?"

"I asked," he said simply. "Please say you'll have dinner with me. Please. It's been a long month with old Nikoli."

"All right," she said finally. "But I can't stay long. I have papers to grade."

Tim ignored her uneven walk, the painful way the shoulders dipped. She was a strikingly handsome woman.

But after dinner, when Nikoli had retired to the back room to clear his throat and collect his thoughts, Tim asked her outright.

Something came over her face, a door snapped shut; but before it did, he saw straight into her pain. Whatever had happened to her was at the center of Jenny.

"It was an accident," she shrugged. "I didn't heal right. The cast came off too soon." She sipped her tea. "Doesn't really matter anymore. I've gotten used to it. What about you? You're not Aleut."

He shook his head. "Eskimo."

"You speak perfect English."

"It's boarding-school English. My father sent me away when I was thirteen." Now it was his turn to back away.

Jenny scrutinized him and suddenly laughed. She set her teacup down and laughed until she held her sides.

"What's so funny?"

"*We* are," Jenny gasped. "You and I. You're right, you know. Quite right. We're alike. We both have 'vast uncharted regions through which strangers dare not tread.' Anyway, your little secrets are safe with me, kiddo, because I don't care to know them. Not any of them. It takes all the energy I can muster to stop thinking about my own. The only thing that really helps me forget is knowing I'm truly lost. Nobody can find me here—not even me." She laughed again.

Tim said, "I went home for the first time in twenty years two years ago."

Jenny smiled. "I don't want to hear it. Pain. All I hear is the pain in your voice. And believe me, Mr. Eskimo—"

"The name's Tim—"

"Mr. Eskimo Tim, I don't want it and I don't need it. So you can quietly get up and do your bleeding elsewhere."

"I live here," he protested.

"All right," she said amiably, and got to her feet, "I'll leave. You don't have to walk me home. I know the way."

At the door she turned and said, "At the risk of sounding like John Wayne, I think the island's not big enough for both of us."

He could hear her uneven steps a long time as she lurched over the wooden planks.

He showed up the next day as she was saying, "If two cans of milk cost ten cents, how much will four cans of milk cost?"

One of the boys who had carried Tim's trunk raised his hand.

Jenny nodded. "Yes. Vasily."

"At the trading store or the co-op?"

The class laughed.

Jenny said sternly, "Vasily, I am not amused."

"But Miss Blue, they're different," Vasily insisted. "At the co-op, you could trade fish for four cans and keep the money; but at the trading store, which is a dumb name because you can't trade there, they'll charge and how."

"And how much will they charge at the trading store?"

"For four cans?"

"If two cans are ten cents."

Vasily pondered it; he scratched his head. He said hopefully,

"You sure you wouldn't rather I caught the fish and took them to the co-op?"

The class guffawed. Jenny cracked her ruler against the desk and the class smartened up in appearance, if not in addition.

"Those of you in the blue book, finish lessons three and four. The red book, go over your subtraction; tomorrow, we're having a drill; and Tasha, do the algebraic equations on page thirty-nine. Now," she said brightly, as if it had been her idea all along, "we have a special guest today. Mr. Tim Snow."

The class stood to the left of the desk and clapped.

"Like a bad penny," she hissed at him. But she kept smiling. "Mr. Snow is going to treat us to a botany lesson, and we will all benefit from it, I'm sure. To assure that we will benefit from it, we will have a test tomorrow morning on everything he said."

She settled behind her desk and folded her hands. "Mr. Snow?"

"May I?" He held his bag over her desk.

"Certainly."

He opened the sack and took out dried plants stapled to a board. "Seaweeds. You eat them. Red dulse, alaria, laminaria, ulva. And wild cow parsnip. Putske. Which one tastes like celery?"

A small girl with enormous black eyes promptly waved her hand.

"Yes, Tanya," Jenny said.

"What does celery taste like?"

"Crisp, with veins that run up and down the stalk, juicy like it's full of water," Tim explained.

Tanya waved frantically.

"Yes, Tanya," Jenny said.

"Putske. My friends and I cut off the shoots with knives and tear back the leaves, and boy, is that ever good. But you stay away from the juice or it gives you a rash."

"Very good." Tim nodded, pleased. He held up a board of dried berries. "Who can tell me the names for these?"

A small youth with long hair and glasses raised his hand.

"Yes, Philip," Jenny said.

"That's an *unignaq*," he said softly.

"Good," Tim said. "Can you tell me the name in English?"

591

Philip studied the floor.

"Can anyone tell me the name in English?" When no one volunteered, Tim said, "It's a blueberry. Good eating."

The class nodded and he pointed. "Cranberry."

"Say it after him," Jenny instructed. "Cranberry."

"Cranberry," the class repeated.

"Crowberry," Tim pointed to a clump of smooth black berries.

"Crowberry," the class said.

"Very good." Tim put down the board. "Miss Blue and I have a surprise for you."

He avoided her eyes. "She has given me permission to take you all on a field trip outside the class. "We'll collect samples and learn their names."

Jenny went rigid with amazement.

He said earnestly, "I think we should all stand and give Miss Blue a big hand. What do you say?"

The class stood and clapped lustily and Tim turned and smiled broadly at Jenny. "Thank you, Miss Blue. I think my botany lesson is done for today."

"I should think so," Jenny agreed. Her voice was ice.

"Now be very good, very attentive, and learn all your lessons, and then Miss Blue will let you come outside with me. Won't you, Miss Blue?"

She smiled thin lipped at him. "Thank you, Mr. Snow. And now it's time for music."

It was the only way he could think of to make sure she saw him again and it worked. Right after school, Jenny hunted him down.

He was at Sandy Beach collecting the long grasses Aleuts wove into fine baskets.

He straightened when he saw her. "Well. How nice."

"You have really taken it too far." It was starting to rain, and Jenny stood in her boots and skirt in the tall grass and pulled her jacket closer. Her hair was damp where it stuck out from the scarf.

"What do you mean?"

"You know exactly what I mean. I should have you shot and stuffed with your own exhibit grass."

592

"Mad, huh?"

"Mad? I am furious. Furious. If I knew your supervisor's name, I'd report you."

"It's Lorkin. Got the address at the house."

"Why don't you leave me alone?" Jenny burst out. "Why do you keep bothering me?"

"Jenny, look at this." He held up a delicate lace fern. "Do you have any idea what this is?"

"Yes. It's an attempt to divert my attention. I'm telling you to leave me alone!"

"It's a *polystichum aleuticum*. Named it myself. As far as I know, they only grow here."

With grudging interest she leaned over to examine it. "Are you serious?"

He nodded. "I think it's indigenous to the chain. Maybe to Atka. When I go to Unalaska for a few days, I could take you along, if you could get away. We'll go hunting the wiley fern."

"Tim," Jenny said, remembering herself. "I'm not interested in you or your fern or for that matter, going to Unalaska. I have my work and my responsibilities and that's enough."

"You are a hard case, aren't you?"

"As nails," Jenny said. "Well. You are finally getting the idea. Since you committed me to a field trip, I have to go along with it, but I don't have to like the idea, or you. So. If we understand each other. You do understand, don't you."

"Quite."

"Good." She extended her hand. "I'll say good-bye."

He grasped her hand, brought it to his mouth and kissed it. She slapped him.

He slapped her back.

"That is quite enough," she shrilled.

"For me, too. You're right. You win. You can go on being rude forever. But you should know something. Someplace along the line, your rudeness soured into downright nastiness. You want to be left alone. Fine. I'll leave you alone with pleasure."

He stomped away from her.

"Tim," she called.

He ignored her.

"Tim." She came closer.

~~He was yanking out samples.~~

"I'm sorry," she said stiffly.

He kept weeding.

"I have soup going, if you don't have other plans."

He straightened. Jenny's hands were cupped together and her body was shifted to take flight, but she held her ground and repeated, "If you aren't busy."

"I'd like that," he said.

He came an hour later, bearing gifts.

"Gertrude Lawrence," Jenny said reverently. It was a recent *Life*, June 13. Gertrude was wearing a mushroom hat and white gloves and making lips at herself in a mirror. "She's stunning."

Tim looked over her shoulder at the cover. "May I?"

She nodded and he thumbed rapidly through it, creased it open and handed it back. "I thought maybe the kids would be interested."

The caption read "Speaking of Pictures . . . a movie sea lion goes to work."

Curley worked for Paramount Pictures, making *Spawn of the North*, with George Raft. The pictures followed him from the time he turned off his alarm clock with a flipper to his first appearance on the set.

Jenny laughed. "Vasily'll want to take the next boat out."

"To volunteer as Curley's trainer?"

"No, to kill him and eat him."

Tim laughed and Jenny said, "I do appreciate it. Thank you. It's been a long time since I've seen one of these."

"There are some other stories you might want to use in class. Pictures of a million-dollar dog show at Madison Square Garden. Breeds the kids have never seen: Great Danes, Cocker Spaniels, Russian Wolfhounds. A Kuvasz. Oh, and there's also a whole story about Marian Anderson performing in Philadelphia at the Academy of Music. If the kids have experienced any prejudice yet."

"Not here." She shook her head. "Most of them will never leave the chain."

She read through it, and Tim said, "She left right afterward for her house on the Riviera, so she's not doing badly for a Negro."

Jenny recited, "The gilt and plush boxes, usually occupied by Drexels and Biddles, were filled with Philadelphia's Negro society, who had come to hear the lovely contralto voice of their race's greatest woman singer." She put the magazine away. "Things really won't be equal until the whites come to hear her, too."

"It won't happen," Tim said bitterly. "At least not in our lifetime."

She went to stir the soup. "Was there a lot of prejudice against you?"

Tim stuck his hands in his pockets and sighed. "Sure you want to hear about it? I thought you said other people's pain was a pain."

"It is," she said calmly.

He laughed and looked out the window. It was blowing outside, quick little gusts that rattled the tin roof and shook the door.

"How did you wind up working with plants?" She carried the soup to the small table covered with oilcloth, got two spoons and a plate of fried bread, along with greens she had picked outside.

Tim adjusted the wick on the oil lamp. He shrugged. "It was my major in college."

He held her chair out and she sat down. "Where did you go?"

"Doane College in Crete, Nebraska, home of Alpo Dog Food and raging desperation. The women lived in Frees Hall, under lock and key and the constant eye of Miss Brooks. They had to sign in and out and be back in the hall by eight o'clock on class nights. The campus had brick buildings and climbing ivy and a footbridge spanning an algae-crusted pond, and on soft spring nights, girls would roll up their blankets outside on the lawn, and watch the fireflies."

"It sounds wonderful."

"We called it 'Deadly Doane where all the Cretins go.' So perhaps I'm not capturing its essence. The place seethed with a last-chance kind of bitterness: the students were farmers' children and knew they would be returned to the farm like cows to their stalls at the end of four years. Escape was brief and poignant. Oh, there were some exotics: an Arabian prince wanted to buy Miss Brooks when he first saw her trotting across campus, breasts rigidly contorted under a tight sweater. But for the most part, they lived and died in Crete or Fremont or Beatrice, sometimes bolting as far as Lincoln to look at a real University, which only enhanced their feelings of inferiority. Even the teachers were sick of it. It was a Congregationalist college, a teacher's college."

He picked up his spoon and stirred.

"Then why aren't you teaching?"

Tim smiled bitterly. "No one would hire an Eskimo. I applied to fifty-nine high schools and received seventy-two rejections. Some high schools got wind of it and rejected me in advance to save time. Finally I threw myself on the mercy of the Interior Department and insisted they give me a job. I made it so awkward they finally did."

"Must have been hard for you in school."

He shrugged. "The dean referred to me at a fall tea as 'the savage.' The worst was the first spring, during the one long, lavender-colored night the freshmen are picked for a fraternity." He sipped, stopped, and leaned on his elbow, staring into space.

"I remember the windows were all up and the room was full of the hazy smell of corn from the dog-food plant, and you could hear the cheering and laughter, the muffled commands, the footsteps on the lawn. My roommate was picked early, and I tried reading a magazine, but I was acutely aware of little sounds. Waiting. Eventually, of course, the night sounds died away, the campus shifted and settled and went to sleep. No one ever came for me. I didn't find out until the next day that I was the only one on the whole campus who wasn't picked. The only one."

He smiled sadly. "They liked me, too. It wasn't that. I was an Eskimo. I had brown skin and a flat face and different memories."

"I would have left," Jenny said flatly, spreading the fried bread with blueberry jam.

596

"I was on a four-year scholarship and had failed to read the fine print. They owned me for four years, Jen. It was part of the deal. The other part was that I would be exhibited whenever trustees came with their checkbooks out. An example of how even the most bestial of men could still have a preppy veneer."

"Did you fantasize revenge?"

Tim laughed. "I *lived* it."

"What did you do?"

"The last day, after I had graduated, with my diploma in hand so there was no way for them to take it back, I streaked the faculty-trustee picnic waving a hatchet, wearing a loincloth and a smile."

"You didn't!" Jenny giggled. "What happened?"

"Miss Brooks asked me for a date."

Jenny laughed. "See, there's some triumph in there."

"Lots of triumph," Tim said seriously. "But I still ended up here."

"You don't like Atka?"

"I love Atka. It's a botanist's paradise. What I mean is, prejudice in America is a deep-rot disease. People give lip service to it, Jen, but things won't be equal as long as the natives have to sit on their own side of the theater in Nome. And the States are ten times worse, with their white drinking fountains and off-limit swimming areas.

"I went home, Jen, and the poverty I saw filled me up. With rage. Most of my family's gone, killed by disease and neglect. My dad wanted me to stay. He has this idea that I was meant to lead our people into some great shining future, but Jen, I knew if I did stay, I'd wind up killing somebody. There is no future for my people. The Eskimos along with the Arctic Ocean are finished, along with the Indians in the interior and the Aleut children stumbling through phonetic English in your class. It's a dying way of life, and the sad thing is, it's dying without a word. The rich variety of history, the tangle of customs—all of it. It will be as extinct as the Aleutian sea cow in a few years."

"How would you like to give a report to my class on growing up Eskimo?" Jenny said suddenly. "The kids would love it. They can't believe your ocean freezes solid in the winter. Please, say you'll do it."

She reached out and touched him with strong, white fingers. "All right," Tim said. "Any time you want."

He got up. It was raining heavily outside. "Thank you for your hospitality," Tim said. "I appreciate it."

He went to the door, and Jenny followed him. "I'm glad you came," she said shyly.

"Thank you for asking me." He didn't try to kiss her.

They call it a williwaw, and it's the strongest wind in the world. It slams down mountains, shifting through the warm currents, and can pick up a grown man and hurl him to his knees. It's as devastating as a hurricane only colder.

This one came up fast in a clatter of hail at the end of the field trip. The students saw it spiraling down Korovino Volcano and got immediately to their knees, covering their heads.

It picked up the samples they had collected and tossed them out to sea. Charlie Korson lifted his head and was bounced end over end toward the bluff. Tim Snow hurtled after him and brought him down.

"Hang on to me," he commanded, and got on his hands and knees, pulling against the wind until he dropped Charlie next to his friends, like a pup.

"Is there any shelter around here?" he yelled to Jenny, over the wind.

She nodded. "About a half a mile—" she screamed. "Over the next bluff."

Single file, adults at the front and rear, they crawled over the muskeg, holding on to each other when things got rough.

It was a barabara, a sod house abandoned before their grandparents were born. They dropped down the roof, toehold notched inside, and dropped through a hole.

A rat scuttled in the corner and disappeared through a hole. Tim patted his pockets for a match, found one and lit the candle he took from his pocket.

They were in a dirt room about twelve by twelve feet, latched with dried reeds. It was bare except for a curious dry mound of earth in one corner. It looked like the hive for an enormous bee. The students clustered around it and Tim commanded,

"Don't touch it." He held the light high and examined it, his voice curiously pitched. "Jenny. Miss Blue. Come here, please."

Jenny limped over.

"Do you know what this is? Do you know what we have here?"

She shook her head.

"It's a mummy. I'm almost positive. The Aleuts along the chain mummified their dead." He raised his candle. "How many of you know what a mummy is?"

Vasily raised his hand confidently.

"Vasily," Jenny said.

"A mummy is a person who is the closest to you in the whole world. She puts you to bed when you're little and never forgets your name, no matter how many kids there are."

"That's a *mommy*, Vasily," Tim said gently. "But that's a good try. No, a mummy is a dead body."

The children stared at it.

"You mean there's somebody in there?" The littlest boy drew back.

"It's possible," Tim admitted. "Long ago, relatives would keep the body inside the house, sometimes for months, and talk to it."

"It bet it never said much back," Vasily said.

"The body would be all folded up, as if the person were sitting with his knees up and his hands covering his face, like this." Tim gave the candle to Jenny, got down on his haunches, drew up his knees and covered his face with his hands.

"Didn't it stink?" Vasily asked.

Tim stood and shook his head. "No. Everything inside was taken out and the bodies were stuffed with straw, like dolls. Sometimes they were put in an ice-cold stream for days, and then dried and taken inside."

"Let's bust it open and see," Vasily suggested.

"No," Tim said sharply. "And this is important. This barabara is off limits now to everybody. Understand? A special kind of doctor has to come and look at it."

"It seems pretty late for that," Vasily said doubtfully.

The storm was easing to a brisk rain, and Jenny said, "I think we should start home, gang. What do you say?"

He made a fire in her stove, and Jenny got down a bottle of wine. "To celebrate," she said. "Do you think it really could be a mummy?"

He took the glass. "I think so." He couldn't keep the excitement out of his voice. "Ales Hrdlicka discovered a large burial site on Kagamil Island. Actually two caves. He found two hundred beautifully preserved bodies going back at least a thousand years. But that was nine years ago. This could be a major find."

"You'll be leaving then, I guess."

He shook his head. "Not until next spring at the earliest. I'm here for the winter."

They drank the wine and the rain fell outside and Tim said, "I never asked you about your folks."

"There's nobody alive in my family," Jenny said. She drank.

"Why don't I believe you?"

Jenny laughed. "Probably because it's a lie. Now drink the wine like a good boy and then you can walk home through the hail and think of me all night."

He drew her to him and kissed her lightly. "Is that my homework?"

"No," she pulled away. "No, that was just a way for me to maintain distance. That old bugaboo. Don't you think you have one or two things you keep relearning in your life, over and over?"

"What do you mean?"

"I keep relearning that I'm really quite alone, and that I had better buck up and learn to live with it."

"You don't have to, you know."

"Learn to live with it?"

"Be alone." He put down his glass of wine. It was deep red in the soft light of the fire.

"Come now, Tim Snow. If you're planning on romance and candlelight, you've picked the wrong woman."

"I have?"

"Pick someone young, with fire in her veins, someone who's not afraid, and willing to risk it all."

600

"I think I picked the right one."

Jenny poured more wine. "We seem to be drifting into something here, Mr. Snow. Would you care to explain it?"

"I think I picked a woman who is exceedingly kind, extremely bright and not a little cautious. She fires my nights with questions."

"Well, as long as that's all she fires." She drank.

"That's not all." Tim gently loosened her hair. "Why is it you go to such enormous lengths, Jenny Blue, to make yourself look dowdy? You are truly the most lovely of women."

Her hair tumbled down her back. Tim caressed her neck.

"Tim." There was fear in her voice.

"What are you afraid of, Jen? What?"

Tears rolled down her face. She got up. "I think it's time you left." She limped over and held open his jacket. "Please. I do. Please."

He got up, sighed, put down his glass. "Jenny Blue, I will not harm you. I have something quite different in mind."

"Please," she said stridently. "Please—"

"It's not what you imagine, either." He took her hand and pressed it to his face. "Jenny, you are a gift from God. I will keep saying that over and over until you finally drop this false twisted thing inside of you that's been tearing you apart. You are a lovely gift from God. And it warms my heart to have you in my life."

He kissed her hand and went out into the stormy night.

Such a cautious courtship. Like a deer, Tim thought, Jenny was always ready to bolt at the least sign of danger. Quiet fencing took them through the winter and into spring. She still hadn't shared anything about herself, but she had stopped flinching when he touched her.

In late March the man from the Smithsonian arrived with calipers and cameras and spatulas and a whole bag of tricks, picked up the mummy pod and left on the next boat.

"Do you suppose we'll ever know what it was?"

Tim tried to hide his disappointment. "Don't know, Jen."

"Why did he bring all that stuff with him if he wasn't going to open it here?"

"Don't know that, either."

"I hope at least he gives you some credit. Calls it *Hominus Snow Erectus,* or something."

Tim laughed. "What? Are you leaping to my defense?"

"Not leaping. I'm afraid that's quite out of my realm. Let's say I'm cautiously coming around."

"To what?" He took her hand.

"To liking you."

"Wonderful. Let's have a party."

The williwaw was butting heads outside but inside, the fire burned hot and bright. One thing led to another. He kissed her.

She tensed. Relaxed. He kissed her again. And again.

Finally he picked her up and carried her to her bed and laid her down and said "Jenny, Jenny" over and over as he took down her buttons and ran his hands down her body.

Her breath heaved, not from passion, but from fear and trying to contain it all, and he finally got her undressed and lay next to her.

"Oh, no," she said. "Oh, no." Her body trembled.

Tim said, "I'd sure like to get my hands on the man who did this to you."

She was rattling and crying and saying over and over "Oh no, oh no," while outside, the wind whistled and the door thudded and the loose tin banged on the roof.

"Jenny, Jenny, I won't hurt you. I won't. Jenny. Talk to me. Tell me what's happening."

"This isn't a good idea and I want you to leave."

"Tell me what happened, Jen." He touched her belly and she buckled away from him.

"Please, please."

"What happened? Were you raped?" He sat up in bed and touched her face with his hand. Her teeth chattered. "Is that it, Jen? Is that what happened?"

"No, no," she thrashed her head and suddenly grew very still. Tears slid down her face. "You really want to know, don't you?"

"Jenny Blue, I've asked for a transfer to stay indefinitely on Atka. I want to marry you."

602

A sob rattled in her throat. "That's not possible," she said finally.

"I want to marry you. I love you."

"I'm damaged goods." She rolled away and buried her face in the pillow.

"What do you mean? Damaged goods? What kind of bull is that?

"Did you kill someone?"

Jenny spoke tonelessly, hopelessly. "No, no. Didn't have to."

"Did you walk the streets? Because if you did, it wouldn't matter. It wouldn't. I love you."

"No. No. Neither of those."

"Then what?"

She shook next to him. He touched her arm, her face, her chest. "Tell me."

"I was in love with a boy through high school," she whispered.

"And after high school? What happened after high school?"

The hail clattered and the wind gusted and grew still.

"I married him. It was at the start of the war. He was going away. We married." Her voice was harsh and low. "We married. And I loved him more than life." She laughed through the tears. "You know, I used to make deals with God. I'd say, 'God, if you bring him home, I'll never ask for another thing, ever.'"

"Did he come home?"

Jenny was silent. She put her hands to her face. Tim took them down, pressed them to his heart. "Did he come home, Jen?"

She shook her head soundlessly.

"Was there something wrong with him?"

Her face collapsed. "Yes," she whispered. "He was my brother."

"Oh, Jen, oh, Jen, oh, sweetheart, oh, my love." He pulled her into his arms and held her.

"I didn't know," Jenny sobbed. "My mother knew. She never told me. I married my own brother—"

He kissed her strongly and long, and reached down his hand

603

and stroked her.

She stiffened and pulled away but he kept saying, "No, Jen, no, Jen, I love you. It's okay, Jen. It's fine."

He stroked her harder and faster, until she reached the point where in all the books she read the woman's heart beat like a dove or a star burst across the sky, only it wasn't like that; it was intense, and sudden and violent and Jenny kept saying, "Ah, ah," over and over and afterwards, he held her and she cried.

In the morning, he said, "Let's get married. Let's go and have the bishop or whoever it is at a Russian Orthodox Church—let's have him marry us. I want to make love to you, Jen, and I want to do it as your husband."

The inside of the church was soft blue with white trim and all the candles had been lit.

The bishop was wearing long gold robes and his assistants were in white. They broke the sacrament and blessed it and Jenny and Tim held hands and spoke their love and afterward, the children ran ahead of them dropping flowers.

He took her home and made love to her and loved her always and in all ways, and in January of 1940, they had a child, a son.

They named him Tommy Ryan Snow, after her mother's father.

He was born with two small birthmarks—a strange purple scar on his shoulder, slightly indented as if it had been gored by a bear, and a small purple line slashing his face.

The same markings as Nuka.

Fifty

In some way, in the fall of 1940, Anchorage was as removed as Atka. The iron boots of Nazis marched across France toward Belgium; Edward R. Murrow interrupted the CBS "World News Roundup" with bulletins from the front; and Walter Lippmann warned America to beef up its navy, but it was all far away and happening to somebody else.

In Anchorage there were streetlights but hardly any streets, cars but no place to go. License plates had four numbers.

It was middle America, set off to one side.

The Cincinnati Reds won the World Series and Anchorage found out a day late. The contests on the back of Wheaties boxes expired before the boxes made it to the grocery shelves; and *Good-bye, Mr. Chips* was welcomed home to the Empress two years after everybody else saw it.

But a can of beets cost only 13 cents, and everybody knew where their kids were. Everybody else's kids, too, for that matter.

It was *Our Town* without the elms; Kansas with mountains and no Auntie Em.

The spring before, in Washington, the army had asked for $12 million to build a base near Anchorage. It was refused. Five days later Hitler pushed into Norway and Denmark, and a senator with an atlas figured out where Alaska was. The money was reinstated. The army moved in with bulldozers and cats, but it was still somebody else's army, out there on the edge of town.

In the fall of 1940 the town was still drifting, like a hypnotist's subject, deeper and deeper into sleep.

Flame balanced the tray on her arm and quietly opened the

door. Jordan slept with one arm flung back and her dark hair tousled a child-like face. Flame put the tray on the top of the bureau and studied her daughter. A lump rose in her throat.

Too soon, she thought. Too soon.

A corkboard of campaign buttons hung next to the sink and Flame stared at it until her eyes cleared.

No More	If I Were	Thanksgiving	NO
Fireside	21	Day	FRANKLIN
Chats	I'd Vote	Nov. 5	THE
	for Willkie		FIRST

And underneath, a neat row of pro buttons:

Two	FDR	Better a
Good Terms	CARRY	Third Timer
Deserve	ON	Than a
Another		Third Rater

She stepped around the Toastmaster waffle iron next to the hope chest and sat on the edge of the bed. "Jordan. Sweetie. Time to wake up. It's the big day."

Puzzled, Jordan opened her eyes, focused on her mother, squeezed her hand. "Are you scared?" she whispered.

"Are you?" Flame asked.

Jordan shook her head. "I love him, mom. I really do. He'll be good to me. You'll see."

"But you're so young!" Flame cried, stopped. She wasn't going to say that. Not today. Not again.

"Mother."

Flame sighed; her mouth trembled. "Forgive me," she whispered. "Today of all days. Well. I brought you breakfast in bed."

She got up briskly and went to the dresser. "Your favorite: orange juice, eggs benedict and coffee. Black." She settled the tray on Jordan's knees.

"I love you, mom," Jordan said.

"I know," Flame said. She clasped her hands together. "Did David's vacation come through?"

Jordan shook her head and dug into the eggs. "Not until after Christmas. The department's short staffed now, anyway, with Capper on leave. We've decided on where, though."

She reached into her nightstand and drew out a brochure. "Southern California. We're going to lie around on the beach and visit Paramount Pictures. I can hardly wait."

"I'm happy for you, Jordan—" She hesitated and Jordan eyed her curiously over the top of her fork.

"What?"

"Do you have any—questions?"

Jordan chewed and swallowed. "You mean about sex?"

"Well, yes. About sex. Do you have any questions?"

"Mother, it's 1940." And then realizing that sounded more curt than she intended, she added gently, "I don't know a lot of things. But I know David will be kind to me."

"Are you planning on having children right away?"

Jordan shook her head. "Not with college correspondence. Of course, David's parents want one a month. Two if the month has thirty-one days."

"You don't think they're going to be—a problem?" She was trying to be so careful.

Jordan shook her head. "No," she said flatly. "And really, mother, you'll like them. Mr. and Mrs. Kobayashi are nisei. Second-generation Americans. The only thing Japanese is their last name."

"So many apartments won't take nonwhites—"

Jordan shrugged. "Then we'll live on the beach. Oh, mother, I don't mean to sound flip, but it's got to stop sometime. It's all so silly. The idea that white is right. David's a policeman, for Pete's sake. He hasn't had trouble making arrests with eyes like slanted almonds"—she paused dramatically and giggled—"lips like pomegranates, teeth like stars—"

"Okay, okay," Flame laughed. "I get the idea. And honey, I am glad for you. Sad for me, I have to admit. But glad for you."

"Oh, mom." She squeezed her hand. "I'll visit. You'll get so sick of me—"

"Only to visit, though. I don't want you coming home to mama when things get rough."

"Ah, tossed from the nest into the arms of the savage beast

of desire."

"You've been reading too many novels." Flame picked up a small box on the nightstand.

"A beauty patch for my breast," Flame explained.

"Times have changed. I can remember when you didn't have breasts."

"That's not hard. It was last week."

"Oh, come on." She smoothed Jordan's hair. "Darn it. When did you grow up? I'll talk to David. There oughta be a law."

Jordan threw her arms around Flame and they held each other. "Wish dad could give me away," Jordan said finally.

"Me, too, honey," Flame whispered.

Jordan pulled away suddenly. "What time is it?"

"Late," Flame pronounced. "Almost eleven."

"You're kidding! How could you let me sleep that long?"

"Because you'll be up all night," Flame kissed her soundly and left the room before Jordan could see the tears.

The rituals. The rites of passage. Why couldn't she watch Jordan floating down the aisle in a billowing cloud of satin and feel only motherly pride?

The dress warranted it: they had paid a fortune, a dollar per square foot of antique ivory satin and had it specially made in California by Philip Mangone. It was drenched in crystal beads and lace and held up as if by magic over Jordan's delicate breasts. The veil in her hair was pinned with satin flowers encrusted with seed pearls, and she carried the family Bible, as she walked down the aisle escorted by a family friend. Flame thought of Batt and the old pain came flooding back.

Now Jordan was detaching herself from Cam's immaculate gray-haired wrist to stand across from David. The row of bridesmaids stretched behind her like turquoise lagoons.

The minister was insisting she love, honor and obey, and Jordan was giving up without a fight.

Obey, Jordan? Obey?

David smiled down at her and told her he would love and cherish her until death took him.

But Jordan, there are so many ways to die, Flame wanted to

explain. It's such a fragile thing, this bond.

But Jordan wasn't listening.

On the groom's side, George Kobayashi glanced down the clean, composed row of his children dressed by Saks Fifth Avenue and back at his oldest son. Pride swelled in his chest for this sansei with the winning smile and firm step.

George was rich. He was a mechanical genius. He had made a fortune patenting his hydraulic gear grinder used for airplanes and now divided his time between the United Aircraft military plant in California and tending flowers in his Anchorage garden. He wanted to buy David his own factory, but David refused, so George bought him a Dodge with fluid drive instead and a matching one for Jordan.

Jordan was frail and lovely as a reed, and she loved his son. George could see it in her eyes.

Perhaps in his secret heart he had desired a more suitable companion, a young woman trained in the art of compliance; certainly he wished the couple had chosen to live with them; but George was a practical man. He knew David had to live his life his own way.

George composed his hands during the minister's prayer for long life and guidance, and added his own silent signal into the swirling jet of spirits. His mother had belonged to the Church of Christ of Japan, and his father practiced ryobu-Shinto. George prayed to them all.

"It has eight hundred parts," he explained over the noise. A swing band was playing at the Elks' Club. It sounded like Woody Herman with a learner's permit.

"It must be fascinating." Flame poured more champagne in George's glass.

He looked at her sharply. "No. Frightening. We have so far to go in such a short time." He led her through the double doors onto the iron-grilled balcony.

"You think we'll get involved, Mr. Kobayashi?"

He nodded. "It's inevitable. Hitler's a madman. Right now we are hopelessly underpowered. We have a naval fleet of twelve battleships, six aircraft carriers, eighteen heavy cruisers—" He shook his head. "Half the destroyers in the fleet are left from the First World War. I served on a ship that's still expected to perform. That's why the impetus to produce more aircraft."

"I keep thinking you're Japanese, but you're not really, are you?"

He laughed. "I was born in Portland. My parents were toddlers when they left Kyoto. I'd like to visit, though, after—the madness."

He drank and patted his mouth with a handkerchief.

Flame said, "I am honored we are related by marriage, and I am looking forward to having your family to dinner."

He bowed slightly, straightened. Erect, he was the same height as Flame.

"The honor is mine, and my family's. You have built Jackson's Flying Air into an empire. If my memory serves me, you have six Vegas, a fleet wing amphibian and S-39 Sikorsky—all with Morse radios—and offer the only reliable daily service to south central Alaska. Most of it accomplished in the last four years."

"Thank you, Mr. Kobayashi. You give me far too much credit. My late husband was the guiding force behind Jackson Air. I picked up whatever fell off his desk."

Kobayashi bowed again. "As you wish, Mrs. Jackson, but you have still accomplished remarkable things."

The orchestra finished "Woodchopper's Ball." "Attention, attention. May I have your attention. I would like to present—" The bandleader curled his hand over the microphone. "Drumroll, Bill." The drum started.

"I would like to present the new Mr. and Mrs. David Kobayashi. A toast! A toast!"

The guests clapped and David pulled Jordan onto the stage. They had both been drinking. David's bow tie was clipped to his pocket and his hair stuck up around his ears. Jordan's face was flushed.

"To my dear wife," he whumped her fanny, giggled and leaned over her, "what did you say your name was?"

"David!"

"To my dear wife, Jordan. Who has made this the happiest

610

day of my life. Happy—'' he added soddenly, ''so happy.''
Tears came to his eyes.

Jordan immediately crossed her arm through his and they
drank from each other's glass, although Flame thought that it
was the last thing in the world they needed.

The guests cheered and Flame clapped, a lump in her throat.

Why did it feel so wrong?

Maybe it was knowing how empty the house would feel.

Stop it, Flame, she thought. This is no time for feeling sorry
for yourself. You've been alone before. You can be alone again.
New beginnings, she thought. I'll drink to that. And she raised
her glass and drank a toast to herself.

Jordan changed into a Lord & Taylor aviator dress and sailor
hat. Flame kissed her daughter one last time, and they gathered
for the ritual throwing of rice. It all had an air of unreality.

The couple ducked heads through the rain of rice, running
to a car doctored by David's younger brothers.

''Not an easy night. Watching Jordan go.'' It was Cam
Combs, Batt's old friend who had first found the body, and the
man who had given Jordan away.

Now he looked like he wanted to take her back.

''Could I drive you home?''

''Thanks, Cam. I brought the Ford. But you're welcome to
stop by for a drink.''

He was agitated and gray and blubbery, all belly and
mustache.

''Whatever are you trying to say?''

He stopped striding, stuck his hands in the pockets of his
gray pinstripe pants and came suddenly to the sofa and knelt
next to her.

''I'm quite attracted to you.'' He threw his arms around her
and muffled himself deep in her chest.

''Please. Cam. Please.'' She whacked him on the back, trying
to get his attention.

''Flame, I—''

''Cam.'' She pulled away, breathless, and leaped to her feet.
''Cam,'' she said, again, regaining her composure.

He was still prostrate, kneeling by the sofa, arms flung over

611

the candy-striped fabric where Flame's bottom had so recently been.

"Cam. I don't feel that way about you." She said it as gently as possible. "I think of you as a friend. That's all."

He raised his head. "But you're alone now," he protested. "You need someone."

"I have someone." She sat down on the rosewood settee.

"What?" He sounded so genuinely amazed that Flame giggled.

"It's true, I do."

"Who?"

"Me."

Cam smiled uncertainly, as if there were a punch line in there someplace. "I don't understand."

Flame got to her feet and handed him his tails and hat. "Somehow, I knew you'd say that."

"But Flame—"

"Good-bye, Cam."

"Flame." He turned nasty. "What about all those times you threw yourself at me?"

"What?"

"The church bazaar. I know you didn't give me a special price on those pot holders for nothing."

"They were priced to move, Cam. You were just the right person at the right time. There's nothing between us."

"Not anymore," he said furiously and banged out the door.

Flame collapsed, giggling. Poor Cam.

She turned the radio up loud and sang along with Arthur Treacher as she changed into gray slacks and an ivory velour top. It was Cole Porter's latest hit, "Panama Hattie."

"You'll head the class when you cut the grass on the outskirts of Honolulu . . ."

She frowned into the mirror. Gray and a sprinkling of auburn. But her bones were still good, her eyes vivid green. Hardly any lines. New beginnings, she reminded herself. Impulsively she went through the house with a box, collecting things she had always tolerated but never liked—a stuffed goat

612

head with one ear missing; a lamp in the shape of a sea lion Batt had found at some auction. She chucked the box up into the attic, then paused on the ladder, frowned, and trained her flashlight into the gloom.

It was a box she had never seen and attached to it was a letter in Batt's handwriting.

It was addressed to her.

She gripped the flashlight under her arm and pulled down the box. She carried it into the living room, fixed herself a drink and opened the letter.

My best friend—my love

This is a box of Jenny's things. Remember the day you told me to get rid of them. I couldn't. I knew someday you would need to hold her things in your hands again. Here they are.

It will never stop hurting, Flame. I guess the most we can do is accept that; that it's always going to hurt. Darling, always know I have loved you without question, without looking back. Darling, my darling Flame.

Your husband,

Batt

Flame pressed the letter to her breast and carefully put it down. Trembling, she opened the box. Here was the five-legged purple moose, Jenny's diploma, a plaster handprint, a string vase she had made for some forgotten Mother's Day: the bits and pieces of Jenny's childhood.

At the bottom was a collection of schoolwork: an essay on "What It Means To Be An American"; Jenny's first A on a spelling test: and a note laboriously printed on the back of an old electric bill:

Dear Mom,

Don't worry.

It is only a little cut in the curten.
We got most of the blud out.

Your fren,

Jennifer

Blood, curtain, cut? Flame didn't remember any of it. She read it again, smiling, then picked up the moose and hung him over the dining-room table.

"Welcome back, my friend."

He carried her over the threshold and set her down with a crash. "Oops," he whooshed. "Uh, oh." He tottered off to the bathroom and Jordan heard the sound of violent retching.

She picked herself off the floor and looked around. They were at the Anchorage Hotel. The room had one double bed, a chair and dresser with a mirror. Over the bed hung a picture of Judge Wickersham, in a Charlie Chaplin bowler hat and mustache, trying to feed a moose.

"Anything I can do?" she called.

"Pray for me." He hiccuped and threw up some more.

Jordan took off her hat and gloves, kicked off her shoes and settled back onto the bed.

Half an hour later, a chastened and subdued David wove his way to the bed and collapsed heavily on the spread.

"David?" She shook him. "David?" Jordan pulled off his shoes and socks and undressed him.

He had a small and compact body, with no chest hair and an enormous penis.

"Honey," Jordan sat next to him. "Honey."

She nudged him. She fondled him. She kissed him with her mouth open; and after a while, she gave up and went to sleep.

"How do you feel?"

He groaned. "Did you catch the man who did it?"

"Did what?"

"Ran me down with his truck. My head is broken. I mean, broken, Jorde."

"Here, honey." She brought him a glass of water and an aspirin.

"Give me all of them," he muttered.

She patted his hand. "You'll feel better in a minute. You'll see."

He tried to get up, groaned, and sank into the pillow. "What happened?"

"You mean last night?"

"Uh, huh."

"Before or after you threw up and passed out?"

"Oh, Jorde."

"It's all right. We're going to be married a long time."

"Starting now," David said. "Come here."

"David. How much do you love me?"

He was holding on to her hips, moving under her. "Lots."

"How much is lots?"

"Up to here." He gently pressed her firm belly and she felt him moving inside.

"How does it feel when you're inside?"

"Wonderful."

"How wonderful?" she persisted.

He brought his fingers to her lips. "Hush," he said gently. "I'll show you."

"How was it?" She kissed him and took his jacket.

It was four-thirty in the morning. He had the graveyard shift during September.

"Okay." He fixed himself a drink. "Ralph Lincoln Stoutimore was acting up at the Frisco Café again. Been drinking and raising hell since six in the morning yesterday, so by ten last night, he was tooted to beat the band. Kept threatening to cut up anybody who touched him."

Jordan dished up the Salisbury steak and peas and got out the French dressing she had made.

"Didn't have a knife, though."

"That's good," Jordan said, and carried the platter to the table. She went back and pulled out the corn muffins.

"Only excitement happened right after I came on.

615

Whitney—remember him—the turnkey?"

"Vaguely," Jordan said, and went to the refrigerator for the butter and jam and salad.

"He came rushing into the office about seven-thirty and told us a prisoner was crawling through the window."

"Crawling through the window?" She picked up the salt and pepper, counted the silverware on the place mats and said, "It's time to sit up, hon."

"Bob Young was his name." David brought his glass to the table and sat down. "We lit out across the yard like a bat out of hell and dashed across the front yard of City Hall."

"You found him, though?" She had clasped her hands, waiting.

"In one of the pits. We borrowed leg irons from the U.S. Marshal and he was quiet the rest of the night." He bowed his head. "For this and all Your gifts, we give thanks. Amen."

"Amen," Jordan said, and shook out her napkin. "Have you found out yet who broke out the windows at the R.R. dining room?"

David shook his head. "Running down suspects." He dug into his meat. "All under ten, too. Somebody's going to cave any day now. We've got the heat on."

"Kids."

"Reminds me," he said, wiping his mouth. "Dr. Wakowsky has quarantined the Higgins house. Scarlet fever. Everybody's got it. She's in your bridge club, isn't she?"

Jordan nodded. "Oh, dear. Everybody? Their littlest is only five months."

"Well, it might pass through. Fever's a bad business."

They ate in silence the rest of the dinner. Jordan said, "You're supposed to ask me what I did today."

"Okay. What did you do today?"

"I washed and ironed and scrubbed the kitchen floor. Exciting stuff, huh?"

He grinned. "*You* are all the excitement this cop needs."

"Good," she said, and put down her fork. "Because I think it's time for dessert." She pushed herself away from the table and danced into the bedroom. "Coming, big boy?"

He grinned. "Sooner than you think."

The newspaper was spread over the bed and David stopped her from picking it up. "Wait a minute."

He looked at the front page. "Well, I'll be damned."

"What is it?" Jordan peered over his shoulder.

"The draft, Jorde. They're starting the draft.

She gripped his arms. "Let's not think about it. Maybe it's going to go away."

"It's not, Jorde. It's not." But he let himself be pulled down to her, and for a while at least, it didn't matter.

Fifty-One

They were sleeping when it happened, and having breakfast when they heard. It was an AP wire radio report:

"War struck suddenly and without warning from the sky yesterday as Japanese bombs took a heavy toll of American lives at Pearl Harbor."

Jordan put down her fork. "I don't believe—"

"Hush." David held up his hand, listening to the crackle over the radio.

"Witnesses counted at least fifty planes which centered their attacks on Hickam Field, the huge army base three miles northwest of Honolulu."

"Dear God!" Jordan cried.

They stared at each other across the table.

President Roosevelt's voice came over the air: "I asked Congress to declare that since this unprovoked and dastardly attack by the Japanese on Sunday, December 7, a state of war has existed between us and the Japanese empire. This is a day that will live in infamy."

David pushed himself away from the table and stumbled into the bedroom, yanking on his pants, hopping on one foot, pulling on his boots.

"Where are you going? Your shift doesn't start until six tonight."

"Mom and dad's."

"Why?"

"I'm going to mom and dad's."

"I don't understand."

He pulled on his jacket and ran to the door.

"Why, David? What's going on?"

"They're *Japanese*." He threw open the door and ran down the steps.

"But David! They were born in Portland! Both of them!" David ran faster.

They were all up. In the tank, a pink-and-orange angel fish swam in leisurely circles around the castle and the sea urchin, watching them.

His sisters huddled like porcelain dolls on the sofa. Jed sprawled on the floor, the red cuffs of his pajamas sticking out from under the blue terry cloth robe.

"We'll take it as it comes." His father shrugged. "That's all we can do. We're Americans. Good solid citizens. And if it weren't for me, the government would be grinding gears for planes by hand, at ten months a crack. Now wouldn't that be something?"

"Listen to me," David said urgently. "I've got contacts in Anchorage. Connections. You sit tight. Take it easy. Just go on about your business, and I'll get things handled. Okay? Mom?"

She was a small, nut-colored woman with enormous brown eyes. She was wearing a tufted satin robe the color of coffee. "Oh, Davey, I'll be brave. I'll try. It's such a dishonor for our family—"

"Listen, ma." David gently took her hands in his. "You didn't bomb anybody. You tell them that when you go shopping the sales. Anybody gives you a hard time, you tell them your son's one of Anchorage's finest."

She wiped her eyes. "Thank you, Davey."

He tousled Jed's hair, clucked Louise under the chin and patted Cora on the cheek. "Kids, don't take any guff at school, but remember the Golden Rule. Turn the other cheek and ignore it. Understand? Ignore it."

"Okay, Davey," Jed said. He was eight and a scrapper.

"I mean *you*," David said.

"I know," Jed said.

David got to his feet. "Call me if anything happens. Even at work."

"Nothing will happen," his father assured him.

"But if it does—"

"If it does, I'll call. But it won't."

Everything changed overnight. The city was blacked out from five in the evening until dawn, which in December didn't come until eleven. Jordan melted acetate records, and applied the paste to the windows. Flame's planes were pressed into service.

Three hundred residents volunteered for the Home Guard, and prowled the alleys at night with loaded rifles, looking for Japanese spies. A locally organized intelligence group met downstairs in the federal building on Fourth Avenue, reviewing tips: Emil Pfiel was a German high-command spy because he had a funny last name, a neighbor insisted. The friendly Japanese cook working for the railroad was accused of thinking about adding cyanide to the corned beef. Charlie Ellsworth had to snowshoe up to the Independence Mines and check the alien cards for miners at the Lucky Shot.

Buckets of sand appeared on the Lathrop roof and in the hallways of buildings. People drove with the red parking lights on.

John D. DeHey, a Naknek hotel operator who had survived minor surgery, died at Providence Hospital from shock during the first air raid siren.

In February, three squadrons arrived at Fort Richardson: the Twenty-eighth Composite, the Twenty-third Air Base group and the Eighteenth Pursuit Squadron, swelling the military population to 3,917—400 more than the entire town.

Nobody was ready for them. There wasn't enough sewage treatment, electricity and water. School population doubled. Prostitution, which David and the four other men on the force had once corralled between A and C Streets along Ninth Avenue, bloomed like a virus.

In March David was classed l-A and left a week later for basic, requesting Fort Richardson. He was shunted through Prince Rupert Staging Area at Port Edward, British Columbia, and was back home by May.

He had lost weight and there were hollows under his eyes.

"David, I've been fine!" Jordan exclaimed when she saw

him. "You needn't have worried about me."

He stared at her in stony amazement.

Worry about her?

He hadn't even thought of her.

It was his family that was in jeopardy.

George Kobayashi jerked startled from sleep, groped into his bathrobe and shuffled through the bedroom to the living room.

Someone was banging down the door.

It was two in the morning. The sun was beginning to come up. It was hot for May. Dust floated down a column of light by the brick fireplace.

"All right, all right," he said good-naturedly. He unbolted the door and opened it.

It was three men with guns.

"Mr. Kobayashi?"

"Yes?" he quavered. "What do you want?"

"FBI." A sandy-haired yellow-eyed kid flipped out his wallet and George examined the seal.

"Yes. What do you want?"

"You have three children living at home, is that correct?"

"What is this? What's going on? My son Davey is an army private."

"Mr. Kobayashi, you and your family have ten minutes to get dressed and packed."

"Where are you taking us? I have rights. I'm an American."

The kid with the flat eyes and identification checked his wristwatch. "Nine minutes, forty-five seconds, Mr. Kobayashi."

George turned and fled into the bedroom. "Nina."

"I heard." Her eyes were huge and terrified. "What are we going to do?"

"Go along with it. Davey will get it all straightened out. Wake the girls and I'll get Jed."

They gathered in the living room. Louise clutched a doll. Jed had his baseball mitt. Nina guarded the two suitcases, remembering everything she had left out.

"Just a few more things—" she cried, standing up.

"No," the spokesman said firmly. "No time."

"Please! A sweater for my youngest!"

"Thirty seconds, Mrs. Kobayashi."

She ran into Cora's room, frantic, and scooped up a drawer full of sweaters and another pair of socks. Pants. Did she have enough pants? On the wall was a picture of Lana Turner in a sweater. She was smiling. Nina yanked open a bottom drawer and added another pair of jeans and some shoes.

The FBI man appeared at the door. "Time's up."

She ran into the living room and flung open a suitcase, cramming in as much as she could. George took out a sweater and sat on it, clicking the locks.

"Now. It's time to go now."

"But our son!" George cried. "Let us call our son. He's a soldier." George started for the phone. "Please."

The FBI man got out his gun. "Now, Mr. Kobayashi."

"Who's going to feed the fish?" Nina wondered.

George said, "Jed, make sure the back door's locked."

"I'll do it." The man had black hair and glasses and walked with a limp through the kitchen.

He came back. "Done."

George carefully took his felt hat from the brass rack, put it on and picked up both suitcases. He patted his pocket for his keys. "Come, family. This will be over soon. You'll see."

He locked the door and the FBI men herded them into a waiting car.

Louise began crying disconsolately.

"Hush, now," Nina commanded. "Things will be fine."

"Shirley was coming for a doll tea party today," Louise cried. "We had it planned for weeks."

"It's a mix-up," her mother said. "You'll see."

The car stopped at the Ship Creek railroad depot.

"I don't understand," George said as the men yanked open the doors and pulled them out.

"Order of President Franklin D. Roosevelt, Number 90066, permitting the relocation and detention of Japanese-Americans."

The suitcases were shoved up to the conductor.

"We're going away? You're taking us someplace?"

The flat-eyed kid with the fancy badge picked up Jed. He

wrestled him, kicking and spitting. "No!" Jed cried. "No! You're not taking me anywhere!"

The man handed him up. "Come on, girls," he said quietly. Louise and Cora crowded around their mother's knees.

"Get them on."

Nina nodded, eyes wide, and took the girls by the hand.

"This isn't right. You know this isn't right," George said.

Nina and the girls climbed the metal stairs slowly. The train rumbled.

"You." George pointed at the kid. "I want your name. I'm going to report you."

"Report me to whom?"

"To somebody high up," George roared. "Now give me the name."

"Mr. Kobayashi, I'm only doing my job." The two others shifted next to him, hands on their guns.

"Yes, yes. That's right." George said heavily. He pulled himself onto the first step.

"Not you."

"What?"

"Not you. The orders were for your family."

"What are you saying?"

Nina knelt on the platform, stretching down her hand. "George!" she screamed. "Hurry."

George jerked his arms free and raced up the stairs. The train started to move. Two men jumped him and pulled him back.

"George!" Nina screamed. The train picked up speed.

"I'm sorry, Mr. Kobayashi. Please. I'm sorry."

George ran along the train, his arms out. Tears streamed down his face. He stopped, panting. The train pulled away.

The flat-eyed kid gently put his hands on the old man's shoulder. "It's a rotten business, this war. Rotten."

Inside Fort Richardson a barbed wire fence had been erected around pyramid tents and a one-story frame stockade. Private David Kobayashi was assigned to guard duty at oh-seven hundred hours the morning of May twelfth.

Dust rose hazily over the enclave as he got out of the truck and went inside. After reporting to the CO, he examined the compound. Besides the mess hall, there were cells with bare mattresses, showers and latrines.

It was breakfast time. David stood at the rear of the mess hall, drinking coffee. He turned pale and put down his cup.

Facing away from him at the first table sat a small, dark-haired man.

"Dad." He slipped across from him, stunned.

"Davey!" his father cried. He gripped his hand. "Do you know what happened to your mother? Have you heard anything?"

"What did they do?"

"They came two nights ago. Took Nina and the kids and put them on a train. I haven't heard anything. Davey, please! You got to find out. Please, Davey!"

"I promise. How are you?"

"Mad as hell. To do this to an American citizen. I don't understand. I was born here. I pay taxes. I sold the military plans for a gear grinder!"

David's eyes grew wet. "I'm sorry, dad."

"I always raised my kids to be good Americans. Good citizens. Jed tried to bite the FBI man. If I'd have known they weren't letting me on that train, I'd have bitten him myself. Ah, but it's not your fault."

David was weeping openly and his father tried to change the subject. He patted David's hand. "Food's good here. And you won't believe some of the characters. See that guy?"

David blew his nose and stared at the man his father pointed out. He was squat and swarthy, with a thick scar around his neck.

"Name's Max Gottchuk and he stole coal along the Bering Sea. He's a pirate, Davey, a real pirate. Got himself locked up in Russia, and he busted out and brought both of his guards to Nome as hostages."

"Dad—"

"It was an international incident. The guys in Washington didn't know what to do. Here was this pirate—"

"Dad, I'm sorry."

George put his head in his hands, composed himself. "Just find out what happened to mom, okay? And Davey, if you

624

can—" he gripped his son's arm. "Get me orders to the same place, okay?"

"Okay," David whispered.

"I made reservations for us at the Lido," Jordan said. "Your old police buddy owns it. Capper."

"You did what?"

"It's a happy day. Four years ago today we were introduced."

David nursed his drink and looked at the radio. "I told you. I don't feel like going out."

Jordan had dressed carefully in a new blue middy blouse with a sailor tie and cuffed sleeves. The anchors on her bracelet clanged as she knelt in front of him and pressed his hand to her face.

"Honey, being miserable won't bring them back any faster."

"What do you know about it?" he jeered. "What do you know about anything?" He pushed her away and went to the kitchen.

"David, you don't need any more to drink."

Ice clattered into his glass.

She went to the door, studied him. "Is it somebody else? Is that it?"

"You mean because we haven't done anything in months?" he leered at her. "Can't accept that maybe it's just you, huh? That it? That what's got you going?"

"David, stop it. It's not my fault your father was arrested."

"You're white, Jordan. What do you know about anything?" He tilted back the glass and made a face as he drained it.

She took the glass away. "Things will get better."

"Why?" he taunted. "Because you say so?"

"Because it can't go on like this!" she burst out.

"That's the first thing you've said that's made any sense."

"Talk to me," she pleaded. "Tell me what's going on."

He got down another glass and poured himself a drink.

"You drink too much," she snapped.

He drained the glass. "I want you to leave."

"What?"

"Leave. I want you to go to Washington or someplace."

"But I live here!"

"The Alaska Defense Command has issued orders evacuating the families of military personnel. It's routine in time of war. I'll be going on twenty-four-hour duty soon. All wives and families are being evacuated."

"That's just for non-Alaskan families of military. I've lived here my whole life! I'll be fine."

"Don't you understand? I don't *want* you here! I want you to leave."

Her cheeks splotched pink. "I don't understand, David."

"I don't understand, David," he mimicked. "That's the whole problem in a nutshell, Jordan. You don't understand. You're a kid. A whiny, sniveling, nineteen-year-old hot-boxed little kid."

"David."

"I never should have married you. Never."

"How can you say that?" She started to cry.

"It's easy." He slammed down his glass. "I'm going back to base, Jordan. Do me a favor."

"What?"

"Don't be here when I get back."

"David!"

He banged the door shut. The ice clinked gently in the glass.

"It's my fault. I never should have allowed the marriage. You were too young."

"Blame it all on me!" Jordan flared and immediately dissolved in tears.

"Oh, honey. Oh, Jordan." Flame held her. Jordan sobbed into her chest.

"We don't talk," Jordan said despairingly. "I try to get him to talk about what happened with his family, and he clams up. We haven't—touched each other in months."

Flame stroked her hair.

"Do you think I should go?" Jordan asked in a small voice.

"Oh, honey. I don't know. You're the only one who can make that choice. How does it feel?"

"Terrible. Did you and dad ever have troubles?"

"Oh, yes. Two people can't live together and not. Oh, I guess

626

they could, but it would be an empty thing. The question is, what do you plan to do about it?"

"I don't want to go. I think it would be bad for our marriage. Something tells me it would change everything."

"Then that's your answer."

Jordan shook her head. "No," she said slowly. "David wants me to. At first, all I could think of was that he doesn't love me anymore. But that's not it. I think he's so wrung out over his family, he's scared to death something might happen to me."

"To you? What could happen to you?"

Jordan avoided her mother's eyes. "David thinks things could get hot here." There was a long silence.

She brightened. "Why don't we leave together? A mother-daughter trip. Wouldn't that be fun?"

"Oh, honey. I can't. I'm involved in the Siberian lend-lease. My pilots are ferrying planes to Russia. I can't leave."

Jordan got up. "Then take care of him for me, mom."

Jordan took a train filled with military wives and children to Seward, where they boarded a military transport ship which took them to Seattle.

The *St. Mihiel* immediately took on passengers for a return trip to Alaska; people who had volunteered for war duty at Fort Richardson.

They were all young and single secretaries.

David met her at the Seven Seas, a bar with fake seaweed, green glass bubbles, and thickets of coconut and bamboo. A stuffed turtle hung over her head. She was very blond and had long, spiky fingernails painted blood red.

"Buy you a drink."

"Yeah, sure, soldier."

"What'll you have?"

"Some Monnet Cognac." Her voice was squeaky and whiny and she was wearing the tightest sweater David had ever seen. Her breasts stuck out in two points, the nipples flat like buttons.

David stared at them frankly. "Haven't I met you before? You seem familiar."

627

She nodded and extended her hand. "Thought I recognized you. I work in the MP office. Name's Trixie. You're David, aren't you?"

He smiled. "Yeah."

She smiled coyly and took out her mirror, painting her mouth in a cupid's bow. "There's a rumor about you going around."

"Really?"

"Yeah, really." She fluffed her hair with the spikes. "They say—I mean, the other guys—" She shrugged.

The drinks came and David gave the waiter two-fifty. On the Wurlitzer, the thin man was playing, "Jingle Jangle Jingle" and everybody was dancing between the tables.

"What do they say?" David prompted. He stroked her wrist.

She stared at him and he stared back. "They say you have the biggest cock in the department."

"Really?" He picked up her hand and kissed her wrist, flicking his tongue back and forth. She closed her eyes and smiled, nodding.

"Nice." She shifted in her seat and her nipples grew.

"How'd you like to see for yourself?"

She opened her eyes. "I thought you'd never ask."

He rented a room at the Lathrop and stripped in the bathroom soaping down his crotch and lathering his penis. It stood rigidly hard in his hand. He studied his face.

No trace of the madness showed. Of his mother and brother and sisters disappearing. Of guarding his own father. Of Jordan. He leaned his head against the mirror. It felt cool against his hot cheek.

Crazy. The world was crazy. He stared at his deflating penis and stroked it back into an erection. He needed to forget. Everything. For one night. For one minute.

Trixie was leaning back against the pillows, her legs open. She had fat knees and soft white thighs and jet black hair tufting around the pink labia.

She whistled when she saw him. "Will you get a load of that."

He sank his mouth over her crotch and she stiffened,

628

rubbing her chest with the flat of her hand. He pulled at her with his lips, his tongue.

"Uhm," she grunted. "Uh huh."

He brought her right to the point where her thighs stiffened and her mouth slacked open and then he yanked away from her and rammed his way inside.

Her eyes widened and she yelped in surprise.

"Is it too big?" He was slamming into her, the noise a wet slapping sound in the quiet of the room.

"It feels"—she was choking— "It feels—" She closed her eyes and groaned deep in her chest and her nipples wobbled in opposite lavender directions. He felt her rippling around him.

"Good, Trixie, good," he murmured. He lifted her bottom high and pounded away. "Do it again," he commanded.

"David," she whined, breathless.

"Again." He lifted one hand and stroked with his thumb. "Now," he ordered. He rocked into her and she cried out and squeezed her eyes tight.

It was a deeper climax than the first, and left her drenched in sweat.

"Again," he said.

"David."

"Do as I say."

She trembled, her mouth slack. Her nipples were hard rosy balls. She clutched his arms weakly and her hands fell to the sheet.

He pumped into her. "It's going to be better this time," he murmured. "Even better. Deeper. Much deeper. You're going to squeeze around me—"

She cried out and raked his back with her nails. She was moaning now, purring deep in her chest. Her hair was sticking to her forehead in damp ringlets.

"David!" she cried. "David."

"That's just the beginning, Trix. That's just for starters."

"I can't anymore," she protested weakly.

He smiled. "Oh, yes, you can."

He counted twenty times before he pulled out and came on her chest in a heaving series of jerks. They lay together, exhausted.

"David, I never—"

"I have a house in town," David said.

"Why did we come here?" she said, surprised.

"I have a wife, too," he went on, as if he hadn't heard.

"Oh," Trixie sniffed and covered herself up.

"I want you to live in my house. Be my mistress."

"What about your wife?"

"She's outside for the rest of the war."

"I hope it's a long war, then." She turned over.

"What are you doing?"

"Going to sleep," she mumbled.

"No," he said. "No, you're not. Turn over. I have something to show you."

"David! Not again."

"Oh, yes," he said. "Oh, yes."

Fifty-Two

Tim Snow fiddled with the radio dials, crouched down and put his ear to the receiver. The signal faded in and out. It was beamed from Seattle and bounced off a tower at Unalaska before getting to Atka. Rain clicked in staccato on the tin roof.

Jenny shushed their son and bounced him on her knee. The peculiar birthmark on his face hadn't faded as she'd hoped; if anything, it had grown more pronounced in the two and a half years since his birth. Tommy rolled off her lap and crawled under the radio wires.

"No, honey." Jenny picked him up, struggling. He had Tim's ivory tan complexion and black hair and Jenny's iron will.

Tim made a delicate adjustment and a voice said clearly: "A large force of Japanese have landed and taken the island at Attu. The discovery was made this morning by a bomber from the 36th Bombardment Squad. Details are sketchy, but both teachers on the island, C. Foster Jones and Etta Jones, are believed captured, along with thirty-nine Aleuts, the entire population. The last broadcast was three days ago."

Tim and Jenny stared at each other, horrified. They had met the Joneses the summer before, during an Aleutian Island teachers' conference. Jones had a kindly horseface, and his soft and gentle wife side-parted her hair over a broad forehead. She wore prints and talked of Picasso.

"The troops marched overland to Chichagof after landing at Holtz Bay. The exact troop location is unknown, but they are believed . . . south . . . Bay."

The signal came in and out. Tim beat his palm against the receiver.

"Damn." He twisted the knob slowly until they picked up

another signal, fainter than the first. Tim adjusted it and they heard:

". . . have occupied the island of Kiska and taken prisoner ten men working at the United States weather station there. It is . . ."

The report crackled and died.

"Jen."

He touched her shoulder. "I've got to, Jen. You understand that, don't you?"

She bowed her head and nuzzled Tommy. "Yes," she said faintly.

She raised her head. "I'll get you packed."

They hiked single file through the sloppy mud, Tommy chortling on his father's shoulders. In the bay twenty Catalinas were lined up like ducks, barely visible through the fog. The military had been moving in the heavy amphibious bombers all week.

"Do you think they'll send you to Kiska?" Jenny asked.

"I don't know, hon. I imagine. Or Attu."

Tim had joined the Alaska Scouts; Castner's Cutthroats, they called themselves. Tim had only used the nickname once out loud. Jenny had burst out weeping.

"War! Again! God, I hate it! Isn't once in a lifetime enough?"

"Jenny, listen to me," he had said. They were doing dishes. Tim picked up another plate and wiped it. "If the Japanese take Attu, they can walk right up the chain to the mainland of Alaska. And from there— Attu is only 650 air miles from the nearest Japanese base. Closer to us than Anchorage. I have to do what I can."

"But think about us! About Tommy." She glanced at their son. Tommy was running a truck up the side of their crocheted spread.

"I am," Tim had said. "The Scouts aren't a regular company. They're the best. Natives from all over the territory. I'll be fine."

"You were raised outside. You don't know the first thing about survival."

"Wrong. I learned a *lot* about survival outside. Besides, I didn't leave Barrow until I was thirteen. I have to go, Jen. I can't stay, with bombs bursting in our backyard."

"They haven't yet."

"They will," he had answered. "And when they do, you have to promise me you'll take Tommy and leave."

"Leave? Go where? This is our home."

She looked around the small room. Herbs bloomed along the south window. Their curtained alcove was separated from Tommy's boxbed and toy chest by a bookcase they had shipped from Seattle. Books, canned fish and jams filled the shelves, along with a partially finished reed basket. Jenny's first. Pregnant Mrs. Tartakoff was showing her how. Slickers dried on hooks by the door, and a box of dried reindeer dung sat next to the stove.

"Where would I go?"

Tim appeared to be absorbed in a spot on the plate. He polished it carefully. "Anchorage."

"Anchorage? Who do I—" Sudden comprehension. Anger flared. "If this is some attempt on your part to fix things between me and my folks, I'm telling you right now, Tim Snow, it's way past the fixing stage."

She drove her arms into the soapy water and furiously scrubbed a pot.

He set the plate down and reached for another. "Isn't twenty years of hating long enough?" His voice was too careful, too controlled.

"No," Jenny said flatly.

"Damn it, Jenny!" he shouted. "Are you going to let this thing cripple you forever?"

"Stop it." She was shocked by the outburst. He had never yelled at her before.

Tommy dropped the truck and looked from one parent to the other.

"It isn't enough it got your leg, is it?"

"I don't want to talk about it."

"Because it did. If you'd stayed in the hospital—if you hadn't been so consumed with hating your mother—"

"I said I don't want to talk about it."

633

Tommy started to cry. "Now look what you did." Jenny limped over and picked him up, wiping her soapy arms on the front of her shirt.

She said gently, "It's all right, honey. It's all right."

She turned her back on Tim and stared out the window. The rain was turning to hail through the bank of gray fog.

He touched her. "Jen. Release it. It doesn't matter anymore. We matter. Us. Right here in this room. The rest doesn't count. Forgive your mother and go on. Give her another chance."

He had gone back to wiping the dishes and Jenny had put Tommy down and finished the pans.

It had been the first real fight of their marriage, and left them both feeling fragile and sad. For the next week they had been overly polite, apologizing for little things.

And now he was leaving, and it still wasn't fixed.

"All right," Jenny said suddenly. He raised his head warily over the duffel bag. "I'll take Tommy to Anchorage. But they might not be there. And if they are, they might not want to see me. So I'm not promising anything."

He came over and held her. "Thank you."

There was nothing left to say. They both knew how the other felt. Delaying only made it worse. Tommy yipped around their knees. Tim slung the duffel bag over his shoulder.

The PBY was roaring to life as they turned down the hill past the cemetery. It was a fat plane with the belly of a compulsive overeater and now it swallowed a group of men and bags and held its mouth open for Tim.

He picked up his son. "You be good, now."

Tommy looked at his father with clear brown eyes. The purple scar ran finely down his face, ending at the chin.

Tommy hugged him and Tim patted the boy briskly on the behind. He embraced Jenny, kissed her and pulled away. He started quickly down the ramp.

"Tim."

He turned back. Her dress was drifting around her knees. Reindeer grazed in gray shadows in the fog by the cemetery crosses. "What, honey?"

She pushed back her hair. "Keep your feet dry."

He nodded and climbed on board.

Jenny took a last look around. She had given the plants to Mrs. Tartakoff, pregnant with her sixth; and left the books on the shelves. Everything else had been packed in three trunks on the floor. The crew would carry them down. The plane was due in an hour.

She took Tommy's hand. He was dressed in long pants, and Jenny had scrubbed him in the enamel tub until he shone.

"Tell you what," Jenny said. "Let's stop by the church and say good-bye to the candles."

He trotted next to her down the muddy street. It would be dark in half an hour. It was raining, and Jenny tightened her scarf. Only a few planes were left in the bay. They had been going on bombing missions over Kiska for three days. The fog was too thick to see the smoke from the bombs, but they could hear the sound over the breakers. A ship was nosing into harbor.

They walked up the path to the church. She pushed against the wooden door. It had been sticking from the rain.

They were alone. Jenny loved the little church. It had hardwood floors and nine paintings of saints. The altar was draped in gold brocade and the heavy gold Russian Orthodox Church cross rose between the two stout solid gold candlesticks. Smaller ones filled the alcoves.

Outside, a whistle blasted. There were shouts, cries. The sound of gunfire. Alarmed, Jenny grabbed Tommy's hand and limped outside.

Vasily Tartakoff raced by. His mother waddled behind him, supporting her belly with her hands. Across the village, people were running toward the harbor.

"What is it? Vasily?"

"Come quick, teacher. The navy says we have to come quick." He sped away.

She glanced back at her house. Her trunks were directly inside the door. She could never lift them by herself.

"Mrs. Tartakoff." Jenny hurried and caught up with her. She was young: mid-twenties, with gaunt features and streaks of gray in her hair. She looked as old as Jenny. She shouldn't be having more kids. This one was due in three weeks.

"I'm fine," Mrs. Tartakoff said. Her face was gray. Jenny gripped her arm and held her up.

Past the cemetery they got their first clear view of it: gray and peeling, a high rail wrapped around the top and a seam of iron near the water line, like a bathtub ring.

A naval officer was speaking through a megaphone: "May I have your attention please. This island will be immediately evacuated. Repeat. Immediately evacuated."

"No!" Mrs. Tartakoff clutched her belly, and Jenny wrapped her hands around her.

"Are you all right?"

"A pain."

"Can you walk?"

She grimaced, dragging her foot. She grunted and sweat came out on her forehead.

A naval officer was running up the path toward them. He had pinched features and small dark eyes.

"This woman can't go anywhere," Jenny said. "She's starting labor."

"Then she's going to have to do it on board," he said sharply.

"I don't understand."

"Lady, this island is about to be hit. The Japanese are coming in. Everybody's going."

"That's impossible. I'm leaving on a plane in an hour."

"You're leaving *now*. By boat."

He raced past her up the street.

"Mrs. Tartakoff. Listen to me. We're going to have to get you on the boat. Put your arm around me."

She moaned and limply flopped her arm. Jenny lifted it around her neck and dragged her toward the ramp. Her husband caught up with them and took her.

"What about my skiff?" asked one man. Nobody answered him.

"What is happening to you is for your own protection."

"What about the dogs?"

"Leave them. Leave them behind."

"Can I take a crib for my child?"

636

Jenny took Tommy's hand. "Do we have time to get anything? We just have what we're wearing."

"Ma'am, that's enough." They climbed up the ramp.

Jenny stood at the rail and watched the sad collection of natives hurrying down the street. Behind them was the officer, brandishing a gun.

Here was Narnia, caught with wet hair. Old Nikoli hobbling on a cane, wearing a battered hat. Timius, who could never pronounce his English g's.

They were herded up the ramp.

Behind her a terrible scream rent the air. "Tommy, listen to me. This is important. I have to help that lady. She's going to have a baby. I want you to stay right here until I get back, understand? Right here. I bet Nikoli would tell you stories about Russia. How does that sound?"

Tommy started to cry. There was another scream.

Jenny hesitated. She spotted Vasily's older sister, Nadia, her small face twisted in misery. She was listening to her mother.

Jenny took Tommy by the hand. "Nadia."

"Teacher." Nadia clung to her. "How is mama?"

"I'm sure she's fine. I'm going right now to see. I need you to watch Tommy. Don't let him out of your sight, Nadia. Not even for a minute. He's very fast. Promise me."

"Yes." She nodded her head. She had her mother's dark eyes and hollow cheeks. Another three years and she would be married and bearing a child a year until exhaustion stopped her.

"Yes." She nodded her serious, dark head.

"Good." Jenny hugged her son. "You listen to Nadia. Don't go anywhere. Promise mommy?"

Tommy arched his back stiffly, then made his legs spaghetti and collapsed to the ground. An enormously funny joke.

"Mommy's serious."

Tommy grinned and a dimple cut into the purple birthmark.

Jenny kissed him and smoothed his collar. "Remember what I said," she told Nadia.

The girl nodded, twisting her fingers in the hem of her skirt.

There was another scream. Jenny ran down the corridor to meet it.

637

Nadia took Tommy by the hand and said, "We'll go stand by the rail and look. But only if you're good."

"Yah, sure." Tommy was willing to promise anything. He was two and a half, and had the moon in his pocket.

He trotted next to Nadia, and when she turned her back for a split second, he slipped through the rail and down the ramp; he was certain someone would stop him. No one did. He ran further, until the fog took him.

"Mommy!" He stopped, chilled. He remembered his mother had packed his heavy coat in the blue trunk. The green trunk? No, the blue trunk. He trotted confidently down the street and went into his house.

The trunks were right where they left them. He browsed around, poked under the bed and retrieved an old car he had lost. He rolled it back and forth, up the trunks and across the floor under the table.

He frowned, stood and looked up through the window. He could only see a patch of sky from his short vantage point, but the sky was orange.

Not a sky color at all.

Tommy frowned and shook his head. No, not a sky color.

He remembered his jacket and shook the locks. Nothing happened. He glanced uneasily at the sky.

It was redder now, and making a crackling sound.

The house was on fire.

Alarmed, he rushed outside.

Everything was burning.

All the houses along the street stood out in fire, like somebody had crayoned outside the lines.

"Mommy." His voice was subdued. His mother was always there when he called. Had he left her someplace?

The *boat*. In relief, he ran through the fog; only it wasn't fog. It was smoke, and it was getting thicker. Tommy couldn't breathe. He choked, stumbled, and dropped to his knees.

The mud was cool and wet.

It was going to be a bad one.

Sweat glazed Mrs. Tartakoff's face and she thrashed from side to side. Her water had broken immediately and the early labor was hard. A bad sign.

Jenny patted her forehead and held her hand.

The door banged open.

"Nadia! I told you—"

Nadia was sobbing.

"What's wrong? Is it Tommy?"

"I looked everywhere for him."

"Mrs. Tartakoff. I'll be right back."

She moaned and closed her eyes.

"What happened?" Jenny closed the door.

"I'm sorry, teacher. I'm sorry."

"Nadia, this is important." Jenny gripped her shoulders. "Do you think he got off?"

"He's not on the boat."

"You're positive."

She nodded, sobbing.

Jenny ran to the deck. The ramp was being raised. The town was a ball of fire. She ran down the ramp and jumped, falling badly.

"You can't do that!" The officer shouted down at her.

"My child is down there!"

"Lower the ramp," he commanded. "I'm coming with her."

Jenny limped up the dock, past the cemetery. Ashes burned her eyes.

"Tommy!" she screamed.

The wind was hot and dry. Sweat broke out.

Only two places Tommy would have gone. Home or the church.

The church was outlined in angry red on the hill and Jenny ran toward home, the smoke thick and black.

She ran faster, her bad leg aching. Past the trading post. Past the co-op. Three houses.

"No!" she cried. She limped closer, disbelieving

The house was fiery coals. The roof and walls hung in shreds. "Tommy!" Was he in there? The trunks were black lumps on the floor.

She stepped onto the floor and reared back. A piece of liquid linoleum stuck to her shoe.

"Tommy." She dropped to her knees in the mud.

"Mommy." It was weak and coming from far away.

"Dear God." Jenny stumbled to her feet and groped her way through the smoke. "Tommy!"

"Mommy." He was starting to cry.

"Stay where you are and I'll find you."

She was going down the street toward the harbor. Had she run right past him in the smoke? He was crouching on his knees, his pants muddy, small arms over his head.

"Mommy!" He scrambled to his feet and threw himself into her arms. Jenny held him tightly.

"Don't you ever do that again. You scared me."

"I did?"

He settled against her chest.

"You did."

Behind them, a building exploded, a ragged ball of red and orange. Jenny limped toward the harbor.

The officer was waiting at the ramp.

"Hurry."

They ran up. The ramp was lifted and the ship pulled away. From the rail, they watched the town burn.

"Fire," Tommy announced, and pointed at Atka.

"I see it," Jenny said.

The villagers were crowded together along the rail, women wailing disconsolately, children crying, men banging clenched fists against the railing.

"Is it the Japanese? Have they landed?" Jenny put both hands on her son.

"It's not the Japanese," one man said. "American soldiers burned Atka."

"Americans? Americans burned our homes? I don't understand."

The man broke down. "They told me—they didn't want the Japanese to use our things." He said the words as if they didn't make sense. "I asked the soldier what would happen to us—now that our homes were gone. He told me it was for our own protection. But teacher, what if the Japanese never land? Everything's gone. And for what? We have no boats? No tools. No guns."

Jenny squeezed Tommy's shoulder. I have my son, she

thought. "We'll be fine. They wouldn't take us away without some sort of plan."

"Teacher!" Nadia ran to her. "Please. You got to come quick. My mom's having trouble."

"Nadia, hold on to Tommy's hand. Don't let him do anything."

"I'll be good," Tommy said. "I promise."

She kissed him. "Promise me."

"Cross my heart and hope to die."

She felt a lump form. "Don't do that."

"Please, teacher." Nadia's face was a thin mask of terror.

Jenny steeled herself and went down the corridor to the room.

Mrs. Tartakoff was panting under a sheet.

Jenny gripped the woman's hand. "Now listen to me, Mrs. Tartakoff. Don't push. I know you feel like it. Don't do it. It's too soon."

The woman was hysterical. "There's something wrong. I can tell. Something."

"It's the beginning of labor. It always feels that way."

"No, no. They've been easy ones before. This one isn't even down where it's supposed to be."

"What do you mean?"

She grimaced and dug her nails into Jenny's palm. Jenny pulled back the sheet.

"Dear God," she whispered.

Her belly was rigid, the infant high next to her breastbone. It wasn't moving down the canal.

"Get up, Mrs. Tartakoff."

"Pains," she muttered. "Can't. Pains."

"Get up. You have to walk. Now!"

Jenny pulled her skirt on, and fastened her boots. Mrs. Tartakoff was curled on her side, panting.

"I'll be right back."

She ran down the corridor. There must be a doctor on board. A medic. Didn't boats always have medics?

"He's on leave," the captain explained, putting his mug carefully down. "What seems to be the problem?"

"The problem seems to be," Jenny said tartly, "that a

641

woman is going to die in labor if we don't get some help."

The man smiled reassuringly. "Women go into labor all the time. It's perfectly natural."

"This one isn't. Do you know anything at all about labor? No, of course not." Jenny answered it herself.

"I have three children," the man protested.

"Your wife had them. Unless you assisted—" Jenny said hopefully. He shook his head, repelled.

"Here's the problem. The woman's water broke. That means that the baby isn't protected anymore from bacteria. The baby's got to come out in the next ten hours, or they both could die."

The man paled. "I'm not very good with female problems."

"Is there a hospital nearby?"

"The closest is Unalaska. It was bombed by the Japanese."

"Get me hot water, clean rags, sterilize a knife. And get two men down to her room. We've got to get her on her feet."

They walked her for hours, up and down the corridor. The white-haired Russian Orthodox priest on one side, her wiry husband on the other.

The baby wasn't moving.

At dawn the pains stopped altogether, and she collapsed from exhaustion. They put her to bed. Her husband held her hand.

By noon she had a raging temperature. By dinner the odor of decay filled the room, and she lapsed into a coma.

Jenny stood in the hallway with the Tartakoff children and Tommy. The door opened and the priest came out.

"No!" Nadia cried. She stumbled down the hallway.

"Nadia." The priest held her.

"I want to see her."

"No, Nadia, no."

Two men in uniforms raced by, carrying a plastic sheet. They opened the door and closed it swiftly behind them.

"The baby!" Nadia cried. "How's the baby?"

"Dead. They're both dead."

Vasily said stoutly, "It's a lie!"

"No," the priest said.

642

The door opened. The men carried out something wrapped in plastic. It was heavy and they shifted it back and forth. "Mother," Nadia cried, following them.

They carried the bundle to the top deck and threw it over the side.

It slipped into the gray and foaming water and was gone.

It was not an easy trip.

The ship stopped at St. Paul and St. George islands, taking on passengers. Almost seven hundred persons were crowded onto a boat that was to carry three hundred. Women lined up to wash out diapers in water that was turned on only an hour a day.

The boat rocked though heavy seas, high winds and pouring rain, heading toward southeast Alaska. After almost a week, it anchored at Funter Bay on Admiralty Island.

The natives from St. Paul and St. George pressed to the rail. "Trees," one of them said.

Spruce stretched to the sandy beach. Behind the forest rose snowcapped mountains. An abandoned cannery sat on the beach, walls sagging, windows broken.

"Too many trees," somebody else agreed.

The officer with the bunched-up features said grandly through the megaphone: "Attention, residents of St. Paul and St. George. This is your new home. Please begin orderly debarkation. You will be supplied bedding, clothes and food. Repeat, bedding, clothes and food."

A navy skiff ferried them to shore and unloaded gear, leaving it on the beach in front of the cannery.

The last thing Jenny saw as they pulled away was a woman crying.

"Won't be long now," she said to Tommy.

"Yep." He pulled his cap down over his eyes.

They unloaded the Atka villagers at Killisnoo at three in the morning on a red scow that smelled of fish and rotting twine. The Tartakoff kids were in the first load.

"I know," Jenny said, hugging Tommy between her knees. "Let's sing 'Cheer for Old Atka.'"

They had written it in school the year before, to the tune of "Roll out the barrel." Jenny started it:

"Cheer . . . for . . . old . . . Atka . . .
It . . . is . . . our . . . home . . . through and through . . ."

She couldn't finish. Vasily Tartakoff took it up, in a higher key:

"Cheer for old Atka . . .
We like it fine . . . so will you . . ."

They stared up the beach; their voices faltered and died.

A rotting herring saltery stretched into the trees, surrounded by sagging cabins.

"Everybody out," the officer said.

Jenny lifted Tommy down and clambered over the side. He pressed into her, suddenly afraid.

"Don't you want to look around?"

He shook his entire body.

Jenny gently took his hand. "Come on, sweetie. Come on."

Not one cabin had a roof or all four walls. The inside of the saltery was divided into small rooms. There was no water, no electricity, no sewage disposal; but there were plenty of rats. The officers dragged canned goods through the door and stacked them up. Potatoes and sauerkraut.

Jenny limped outside and approached the officer hauling dirty army surplus mattresses up the beach. He had red hair and orange freckles on his arms. "Excuse me, but where are we supposed to live?"

"Anywhere you want."

"But there's nothing here! No stove. There are eighty-three of us."

"I have to go." He strode down the beach and picked up another mattress.

"Wait! How are we going to live!" She followed him.

"Any way you want, lady."

"We don't have guns. No boats to fish with. No medicines. What if somebody gets sick?"

"Look." He thumped down the mattresses. "There's a war going on. The Japanese were going to bomb Atka."

"Did they?"

"Did they what?"

"Did they bomb it?"

He picked up the mattress and went inside, dropping it in a pile of plaster.

"You haven't answered my question."

"If they didn't, it's because there was nothing left. Does that answer your question?" He walked outside.

"I was supposed to be taken in a plane to Anchorage. I'd like to know how long you plan on keeping us here."

"You tell me."

"Tell you what?"

"Tell me how long the war's going to last, lady, and then I'll tell you how long you'll stay."

There weren't enough mattresses or blankets. The roof leaked in the rain. They collected water in a barrel and immediately dumped it. It was thick with roaches. Ten people slept to a room.

The first week, they were infested by lice.

The second week, stomach flu swept through the cannery. An old man died.

And then the plagues started.

Fifty-Three

It was a Victorian house with a peaked roof and porch, at the end of a quiet street, set back in a riff of flowering trees. Tim straightened his hat and pressed the Whitman Sampler under his arm to open the gate.

A dog yapped to meet him. It was a mix—terrier and collie, Tim guessed—with curly tan hair and shaggy heels.

"Easy, fella. Easy." He extended his hand. The dog nosed it gently and tried to bite his ankle.

He rang the buzzer. Chimes sounded. Behind the house, the inlet spread in gray-and-purple patterns. Snow was melting on the Chugach.

The door opened. Tim stared.

She was small, with brilliant green eyes and a full mouth. Her hair was piled up in a loose bun that ordinarily would make a graying woman look grandmotherly; but on her it was stunning. Her eyebrows were still dark, and her hair glinted with auburn highlights. She was wearing oyster-colored wool slacks and a rich, wine turtleneck. Around her neck was an antique ivory necklace of small beads and matching earrings.

"Yes?" Her voice was curious and polite. She opened the screen to let the dog in and closed it.

Tim smiled. "You must be Jenny's mother."

She began trembling uncontrollably. She clutched her chest. Her eyes fluttered. She dropped to the floor.

Tim yanked open the screen door and picked her up. She was light. He carried her into the living room and checked her pulse. Speeding wildly. He found the kitchen and got her a glass of water.

She was sitting up, dazed, when he came in.

"I'm terribly sorry for the shock. Please forgive me."

"Who are you?" she cried. "How do you know Jenny?"

"You mean she's not here?"

"Jenny's coming here!" She burst into tears. "Thank God." She clutched his hand. "Thank God. Jenny's coming home." She drew the last word out, and Tim saw with terribly clarity how it had been. He was suddenly ashamed. He should have insisted Jenny go home years ago.

"Please forgive me."

"For what? Springing it on me? You don't know how it's been. So many years I prayed—" She wiped her eyes.

"My name is Tim Snow. Jenny and I married three and a half years ago."

"She's here in Alaska?" Flame covered her face with her hand, sobbing.

"We were on Atka together. She's a teacher."

"A teacher?"

"You have a grandchild. She called him Tommy Ryan Snow. After your dad."

It was too much. She clutched at her chest and Tim leaned over her, suddenly concerned.

"Medicine. I have pills. Counter."

He found them and thumbed open the bottle. "How many?"

"Two." It was getting worse. She swallowed them dry and immediately her breathing slowed, her pulse calmed. "Just let me sit here a minute. I'll be fine."

He stared at the room. It had none of the busy bits and pieces he associated with fussy old women living alone: too many cats and statuettes. Instead, there were clean bold lines: lots of brass, plants and stained glass.

"I haven't offered you anything. Scotch? Is it too soon? To hell with it. Let's celebrate." She went to a wine rack and pulled down a bottle, wiped it, opened it and sniffed the cork.

"1901. A very good year. Carrie Nation shot her way through the best bars in Chicago in 1901, haranguing city hall about the evils of alcohol." She poured a glass and gave it to him.

"To my son-in-law. And for bringing Jenny back."

"To you." He raised his glass. "For having stood it all these years."

Flame's eyes gleamed and she turned toward the window. The sun was setting, dyeing the water a deep rose.

"You know—about what happened?"

"All of it."

Flame took a deep pull of wine. "Yes. Well." She sat in the Chippendale by the stone fireplace, rubbing her palm along the rosewood arm. "How—how is she?"

"You mean is she finally over it?" Time was so short; he was on twenty-four-hour leave.

"Yes. Has she forgiven me?" Flame's voice was husky.

Forgive me, Jen, for writing the script for you. But if you were here, and could see her face—see the effect the whole thing's had—

"It was never your fault, Mrs. Jackson."

"Please, call me Flame."

"Flame, Jenny loves you very much."

Flame lowered her head.

"She was coming home to tell you that. She wanted to make up for all the years of silence. But the silence grew—"

"I understand—" Flame said loyally.

"—the silence grew until facing you became hard. Something she put off. She was young when she said those things. Afraid and in shock. But she loves you. Know that. And know that she's alive and happy. She tells Tommy stories about you."

"She talks about me?"

"All the time."

"When are they getting here? Tomorrow? Should I air out—"

"I don't know, Flame. I thought they'd have been here months ago."

"Dear God. Do you think something's happened?"

He looked out the window, "I'm worried myself," he admitted. "Atka's been evacuated."

Flame put her glass down and stood up. "What can I do?"

His eyes met hers. "Find them."

"I don't care if it is two o'clock in the morning, I've been trying to put this call through since six o'clock. Six o'clock last February," she snapped. "No, I don't know six o'clock whose time." She listened.

"Yes, I'll hold."

It was dark outside and Flame groped for the string on the lamp and yanked it down. Her voice deepened.

"Hello, Harry? Yes, I know. It is a surprise. After all these years. I'm fine, thank you. And how's your wife? Those lovely children? Wonderful."

She laughed. "Yes, I quite agree. You're still doing great things in the legislature. I read about you all the time. You're welcome. Well, yes, there *is* something right down your alley. I'm trying to locate my daughter, Jenny."

She picked up the phone and carried it to the chair. "Jenny Jackson. Her last name's Snow now. I think she was on Atka when it was evacuated. Yes. I know things are in an uproar." "I understand. Certainly. I'll wait."

She realized now why Batt smoked. Something to do in the gap between lives.

She rummaged through the rosewood escritoire, found a pen and pad. Drummed her fingers. Sighed. Examined the ovals in her nails.

"Yes? You found it? Killisnoo. Can you spell it. Thank you, Harry. Thank you. Oh, and Harry? Where is Killisnoo?"

They carried her outside into the sun, and brought her son close to her head. Jenny feebly squeezed his hand.

Tommy wouldn't look at her.

Jenny was covered with boils. Sixty on her face and chest alone. "Honey, mommy loves you."

"Yes," he whispered. She could see the sharp pricks of white flesh between the black lashes. His hand was limp in hers. Jenny shifted it off the most painful boil in her palm.

"You know your name?"

He nodded and recited it. "Tommy Ryan Snow."

"And your father's name?"

"Tim Snow."

"Where did he come from?"

"Barrow."

"Good." She sank backward and stared at the blue sky. Tears ran out of the corners of her eyes. "Tommy."

"Yes, mom."

"Promise you won't forget me."

"I promise." He seemed surprised. "Where ya going? To a fire?" One of the older boys had taught him to say that.

"No," Jenny whispered. "No, Tommy. Not to a fire."

"Mommy, I'm going to go play now. Okay?" He got up and darted away. She turned her head and followed him with her eyes, until he flashed around the building; gales of laughter, whoops of delight.

It happened then.

First the localized pain of the boils, then the fiery flash as the bacteria leaped across the healthy skin.

"Mama," Jenny said. She started to cry. "Mama."

It was the worst way to die. The slowest. In a glaze of pain, Tommy faded in and out. Tim. Logan visited once, but he saw her and went away.

It was raining. No, no. It was the putrescence of the boils.

The third day, things worsened. They fed her a sponge soaked in water. She could barely squeeze it with her tongue.

Is this it? she wondered. All there is?

She closed her eyes. The last thing she saw was her mother's face.

"Not good," the medical man said, shaking his head. "Not good at all." He had lined them all up, deloused them, dispensing a pharmacy worth of drugs. Now it was the government man's turn.

"There is nothing to fear." He had a mournful voice that he doctored by turning it up at the end, in a phony lilt. "They'll be well taken care of."

He looked over his five small charges, huddling together—one little boy, about three, with a funny scar on his face; three sisters and a brother.

"Where are you taking them?" Vasily asked.

"They're orphans," the man explained. "It means they don't have any relatives. They're going to an orphanage."

"Tommy has a father. He's in the service."

"I understand that. But he doesn't have a father here." He smiled gently. "It's a difficult concept. Hard to understand."

"Where are you taking them?"

"Away," the man replied, and herded them onto a boat.

At least the Scouts were wearing the right kind of clothes. The poor slobs from the Seventh Mechanized Infantry had done hard time in the Mojave Desert, training for Africa. They had been lectured on tropical diseases and issued short-sleeved shirts and ventilated leather boots, right before they hopped onto military transports bound for the Aleutians: land of spring snows and freezing mud.

The plan was to take Attu away from the Japanese the first part of May and be home in time for coaching little league.

The experts had it all figured out. The Japanese had dug into the hogback ridge that humped over the back of Attu, and the Scouts and the infantry were going to dig them out.

Simple campaign; three days, max. But the experts had it figured wrong.

That first occurred to Tim on the sixth day of the three-day campaign when his stomach fluttered from hunger and he noticed the raggedy boxes of food still on the beach, two hundred feet under him.

They had landed at Red Beach on Holtz Bay, packing C-rations for two days of hard climbing. Plenty of food to last until they met up with the infantry, coming the opposite direction. But from their vantage point on the ridge, the Japanese saw them all and picked them off like ducks.

It had looked so good on paper.

The experts hadn't figured on how useless a howitzer would be, sitting in a Cat tank that was stalled in the mud. They had forgotten what cold and constant wet can do to a man's feet.

The commanding officer was curtly dismissed on the sixth day, but Tim was still just as hungry under the new commander, and when he dozed, every shape was a boiling hot dog.

The Japs wouldn't give in, was the thing.

The Americans dumped more men and supplies on the beach, but the food sat there, making a run for freedom every time the tide came in.

The Americans outnumbered them eight to one, but the Japs

were there first. Two miserable weeks later, ten Scouts were left out of two hundred. The Japs had joined forces with trench foot and gangrene.

And then superior numbers finally started to grind the enemy down. Tim and the men from Alaska's Fourth Infantry regiment, and the tattered remnant of the Seventh Infantry, knocked the Japanese back to Chichagof Valley.

It was the third Sunday in May, and it was snowing hard. Engineers had carved a jelly-belly road out of the quivering muskeg, and the Cats had started up the hill with the howitzers. The fog sifted away long enough for the Air Force to thunk the Japanese on the head and get their attention.

The Americans were going to win the war. Or at least the battle, which to Tim was the same thing. After Attu he had two weeks leave and he would spend it finding Jenny. The rumors had already started that the Japanese were killing themselves rather than fall to the enemy, and midweek, Tim had stumbled on a field of them.

They had pulled the pins on grenades up close to their chests, and the field was sodden with blood and body parts.

One severed hand has almost more impact than an acre of them: the mind reels away from enormous horrors. Tim looked at the field until he composed himself. He turned and went down the hill.

He was assigned to a small medical attachment, ferrying wounded away from the main action. It was Sunday. He was sleeping.

The flap on his tent raised.

He opened his eyes.

It was snowing outside. Facing him was a Japanese soldier. He was middle-aged, with wire glasses and a pleasant face.

In his hand he held a grenade.

"No!" Tim screamed, and rolled out of his sleeping bag.

The man said in perfect English, "We die. Yanks die too."

He smiled sadly and pulled the pin.

Nobody asked Tommy how he felt and he felt awful. His tummy hurt all the time, and he was afraid to close his eyes to go to sleep.

His mommy did that once and they took her.

Every morning after cold mush, he'd go to the high wire gate and look down the road. He was waiting for his dad.

While he waited, he repeated his name and his father's name and Barrow. Barbed wire hung on top of the fence. Sometimes a car would come in, or a truck.

But nobody ever left.

Tommy slept in a bed with sheets, and nobody had scabs on their face like his mom, but he wished she were there to hug him.

One day it started raining, and everybody stayed inside. They didn't make Tommy or the other little kids go to the classroom, but there was nothing to play with so they might as well have. Right around dinner time the rain stopped, and Tommy raced outside.

A bird was lying next to the flagpole and Tommy picked it up and petted it. It was sleeping and its fur was wet, so he carried it inside to the kitchen and asked the cook to warm it up.

She screamed and called in the super, and the super whacked Tommy up one side and down the other and called him a dirty savage. He tried to tell them they'd wake the bird, with all that yelling, but they picked it up in a towel and threw it outside.

"It's dead, Tommy. Dead."

Afterward, when Tommy thought of his mother, he saw her with a bird on her chest.

A day later they gave him a shower even though it wasn't Saturday and dressed him up in clothes from the church box and let him ride on the fuzzy backseat of the Nash out through the gate. They put him on a bus and he went to another place with kids.

He wondered if it was because of the bird.

But then they explained that nobody had room for him because of the war and his being ugly and still wetting his pants, and he understood better.

He still remembered his dad's name and Barrow, but when they put him on a boat and took him to another place, he got too excited to remember; and then when he tried, he realized he'd forgot.

*　　　*　　　*

In the bottom of the white marble federal building on Fourth Avenue, an office had been set up in the far southeast corner. The sign on the clouded door said simply Relocation, and was an attempt on the territory's part to keep track of the countless people who had been uprooted by the war.

It was staffed by a single man on loan from Alaska Defense. Next to the door inside, a church pew had been set up for people waiting in line.

The man was polite and extremely kind. "It's the same for everybody," he was saying. "I really am sorry. The records we do have from the Aleutians are dreadfully incomplete."

He took a deep breath and tapped his pencil against the page in front of him. He had pulled it from a manila file that he had found in an overflowing box on the floor behind him. It had taken forty-five minutes of hunting.

"There is one thing we do know for certain, Mrs. Jackson." She leaned forward.

Oh, he hated this job. "Your daughter had a serious illness."

Flame groped for her purse, pulled out her pills and swallowed. "What kind of illness?"

Her voice trembled. Behind her on a pew, an infant wailed against his mother's shoulder and a white-haired man leaned on his hand, snoring.

"It doesn't sound serious except that the conditions were rather—primitive. Boils, Mrs. Jackson."

"Boils?" She sounded puzzled. "You mean one? Two?"

He looked her full in the eyes. "Hundreds."

She flinched. "No," she said quietly.

"As I said—things were primitive, the illness got out of control—"

"No—"

"Your daughter passed away very suddenly, Mrs. Jackson. There was that, at least. After things—deteriorated, she went quickly."

"I needed to see her—" Flame whispered. "Hold her in my arms."

He needed a transfer. A vacation. "I'm sorry."

"You don't understand." She raised her voice. "I needed to see my daughter! We had important—" she sobbed into her

654

hands. Ten minutes went by on the clock.

He handed her a Scott tissue.

She dabbed her eyes and said in an even voice, "I don't believe it. There's been some mistake."

They all said that, but he never got used to it.

"There's been no mistake, Mrs. Jackson."

The air went out of her. Her eyes dulled, her mouth. "I see."

"She was given a Christian burial at Killisnoo."

"Tommy," Flame said suddenly. She looked up. "What happened to the boy?"

"The boy?" He examined the paper again. "There's no record of a boy."

"My grandson!" She gripped the table. "Where is my grandson? Dear God, if my grandson is gone—"

The man thought quickly. "Was his father there?"

Flame shook her head. "He's in the Scouts. Tim Snow."

"That's your answer," the man said, relieved. "The Scouts are being rotated out. He's probably with his father this very minute."

"Do you think so?"

His heart hurt. He didn't have the skin for this job. "Right this minute."

Dazed, she picked up her bag, draped her sweater over her arm.

"Do you need a ride? I could call a cab."

"No. Thank you, young man. You've been very kind."

She hobbled to the door, opened it.

Very kind. He closed the file and shoved it into the box.

Fifty-Four

In the summer of '43, George Kobayashi was transferred from the Fort Richardson stockade to an internment camp in California. He died there two months later, never seeing his wife and children. They had been sent to a camp in New Mexico, where a daughter and son died during an outbreak of scarlet fever. His wife and remaining daughter lived in the camp two more years.

Jordan came back to Anchorage ahead of schedule that summer, and found her husband David living with another woman in their house. David had fathered a daughter and Trixie was expecting a second child. Jordan filed for divorce.

That was the summer Flame received verification of Tim Snow's death. She immediately began looking for Tommy. She traced him as far as an orphanage in Juneau.

After that—nothing.

Fifty-Five

Right from the start, they were told they were stupid. That was the primary lesson. All the other lessons—the names of the states, the multiplication tables—took a backseat to that.

"If you work very hard, learn your lessons, maybe you will get a good job, like a janitor. Hang on to it," Tommy's teacher counseled.

Along with practicing table manners and how to shift through the gritty jungle of schoolyard etiquette, they also practiced ducking and bowing and staring at the feet of the white person speaking.

It was called the Eppie Mayer Home, and it was the only home Tommy remembered. It was brick and three stories high and faced a house that kept goats. The home had a high fence and a broken swing in the dirt behind the kitchen door. There was an enormous garden, but hardly any laughter and love.

He couldn't remember his parents. Tommy had a sharp memory of a reindeer, grazing against a green hill in the rain, and strong sense of arms hugging him, but no face stood out clearly from his childhood, like a person illuminated in a dark hallway under a light.

He felt his mother's presence through her absence.

There were seventy-five kids, eleven adults and two cows. Everything was structured by a gong, signaling the end of one activity and the beginning of another. The girls and boys were separated, and the older boys ate together at a different time. The boys cut wood for all the stoves in the dormitories and classrooms. They milked the cows and picked vegetables and shoveled sidewalks.

The girls learned to cook and sew. They ripped apart clothes from the church box and used them as patterns. They knitted mittens and socks for themselves and a pair each for some anonymous boy, using string they unwound from a flour sack.

Everybody had a number. Tommy's was 649. The numbers first started in 1925, when the home was built. This was 1950, which meant that a lot of kids had passed through.

When he was smaller, Tommy had hoped that he'd pass through too.

On visiting days, couples came to look the kids over and take one home, but Tommy was a long way from the pick of the litter. He had those funny birthmarks, for one thing. The one on his shoulder didn't matter, since nobody looked at his shoulders anyway, but the other one was as plain as the nose on his face. Plainer. It was purple and jagged, like a spider leg, and ran down his face from his forehead to his chin, cutting through his cheek.

A strawberry, the civics teacher called it; only it was the color of raspberries. Couples weren't looking for kids with raspberries; only peaches and cream.

The Eppie Mayer Home was built on a street next to the harbor, and Tommy went to sleep dreaming of trains and ships; listening to the mournful mix of male flight sounds that urged him to ride the rails or join the navy. When he wasn't working and wasn't in school, he would sometimes lope down the street which even in summer was damp, and slouch on the fringe of dock workers, inhaling the heady smell of salt and sea, his hands flexing to grip the guide wires or steady a bale.

The railroad started in Whittier, and everything going north first was dumped on the docks, to be loaded. There were Campbell Soup cans and Wurlitzer organs; plane parts and train sets; erector toys and ejector blades.

And it was all *going* somewhere.

The teacher said Tommy was going somewhere too, going to hell in a hand basket, but he wished he were going to Anchorage instead.

In the Eppie Mayer Home the older boys had their own dormitory. It had long rows of enamel beds and thin woolen blankets covering a bottom sheet and a lumpy mattress. At

658

night the boys whispered to each other under the cover of darkness, before the sharp command from the super shut them up.

It's a terrible thing to grow up without a family. Children without mothers grow up always hungry. They spend an enormous amount of energy shoring themselves up. They have thin arms and tough hides and they never talk about it. Ever.

The closest they might let themselves come to it is on Sundays, watching the clean, pressed families troop out of church, faces happily relaxed, smiling to themselves about the roast browning in the oven. Then the kids from Eppie Mayer might deliberately pick a fight or scowl viciously or ping rocks into a tree, trying to hit something alive.

But if they talked about it, the shell would shatter and the howling blood-curdling wail that had been building forever would come twisting out and swallow everybody up.

The little kids on the babies' side still crawled easily into laps, needing it, but the older boys would stand up suddenly and send them sprawling across the floor, not from meanness, but from a sad certainty that the world would do that to them sooner or later anyway.

They were not permitted to touch each other, hug, slap, bite or kick. But the most stringent rule was against secrets.

They couldn't have any.

These kids without homes were forbidden to have friends.

It was one rule too many, and the kids ignored it. They got up at six and went to church. Then there was breakfast and chores and school until noon. After lunch the boys worked on the director's car, in shop, or learned to make bookends, and then they went back to school until supper.

Everybody was always trying to figure out ways to earn money, but if they did, they could never keep it. It all went back into the Eppie Mayer Home, for the good of the community.

Tommy and the other kids sat down the week before Christmas every year and asked Santa for three things. It was a big joke, since there was a limit to Santa's budget, and all the presents came out of the mission box anyway, but it was a nice thought.

Tommy stopped believing in Santa the same year he stopped believing in God. He had asked both of them for a family and nothing happened.

But he had friends, boys he could count on, and did.

There were three of them and they ran together. Tommy was ten and in the fifth grade. Education for the kids didn't stop until after the eighth grade, so he still had some time to decide what he wanted to do. The other guys were older and it was right around the corner.

Even though the three of them couldn't expect any good jobs since they were stupid, at least they weren't female and native and stupid.

Tommy sensed that was worse.

The girls in the seventh and eighth grades would all be required to sing in the church choir and the men from Whittier would come over and listen. If they saw one they liked, they would ask the super for a meeting and then the girl married him.

She was never asked.

Tommy burned to know how these marriages worked out, but the girls just faded away, getting more faded by the year. At least they had someone to hold.

That was the real thing Tommy wanted—above earning money he could keep or going to Anchorage—he wanted to be a part of a real family, with uncles and old folks and babies in smelly diapers crawling over the linoleum. Where people burst out with sudden arguments and fixed things afterward. He wanted to belong.

It had taken years for the letter to catch up. Nuka sent a grandson to the teacher, who came to the hut in deference to Nuka's age.

They had run through nine teachers in ten years. This one was small and intense and determined to stick it out. Nuka gave him six months.

The teacher turned the letter over and said, "It's from the Alaska Defense Secretary. Do you want me to open it?"

Nuka nodded. His hair had turned completely white.

"Interesting," the man muttered. "There is no Alaska Defense Command anymore, you know." He ripped it open and pulled out the letter.

It was dated June 2, 1945.

Dear Nick Snow:

We regret to inform you that your son, Timothy Snow, was killed in action on May 30, 1943. He died honorably, defending his country during the battle to retake the Island of Attu.

Nuka sighed, his hands clasped together.

"Is that all?"

"No." The teacher's voice was subdued. "There's more." He bent down and said:

His wife, Jennifer Snow, died on the Island of Killisnoo following the evacuation of Atka. Their son, Tommy, has been placed in a territorial orphanage in Juneau. May we hear from you concerning this matter? If you fail to reply, we will assume you have no interest in the boy and he will be available for adoption by others at the Eppie Mayer Home in Whittier.

Sincerely,

The signature was smudged.

"I have a grandson?"

"Nick," the teacher was uncomfortable. "He might have already been adopted. You may never find him."

"Where is this Whittier?"

"It's about as far away from Barrow as it can be and still be part of Alaska."

"It doesn't matter. I am going there."

"You are? How?"

"You are going to take me," Nuka said confidently, and pulled himself up by his cane. "Now come. We must

661

get ready."

They came for Tommy in the middle of Reading and told him to go to the office. On the way he went back over everything he had done wrong that week. The list was longer than the walk.

There were two men in the super's office, a short man with cropped white hair and a younger man. They turned when Tommy walked in.

The old man had the mark on his face. A scar running down his cheek and ending in his chin.

"Tommy?"

Tommy was suddenly afraid.

The old man went over to him, carrying the weight off his fragile knees. "Don't be afraid," he said softly. "I see it, too. So you are the one."

Tears coursed down the old man's face.

The super said, "This man is your grandfather, Tommy. He's come from Barrow to take you home."

Home. The boy stared into the old man's eyes. "You really are my grandfather?"

"You know that."

Tommy flew into his arms and buried his face in his chest. "I've waited so long."

"And I've waited a lifetime for you," Nuka said in a choked voice.

They were walking along the beach. Nuka was saying, "Don't expect to see the end. Know that it is enough to have the beginning firmly in mind. The next step will open itself to you when you have prepared yourself."

"But, grandfather!" Tommy cried. "I am a boy. How will I lead our people into greatness?"

"You see this hand?" Nuka squeezed his own gnarled fingers around the boy's.

Tommy nodded.

"No, I'm talking about your hand, inside of mine. You have everything you need already. It's right inside of you. But you have to trust it. That's the key. You have to trust your instincts. Open your hand."

Nuka took away his hand and Tommy opened his. Inside was a small white stone.

"How did you do that, grandfather?"

"You did it. You're just not attuned to your own power yet."

He picked up the stone and threw it into the ocean. "What do you see?"

"A stone falling," Tommy answered promptly.

"And now?"

Tommy strained, trying to see with his heart. "Ripples."

"And now?"

"There is nothing. The water is still."

Nuka smiled. "Then why is it the ripples are seen in the mind of your son, and his beyond him? Everything you do touches something else. Someone else. Within you this moment is the seed of the future. I have been waiting all my life to tell you. For years I put those visions away. I could not share them with anyone but you. You are the next in line, you are the one who will lead our people to greatness."

Tommy mulled it over in his mind. "Why do you suppose I was chosen?"

Nuka's voice grew fierce. "Because you are special, Tommy. You see things with your heart. Never question that. Never waste time questioning your talent. Only use it. That's what the Great Spirit intended."

"You speak of the Great Spirit, and yet you wear a Christian cross."

"It comes from the same source, Tommy. It doesn't matter what name you give it, or how you summon it up. In this world are great powers for good—and awful temptations to do evil. Align yourself right now on the side of good, throw your heart and mind and efforts into it, and great things will come back. But you have to trust yourself and trust the Great Spirit, however it is called, and make your faith work for you."

"I'm only one person!" Tommy cried. "There are so many whites. So many tribes and nationalities of natives. Grandfather, in Juneau at one orphanage were Tlingit-Haida kids who carved tall totems."

663

"What's a totem?" Nuka asked.

"It's a tall column of wood with figures on it. But that's what I mean. They are different than the Eskimos—than us—and the Aleuts are different and so are the Indians in the interior. They all have different languages—customs. How can I pull them together?"

"Start by pulling yourself together. Things will fall into place. You're trying to see the whole picture again, Tommy. Concentrate on this particular step. Make sure the direction you're going is correct. By correct, I mean ask for guidance. Make sure you're not falling off the track. But then trust it and go with it. Put your whole heart into it. Amazing things will happen."

They were coming up on a slight rise overlooking the ocean. Far out to sea, whales spouted in the gray-and-mauve ocean.

"Great changes are coming over the land," Nuka said. He sat down. "Men with spikes have been going out into the ocean, looking for something. Oil. I used to think, when I was very young, that the answer lay in avoiding the whites. But that is not possible. They come and take what they want, and unless we're very fast and very good at protecting ourselves, they're going to take away the land."

He scratched in the sand. "See this?"

It cascaded from his hand. "The land, Tommy. You have to hold on to the land. And in order to do that, you have to go to school. Learn about the white man. But never forget where you came from, Tommy. Or who you are. You're native. And your roots go back into the dark days. Can you feel it in your blood, Tom? Do you see it?"

Tommy stared at his grandfather. Nuka stood with an exalted look in his eyes, staring at the sky. His body began to shimmer with light.

"Grandfather," Tommy cried.

"Remember: you have everything inside of you that you need. Everything. The light is in you, Tom. And the future of the People of the Whale you hold in your hands."

"But I'm only ten!" Tommy cried.

"You wear the mark," his grandfather said. His voice was airy, light. Tommy could see the sweep of ocean through it.

"I'll always be here. Always. You have nothing to fear."

"Grandfather!" Tommy cried. He ran blindly up and down the beach.

Nuka's body became fainter and fainter, until it was only a tracing of light over the ocean. Then he held up his hand in farewell, and was gone.

Fifty-Six

Everybody liked Ike, even Adlai Stevenson after the election. He had a bald, shiny face the camera crew could never completely mop dry, and a grandfatherly way of clouding the issues with a lot of knee bouncing and story telling. Everybody felt safe with him.

Especially the Alaskans working for statehood. Even before he won, he had urged quick statehood for Hawaii and Alaska, saying it would show the world that Americans practiced what they preached.

As mere residents of a territory, the Alaskans couldn't vote in presidential elections, had no power to choose their own governor—he was an appointed official—and they had no power in Congress. The Alaska delegate couldn't make laws.

Congress decided what to do with a territory's natural resources. And it could make laws that discriminated against the territory, if they benefited some states. In Alaska's case there was the Jones Act. It singled out Alaska in shipping laws, stating that any goods entering or leaving the territory must be carried on American ships. The Canadian ships were cheaper; even the shippers in the States were using them, but Alaska alone had to use American ships. The law specifically benefited the state of Washington, since it was the closest American port. Wesley Jones, who pushed the law through Congress and later named it after himself, was a senator from Washington.

Judges were appointed by the federal government.

The ability to raise taxes was limited. In order to create a bond issue for a high school, for example, it took the approval of Congress.

Improvements within a territory required congressional approval, which was slow in coming. In 1953, the year

Eisenhower was inaugurated, there was no road extending even from south to north across Alaska. In order to reach villages in the north, you could fly, use a dogsled in winter or go around by ship. The railroad didn't go that far; it ended halfway through the territory in Fairbanks.

But the main thing that had the Alaskans upset was the way the federal government treated Alaskans like children, like they didn't have a brain in their heads, and certainly couldn't control their own affairs.

Everybody, that is, but Ike. So, in February, when the first green was leafing on the trees around the Capitol, Alaskans gathered to honor him.

The Alaska Statehood Committee had rented a suite of rooms near the Capitol for the inauguration and brought in extra television sets, turning them up over the noise of two hundred people talking at once.

The crowd consisted of everybody who worked toward statehood who wasn't sufficiently far enough up the scale to be invited to listen to Eisenhower speak personally. There were aides to delegate Bob Bartlett, territorial attorneys, executive assistants and researchers assigned to the House Subcommittee on Territorial and Insular Affairs.

This was a lot more fun. You could drink, for one thing, and eat. It was a catered buffet, and everyone had a small plate of sandwiches and dip.

The speech hadn't come on yet, and the televisions were tuned to "You are There." This time they were there with Charles A. Lindbergh in the *Lucky Lady* at 12:52 P.M., over Nova Scotia. His map started to blow out the window and he jerked it back, while a voice intoned: "This is the key to Paris. If I lost this, the trip would be over."

"You're new here, aren't you?"

Jordan looked up from her chicken salad and shook her head. "What's new?" He was pleasant looking in a serious way, with horn-rimmed glasses and a sharp, fine mouth.

"Couple months?"

She nodded and her curls bounced. She had cut it in a poodle, and was one of the few women who didn't look ridiculous. It accented her almond-tipped eyes and high cheekbones.

He stuck out his hand. "Al Britton. And you're—?"

"Jordan Jackson." She shook it.

"Mrs. Jordan Jackson?"

"I'm divorced."

The actor playing Charles Lindbergh was stumbling off his plane in Paris and was being lifted up like a prizefighter, confetti sprinkles across both shoulders. The credits rolled across the top and then they cut jerkily to Eisenhower. The camera panned the audience. Everybody was clapping.

"There's a deepie playing at the Capitol tonight. *Bwana Devil.*"

"It sounds terrible."

"It is," Al said agreeably. "I've seen it twice. It was better the second time. My three-D glasses fell off during the part where the lion ate the railroad, and the lenses got soaked in a puddle of root beer. Everything was orange after that. You want to go?"

On the screen Eisenhower was shuffling papers on a podium festooned with I LIKE IKE buttons. He was dwarfed by a satin flag backdrop. Mamie stood next to him, in pink.

"All right."

She had no idea what made her say that, except she hadn't been out of her hotel room since she came, except on business, and was lonely.

President Eisenhower went through the Korean War, the bomb, the Communist threat, and then gave his unequivocal support for statehood for Hawaii.

He urged that it be granted before the senate races in 1954.

Everybody in the room was quiet, waiting. Alaska and Hawaii had always been lumped together in the bid for statehood. Eisenhower moved on to unemployment.

The Alaskans were stunned.

"I don't believe it!" Al shook his head.

"The speech isn't done. He'll come back to it."

But he didn't. It was a bitter blow.

Alaska had already waited eighty-six years since the time America had purchased it from Russia.

"I can't believe it—*Ike*—" someone said.

It didn't take them long to figure out why. Hawaii traditionally voted Republican. Alaska usually went Democrat. Eisenhower was facing a wobbly balance in Congress and needed another Republican state to bolster his edge.

The silence in the room was as flat as the champagne.

Someone switched off the television and put a record on the player. It was Perry Como singing about lost love.

Al grinned ruefully. "Politics." He took Jordan's plate and set it down on the table. "Care to dance?"

He was easy and graceful and didn't try any fancy maneuvering.

"You know what's so curious?" Jordan stared up into his gray eyes. "It's a Republican legislature in Juneau this time. It doesn't make any sense."

"We should send him a wire. Tell him so."

The song ended and they broke away self-consciously. "Let's see about that movie," Al suggested.

"All right."

The air smelled of spring and exhaust fumes. It was cold, and Jordan adjusted her stole. The lights were coming on along the Lincoln Memorial.

"So." He stuck his hands in the pockets of his trench coat. "What's a gorgeous girl like you doing in a place like this?"

"I'm a researcher attached to the Statehood Committee, lobbying in Washington. Digging out horror stories about other territories' problems in becoming states. Did you know Andrew Johnson tried to stop Nebraska?"

"Really?"

"He vetoed its statehood bill. It was 1867. The same year Alaska was bought from the Russians. His head was on the block anyway. One more vote and he would have been impeached. The House ran over the veto and Nebraska got in."

They stopped at a light. In the corner of a bookstore window stood copies of *The Old Man and the Sea*, *The Silver Chalice*, *The Holy Bible* and a paint-by-numbers of the *Last Supper*.

1953 was a big year for religion and fish.

"How about you?"

Al shrugged. "I'm one of Bob's boys."

"Bartlett?" He was the Alaskan delegate to Congress.

Al nodded.

"How's he going to take Eisenhower's defection?"

"Hard to say. He's introduced a bill every session since he took Dimond's job." The light changed and they crossed the street. It was starting to rain. "My apartment's only two blocks away. We could go in until the rain lets up."

"All right."

They ducked their heads and ran.

Al's apartment was like him, clean and tidy and comfortable looking without being wildly attractive. Jordan looked around and sat down on the sofa next to the television.

"Are you hungry? I could scramble some eggs."

She shook her head. "Not after all those sandwiches."

"Then how about a drink. Scotch?"

"Please."

He went into the kitchen, humming to himself and called, "'What's My Line' is on."

Jordan got up and turned it on. Dorothy Kilgallen was asking a man whose job was polishing jelly beans if he needed a college education to do what he did. He had to think about it before answering no.

Jordan wasn't in the habit of going to strange men's apartments, drinking their Scotch and watching Bennett Cerf polish his glasses. But it all felt perfectly comfortable. She took off her shoes and rolled the balls of her feet across the carpet, idly sectioning her pop-bead necklace into two small bracelets.

Al came back with her drink and sat in the armchair.

Arlene Francis was saying, "Is the product you work with bigger than a bread box?"

"Did you grow up in Alaska?" Jordan asked.

Al shook his head. "But please don't hold that against me. I know how territorial Alaskans are."

"Terrible pun," Jordan laughed. "Rubbing salt in the wound. Besides, no one is more of a fanatic about Alaska than transplanted easterners."

"I'm from the Midwest. The accent came from Harvard and

the law degree from Notre Dame. And you?"

"Political science, class of '45, University of Washington. Master's in business administration from USC." She sipped her drink. "Do your parents still live in the Midwest?"

"Both of them are dead. And yours?"

"My dad and a brother died when I was thirteen. My mother's alive. *Very* alive. She owns a private air-carrier service that's about to be bought by Western Airlines. She's going to be rolling in money."

"Does she want to get married?"

Jordan laughed. "You're not her type. How about you? Have you ever been married?"

"I came close once. A Vassar woman. But no."

"It doesn't come highly recommended."

"I take it you weren't happy?"

"I was very young. Only seventeen. It was right before the war."

"What happened to him?"

"He's already married and divorced. Twice more. Has a passel of kids. Trying to populate an entire Southeastern village by himself, I guess."

"I'm sorry."

She shrugged and pulled her legs under her. "It doesn't hurt anymore."

Her face was small and young under the cap of curls, the eyes dark. Steve Allen had just guessed the guest's occupation and the man was passing out an Easter basket of jelly beans. It had stopped raining.

Al put his drink down. "Well. *Bwana Devil* has gone on without us. May I walk you home?"

"I insist."

At the door he chucked her under the chin and drew her mouth up to his. It was a brief, friendly kiss. Not passionate, Jordan decided, but nice. Warmed the innards.

"Tomorrow night for the movie?"

"Sure," she said.

He had a good mind, a sense of humor and he listened to

671

what she said. They worked together on a proposal to the House Subcommittee on Territorial and Insular Possessions; it would increase the amount of land the federal government awarded Alaska from 40 to 100 million acres, if it became a state.

When the measure passed and disappeared into the House Rules Committee, they celebrated at a fancy restaurant. There were pictures of horses and hounds on the wall, and one of Willie Mays whacking a ball. Above the cashier hung a long brass hunting horn and a signed picture of Elizabeth Taylor. The silverware clinked expensively on the red linen tablecloths and the waiters were dressed in black velvet hunting jackets and red bowties.

They were taken to a corner booth overlooking the kitchen.

"That's what I love about Washington," Al said cheerfully. "If you get any grandiose ideas about where you fit into the scheme of things, you come to a fancy place and they'll remind you."

They ordered from the red tufted menu with reckless disregard for price. On the tray with their oysters on the halfshell, the waiter carried a tall drink for someone at the next table: two scoops of pineapple ice cream in a base of pina colada. As they watched, he leaned over and torched it. It flamed prettily as he put it down in front of the customer.

"It's called a reincarnation cocktail," Al explained. *The Search for Bridey Murphy* had just come out and 100,000 copies had already been sold. It described how an amateur hypnotist reportedly took an everyday Colorado housewife back through a previous life in Ireland. "Do you believe in that kind of stuff?"

"Absolutely not!" Jordan laughed. "It's really rubbish. I have trouble enough getting through *one* life."

"I agree. Funny how some people develop peculiar ideas." The waiter brought the oysters, and he washed one down with white wine. "You know, some people—people you even might know and respect, Jordan—believe the only appropriate place for sexual experimentation is within the confines of marriage." The farthest they had gone was kissing and

672

holding hands.

She laughed. "Funny guy. What are you doing—feeling me out?"

"You mean instead of up?"

"It had occurred to me." They devoured the oysters and started on the rolls as they waited for the entrée. They had ordered a medium-rare New York cut, baked slowly in rock salt. It took forever but it was worth it. The salt was chipped away at the table and the meat was sliced into thin pink strips and slathered with a choice of three sauces.

"You know I am not interested in casual groping."

"Then how about serious groping?"

She shook her head. "No, thank you. I'm thirty years old and heavy breathing went out when I was seventeen."

"You mean you never—? Since then?" He was amazed.

Her chin went up. "No, as a matter of fact, I haven't."

"I see."

She finished her roll. It tasted like dough.

"It seems like a terrific responsibility for some guy."

"What do you mean?"

"I mean, anybody who wants to get serious with you had better be serious. And not just serious for a couple of weeks, either."

She stared at him. She could sense a coolness, a pulling away. "That's right," she said gently.

After dinner he took her home and brushed her mouth with his lips. "See you around."

"Probably not." She closed the door quickly.

During the next two years, she ran into him occasionally, once at a Jackson Pollock art opening, later at a symphony concert and again at a touring company performance of *Three Penny Opera*. He was always squiring a different, vapid-looking child on his arm, each distinguishable from the last only by hair color. Jordan had started dating a Washington corporate attorney. He was steady and sincere, but nothing moved inside when he kissed her.

In 1955 fifty-five Alaskans were chosen to write a

constitution for the territory. It was the territory's way of showing the federal government they were serious about statehood. Jordan had been one of those elected, and left Washington gladly. Robert had asked her to marry him, and she needed time to think it over.

The delegates met at College, Alaska in November. Jordan signed up to work on the local government provision of the constitution. Half of the committee members she recognized on sight: an attorney practicing in Anchorage who had given legal counsel to her mother during the FCC hearings on the sale of her airline; a school teacher from Juneau. There were six working on her committee. Five of them waited ten minutes before the last member showed up and slid into the seat next to Jordan. It was Al.

"Well. We seem to have chosen the same committee."

"Same committee. Different commitment."

"What do you mean?"

"*I'm* on time."

"Did you bring your friend?"

"You mean the promising young attorney?"

"Is that what he is? He looks like a lizard in a Brooks Brothers suit."

"At least he doesn't need his mother's permission to stay out past eight."

He smiled. "I didn't think you cared."

"I don't."

They set up provisions to avoid overlapping taxes, created borough governments and shifted an enormous amount of power to the local government. Alaskans had learned the lesson well of home rule, after being ruled for so long by outsiders.

Other committees lowered the voting age to nineteen; created a provision giving Alaskans a means for overthrowing martial law; created a bill of rights, a system of financial checks and balances; and set up specific methods for handling natural resources to insure supply and give Alaskans access.

At Christmas the convention broke for a three-day holiday, and Jordan took the train to Anchorage. Flame was waiting at the depot in a blue fox coat and matching hat, her hair a soft white and her cheeks pink from cold.

"You look terrific!" Jordan kissed her.

"I feel terrific. The sale went through. Come on, I'll tell you all about it over a hot toddy."

Home looked just as Jordan remembered it: the fire crackled in the hearth and Flame had bought a blue spruce from a lot on the corner. They had been shipped up the Alcan from Minnesota. It was too cold in Anchorage to grow decent Christmas trees. She had waited for Jordan so they could decorate it together. She put Bing Crosby on the record player, singing "White Christmas," the song sweetly reminding them of how much was right in the world.

Jordan lifted the flaps on the Christmas-ball box. The cardboard was battered with age. She lifted out a ball she had made in grade school. It had green and red sequins and a rhinestone button of Flame's.

Bing was singing . . . "Where the treetops glisten . . . and children listen . . . to hear . . . sleigh bells in the snow."

Jordan hung it first. Flame brought her a cup of hot buttered rum, her face barely suppressing her excitement.

"Out with it," Jordan commanded.

Flame said, "You are looking at a multimillionaire."

Jordan crowed and kissed her. "How much?"

"Four million dollars."

"My heart," Jordan said, staggering backwards.

"My feeling exactly. When they offered it, I kind of paused, and they thought *I* thought it was too little. So the chairman of the board says, 'Don't worry. Of course that's not all.'"

"I don't believe it!"

"It was great. By this time I had regained my composure enough to say, 'Of course.' He answered, 'We're prepared to offer you stock.' I said, 'Twenty thousand shares.' 'Twenty thousand,' he says, and his voice squeaks. 'And an option to buy twenty thousand more,' I say, 'at five dollars a share.' For a minute we were just looking at each other, like two old grizzlies, and then he said, 'George, draw up the papers.'"

"Oh, mother! It's wonderful! What are you going to do?"

"You mean first?"

"Yes, the very first thing."

"I'm going to put it all on the floor and sit in it."

Jordan laughed, and hooked her arm around her mother. "Then what? Are you going to visit Egypt? You've always wanted to see the pyramids."

"Visit, hell. I think I'll have it gift wrapped and sent home." Jordan laughed.

"No, really, I'm going to find Tommy Ryan Snow."

Jordan set her drink down carefully. Her face grew watchful. "You mean Jenny's child?"

Flame nodded. "The grandson I've never seen. I know all the pitfalls, believe me. I'm prepared to exercise some common sense. I know how money can and will bring a million imposters creeping out of the woodwork. I don't care. And I'm not obsessed with it, Jordan. I want you to know that. I'm not going to squander my entire fortune chasing down a dream. It's just this—this unfinished business. If I had had a chance to square things with Jenny before she died, maybe I could let Tommy go. But he's the only person now that can help. You understand, don't you?"

Jordan reached out to her. "Mother, I love you. You spend it on whatever makes you happy. And yes. I can see how meeting Tommy would help. I just don't want you to be hurt."

The phone rang and Flame said, "This will help. Believe me."

She answered it and came back into the living room. Her voice was puzzled, "It's for you. Al Britton?"

Jordan took the phone and leaned against the refrigerator. "Long distance from Fairbanks. Is this my Christmas present?"

"I'm in Anchorage at the depot." He sounded strained.

"Anchorage?"

"Yes. I came to meet your mother."

Jordan glanced into the living room and at Flame stretched out in front of the fire with an afghan over her knees. "Whatever for?"

There was a beat of silence and then Al said, "That's

generally what one does before one marries the daughter, isn't it?"

"Oh," Jordan said.

"Does that mean you're saying yes?"

"Yes."

And that was that.

Fifty-Seven

Flame pulled her granddaughter onto her lap. The girl automatically nestled back into the warmth of Flame's body. "The choo-choo one," she commanded.

Only two years old, and already a mind of her own! Mandy was tall for her age, like Jordan had been, but she had her father's weak eyes. Small, horn-rimmed glasses slipped down her nose. Mandy continually pushed them back up impatiently, or lost them altogether under teddy or the tights she had thrown on the floor. In the morning the glasses were always the first thing she hunted for. Now she gripped the book in both her hands and opened it to the middle.

"You don't want me to start at the beginning?"

Mandy shook her head. "Too sad. Start where he's feeling better."

So Flame read all about how the little train thought and thought it could and said, "I think I can I think I can" all the way up the hill.

Afterward Flame closed the book firmly and said, "Nap time."

Mandy got up without a fuss, knowing from previous visits it was a nonnegotiable issue. They climbed the stairs slowly, Mandy because her legs were short and Flame because that was the only way she climbed stairs now. Mandy slept in Jordan's old room. It still had the same flowered wallpaper and boxbed with a second one under it that you could roll out for slumber parties. There was a child's rocker under the white curtained window and a toy box full of dolls in old-fashioned dresses. Pancake berets and chin-collar shirtwaists had been quite the rage when Mandy's mother was a girl, but now they gave the dolls a sweetly impoverished appearance, like a maiden aunt

678

who wears the same good dress to family gatherings for twenty years.

Mandy sat in the rocker and unbuckled her shoes. Flame always left Mandy's favorite doll propped up in the corner of the bed. Mandy had named her Charlie and thought it was a big joke.

Charlie had soft red bangs and a page-boy and huge eyes that closed and small yellowed teeth under the perfectly done mouth. Mandy crawled under the quilt and made Charlie put her head down, too.

"When you get up, we'll put on our boots and go to the drugstore," Flame promised.

Mandy's eyes were closing heavily, snapping open and closing again. "'Kay," she said drowsily. She turned her head toward Charlie. One dark pigtail fluffed in the air, the other was mashed into the pillow. Her bottom went up.

So like Jordan! Flame closed the door. No one had told her being a grandmother was going to be such fun. She went down the steps and into the living room. Mandy's small suitcase was still next to the dormer window. They could put it away later. That was the nicest thing about being a grandmother; there was always enough time for the important things. She had been so preoccupied when Roy and Jordan were growing up. Of course, they'd had a business to raise, too, and that had been a big worry.

But what a nice system! Grandparents and children. Quiet, warm laps that adjust to the size of the child being held.

They could take the tree down today. Mandy would enjoy that. It was New Year's Eve, and she was spending the night so Jordan and Al could celebrate, although Flame suspected it would be a short celebration. After the sixth month, a woman doesn't dance all night, only sleep.

One more year and they'd be into the sixties. So many changes in her life! From bustles to bikinis.

The chimes rang, and Flame went to the door. She wasn't expecting anyone. Maybe it was Al with something Mandy had forgotten. He was a good father and fine husband. Some men only tolerated family responsibilities, but Al loved them. A much better match, too, for Jordan. Al was strong, without

679

being a tyrant, and encouraged Jordan's talents. They were partners.

Flame opened the door.

It was Cahill.

His cheeks and nose were bright pink and his breath puffed out in gray clouds. He was wearing an aviator hat with earmuffs and a long handmade scarf under his wool coat. In his gloved hands he carried red roses, seared at the edges.

"Happy statehood." He thrust the flowers into her hand.

"Cahill." The strap on his hat dangled, and Flame stopped herself from buckling it under his chin.

He blinked under the glasses. "Well, aren't you going to ask me in?"

"Of course. Where are my manners."

He came into the entryway. His glasses immediately fogged and he took them off and polished them before stooping over his galoshes. He settled them on a newspaper next to Flame's fur boots.

Flame put the roses in water and found him in the living room, looking around. "So this is what you did with it."

They both were remembering how it had looked over forty years before, with the rain riffling down the roof and the windows not yet in.

"Would you like something to drink?"

"A double martini on the rocks. With vodka," he said as he unwound his scarf and took off his coat and gloves and hung up his hat. "Doctor says I'm not supposed to drink. But being a retired doctor myself, I can tell you he doesn't know a damn thing. I've lived seventy-eight years, and I expect to go on a few more."

She went to the kitchen for ice and came back with two drinks. "I didn't ask if you liked olives or onions, so I put in one of each."

"Both. But my stomach doesn't. Thanks, anyway." He took them out and put them on the napkin.

She perched on the arm of the Chippendale, smiling at him. "I can't get over how well you look." Alert. That was the word. Erect posture. Light step. Clear blue eyes under his bifocals and full white hair.

"I could say the same about you. The years have agreed with you." She still had a firm-looking body and luxuriantly thick white hair. Her eyes were still the deepest green he'd ever seen.

"How long has it been? Twenty years?"

"No, no. Longer than that. It was in '37 Sadie and I saw you and this is almost '59."

"How is Sadie?"

"She died last year. Heart attack." His face grew soft. "We had a lot of good years together. Three kids. All grown. Happens fast, doesn't it, Flame? It's funny, I always thought there'd be so much time. Now I look back and it's a blur. A *good* blur for the most part, but a blur all the same." He sipped his drink.

She smiled tenderly at him. "We are old friends, aren't we?"

She reached out her hand, and he gripped it across the expanse of rose carpet, but gently; they both had swollen knuckles. "Did you ever hear from Jenny?"

She got up then and went to the window. It was cold outside, below zero, and ice fog hung like a pall over the street. "Not directly." He turned and her eyes were clear. "She remarried and had a child. Both she and her husband died during the war. I never met Tommy."

"Your grandson?"

She nodded.

"What happened to him?"

She rolled her glass thoughtfully between her hands. "I tracked him to an orphanage in Whittier. The Eppie Mayer Home. They only keep records five years, but I found a man who had worked there. An old man. He remembered Tommy. I guess Tommy has a birthmark on his face and that's what the man remembered. Anyway, he said he thought Tommy was adopted, but he couldn't remember anything else. With so little to go on—"

"I'm sorry."

"I lost a son, too, when he was still a boy. In one of those freak things. A terrible thing." She shook her head. "That's the worst. Losing a child. You always think they'll be there, growing up. In your mind's eye, you see them going off to college and getting married and having children of their own.

681

It's a terrible thing when it happens. The saddest thing. Maybe that's why I needed to find my grandson. Be wonderful to find a child after losing so many." She shrugged. "Some things you have to learn to live with, I guess. And I've still got Jordan. She's due again in the spring. How about you? Did you ever hear from Logan?"

He rolled up a fraying blue cuff. His arms looked frail under the sweater. "No." He picked up his drink abruptly. "But I had three others. One of them Sadie's, whom I adopted. Emily's her name. She and her husband and kids live close by and that's a comfort. The other two are in college outside. Life goes on somehow."

"It never goes away, does it?" she said softly.

"No. But I've stopped thinking about it all the time."

They were quiet, listening to the fire pop. "What kind of person are you now?" she said quietly.

"What?"

She laughed. "How are you?"

"Fine, fine."

"You know that's not what I meant."

"What kind of a question is that?" he grumbled good-naturedly.

"A good one," she grinned. "Okay. I'll start. I don't remember things as clearly as I used to; I need help bringing the grocery bags in from the car, and I need a nap just to make it to my regular nap. But I don't feel older, that's the curious thing. I was going by Koslosky's the other day and saw myself in the mirror and didn't recognize me. I'm thinking of using Lady Clairol, except my hairdresser wouldn't be the only one who knew for sure. The whole town would talk. I am still vain and petty sometimes, but find myself fired up by life. And I think that's a good thing. Getting fired up. I still make plans. Life still amazes me. Things mean less all the time. Jordan— she's my other daughter—Jordan's married now. I have a beautiful granddaughter. Suddenly I am the resident ancient—"

"The what?"

"The resident ancient. The keeper of old tales, the hoarder of history. And I enjoy that. I hold this child in my lap, and we

682

rock and talk. I still miss Batt, after all these years. Miss his wisdom and counsel and being able to reach across the bed and hold his hand. But I'm happy. It's been a short ride, Cahill. And a rich one."

"Funny."

"What's that?"

"How we could have gone completely different directions and ended up the same place." He put down his drink and held out his arms. "Come here. I want to hold you."

They rose and met each other halfway, each startled by how familiar the other was, after so many years. The bodies still fit together a certain way, his arms still held her at a specific angle, and her head fit under his chin.

Tears came to their eyes.

"Cahill!" she cried.

"I know, I know."

"I've never stopped loving you," Flame said. "All these years."

"And why do you think I came back? You have always been the one person in the world most like me." He took off his glasses and wiped his eyes. "Remember when I left you on the dock that day? It was like leaving my arm. I never should have—"

"It doesn't matter anymore. The only thing that matters is that we're here, right now. And we're not hurting anybody else."

They sat down in front of the fire, using the sofa to support their backs. He put a bony arm around her.

Flame said, "A lot of miles, my friend. We've come so far."

He stroked her hair. She put her hand in his. They watched the fire.

"When do you want to get married?"

She looked up at him. "How did you know that's what I was thinking?"

"Because you're the other half of me. And I was thinking it, too."

He blinked his eyes behind the glasses. They stared at the fire. "Do you want to take a nap first?" she asked.

"Do you?"

"No, I'm fine."

"Well then, let's get married."

"It takes three days to get a blood test done," she said. "We could have the wedding on the day Eisenhower signs the statehood bill."

"That's appropriate. A new beginning for everybody." He bent and kissed her and pressed his cheek to hers. His skin was papery thin and dry.

"Let's keep it small. Just our families."

"I only have Emily and Arthur in Alaska and the four grandchildren."

"I'll tell Jordan and we'll have it here. Nice and simple."

He kissed her again. "Remember the first time I asked you to marry me? And how we almost did before I left? Things would have been so different, Flame."

"Hush, now. Things are exactly the way they're supposed to be. Perfect."

Jordan was beside herself with excitement. "Mother! It's so unexpected."

"Well, you had to be there, I suppose." Flame's voice quivered with age. "Anyway. There'll be about ten of us. You'll stand up with me, won't you?"

"Of course! And Mandy—let's have her be the flower girl. Is that all right?"

"Flower girl—I hadn't thought—certainly."

"What are you going to wear? We have colors to pick—food to prepare. Sure you wouldn't rather wait a week?"

"Jordan, when you get to be my age, a week can be a very long time. No, we'll keep it simple and have it here in the living room."

"It was funny, mom. Remember that day at the fair when I asked you who he was and you said he was your oldest friend?"

"That's right," Flame said wonderingly. "You were there. I'd forgotten."

Jordan nodded vigorously. "I could feel it then. That something between you. Mother, I am so very glad! What a wonderful thing!"

"It is," she said, her voice barely holding up. "You can't

know how wonderful. Nobody does but Cahill."

The statehood ceremony started at Sydney Lawrence Auditorium when the doors closed at 10:45 A.M. on January 3, 1959. It was being broadcast live by KENI-TV, Channel 2, and filmed for a later newscast by KTVA. Onstage, Reverend Paul F. Evans clasped his hands together and bowed his head. The audience did the same.

He prayed for guidance for this new state on this great and glorious day—This sacred day, when a tumbling, roaring, green spill of land became part of something bigger, this something called America.

Everyone stood in the warm darkness facing the hotly lit stage and joined in the "Star Spangled Banner," and not as beggars with noses pressed against the glass, not as poor relatives never quite included, but singing with their hearts and souls on fire, because this was their song, finally, and their country. America! How beautiful you are, with your vast gritty cities and your humming hives of steel; your secret flowering cliffs and fragile hopes. America. We bring you our finest, our best: our foaming rivers and towering mountains; the thin whine of railroad songs, sung on a day so cold the bones ache with it; we bring you our hands spilling with summer, with ripe fruit and sweet vegetables. We bring you our harvests and hopes, our strong backs and sturdy minds; we bring you a land fragrant with possibilities. For ninety-two years we have held out our hands to you, and now you have taken them, finally, and we will never let you go. We will make you so proud of us, America! Proud because we are proud, and proud because we have plans here, great plans, plans for cities and clean factories and great sweeps of green silence. .

You do not understand us; we know that. But do not fear for us, or this land. We love her. We need her. And we will always protect her. We need the spaces, we need the clean bite of wind blowing off an empty snowfield; but we need roads, too, and the warm comfort of concrete when the thermometer cracks and explodes from cold. And there's room for both, here! There is. That's what we want to tell you when we sing this song. That's what we're saying when we raise our voices. That we know your fears, but we know this land better than anybody in Washington, anybody in New York, anybody else. It's our land, and now we're sharing it with you.

It was a tremendously moving moment. They sang their hearts out and tears ran down their eyes. Rows of people gripped hands together, next to one another in the darkness, reaching across the backs of seats, joined together in a great hymn of thanksgiving.

Afterward they listened by a telephone hookup to Washington as President Eisenhower signed the bill creating the forty-ninth state. They sang "Alaska's Flag," and then they walked home through a blizzard of noise, as Americans.

The minister surveyed the small knot of family gathered together for this ceremony as old as recorded time: the adult children, the grandchildren shivering with excitement, the elderly couple.

He was pastoring his first church, and this was his first wedding. He blurted out, "You know a lot more about life than I do. You've known each other longer than I've been on this earth, and I thank God I'm the minister who gets to marry you. It reminds me that things are going to be all right in this world, after all."

Cahill moved closer and took her hand. He was wearing a beautiful soft gray wool suit and silk shirt and cravat and his white hair had been cut.

Flame's dress was hand-stitched raw silk that came to midknee. It was a soft pale green that made her eyes look enormous under the white hair.

The minister said, "God has created this holy arrangement of marriage, as a state most to be desired."

Emily started to weep into her hanky and next to Jordan, Mandy scratched her leg with the toe of her patent-leather shoe, leaving a black smudge on the pink tights.

Flame squeezed Cahill's hand. Thank you, God, she thought. A hymn of praise filled her. Thank you for letting this come to pass. For giving us both another chance to be together. We still found each other. We still created a beautiful thing. This sacrament. This privilege.

686

Across Alaska, there is this humming current of life. It crackles through little towns, into valleys, it holds us and sweeps us before it with its magnificence. Life, there is only this: you repeat yourself, with boundless joy, with enthusiastic practice riffs of rainbows and chittering birds flung against a sky nobody sees. Life: you are beautiful, and I have never been so much a part of you as now.

They exchanged rings and kissed. Behind them Emily's youngest child shifted and whispered urgently to his mother, and Emily took him to the bathroom, while everybody clapped and cheered and Al broke open the first bottle of champagne.

After a while, the middle generation did the dishes and visited, while Emily's children fought with Mandy and each other and made up and then ate every scrap of cake left on everybody else's plate, and all the peanuts and sandwiches and mints. The oldest threw up, and then it was time to go.

The minister shook Cahill's hand and kissed Flame on the cheek. "Congratulations. Call me for your fiftieth anniversary."

Cahill and Flame linked arms, and their children lined up for hugs and to give good wishes. Everybody drove away in a puff of gray ice.

Cahill said, "Flame Jackson Blue." His voice choked up.

She leaned against him. "When I was younger, I spent years practicing writing 'Flame Blue' in a purple script—when my family still lived on the hill in Seattle and we played in the pond."

"I never knew that."

She nodded. "I had our children's names all decided, too. We would have three. A boy first, then the girl, then the baby. And we would be very happy."

"At least that part came true." He kissed the top of her head. "Sometimes things end well, don't they? Sad movies seem to be *in* today. Have you noticed? The heroine and hero miss each other by a mile and the audience weeps. Sad books, too. If they mirror life, I'm very grateful they're mirroring somebody else's."

"Me, too."

His eyes grew soft. "Do you have a bedroom in this place,

Mrs. Blue?"

She undressed in the bathroom and put on a soft long nightgown. He was already in bed. He was wearing flannel pajamas and the hair on his chest was white.

She crawled in next to him and he put his arm around her. "You know what I was remembering?"

"What's that?"

"How we used to lie up here when they were building this place. Watch the clouds collide. We were full of fire then. Everything mattered."

"Ah, but we're still full of fire," she said quietly. "It's only been tempered. That's all. It's still there. I think of you, and I still feel that old rush of emotion. That hammering of my heart."

"You do?" He looked at her and took off his glasses. He nestled next to her. They felt each other's knees, the toughness of the bodies. "I think I could die in your arms a happy man."

"Not today!"

"No, not today." He kissed her throat. "Today I just want to hold you."

It started out that way, but it ended up as more.

It was slower than it once was, and gentler; but there was still that miracle of flesh touching flesh, better almost than how it was when they were young because the very old know how fragile it is—this life, this chance to love.

So that's it, Flame thought afterward, drifting into sleep. That's it. Those feelings never go away. It never stops. Ever. It only gets sweeter.

Fifty-Eight

On the outskirts of Niagara Falls is a university run by the Vincentian Order of Catholic priests. The students said the place was built on a bluff and then run on one; but it was a good solid school, featuring law and order.

On Statehood Day Tom Snow was still in his room at Lynch Hall. It was between semesters, and almost everybody else had left. He couldn't afford to go home, and even if he could, he had a job in Lewistown that started in three days, working at a sporting-goods store.

The student supervisors had abandoned the hall, and Tom was stretched out on a bed. On television a special news bulletin of the president signing Alaska into statehood had given way to "I Love Lucy."

His room faced over a snow-covered lawn and highway. Cars glittered like jeweled bugs, and beyond it was the black angle of the Niagara River.

He had been dating a sophomore, Tammy, and she rolled off the single bed next to him and handed him back his paper. It was a Sociology 319 report on growing up Eskimo.

She trotted over to the television set and turned it down. On the screen, Lucy had her leg stuck in a ballet bar.

Tammy had tawny hair and wide blue eyes and a small gap between her teeth. She was going to be a preschool teacher and already had made noises about wanting a "future" with Tommy. The word always appeared in the air as a word of substance, as big as a two-car garage, and as solid and heavy as her cooking.

She curled next to him on the bed. Naturally, they weren't supposed to be curling next to each other anywhere, least of all in Lynch Hall, but the door was locked and they were taking their chances.

She had tears in her eyes. "I can't believe how hard it was. Growing up Indian."

Something snapped in Tom.

He got up and went to the window, putting his palms on the wire latticework. Two priests were walking from O'Donahue Hall to their quarters, passing directly in front of Lynch Hall. They looked like enormous black ravens in the snow.

"I am not Indian," Tom said.

"Eskimo, then. You know what I mean."

"Tammy, Indians and Eskimos are completely different races in Alaska. They look different. Have different languages, gods, customs. Everything is different. You read my report."

"You don't have to get so upset. What I mean is—you grew up on the outside. And now Alaska's a state. So you must have some legitimacy. Things must be going your way now."

"They're not. Statehood is the worst possible thing that could happen to the natives."

"I don't understand."

"The federal government is going to start transferring land to the state."

"What's so bad about that?"

"Some of that land is stuff the natives have been living on for thousands of years. They don't have title to that land. The federal government has never passed a law about natives that would give them the land, free and clear."

"What's going to happen to them?"

"I don't know. I fear for my people. They're poor. They're so poor. Do you know I grew up in a one-room house with a chamber pot in one corner and crates for chairs? But yes, you read the report. Every family's hit with TB or worse."

"Maybe the state will do something for them."

"Standard Oil is already sinking wells in the south central part of Alaska. What's going to happen when they start getting hungry? I'll tell you. They're going to move their drills and platforms out into the oceans. I can feel it. It's coming. And then the whales will stay away, the seals will stop multiplying, and the fragile system that's been keeping my people going for thousands of years will start breaking down."

"Okay," Tammy said.

"What do you mean, 'okay'?"

"I mean, 'Okay, now what do you plan to do about it?'"

She sat back on her heels in her black toreador pants, her hair pulled back into a soft ponytail.

"Well, I'll be a sonofabitch." He sat down slowly. "That's really it, isn't it? It's back to that."

"To what?"

He grinned. "If you don't like it, change it."

"Absolutely."

"You know, I'm starting to like you more all the time."

"Of course." She crossed her feet. "What's not to like?"

Fifty-Nine

Tom got the letter after Christmas in his first year of law school and immediately made plans to go home during spring break. It was from a cousin still living in Barrow:

Dear Tom:

We need your help. The government has us all worried here, but good. The Atomic Energy Commission is planning on testing five atomic bombs right on top of Point Hope. The natives aren't any too happy about it; you better believe it. The government says there aren't enough natives to worry about, and that everything will be safe. But we've started doing some reading about a place called Hiroshima and don't think the federal government knows its ass from a hole in the wall.

The government is drawing up the paperwork to take our land away up here and just move us over. They say it's because of the blasting, but we know it's because they've found all that oil they've been looking for.

   Plus there's another problem. Some police guy—only he's an international police guy, came to Barrow and said we can only hunt birds for our family between certain days. I personally know of 100 men who plan on killing birds on the wrong days, just to see what happens. It could get ugly. You gotta come home and help, Tom. We're counting on you.

Your cousin,

Willie

Dr. Edward Teller was the father of the H-bomb but there was nothing fatherly about the way he was looking at Tom.

"You haven't answered my question," Tom said. The room was deathly still. "Why is it that you and this room of eminent scientists are only now getting around to visiting the people who will be the most affected by the blasting? You've been working on Project Chariot for three years, is that not correct? Selling it to everyone from the Fairbanks Chamber of Commerce to the Lawrence Radiation Laboratory of the University of California. So I ask you, is it not time—no, *past* time, to put it to a vote?" Tom looked around the community-center room at the faces of the villagers. The scientists all had on suits and sat at the only table, their hands talking a separate, busy language: folding paper, smoking, flicking ashes, popping knuckles. But the villagers were as silent as three thousand years of history.

"Fine," Dr. Teller said. "We're prepared to present our side and have it put to a vote. But we must warn you—you're not the only one voting."

"That's true," Tom replied. "The Point Hope Eskimos aren't the only ones voting. But they're the only ones whose vote *counts*, Dr. Teller. They live here. It's their home."

"Don't prejudice our side," Dr. Teller snapped. He got up and went to a hanging chart, riffled through it until he found what he was looking for, smoothed it down and said pleasantly, "As you can see, we're planning on setting off all the bombs at once."

The chart looked like one of those commercials for removing warts: there were five deep pockets dug into the flat finger of land.

"We're going to build you a harbor. The blasts will move about thirty million yards of silt and sand at Cape Thompson in the Chukchi Sea. And the channel will be about nine hundred feet wide and two thousand feet long."

Someone in the back raised a hand.

Teller frowned. "Yes?"

"What about the fish? The whales?"

"Glad you asked," Teller said heartily. He thumped the charts and they swung wildly. "We've done tests—and not just on fish and whales, but on ringed seals, spotted seals, walrus, bear, caribou, birds—the whole nine yards—and the answer is—nothing."

There was a doubtful silence.

"You heard me! Nothing. Oh, maybe a little migratory upheaval of caribou, but nothing major. No, this Project Chariot is going to funnel a major source of money into Alaska, and give the villagers—all of you—a nice harbor to use." He fondled the charts. "We've got it all down here, you better believe it: how much meat a day you eat—five pounds, if you're interested; even your favorite spots for fishing polar cod in January. And the answer is—all that is going to stay just exactly the same."

Tom said, "We know about strontium ninety. We know enough to know scientists *don't* know enough about the cumulative dangers."

"Get to the point," Teller said.

"I'm asking you what you have to back up your position that a negligible amount of radiation will be released into the atmosphere."

"We've been working with the Division of Biology and Medicine, University of Washington Laboratory of Radiation Biology. Everything points to a fission escapement of less than 5 percent. Now—if there are no further questions, let's put it to a vote."

The village council stood and politely, each having a turn, they voted no.

Teller and his crew took down their charts and packed their graphs and left hurriedly.

The villagers had won; but it was only the first battle. They knew the scientists and federal government spokesmen would be back, only with bigger words and stronger arguments.

"How much longer for that school of yours, Tom?" Willie asked.

"Two years."

"You hurry, huh?"

"I'll hurry."

The next fall during Thanksgiving break, Tom flew to

Barrow. It was November of 1961, and the first time that all the Eskimos were meeting in one place. It was sponsored by the American Association on American Indian Affairs. They drafted a letter to the Department of the Interior, urging that it stop Project Chariot and bar the Atomic Energy Commission from conducting any more studies:

> We, the Inupiat, have come together for the first time ever in all the years of our history. We had to come together in meeting from our far villages, from Lower Kuskokwim to Point Barrow. We always thought our Inupiat heritage was safe to be passed down to our future generations as our fathers passed down to us. Our heritage is our land around the whole Arctic world where the Inupiat live.

The land, his grandfather had said. Protect the land. They sent the letter. They organized. They made demands and became activists. They stopped Project Chariot and formed the first regional native association in fifty years.

Can you feel it, Tom? Can you feel it? The plane bumps you down in villages and drops you in Fairbanks, where you take a larger plane to increasingly larger cities. Your head pounds from the volume: too much noise, too many harsh smells, too many distractions. Can you feel it? They're pulling together up north, Tom. It's starting. But the other side is pulling together too.

The problem was entitlement. They had no title to the land. Only promises.

Tom raced through law school.

"Do you want to? It would be fun. Especially with Cahill at the AMA Convention. Give you an idea of what your son-in-law does to earn his salary."

"I'd love to!" Flame said. "Do you know I've never been up there?"

"Really?" Jordan combed Alice's hair and snapped a rubber band around it. "There you go. Go find Mandy." Alice bounded away.

Flame shook her head. "I own a claim I've never seen. 'The Frozen Lady.' I always thought it was such a picturesque name. I guess I always imagined somebody frozen down there, a small, sweet, utterly sad face." She laughed. "It's going to be a big disappointment, I'm sure."

"What we'll do is, we'll charter a plane to take us straight to Fool's Creek. That way we can get a good perspective of the area that's going to be flooded for the dam, and you can finally see your claim."

"Promise me you won't fall in love with it, though," Al said. "It's going to be one hundred feet under water next year."

Al was an attorney working on a proposal for the U.S. Army Corps of Engineers to build a hydroelectric project at Rampart Canyon. It would bury the entire Yukon flats under water, and generate 5 million kilowatts of power. In the spring he and Jordan were taking the girls to Washington, where he would lobby for the project in Congress. It was all very exciting.

"I can't promise anything."

"Mother!"

"I can't. Except that I'm taking you all out to dinner tonight at a fancy place when we get home."

"Deal."

Funny how time shifts things in your mind. Was the town of Rampart really so small? They walked through buildings rotting in the damp, flowers coming up through the broken floorboards, the sound of a swing somewhere, and sudden bursts of laughter that stopped the instant they poked their heads in. Ghosts, all. Julius Ramsdorf's store was still standing, windows long broken, door twisted off, but his fine house on the hill was gone, and there was no trace of the first night Cahill and Flame had spent together. No small cabin, no large garden. Where did they all go? Mercifully the whorehouse had been burned, but part of the nymph was still hanging on the wall, her strange smile intact through the curling paint. Gone. All of it.

The Dealy Sisters and the bathhouse with the ticking pipes; old Wyatt Earp slinging drinks and looking behind him for some hot-fingered kid wanting to make a name.

The schoolhouse still stood on the hill, and in the middle of town, where the general contractor's office had been, a funny, white-haired man had put up a sign proclaiming the place was now Ira Weisner Trading Co.

Ira kept a cat that was as fat as he was, and the shelves were stocked with staples and candy. Under a stack of crates and cartons, Flame saw the tip of a pool table, as swaybacked as an old horse.

A stove in the middle belched oil and smoke, and the place smelled like a tire factory sprayed with Lemon Pledge.

"Who's here anymore to buy this stuff?" Flame asked.

"Be surprised. Got a load of heavy dressers through this morning. Some of those boys working on that damn dam, I guess."

Al was used to the profanity and only said, "Must be Baxton's team. They're doing some surveying."

Jordan bought candy sticks for the kids, and Al took a picture of Flame outside before they climbed back into the Cessna on floats and lifted into the sky.

They followed the Yukon until it cut off into the Little Minook, and they lifted up over the divide. The country rolled out in a thick mat of trees and glints of creeks.

Al was saying, "You couldn't find a better area to flood. In the whole basin, there can't be more than ten flush toilets."

The plane tipped over a flash of stream, and the pilot put her down gently. Flame peered out the window.

It was beautiful.

The Frozen Lady. Al helped her out and she walked slowly up the faint path to a cabin. Through a notch in the trees, she could see sky and a gray cliff of mountain. Fool's Creek was running high and the sound roared in her ears. The ground was matted with cranberries.

She shoved open the door. Mandy had come with her and stamped her foot indignantly. "There's nothing in here, grandma!"

The room was bare except for a metal box on the floor in the corner. Flame hauled it outside and opened it.

"Forgive me," she said, "but I can't help myself. Old age and all."

The lock crumbled in her hands, and she opened the lid. It was a letter, written over sixty years before and never mailed. She put on her glasses and scanned it for a signature. Ely Harrison. The man who had sold her father the claim. Ely wrote:

My dear brother:

My health is failing and even as I write this, I know I am finally leaving. At last! My plan is to find some poor sucker on which to foist off this worthless piece of junk. I am an old man, superstitious to a fault; yet it's the only way to free myself of this terrible curse—by putting another in my place. Ah, but she's a cruel and frozen lady, Alaska! She wraps her hands around your heart with her beauty, and when you can't breathe, from loving her so, she squeezes harder, until the life and dreams are all squeezed out. And when there's nothing left to give, she leaves you—staggering and blind and wanting her still. You can never worship her enough, and you can never win. I've tried to leave her while there's still time. I have tried. But she haunts my dreams. Now it is time, dear brother, for another to suffer as I have.
See you in the spring or see you in hell.

Ely Harrison

Poor Ely. So there was no gold. No chance for gold. But what difference did it make, anyway? It was always the dream of Alaska that had kept her going—not the dream of getting rich. And along the way, that had happened too.

She put the letter in the jacket of her coat and rose stiffly to her feet.

A plane chattered across the sky, following the river. It dropped lower and smoothly taxied to a stop two hundred yards behind them. Three men got out, and Al went over and met them.

Flame could tell by the way he was standing there was some

698

kind of trouble. She walked over.

They were native, nicely dressed, with short clipped hair. One of them had a scar on his face. It ran from the top of his head through his cheek and down his chin.

Al was saying, "Flame, these men represent the United States Fish and Wildlife Service and the natives in the area. They are fighting the dam."

Flame had started to cry.

"Mother, what is it?" Jordan ran over. "Do you need your pills?" Flame nodded, weeping, unable to speak. Jordan said, "I don't know what you've done to upset her, but whatever it is, stop it. She's an old woman."

Flame swallowed the pills. She tried to speak and couldn't.

"Come on, mom. Come on." Jordan took her arm and Flame pulled away.

She lurched toward the men. "You're Tom Snow, aren't you? Tommy Ryan Snow." Tears rolled down her face. She didn't try to wipe them away.

"How did you know my name?"

"And your father's name was Tim. Tim Snow. Isn't that right? And he was killed in the battle of Attu."

"Who are you? Who are you?"

Flame held out her hands. "I'm your grandmother."

"That's not possible! I'm native."

"Half-native. Your mother was my daughter, Jennifer. I've been looking for you, Tom, for over twenty years."

He staggered backward, forward, and fell into her arms.

His heart beat wildly. Everything was numb. *White.* He was half-*white.* And a family. These wide-eyed children staring at him and this kindly looking man in glasses with his arm around his dark haired wife. Related? These were his people, too?

Then what of the dream?

From your seed will spring the rebirth of your people. The rebirth of white people, too? Of those, too?

His grandmother was saying, "Come. I want to talk to you alone."

They walked back toward the woods and passed the main shaft. Flame sat down.

"Tom, let me look at you, Tom. Let me say your name."

He thought of something. "Is that attorney—is he related to me?"

"By marriage. Indirectly. He's your aunt's husband."

Husbands. Aunts. Uncles. He had lived so long without. All those years in the orphanage. And now it had come to this.

"What are you thinking? Something. Tell me."

"I'm going to have to kill him in court. Whoever he is. Kill him. The dam can't be allowed to go through. It can't."

Suddenly it was important for him to make her see. "Over twelve hundred natives live here, up and down the small rivers. They'd all lose their homes. They'd all be flooded. And the birds! It's a breeding ground for waterfowl. The biggest breeding ground in the nation—almost in the world. Gone. All of it would be gone. The salmon run would stop; the moose would leave."

"You believe it very strongly, don't you?"

"Yes." Then he thought, "What should I call you?"

"Anything you like. My given name is Flame."

"Flame, it can't go through. For one thing we don't *need* all that kilowatt power. It's more bureaucratic overkill. And once it's gone, how can we fix it? We can't. It's ruined, then. Ruined."

"Tom Snow," Flame said firmly. "You do what you need to do. You'll always have family. Always."

"You mean that, don't you?" It was almost like this old white-haired woman could see the boy in Tom, see how it had been to be hungry and starved for affection, for arms holding him and people caring.

She reached out and squeezed his hand. "You are my grandson. And I will always love you. Your star is going a different direction, is all. Move across the sky."

"Now you sound like my grandfather from Barrow. It's true, though. I'm not afraid of it anymore. I see things coming. Wonderful things for my people. A gathering of tribes. A pulling together. We're going to march to Washington, Flame, some day! Thousands strong: the Tlingit-Haidas from south-east, the Athapaskans from around here, the Eskimos from Barrow, the Aleuts from the chain. We're going to use words for bullets and win our land. It's coming. I can feel it. I'm part

700

of it."

"Oh, Tom! Follow it! Do it!" Flame cried. "But remember, you're half-white. Remember that once you get the natives working together, then it's time to gather the whites and natives. There's been too much bitterness. Too many private wars. We need each other. All of us."

"Grandmother," Tom cried, the word coming out easily. "Grandmother, live a long time."

"Through you, I'll live forever."

And they walked through the trees to the others.

EXCITING BESTSELLERS FROM ZEBRA

STORM TIDE (1230, $3.75)
by Patricia Rae

In a time when it was unladylike to desire one man, defiant, flamehaired Elizabeth desired two! And while she longed to be held in the strong arms of a handsome sea captain, she yearned for the status and wealth that only the genteel doctor could provide—leaving her hopelessly torn amidst passion's raging STORM TIDE . . . .

PASSION'S REIGN (1177, $3.95)
by Karen Harper

Golden-haired Mary Bullen was wealthy, lovely and refined—and lusty King Henry VIII's prize gem! But her passion for the handsome Lord William Stafford put her at odds with the Royal Court. Mary and Stafford lived by a lovers' vow: one day they would be ruled by only the crown of PASSION'S REIGN.

HEIRLOOM (1200, $3.95)
by Eleanora Brownleigh

The surge of desire Thea felt for Charles was powerful enough to convince her that, even though they were strangers and their marriage was a fake, fate was playing a most subtle trick on them both: Were they on a mission for President Teddy Roosevelt—or on a crusade to realize their own passionate desire?

LOVESTONE (1202, $3.50)
by Deanna James

After just one night of torrid passion and tender need, the dark-haired, rugged lord could not deny that Moira, with her precious beaty, was born to be a princess. But how could he grant her freedom when he himself was a prisoner of her love?

Available wherever paperbacks are sold, or order direct from the Publisher. Send cover price plus 50¢ per copy for mailing and handling to Zebra Books, 475 Park Avenue South, New York, N.Y. 10016. DO NOT SEND CASH.